the Golden Hour

NIKI SMITH

the Golden Hour

NIKI SMITH

LB

Little, Brown and Company
New York Boston

About This Book

This book was edited by Rachel Poloski and designed by Ching N. Chan. The production was supervised by Bernadette Flinn, and the production editor was Lindsay Walter-Greaney. The text was set in Sketchnote, and the display type is RestlessSoul.

Little, Brown and Company
Hachette Book Group
1290 Avenue of the Americas, New York, NY 10104
Visit us at LBYR.com

First Edition: October 2021

Little, Brown and Company is a division of Hachette Book Group, Inc.
The Little, Brown name and logo are trademarks of Hachette Book Group, Inc.

The publisher is not responsible for websites (or their content) that are not owned by the publisher.

Library of Congress Cataloging-in-Publication Data
Names: Smith, Niki, author, illustrator.
Title: The golden hour / Niki Smith.
Description: First edition. | New York : Little, Brown and Company, 2021. | Summary: After witnessing a violent attack at school, Manuel struggles with anxiety but his cell phone camera helps him find anchors when he dissociates, and an unexpected friendship opens up new possibilities.
Identifiers: LCCN 2020005070 | ISBN 9780316540377 (hardcover) | ISBN 9780316540339 (paperback) | ISBN 9780316540315 (ebook) | ISBN 9780316540353 (ebook other)
Subjects: LCSH: Graphic novels. | CYAC: Graphic novels. | Anxiety—Fiction. | Friendship—Fiction. | Photography—Fiction. | Gays—Fiction. | Schools—Fiction. | 4-H clubs—Fiction.
Classification: LCC PZ7.7.S6425 Gol 2021 | DDC [Fic]—dc23
LC record available at https://lccn.loc.gov/2020005070

ISBNs: 978-0-316-54037-7 (hardcover), 978-0-316-54033-9 (pbk.), 978-0-316-54031-5 (ebook), 978-0-316-54034-6 (ebook), 978-0-316-54036-0 (ebook)

PRINTED IN CHINA

1010
Hardcover: 10 9 8 7 6 5 4 3 2 1
Paperback: 10 9 8 7 6 5 4 3 2 1

To all the teachers who believed in me.

chapter one

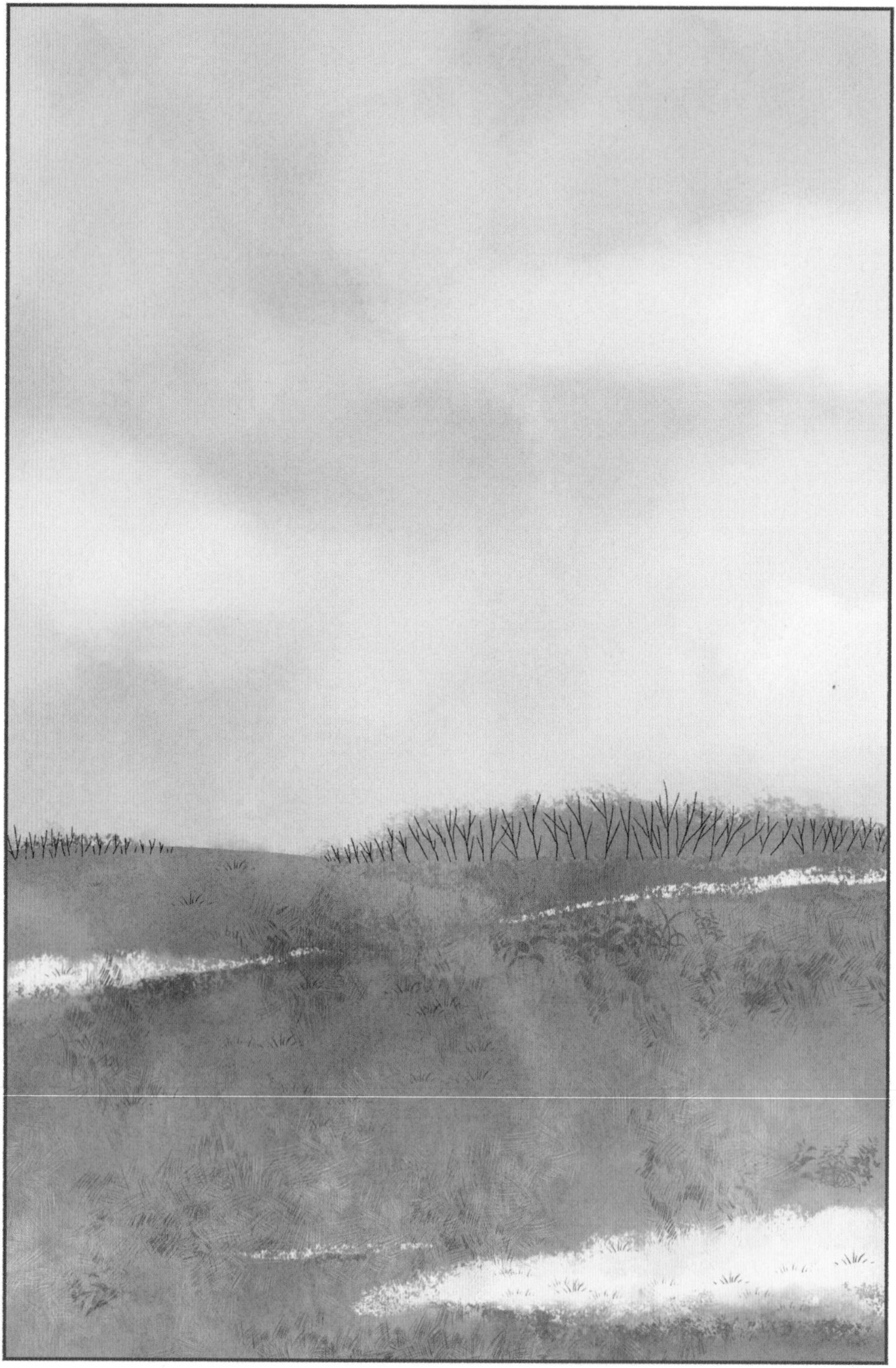

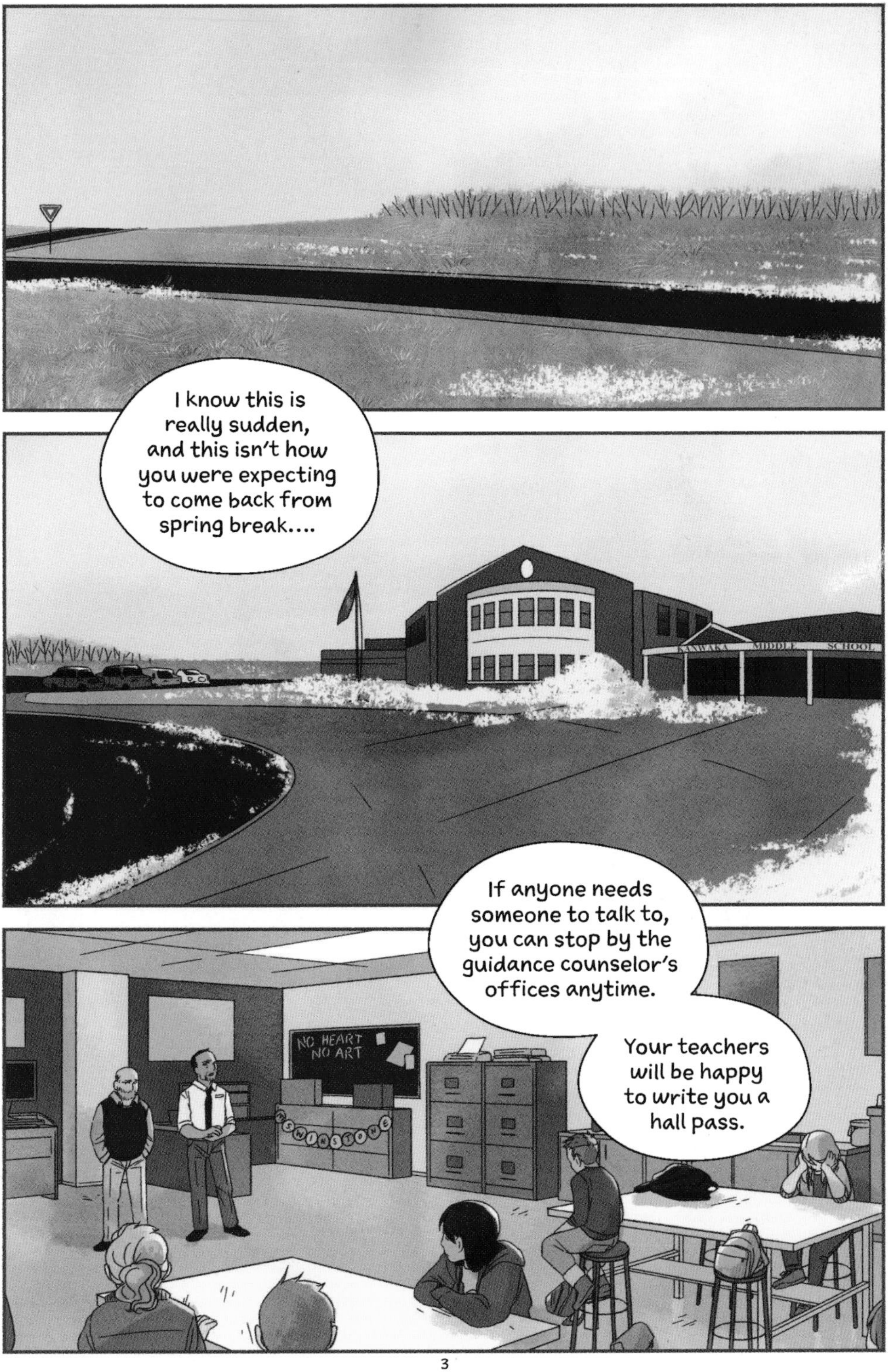
I know this is really sudden, and this isn't how you were expecting to come back from spring break....
KANWAKA MIDDLE SCHOOL
If anyone needs someone to talk to, you can stop by the guidance counselor's offices anytime.
NO HEART NO ART
MSWINSTONE
Your teachers will be happy to write you a hall pass.

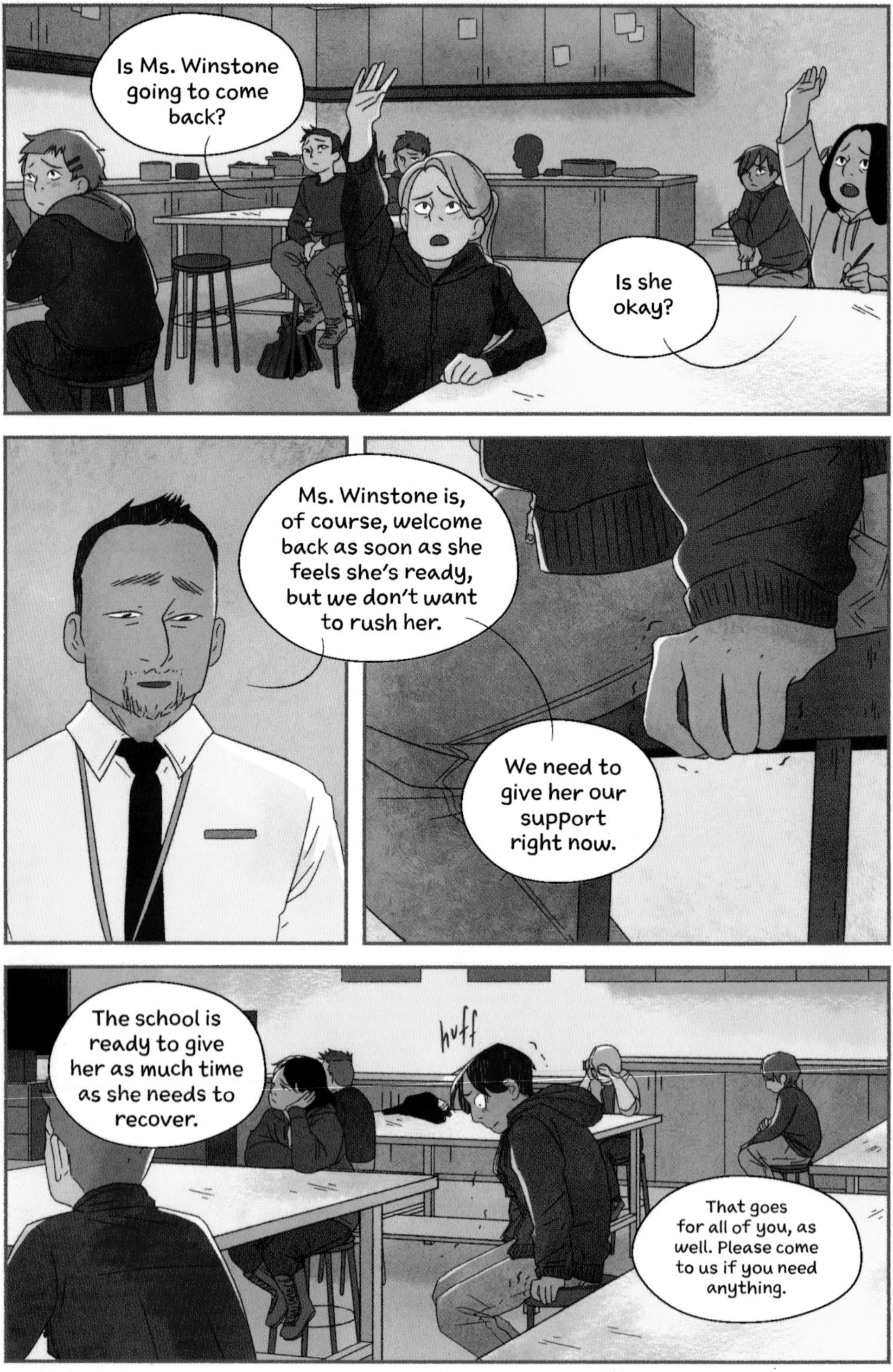
Is Ms. Winstone going to come back?
Is she okay?
Ms. Winstone is, of course, welcome back as soon as she feels she's ready, but we don't want to rush her.
We need to give her our support right now.
The school is ready to give her as much time as she needs to recover.
huff
That goes for all of you, as well. Please come to us if you need anything.

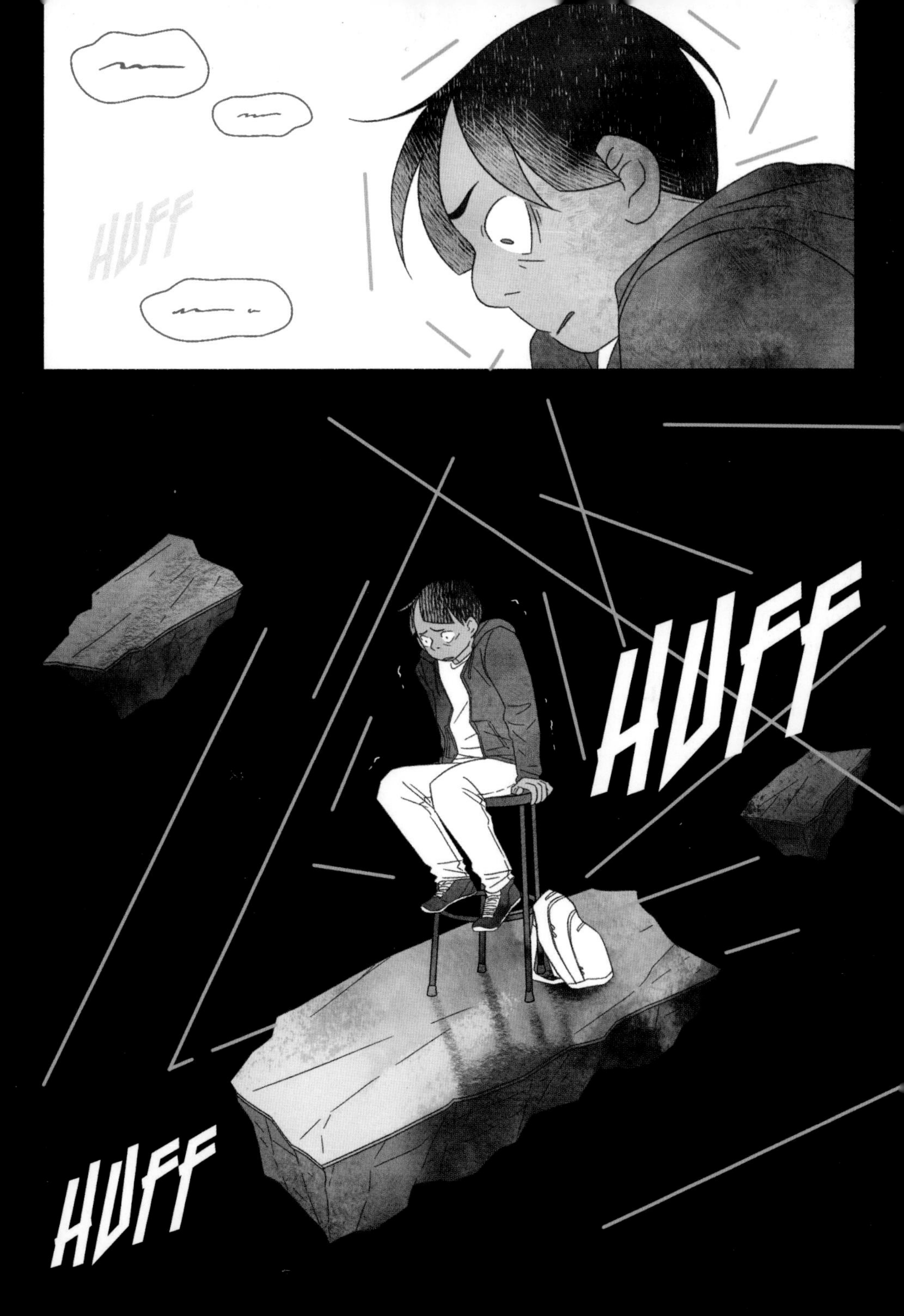
HUFF
HUFF
HUFF

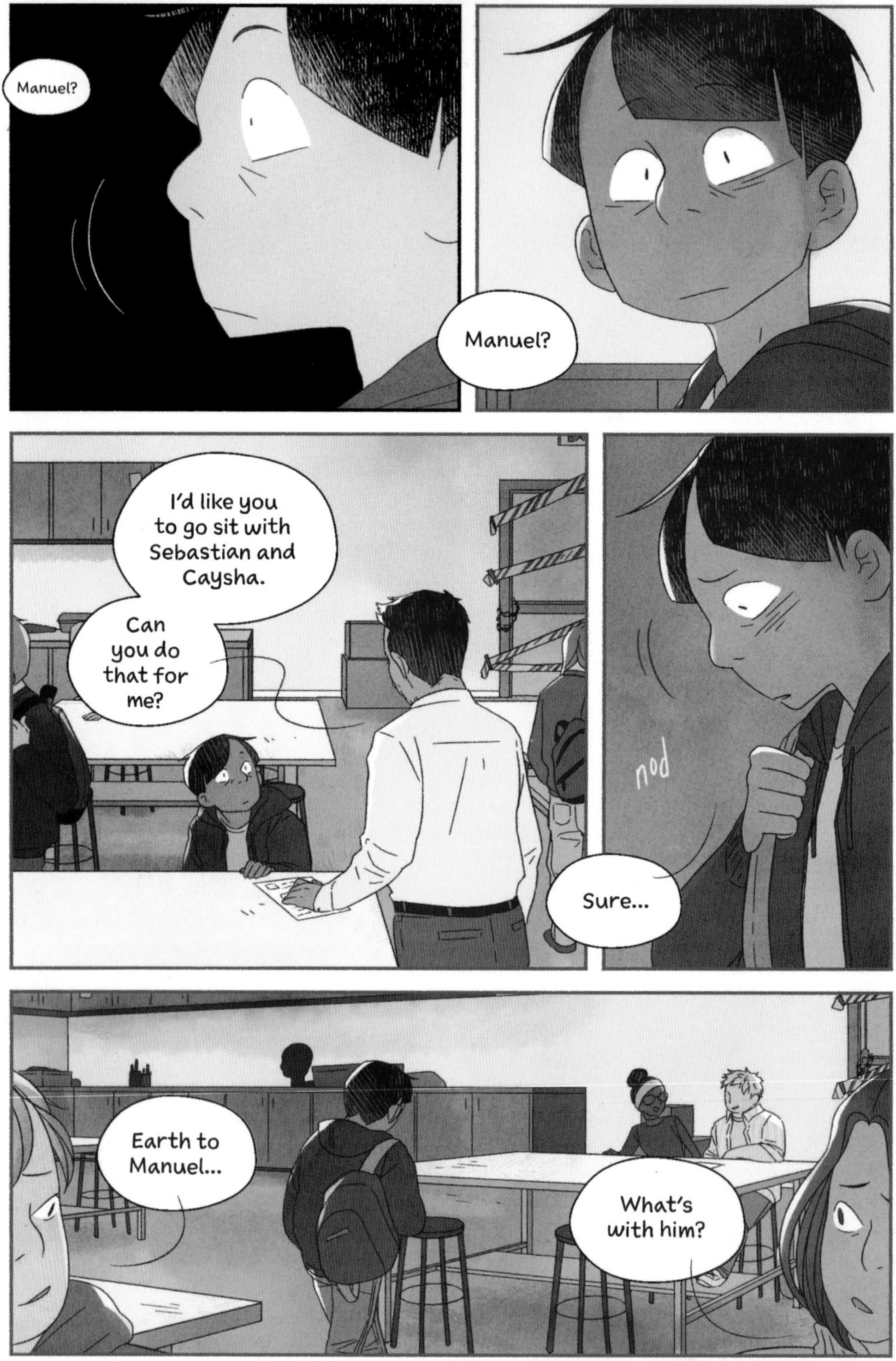
Manuel?
Manuel?
I'd like you to go sit with Sebastian and Caysha.
Can you do that for me?
nod
Sure...
Earth to Manuel...
What's with him?

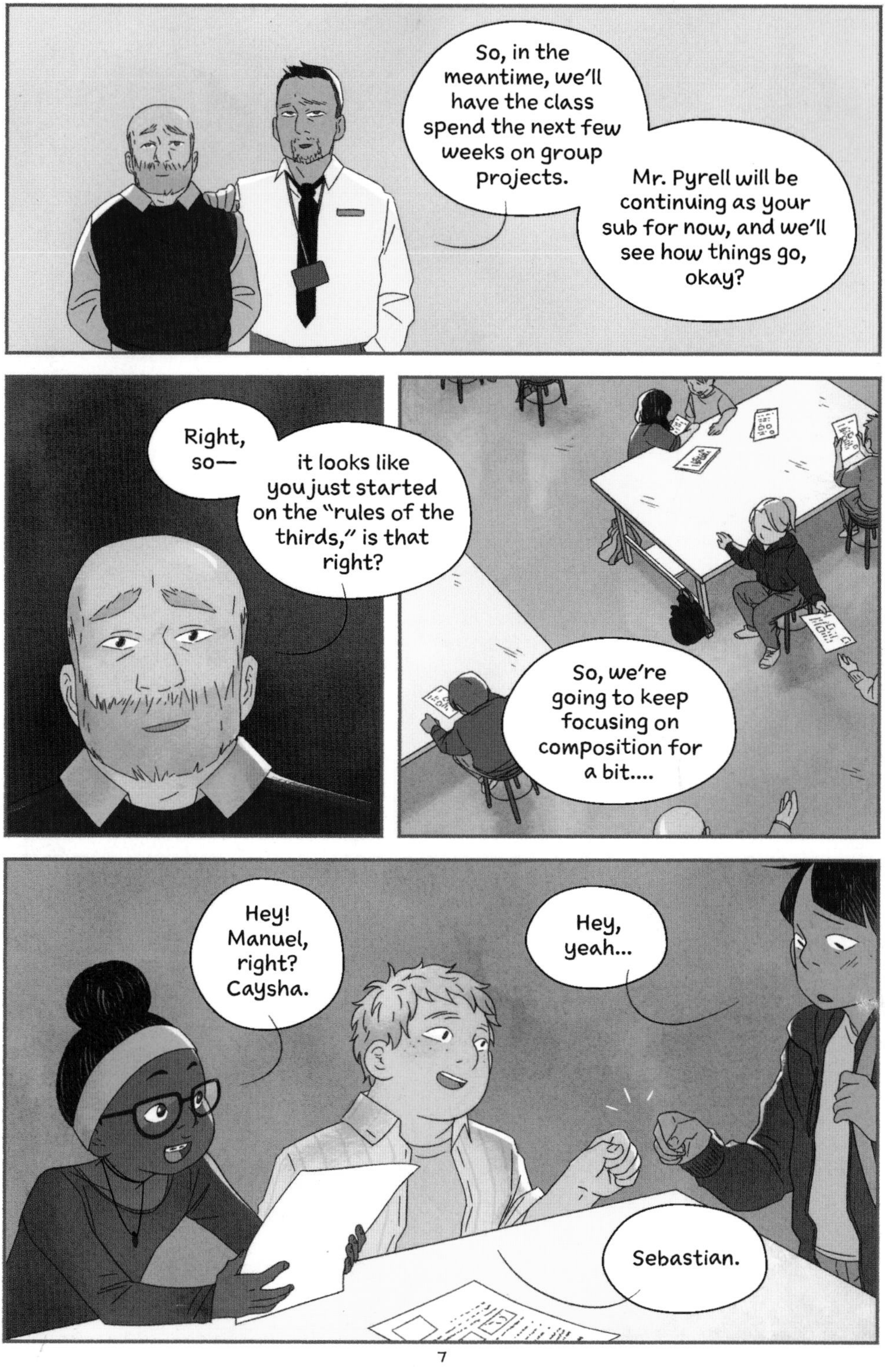
So, in the meantime, we'll have the class spend the next few weeks on group projects.
Mr. Pyrell will be continuing as your sub for now, and we'll see how things go, okay?
Right, so—
it looks like you just started on the "rules of the thirds," is that right?
So, we're going to keep focusing on composition for a bit....
Hey! Manuel, right? Caysha.
Hey, yeah...
Sebastian.

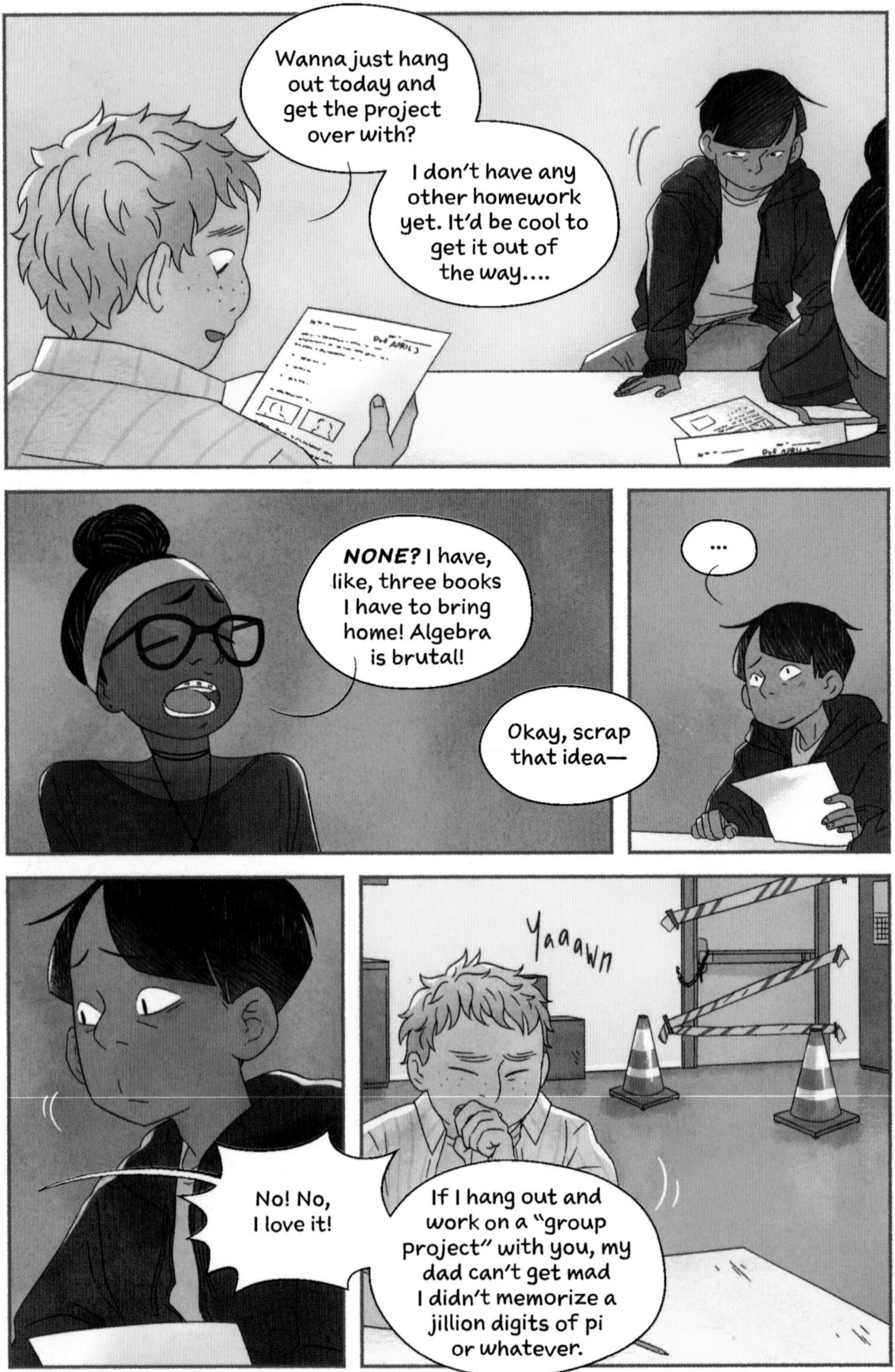

Wanna just hang out today and get the project over with?
I don't have any other homework yet. It'd be cool to get it out of the way....
DUE APRIL 3
NONE? I have, like, three books I have to bring home! Algebra is brutal!
...
Okay, scrap that idea—
Yaaawn
No! No, I love it!
If I hang out and work on a "group project" with you, my dad can't get mad I didn't memorize a jillion digits of pi or whatever.

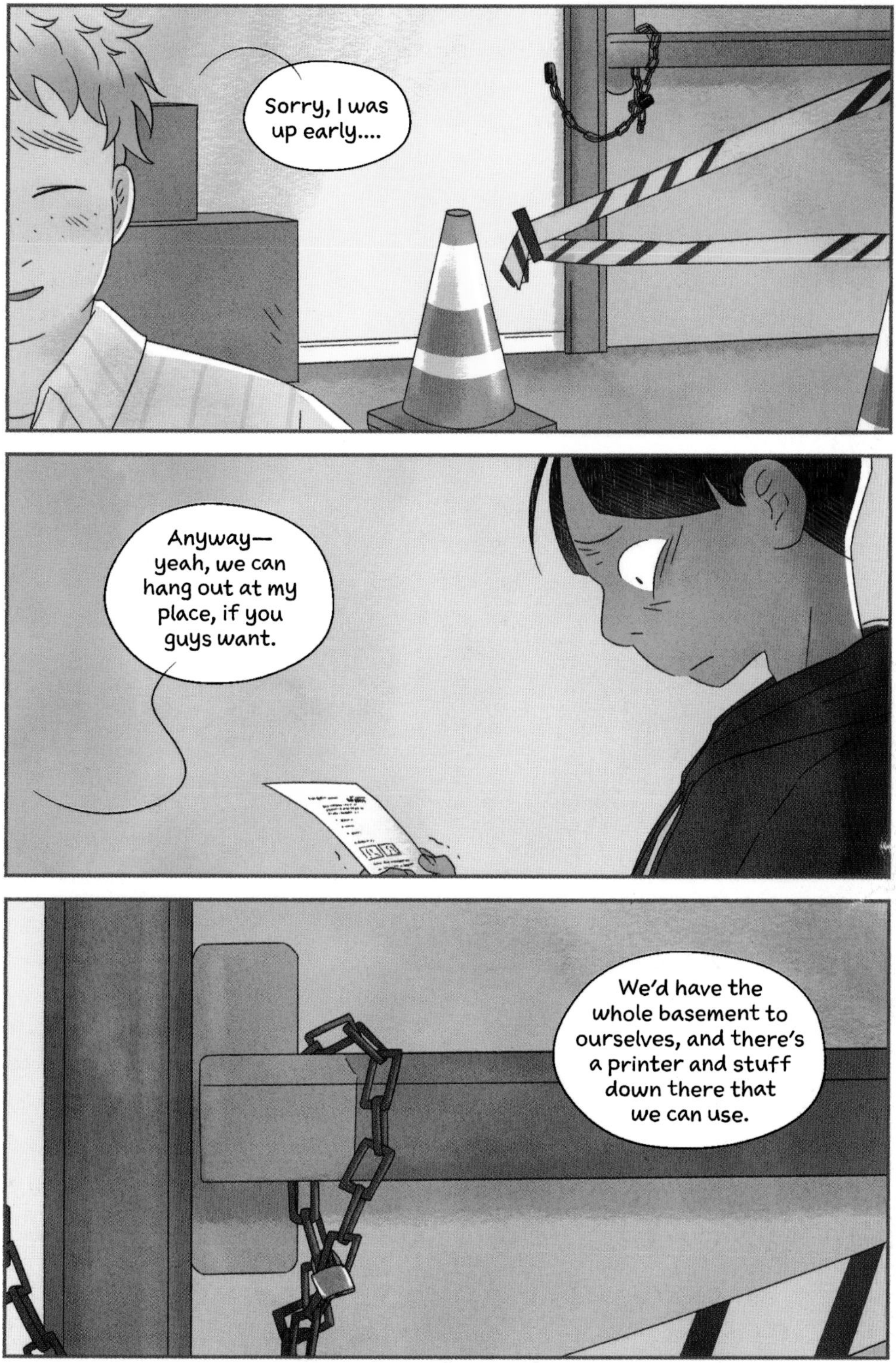
Sorry, I was up early....
Anyway—yeah, we can hang out at my place, if you guys want.
We'd have the whole basement to ourselves, and there's a printer and stuff down there that we can use.

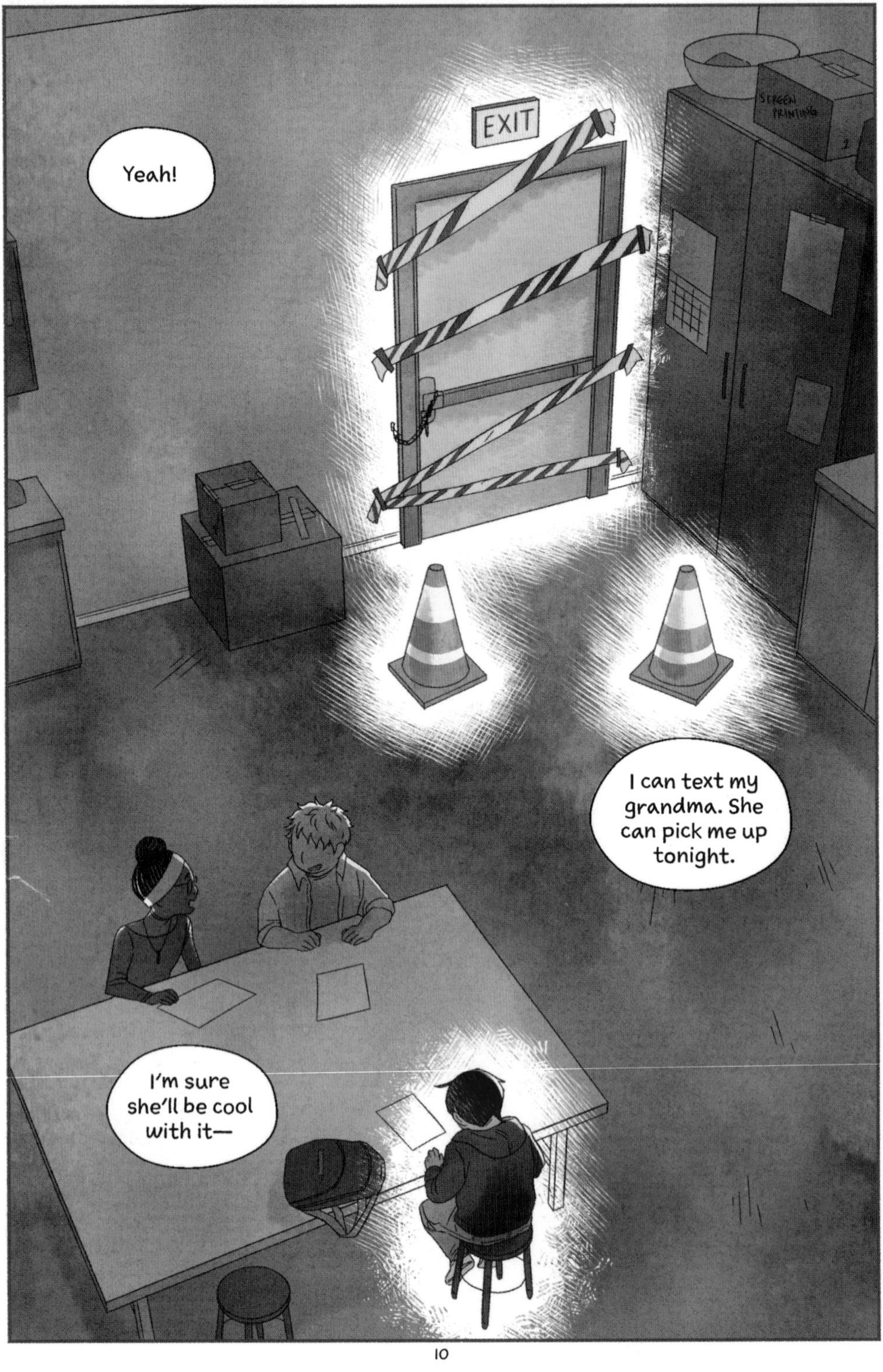
Yeah!
EXIT
SCREEN PRINTING
I can text my grandma. She can pick me up tonight.
I'm sure she'll be cool with it—

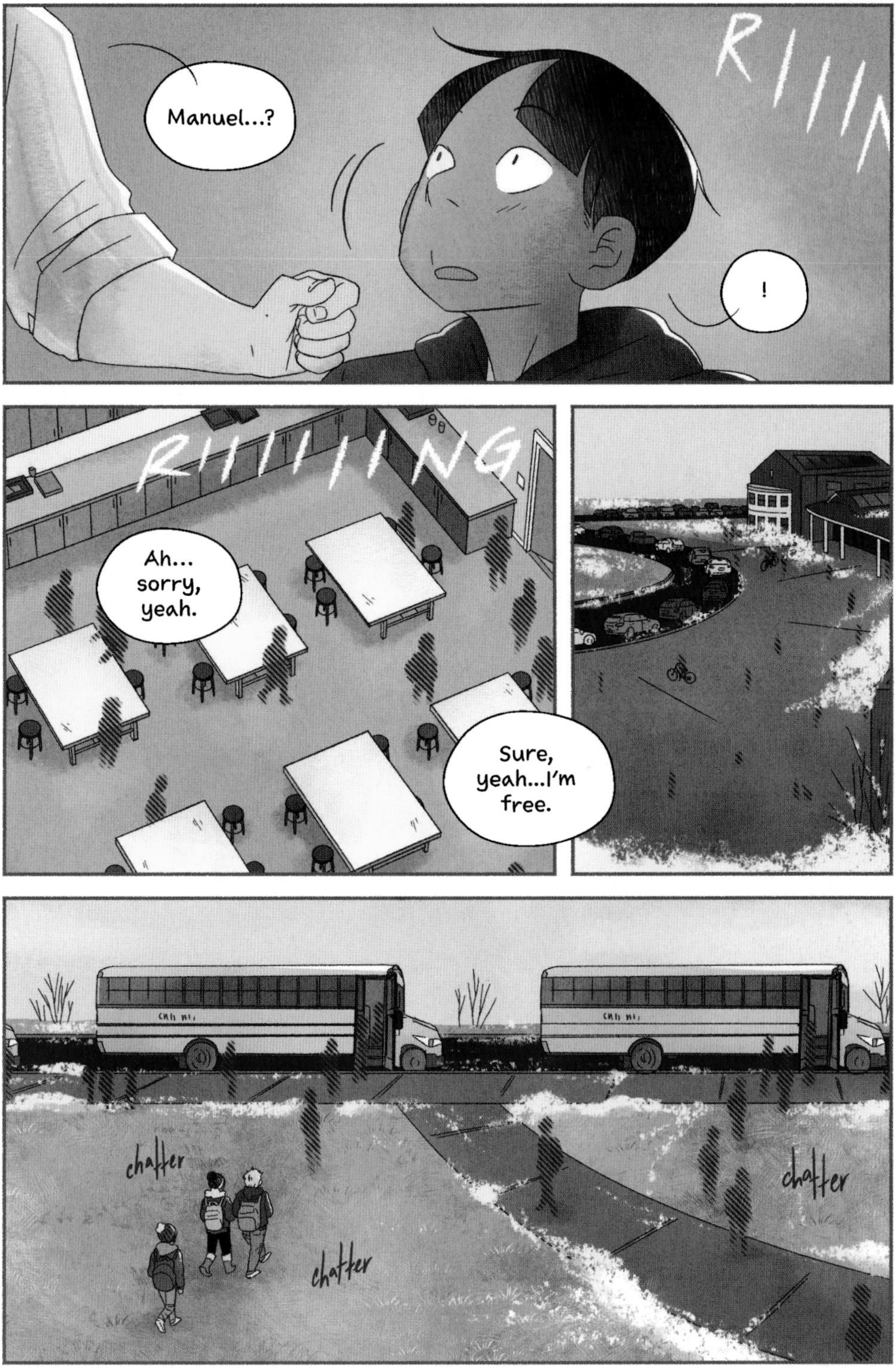
Manuel...?
RIIIN
!
RIIIIING
Ah... sorry, yeah.
Sure, yeah...I'm free.
chatter
chatter
chatter

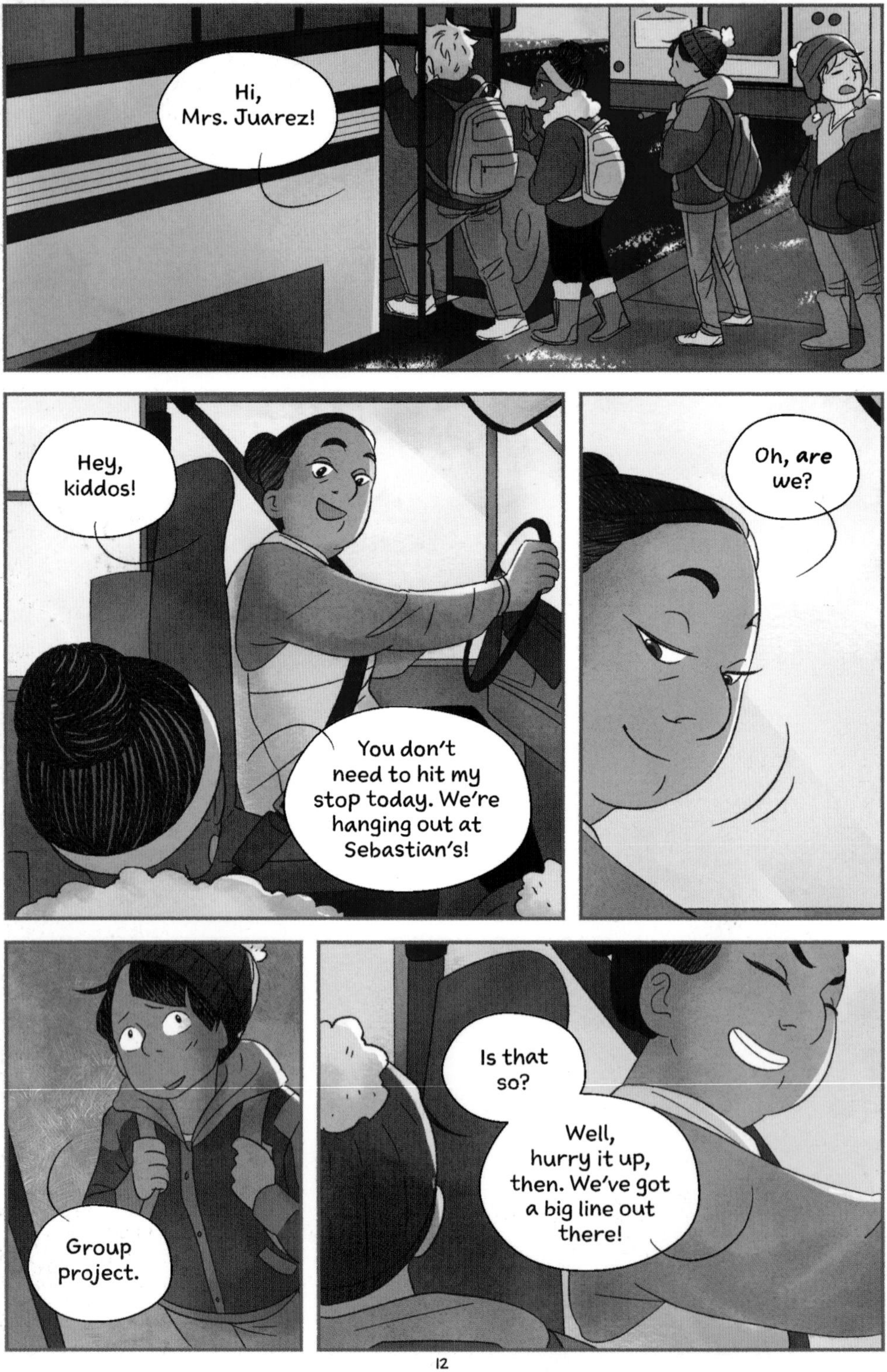
Hi, Mrs. Juarez!
Hey, kiddos!
You don't need to hit my stop today. We're hanging out at Sebastian's!
Oh, **are** we?
Group project.
Is that so?
Well, hurry it up, then. We've got a big line out there!

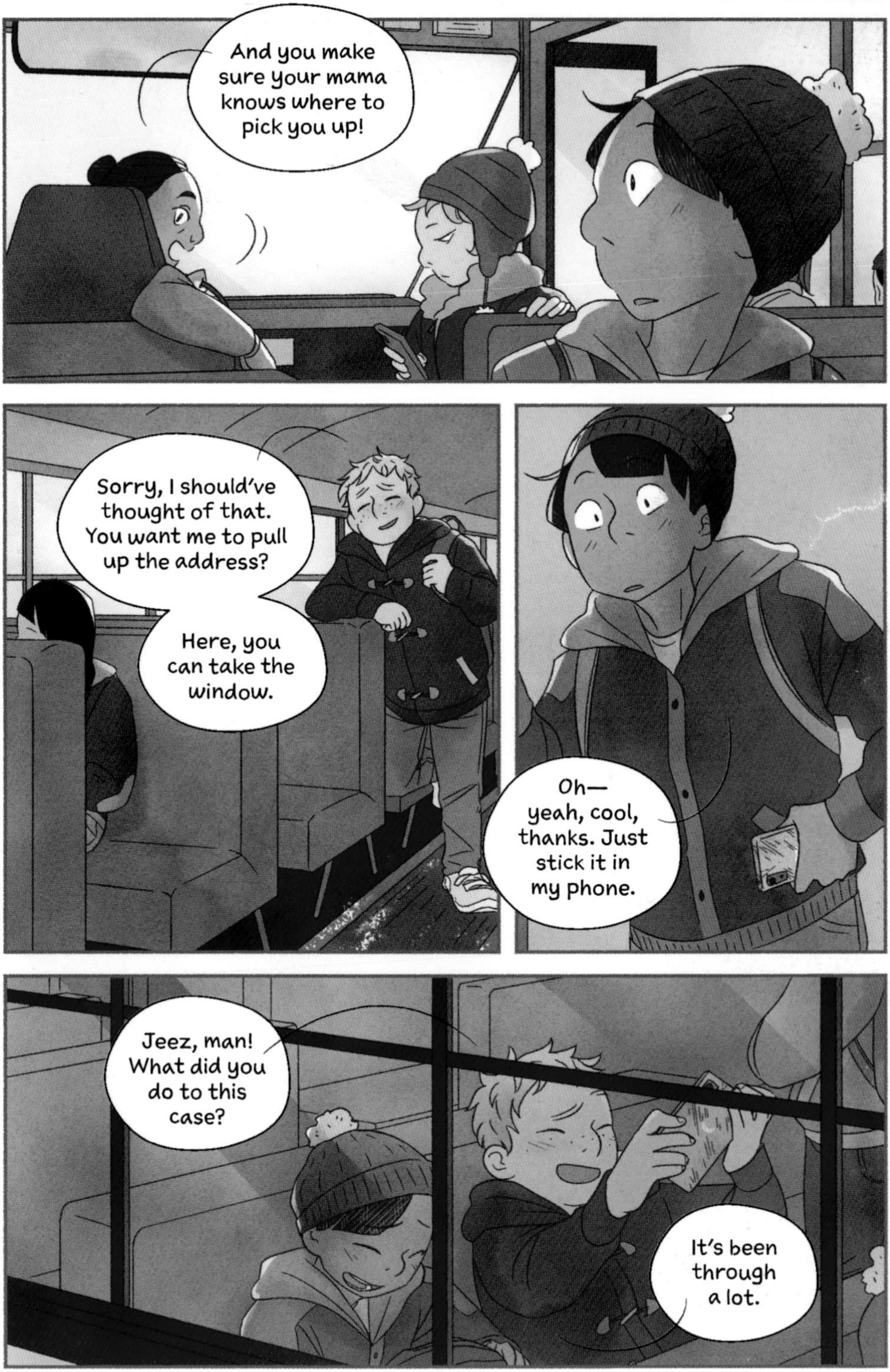
And you make sure your mama knows where to pick you up!
Sorry, I should've thought of that. You want me to pull up the address?
Here, you can take the window.
Oh—yeah, cool, thanks. Just stick it in my phone.
Jeez, man! What did you do to this case?
It's been through a lot.

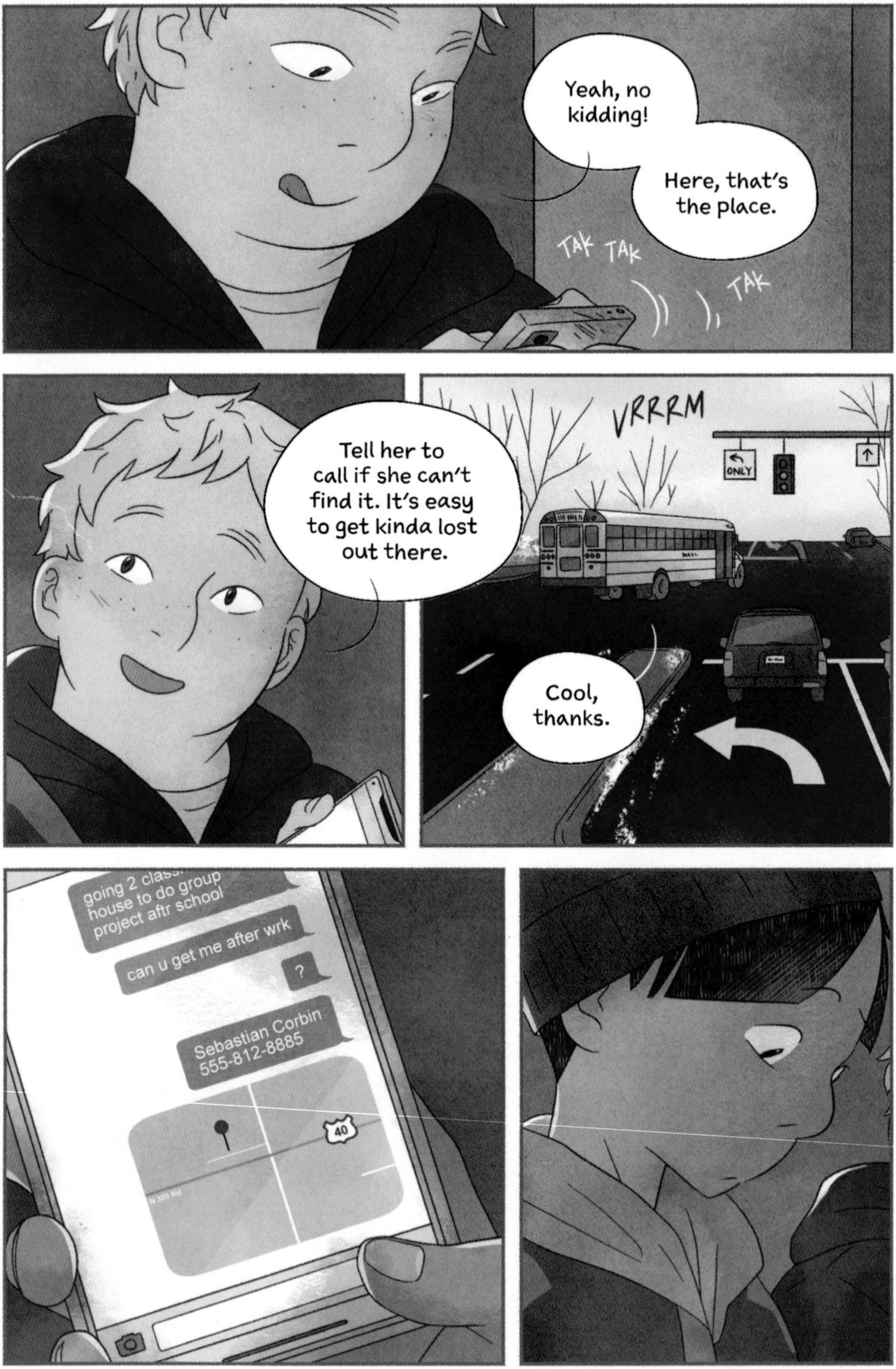
Yeah, no kidding!
Here, that's the place.
TAK TAK
TAK
Tell her to call if she can't find it. It's easy to get kinda lost out there.
VRRRM
ONLY
Cool, thanks.
going 2 class
house to do group project aftr school
can u get me after wrk
?
Sebastian Corbin
555-812-8885
40

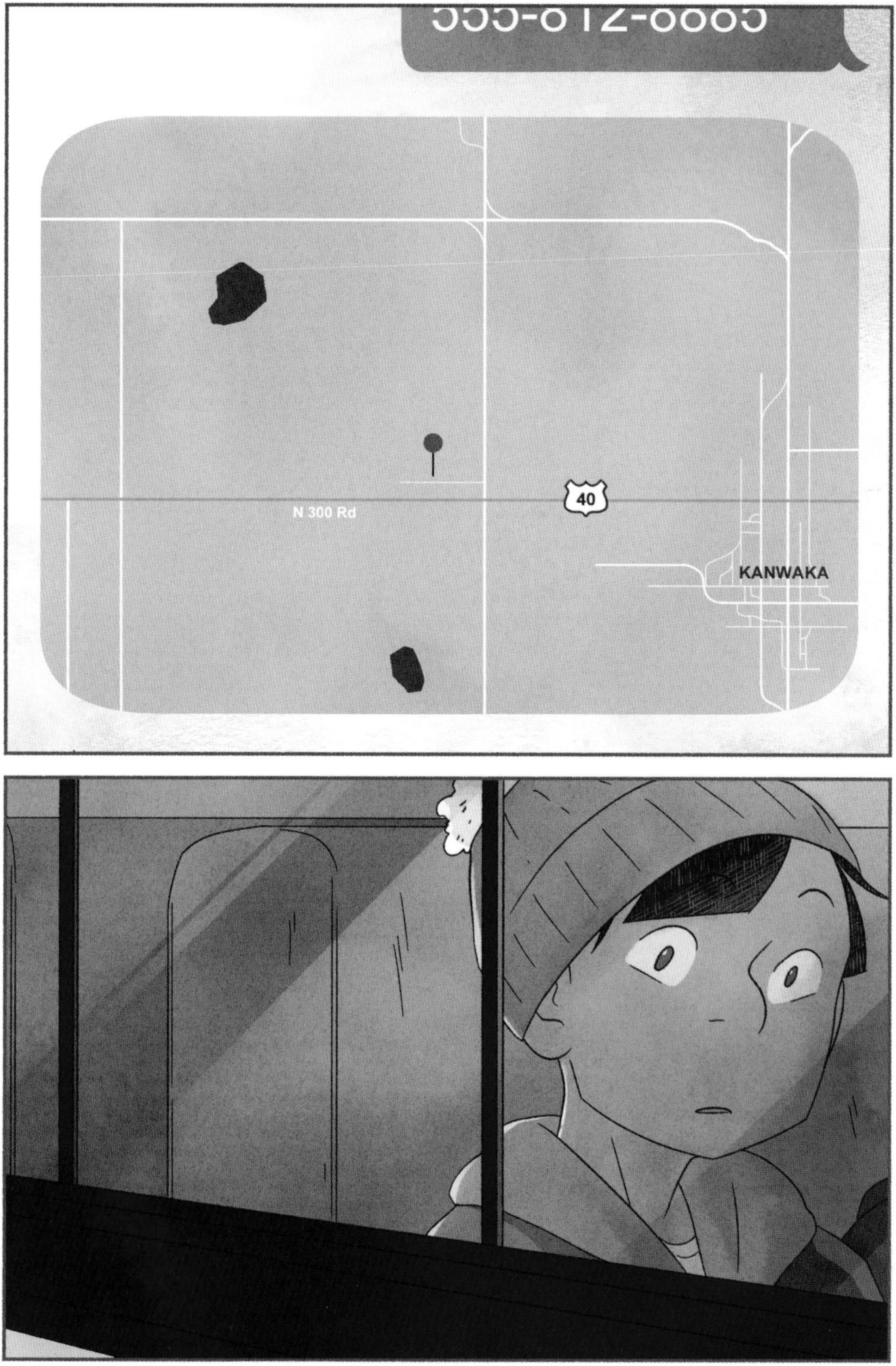
N 300 Rd
40
KANWAKA

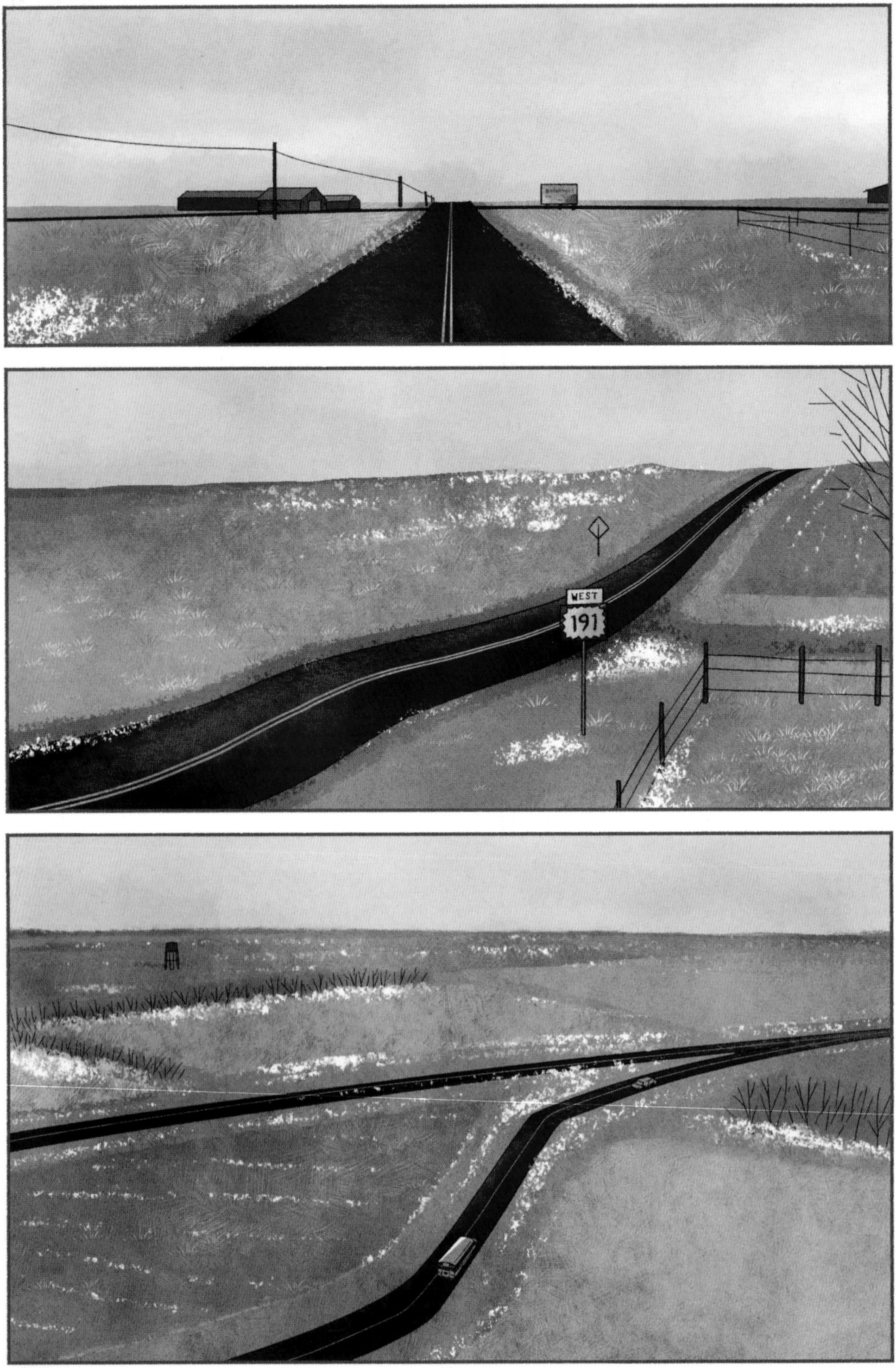
WEST
191

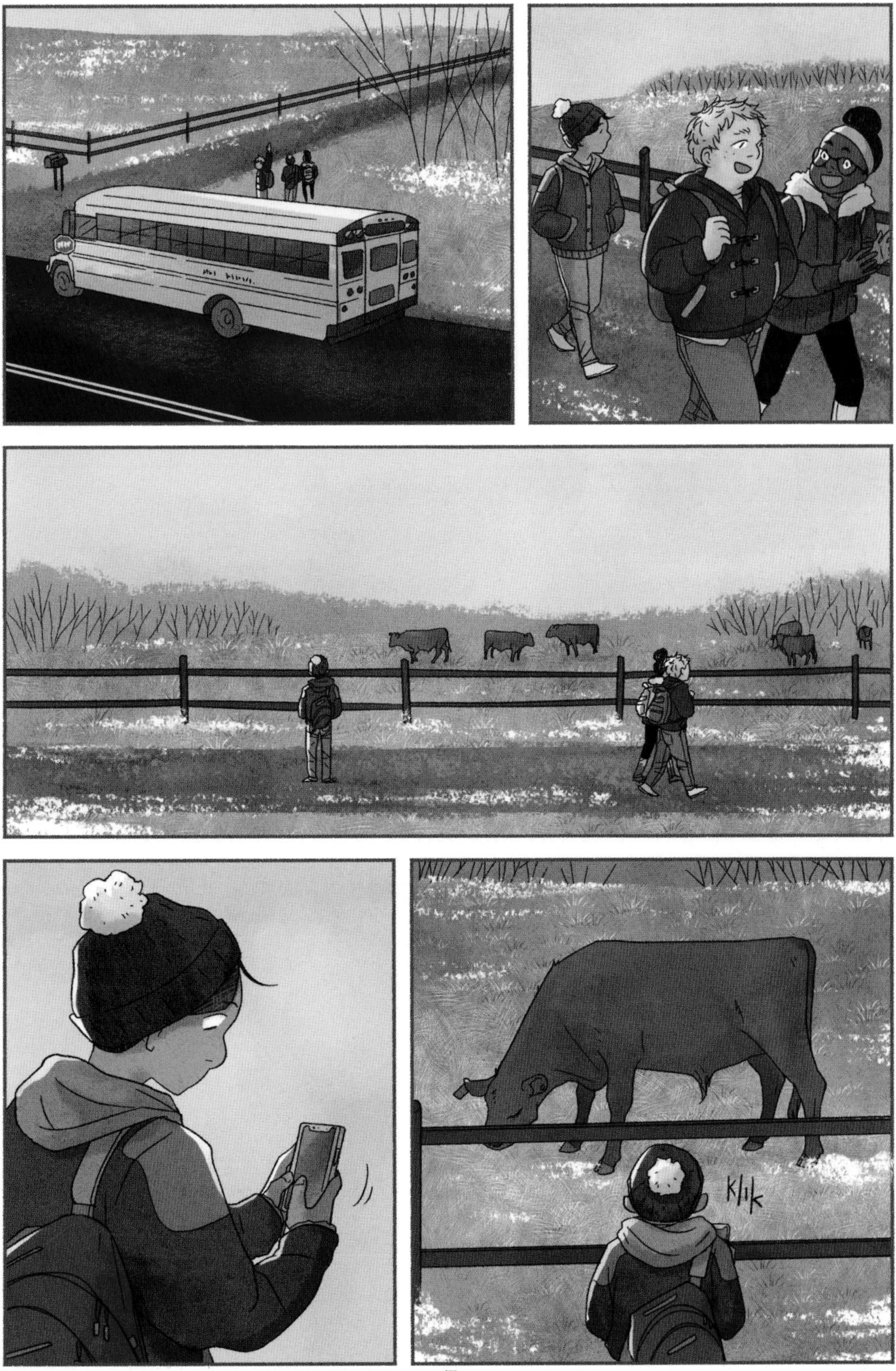
KLIK

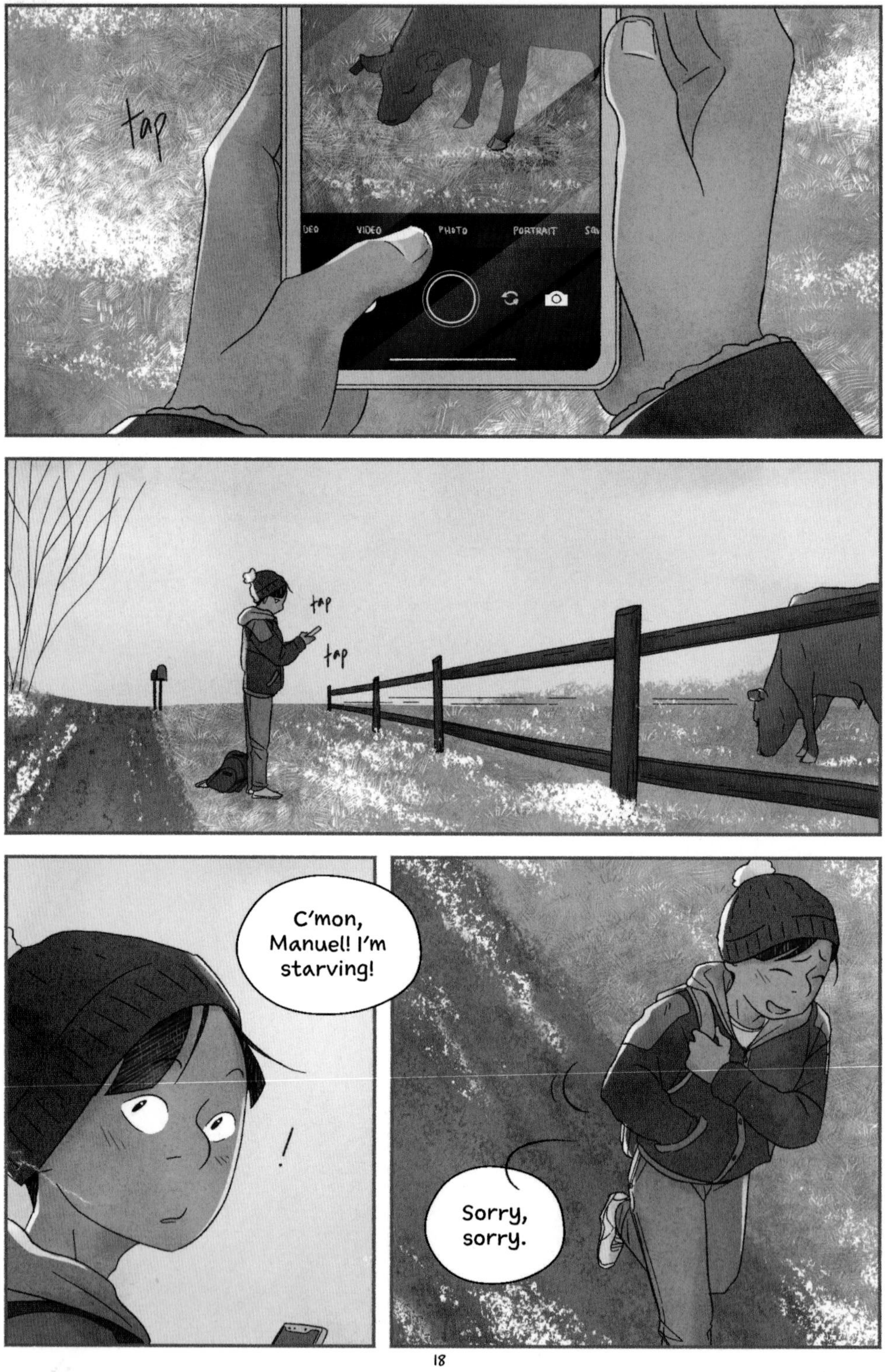
tap
VIDEO
PHOTO
PORTRAIT
tap
tap
C'mon, Manuel! I'm starving!
!
Sorry, sorry.

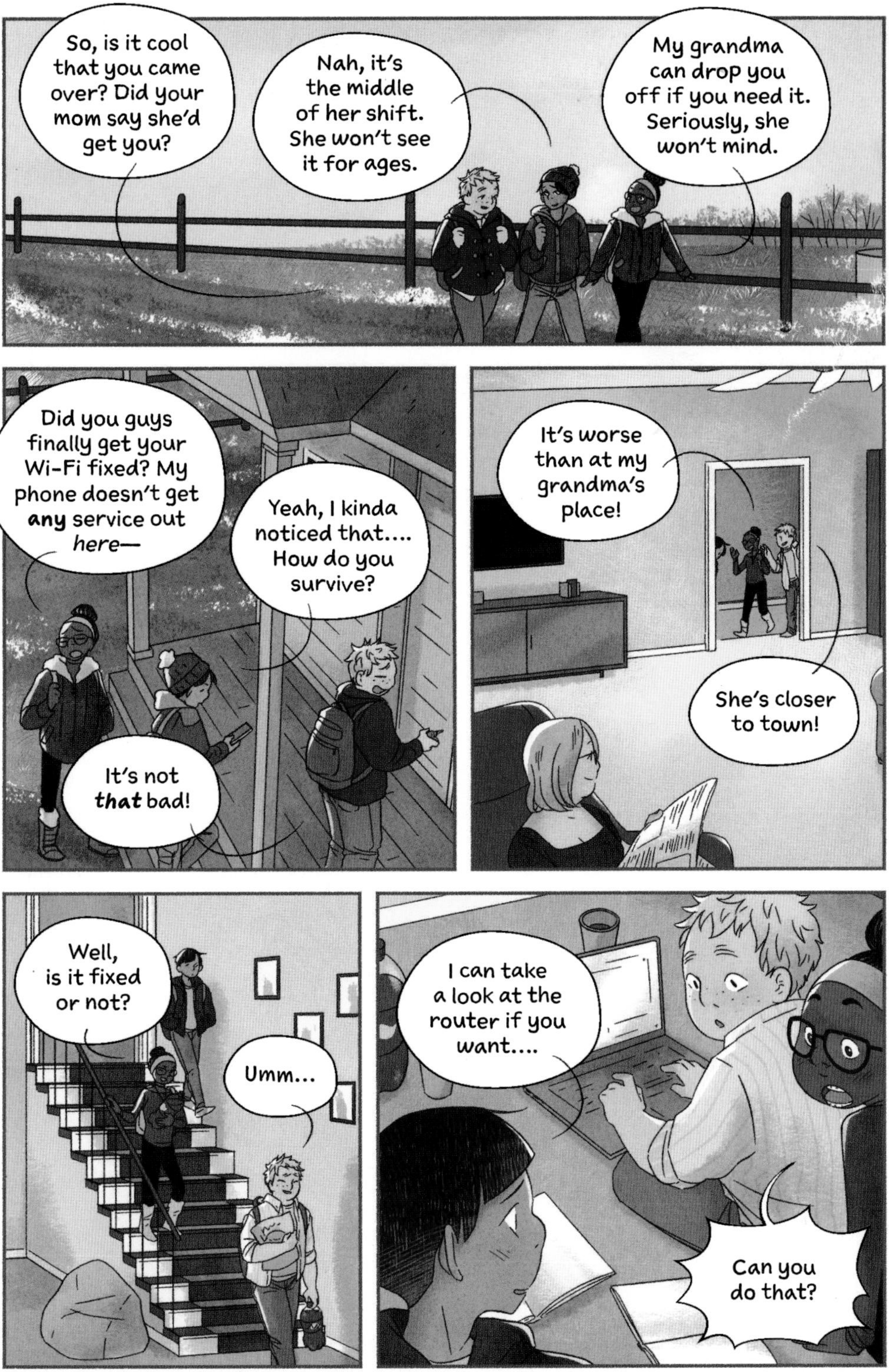
So, is it cool that you came over? Did your mom say she'd get you?
Nah, it's the middle of her shift. She won't see it for ages.
My grandma can drop you off if you need it. Seriously, she won't mind.
Did you guys finally get your Wi-Fi fixed? My phone doesn't get **any** service out *here*—
Yeah, I kinda noticed that.... How do you survive?
It's not **that** bad!
It's worse than at my grandma's place!
She's closer to town!
Well, is it fixed or not?
Umm...
I can take a look at the router if you want....
Can you do that?

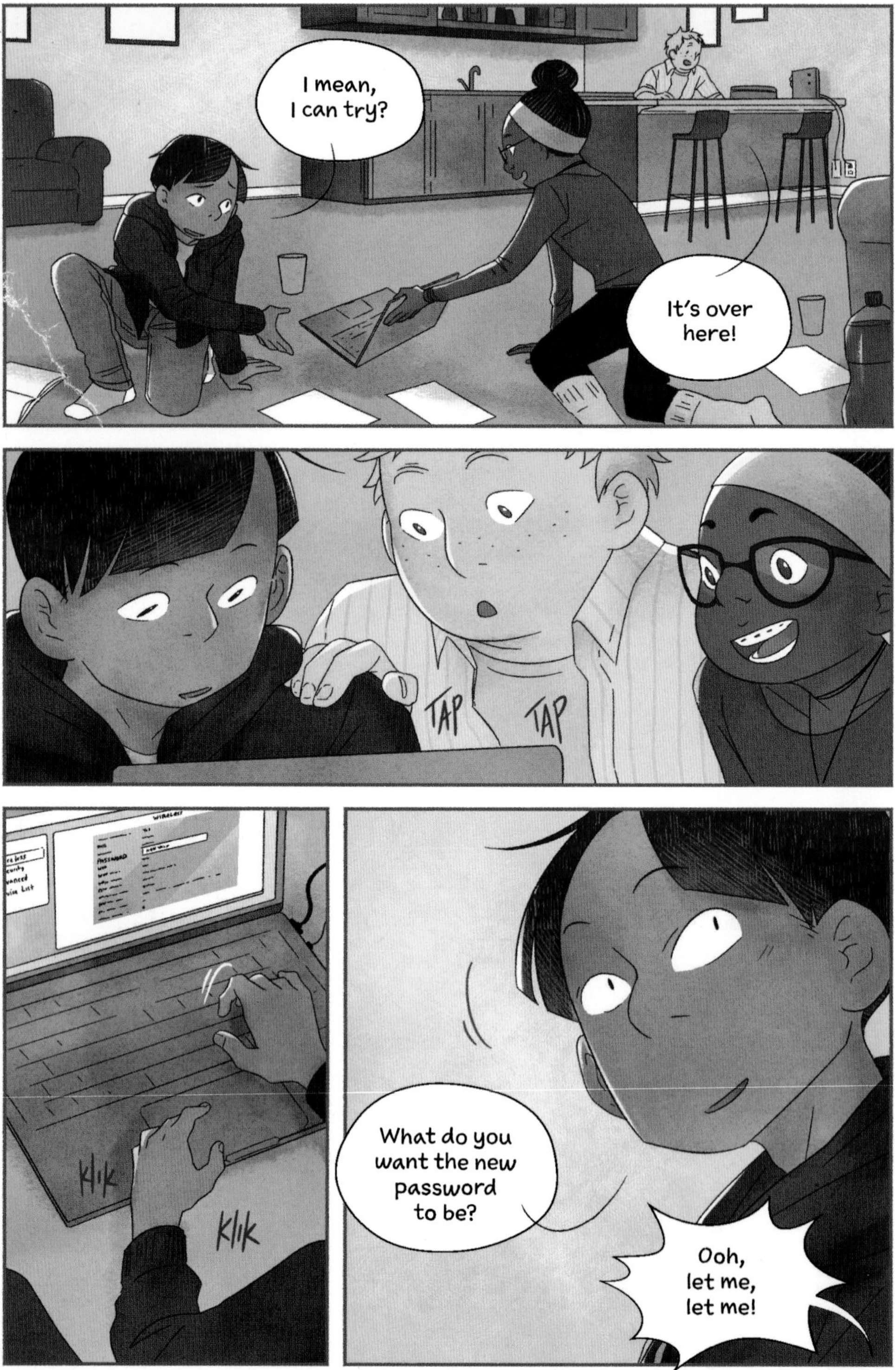
I mean, I can try?
It's over here!
TAP
TAP
KLIK
KLIK
What do you want the new password to be?
Ooh, let me, let me!

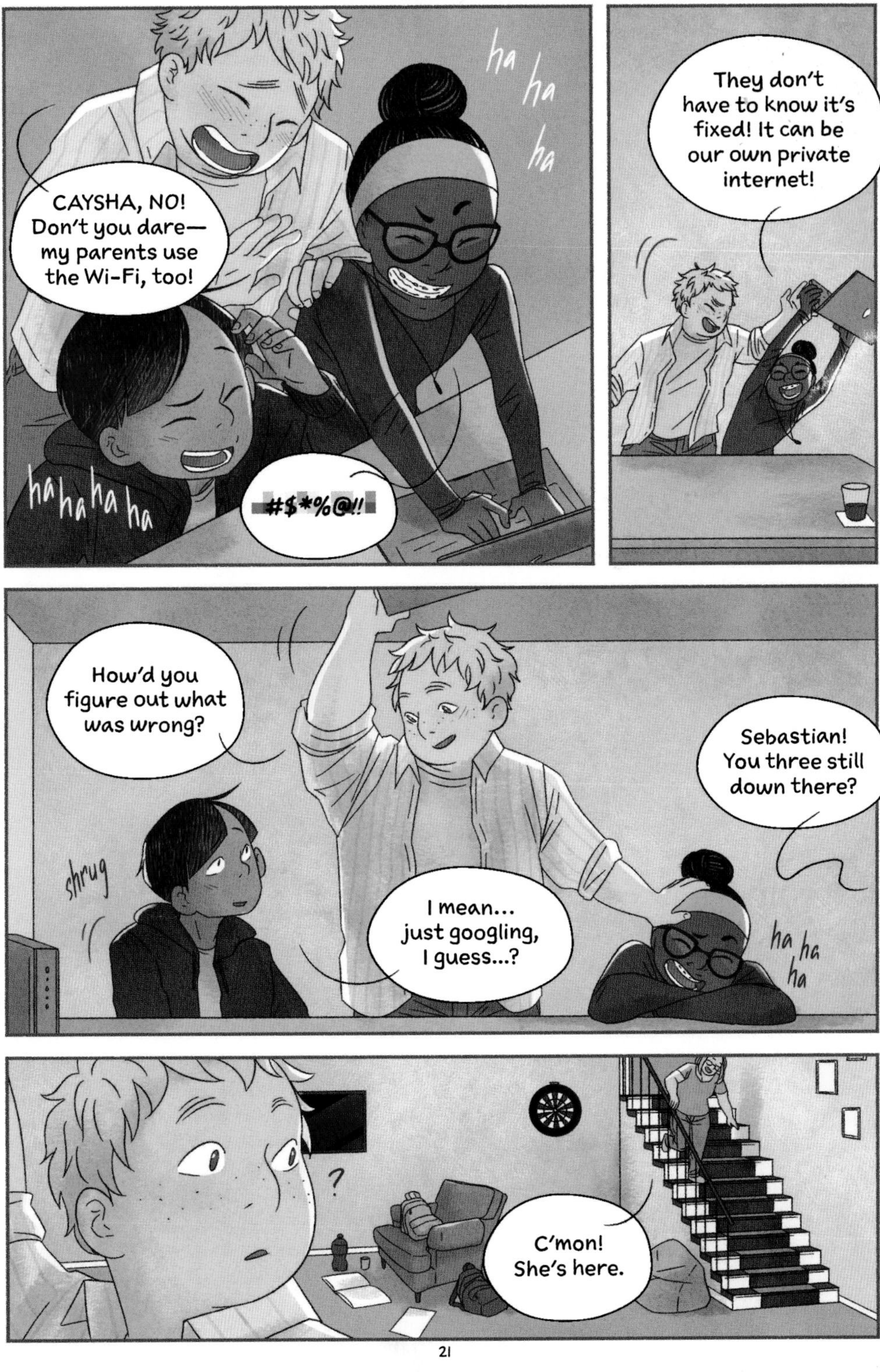
ha ha ha
CAYSHA, NO! Don't you dare— my parents use the Wi-Fi, too!
ha ha ha ha ha
#$*%@!!
They don't have to know it's fixed! It can be our own private internet!
How'd you figure out what was wrong?
Sebastian! You three still down there?
shrug
I mean... just googling, I guess...?
ha ha ha
?
C'mon! She's here.

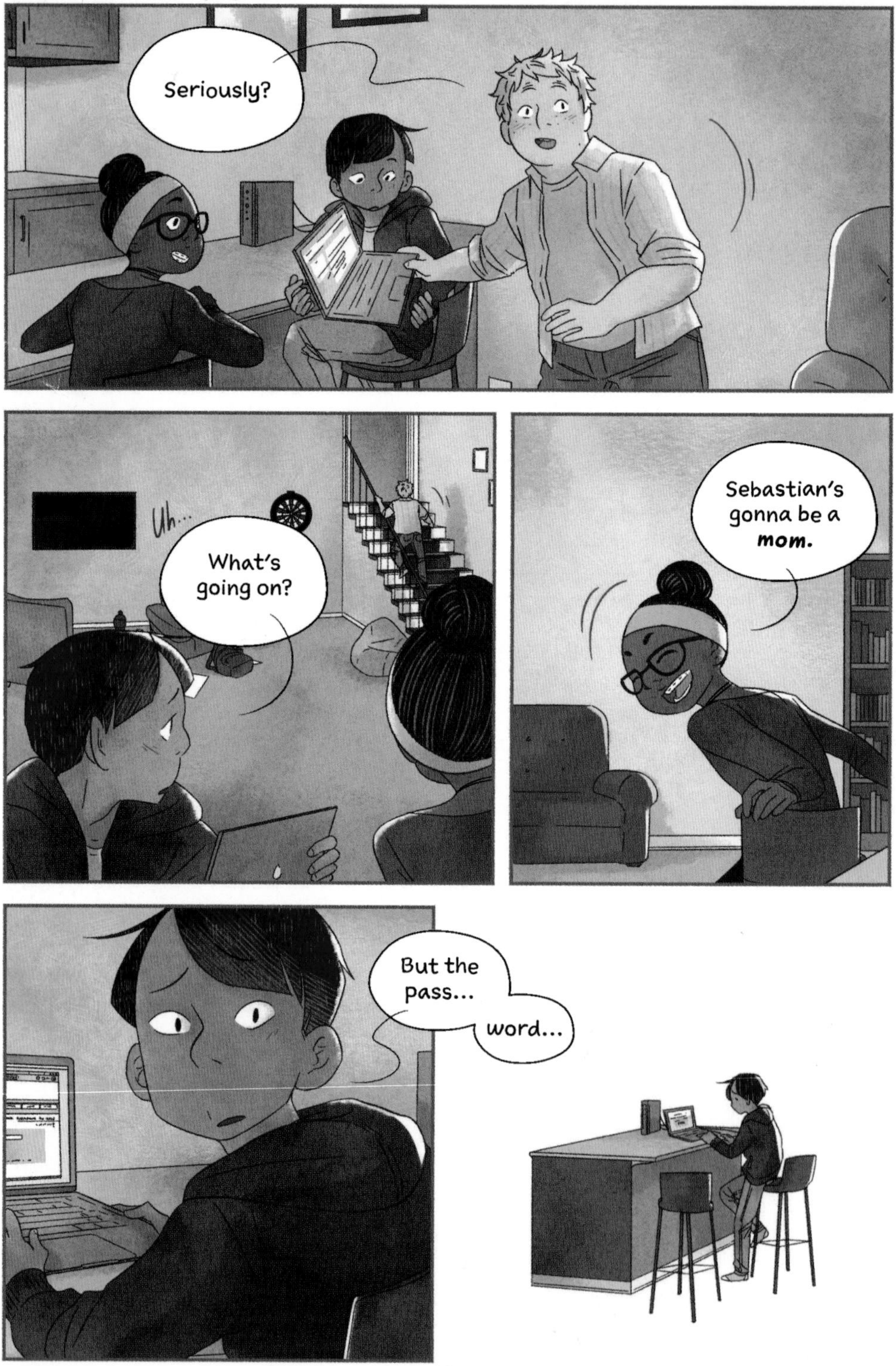
Seriously?
Uh...
What's going on?
Sebastian's gonna be a **mom.**
But the pass...
word...

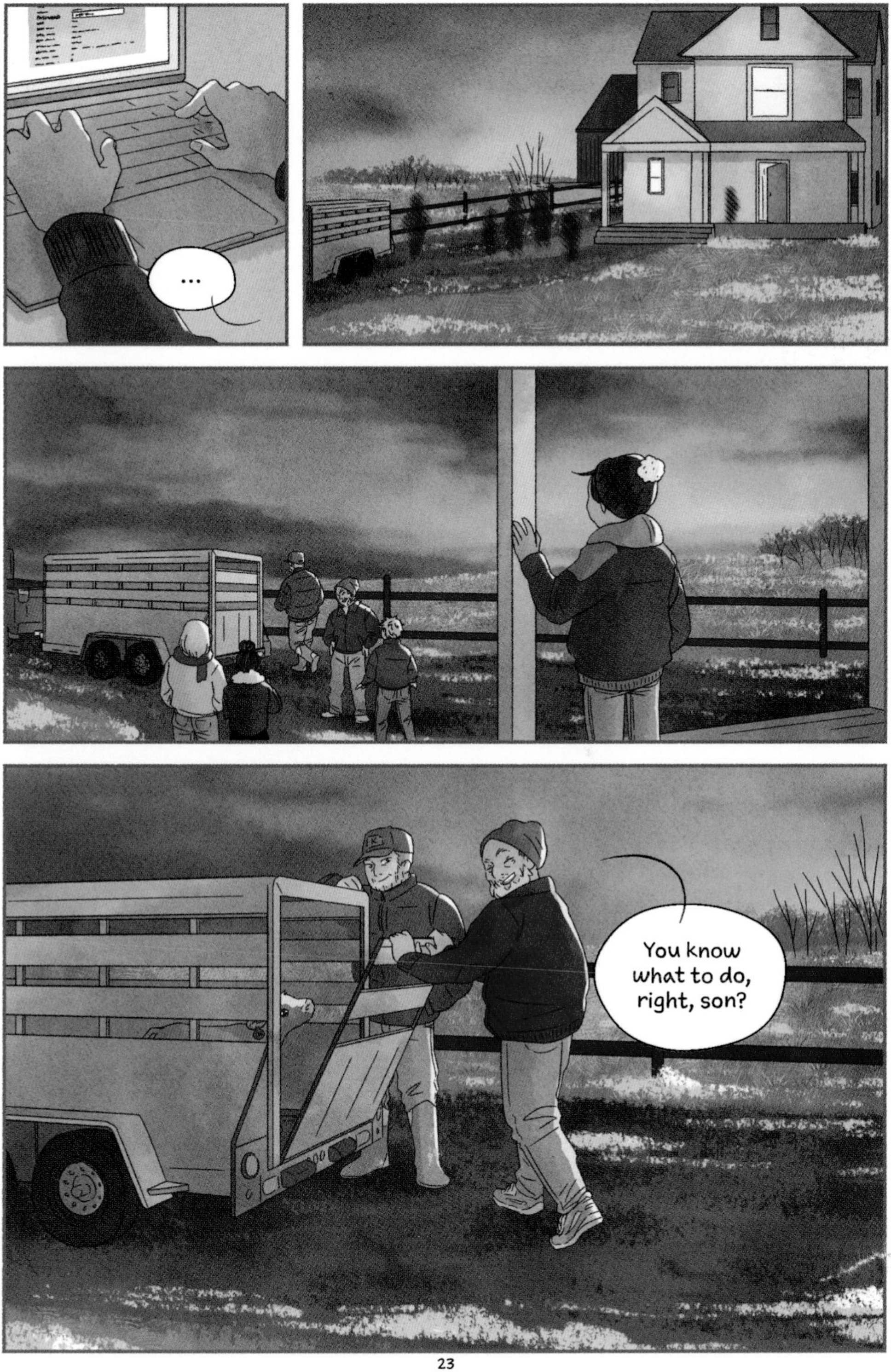
...
You know what to do, right, son?

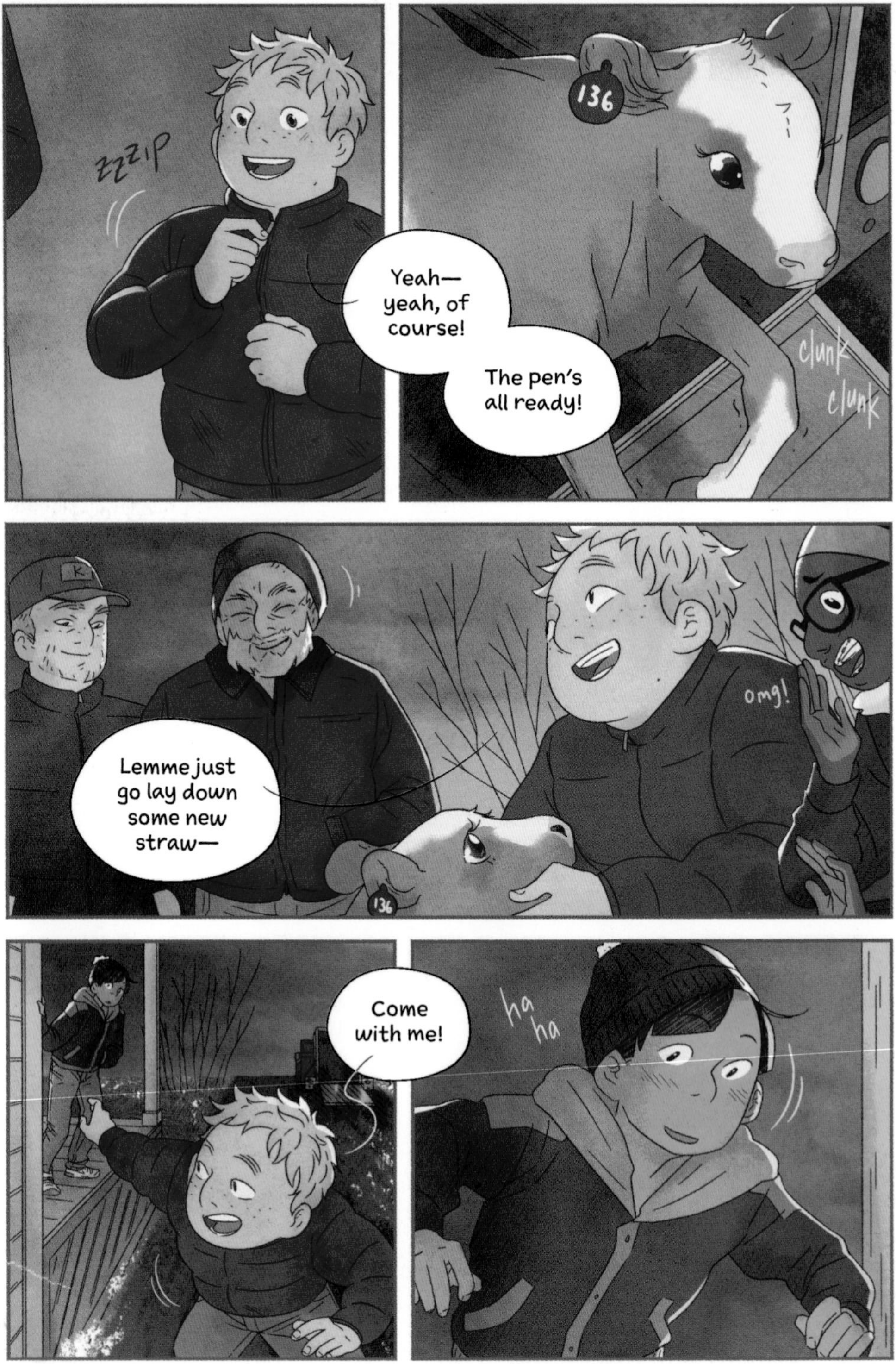
zzzip
Yeah—yeah, of course!
136
The pen's all ready!
clunk
clunk
Lemme just go lay down some new straw—
omg!
136
Come with me!
ha ha

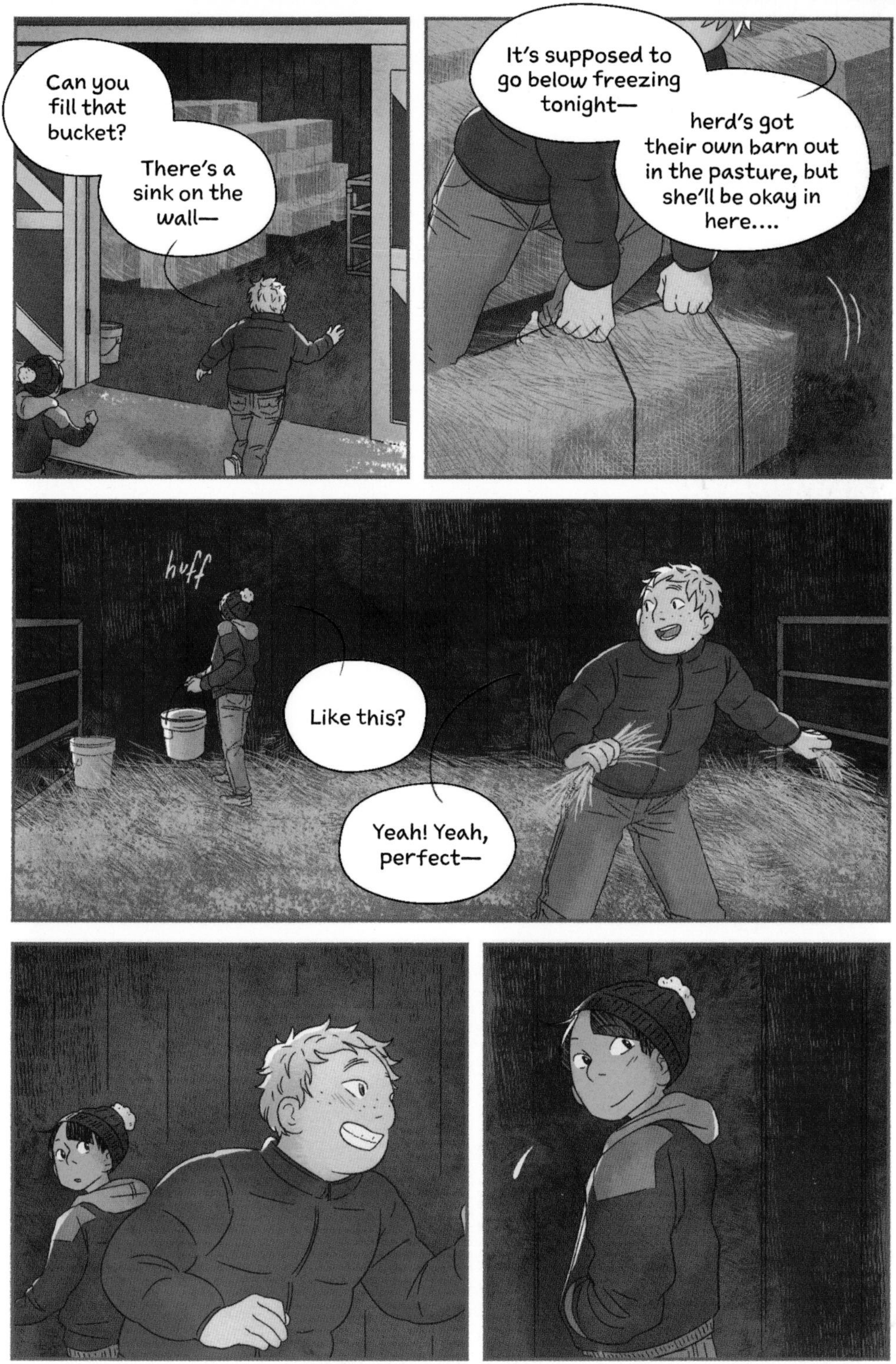
Can you fill that bucket?
There's a sink on the wall—
It's supposed to go below freezing tonight—
herd's got their own barn out in the pasture, but she'll be okay in here....
huff
Like this?
Yeah! Yeah, perfect—

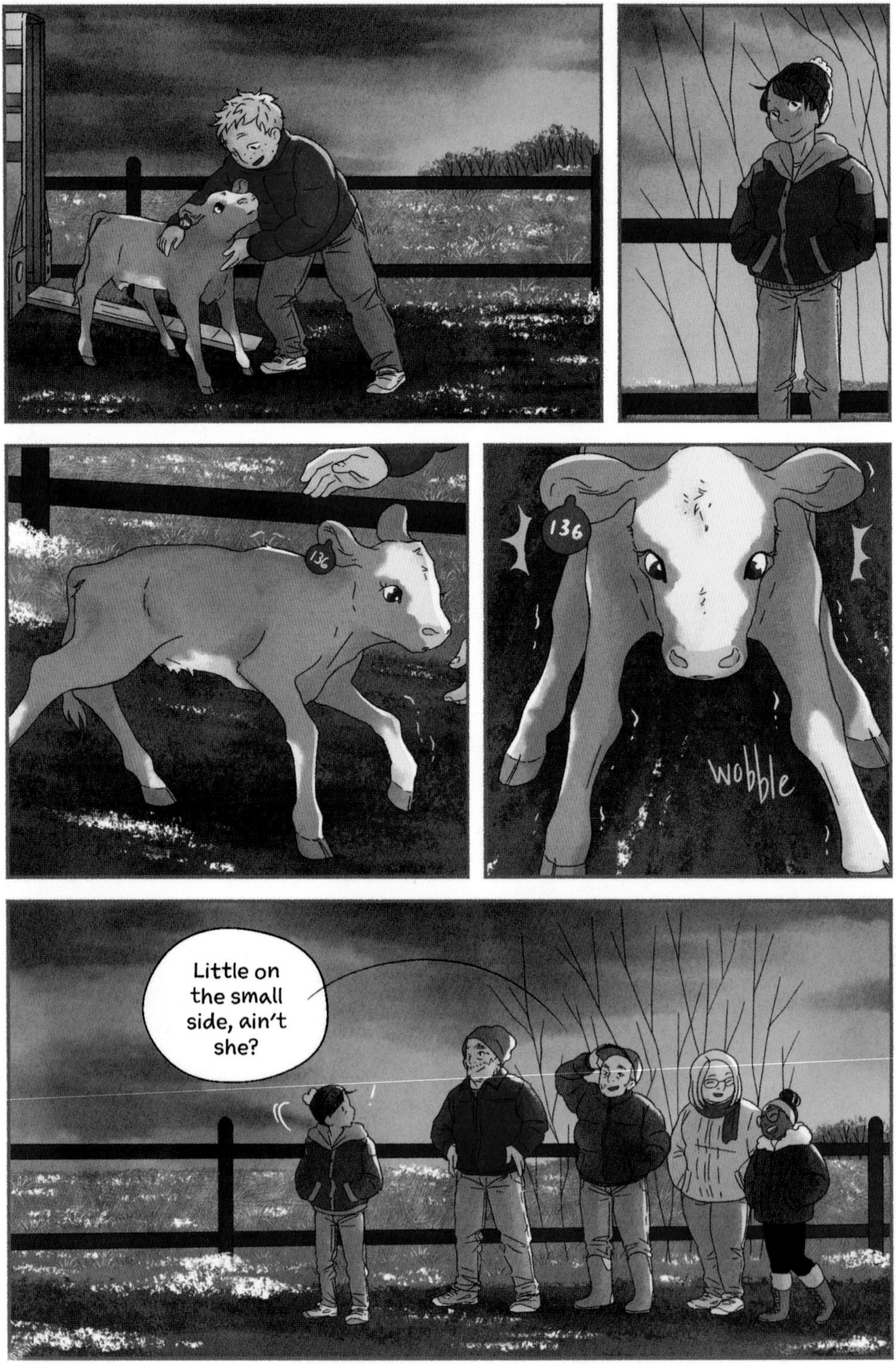
136
136
136
wobble
Little on the small side, ain't she?

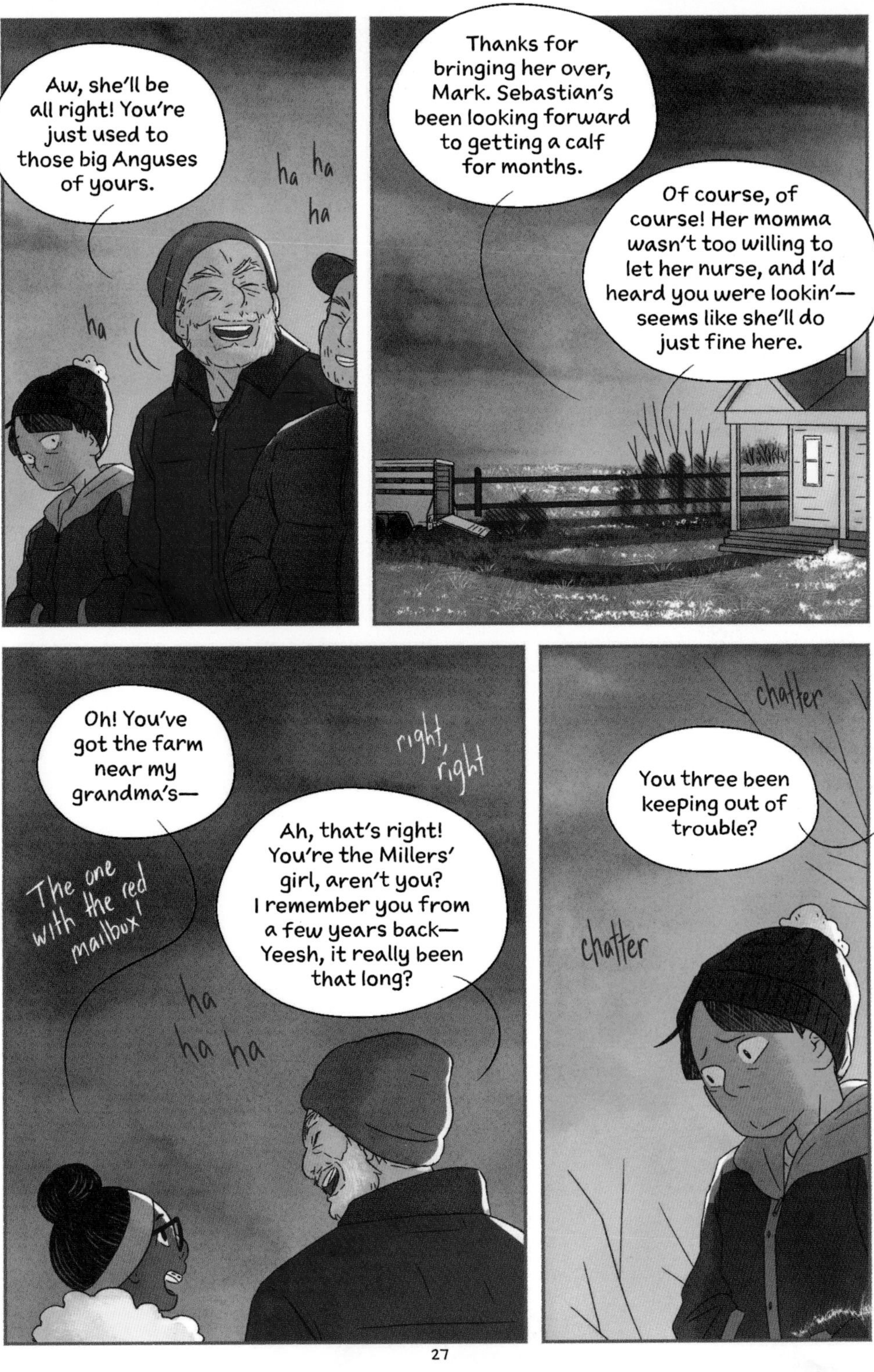
Aw, she'll be all right! You're just used to those big Anguses of yours.
ha ha ha
ha
Thanks for bringing her over, Mark. Sebastian's been looking forward to getting a calf for months.
Of course, of course! Her momma wasn't too willing to let her nurse, and I'd heard you were lookin'— seems like she'll do just fine here.
Oh! You've got the farm near my grandma's—
The one with the red mailbox!
right, right
Ah, that's right! You're the Millers' girl, aren't you? I remember you from a few years back— Yeesh, it really been that long?
ha ha ha
chatter
You three been keeping out of trouble?
chatter

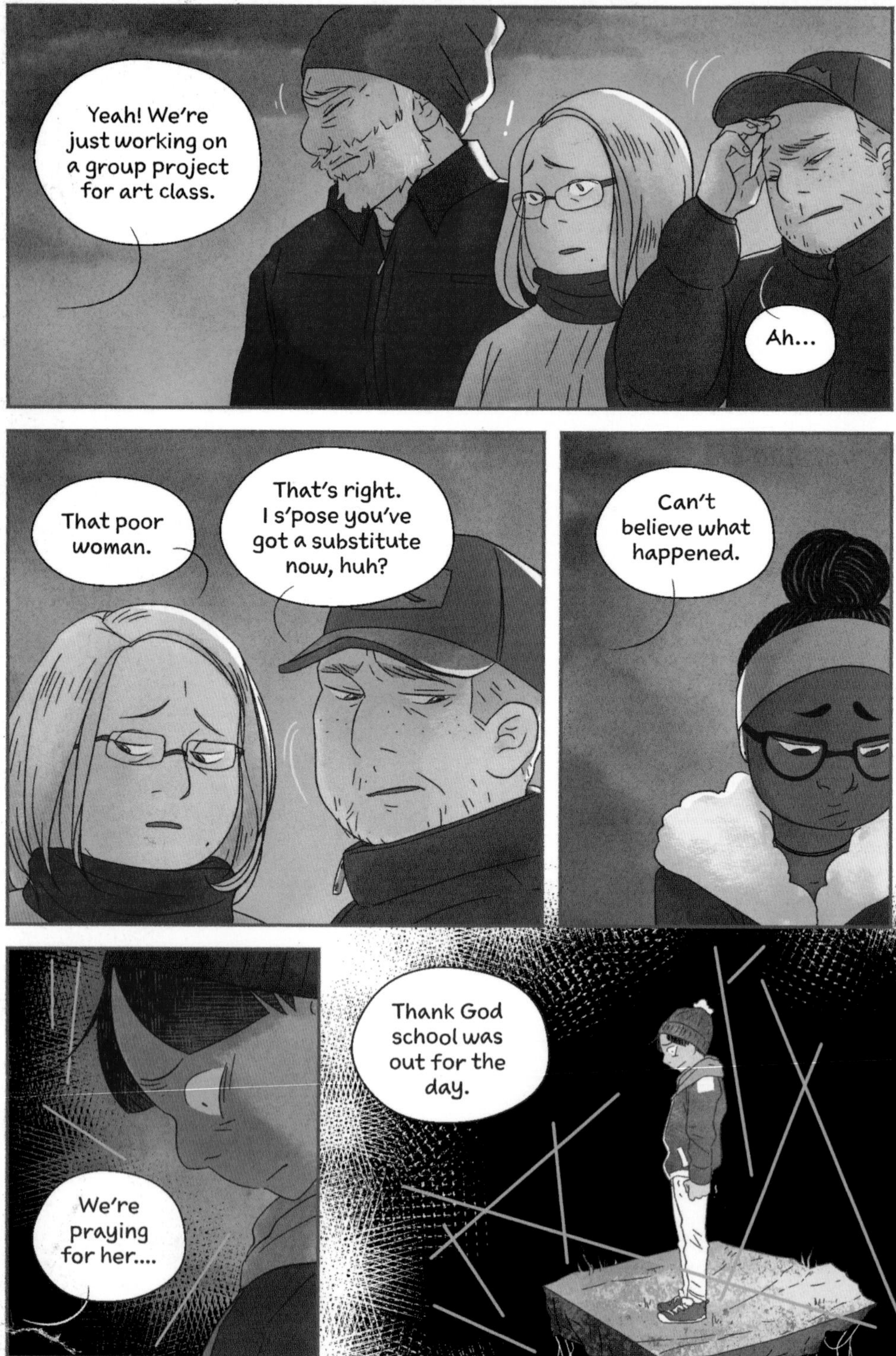
Yeah! We're just working on a group project for art class.
Ah...
That poor woman.
That's right. I s'pose you've got a substitute now, huh?
Can't believe what happened.
We're praying for her....
Thank God school was out for the day.

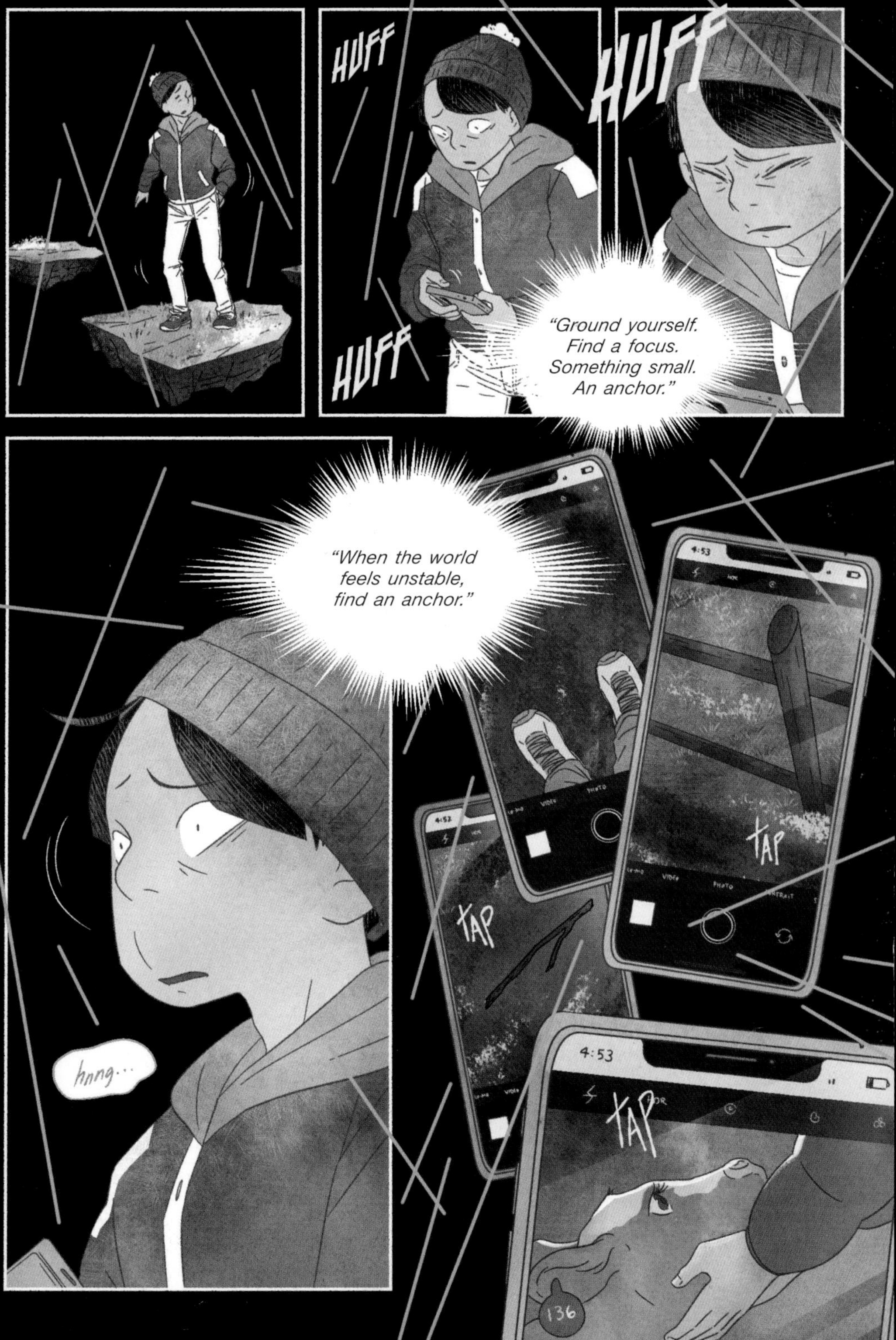
HUFF
HUFF
HUFF
"Ground yourself. Find a focus. Something small. An anchor."
"When the world feels unstable, find an anchor."
hnng...
TAP
TAP
TAP

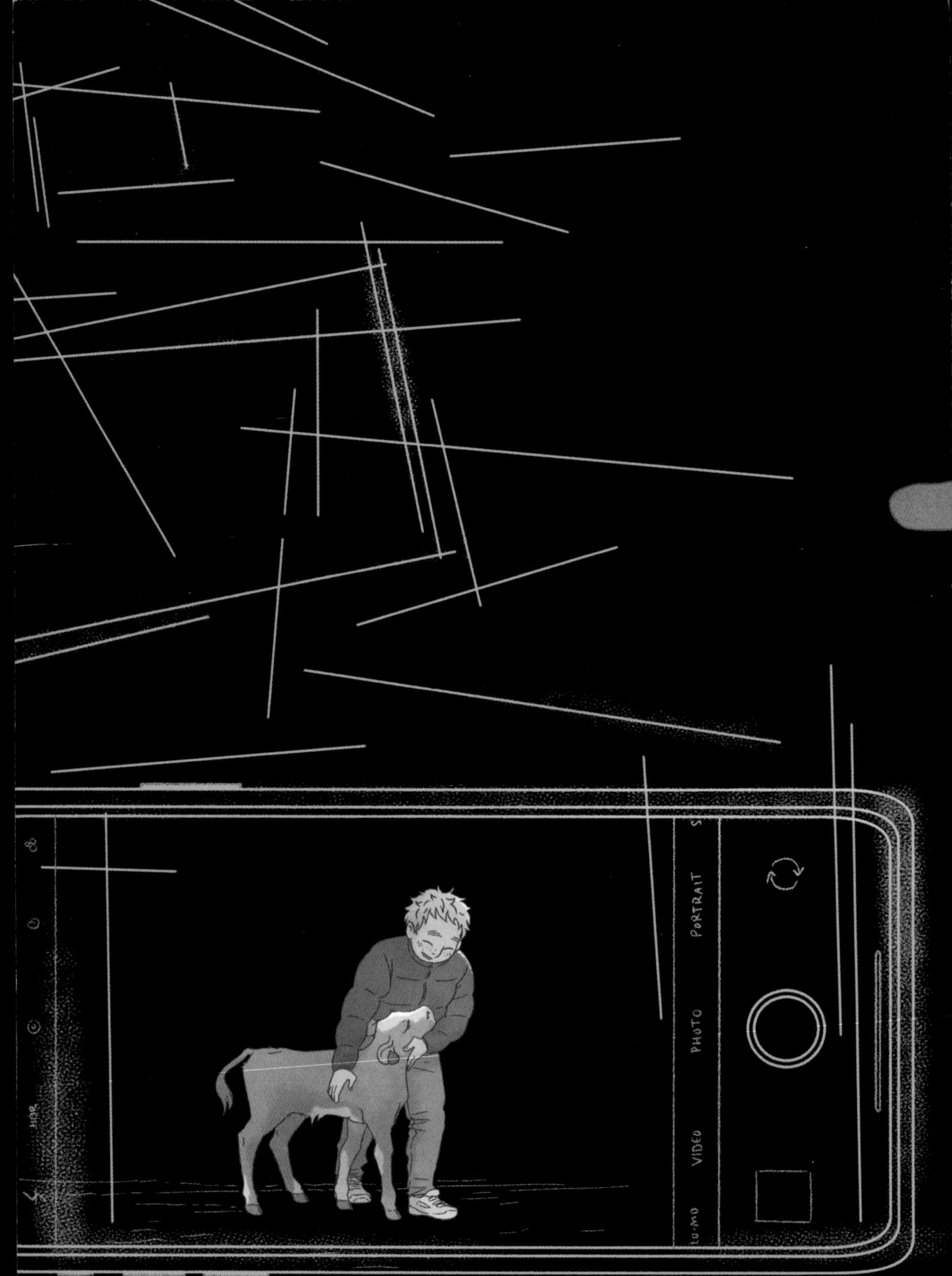
HDR
VIDEO
PHOTO
PORTRAIT

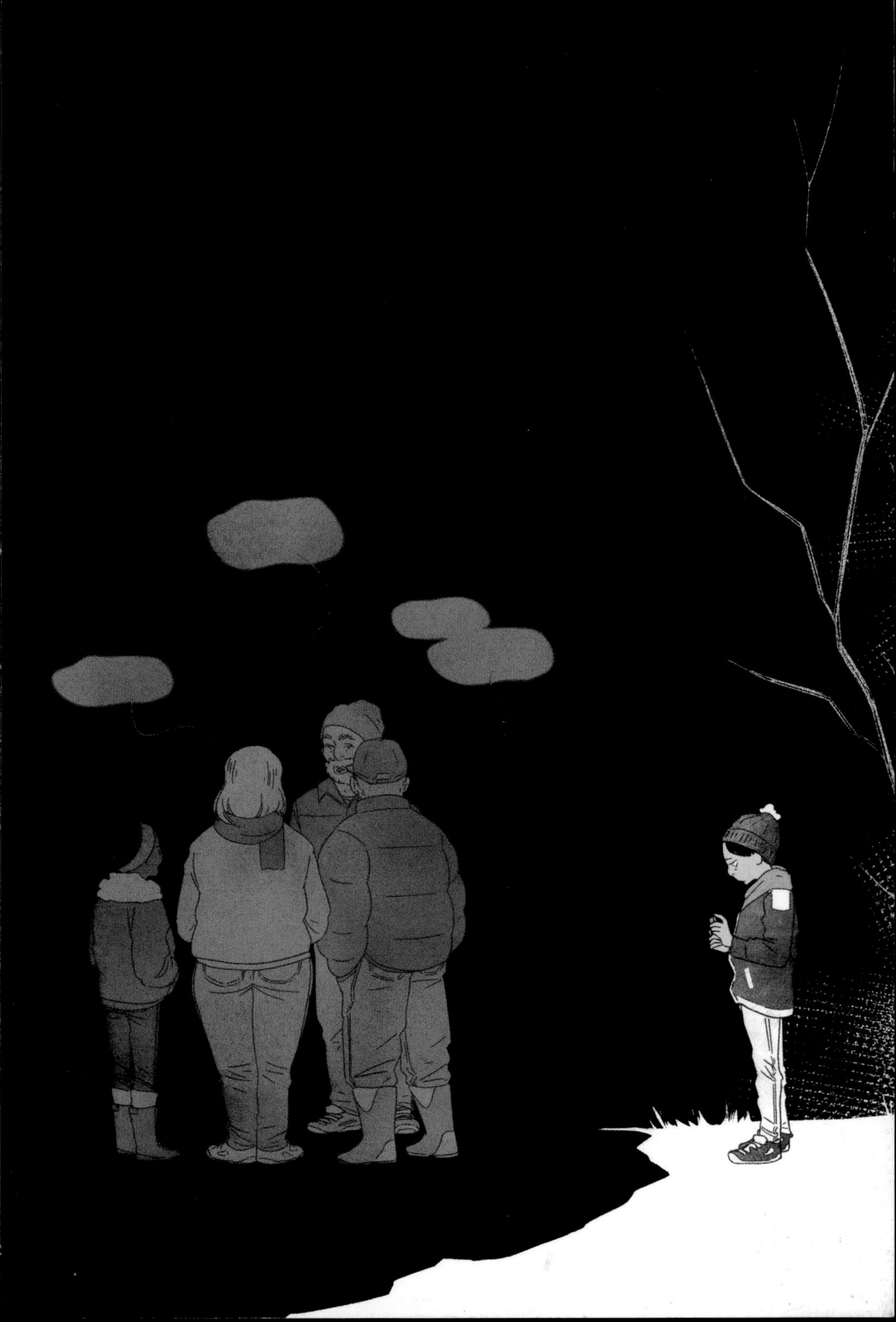

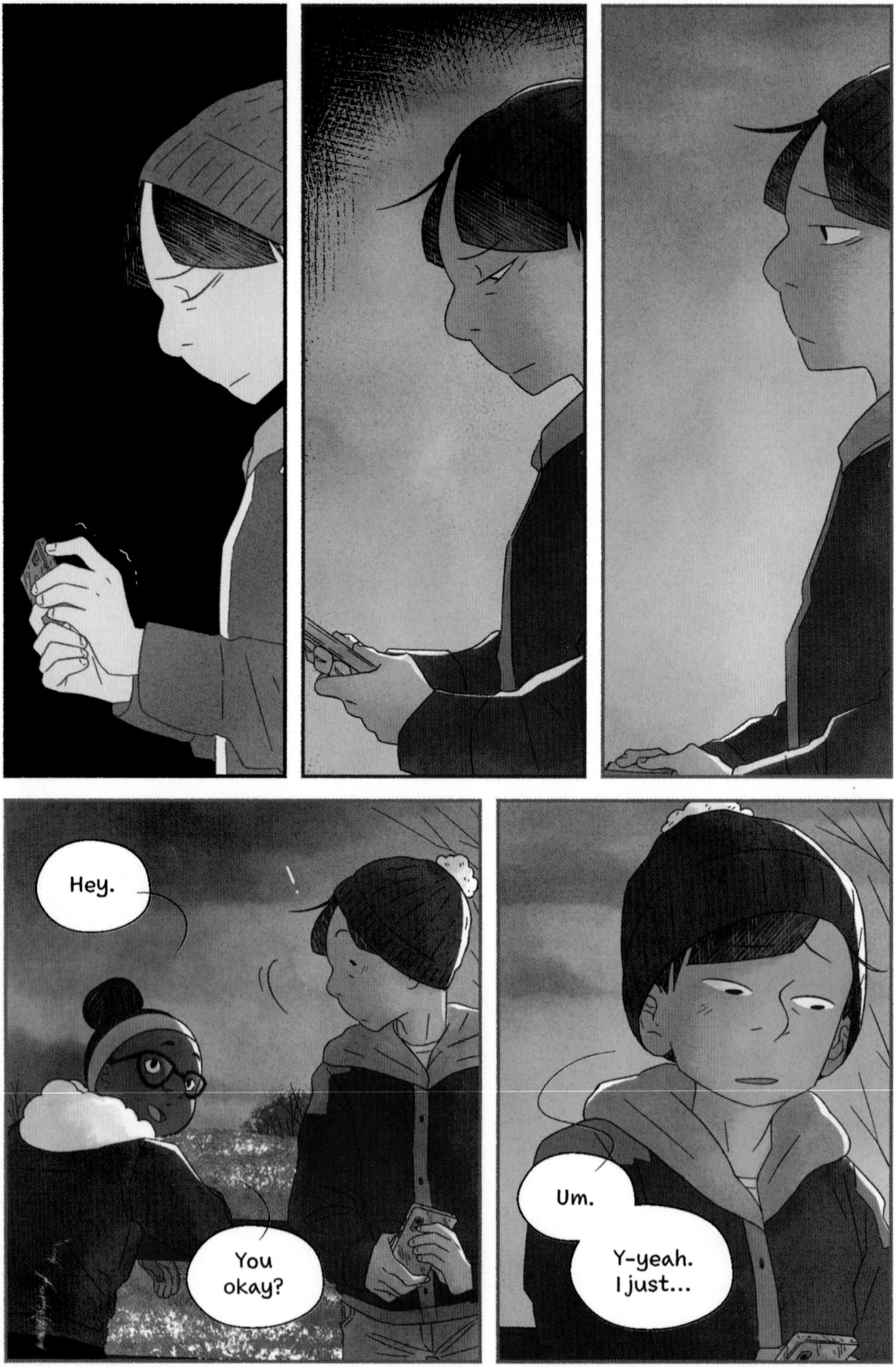
Hey.
!
You okay?
Um.
Y-yeah. I just...

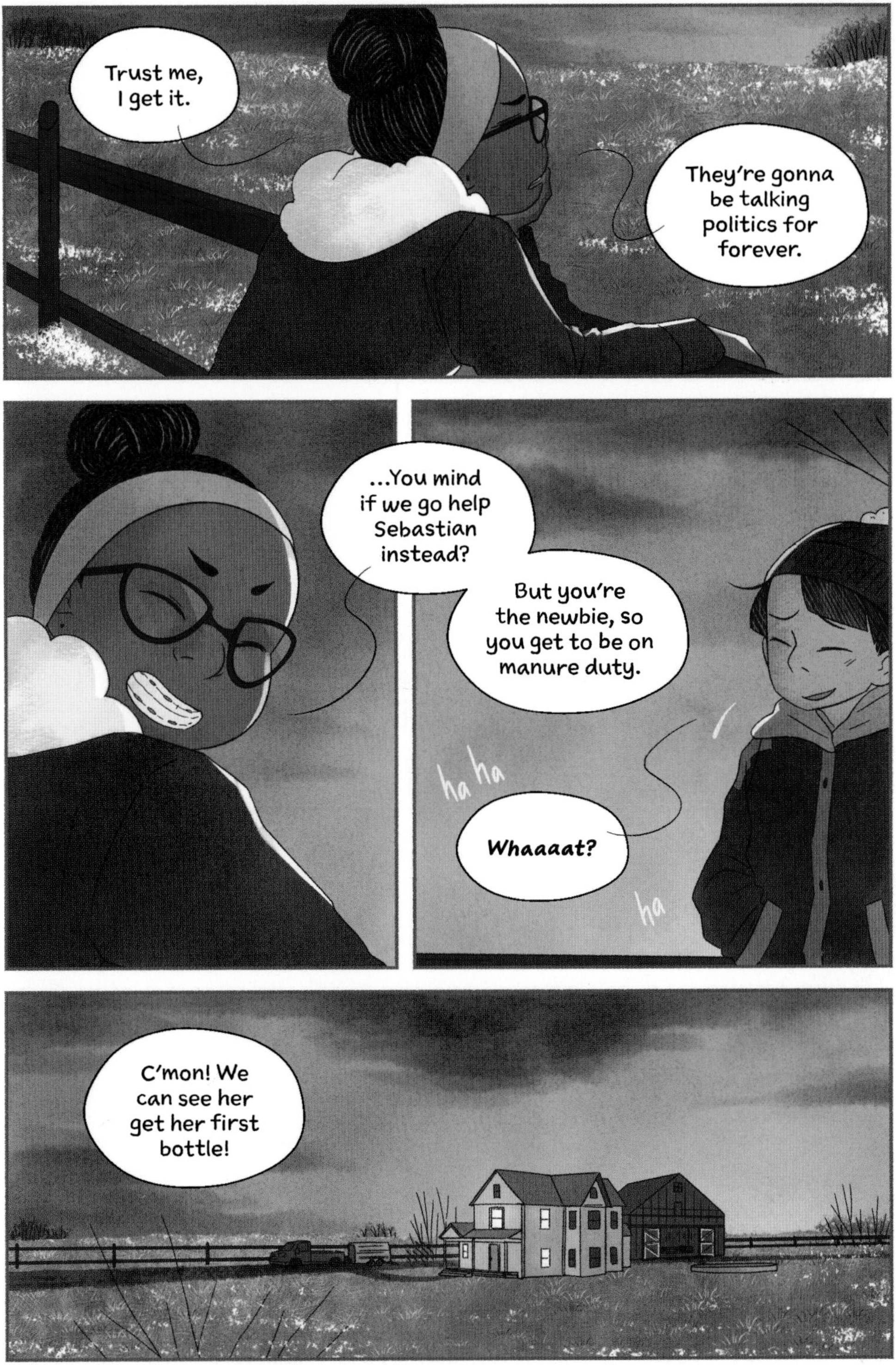
Trust me, I get it.
They're gonna be talking politics for forever.
...You mind if we go help Sebastian instead?
But you're the newbie, so you get to be on manure duty.
ha ha
Whaaaat?
ha
C'mon! We can see her get her first bottle!

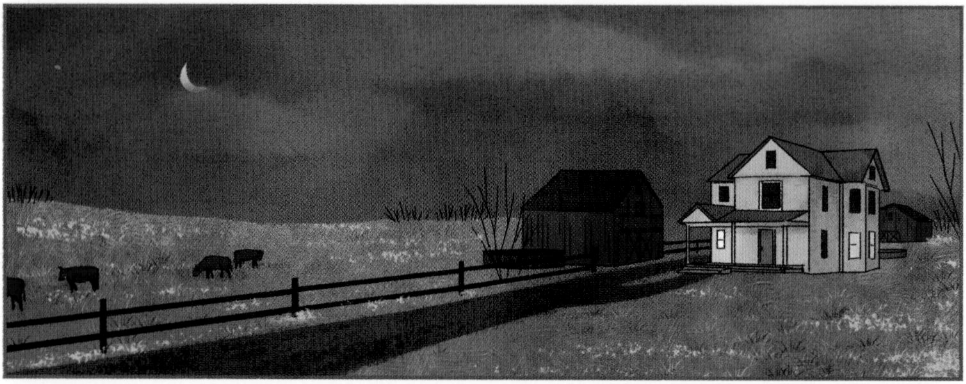

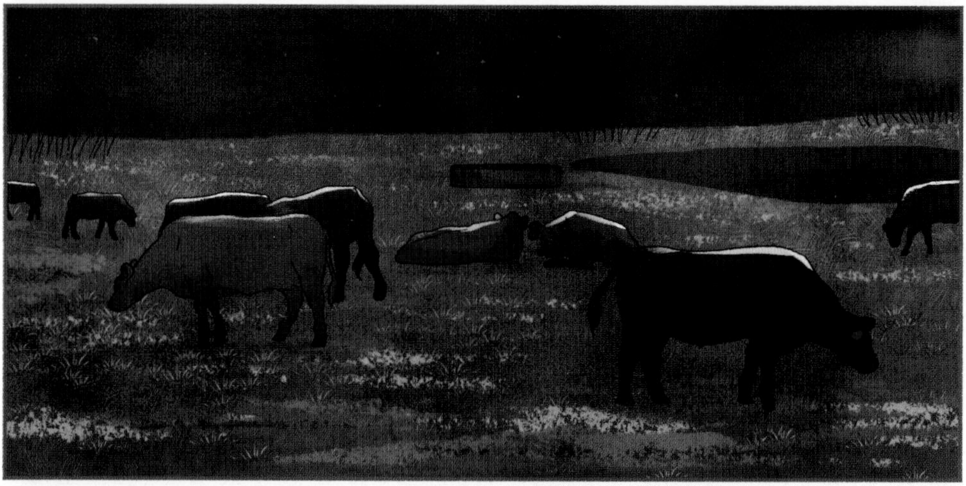

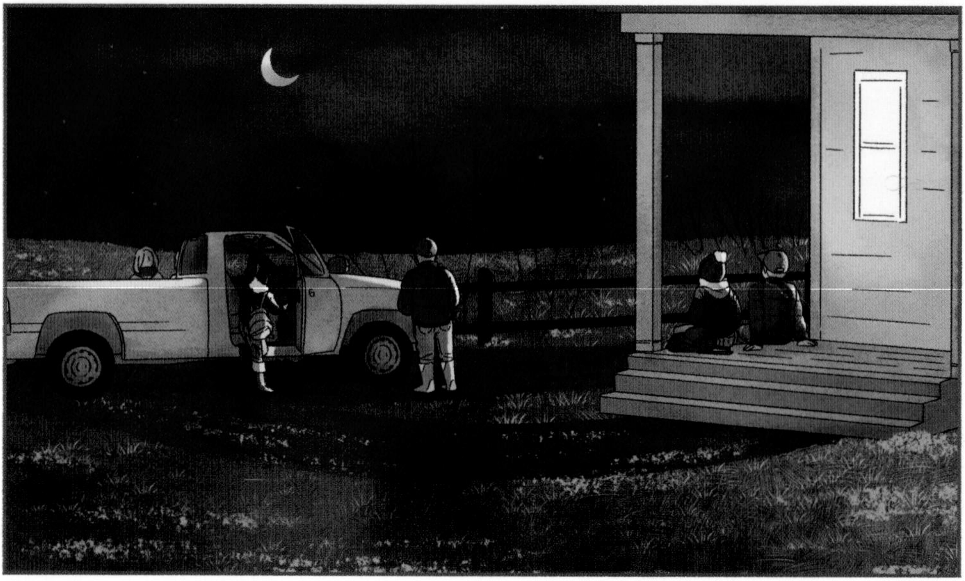

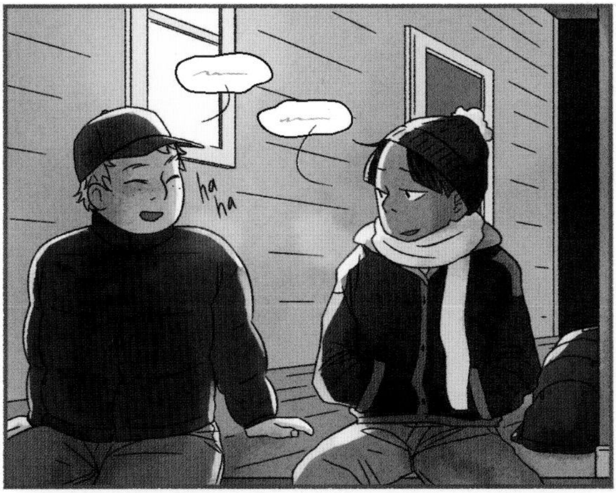
ha ha

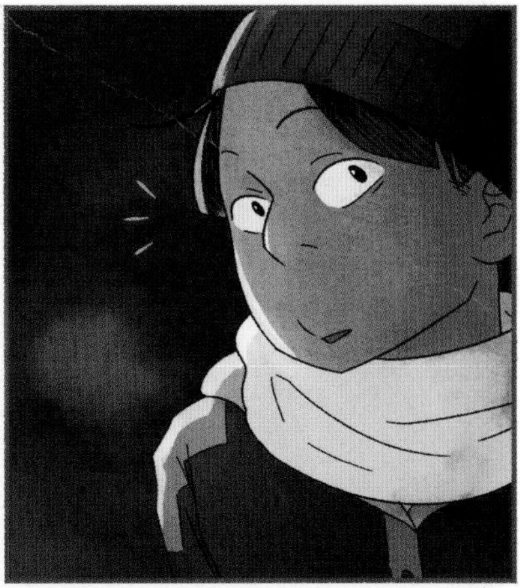

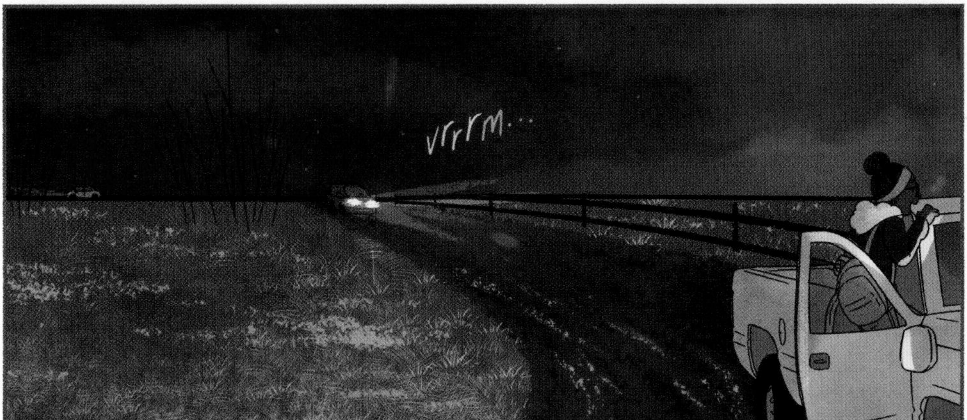
vrrrm....

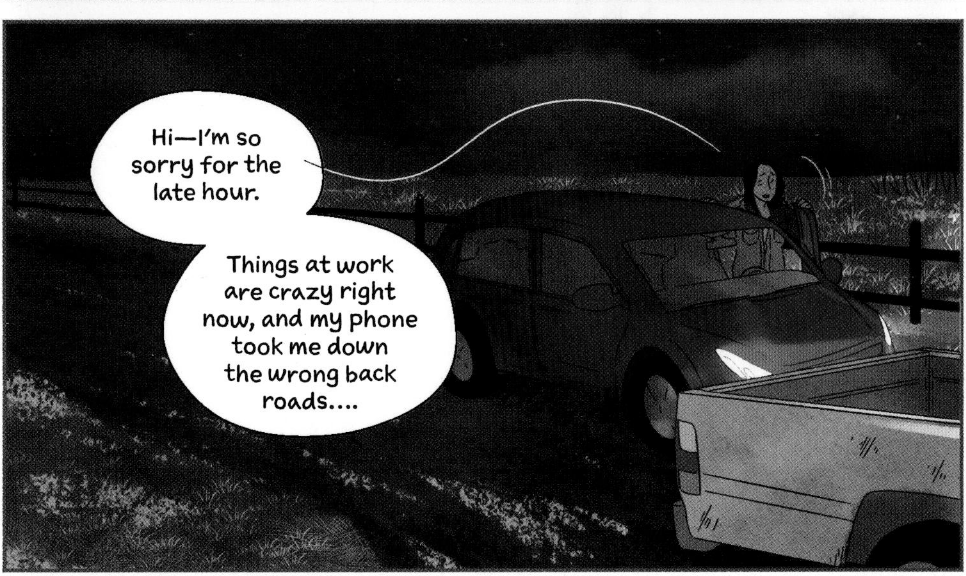
Hi—I'm so sorry for the late hour.
Things at work are crazy right now, and my phone took me down the wrong back roads....

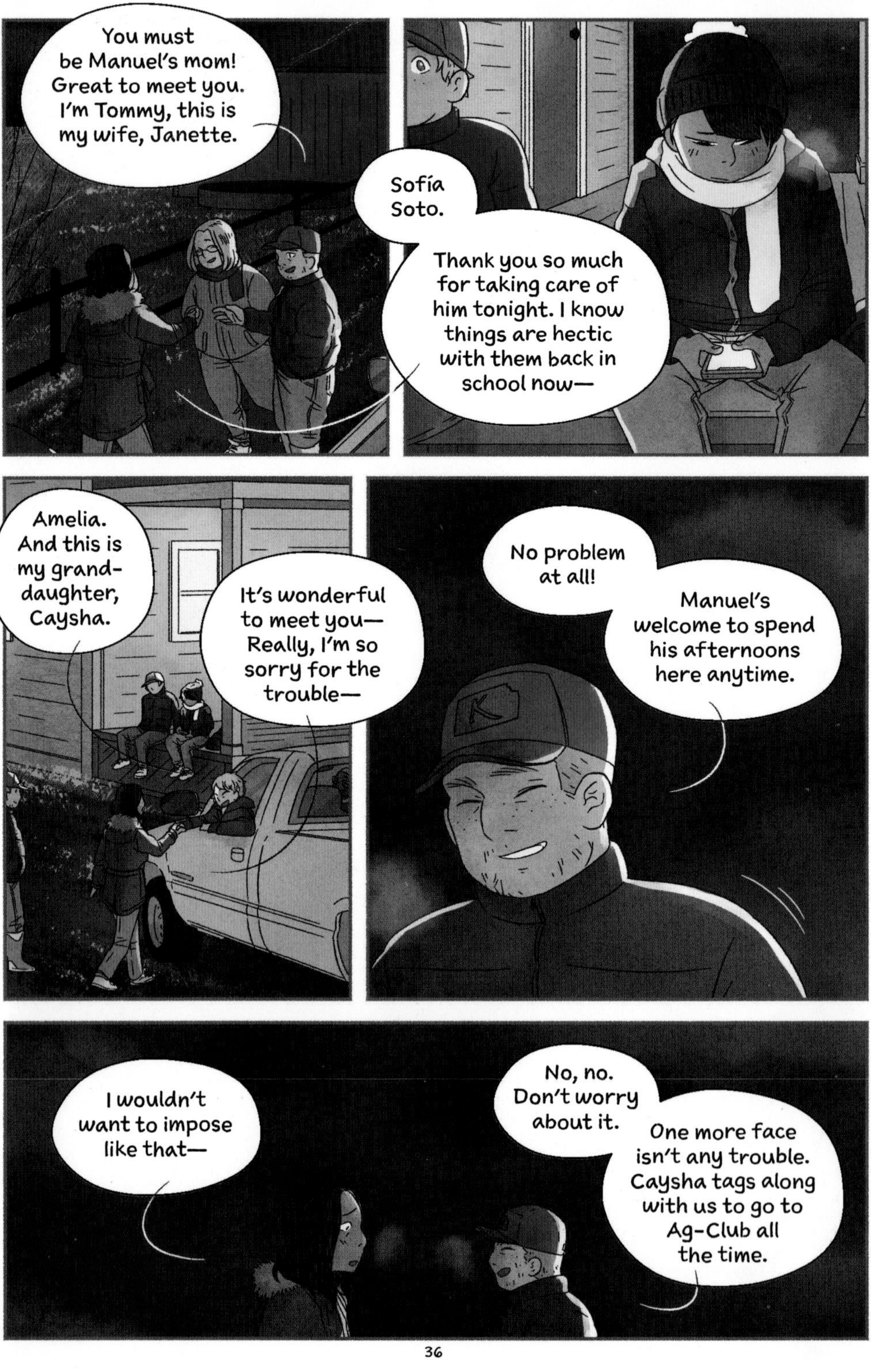
You must be Manuel's mom! Great to meet you. I'm Tommy, this is my wife, Janette.
Sofía Soto.
Thank you so much for taking care of him tonight. I know things are hectic with them back in school now—
Amelia. And this is my grand-daughter, Caysha.
It's wonderful to meet you— Really, I'm so sorry for the trouble—
No problem at all!
Manuel's welcome to spend his afternoons here anytime.
I wouldn't want to impose like that—
No, no. Don't worry about it.
One more face isn't any trouble. Caysha tags along with us to go to Ag-Club all the time.

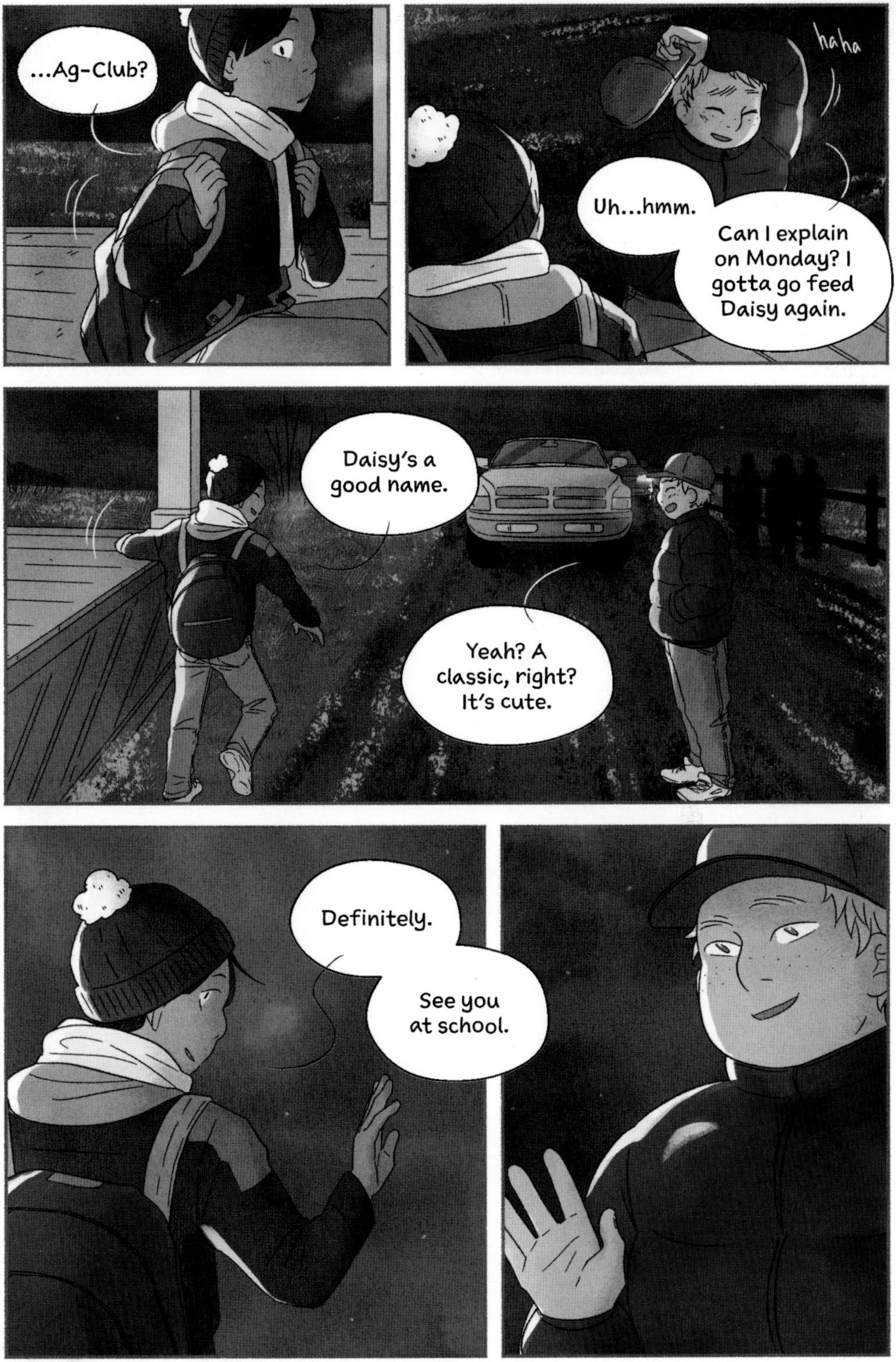
...Ag-Club?
haha
Uh...hmm.
Can I explain on Monday? I gotta go feed Daisy again.
Daisy's a good name.
Yeah? A classic, right? It's cute.
Definitely.
See you at school.

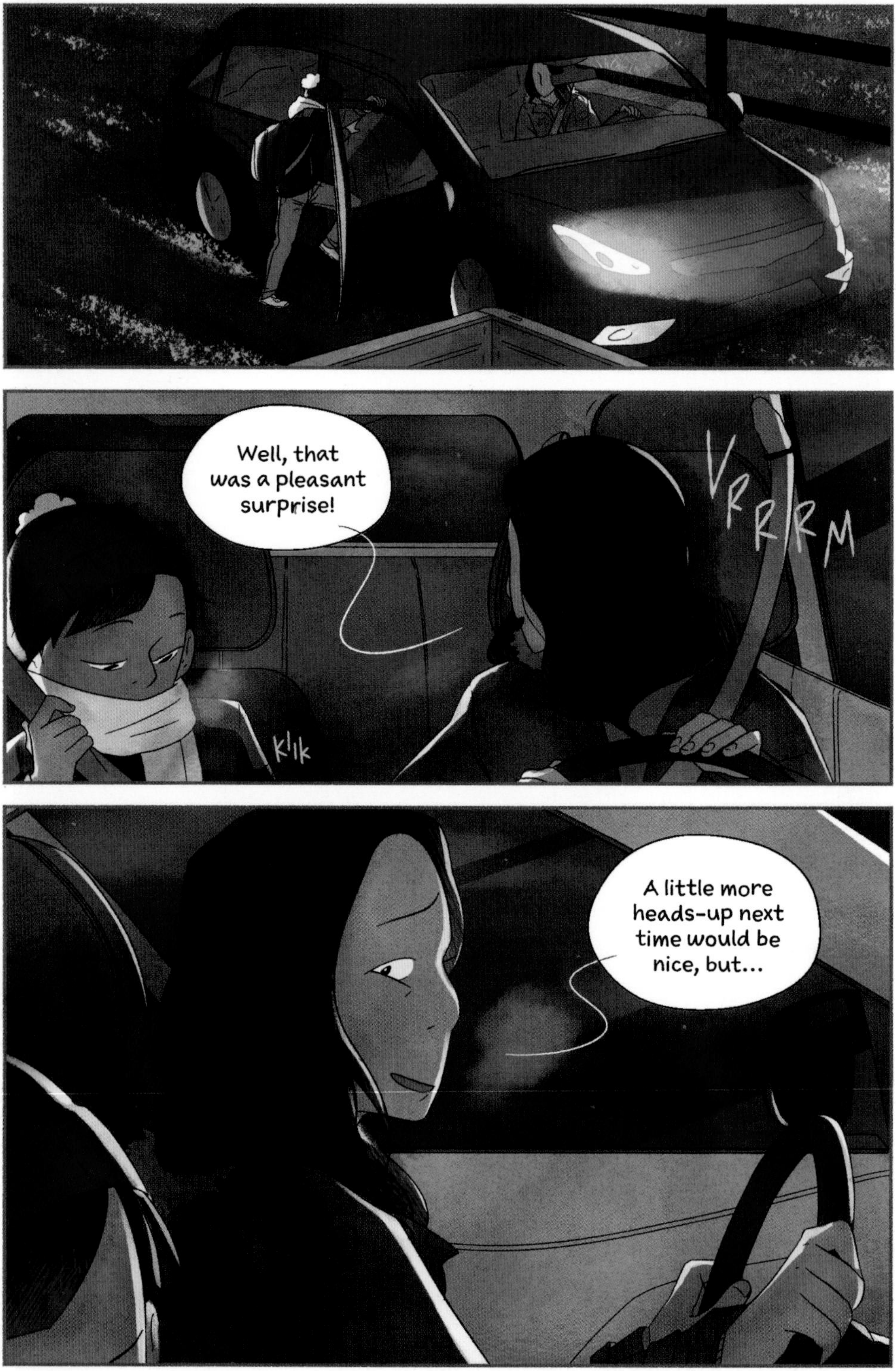
Well, that was a pleasant surprise!
VRRRRM
K'LK
A little more heads-up next time would be nice, but...

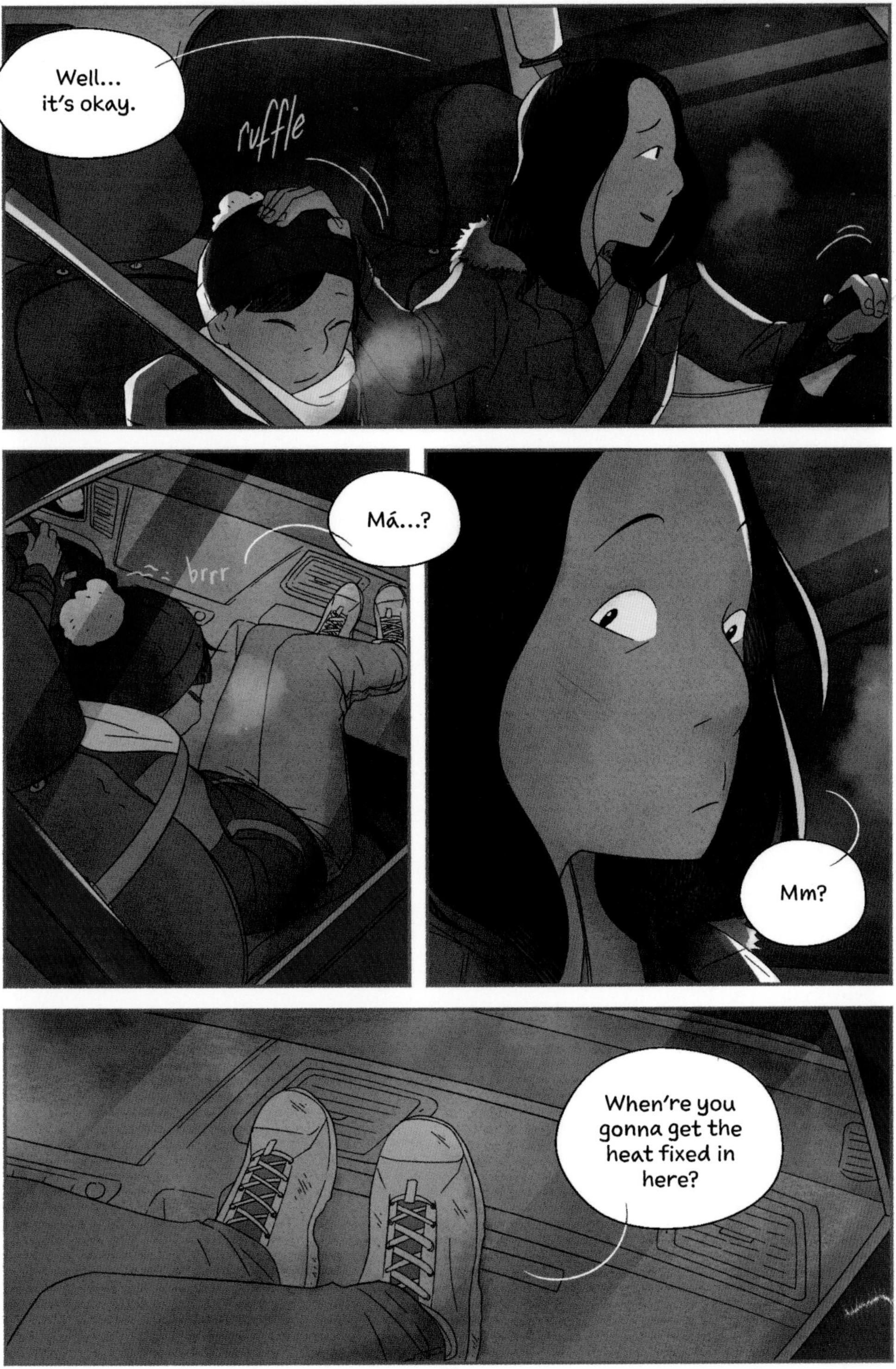
Well...
it's okay.
ruffle
brrr
Má...?
Mm?
When're you gonna get the heat fixed in here?

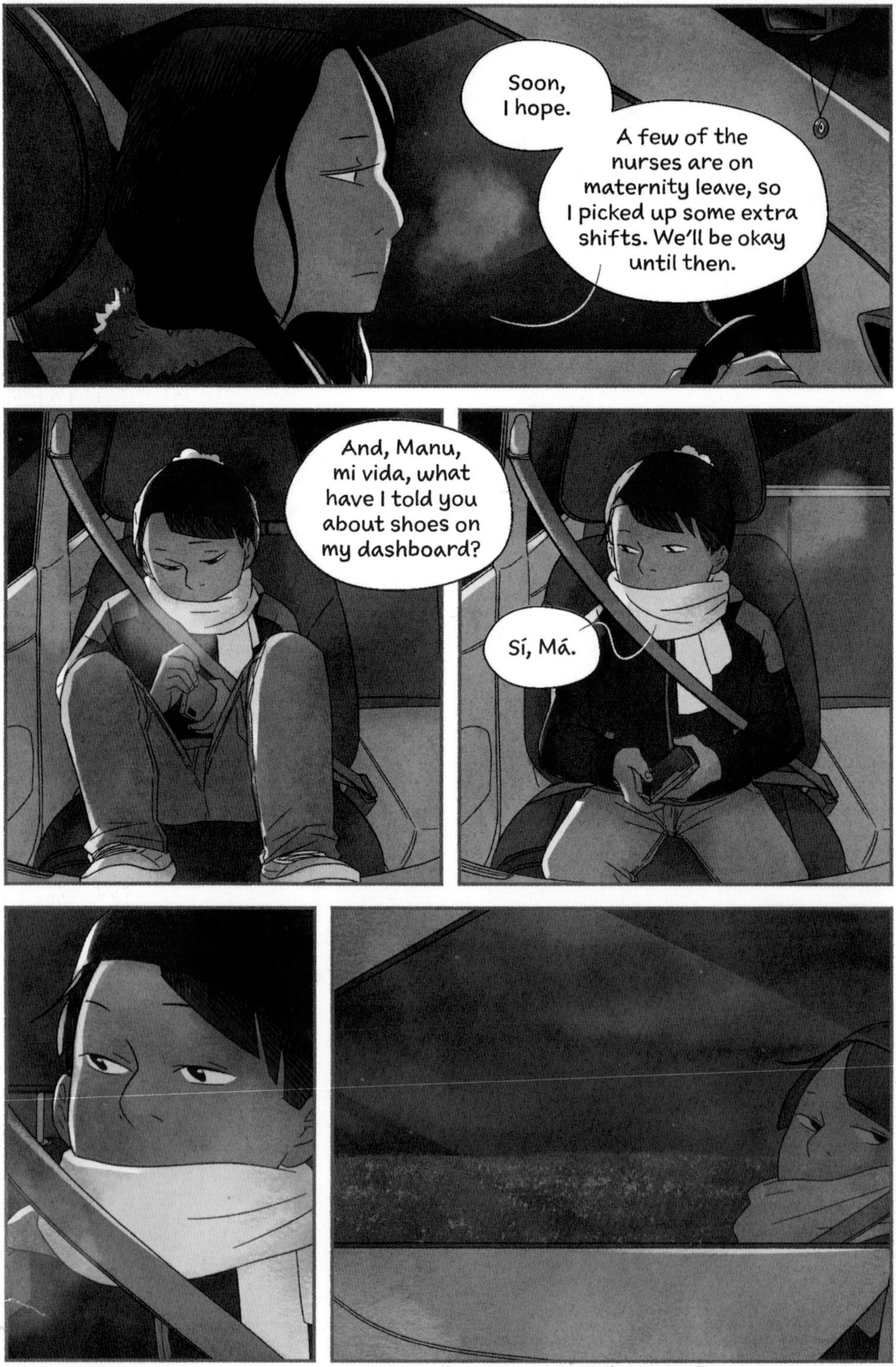

Soon, I hope.
A few of the nurses are on maternity leave, so I picked up some extra shifts. We'll be okay until then.
And, Manu, mi vida, what have I told you about shoes on my dashboard?
Sí, Má.

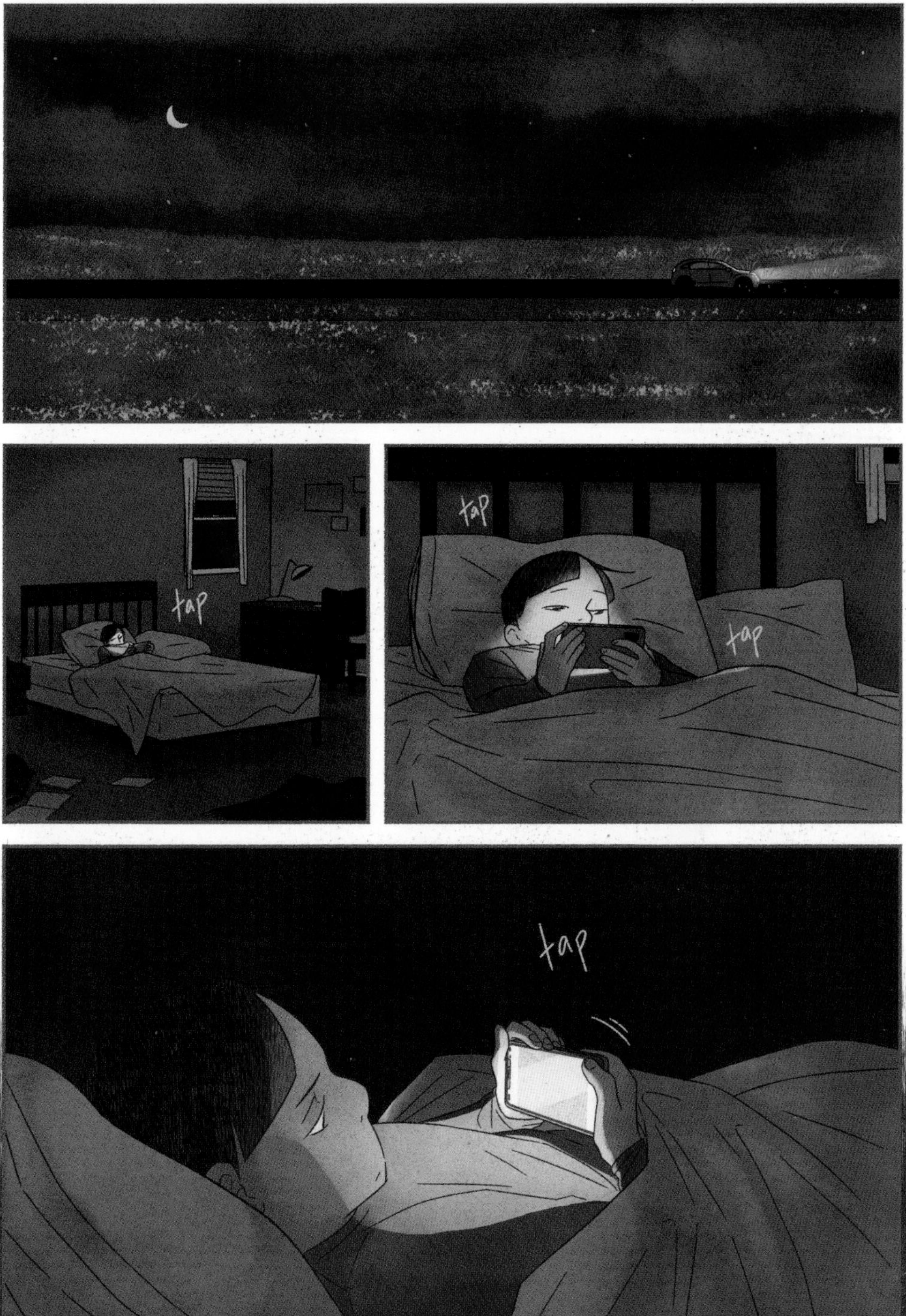
tap
tap
tap
tap

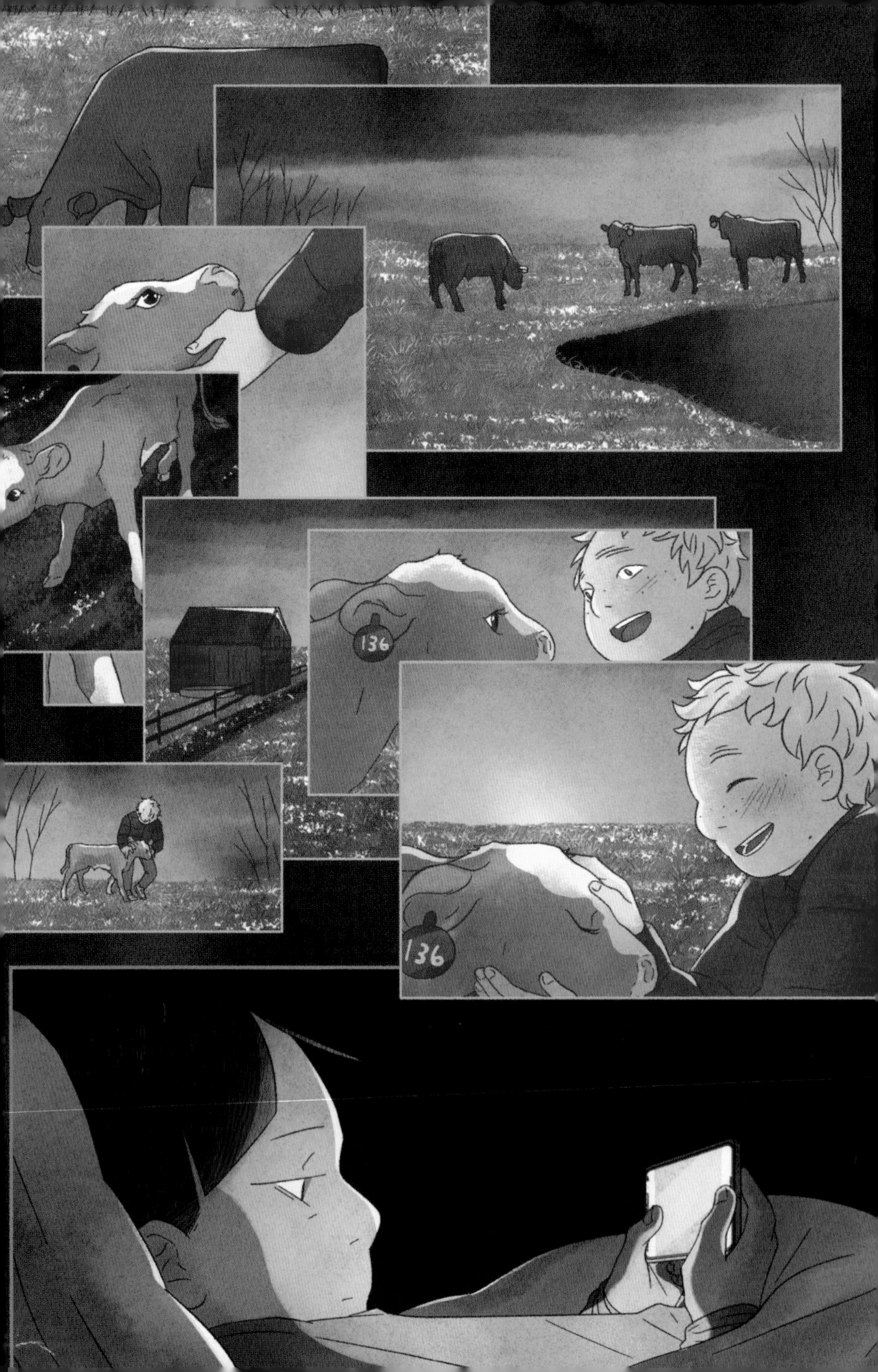
136
136

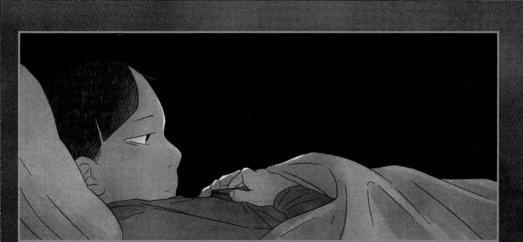

chapter two

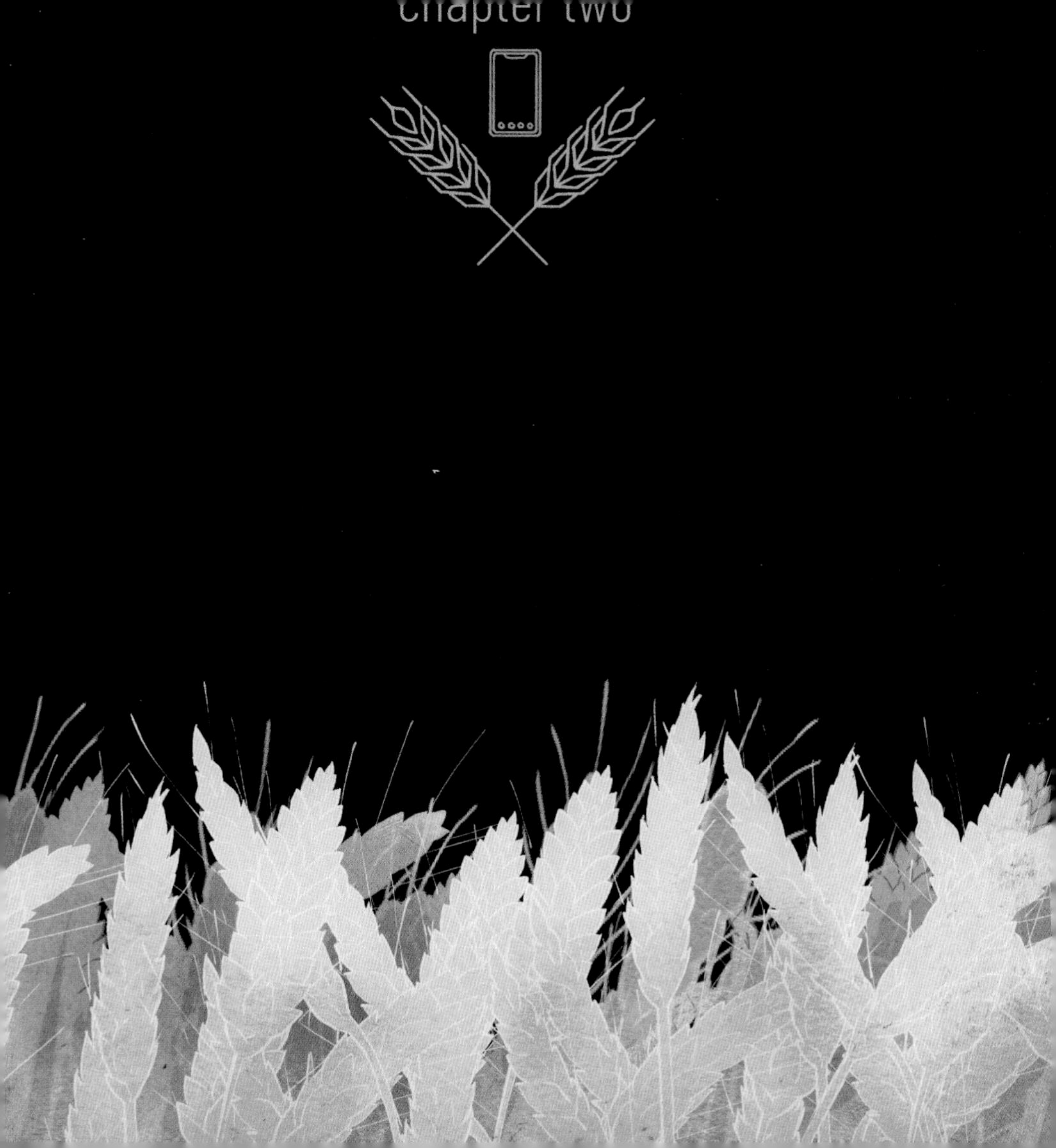

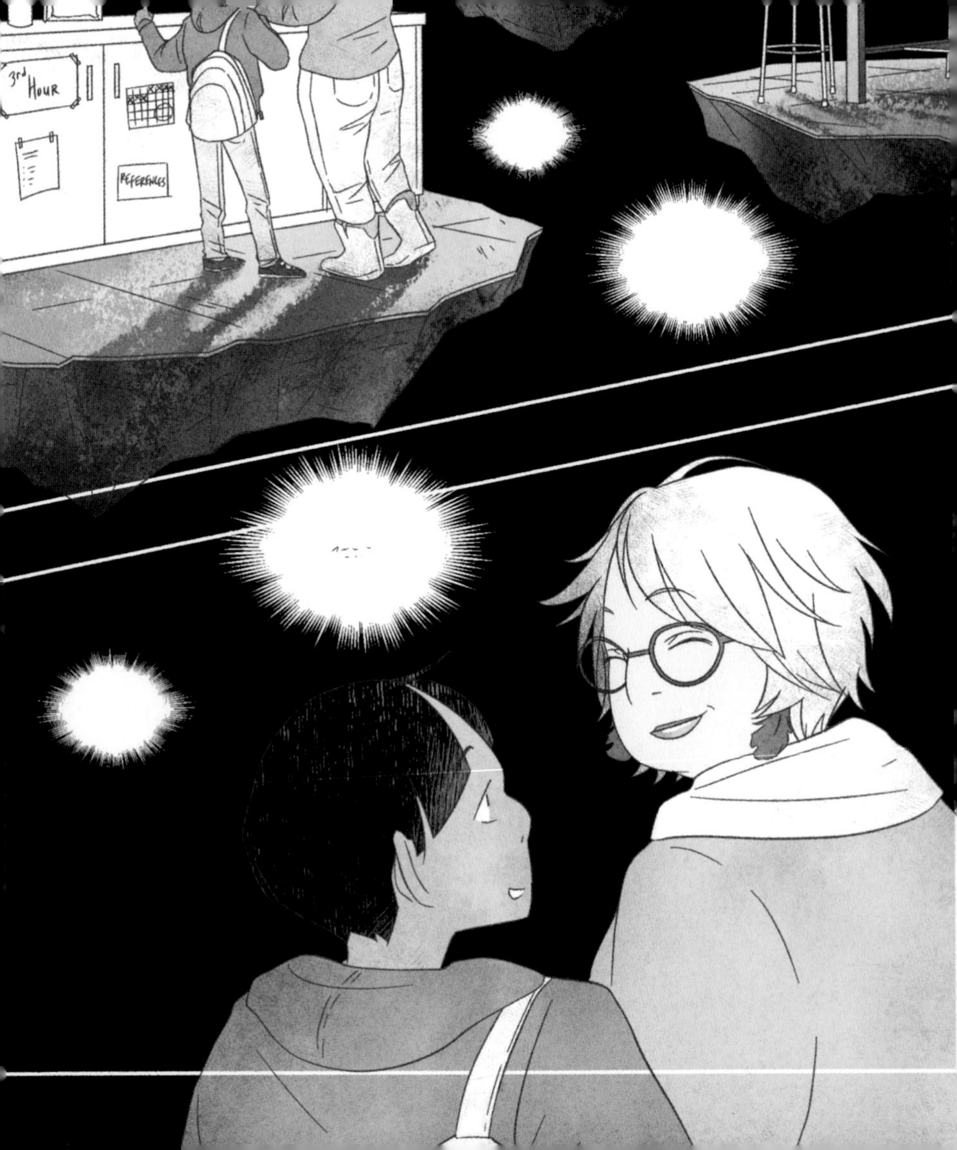
3rd HOUR
REFERENCES

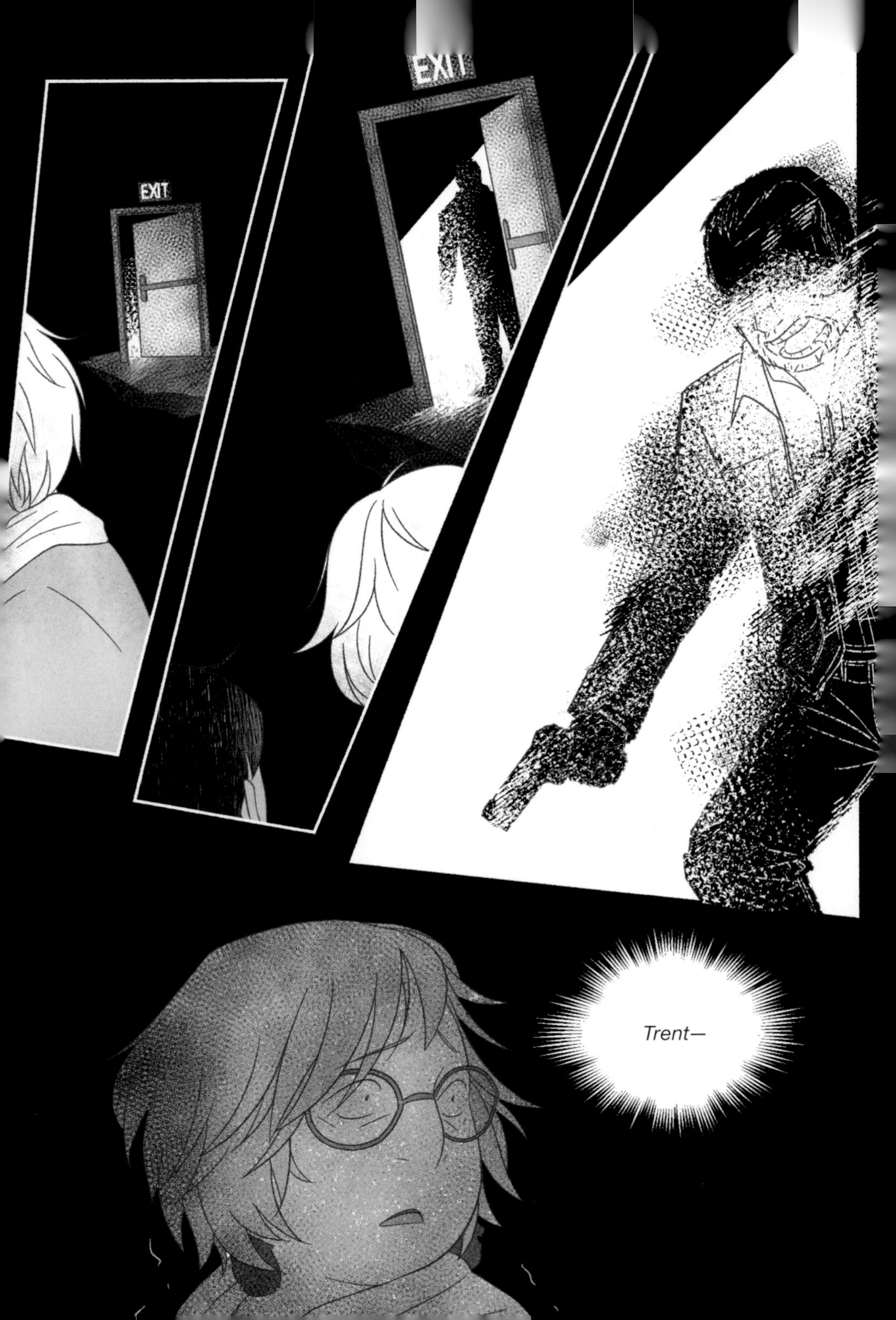
EXIT
EXIT
Trent—

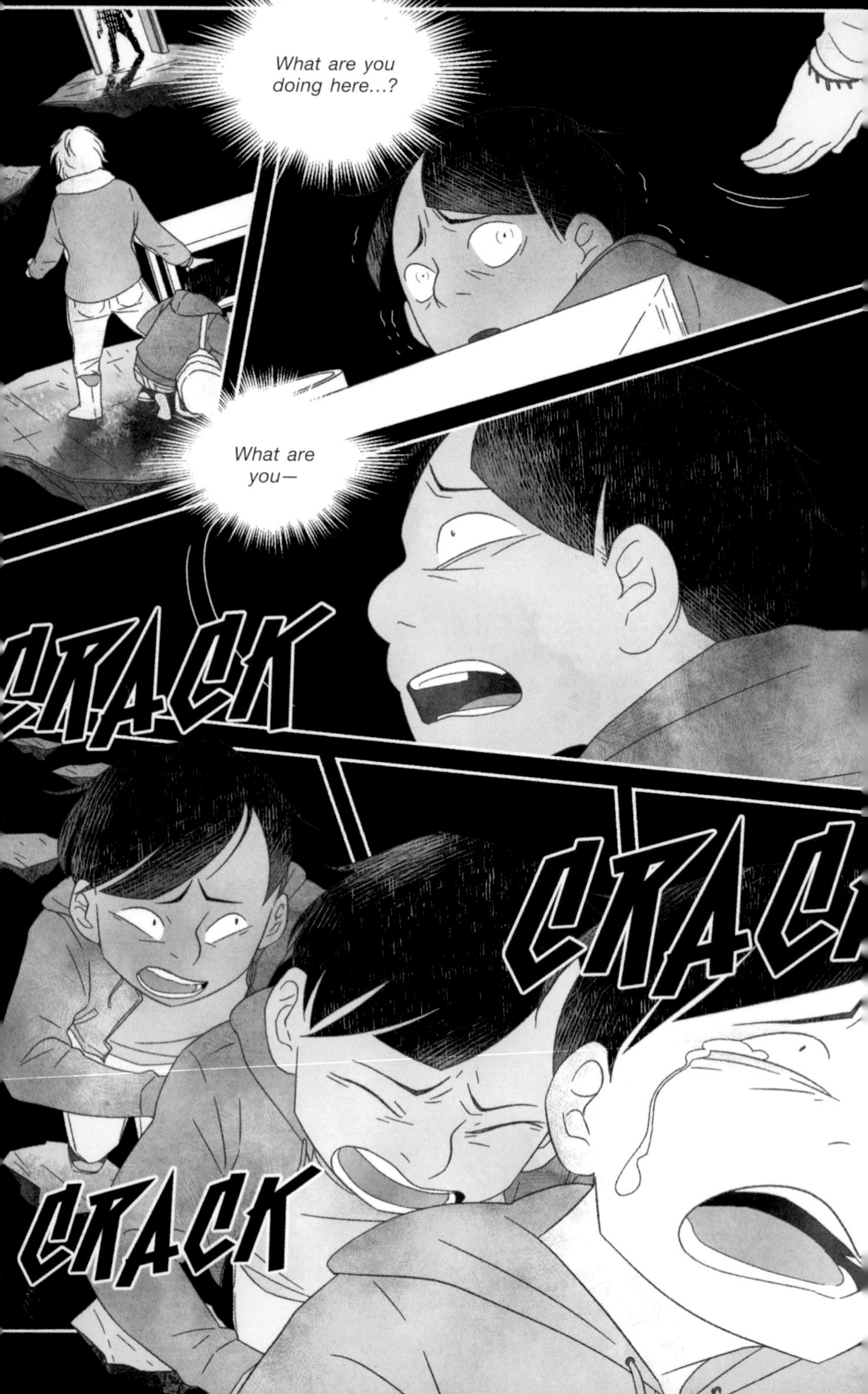
What are you doing here...?
What are you—
CRACK
CRAC
CRACK

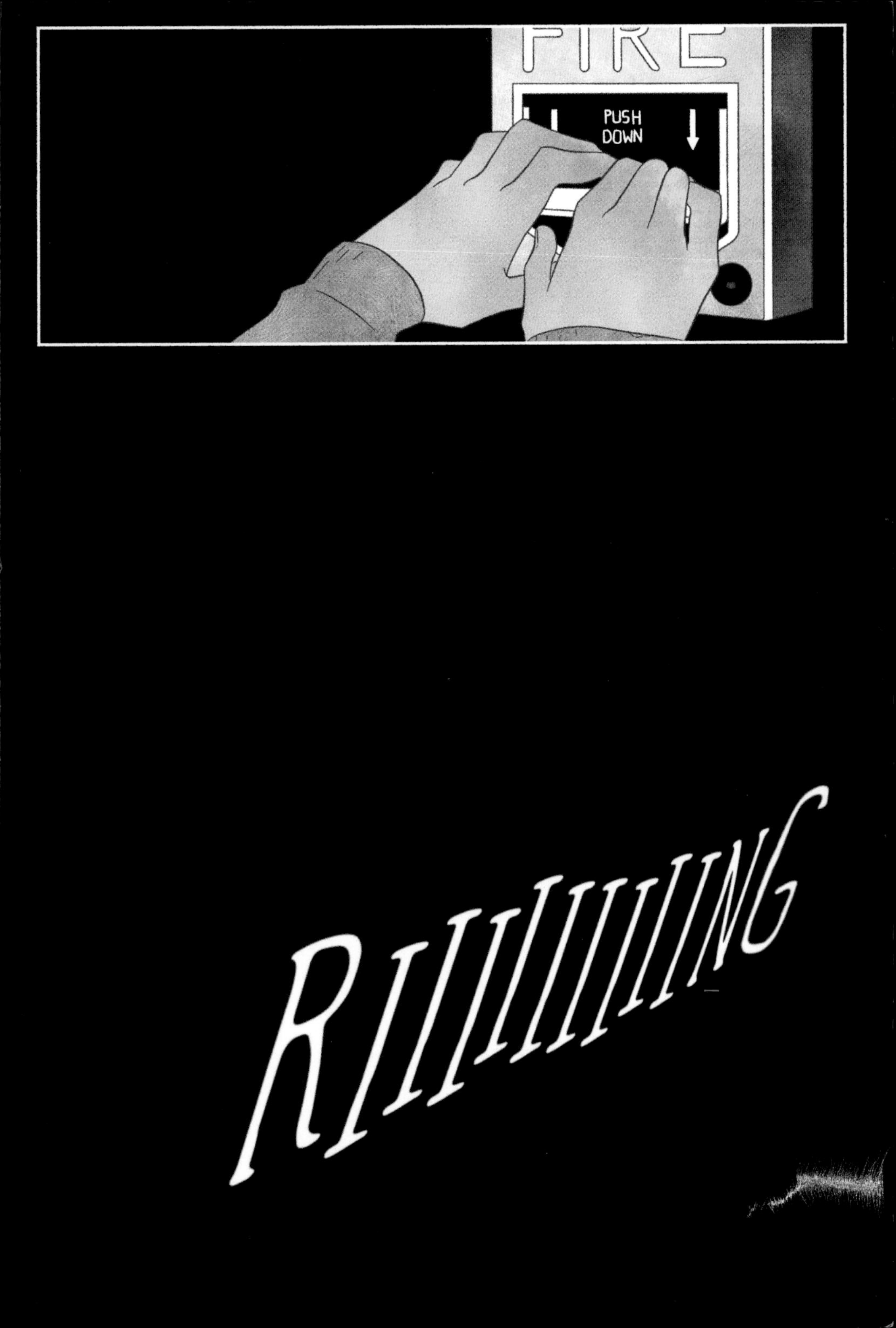
FIRE
PUSH DOWN
RIIIIIIIIING

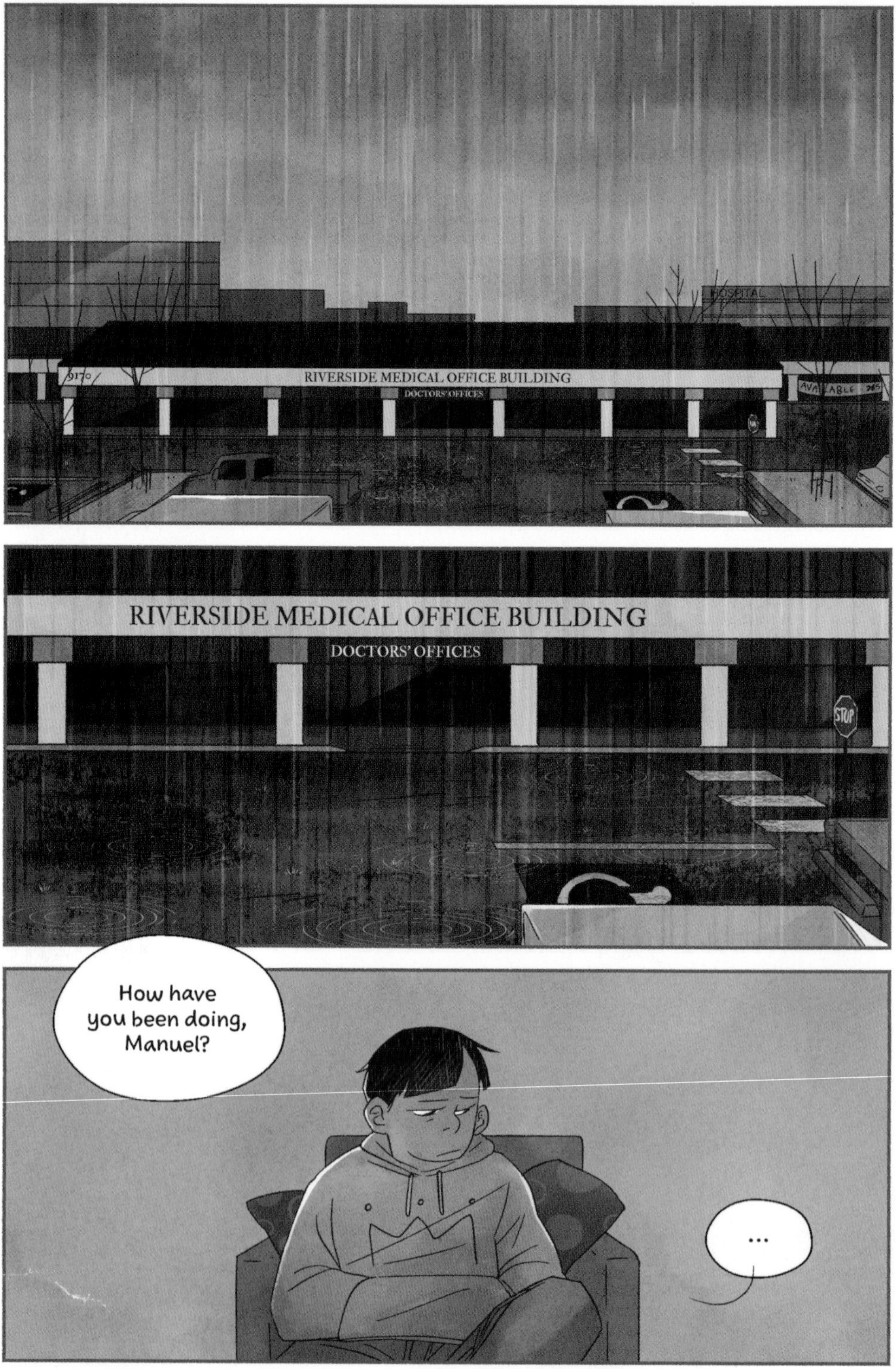
RIVERSIDE MEDICAL OFFICE BUILDING
DOCTORS' OFFICES
HOSPITAL
RIVERSIDE MEDICAL OFFICE BUILDING
DOCTORS' OFFICES
STOP
How have you been doing, Manuel?
...

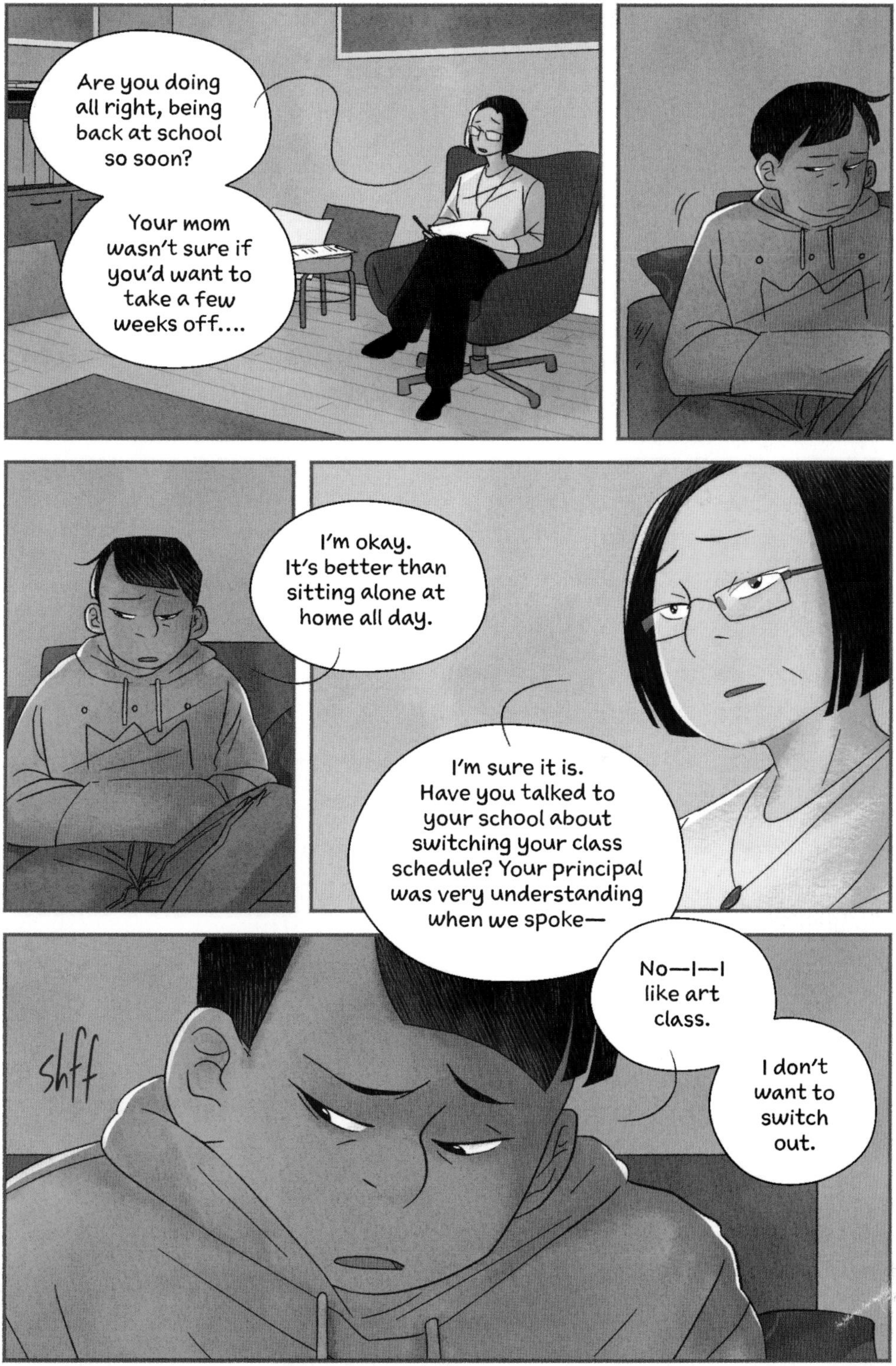
Are you doing all right, being back at school so soon?
Your mom wasn't sure if you'd want to take a few weeks off....
I'm okay. It's better than sitting alone at home all day.
I'm sure it is. Have you talked to your school about switching your class schedule? Your principal was very understanding when we spoke—
shff
No—I—I like art class.
I don't want to switch out.

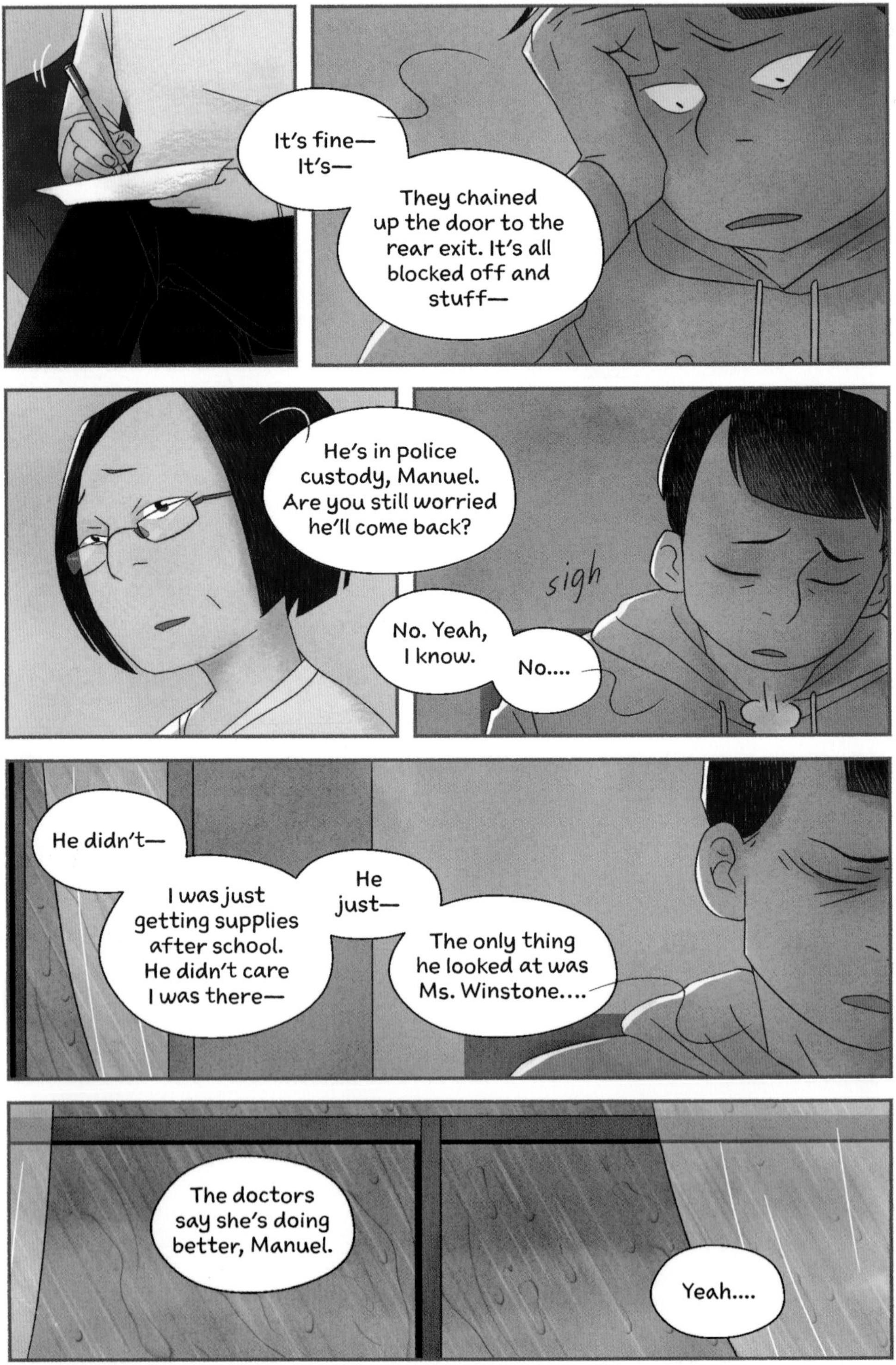
It's fine—
It's—
They chained up the door to the rear exit. It's all blocked off and stuff—
He's in police custody, Manuel. Are you still worried he'll come back?
sigh
No. Yeah, I know.
No....
He didn't—
I was just getting supplies after school. He didn't care I was there—
He just—
The only thing he looked at was Ms. Winstone....
The doctors say she's doing better, Manuel.
Yeah....

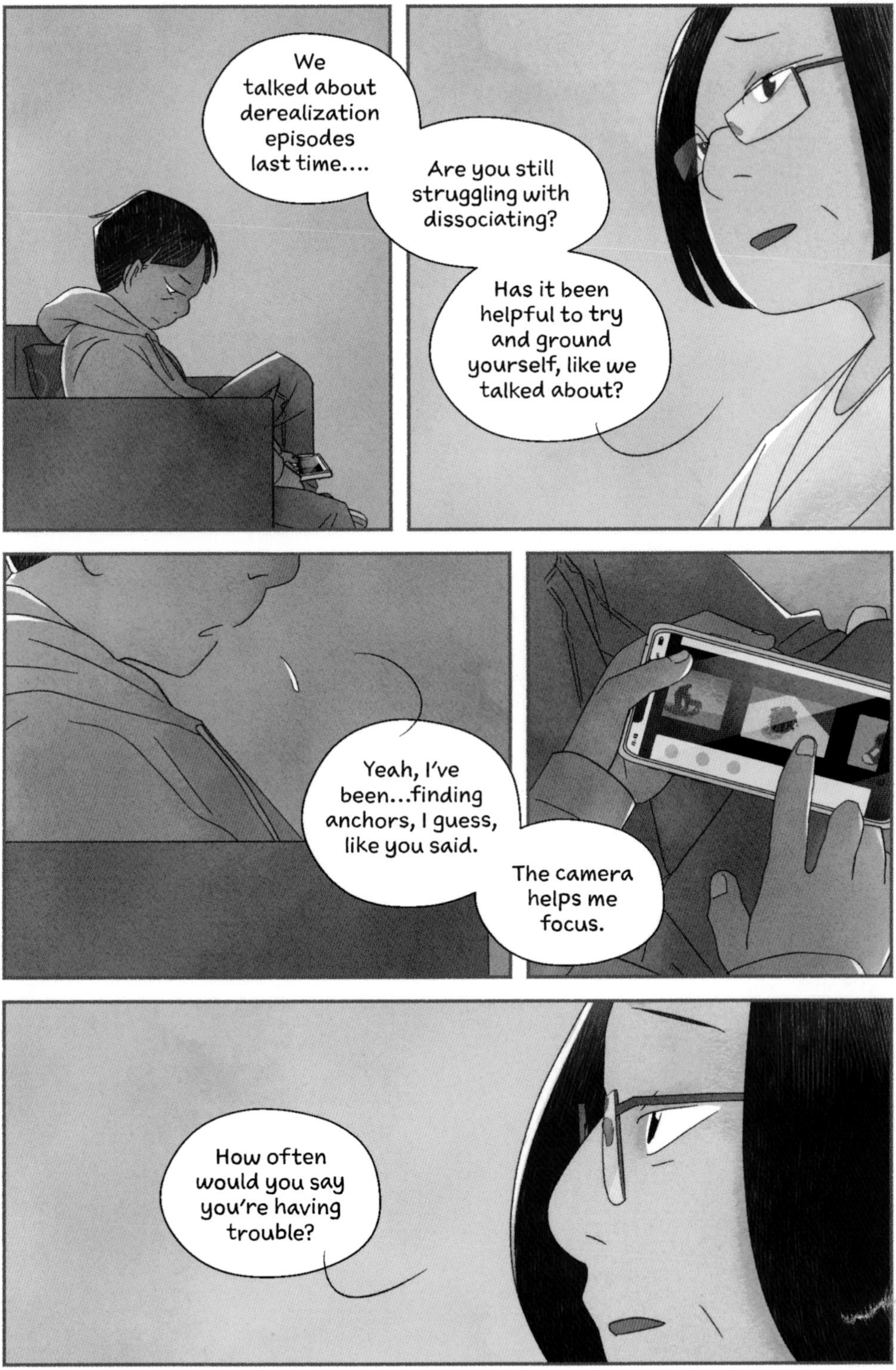
We talked about derealization episodes last time....
Are you still struggling with dissociating?
Has it been helpful to try and ground yourself, like we talked about?
Yeah, I've been...finding anchors, I guess, like you said.
The camera helps me focus.
How often would you say you're having trouble?

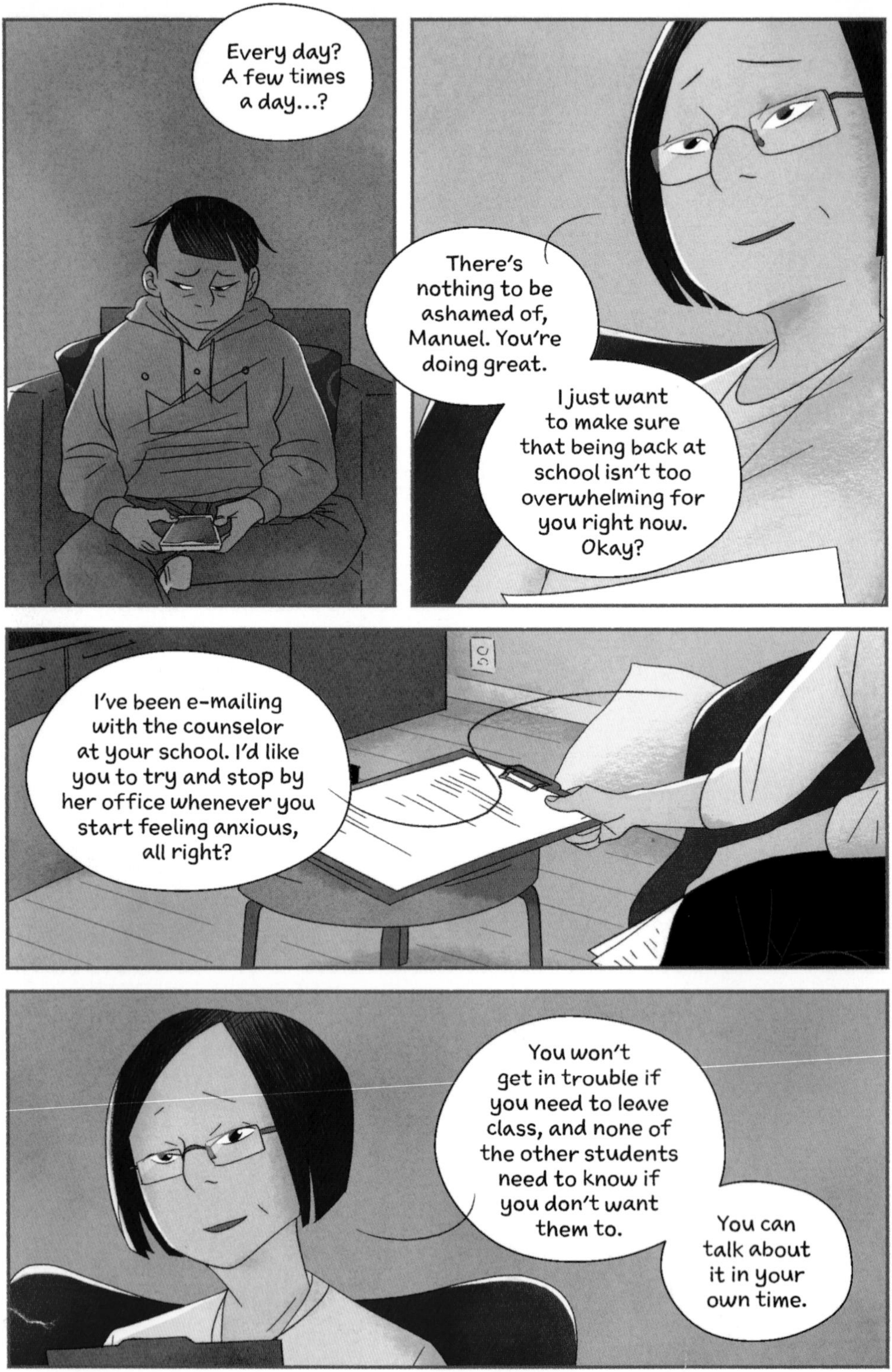

Every day? A few times a day...?
There's nothing to be ashamed of, Manuel. You're doing great.
I just want to make sure that being back at school isn't too overwhelming for you right now. Okay?
I've been e-mailing with the counselor at your school. I'd like you to try and stop by her office whenever you start feeling anxious, all right?
You won't get in trouble if you need to leave class, and none of the other students need to know if you don't want them to.
You can talk about it in your own time.

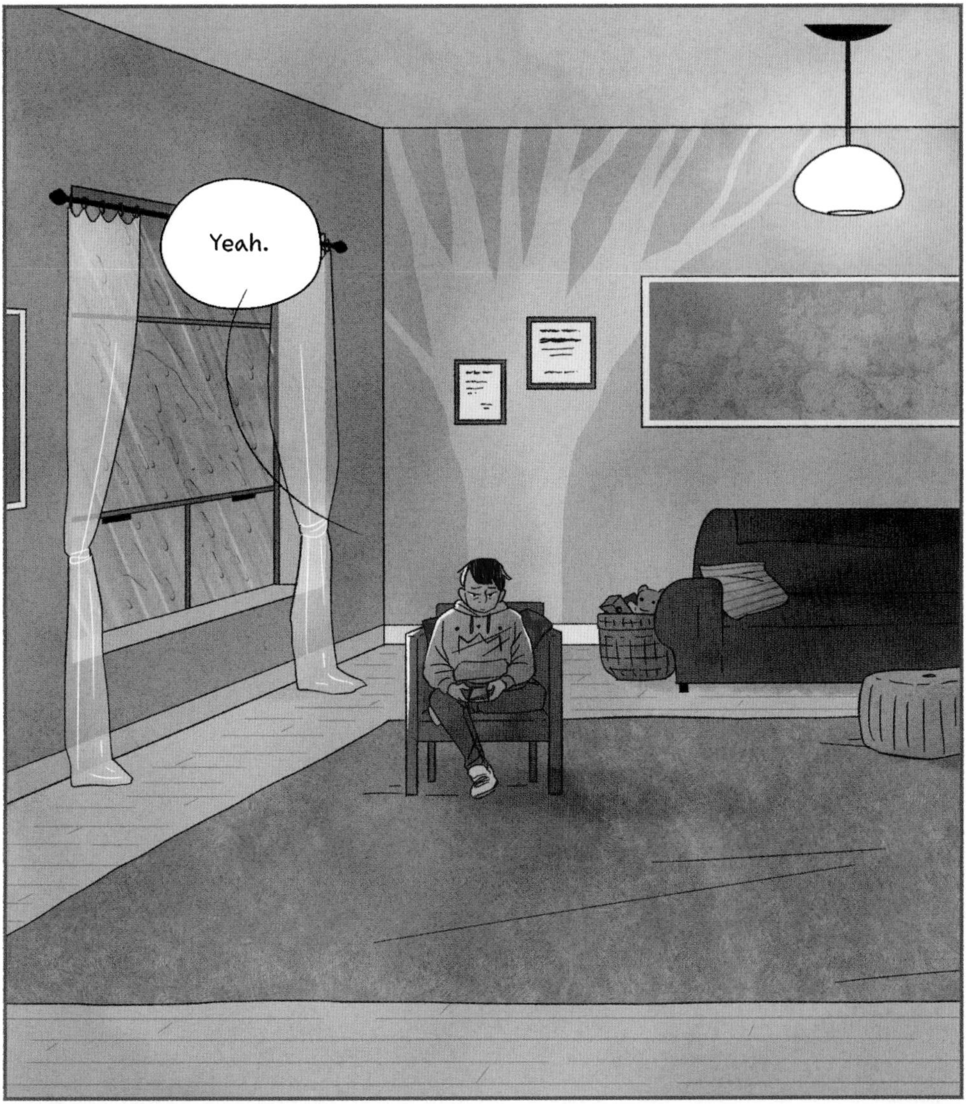
Yeah.
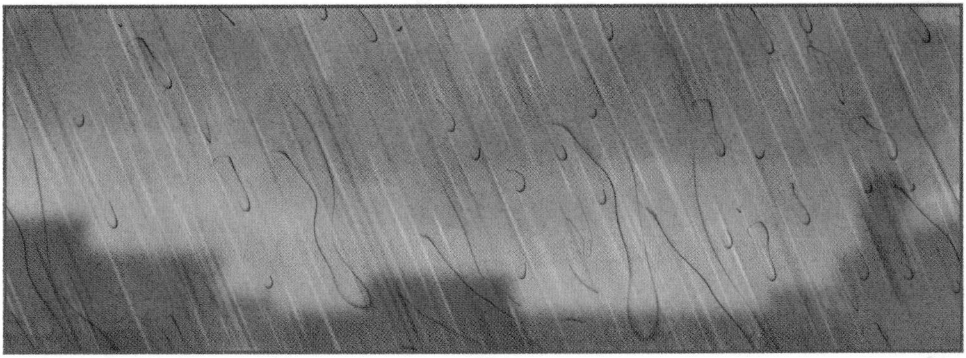

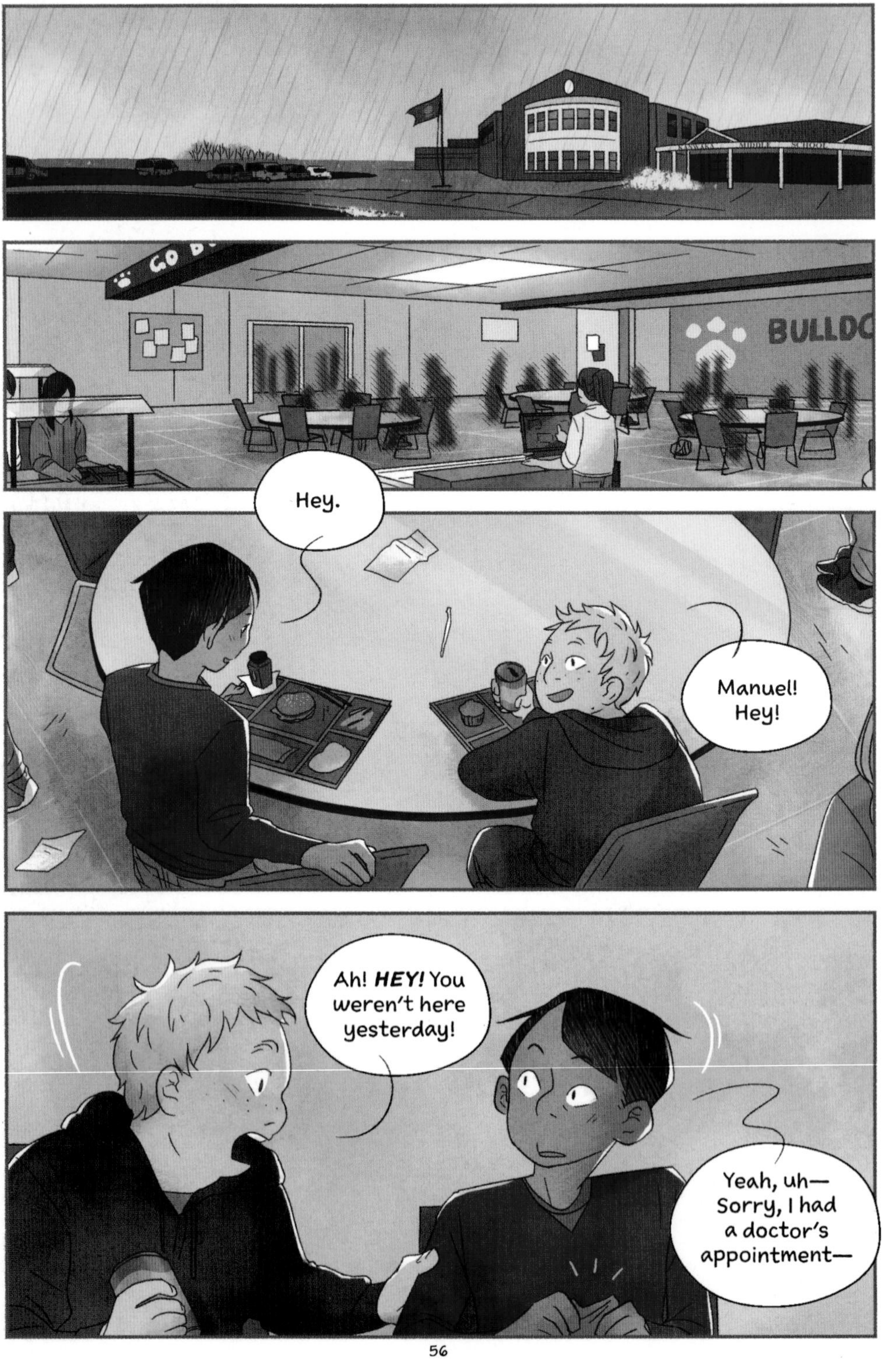
Hey.
Manuel! Hey!
Ah! **HEY!** You weren't here yesterday!
Yeah, uh— Sorry, I had a doctor's appointment—

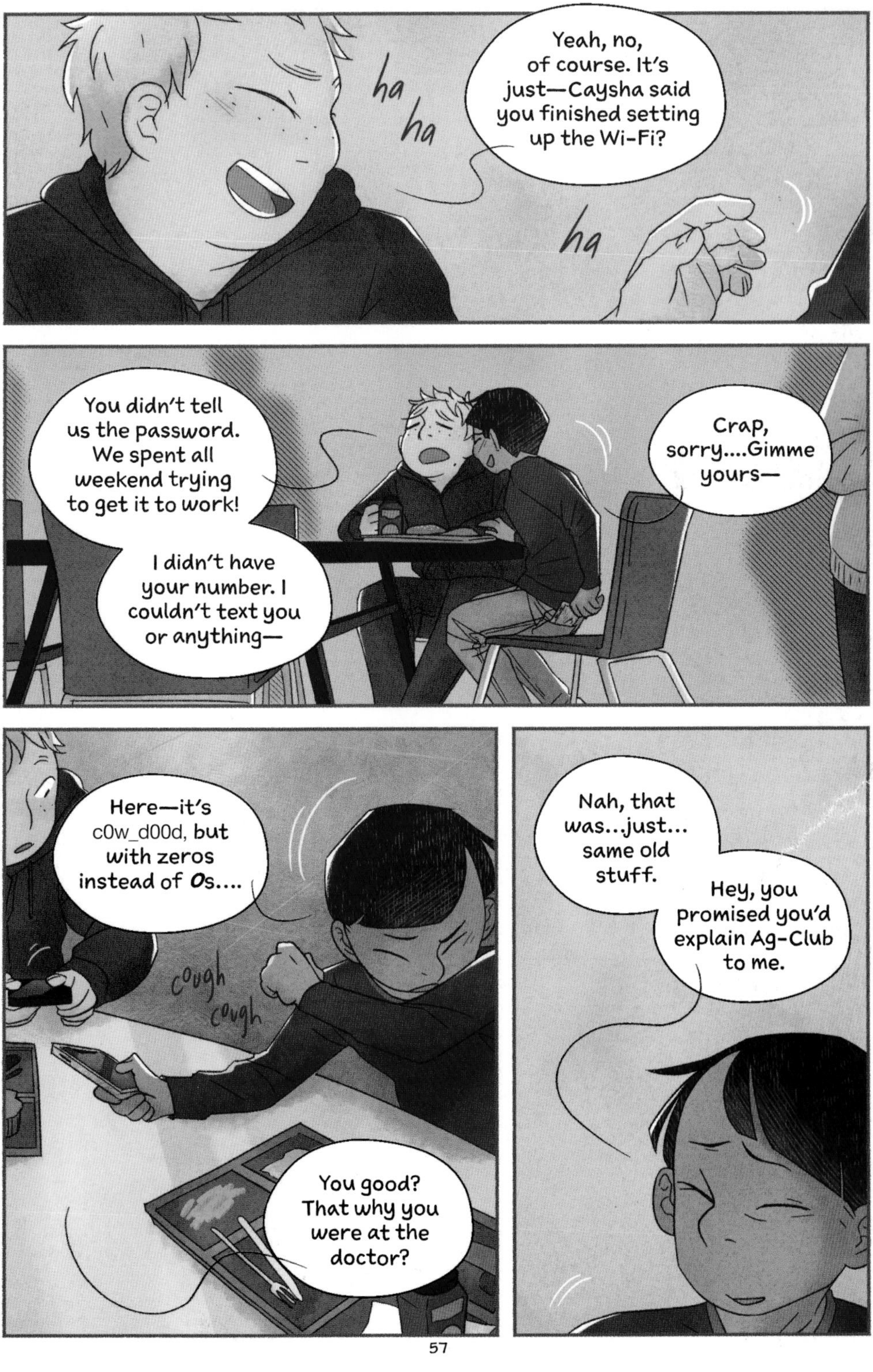
ha
ha
Yeah, no, of course. It's just—Caysha said you finished setting up the Wi-Fi?
ha
You didn't tell us the password. We spent all weekend trying to get it to work!
I didn't have your number. I couldn't text you or anything—
Crap, sorry....Gimme yours—
Here—it's c0w_d00d, but with zeros instead of Os....
cough cough
You good? That why you were at the doctor?
Nah, that was...just... same old stuff.
Hey, you promised you'd explain Ag-Club to me.

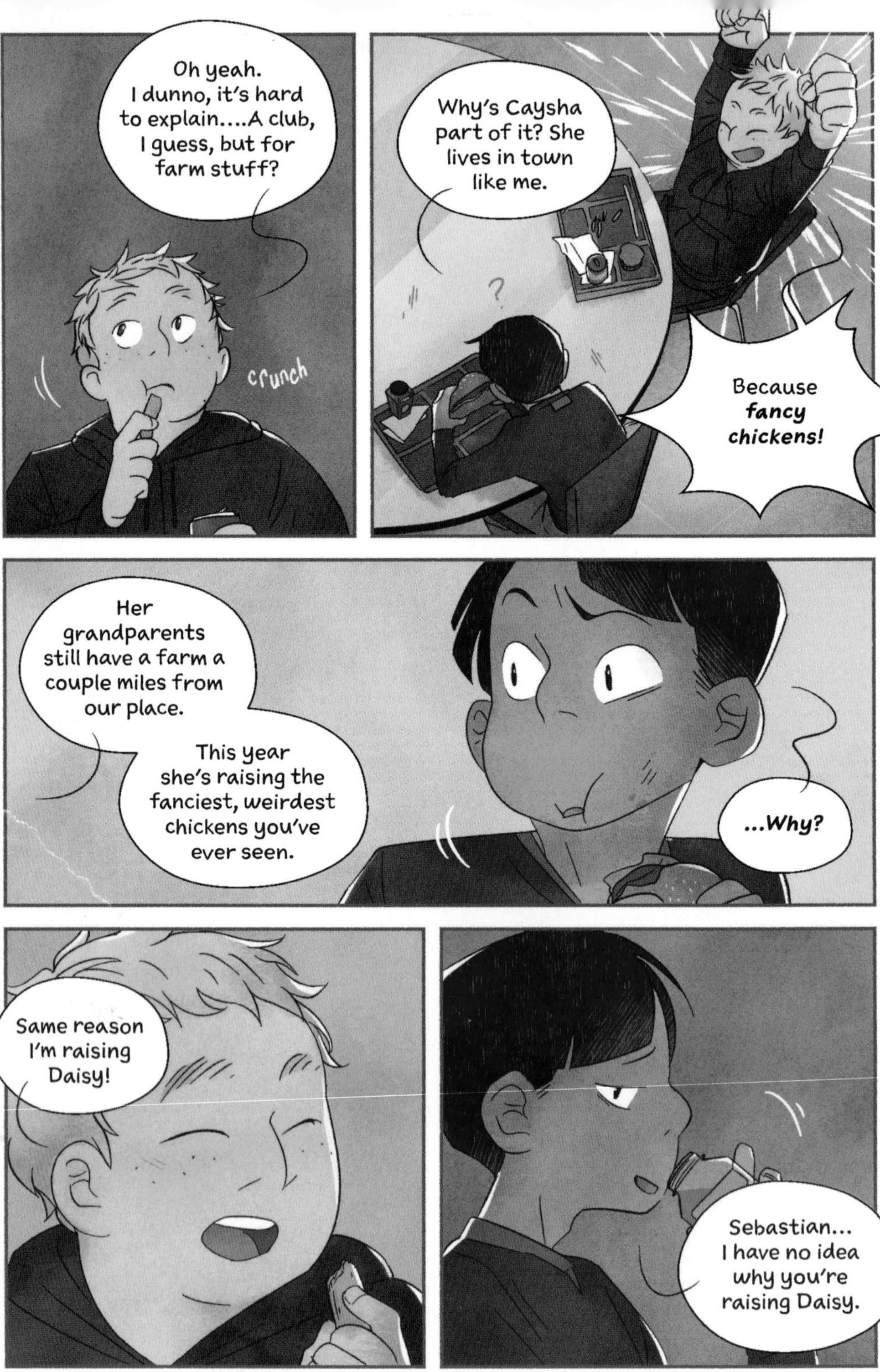
Oh yeah. I dunno, it's hard to explain....A club, I guess, but for farm stuff?
crunch
Why's Caysha part of it? She lives in town like me.
?
Because fancy chickens!
Her grandparents still have a farm a couple miles from our place.
This year she's raising the fanciest, weirdest chickens you've ever seen.
...Why?
Same reason I'm raising Daisy!
Sebastian... I have no idea why you're raising Daisy.

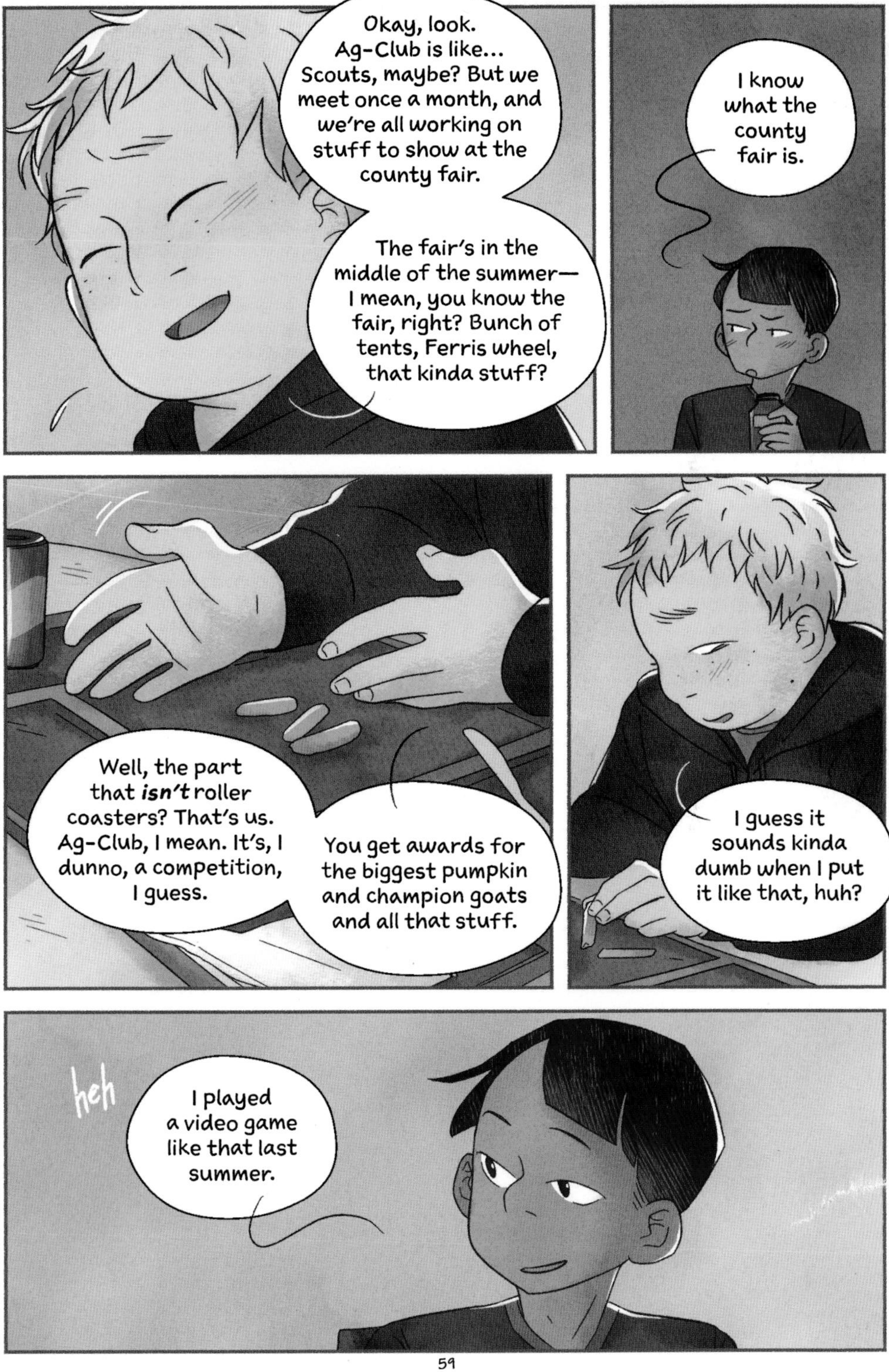
Okay, look. Ag-Club is like... Scouts, maybe? But we meet once a month, and we're all working on stuff to show at the county fair.
The fair's in the middle of the summer— I mean, you know the fair, right? Bunch of tents, Ferris wheel, that kinda stuff?
I know what the county fair is.
Well, the part that *isn't* roller coasters? That's us. Ag-Club, I mean. It's, I dunno, a competition, I guess.
You get awards for the biggest pumpkin and champion goats and all that stuff.
I guess it sounds kinda dumb when I put it like that, huh?
heh
I played a video game like that last summer.

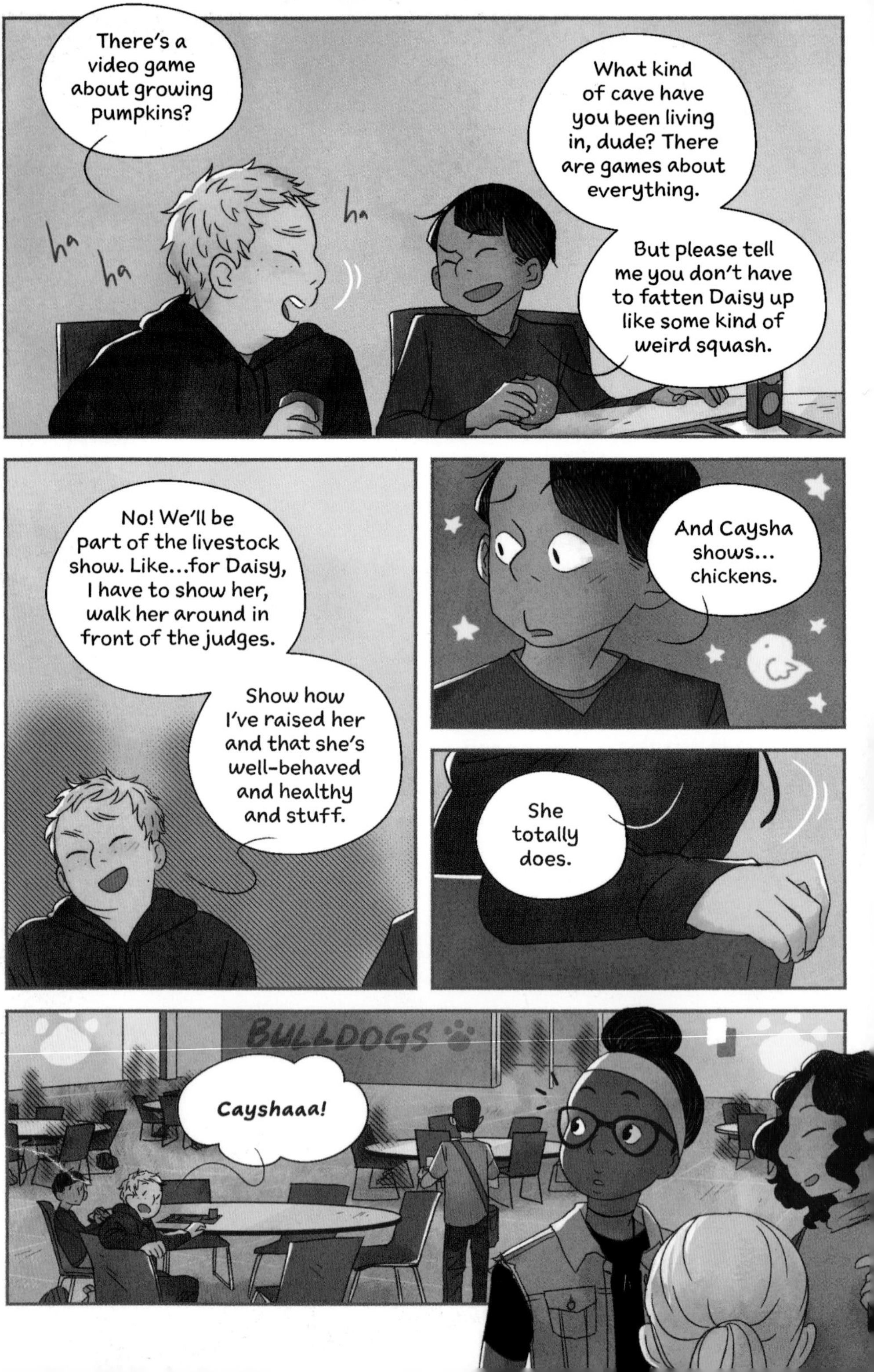
There's a video game about growing pumpkins?
ha
ha
ha
What kind of cave have you been living in, dude? There are games about everything.
But please tell me you don't have to fatten Daisy up like some kind of weird squash.
No! We'll be part of the livestock show. Like...for Daisy, I have to show her, walk her around in front of the judges.
Show how I've raised her and that she's well-behaved and healthy and stuff.
And Caysha shows... chickens.
She totally does.
BULLDOGS
Cayshaaa!

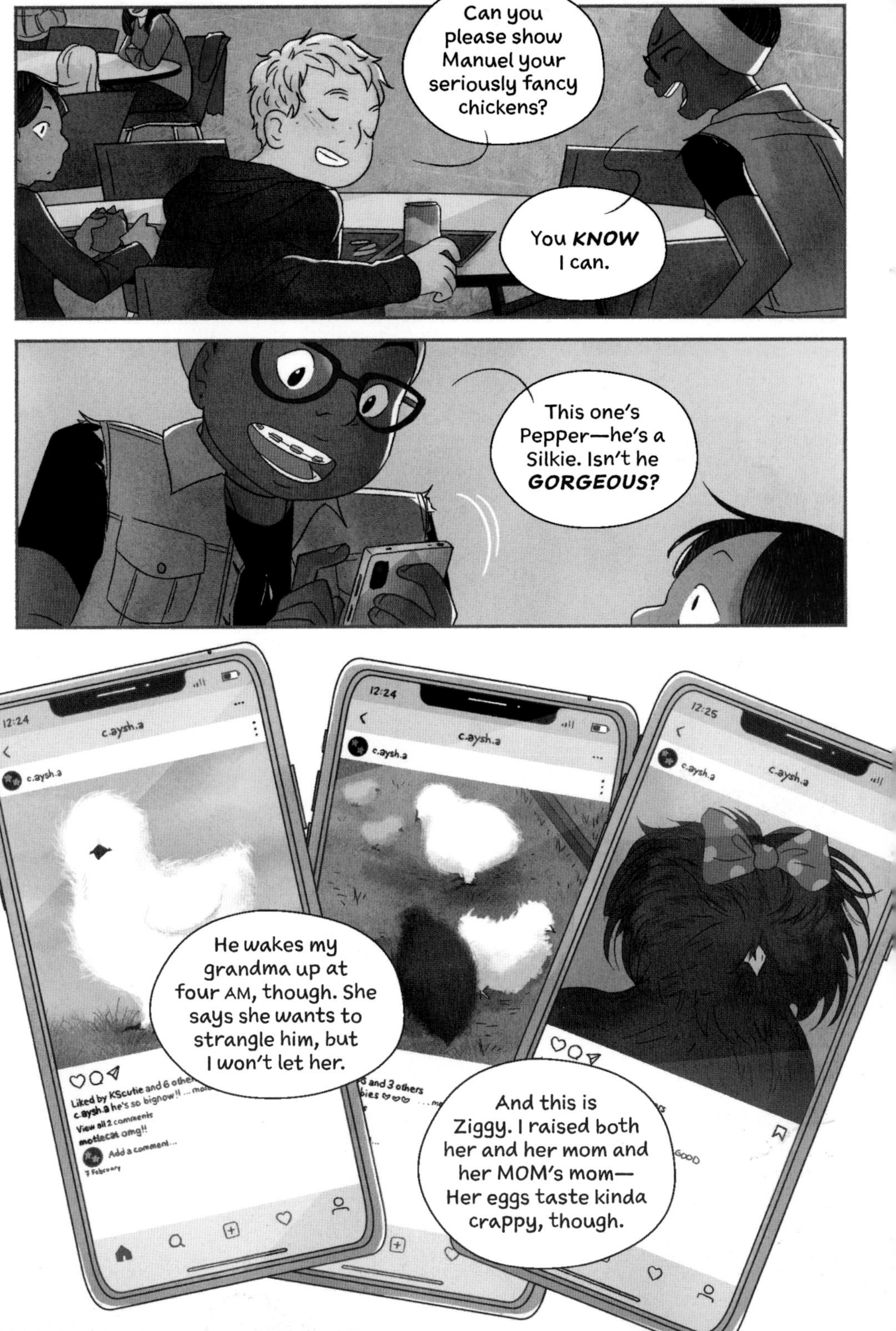
Can you please show Manuel your seriously fancy chickens?
You KNOW I can.
This one's Pepper—he's a Silkie. Isn't he GORGEOUS?
12:24
c.aysh.a
c.aysh.a
He wakes my grandma up at four AM, though. She says she wants to strangle him, but I won't let her.
12:24
c.aysh.a
c.aysh.a
12:25
c.aysh.a
c.aysh.a
And this is Ziggy. I raised both her and her mom and her MOM's mom—Her eggs taste kinda crappy, though.

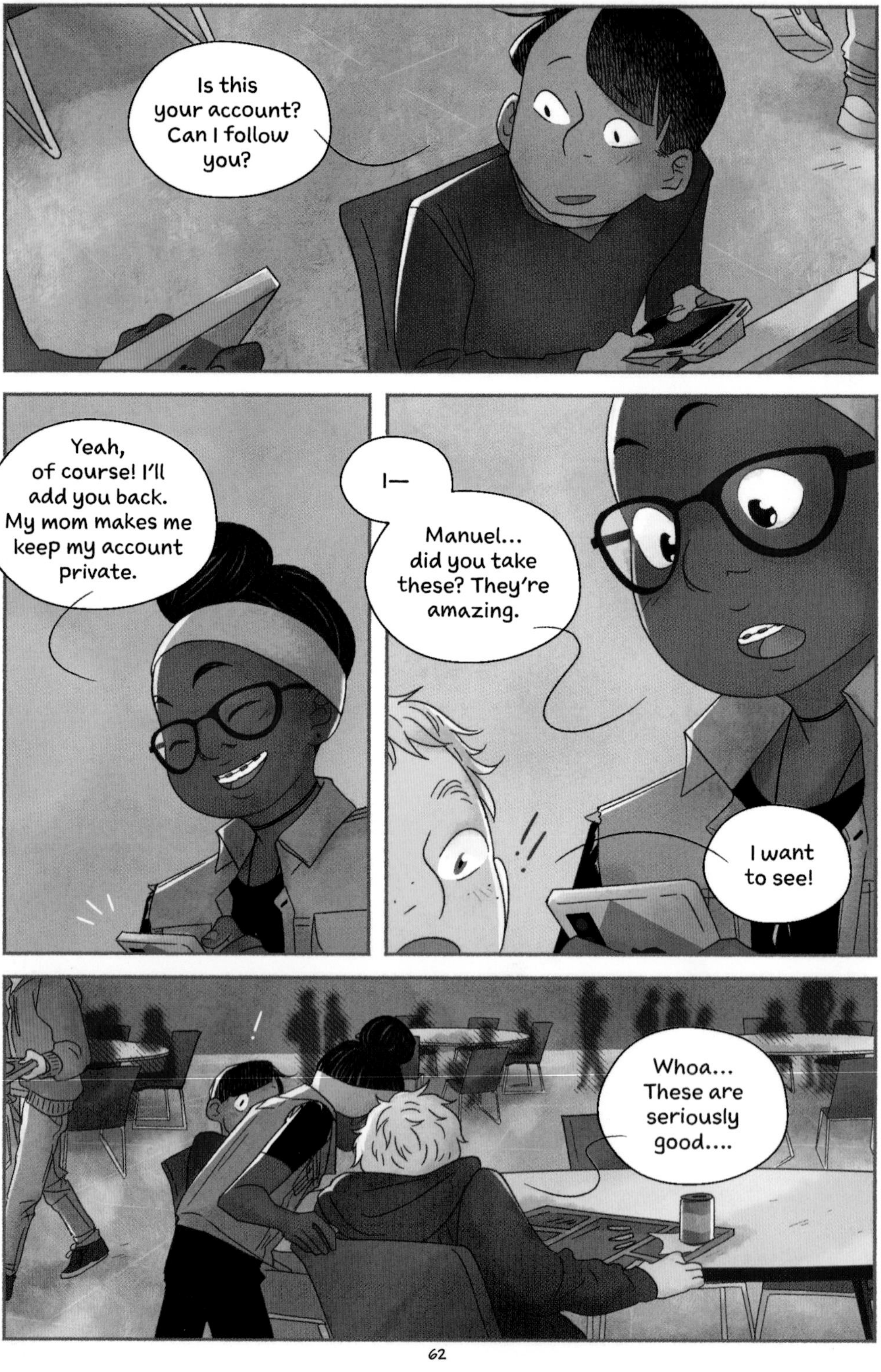
Is this your account? Can I follow you?
Yeah, of course! I'll add you back. My mom makes me keep my account private.
I—
Manuel... did you take these? They're amazing.
!!
I want to see!
!
Whoa... These are seriously good....

Ahh! Look!

SWIPE

12:27

finding_anchors

finding_anch

ed by urbncoyote_ and 36 others
ding_anchors #sky.
all 3 comments
st year. Great
Add a commen

Oh my God, it's me!

I'm sorry, I didn't— I should've asked— If it was okay, I mean— I'm sorry—

No, no, it's cool, it's an awesome shot! When did you even take this?

Man, look at Daisy....It's been, what, four days? She's already put on five pounds, y'know. Just wait till you see her....

?

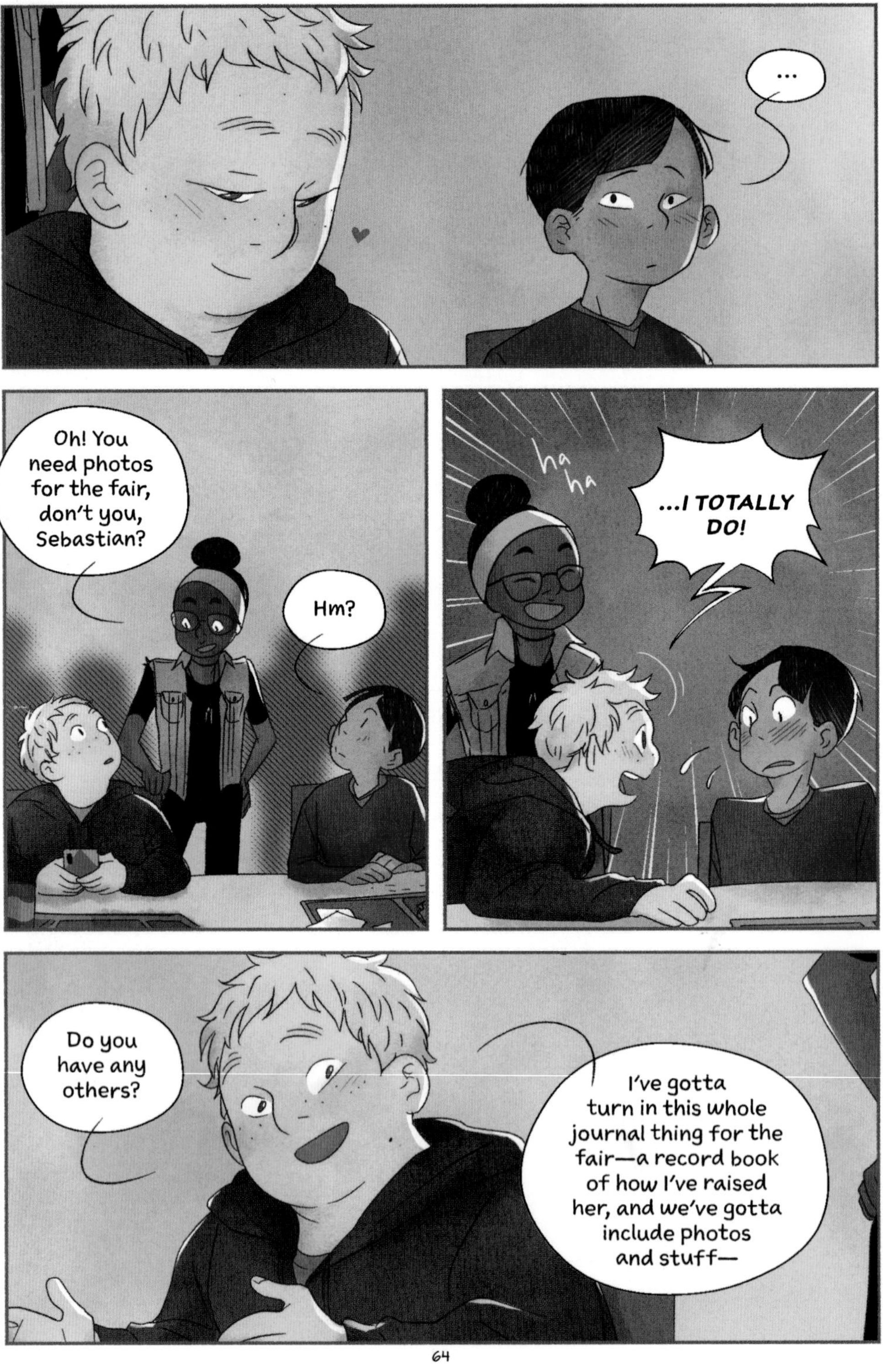
...
Oh! You need photos for the fair, don't you, Sebastian?
Hm?
ha ha
...I TOTALLY DO!
Do you have any others?
I've gotta turn in this whole journal thing for the fair—a record book of how I've raised her, and we've gotta include photos and stuff—

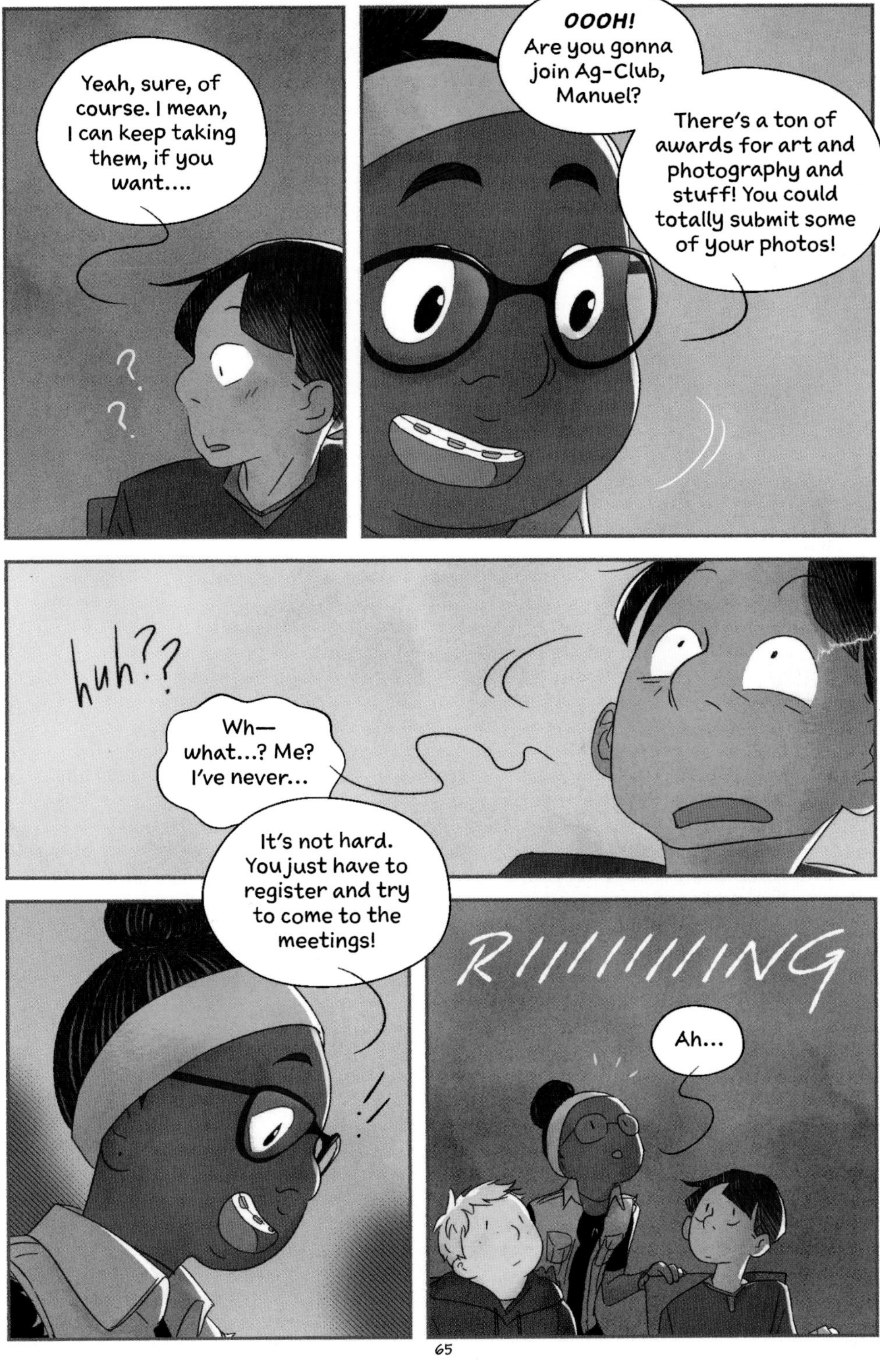
Yeah, sure, of course. I mean, I can keep taking them, if you want....
OOOH! Are you gonna join Ag-Club, Manuel?
There's a ton of awards for art and photography and stuff! You could totally submit some of your photos!
huh??
Wh— what...? Me? I've never...
It's not hard. You just have to register and try to come to the meetings!
RIIIIIING
Ah...

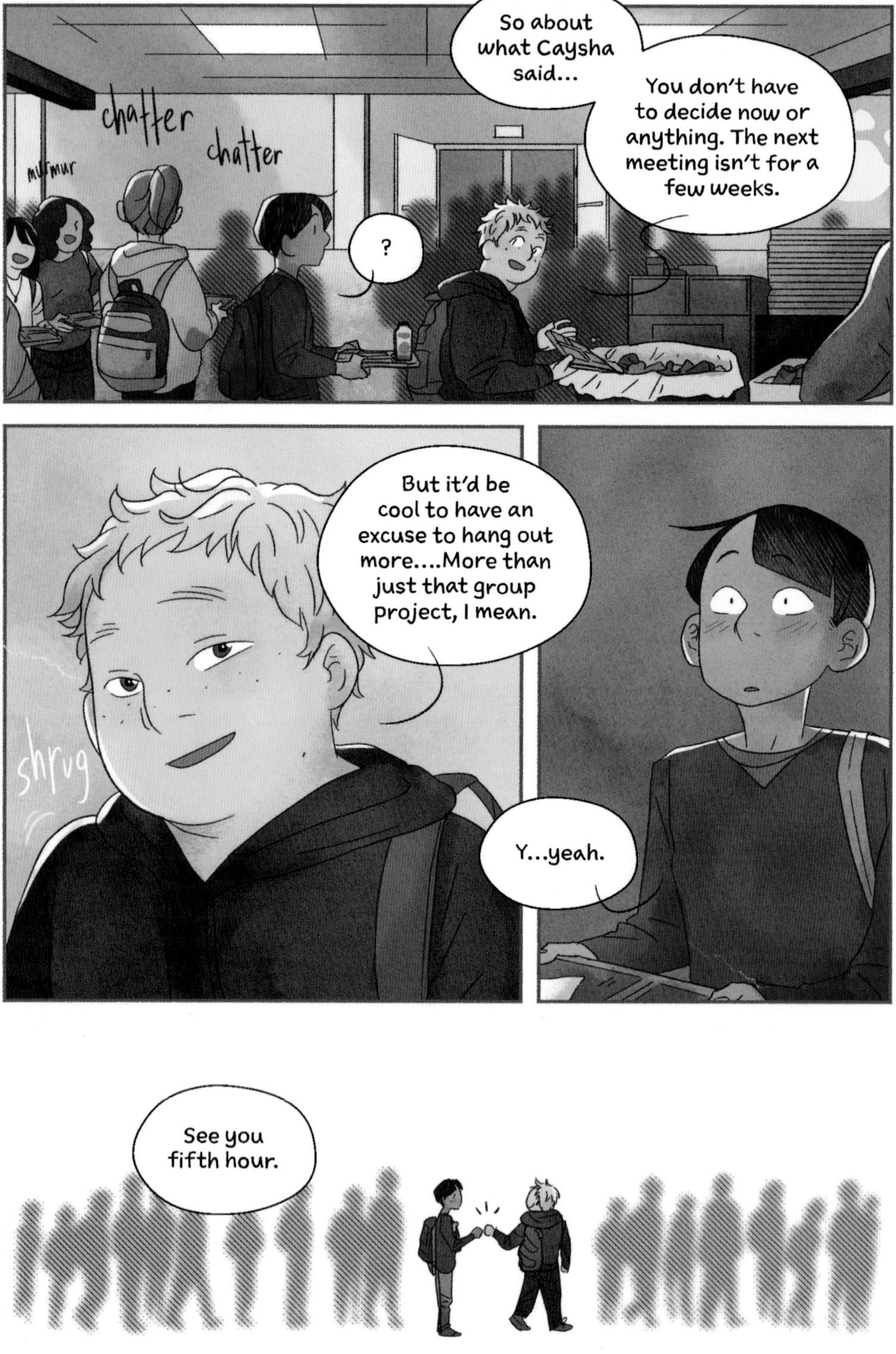
chatter
chatter
murmur
So about what Caysha said...
You don't have to decide now or anything. The next meeting isn't for a few weeks.
?
But it'd be cool to have an excuse to hang out more....More than just that group project, I mean.
shrug
Y...yeah.
See you fifth hour.

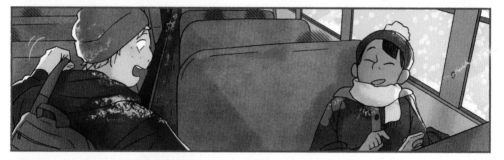

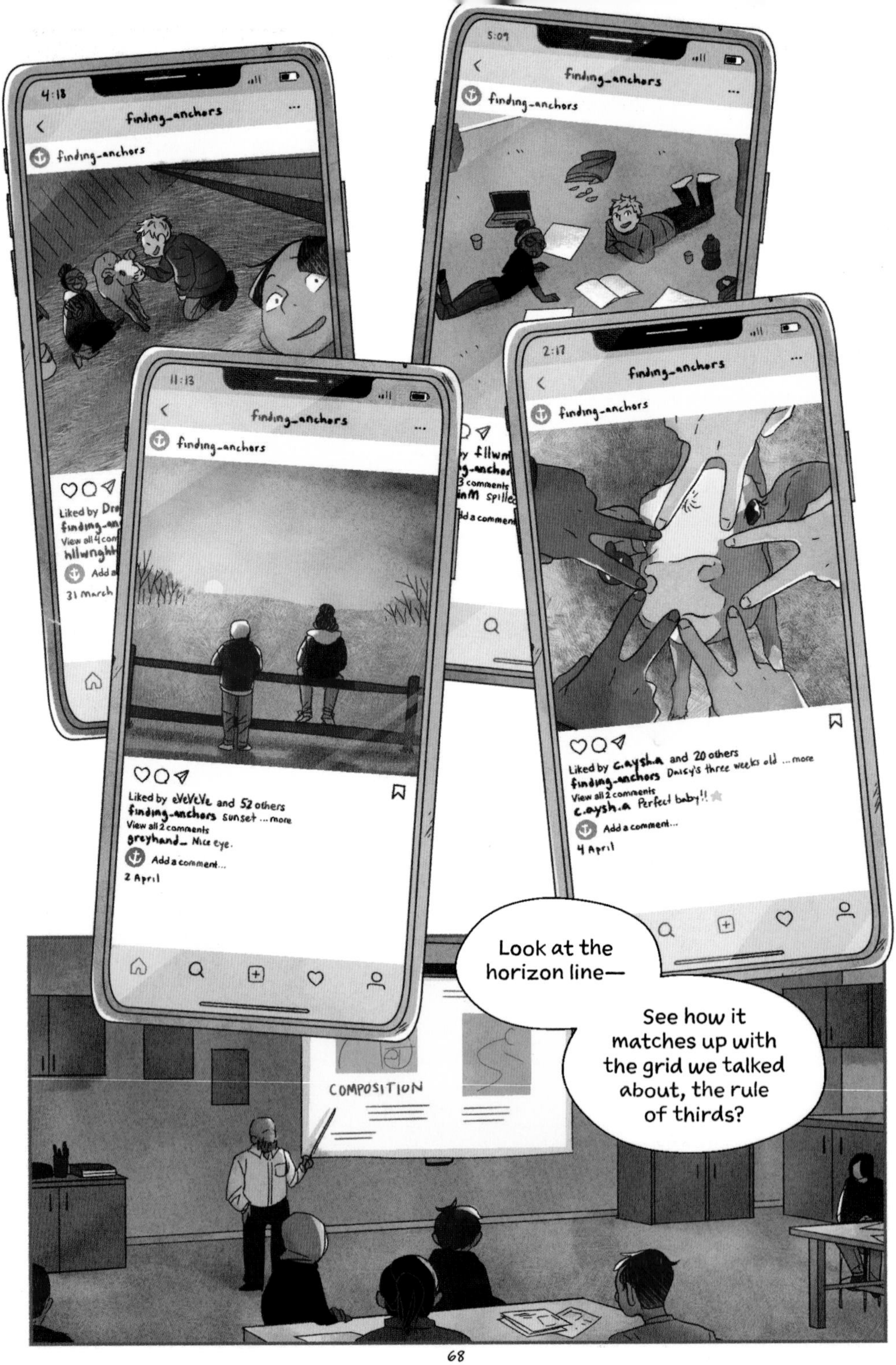
4:18
finding_anchors
finding_anchors
31 March
5:09
finding_anchors
finding_anchors
11:13
finding_anchors
finding_anchors
Liked by eVeVeVe and 52 others
finding_anchors sunset ... more
View all 2 comments
greyhand_ Nice eye.
Add a comment...
2 April
2:17
finding_anchors
finding_anchors
Liked by c.aysh.a and 20 others
finding_anchors Daisy's three weeks old ... more
View all 2 comments
c.aysh.a Perfect baby!!
Add a comment...
4 April
COMPOSITION
Look at the horizon line—
See how it matches up with the grid we talked about, the rule of thirds?

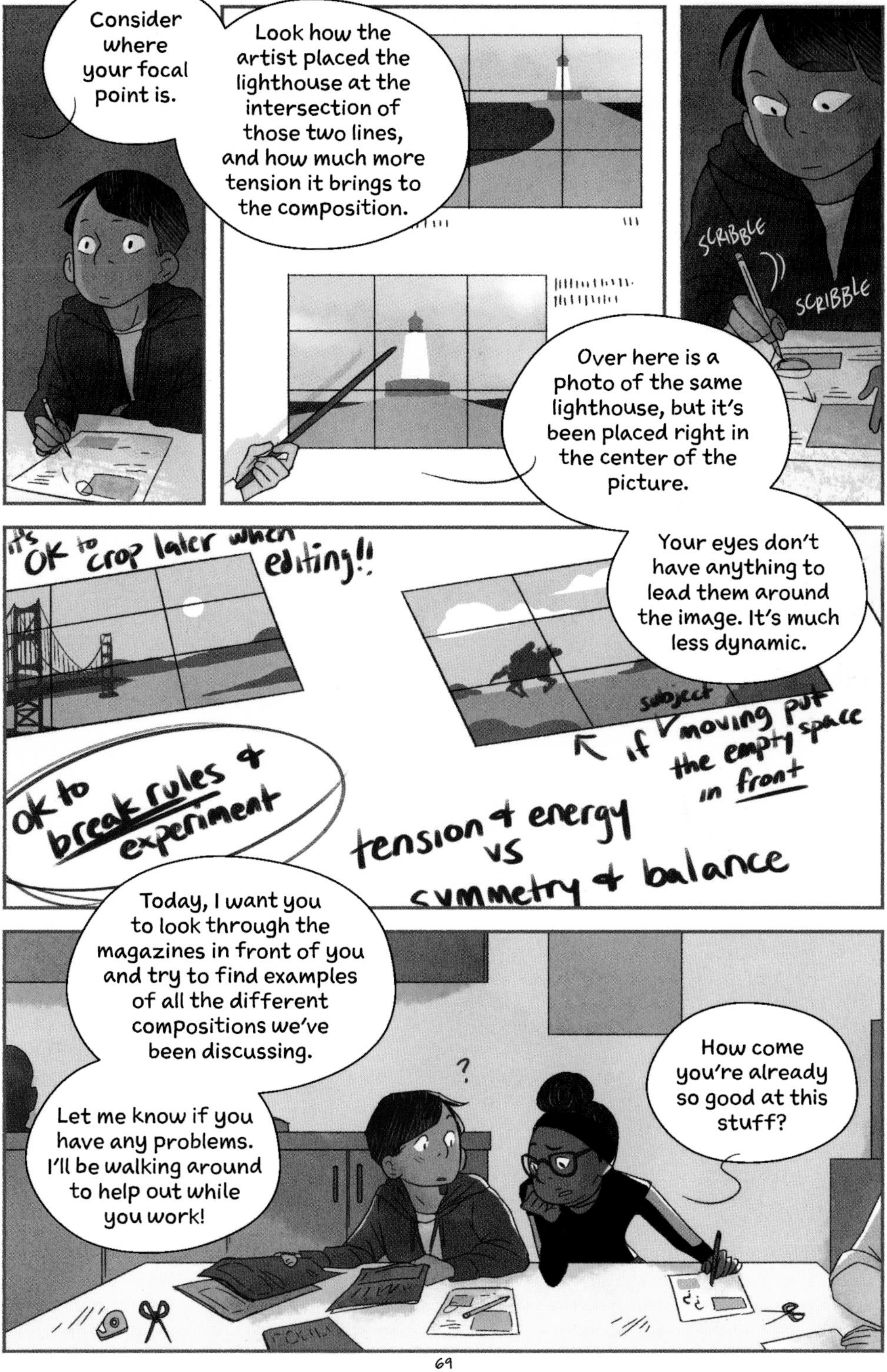
Consider where your focal point is.
Look how the artist placed the lighthouse at the intersection of those two lines, and how much more tension it brings to the composition.
SCRIBBLE
SCRIBBLE
Over here is a photo of the same lighthouse, but it's been placed right in the center of the picture.
Your eyes don't have anything to lead them around the image. It's much less dynamic.
it's OK to crop later when editing!!
ok to break rules & experiment
if subject moving put the empty space in front
tension & energy vs symmetry & balance
Today, I want you to look through the magazines in front of you and try to find examples of all the different compositions we've been discussing.
Let me know if you have any problems. I'll be walking around to help out while you work!
?
How come you're already so good at this stuff?

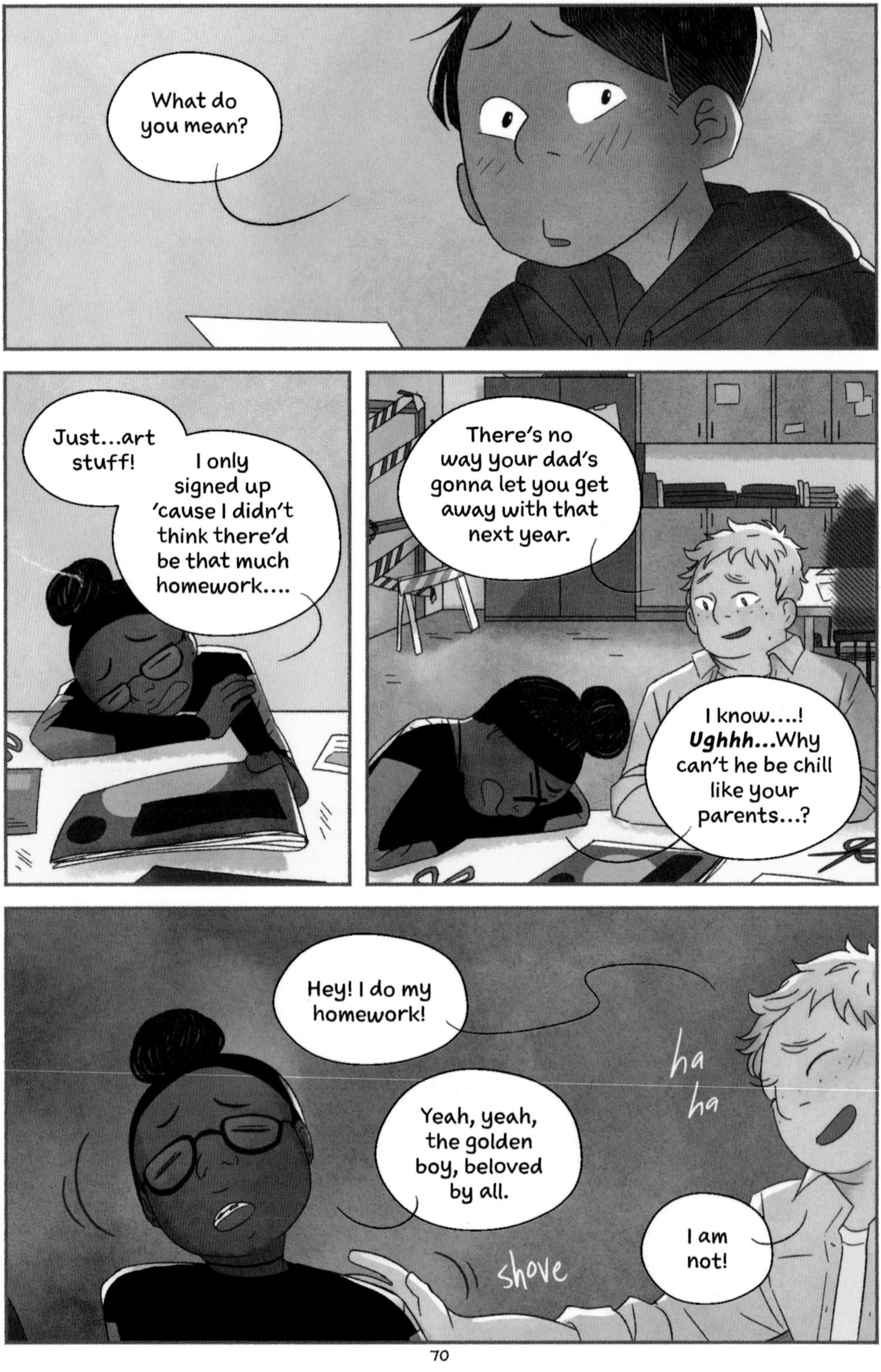
What do you mean?
Just...art stuff!
I only signed up 'cause I didn't think there'd be that much homework....
There's no way your dad's gonna let you get away with that next year.
I know....! **Ughhh...**Why can't he be chill like your parents...?
Hey! I do my homework!
ha ha
Yeah, yeah, the golden boy, beloved by all.
I am not!
shove

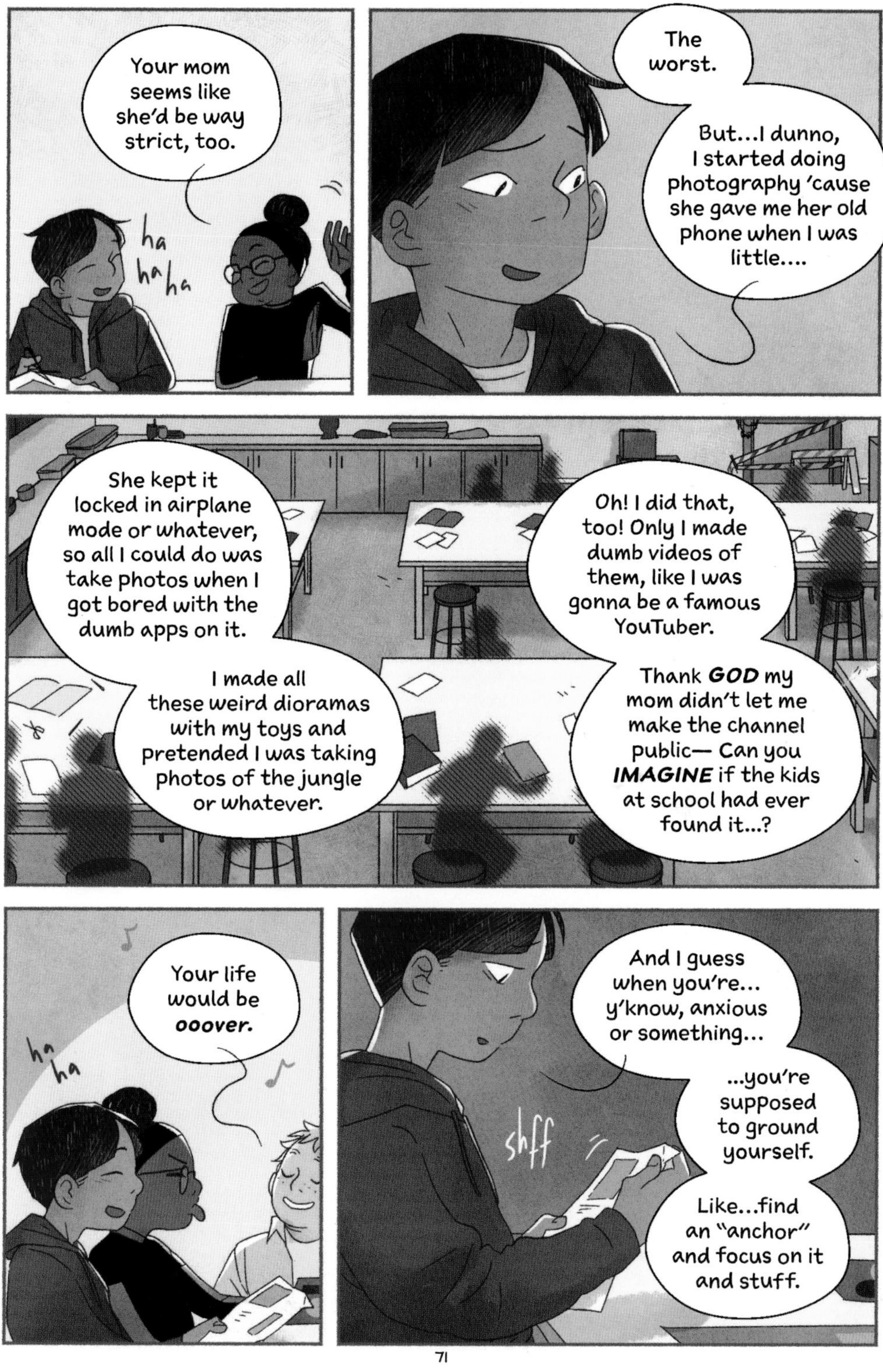
Your mom seems like she'd be way strict, too.
ha haha
The worst.
But...I dunno, I started doing photography 'cause she gave me her old phone when I was little....
She kept it locked in airplane mode or whatever, so all I could do was take photos when I got bored with the dumb apps on it.
I made all these weird dioramas with my toys and pretended I was taking photos of the jungle or whatever.
Oh! I did that, too! Only I made dumb videos of them, like I was gonna be a famous YouTuber.
Thank **GOD** my mom didn't let me make the channel public— Can you ***IMAGINE*** if the kids at school had ever found it...?
Your life would be ***ooover.***
ha ha
And I guess when you're... y'know, anxious or something...
...you're supposed to ground yourself.
Like...find an "anchor" and focus on it and stuff.
shff

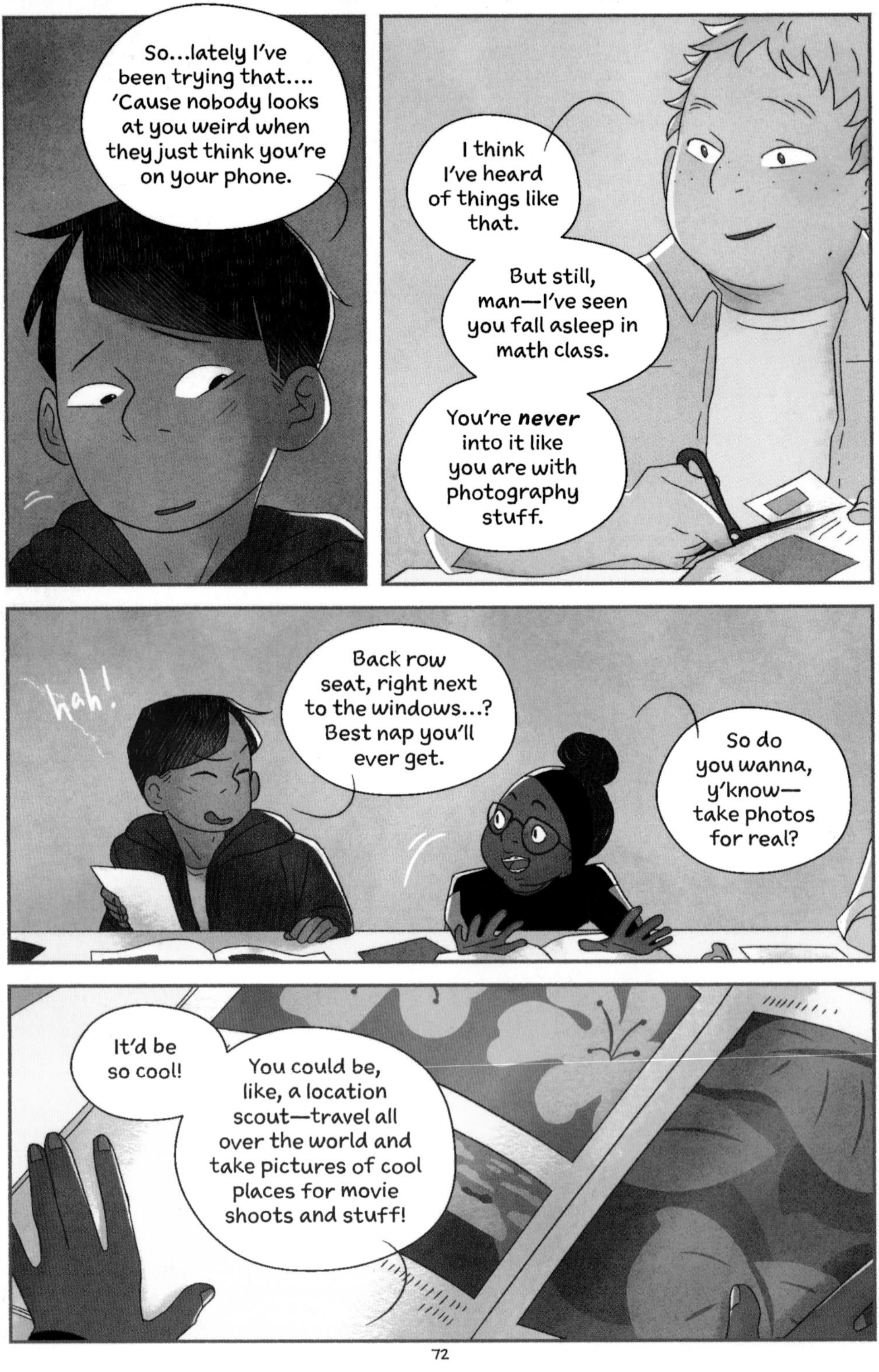

So...lately I've been trying that.... 'Cause nobody looks at you weird when they just think you're on your phone.
I think I've heard of things like that.
But still, man—I've seen you fall asleep in math class.
You're ***never*** into it like you are with photography stuff.
hah!
Back row seat, right next to the windows...? Best nap you'll ever get.
So do you wanna, y'know—take photos for real?
It'd be so cool!
You could be, like, a location scout—travel all over the world and take pictures of cool places for movie shoots and stuff!

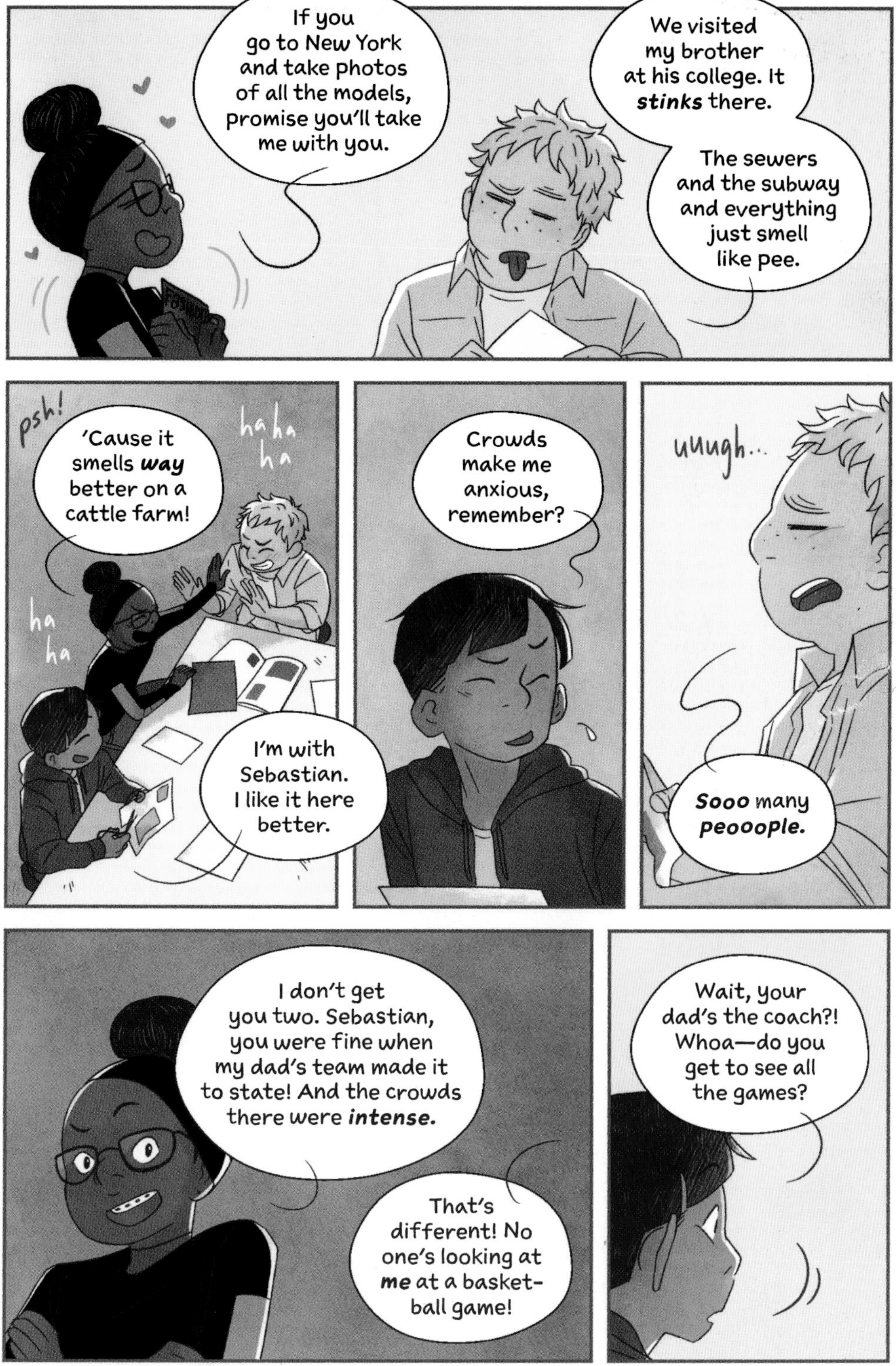
If you go to New York and take photos of all the models, promise you'll take me with you.
We visited my brother at his college. It **stinks** there.
The sewers and the subway and everything just smell like pee.
psh!
'Cause it smells **way** better on a cattle farm!
ha ha ha
ha ha
I'm with Sebastian. I like it here better.
Crowds make me anxious, remember?
uuugh...
Sooo many **peooople.**
I don't get you two. Sebastian, you were fine when my dad's team made it to state! And the crowds there were **intense.**
That's different! No one's looking at **me** at a basket-ball game!
Wait, your dad's the coach?! Whoa—do you get to see all the games?

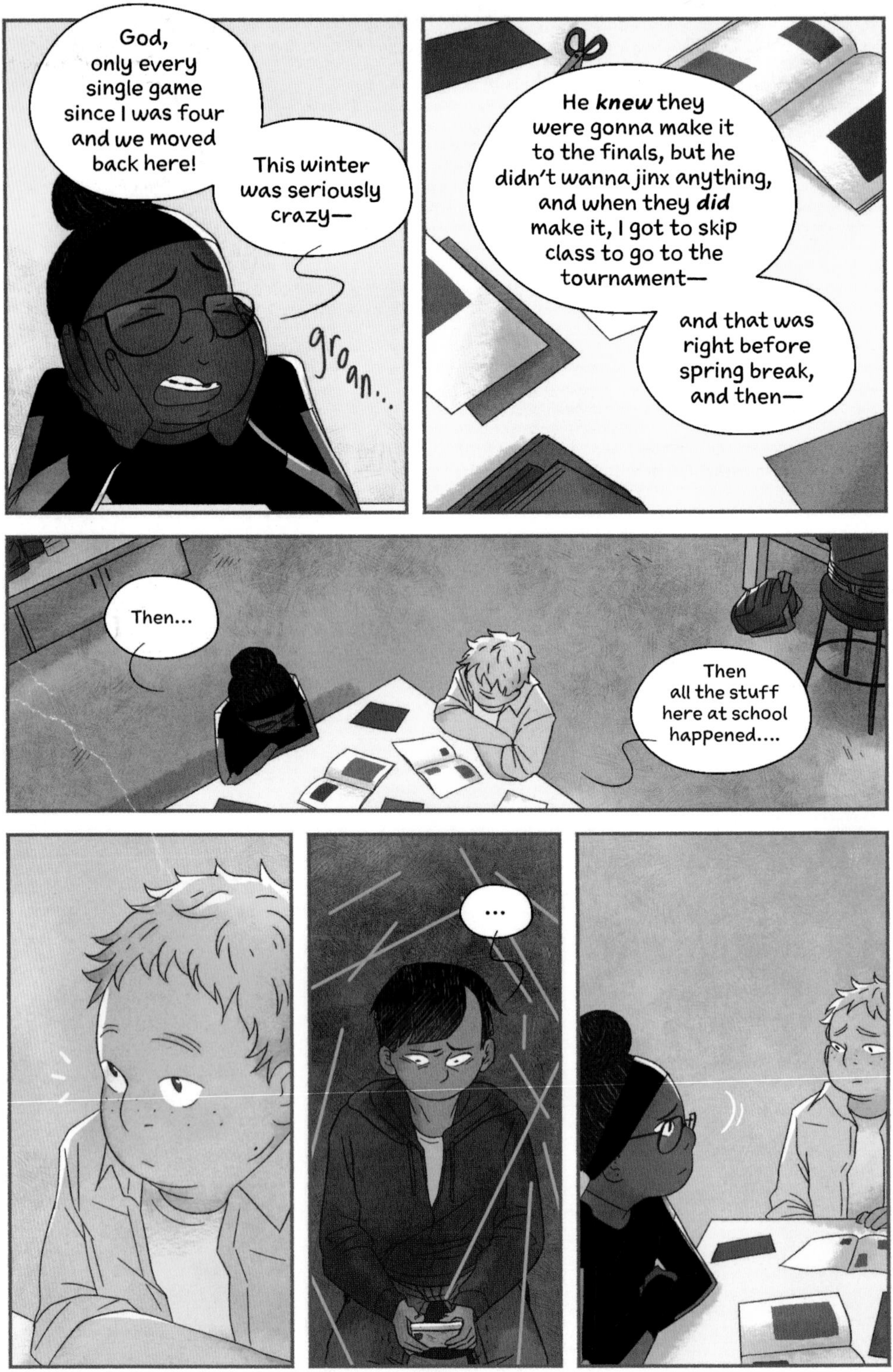
God, only every single game since I was four and we moved back here!
This winter was seriously crazy—
groan...
He *knew* they were gonna make it to the finals, but he didn't wanna jinx anything, and when they *did* make it, I got to skip class to go to the tournament—
and that was right before spring break, and then—
Then...
Then all the stuff here at school happened....
...

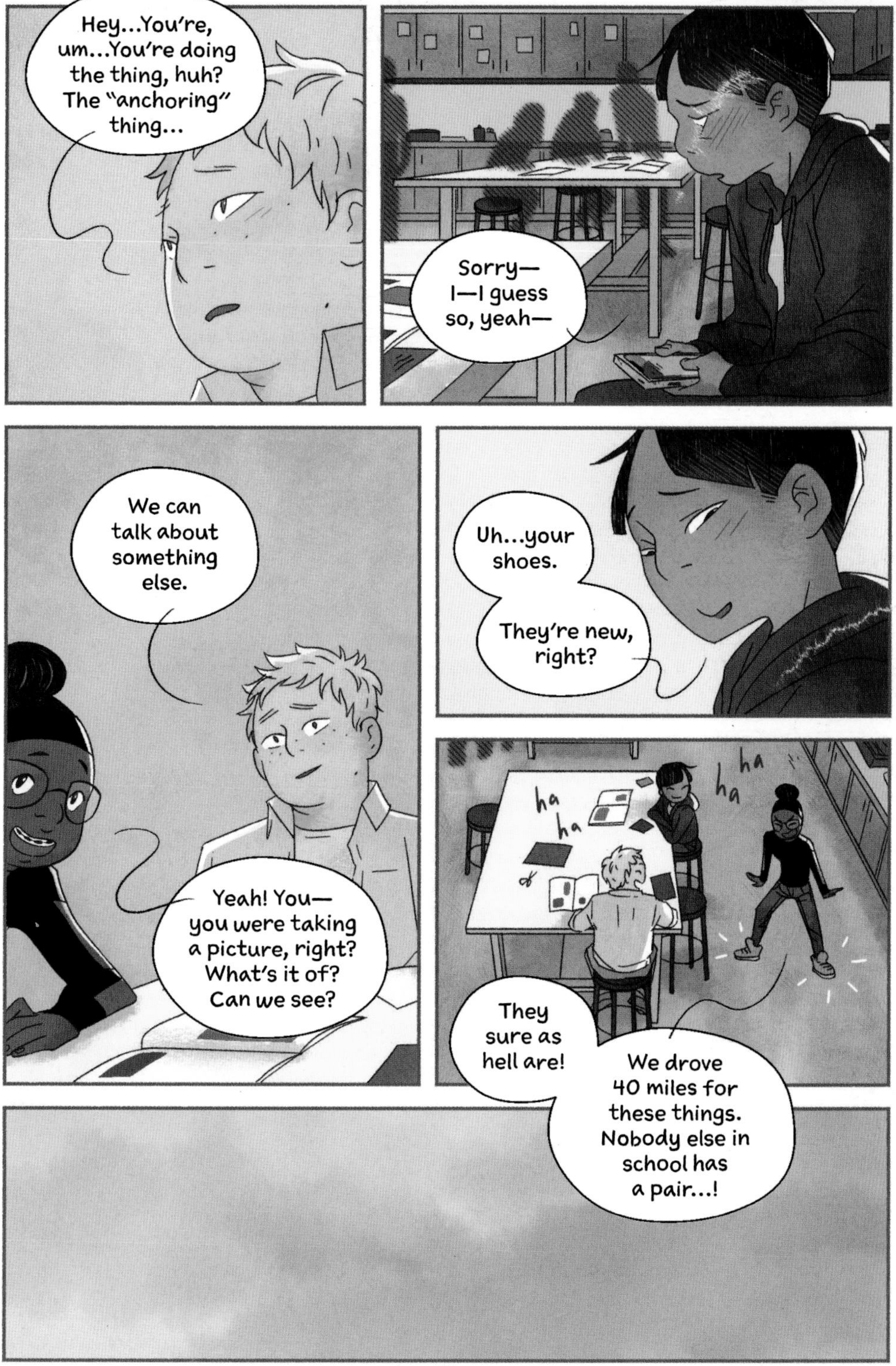

Hey...You're, um...You're doing the thing, huh? The "anchoring" thing...
Sorry— I—I guess so, yeah—
We can talk about something else.
Yeah! You— you were taking a picture, right? What's it of? Can we see?
Uh...your shoes.
They're new, right?
ha ha
ha ha
They sure as hell are!
We drove 40 miles for these things. Nobody else in school has a pair...!

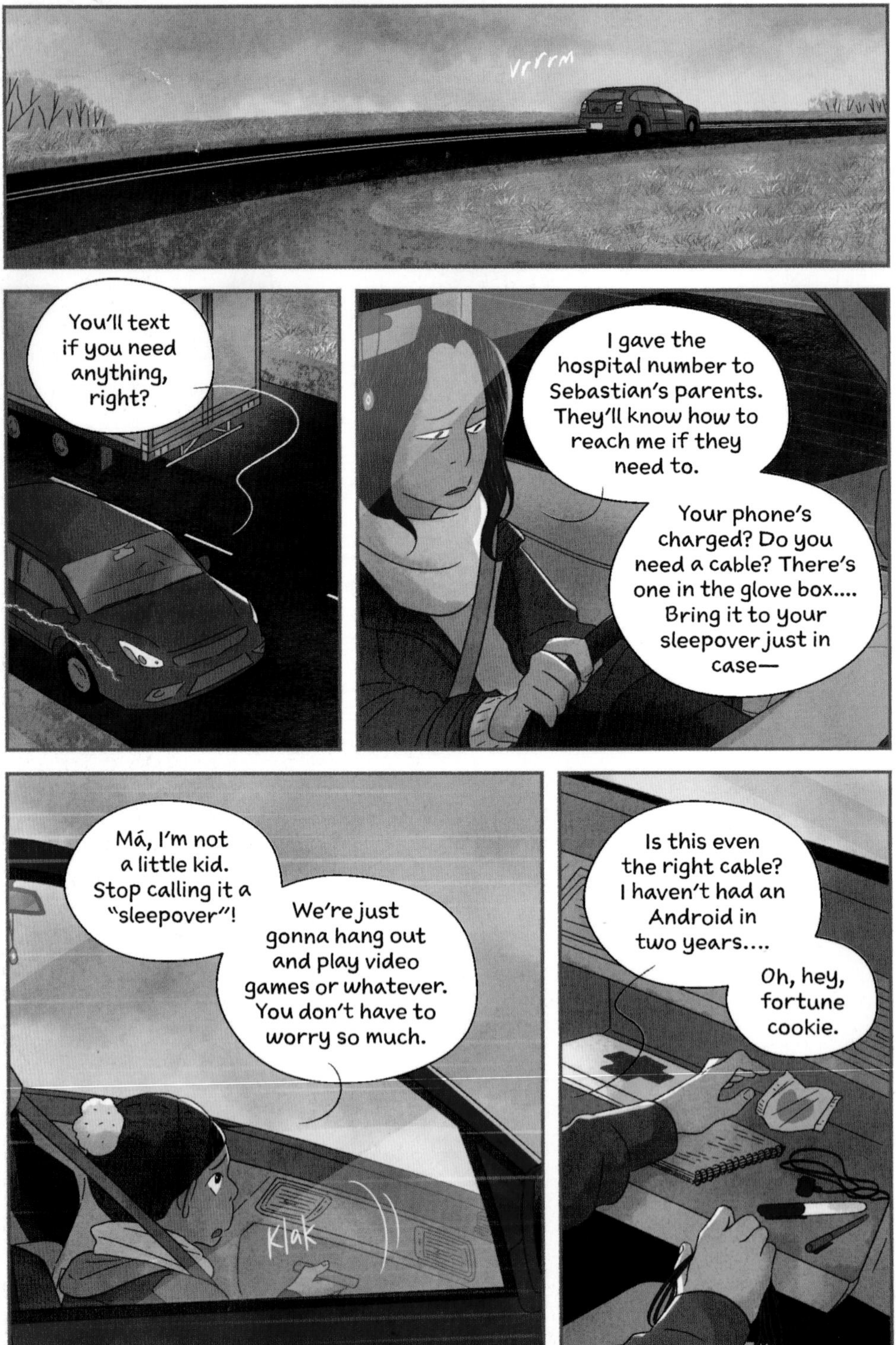

Vrrrm
You'll text if you need anything, right?
I gave the hospital number to Sebastian's parents. They'll know how to reach me if they need to.
Your phone's charged? Do you need a cable? There's one in the glove box.... Bring it to your sleepover just in case—
Má, I'm not a little kid. Stop calling it a "sleepover"!
We're just gonna hang out and play video games or whatever. You don't have to worry so much.
Klak
Is this even the right cable? I haven't had an Android in two years....
Oh, hey, fortune cookie.

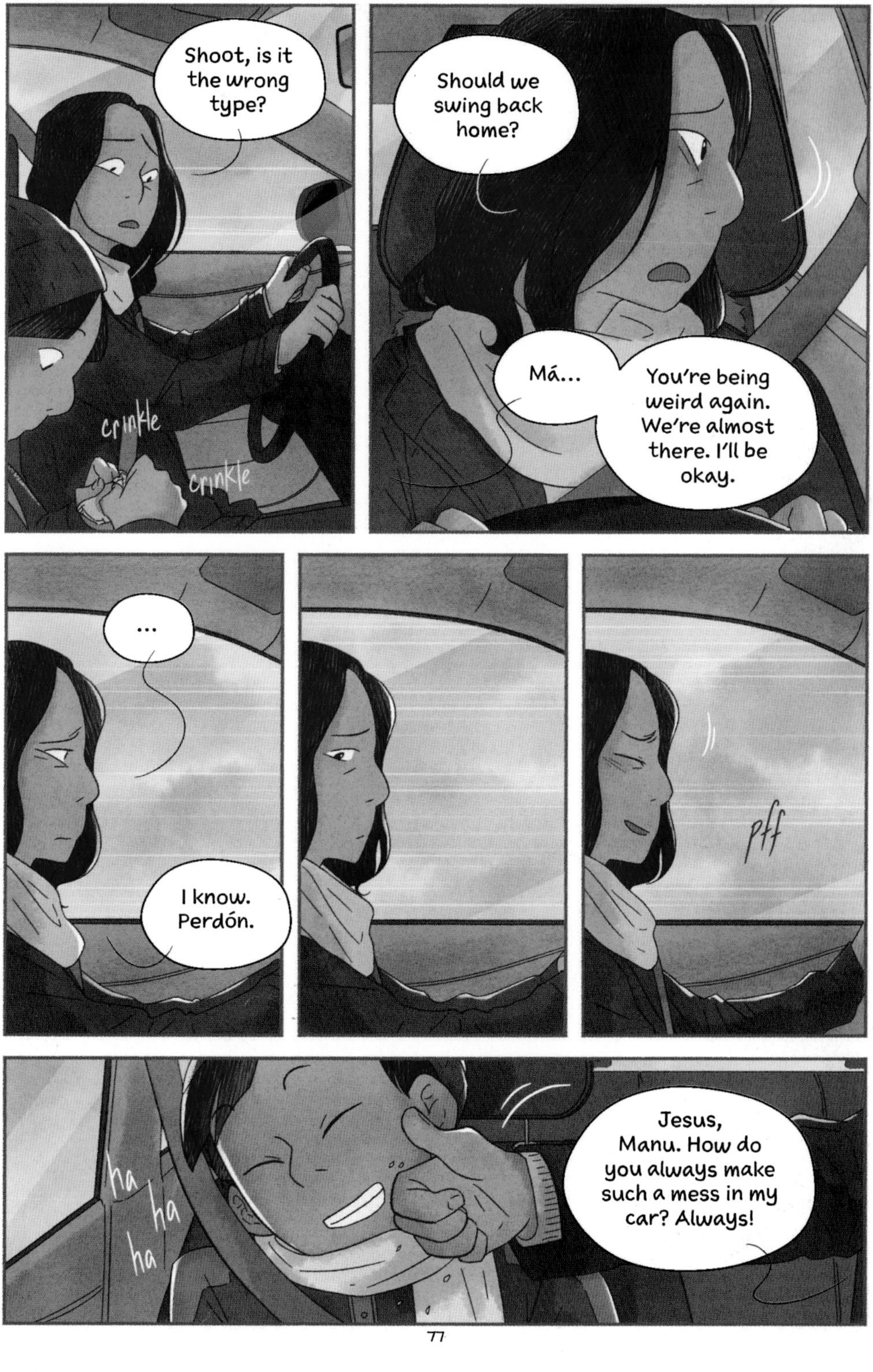
Shoot, is it the wrong type?
crinkle
crinkle
Should we swing back home?
Má...
You're being weird again. We're almost there. I'll be okay.
...
I know. Perdón.
pff
Jesus, Manu. How do you always make such a mess in my car? Always!
ha
ha
ha

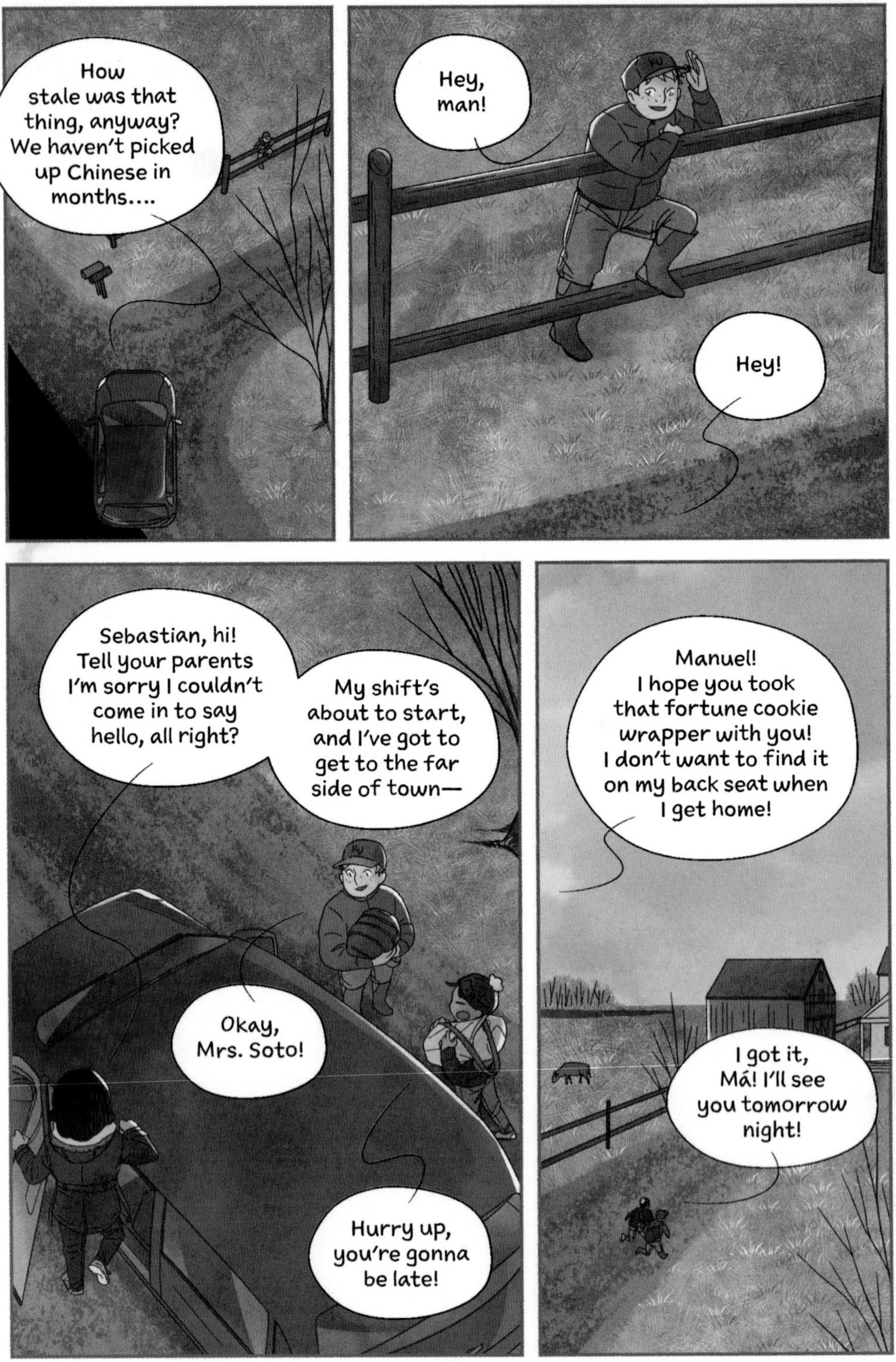
How stale was that thing, anyway? We haven't picked up Chinese in months....
Hey, man!
Hey!
Sebastian, hi! Tell your parents I'm sorry I couldn't come in to say hello, all right?
My shift's about to start, and I've got to get to the far side of town—
Okay, Mrs. Soto!
Hurry up, you're gonna be late!
Manuel! I hope you took that fortune cookie wrapper with you! I don't want to find it on my back seat when I get home!
I got it, Má! I'll see you tomorrow night!

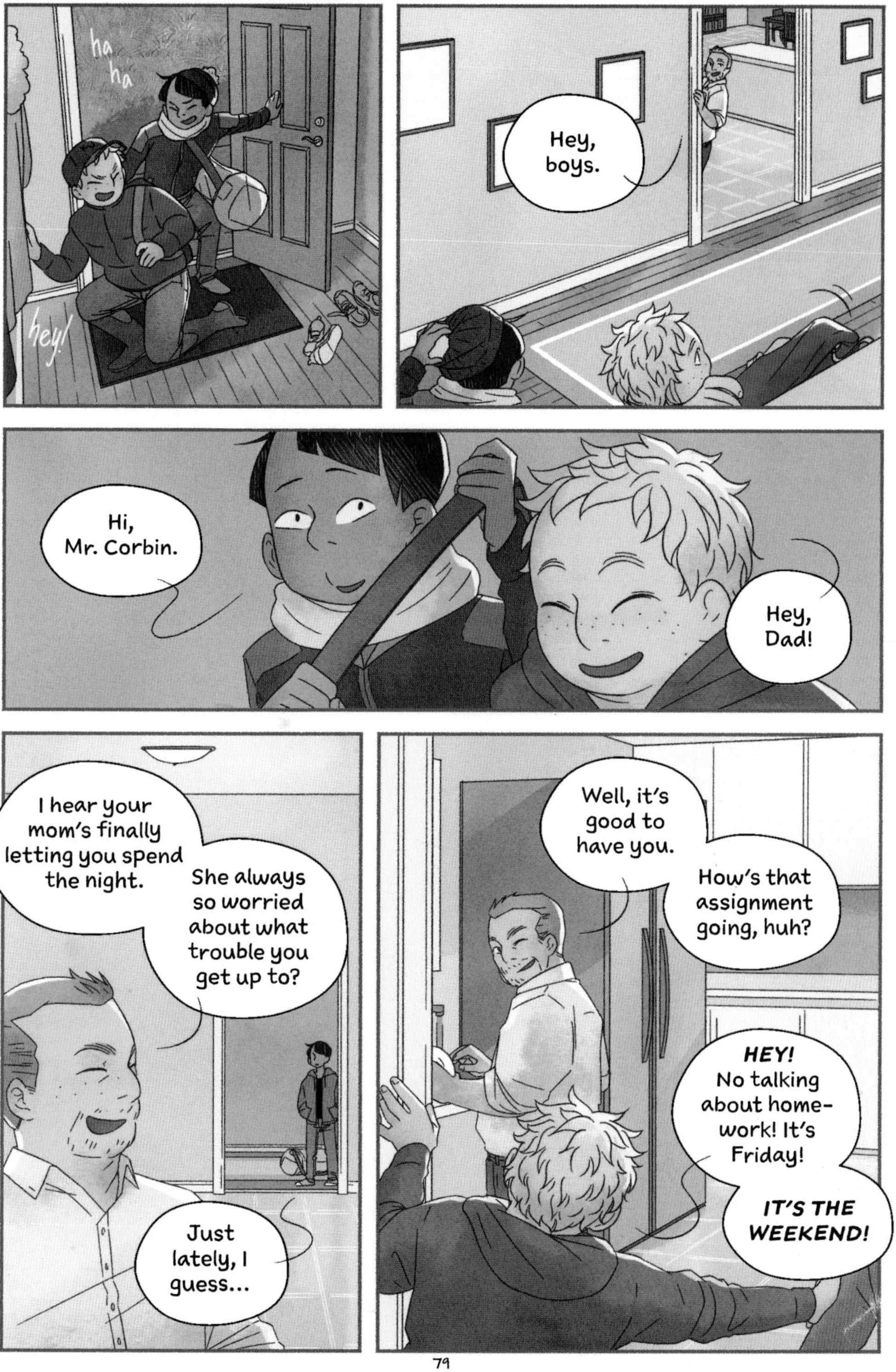
ha
ha
hey!
Hey, boys.
Hi, Mr. Corbin.
Hey, Dad!
I hear your mom's finally letting you spend the night.
She always so worried about what trouble you get up to?
Just lately, I guess...
Well, it's good to have you.
How's that assignment going, huh?
HEY! No talking about home-work! It's Friday!
IT'S THE WEEKEND!

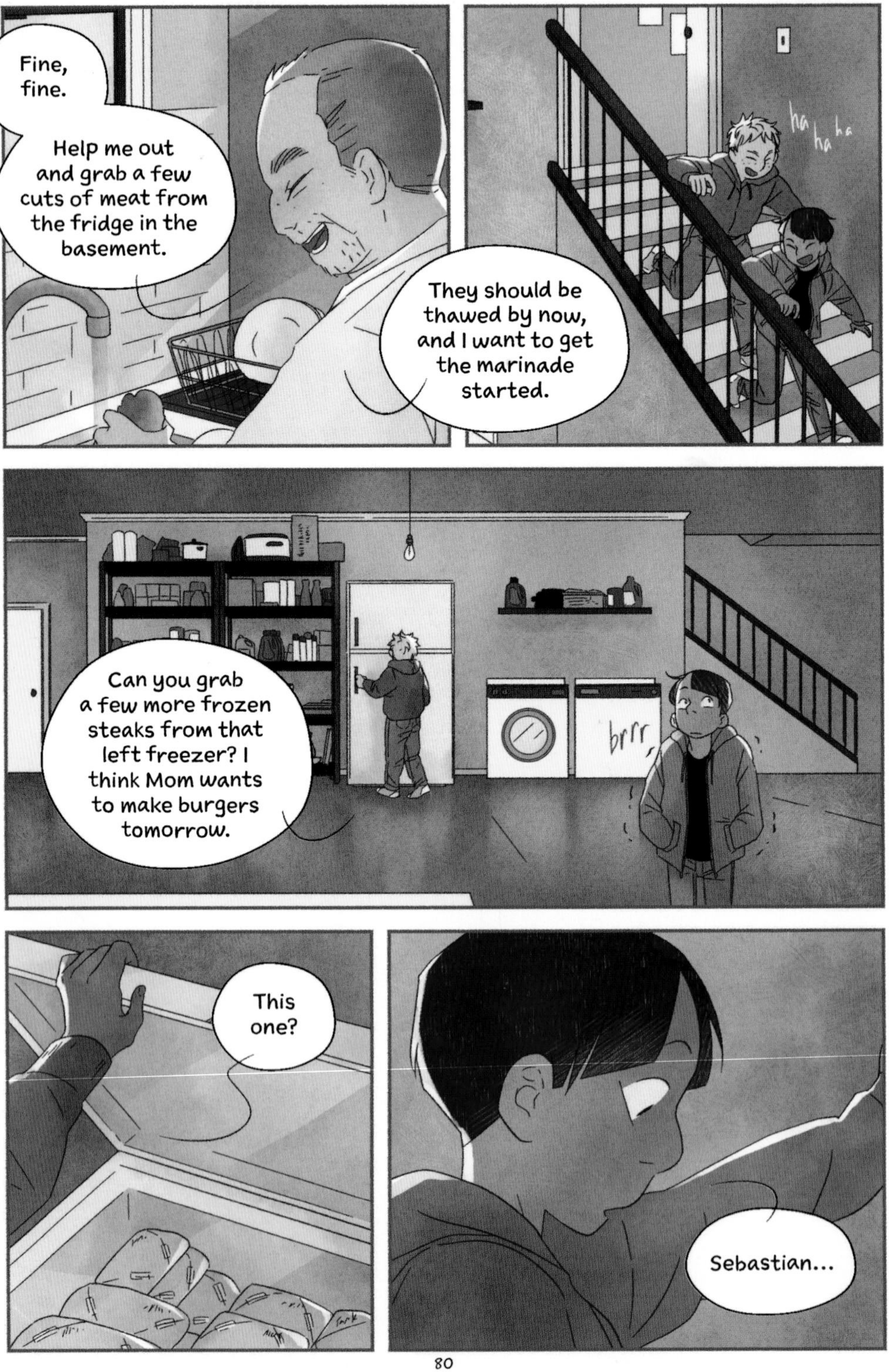
Fine, fine.
Help me out and grab a few cuts of meat from the fridge in the basement.
They should be thawed by now, and I want to get the marinade started.
ha ha ha
Can you grab a few more frozen steaks from that left freezer? I think Mom wants to make burgers tomorrow.
brrr
This one?
Sebastian...

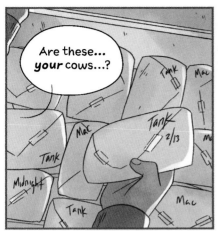

Are these... *your* cows...?

Steers.

Huh?

Steers.
Cows are—

Never mind.

Yeah. My folks
run a cattle farm,
Manuel. That's...
where steak
comes from.

I know
that— I
just—

Isn't it...
Isn't it hard?
I mean...

...naming them
and everything
like that.

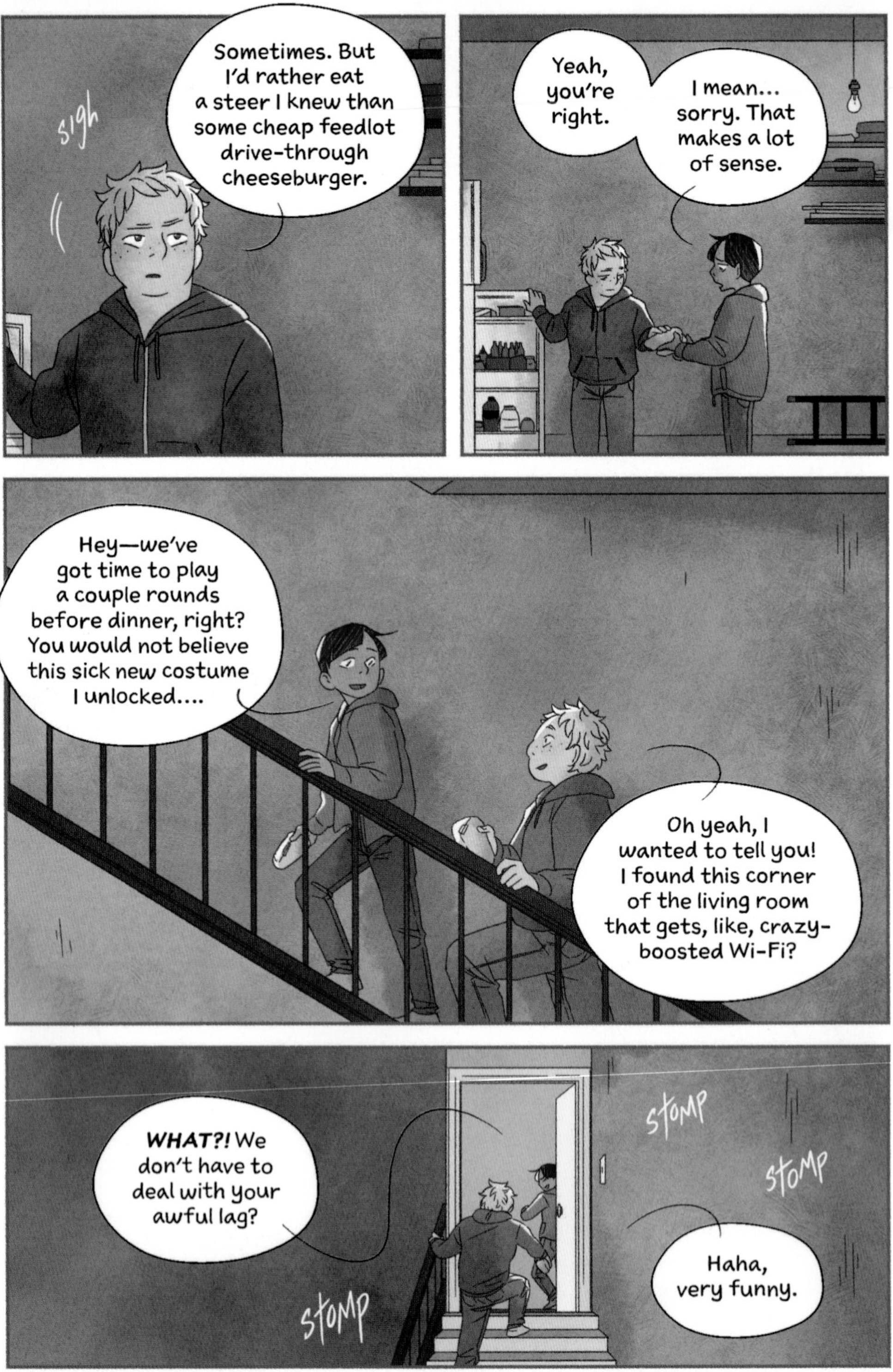
sigh
Sometimes. But I'd rather eat a steer I knew than some cheap feedlot drive-through cheeseburger.
Yeah, you're right.
I mean... sorry. That makes a lot of sense.
Hey—we've got time to play a couple rounds before dinner, right? You would not believe this sick new costume I unlocked....
Oh yeah, I wanted to tell you! I found this corner of the living room that gets, like, crazy-boosted Wi-Fi?
WHAT?! We don't have to deal with your awful lag?
STOMP
STOMP
STOMP
Haha, very funny.

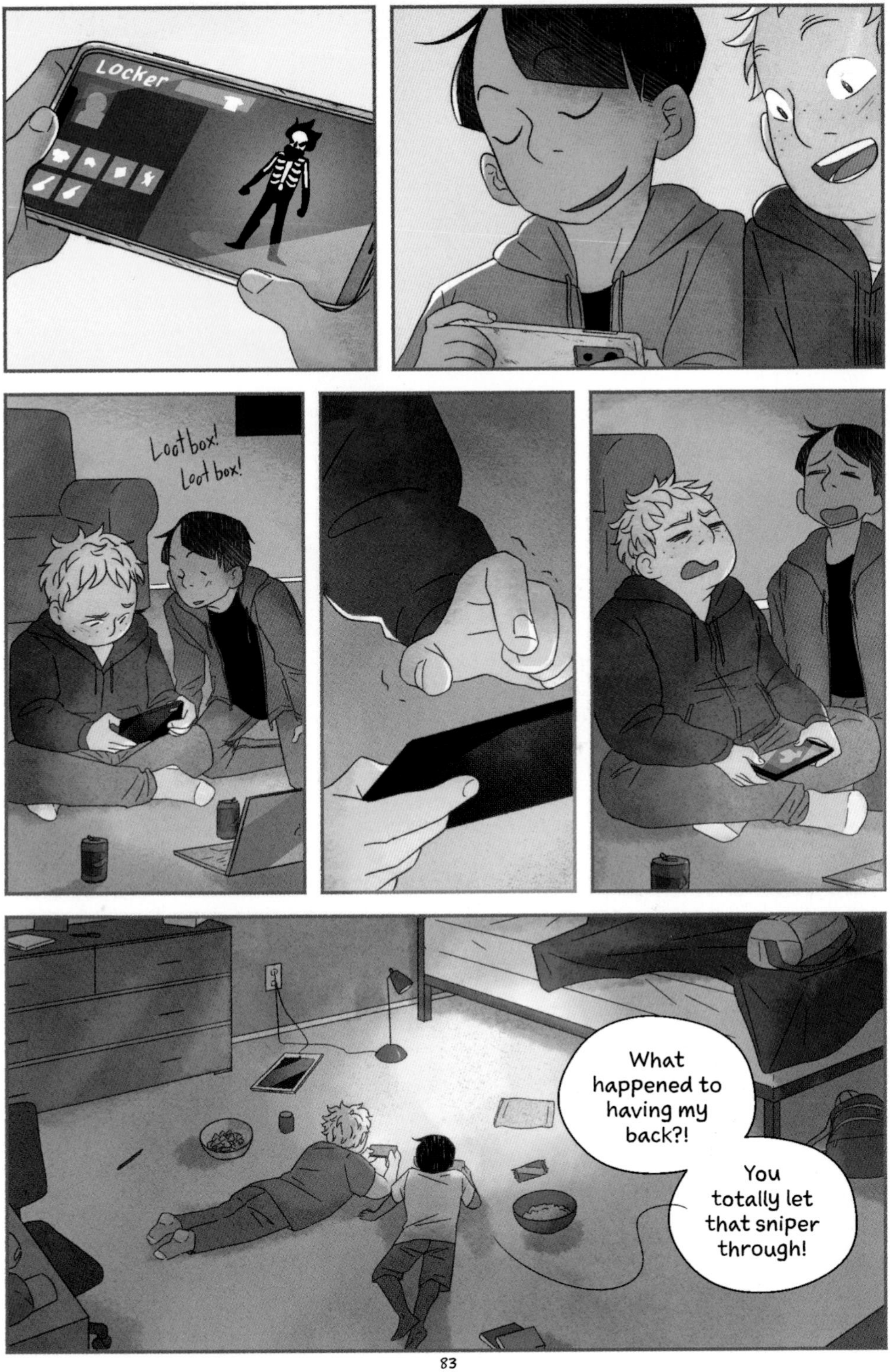
Locker
Loot box!
Loot box!
What happened to having my back?!
You totally let that sniper through!

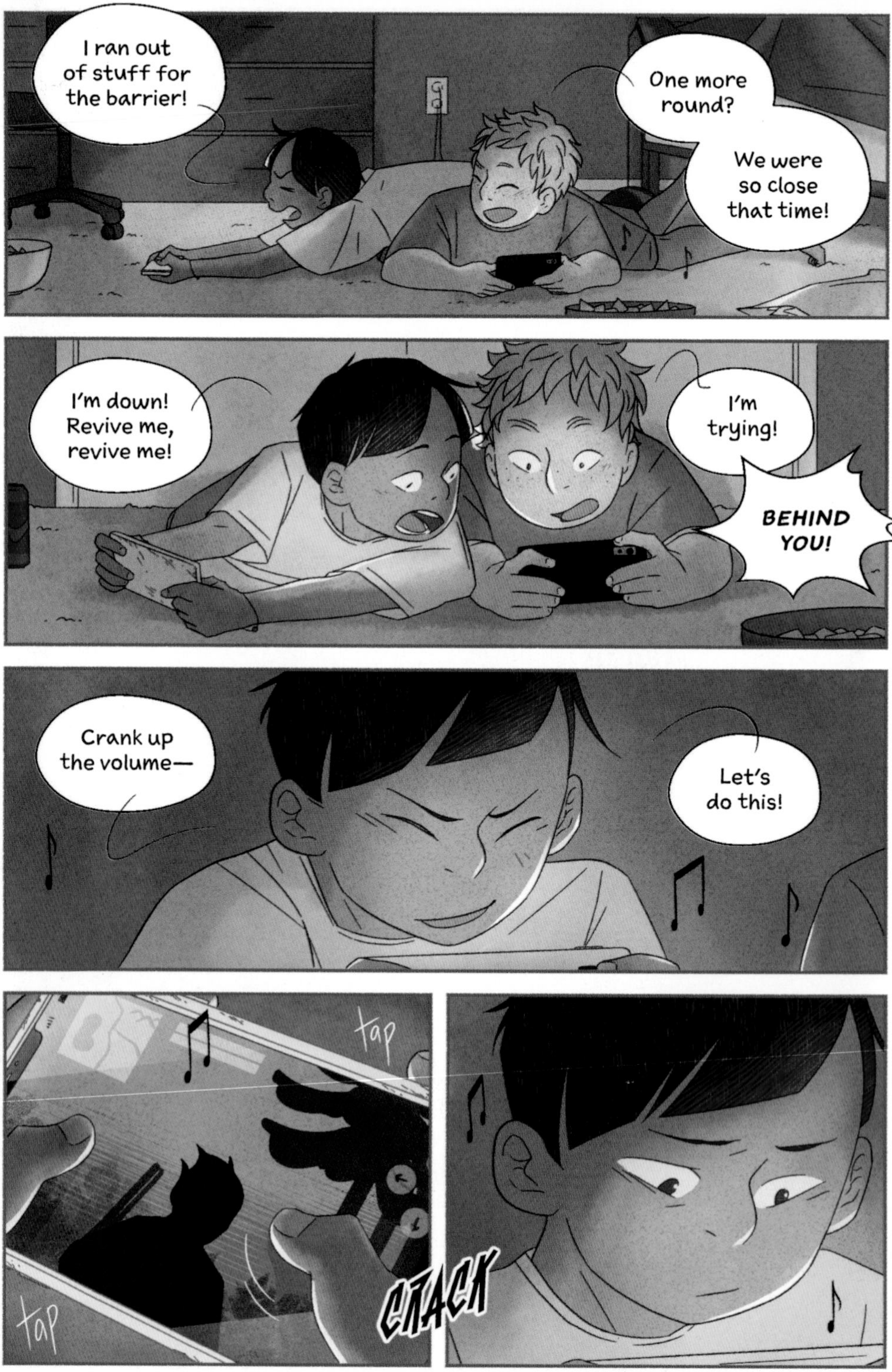
I ran out of stuff for the barrier!
One more round?
We were so close that time!
I'm down! Revive me, revive me!
I'm trying!
BEHIND YOU!
Crank up the volume—
Let's do this!
tap
tap
CRACK

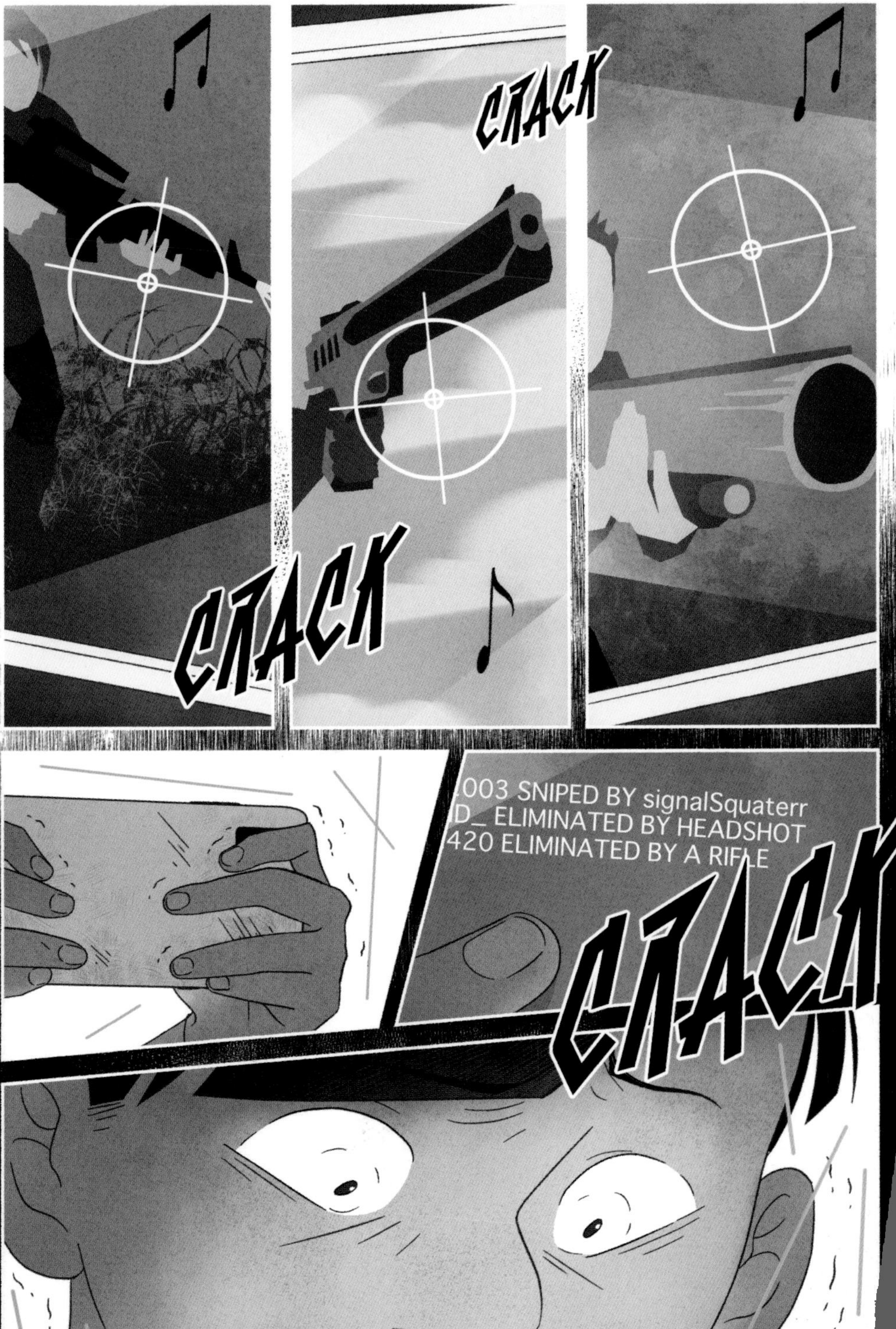
CRACK
CRACK
2003 SNIPED BY signalSquaterr
D_ ELIMINATED BY HEADSHOT
420 ELIMINATED BY A RIFLE
CRACK

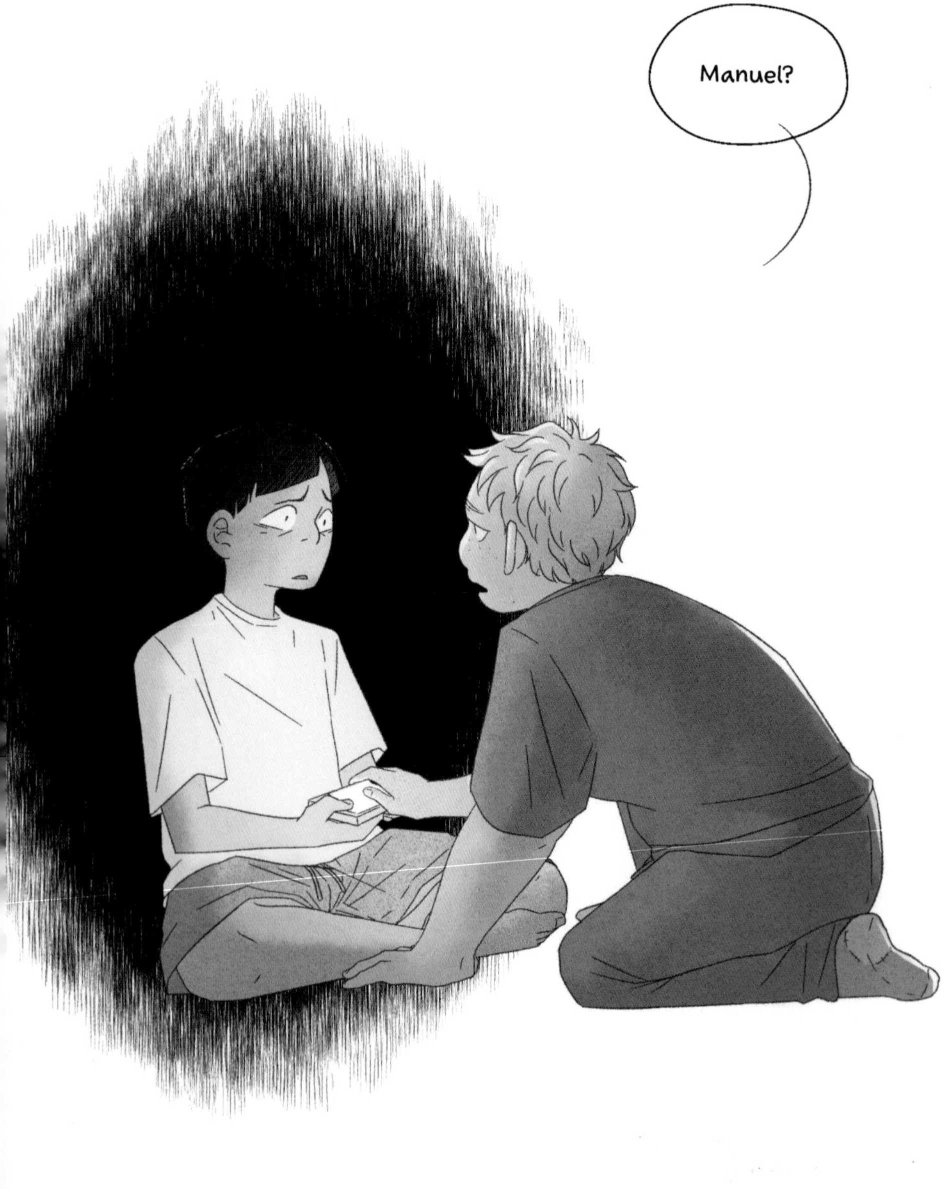
Manuel?

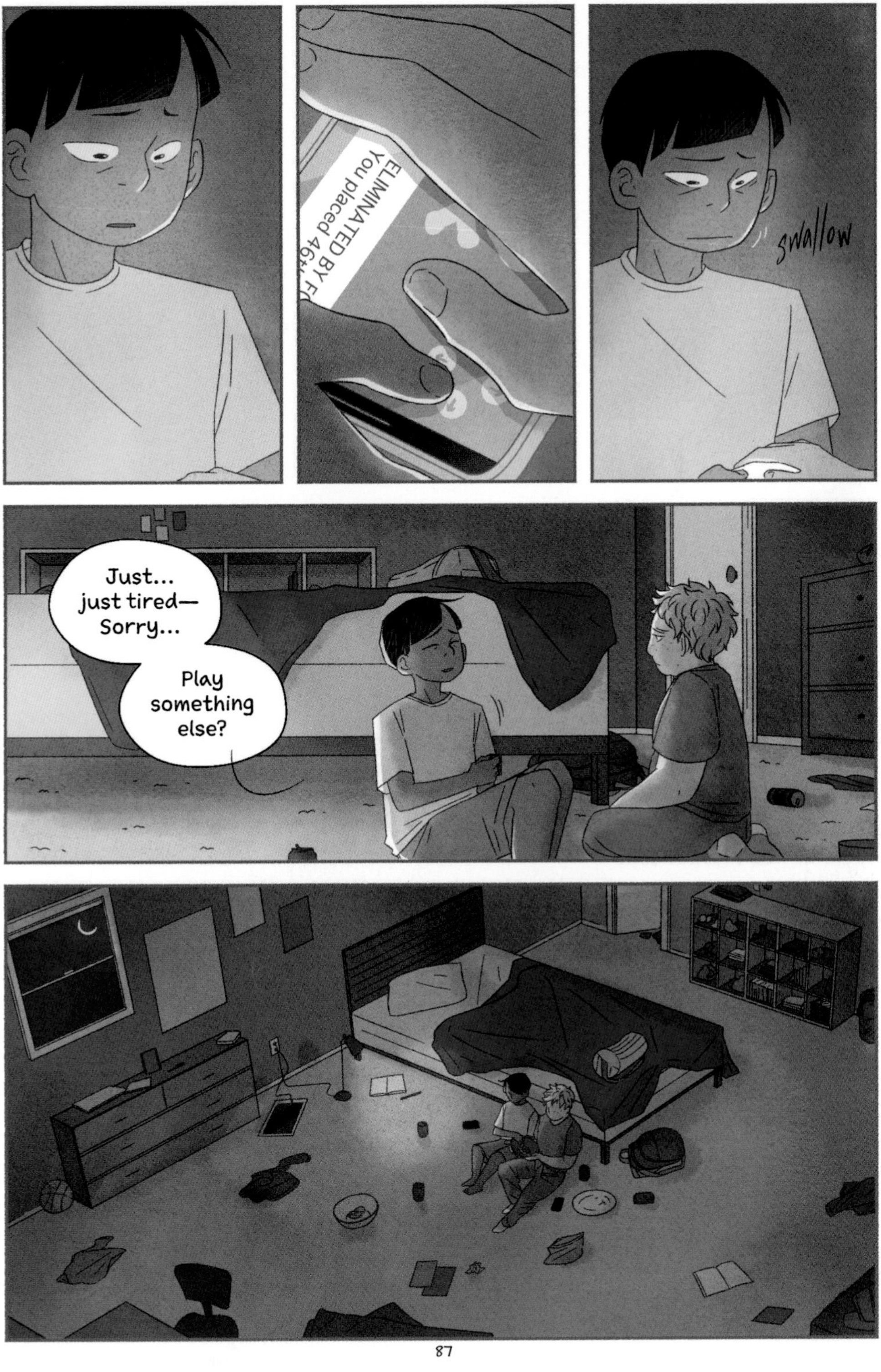
ELIMINATED BY F
You placed 46t
swallow
Just... just tired— Sorry...
Play something else?

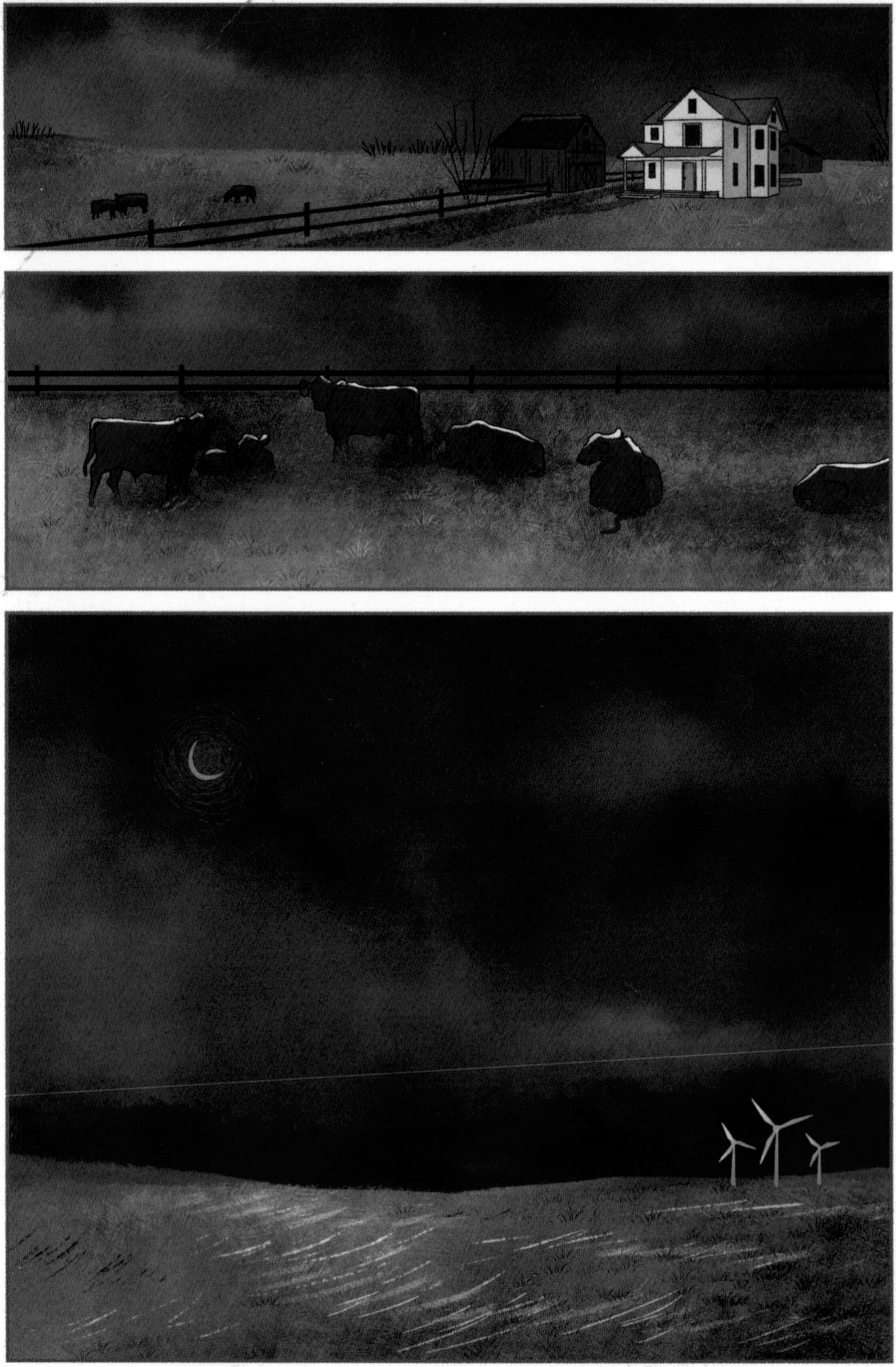

chapter three

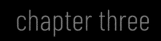

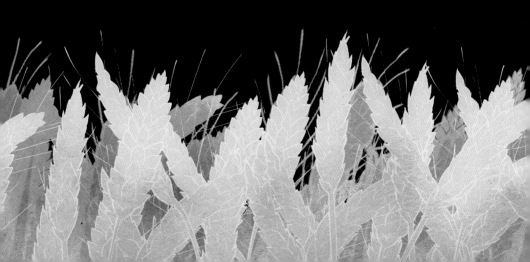

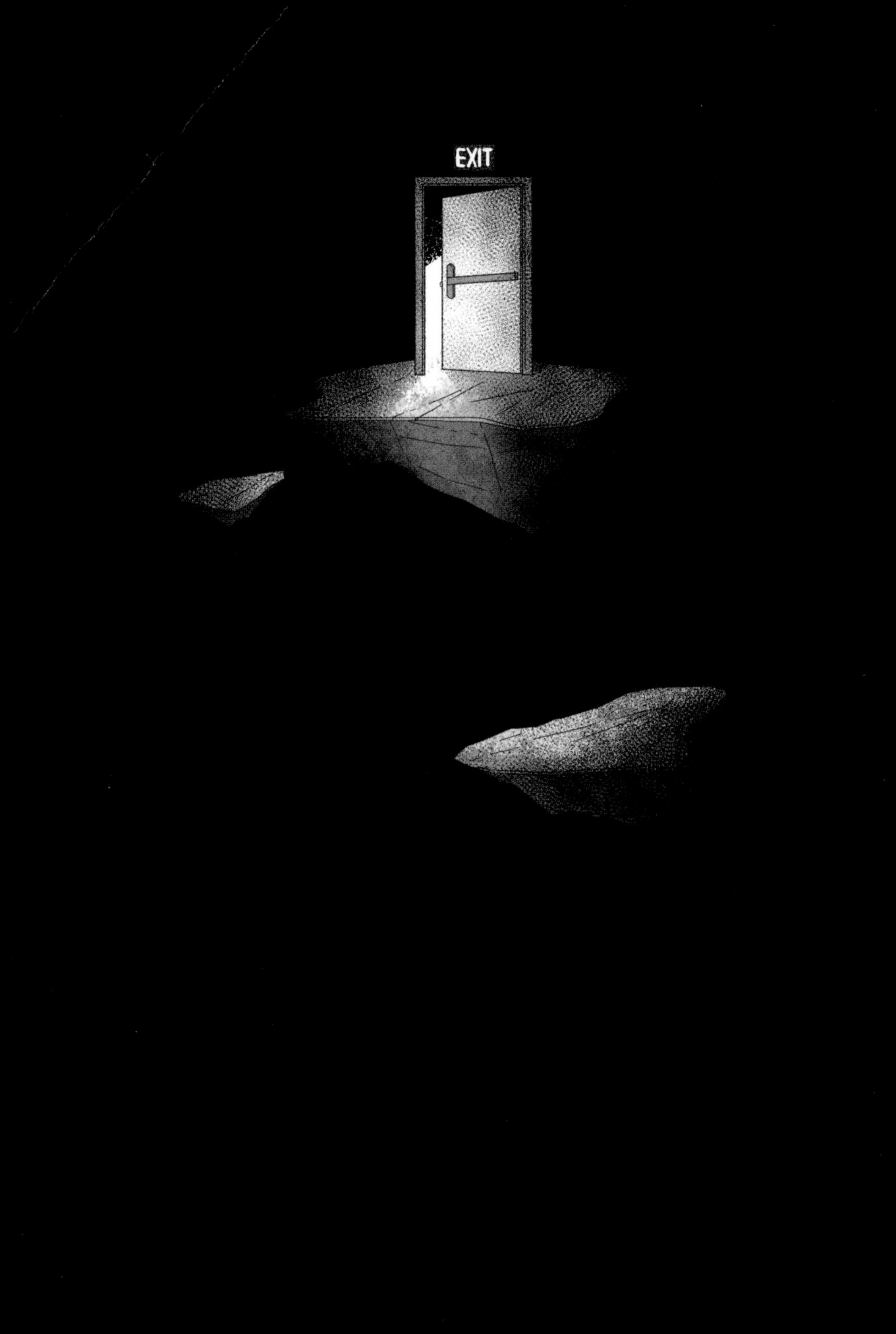
EXIT

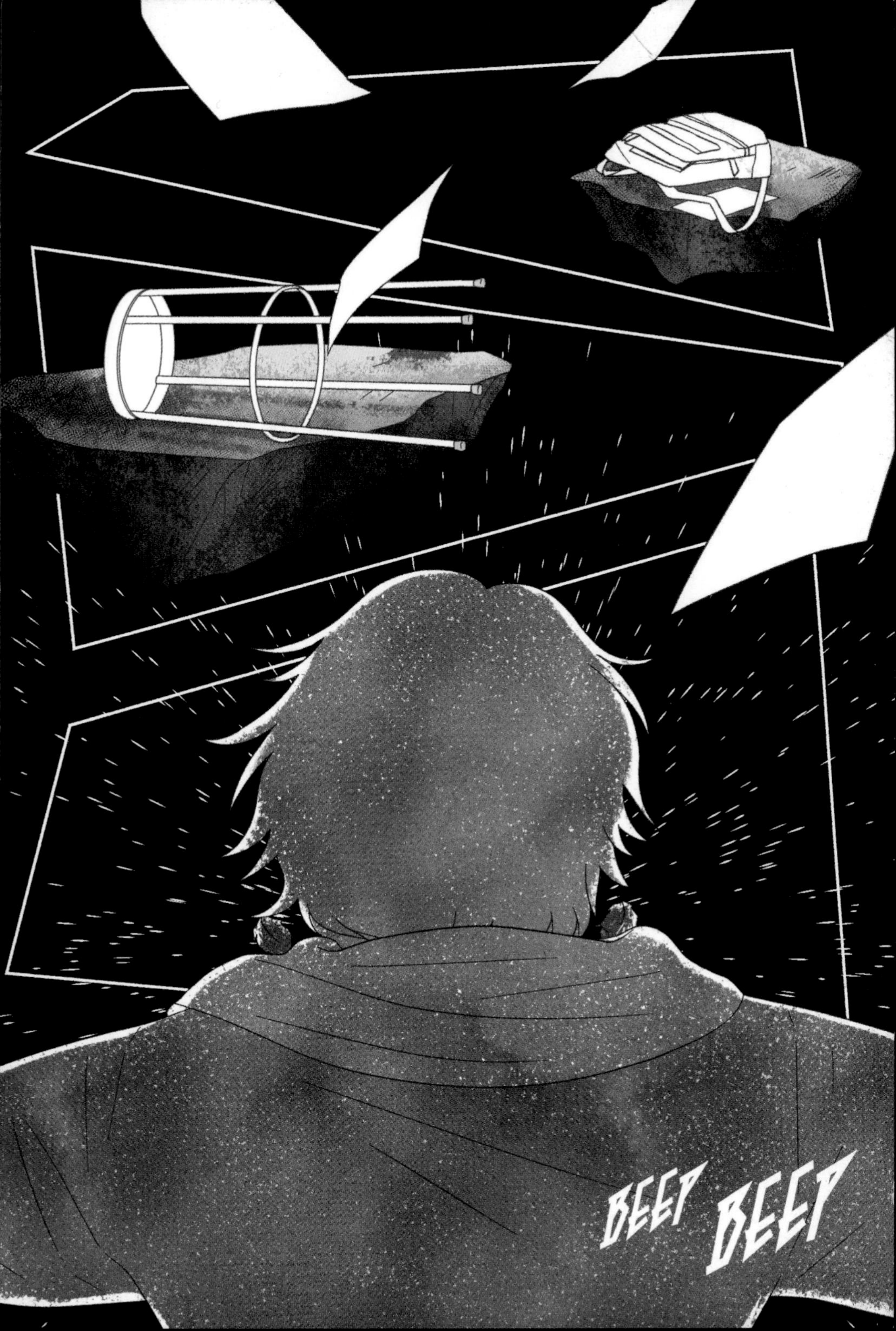
BEEP BEEP

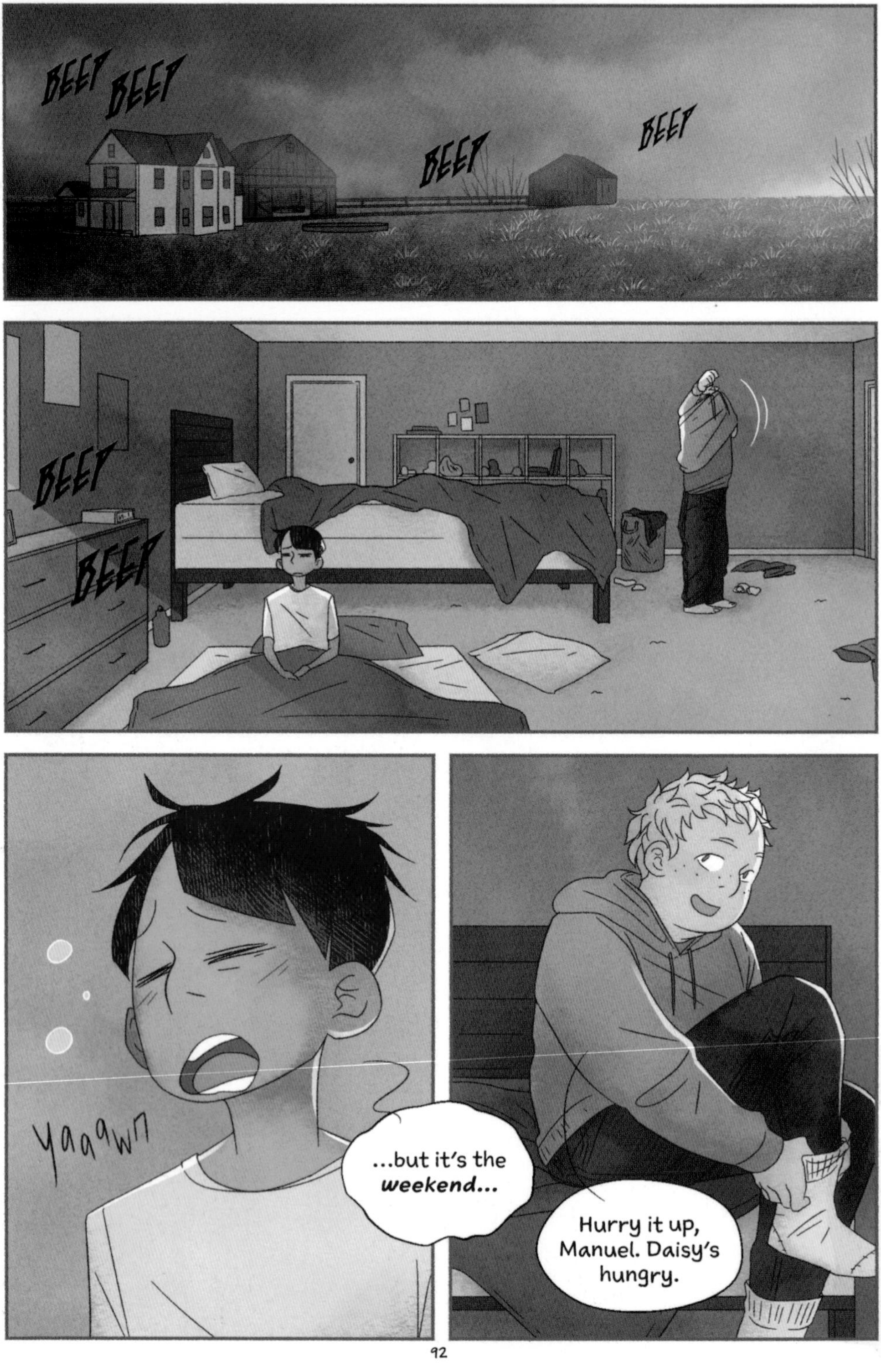
BEEP
BEEP
BEEP
BEEP
BEEP
BEEP
yaaawn
...but it's the *weekend*...
Hurry it up, Manuel. Daisy's hungry.

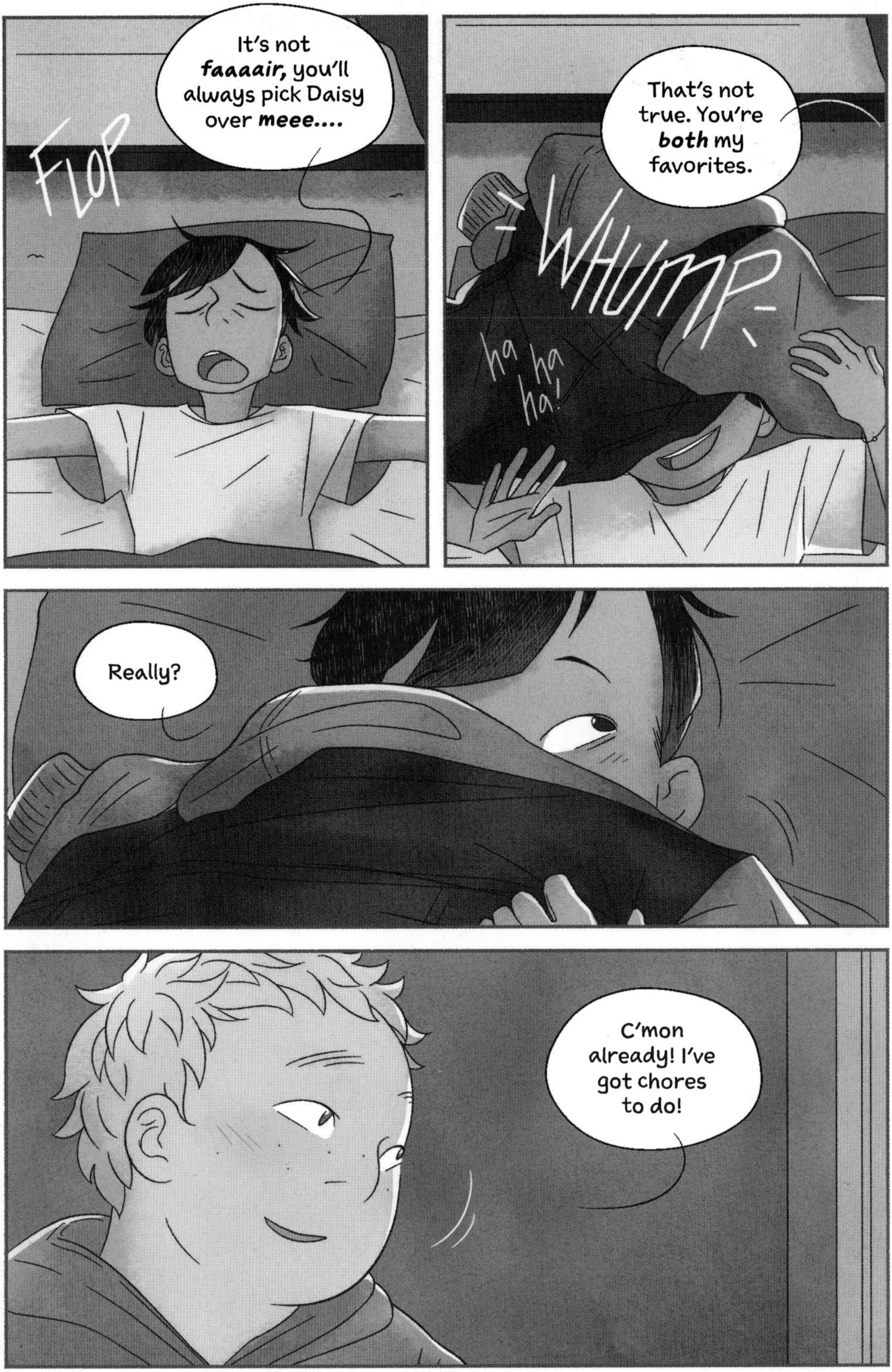

It's not **faaaair,** you'll always pick Daisy over **meee....**
FLOP
That's not true. You're ***both*** my favorites.
WHUMP
ha ha ha!
Really?
C'mon already! I've got chores to do!

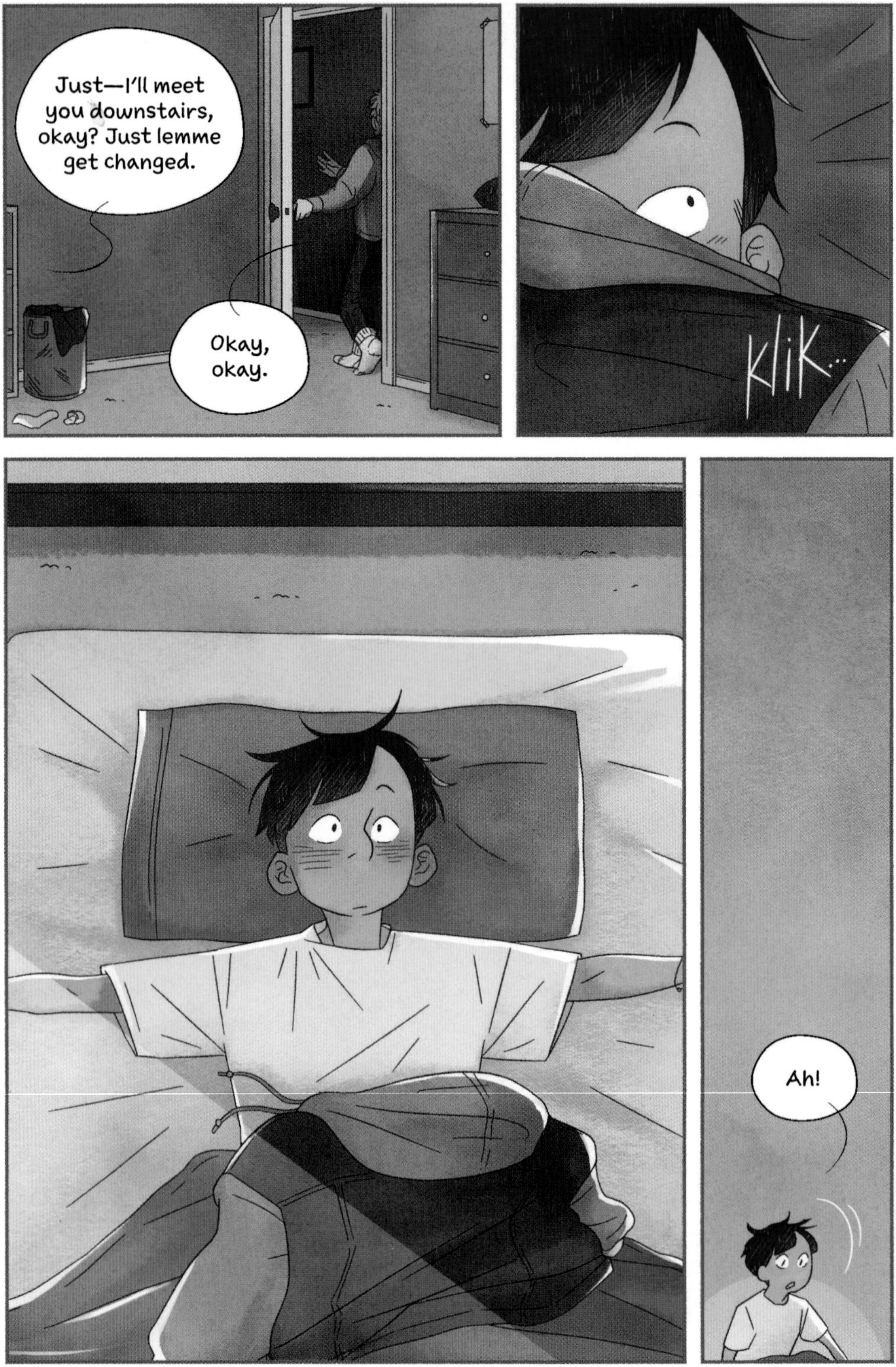
Just—I'll meet you downstairs, okay? Just lemme get changed.
Okay, okay.
KliK...
Ah!

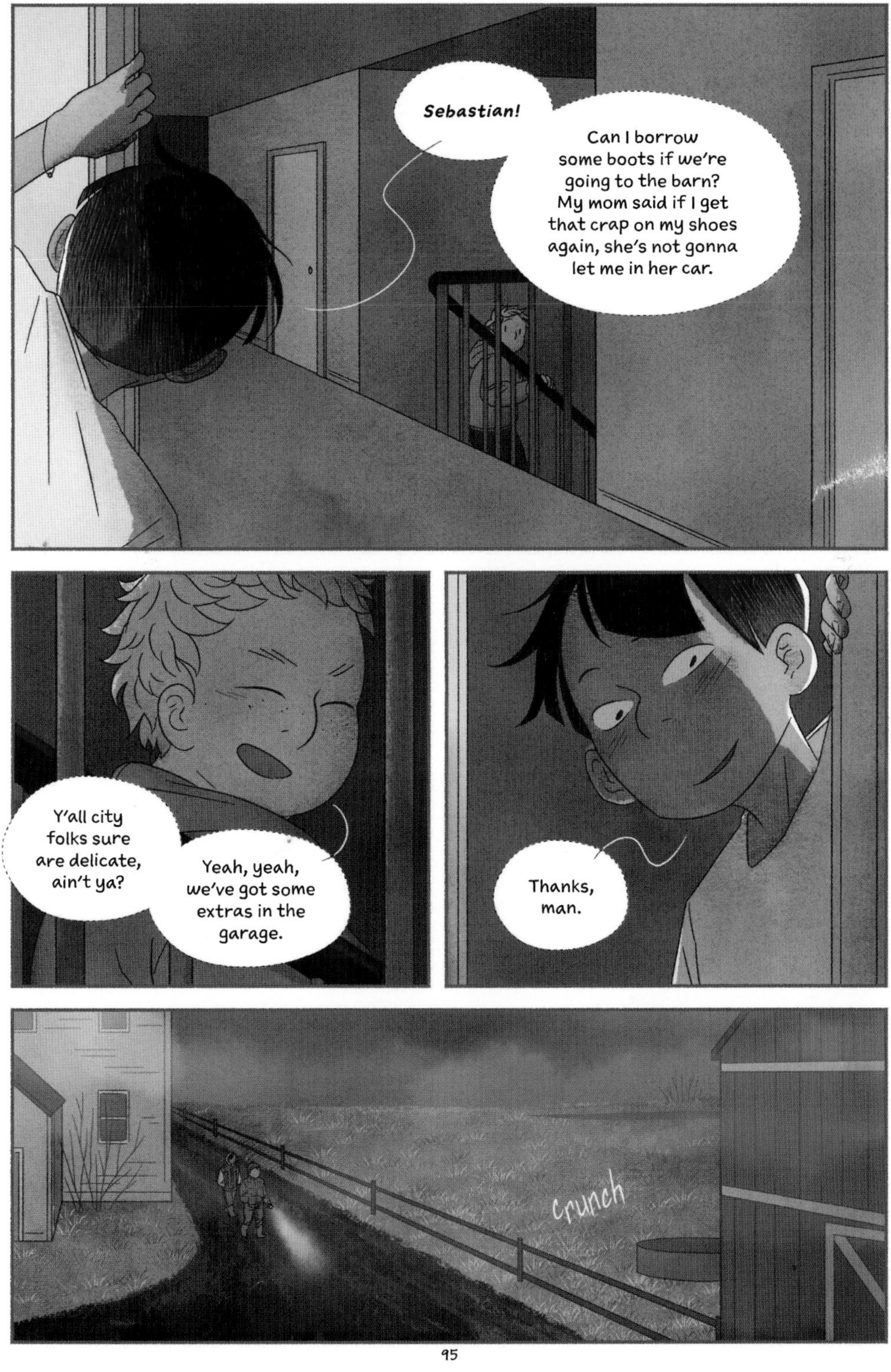

Sebastian!
Can I borrow some boots if we're going to the barn? My mom said if I get that crap on my shoes again, she's not gonna let me in her car.
Y'all city folks sure are delicate, ain't ya?
Yeah, yeah, we've got some extras in the garage.
Thanks, man.
crunch

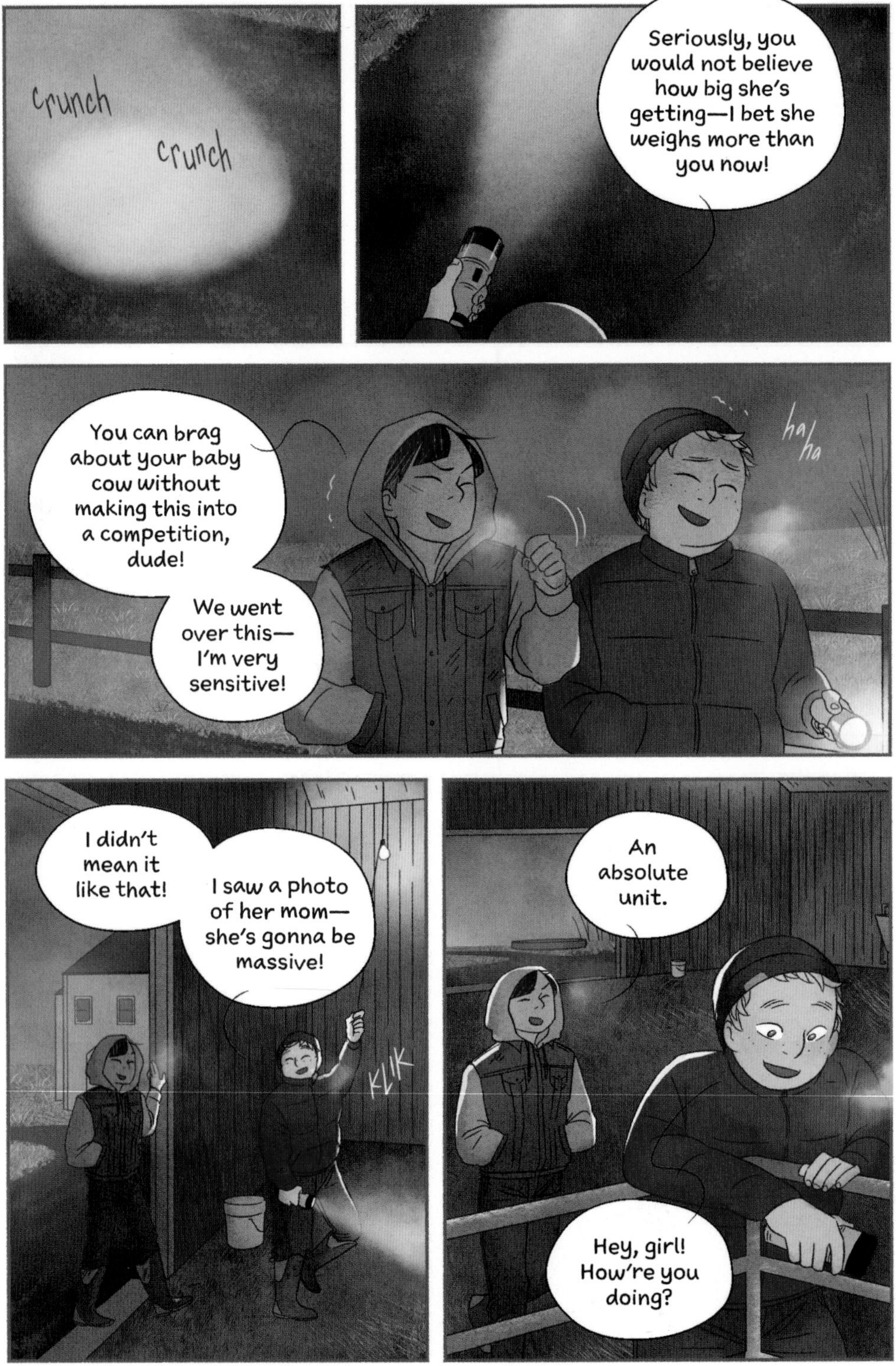
crunch
crunch
Seriously, you would not believe how big she's getting—I bet she weighs more than you now!
You can brag about your baby cow without making this into a competition, dude!
We went over this— I'm very sensitive!
ha ha
I didn't mean it like that!
I saw a photo of her mom— she's gonna be massive!
KLIK
An absolute unit.
Hey, girl! How're you doing?

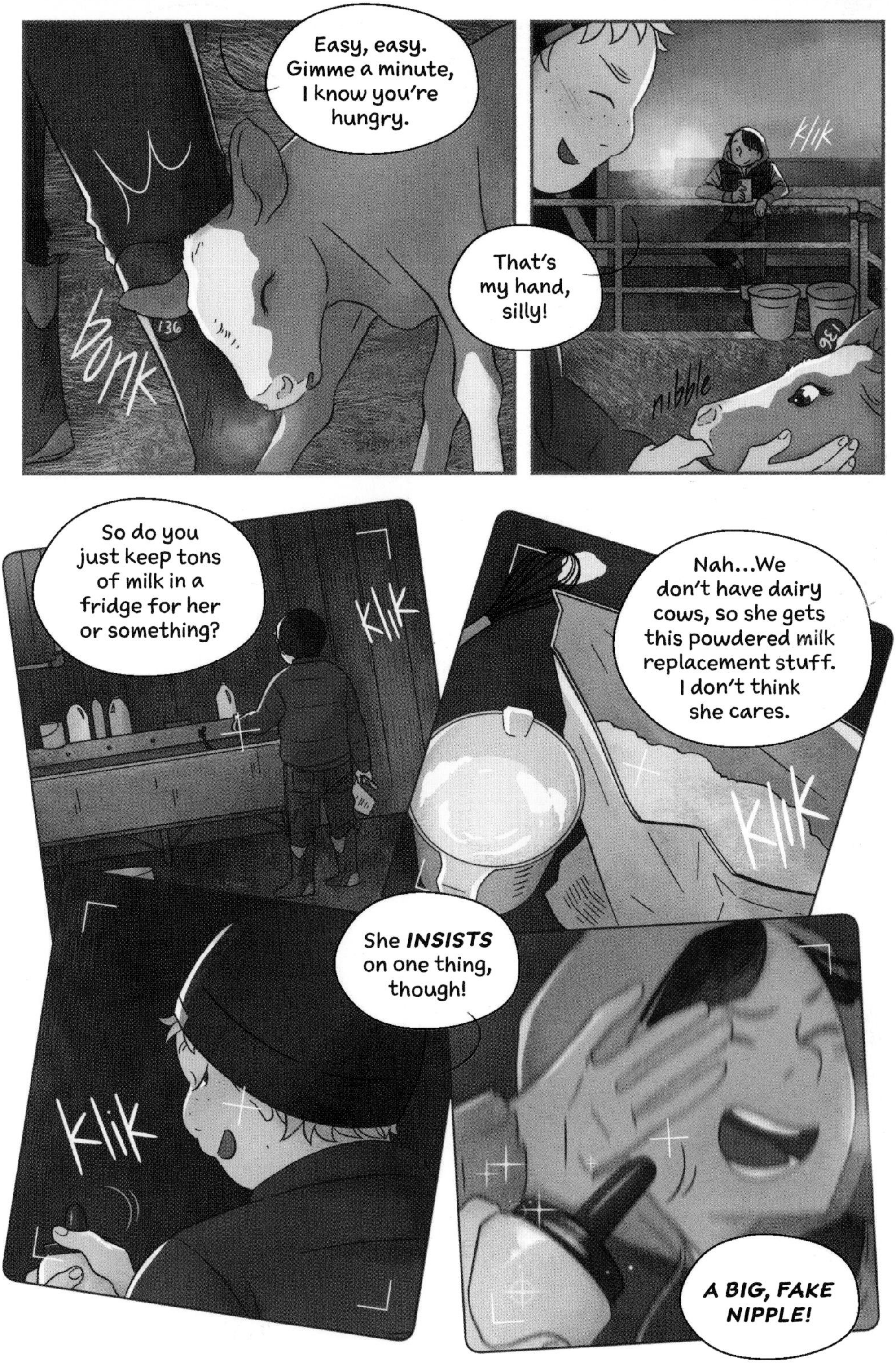

Easy, easy. Gimme a minute, I know you're hungry.
bonk
136
klik
That's my hand, silly!
136
nibble
So do you just keep tons of milk in a fridge for her or something?
klik
Nah...We don't have dairy cows, so she gets this powdered milk replacement stuff. I don't think she cares.
klik
She INSISTS on one thing, though!
klik
A BIG, FAKE NIPPLE!

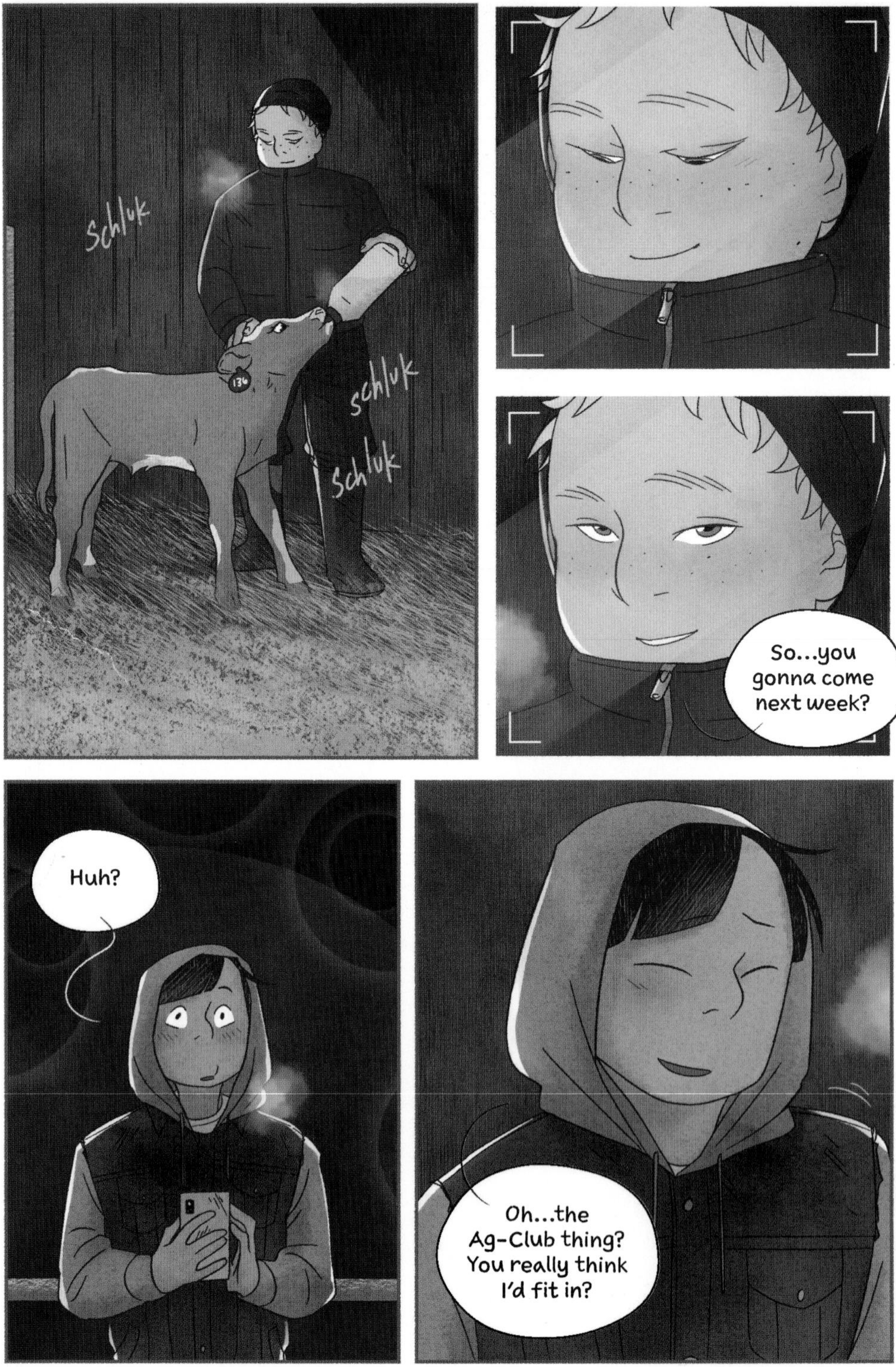
schluk
schluk
schluk
136
So...you gonna come next week?
Huh?
Oh...the Ag-Club thing? You really think I'd fit in?

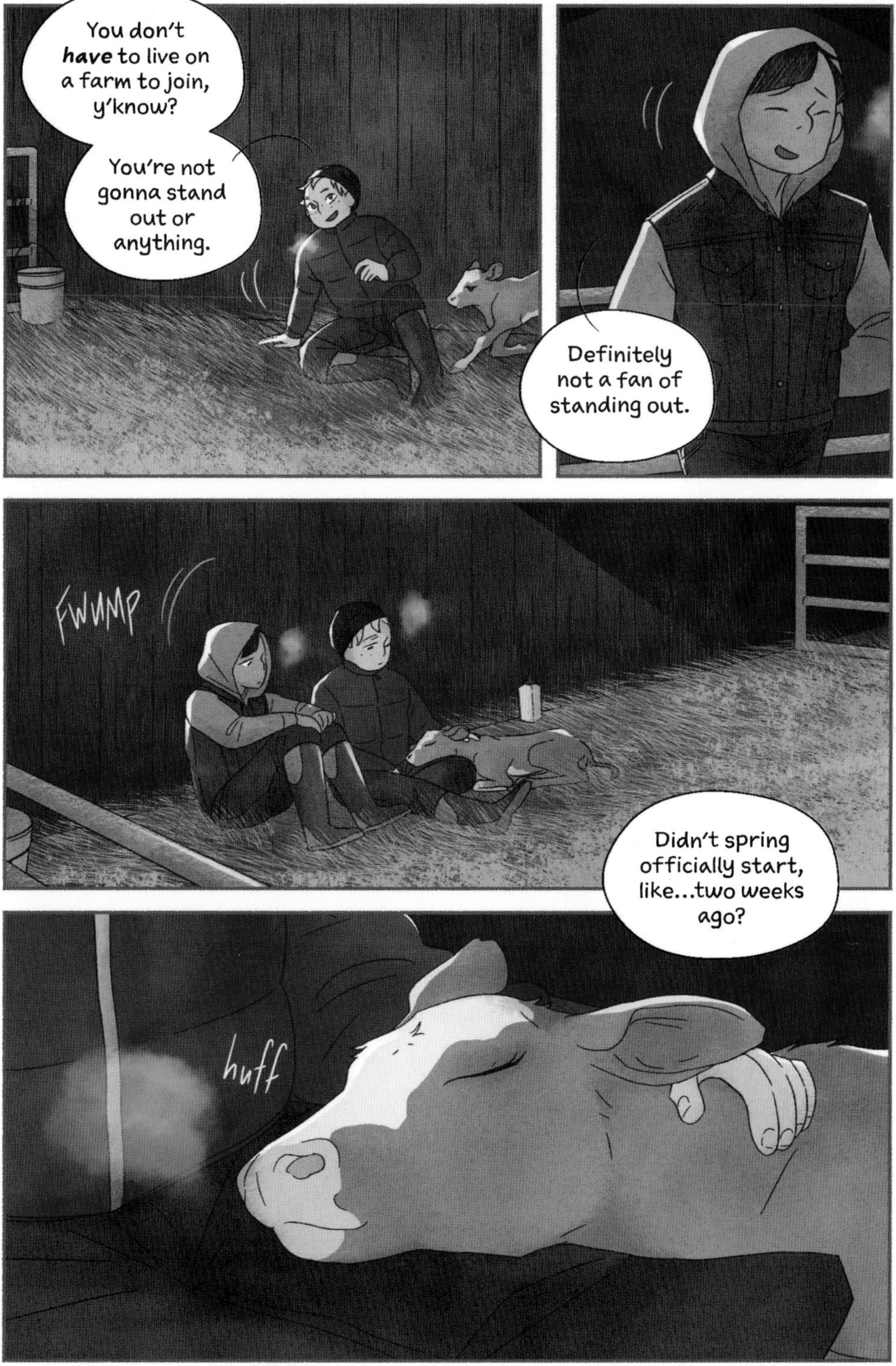

You don't **have** to live on a farm to join, y'know?
You're not gonna stand out or anything.
Definitely not a fan of standing out.
FWUMP
Didn't spring officially start, like...two weeks ago?
huff

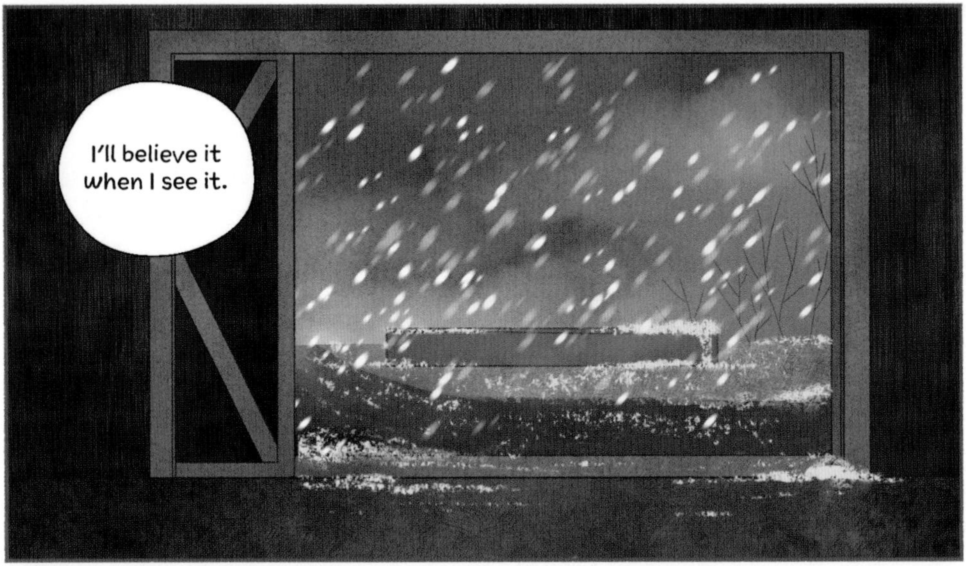
I'll believe it when I see it.

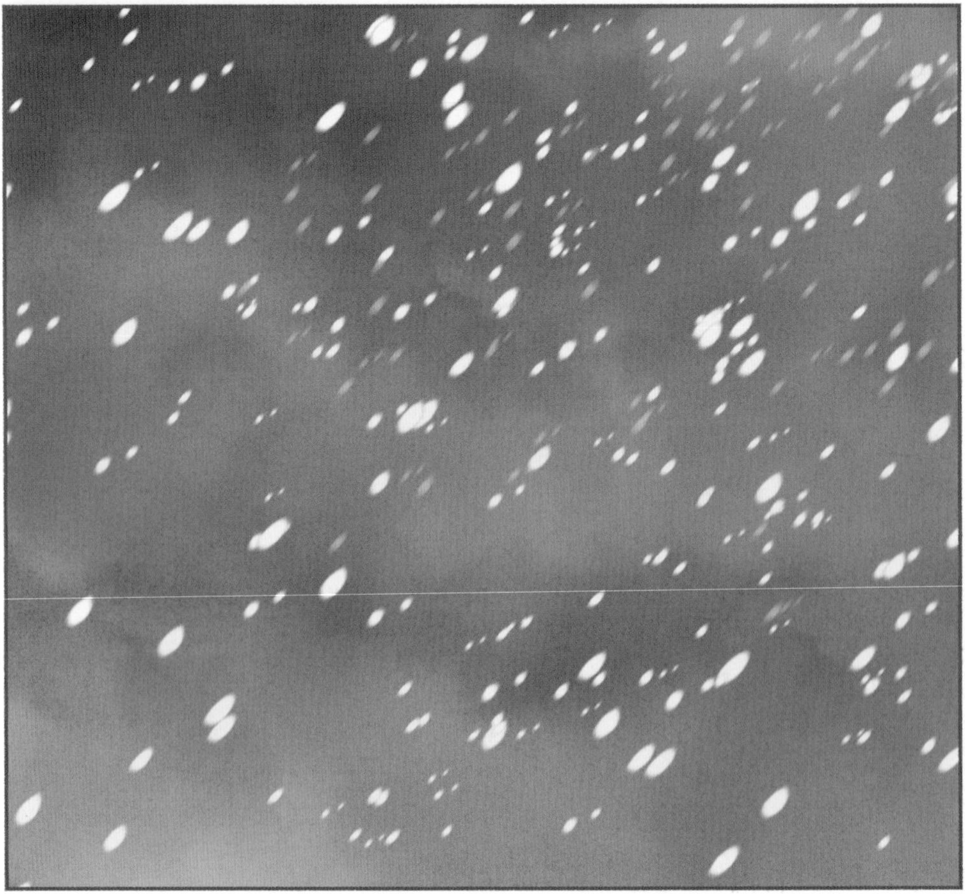

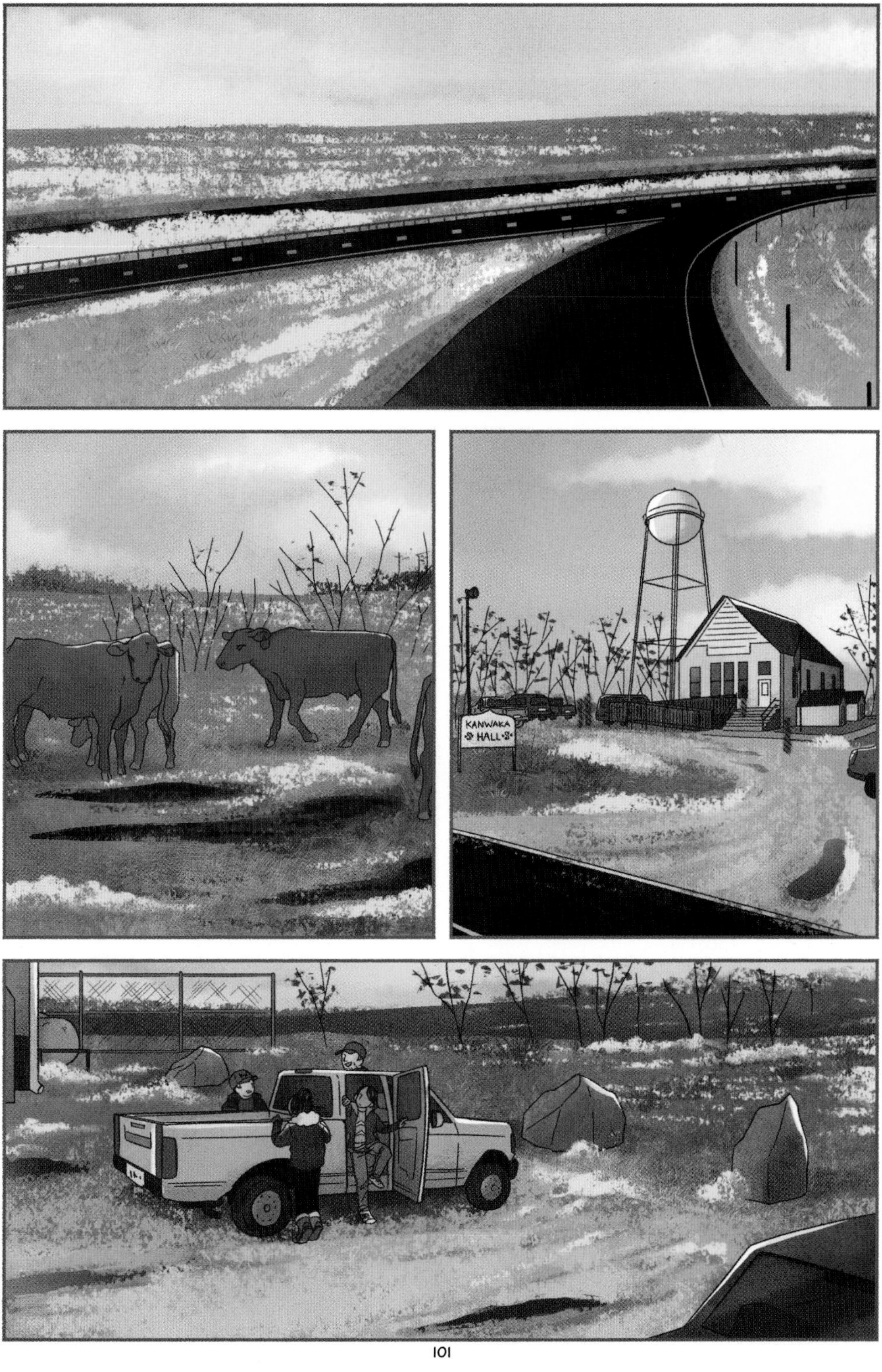
KANWAKA HALL

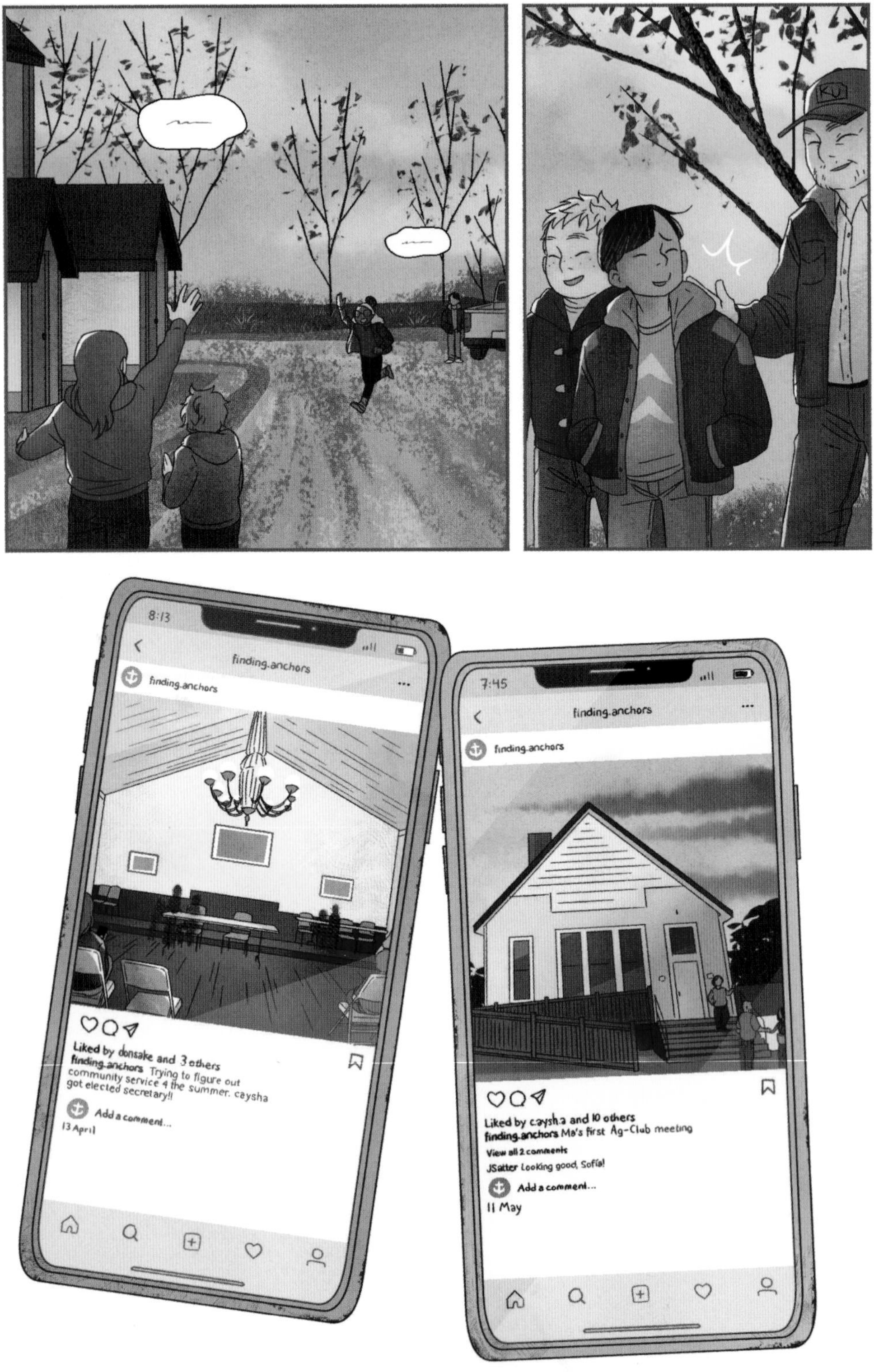

8:13
finding.anchors
finding.anchors
Liked by donsake and 3 others
finding.anchors Trying to figure out community service 4 the summer. caysha got elected secretary!!
Add a comment...
13 April
7:45
finding.anchors
finding.anchors
Liked by caysh.a and 10 others
finding.anchors Ma's first Ag-Club meeting
View all 2 comments
JSatter Looking good, Sofía!
Add a comment...
11 May

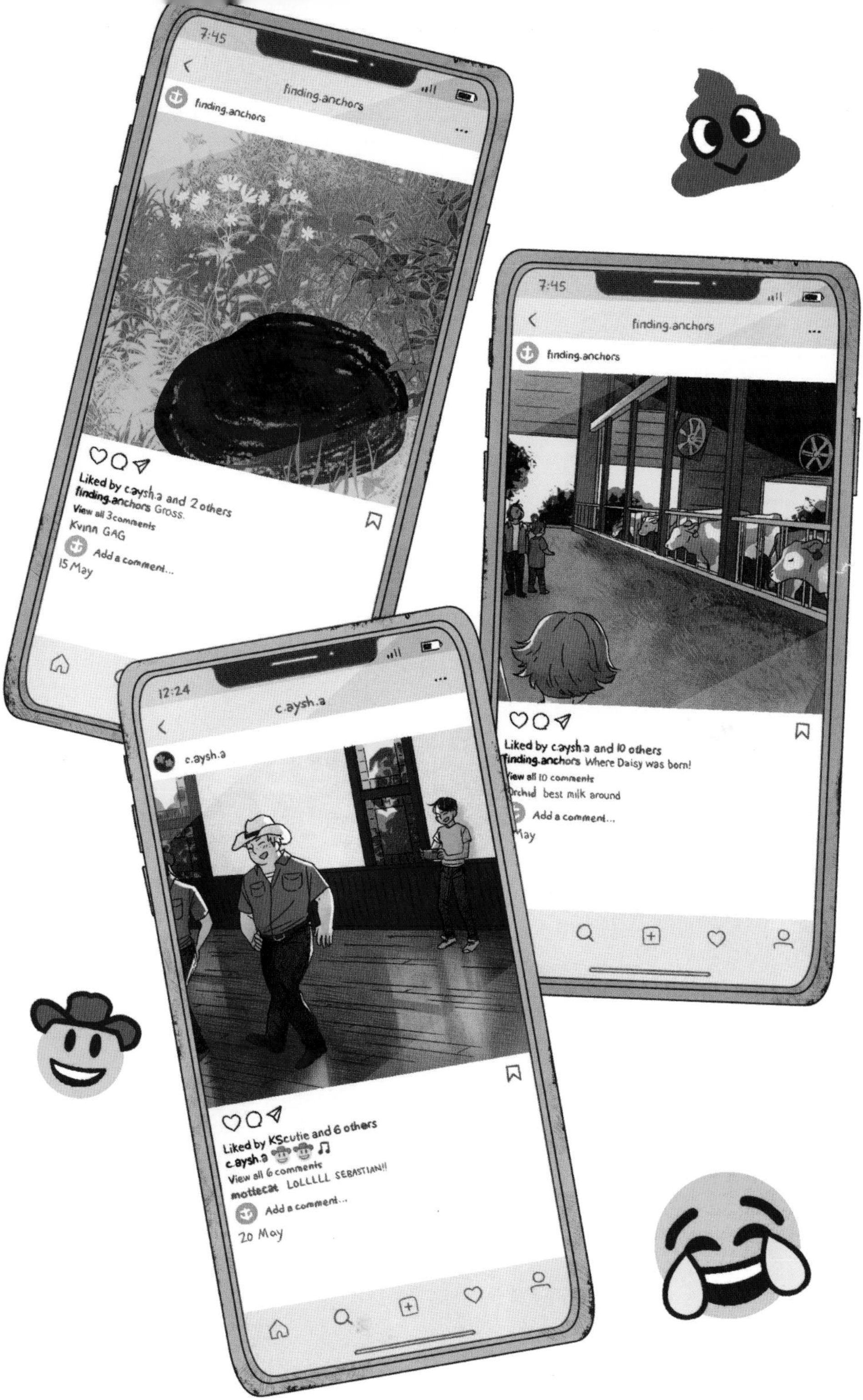
7:45
finding.anchors
finding.anchors
Liked by c.aysh.a and 2 others
finding.anchors Gross.
View all 3 comments
Kvinn GAG
Add a comment...
15 May
7:45
finding.anchors
finding.anchors
Liked by c.aysh.a and 10 others
finding.anchors Where Daisy was born!
View all 10 comments
Orchid best milk around
Add a comment...
May
12:24
c.aysh.a
c.aysh.a
Liked by KScutie and 6 others
c.aysh.a
View all 6 comments
mottecat LOLLLLL SEBASTIAN!!
Add a comment...
20 May

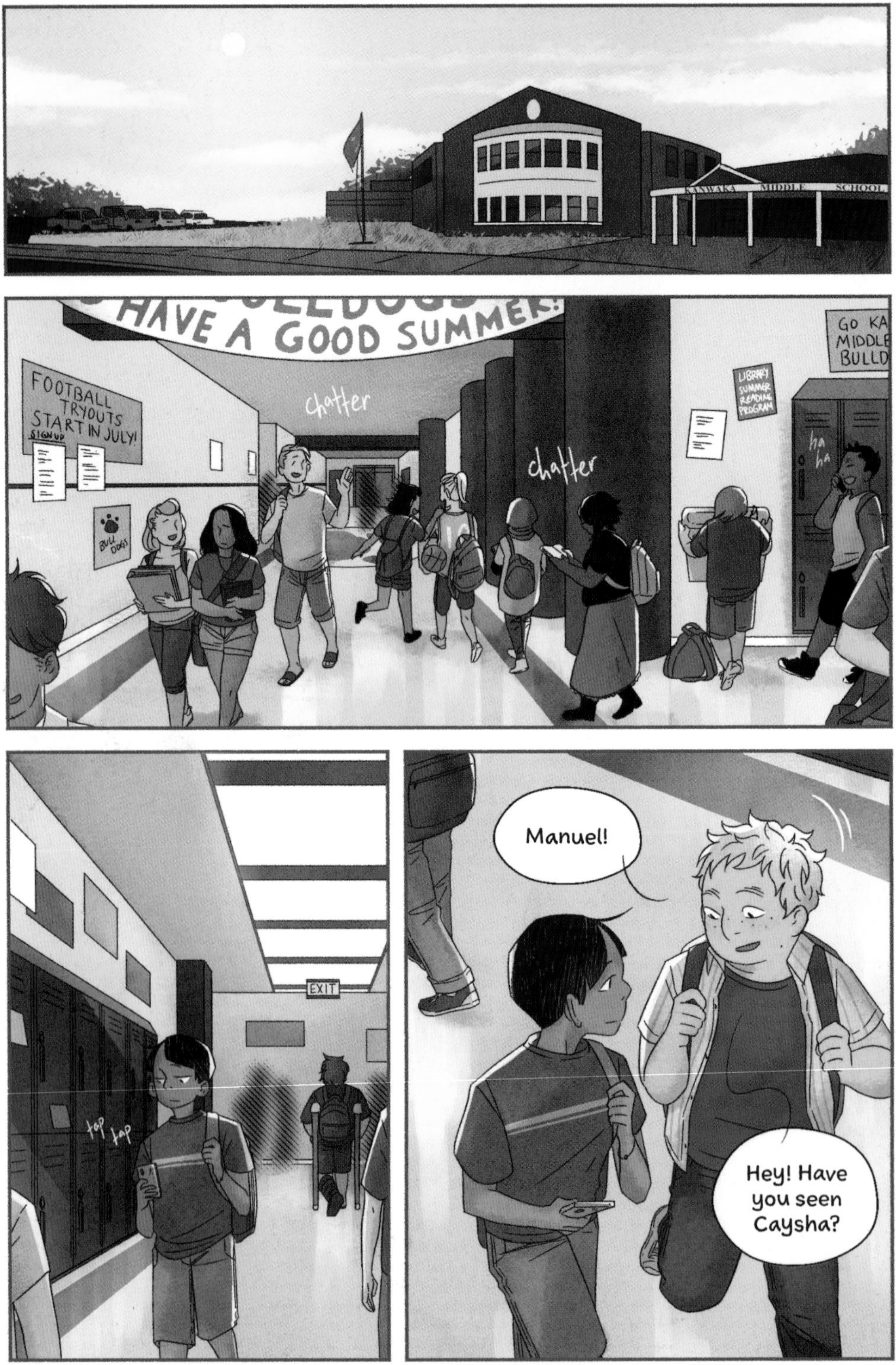
HAVE A GOOD SUMMER
FOOTBALL TRYOUTS START IN JULY!
SIGN UP
BULLDOGS
chatter
chatter
LIBRARY SUMMER READING PROGRAM
ha ha
tap tap
EXIT
Manuel!
Hey! Have you seen Caysha?

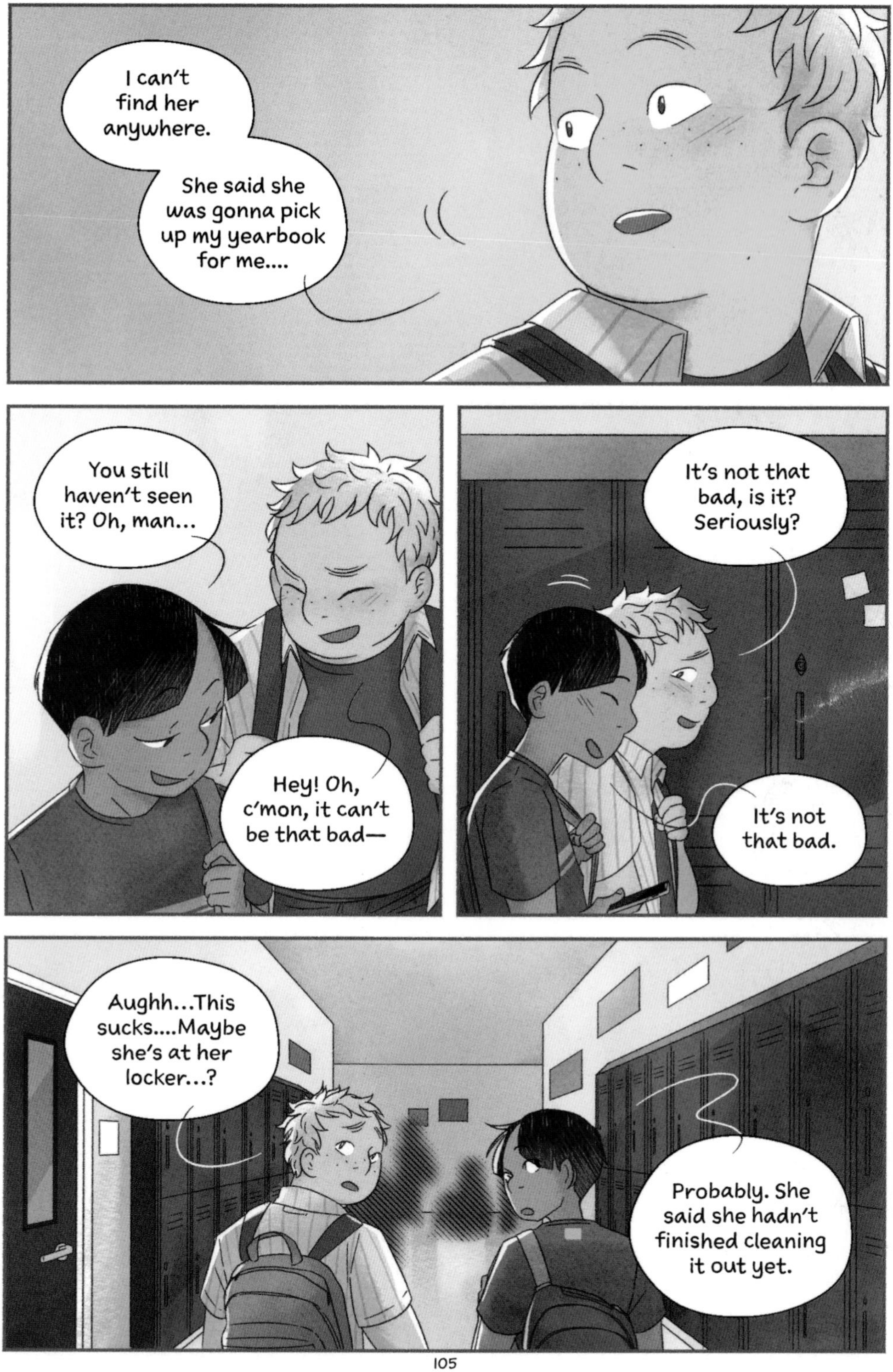
I can't find her anywhere.
She said she was gonna pick up my yearbook for me....
You still haven't seen it? Oh, man...
Hey! Oh, c'mon, it can't be that bad—
It's not that bad, is it? Seriously?
It's not that bad.
Aughh...This sucks....Maybe she's at her locker...?
Probably. She said she hadn't finished cleaning it out yet.

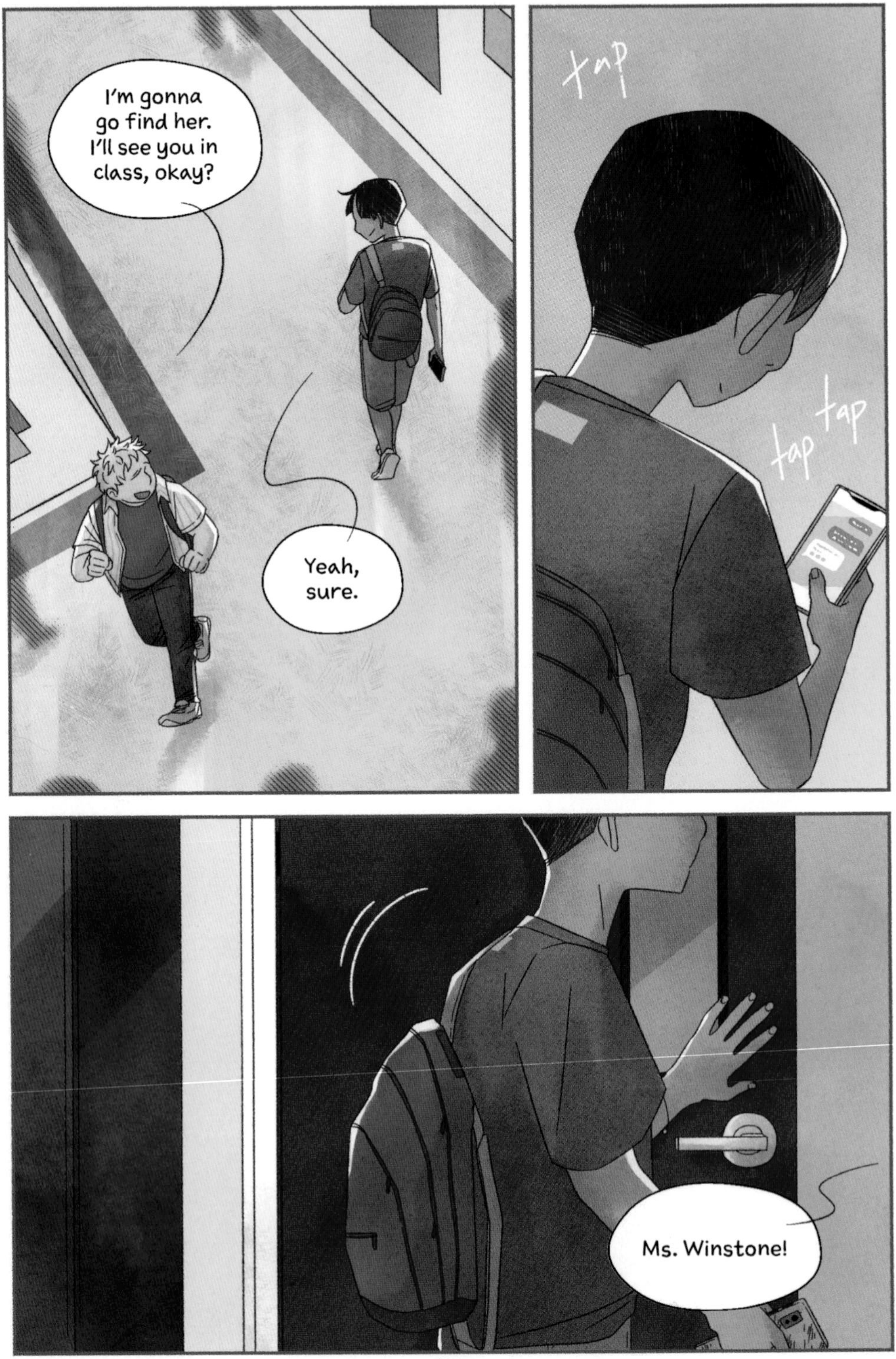
I'm gonna go find her. I'll see you in class, okay?
Yeah, sure.
tap
tap tap
Ms. Winstone!

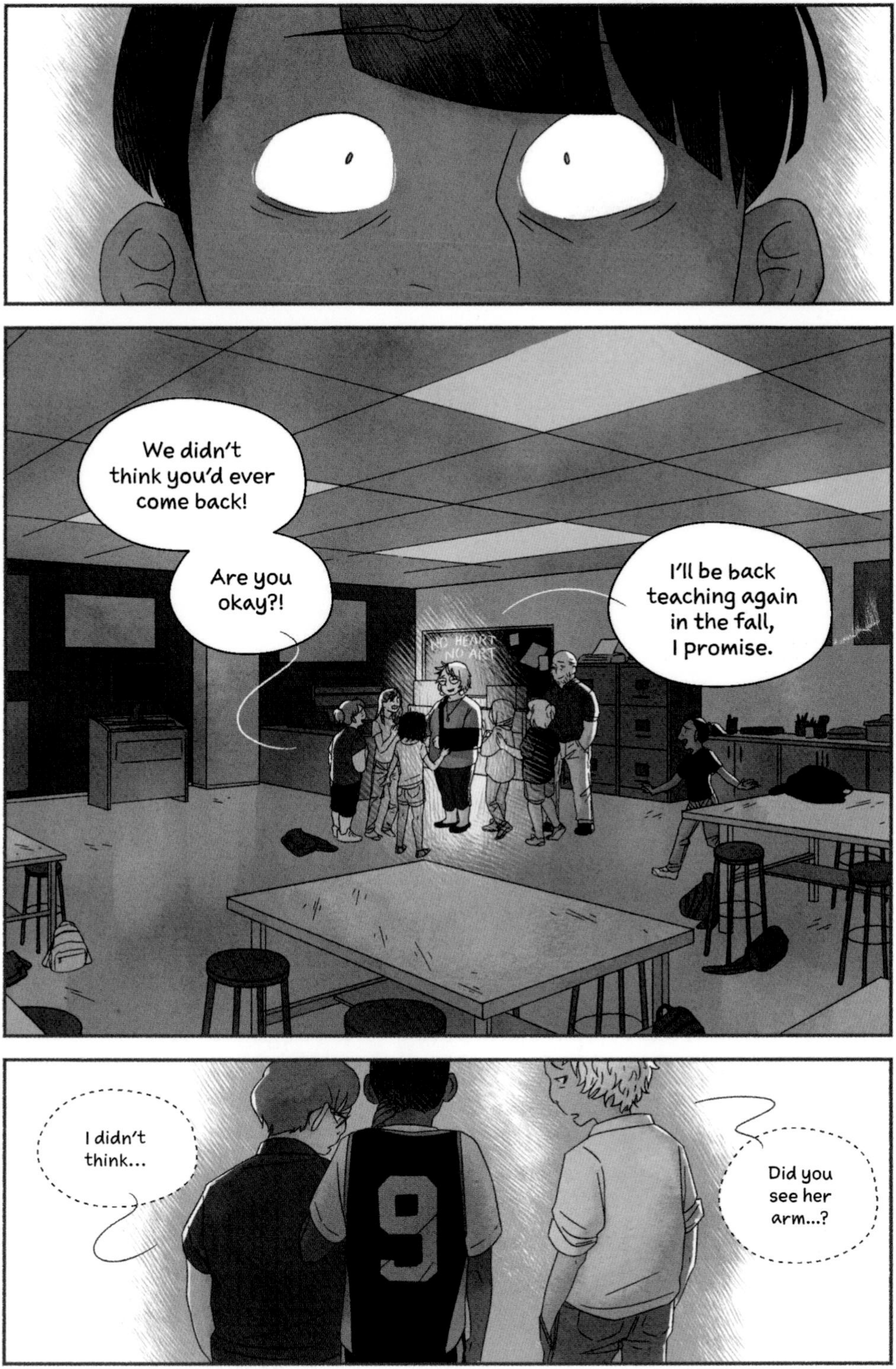
We didn't think you'd ever come back!
Are you okay?!
I'll be back teaching again in the fall, I promise.
NO HEART NO ART
I didn't think...
Did you see her arm...?

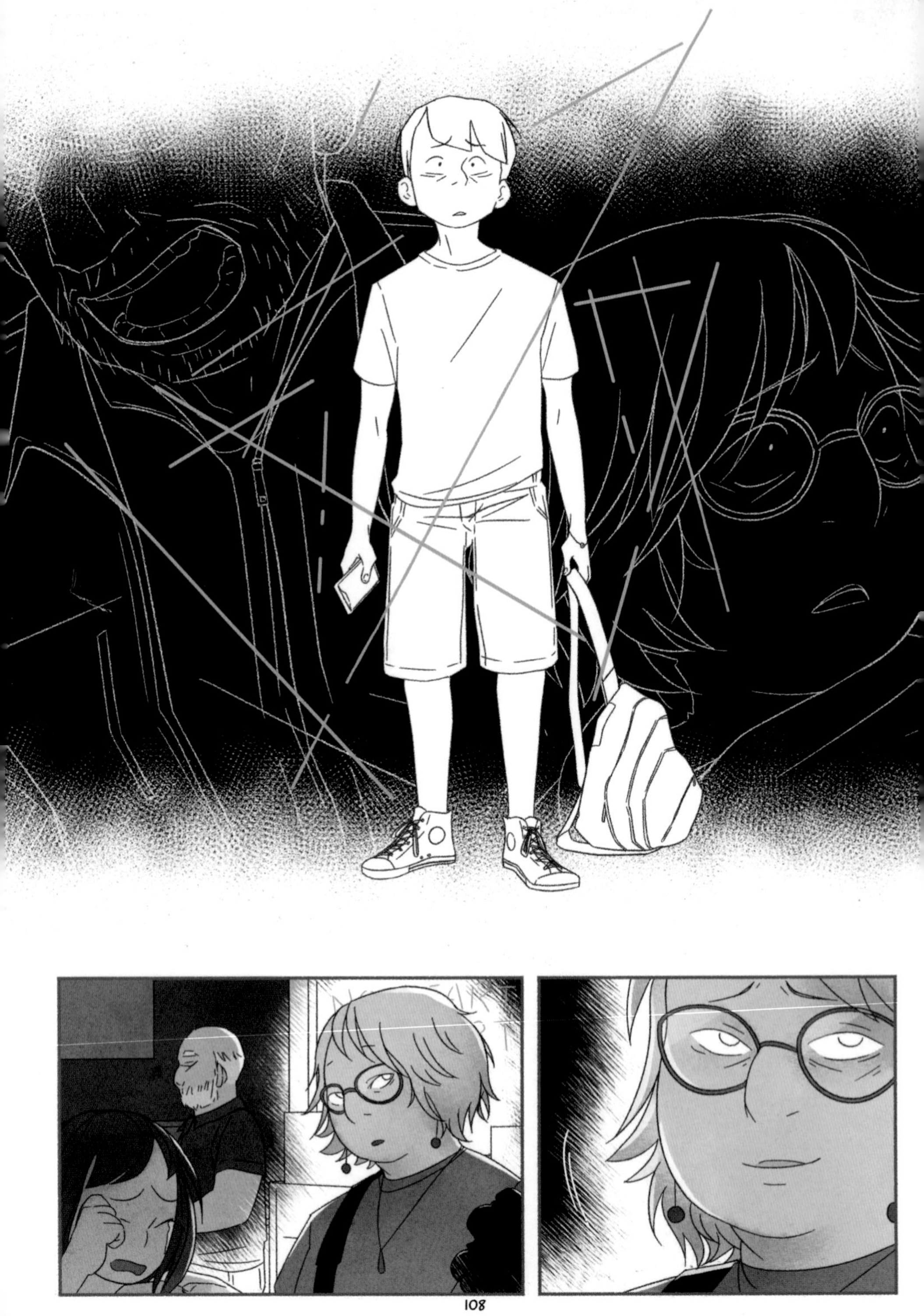

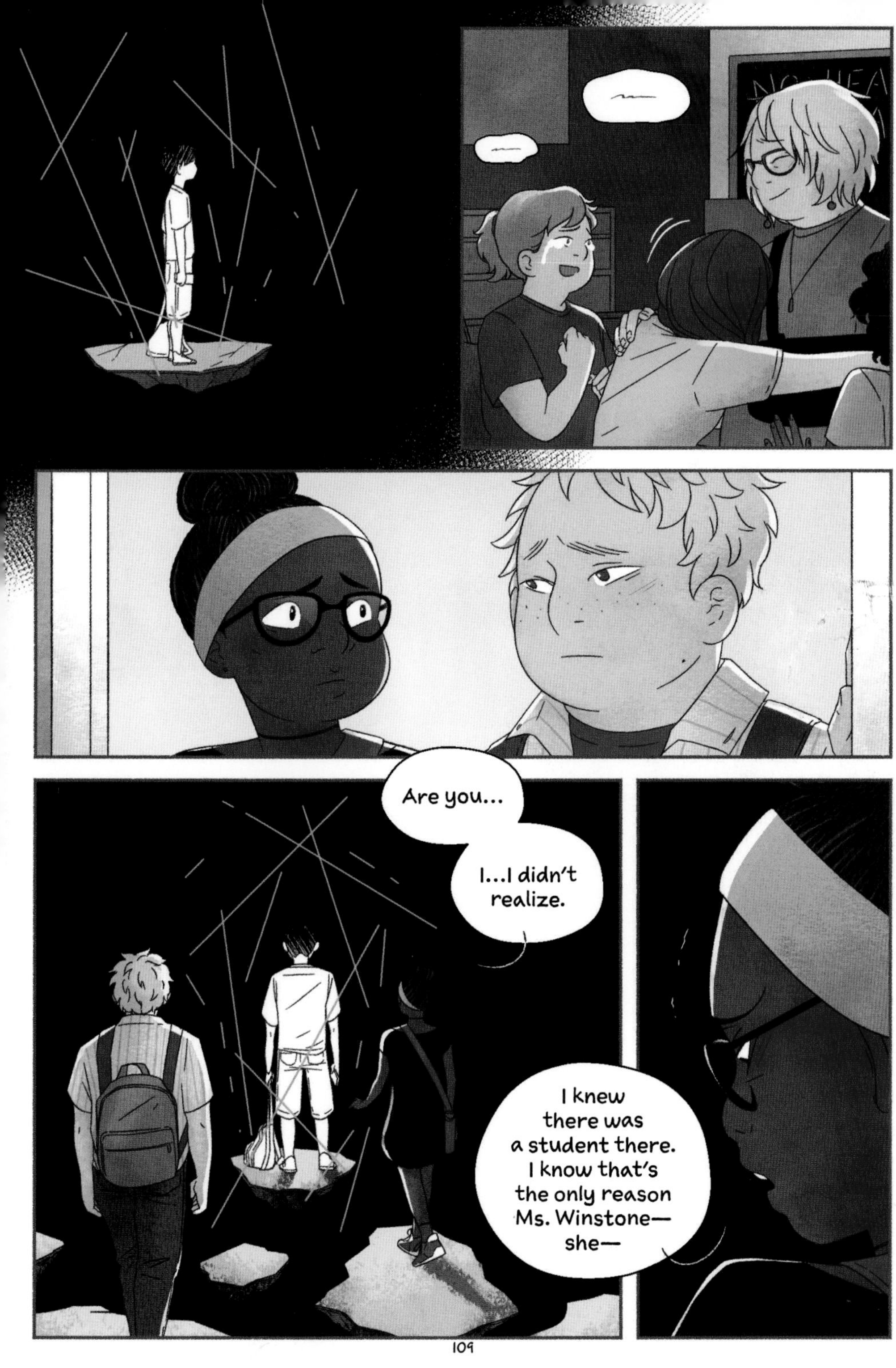
Are you...
I...I didn't realize.
I knew there was a student there. I know that's the only reason Ms. Winstone— she—

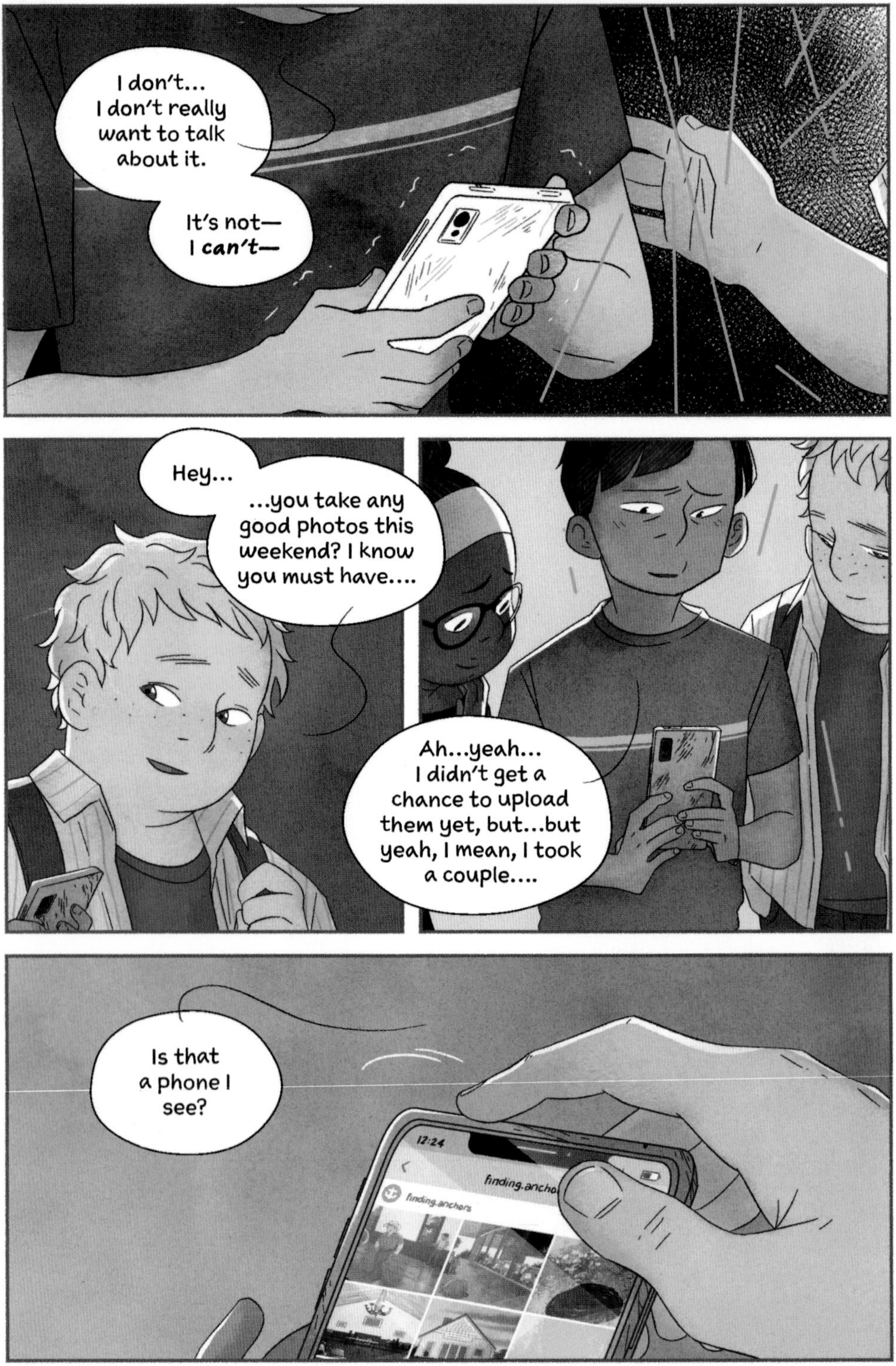
I don't...
I don't really want to talk about it.
It's not—
I **can't**—
Hey...
...you take any good photos this weekend? I know you must have....
Ah...yeah...
I didn't get a chance to upload them yet, but...but yeah, I mean, I took a couple....
Is that a phone I see?
12:24
finding.anchors

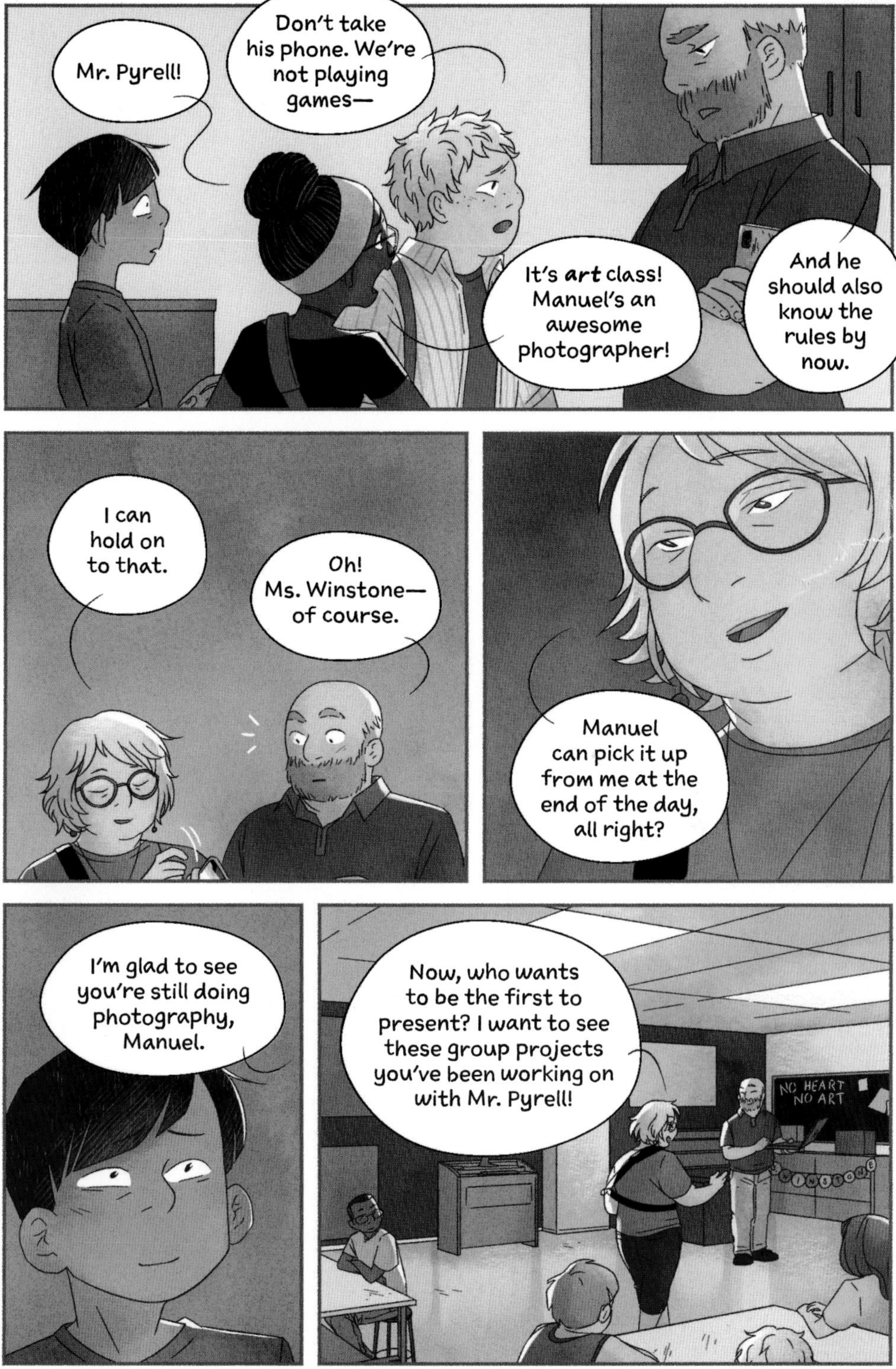
Mr. Pyrell!
Don't take his phone. We're not playing games—
It's **art** class! Manuel's an awesome photographer!
And he should also know the rules by now.
I can hold on to that.
Oh! Ms. Winstone—of course.
Manuel can pick it up from me at the end of the day, all right?
I'm glad to see you're still doing photography, Manuel.
Now, who wants to be the first to present? I want to see these group projects you've been working on with Mr. Pyrell!
NO HEART NO ART

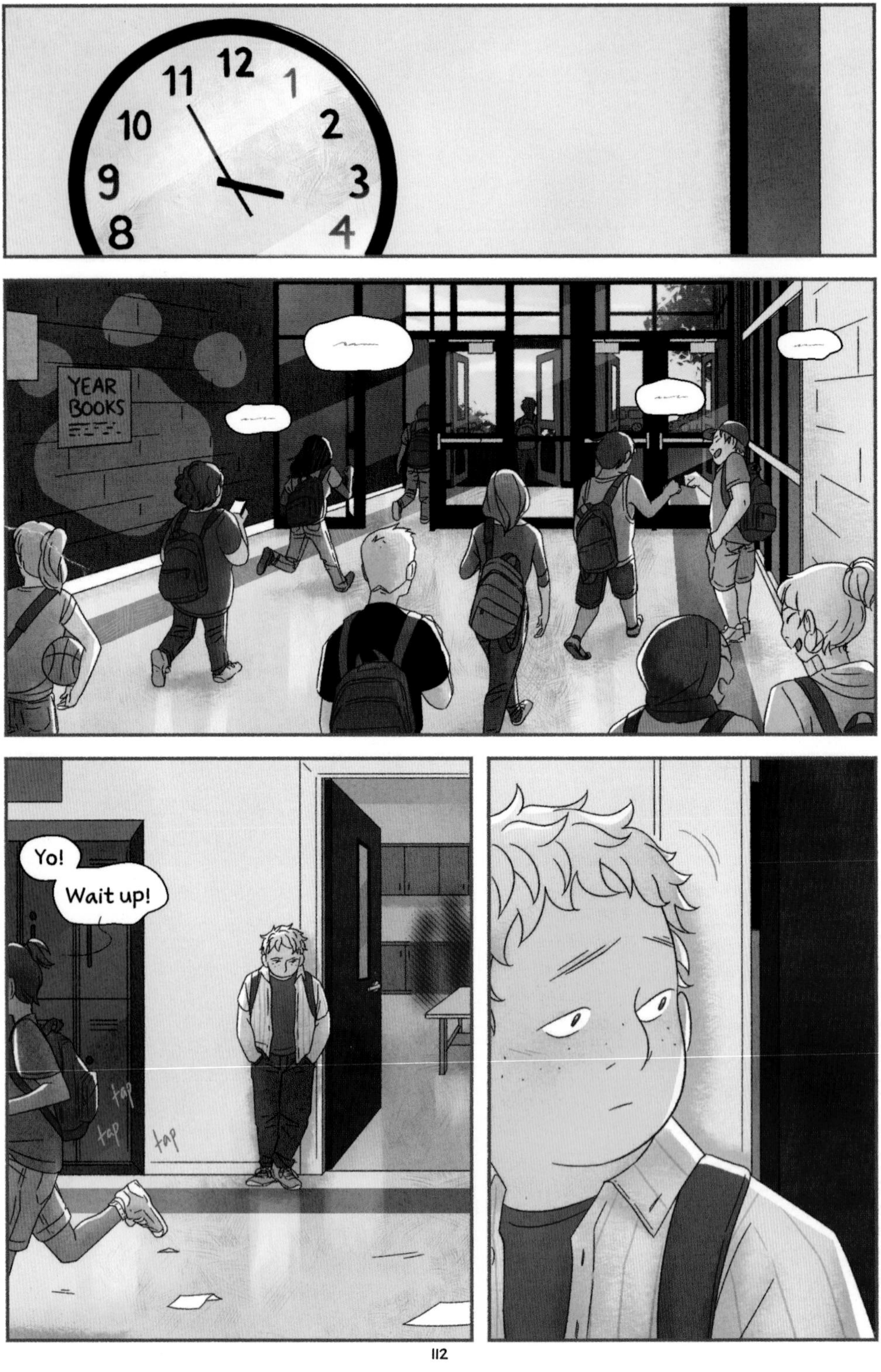
YEAR BOOKS
Yo!
Wait up!
tap
tap
tap

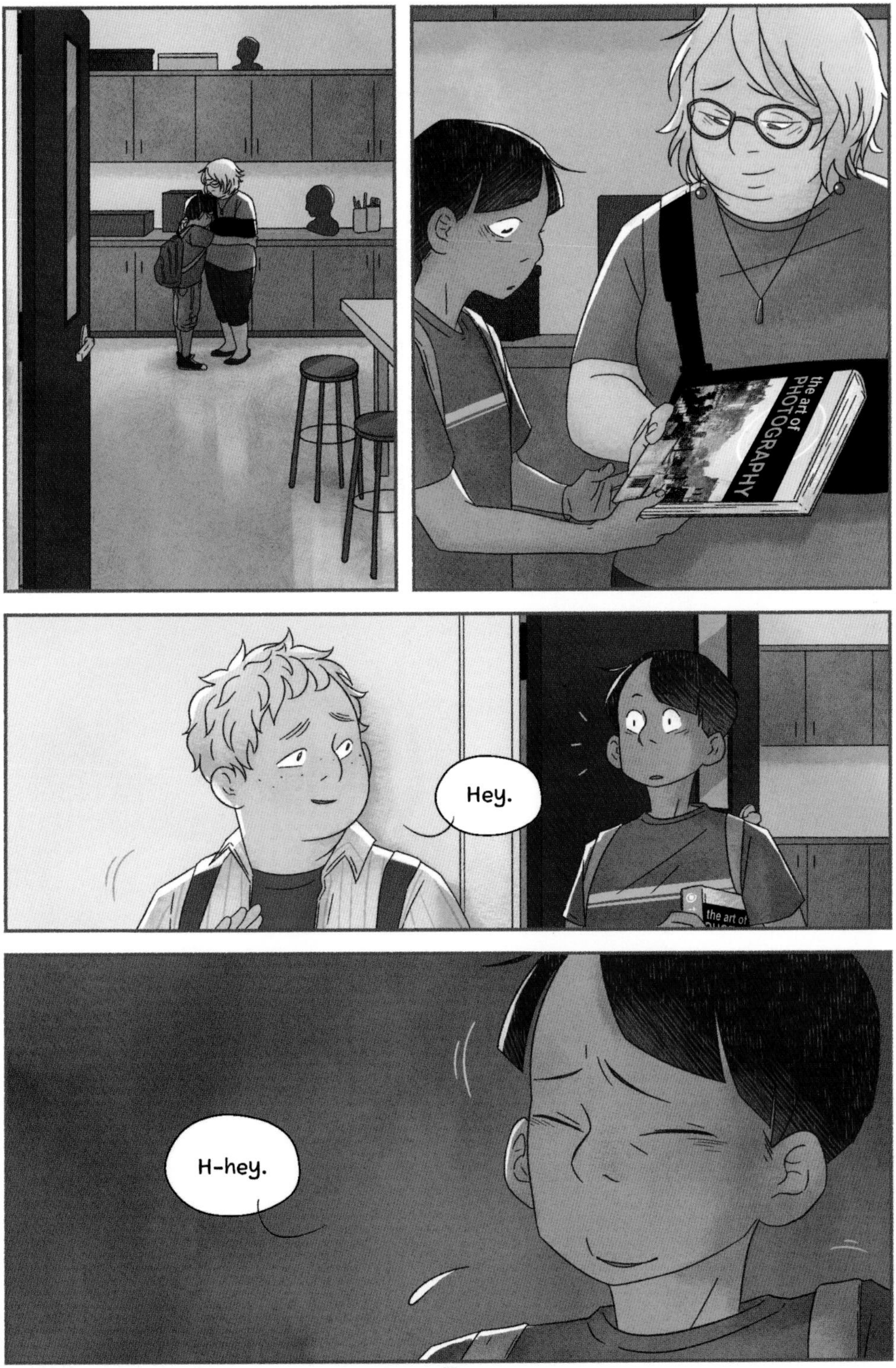
the art of
PHOTOGRAPHY
Hey.
the art of
H-hey.

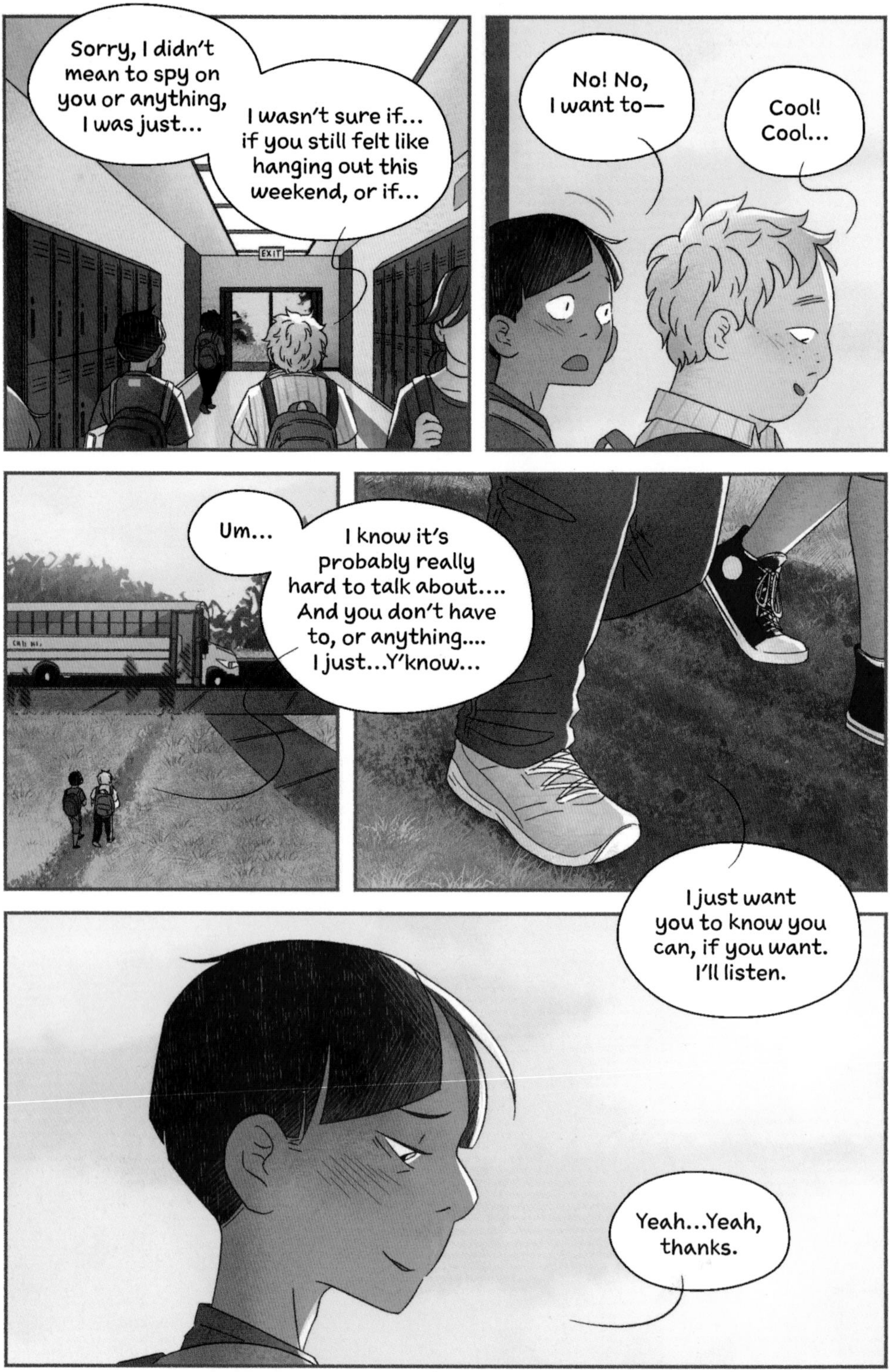
Sorry, I didn't mean to spy on you or anything, I was just...
I wasn't sure if... if you still felt like hanging out this weekend, or if...
EXIT
No! No, I want to—
Cool! Cool...
Um...
I know it's probably really hard to talk about.... And you don't have to, or anything.... I just...Y'know...
I just want you to know you can, if you want. I'll listen.
Yeah...Yeah, thanks.

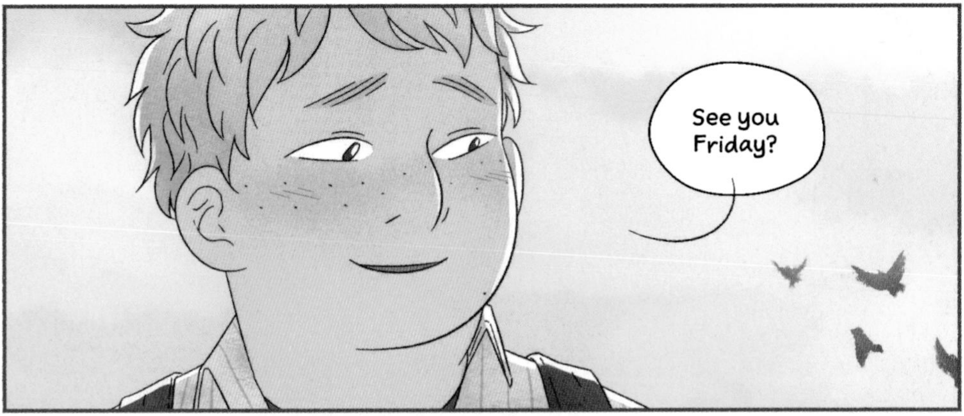
See you Friday?

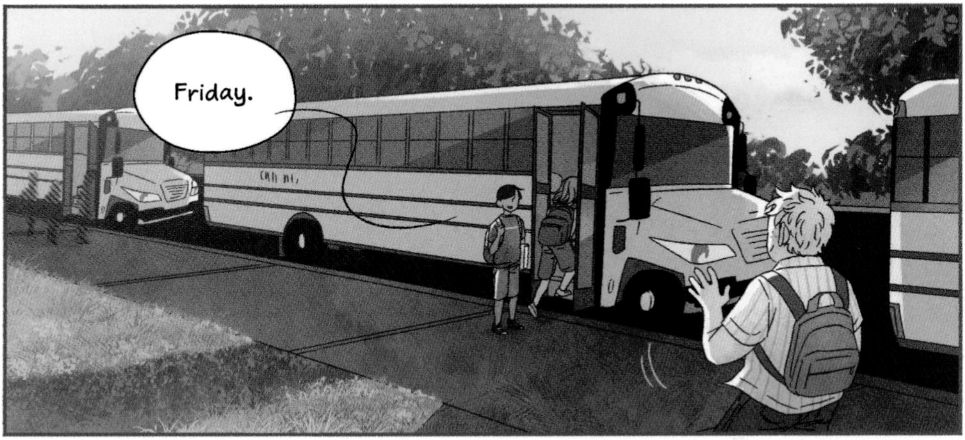
Friday.

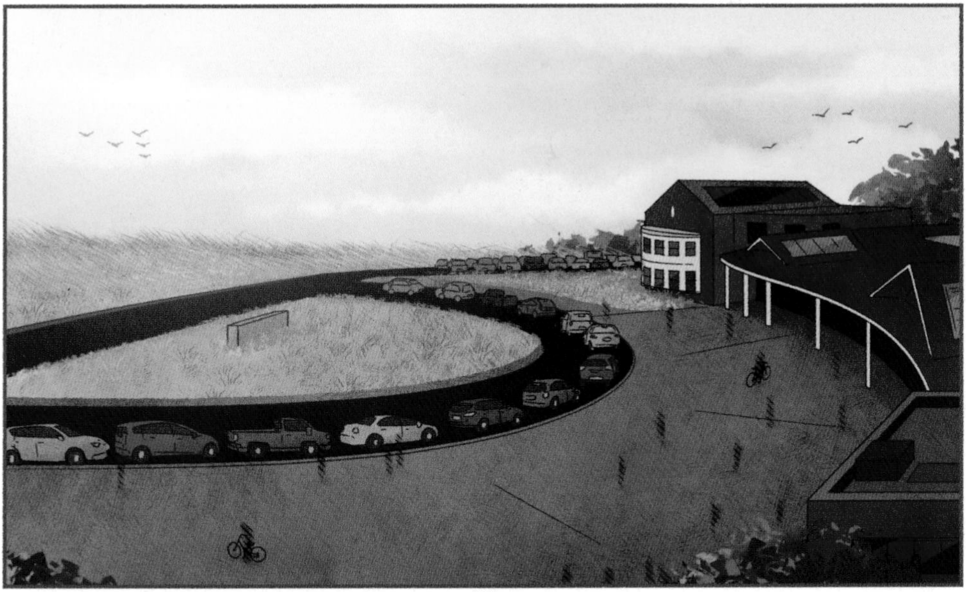

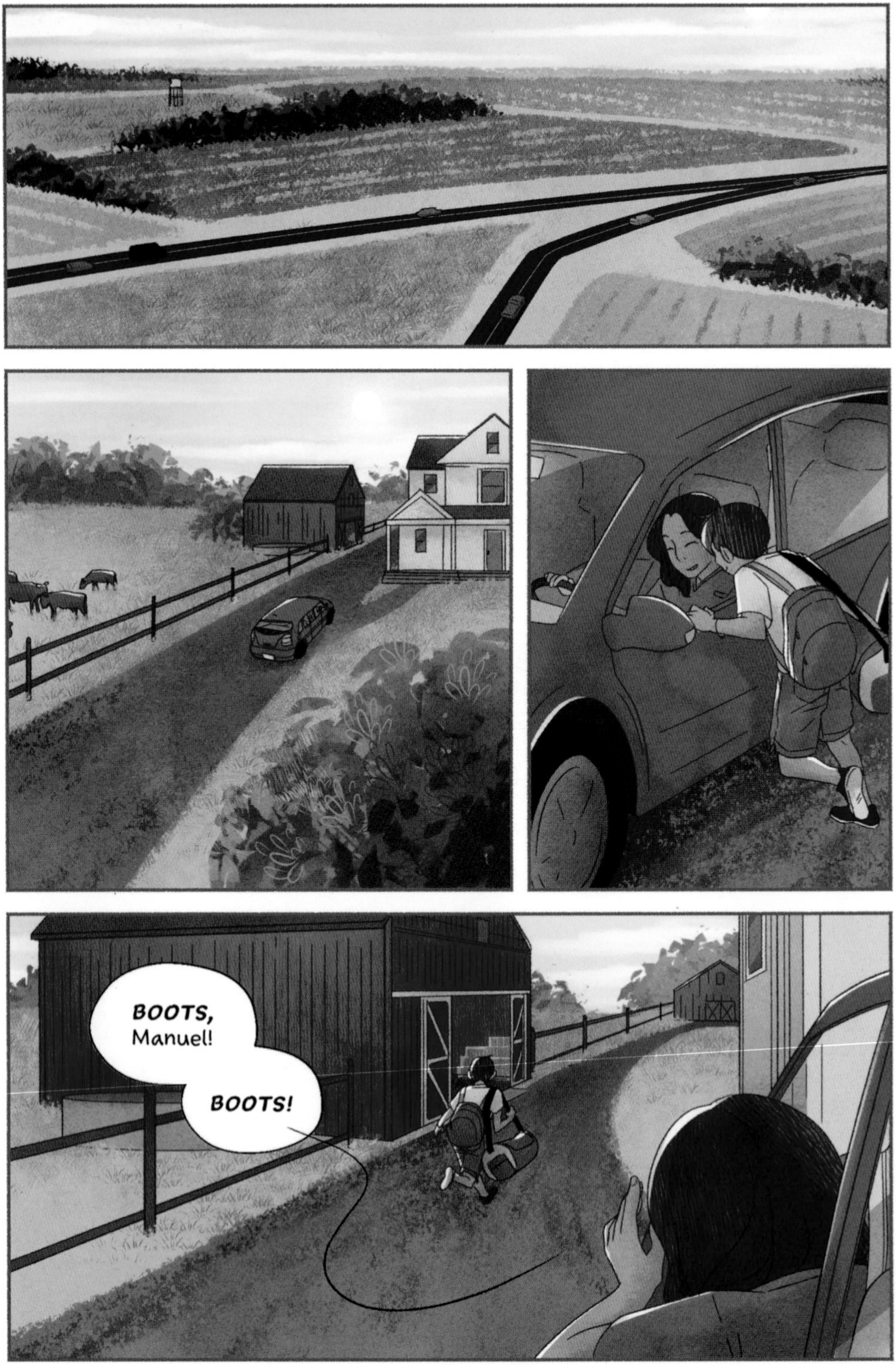
BOOTS, Manuel!
BOOTS!

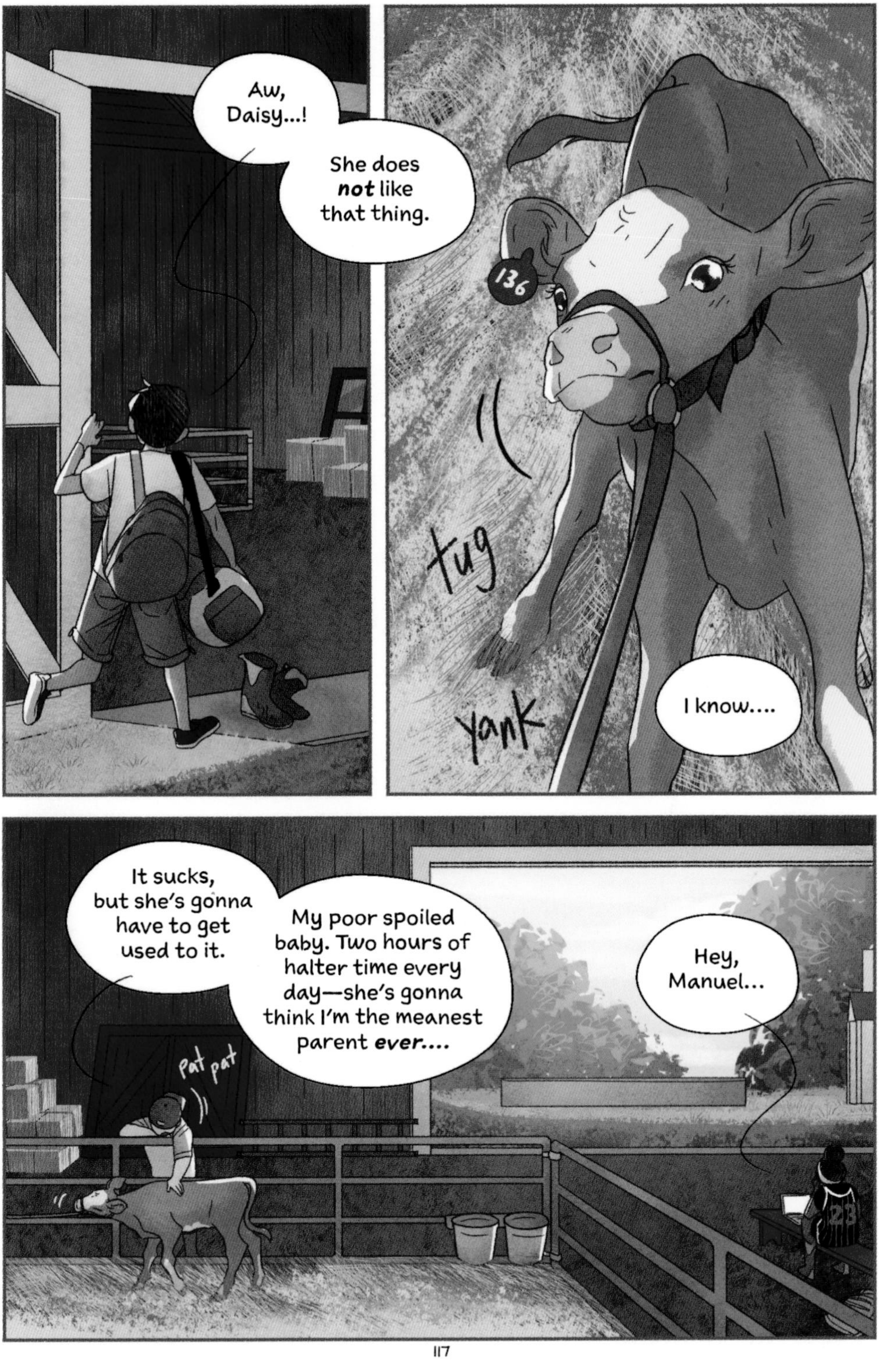

Aw, Daisy...!
She does **not** like that thing.
tug
yank
I know....
It sucks, but she's gonna have to get used to it.
My poor spoiled baby. Two hours of halter time every day—she's gonna think I'm the meanest parent **ever....**
pat pat
Hey, Manuel...

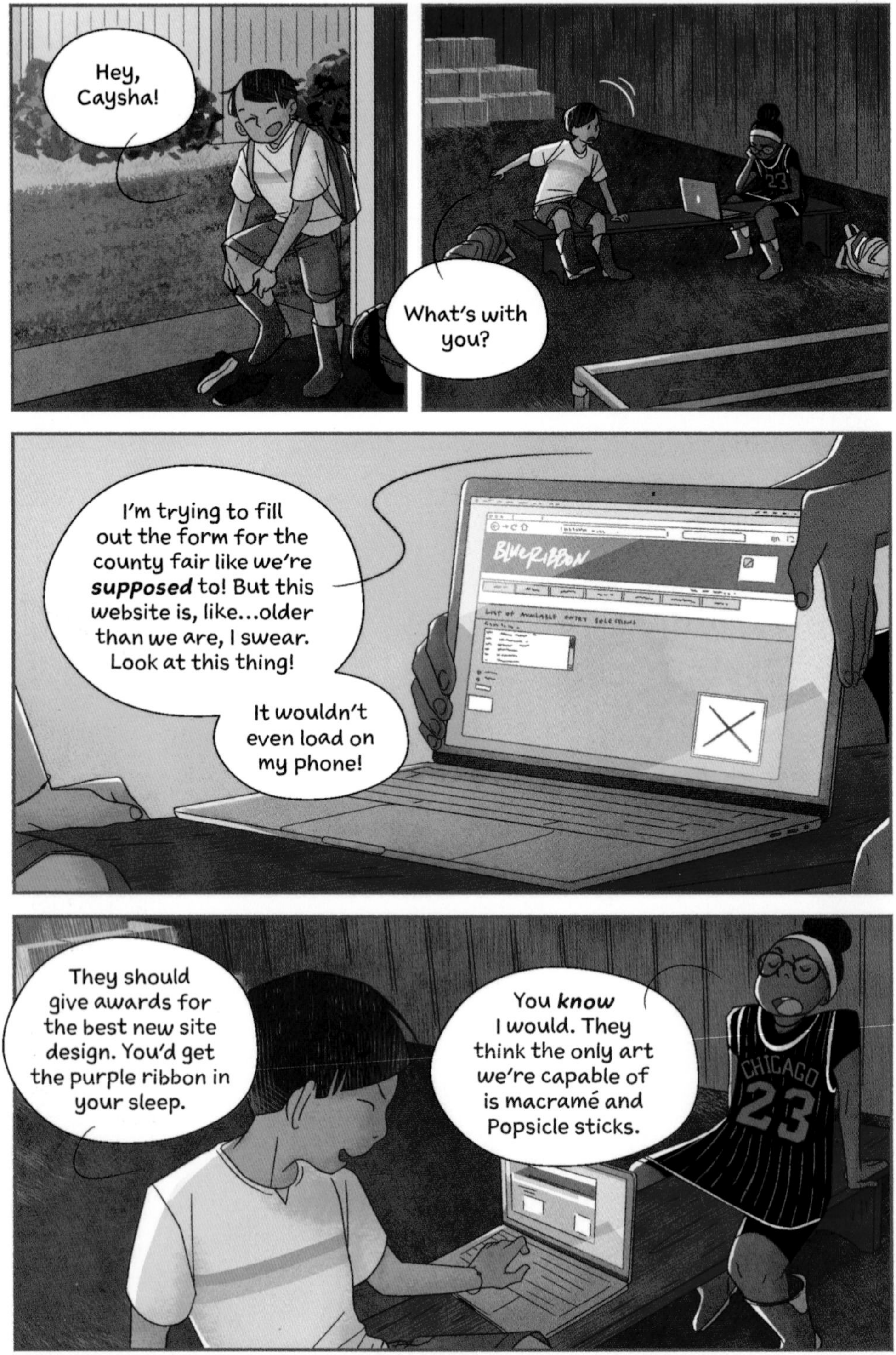

Hey, Caysha!
What's with you?
I'm trying to fill out the form for the county fair like we're ***supposed*** to! But this website is, like...older than we are, I swear. Look at this thing!
It wouldn't even load on my phone!
They should give awards for the best new site design. You'd get the purple ribbon in your sleep.
You ***know*** I would. They think the only art we're capable of is macramé and Popsicle sticks.
CHICAGO
23

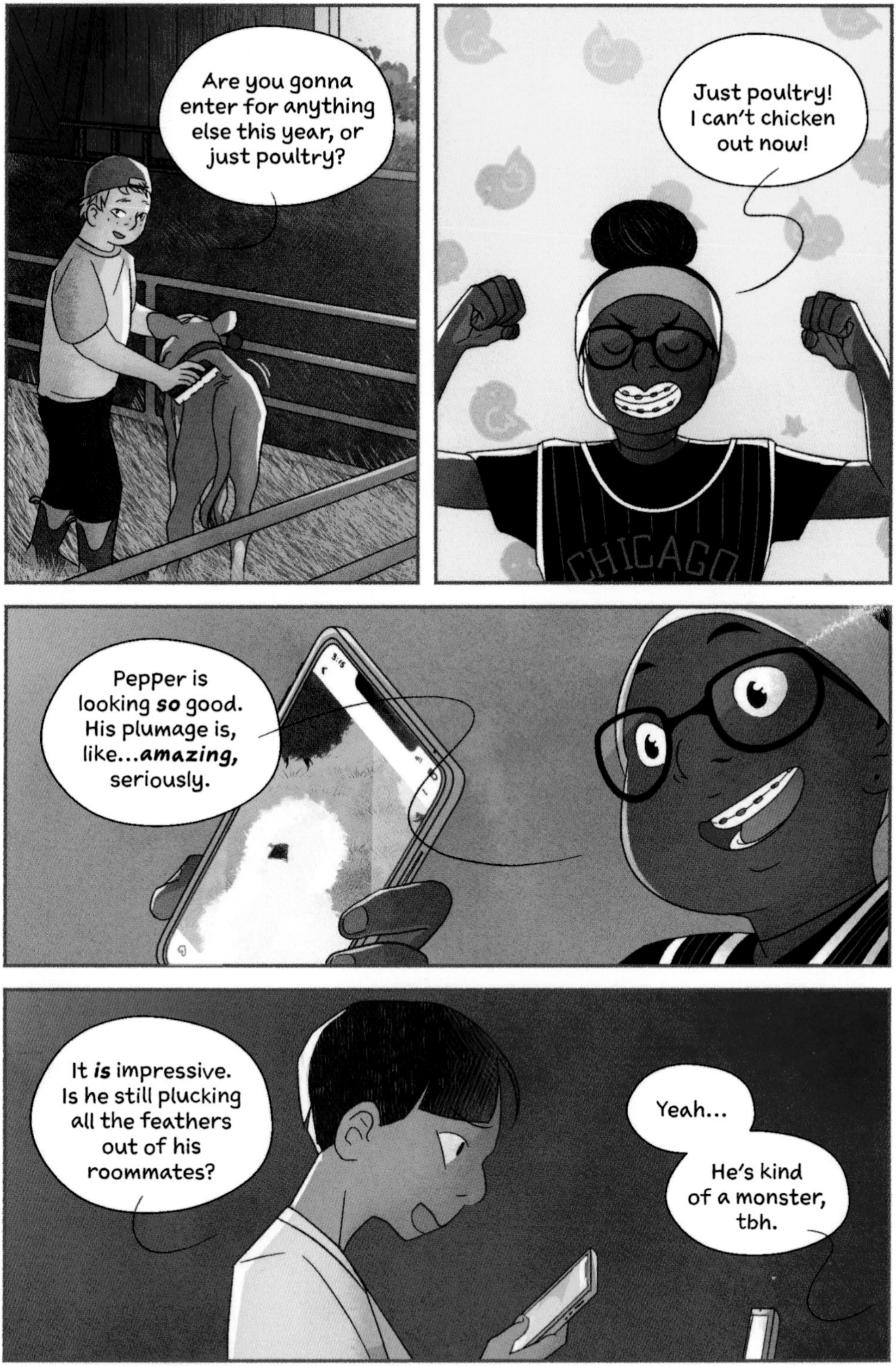
Are you gonna enter for anything else this year, or just poultry?
Just poultry! I can't chicken out now!
CHICAGO
Pepper is looking **so** good. His plumage is, like...***amazing,*** seriously.
It ***is*** impressive. Is he still plucking all the feathers out of his roommates?
Yeah...
He's kind of a monster, tbh.

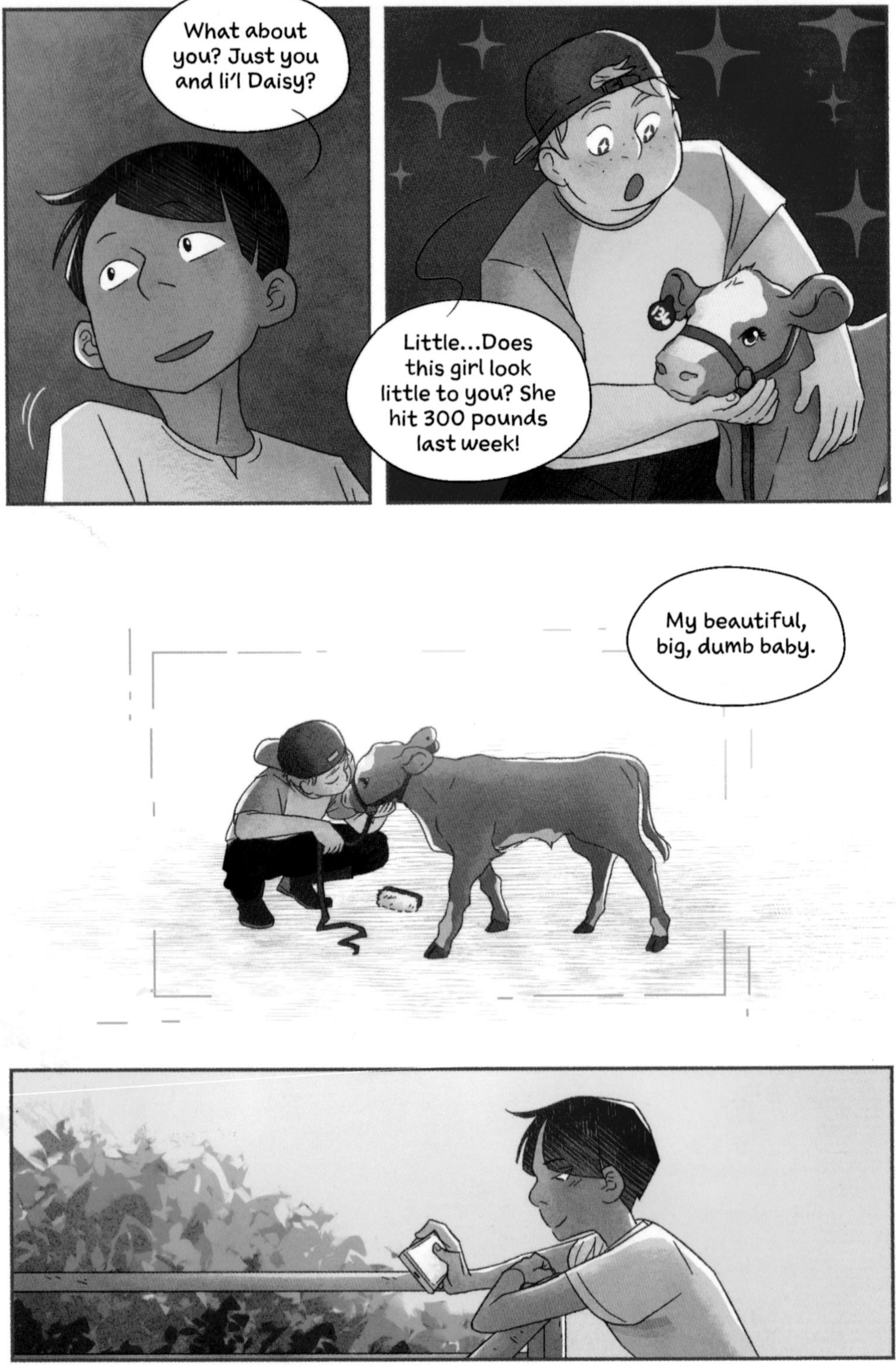
What about you? Just you and li'l Daisy?
Little...Does this girl look little to you? She hit 300 pounds last week!
My beautiful, big, dumb baby.

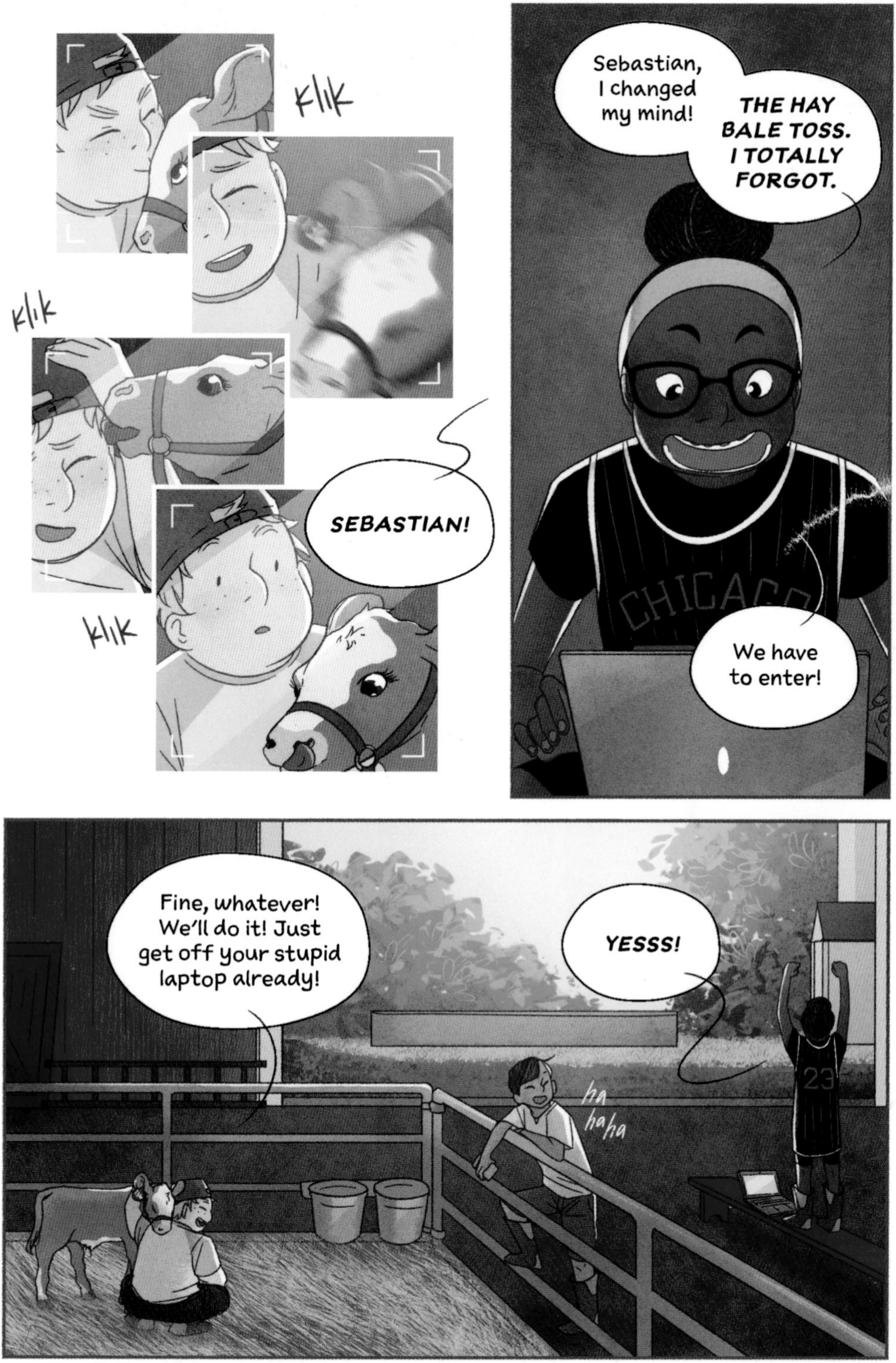
KLIK
KLIK
KLIK
SEBASTIAN!
Sebastian, I changed my mind!
THE HAY BALE TOSS. I TOTALLY FORGOT.
We have to enter!
Fine, whatever! We'll do it! Just get off your stupid laptop already!
YESSS!
ha haha

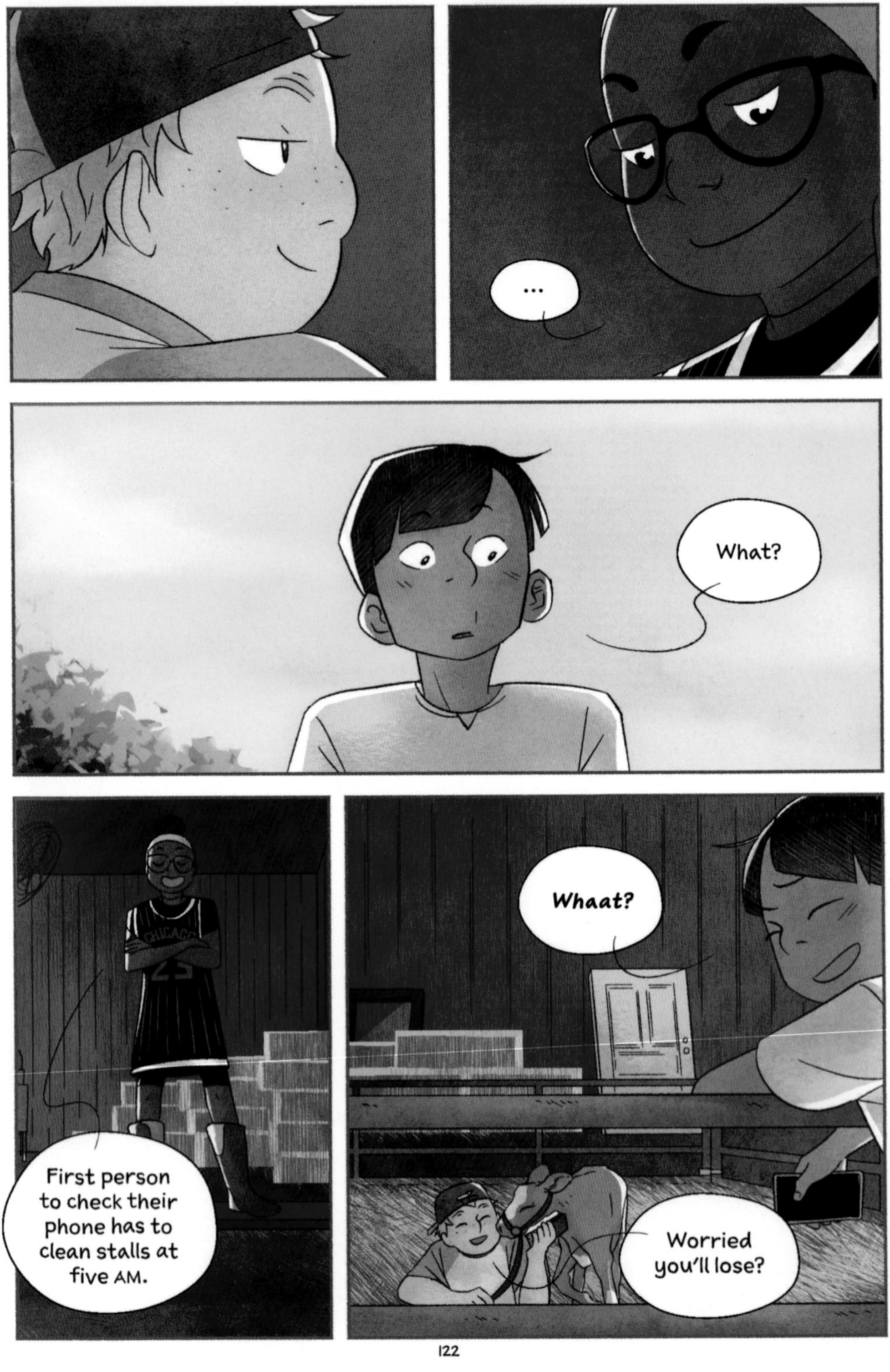
...
What?
First person to check their phone has to clean stalls at five AM.
Whaat?
Worried you'll lose?

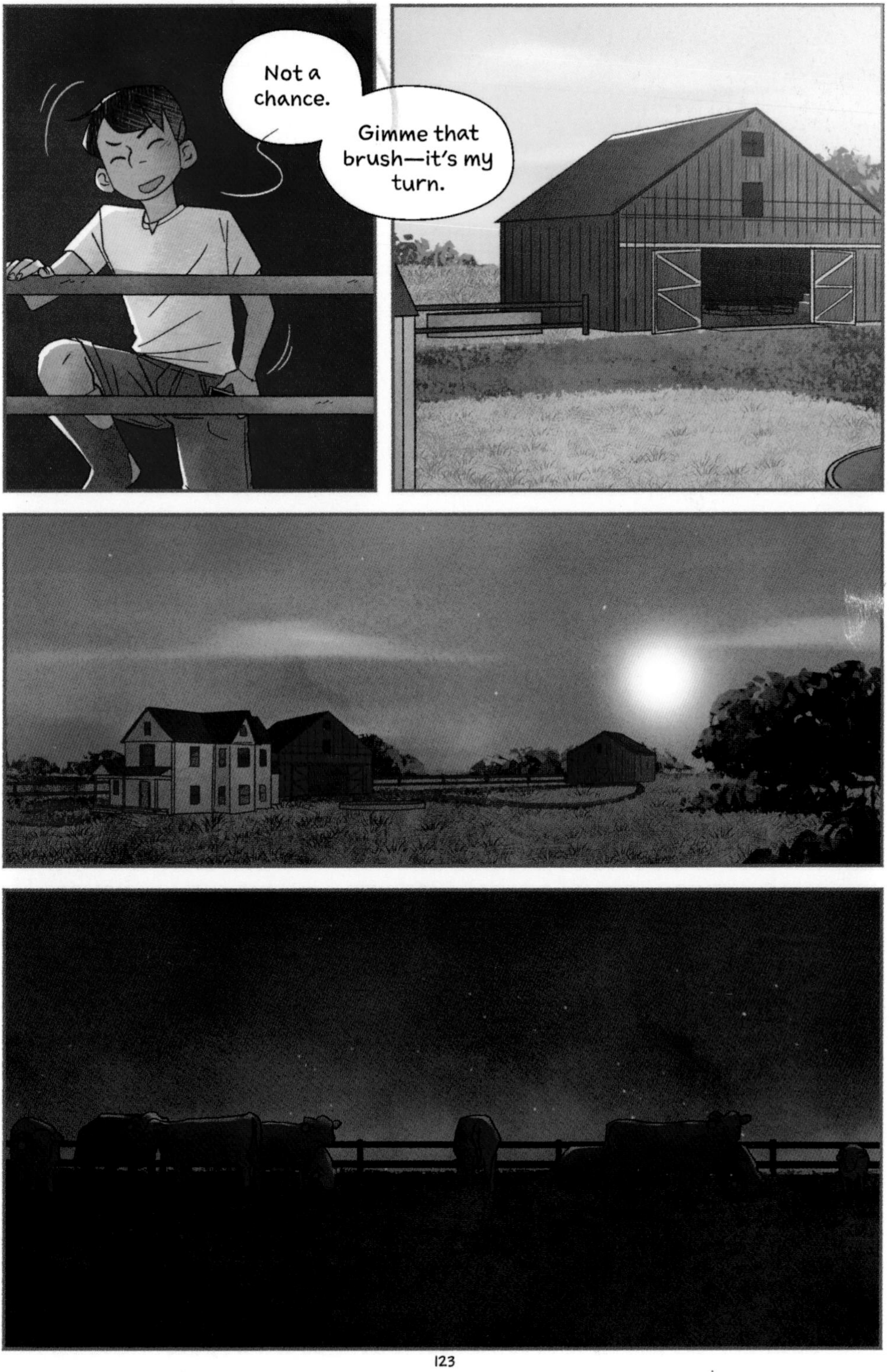
Not a chance.
Gimme that brush—it's my turn.

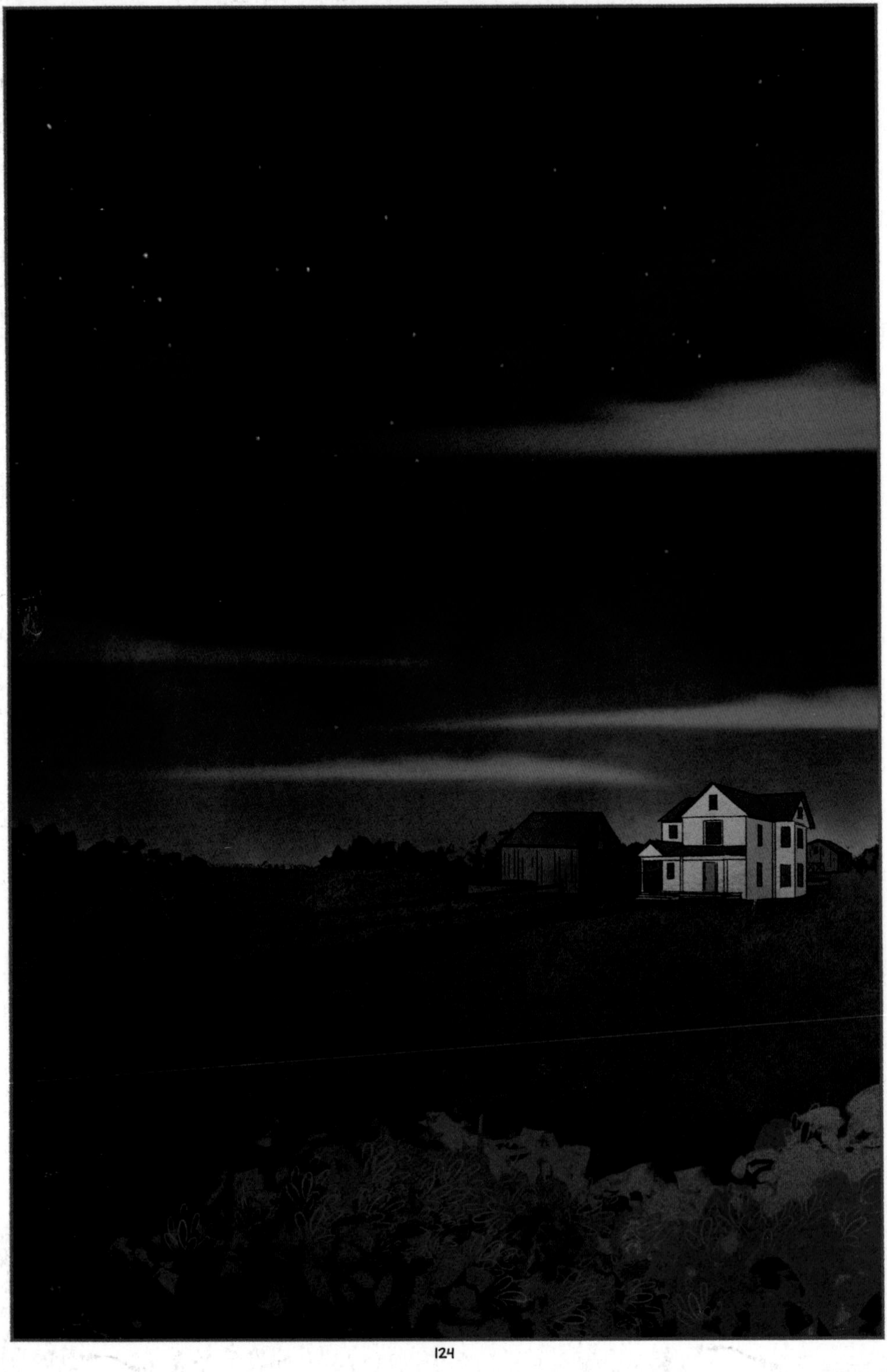

chapter four

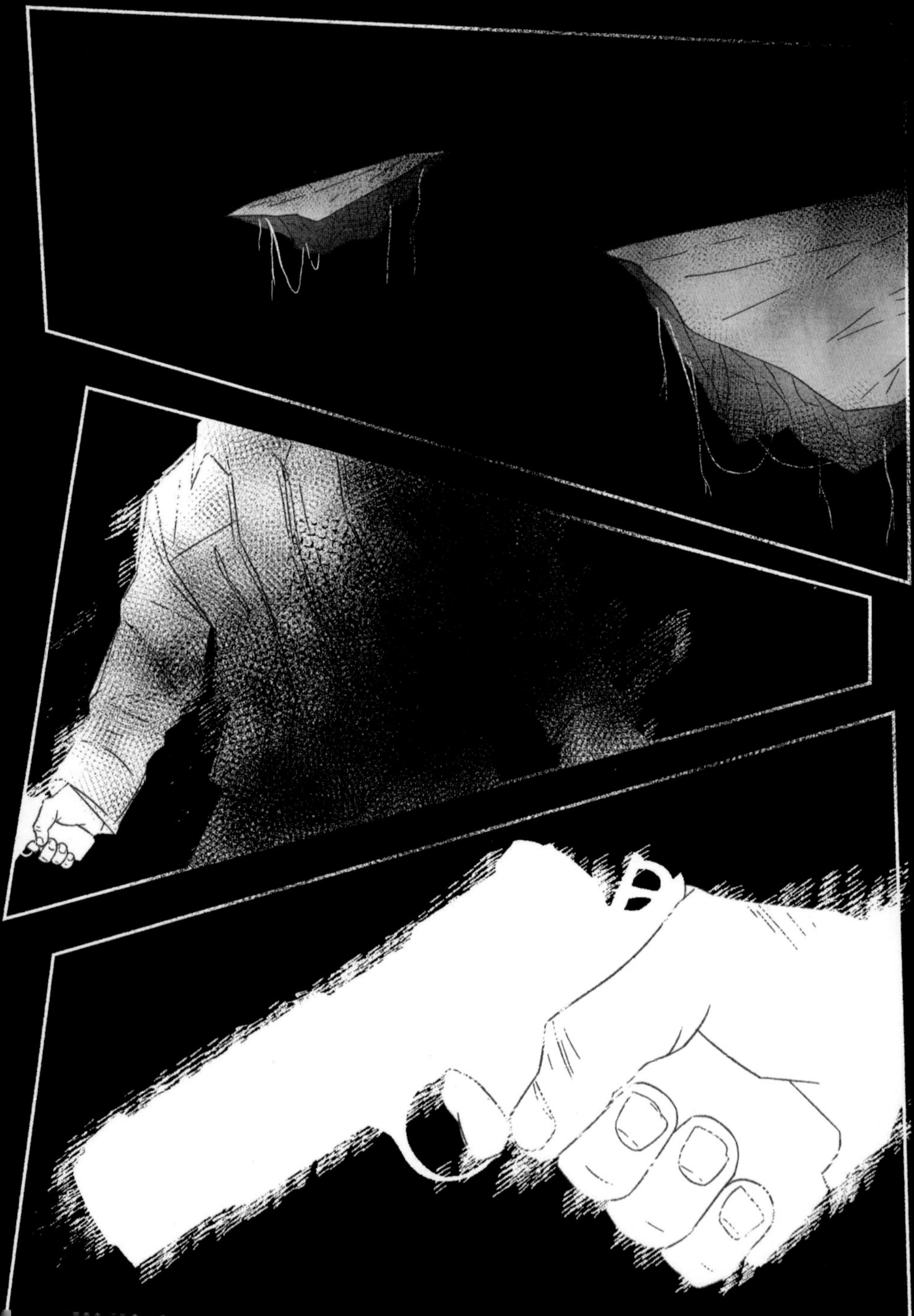

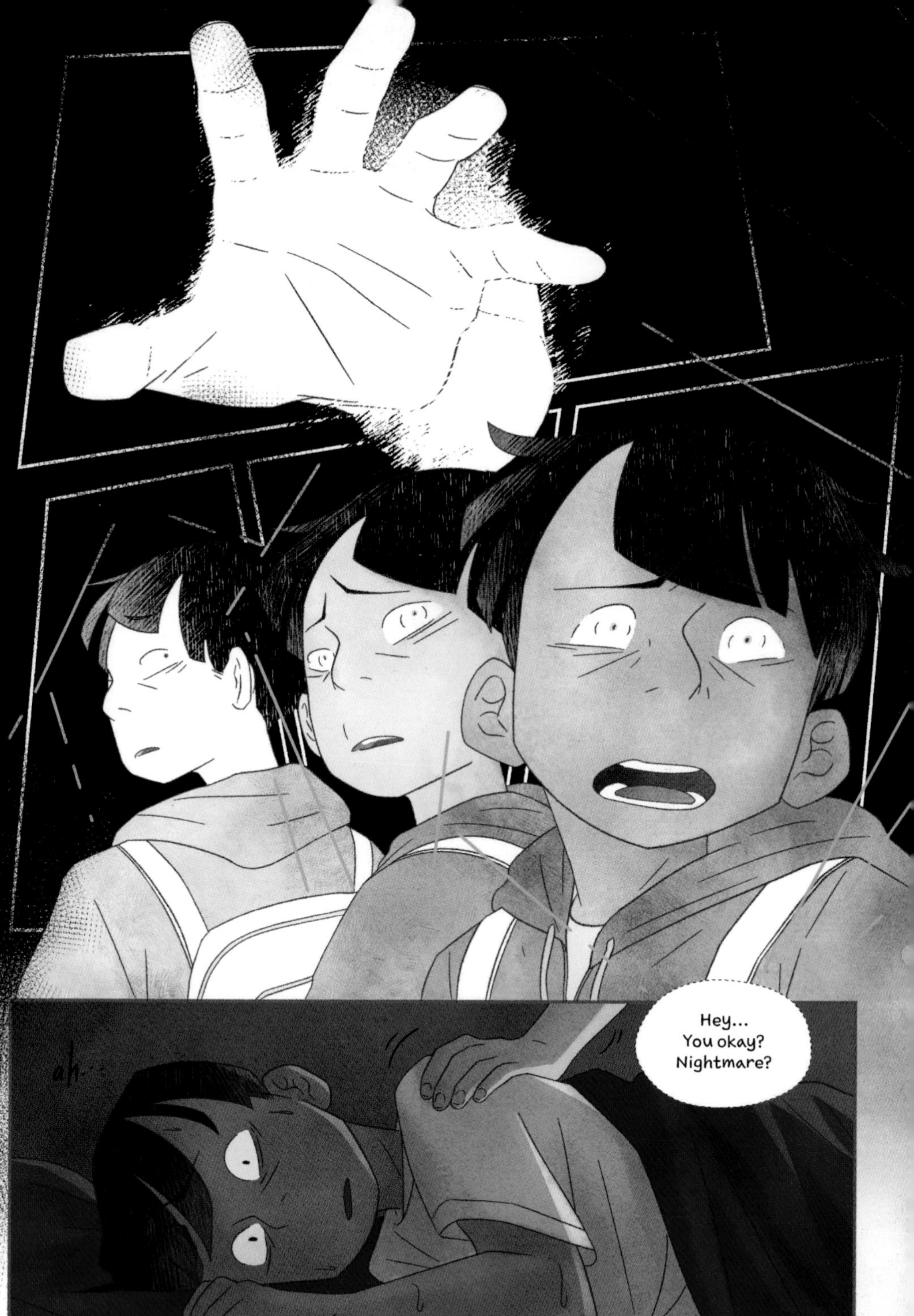
ah
Hey...
You okay?
Nightmare?

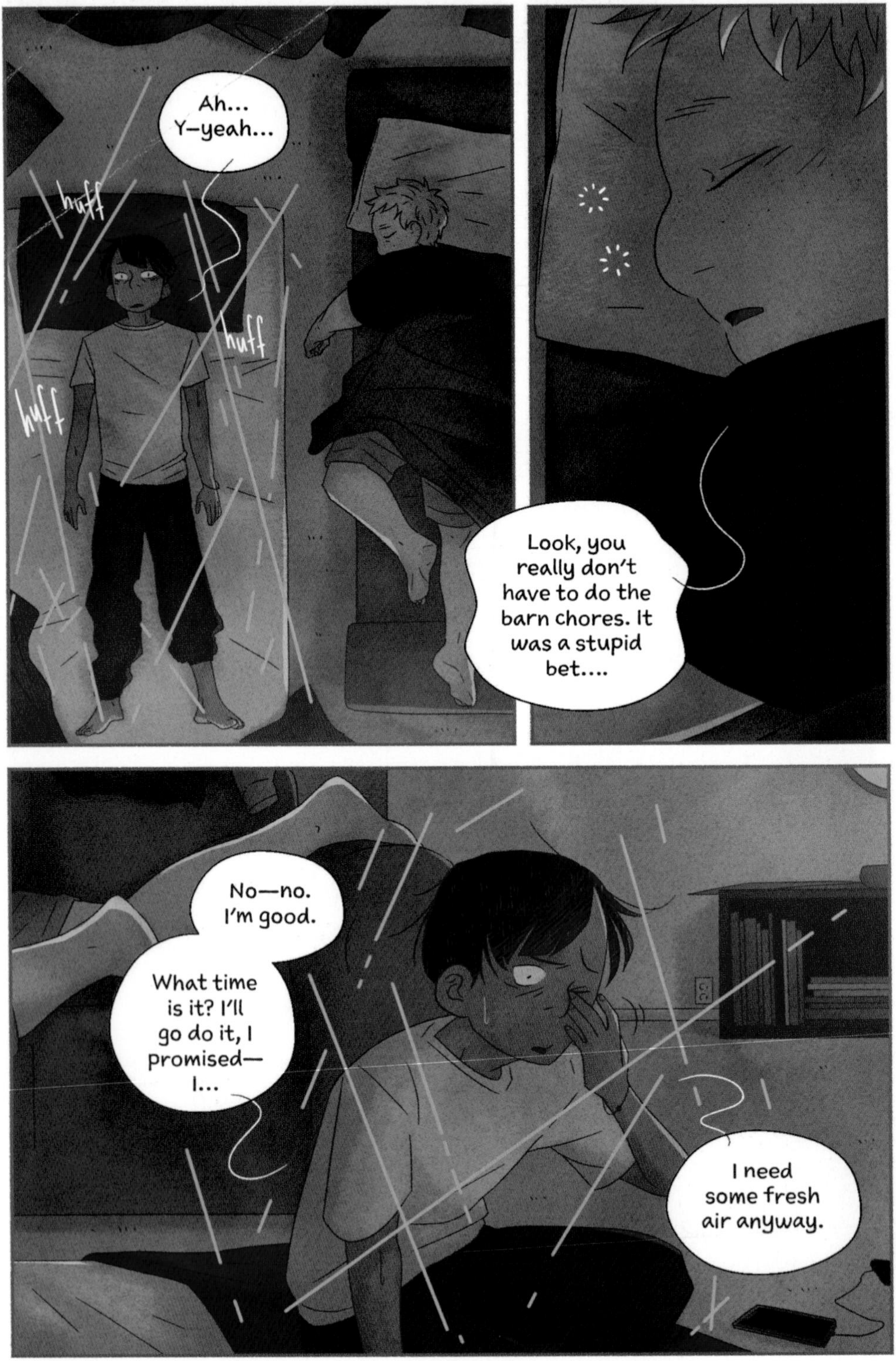
Ah...
Y-yeah...
huff
huff
huff
Look, you really don't have to do the barn chores. It was a stupid bet....
No—no. I'm good.
What time is it? I'll go do it, I promised— I...
I need some fresh air anyway.

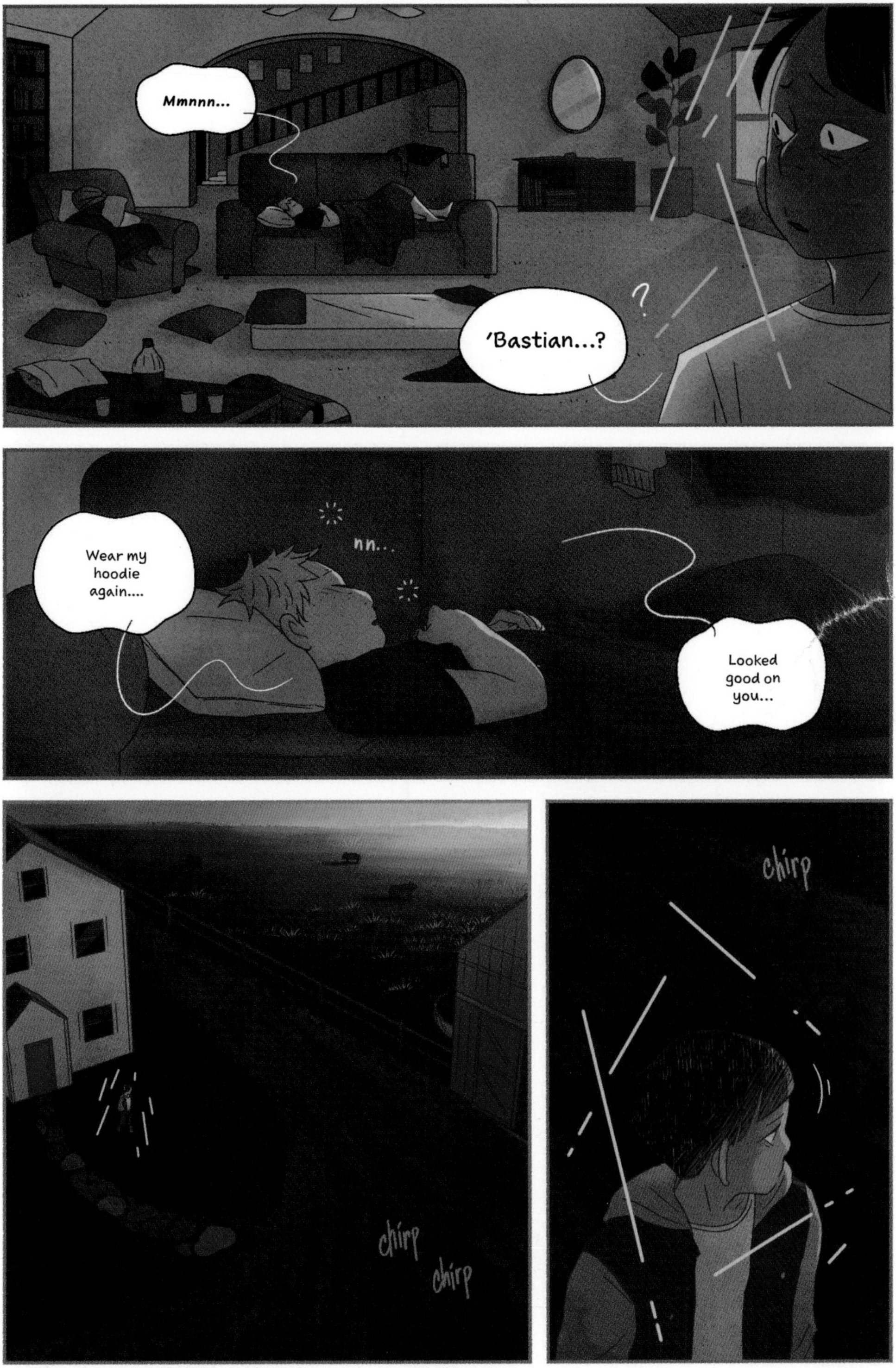
Mmnnn...
'Bastian...?
nn...
Wear my hoodie again....
Looked good on you...
chirp
chirp
chirp

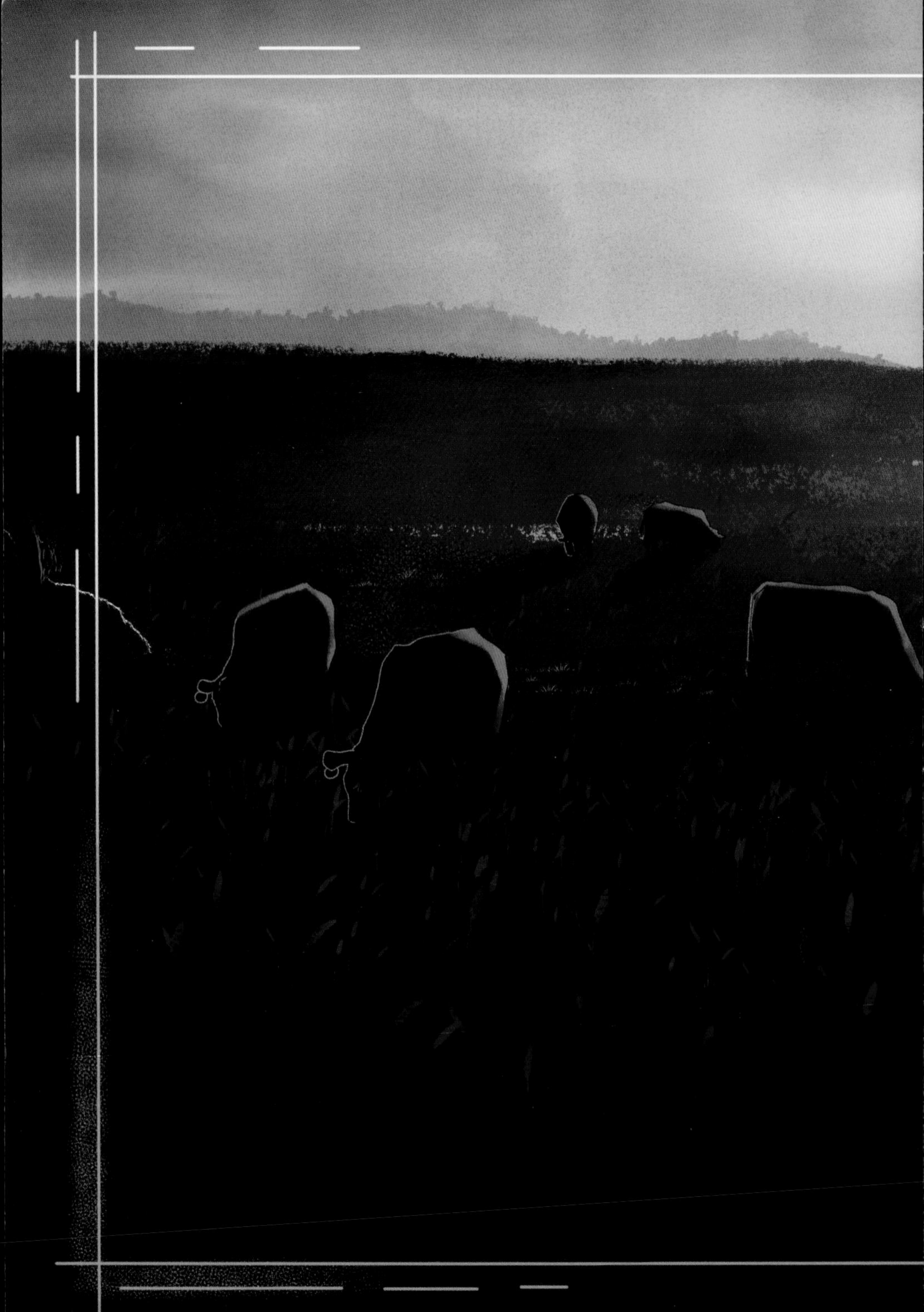

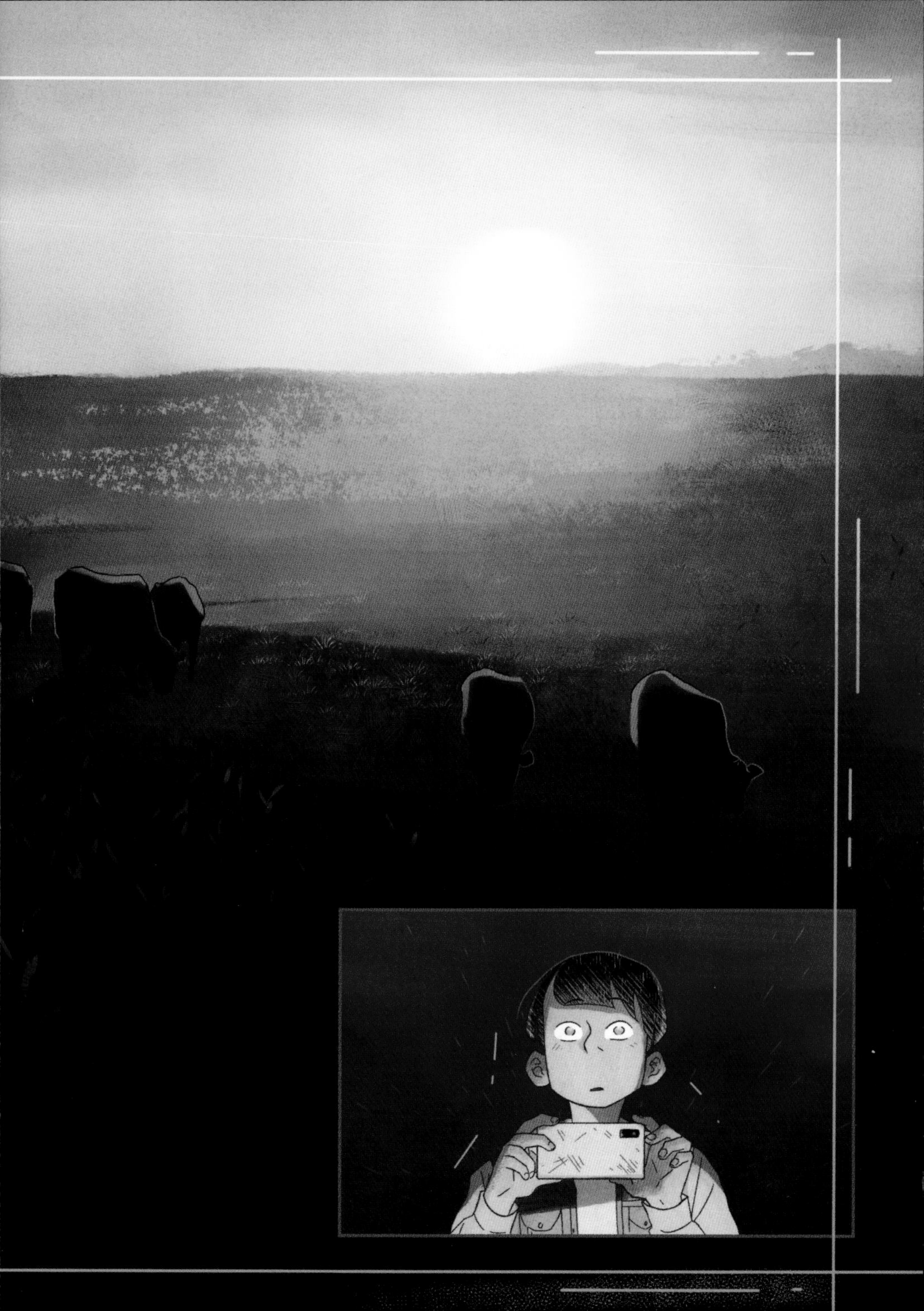

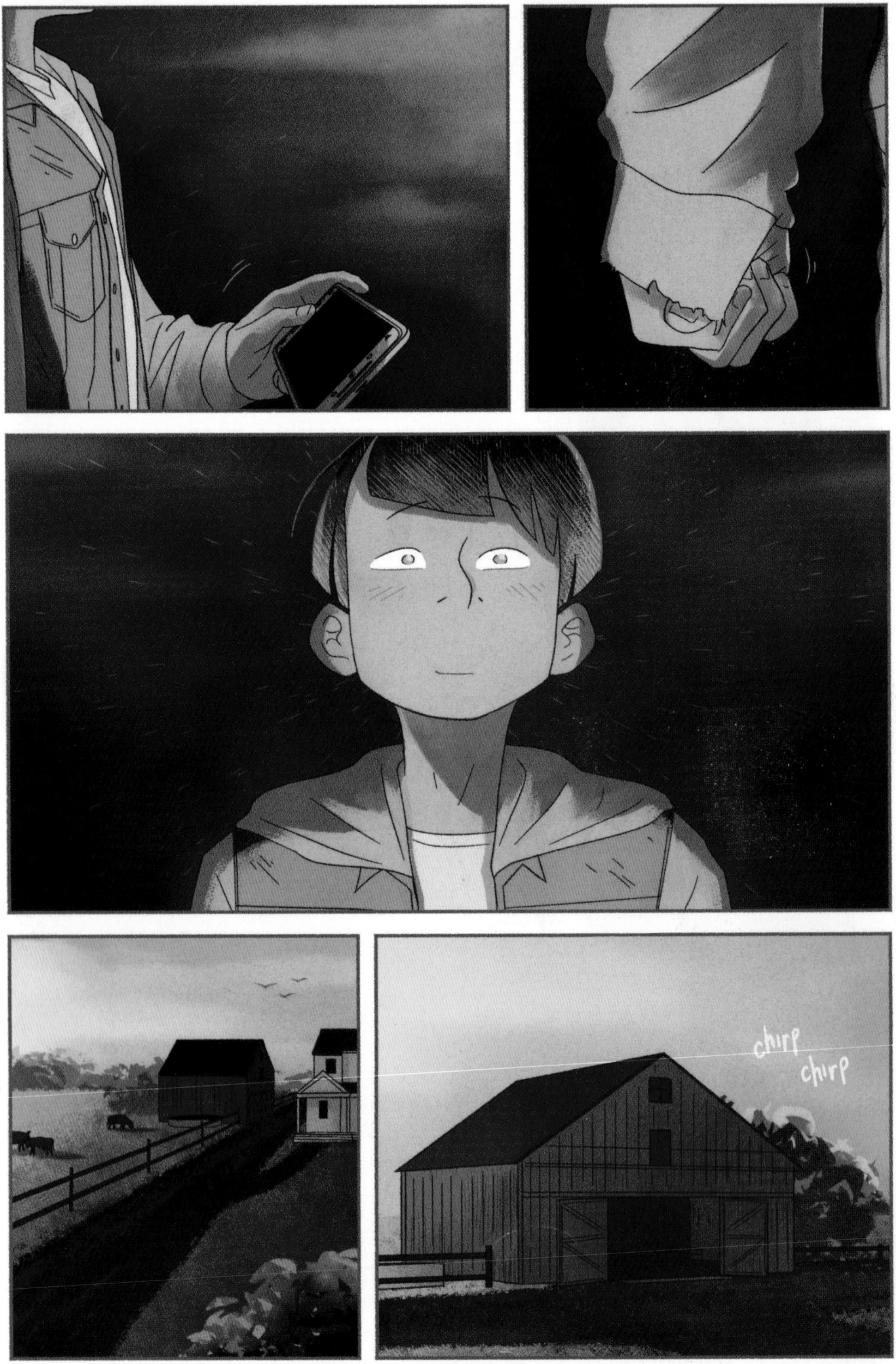
chirp
chirp

shff

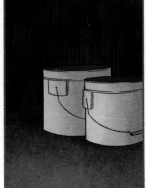

clatter

Hey.

Hey!

Sorry.
I felt bad
making you
be out here
alone....

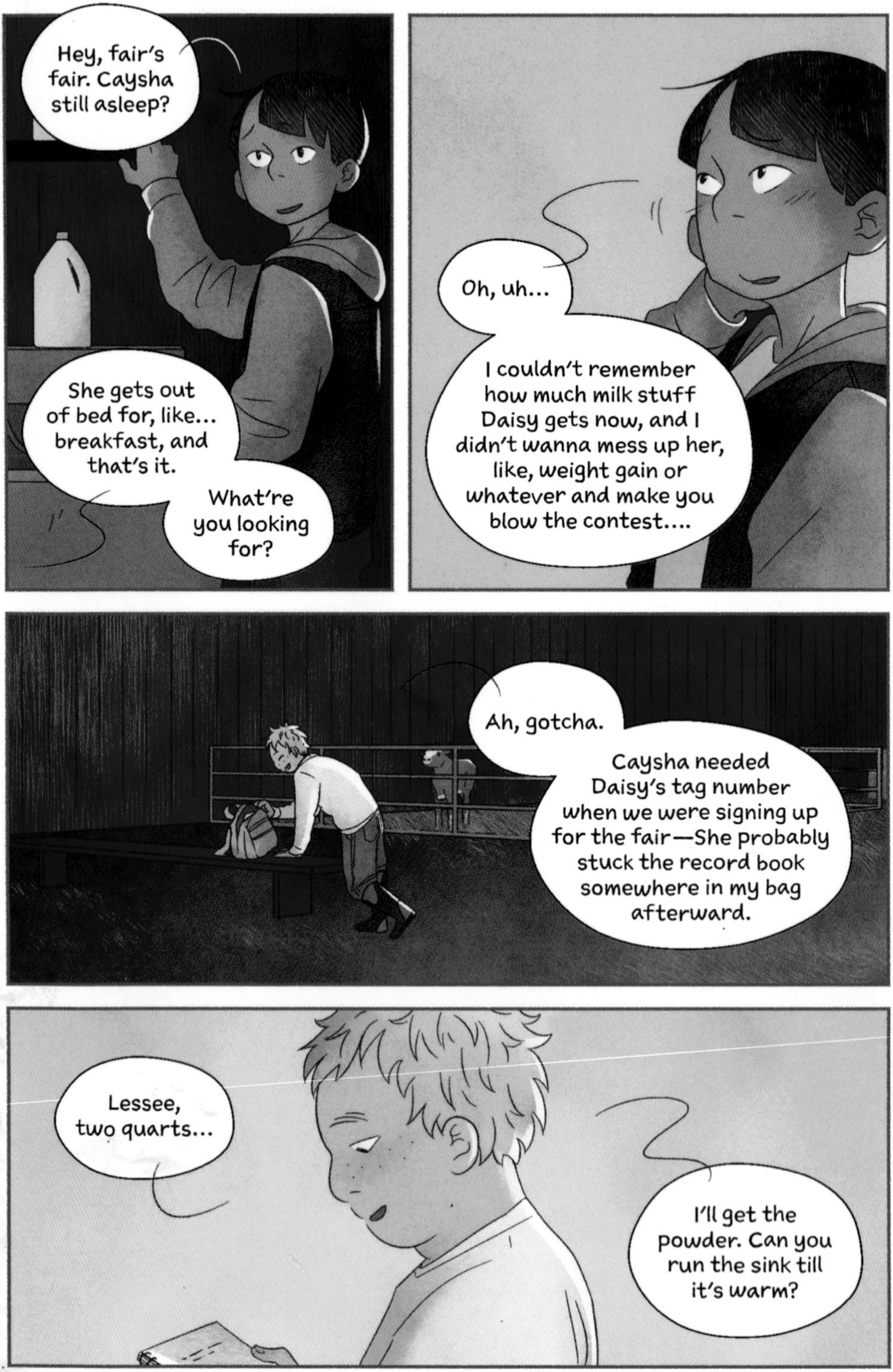
Hey, fair's fair. Caysha still asleep?
She gets out of bed for, like... breakfast, and that's it.
What're you looking for?
Oh, uh...
I couldn't remember how much milk stuff Daisy gets now, and I didn't wanna mess up her, like, weight gain or whatever and make you blow the contest....
Ah, gotcha.
Caysha needed Daisy's tag number when we were signing up for the fair—She probably stuck the record book somewhere in my bag afterward.
Lessee, two quarts...
I'll get the powder. Can you run the sink till it's warm?

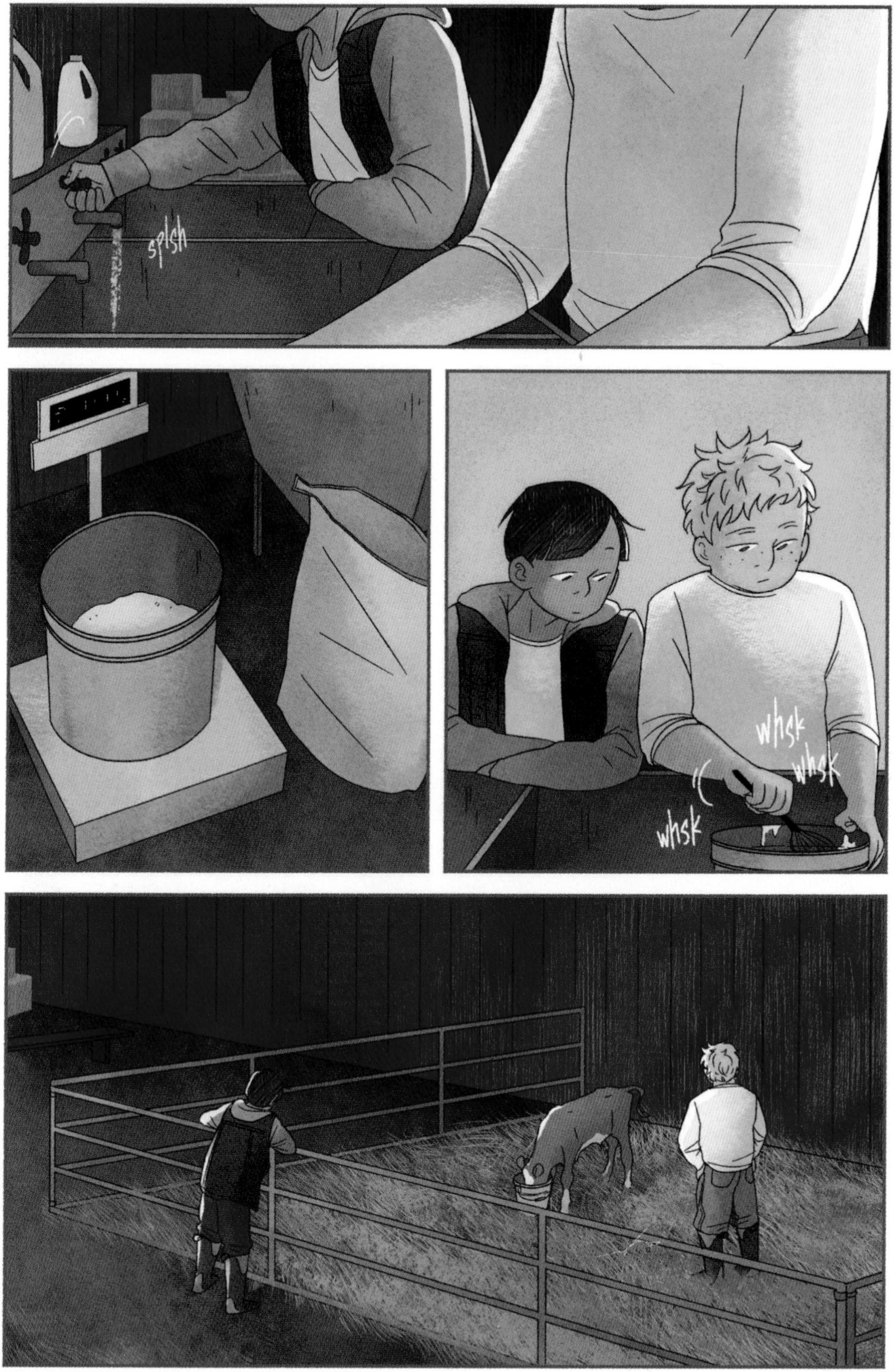
splsh
whsk
whsk
whsk

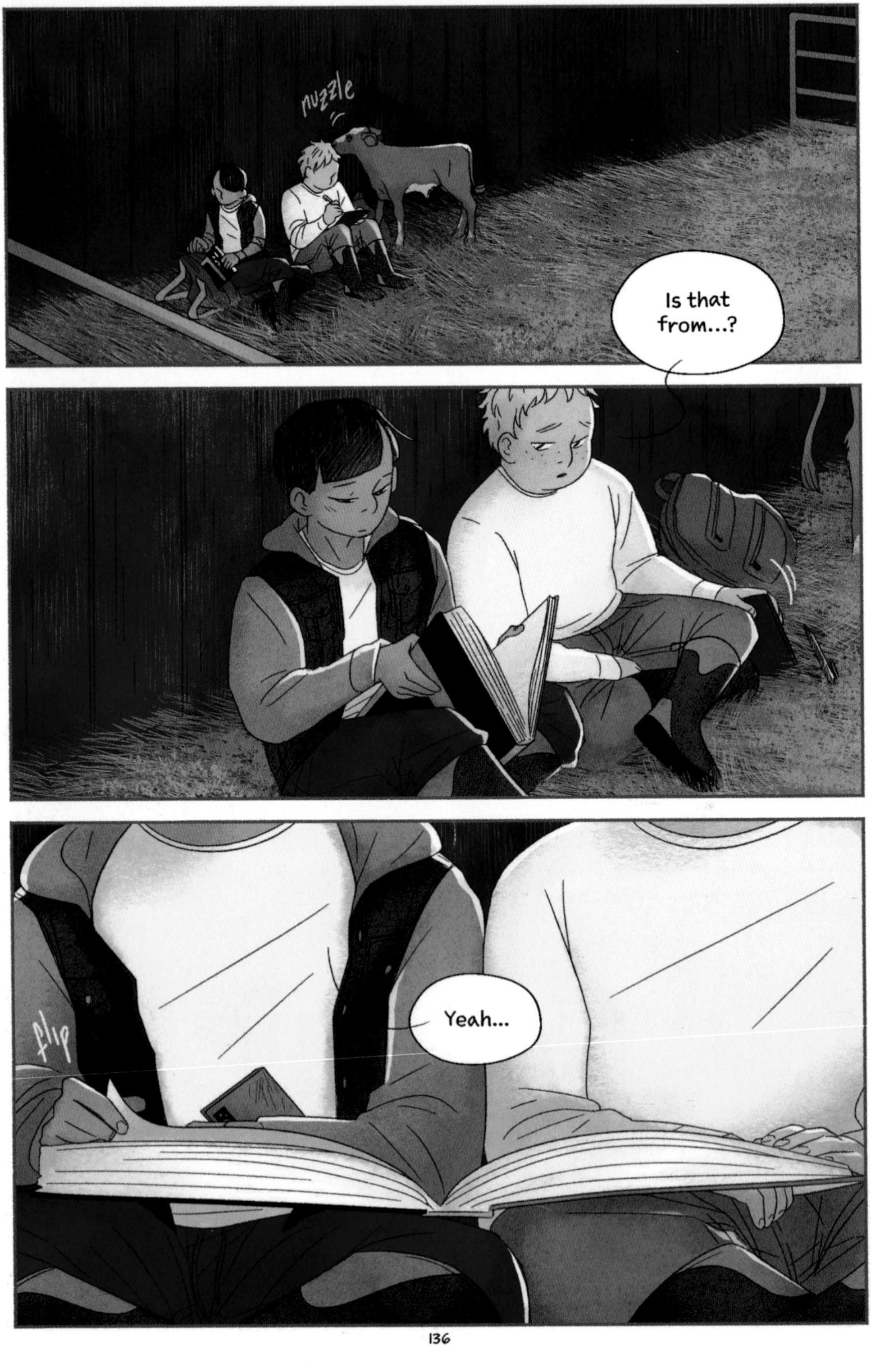
nuzzle
Is that from...?
Yeah...
flip

During the 20th century, both fine art photography and documentary photography became accepted by the English-speaking art world and the gallery system.

At first, fine art photographers tried to imitate painting styles, often using soft focus for a dreamy 'romantic' look. In reaction, Weston, Ansel Adams, and formed the Group f/6 'straight photo an imitation

4x5 Speed Graphic Camera

Weegee (Arthur Fellig)
Coney Island Crowd

...Too many people.

137

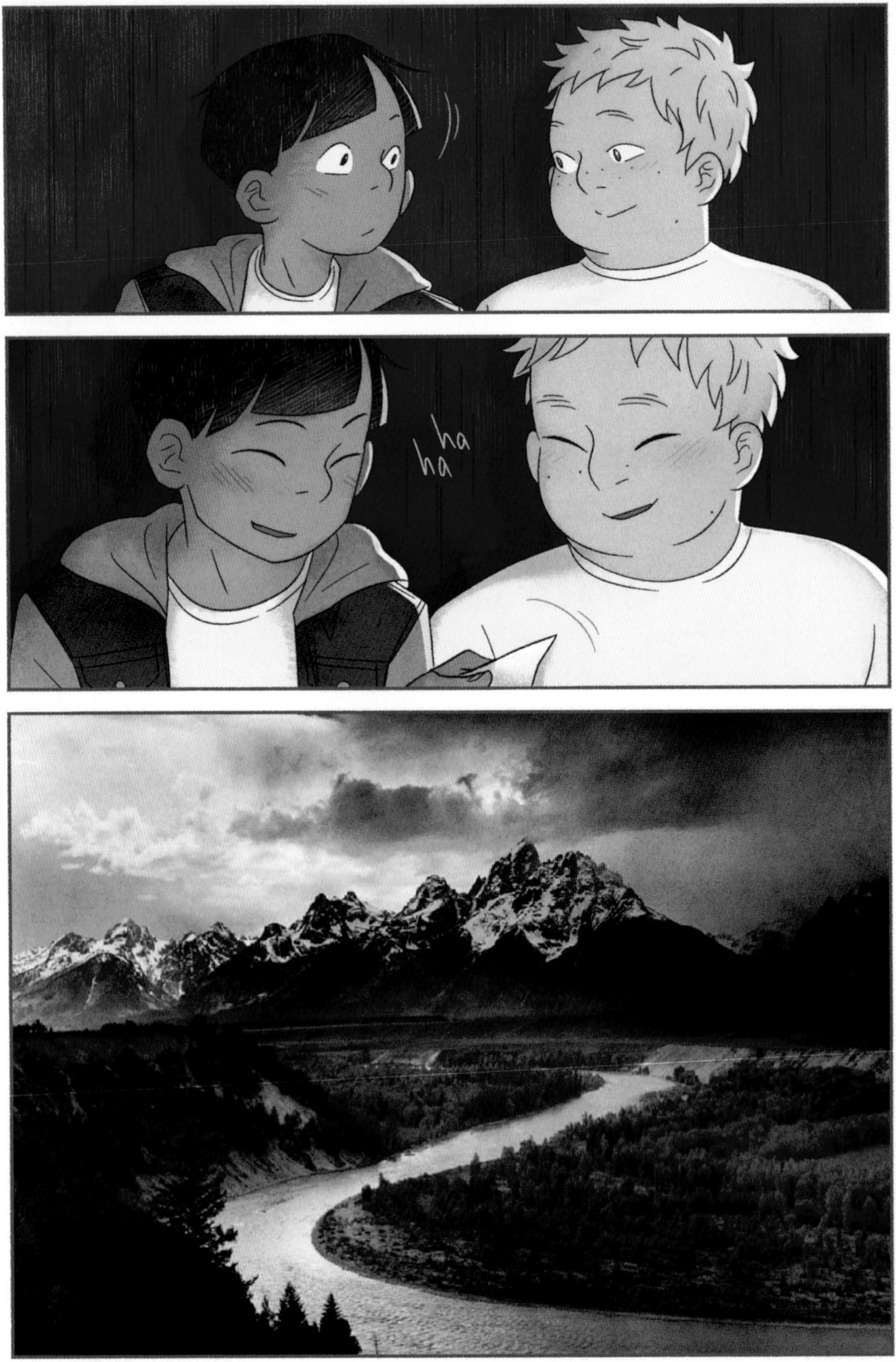
ha
ha

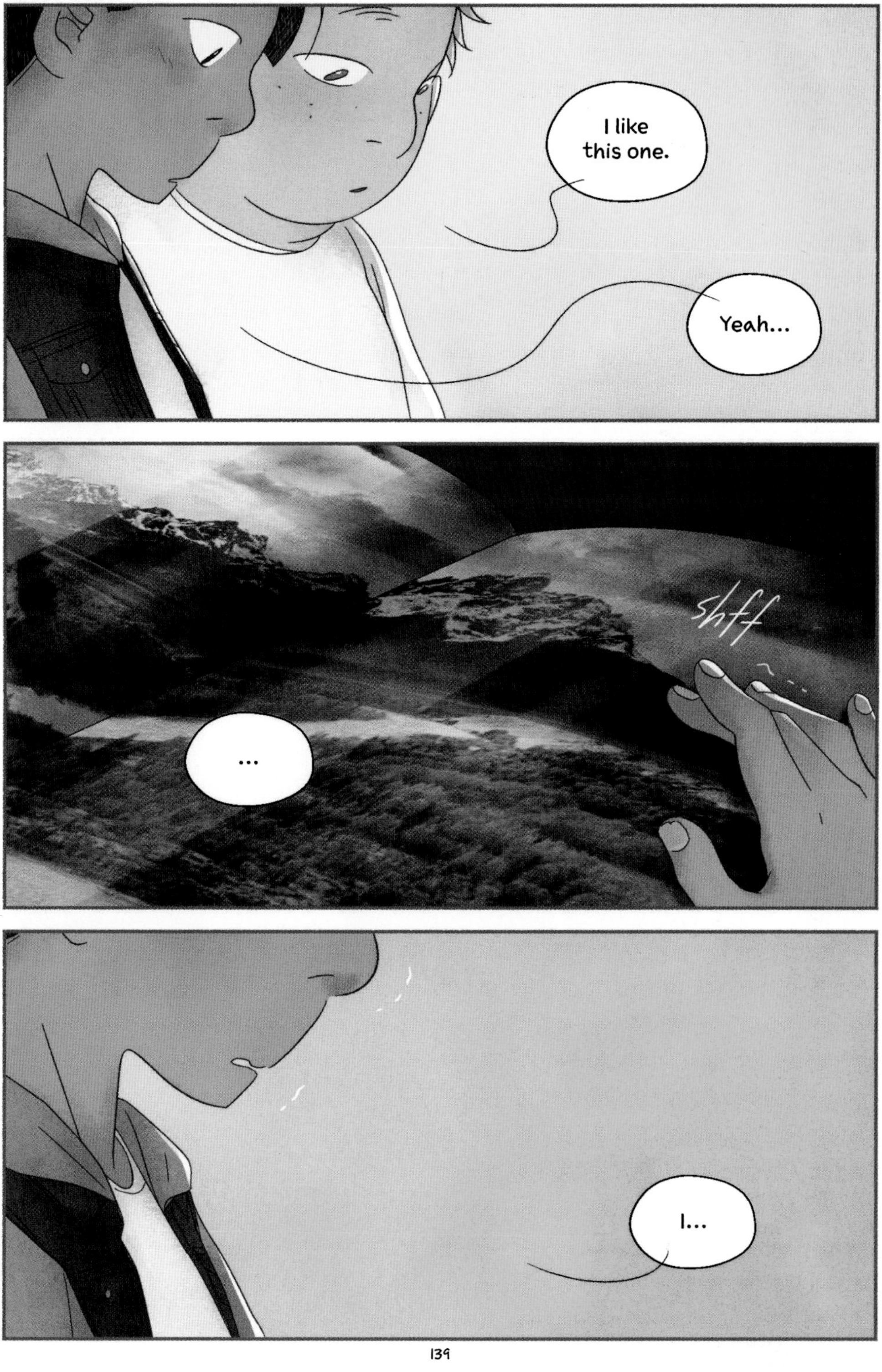
I like this one.
Yeah...
...
shff
I...

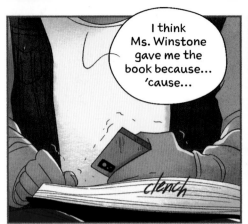

I think Ms. Winstone gave me the book because... 'cause...

She wanted to say thanks, she said.

I didn't— I couldn't visit her when she was in the hospital. It was— She was there for two months and I couldn't—I couldn't face her—

I didn't do anything worth thanking, Sebastian. *All I did was run away.*

Manuel...

You're the only reason the cops were able to catch that guy.

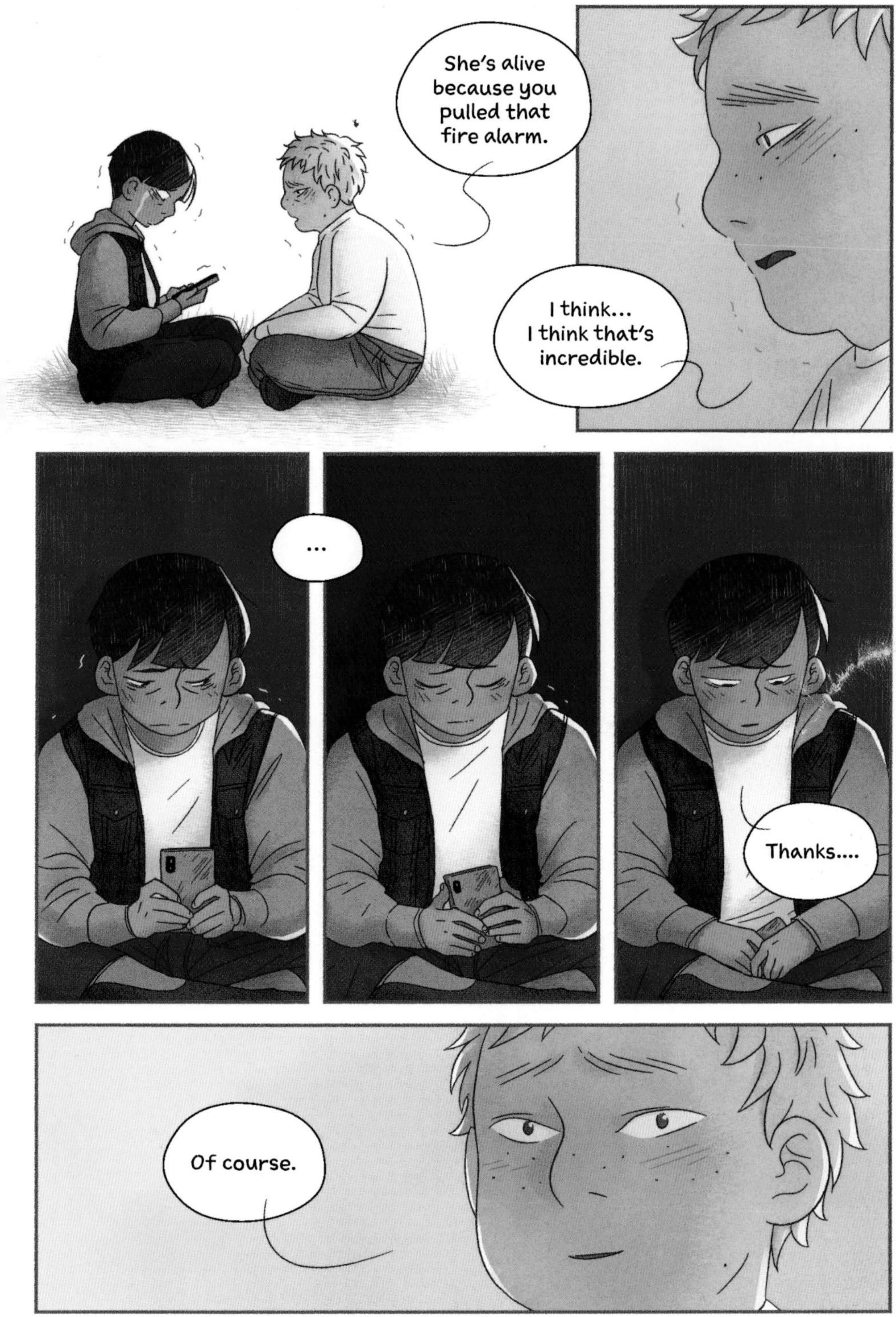
She's alive because you pulled that fire alarm.
I think... I think that's incredible.
...
Thanks....
Of course.

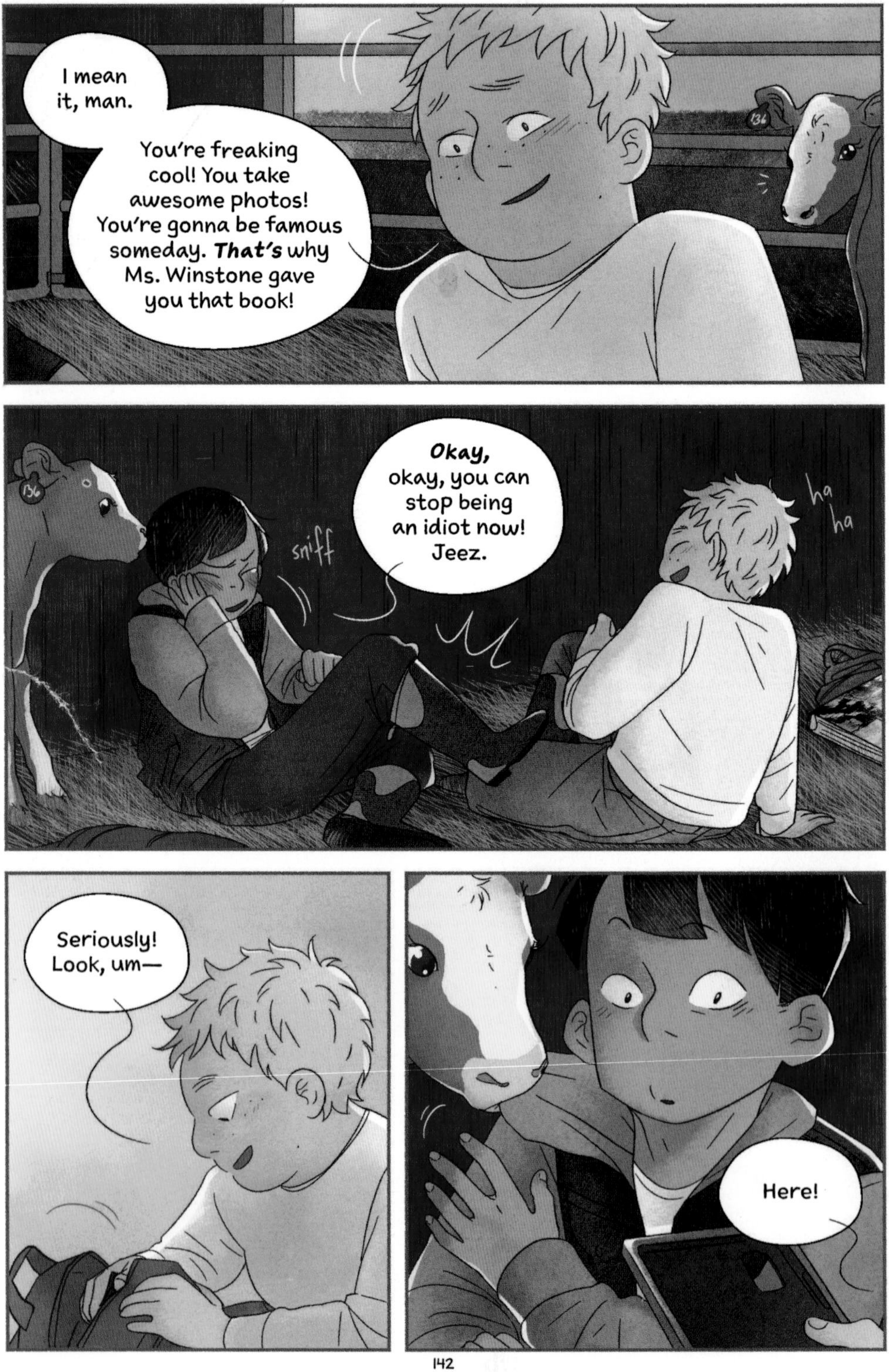
I mean it, man.
You're freaking cool! You take awesome photos! You're gonna be famous someday. **That's** why Ms. Winstone gave you that book!
sniff
Okay, okay, you can stop being an idiot now! Jeez.
ha ha
Seriously! Look, um—
Here!

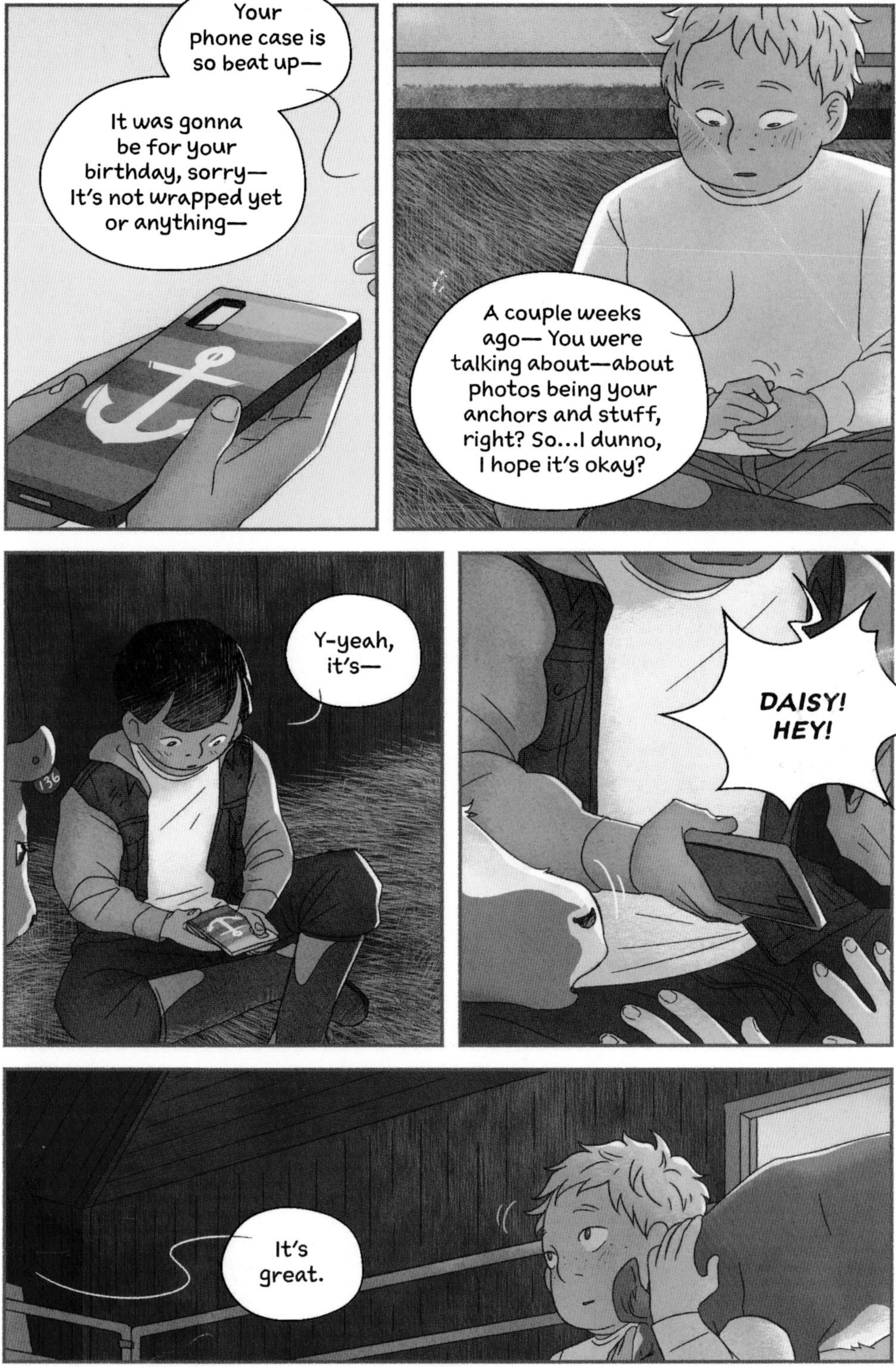
Your phone case is so beat up—
It was gonna be for your birthday, sorry— It's not wrapped yet or anything—
A couple weeks ago— You were talking about—about photos being your anchors and stuff, right? So...I dunno, I hope it's okay?
Y-yeah, it's—
DAISY! HEY!
It's great.

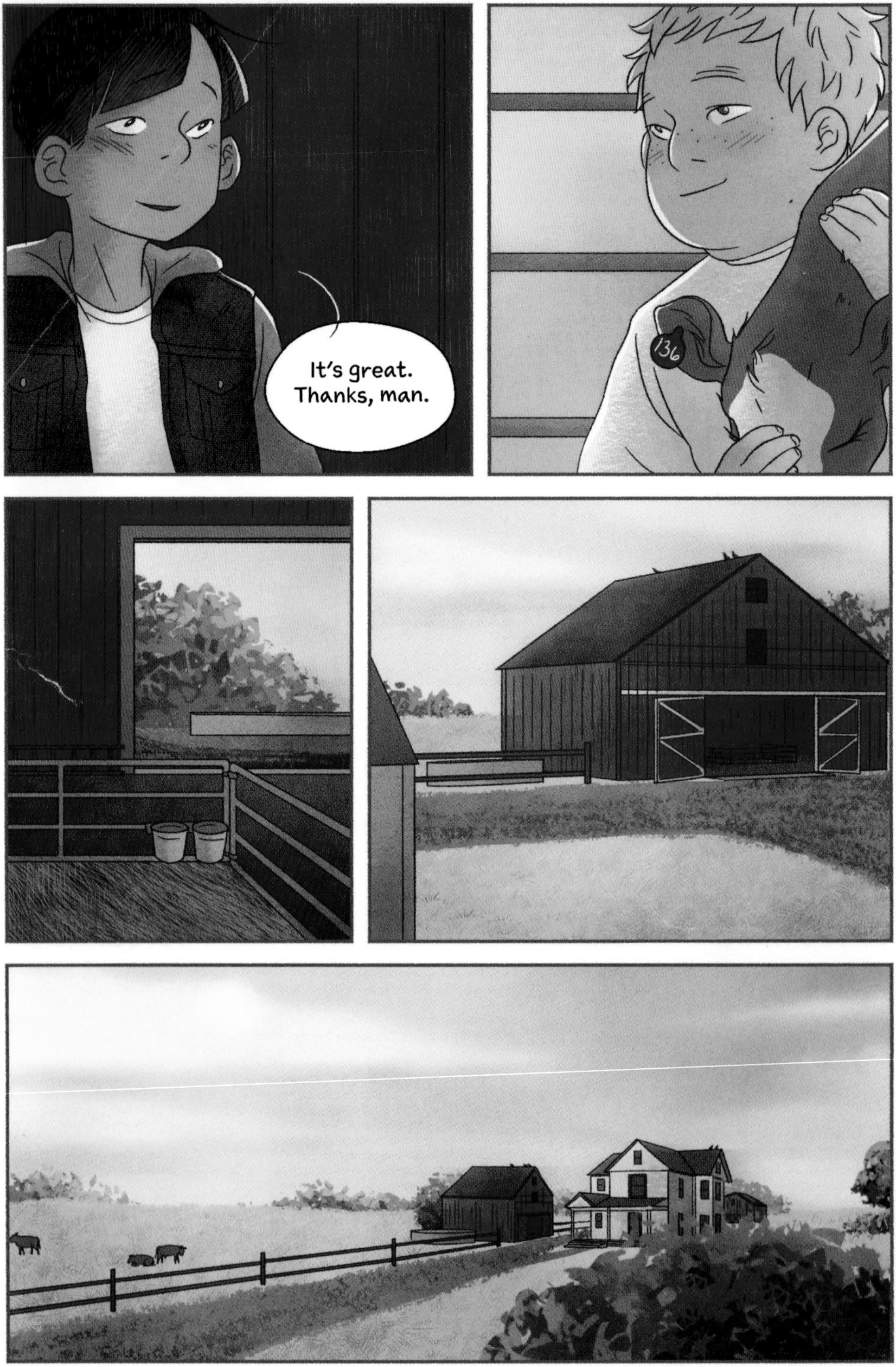
It's great.
Thanks, man.
136

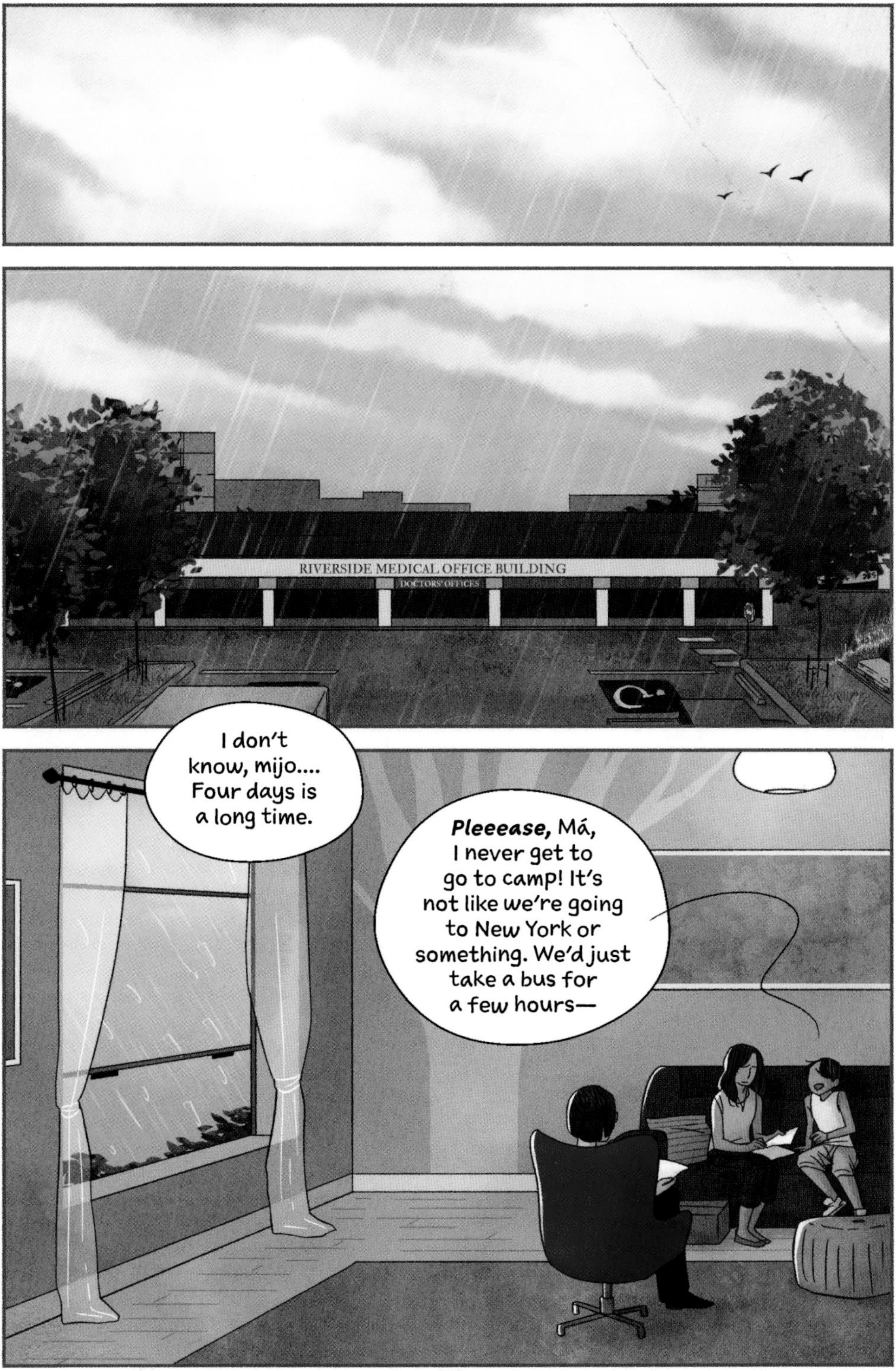
RIVERSIDE MEDICAL OFFICE BUILDING
DOCTORS' OFFICES
I don't know, mijo.... Four days is a long time.
Pleeease, Má, I never get to go to camp! It's not like we're going to New York or something. We'd just take a bus for a few hours—

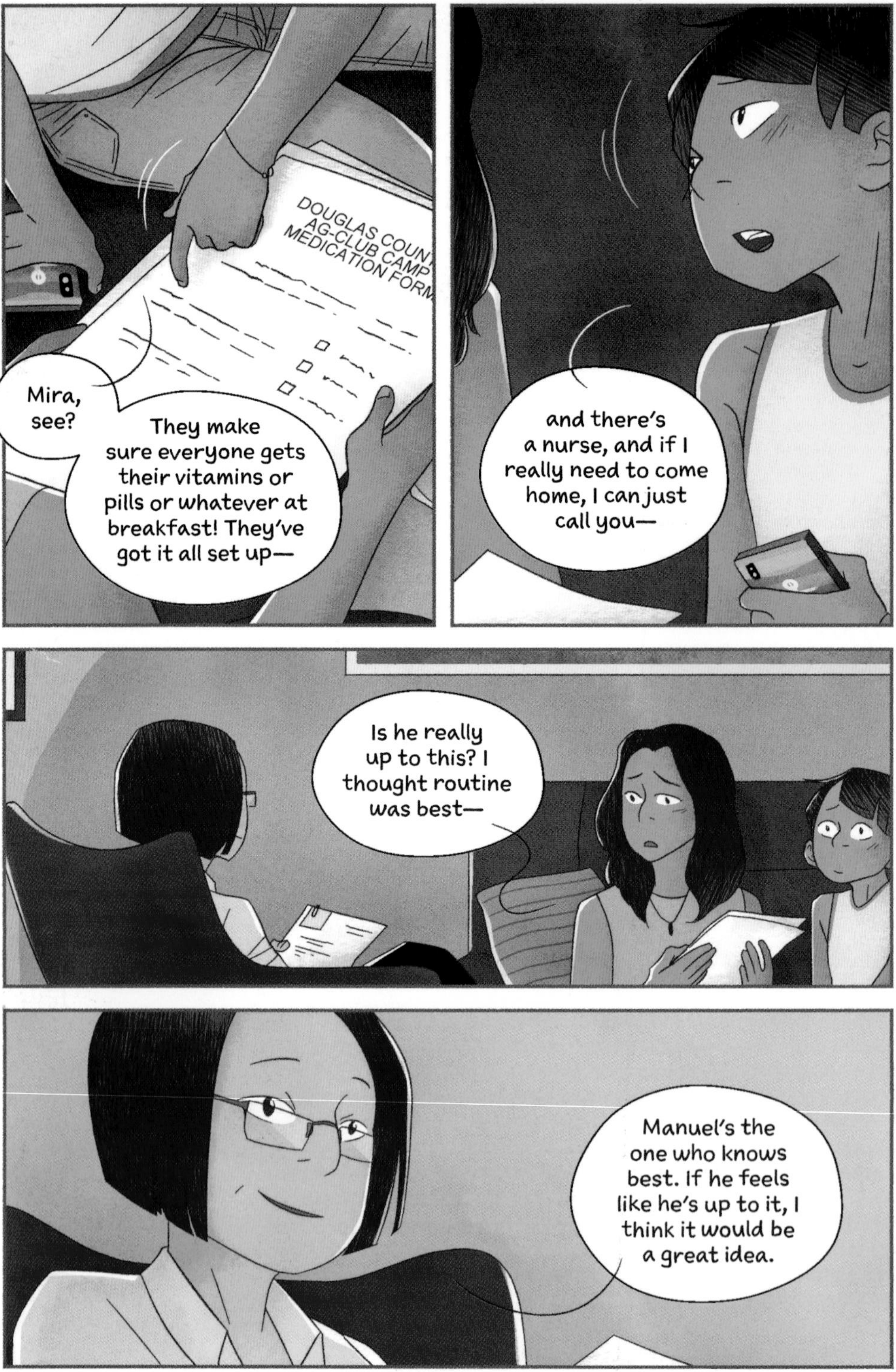
DOUGLAS COUNTY AG-CLUB CAMP MEDICATION FORM
Mira, see?
They make sure everyone gets their vitamins or pills or whatever at breakfast! They've got it all set up—
and there's a nurse, and if I really need to come home, I can just call you—
Is he really up to this? I thought routine was best—
Manuel's the one who knows best. If he feels like he's up to it, I think it would be a great idea.

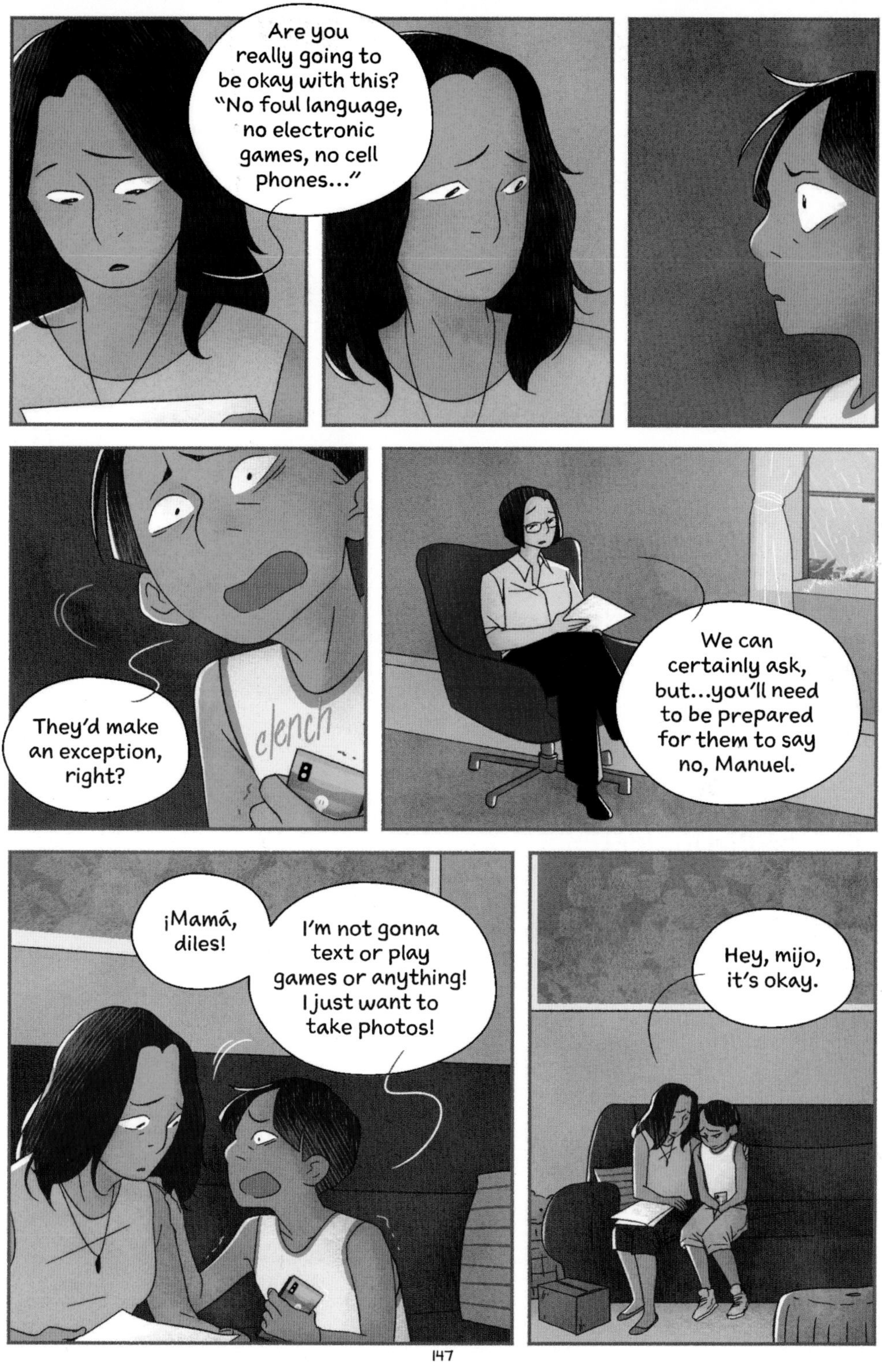
Are you really going to be okay with this? "No foul language, no electronic games, no cell phones..."
clench
They'd make an exception, right?
We can certainly ask, but...you'll need to be prepared for them to say no, Manuel.
¡Mamá, diles!
I'm not gonna text or play games or anything! I just want to take photos!
Hey, mijo, it's okay.

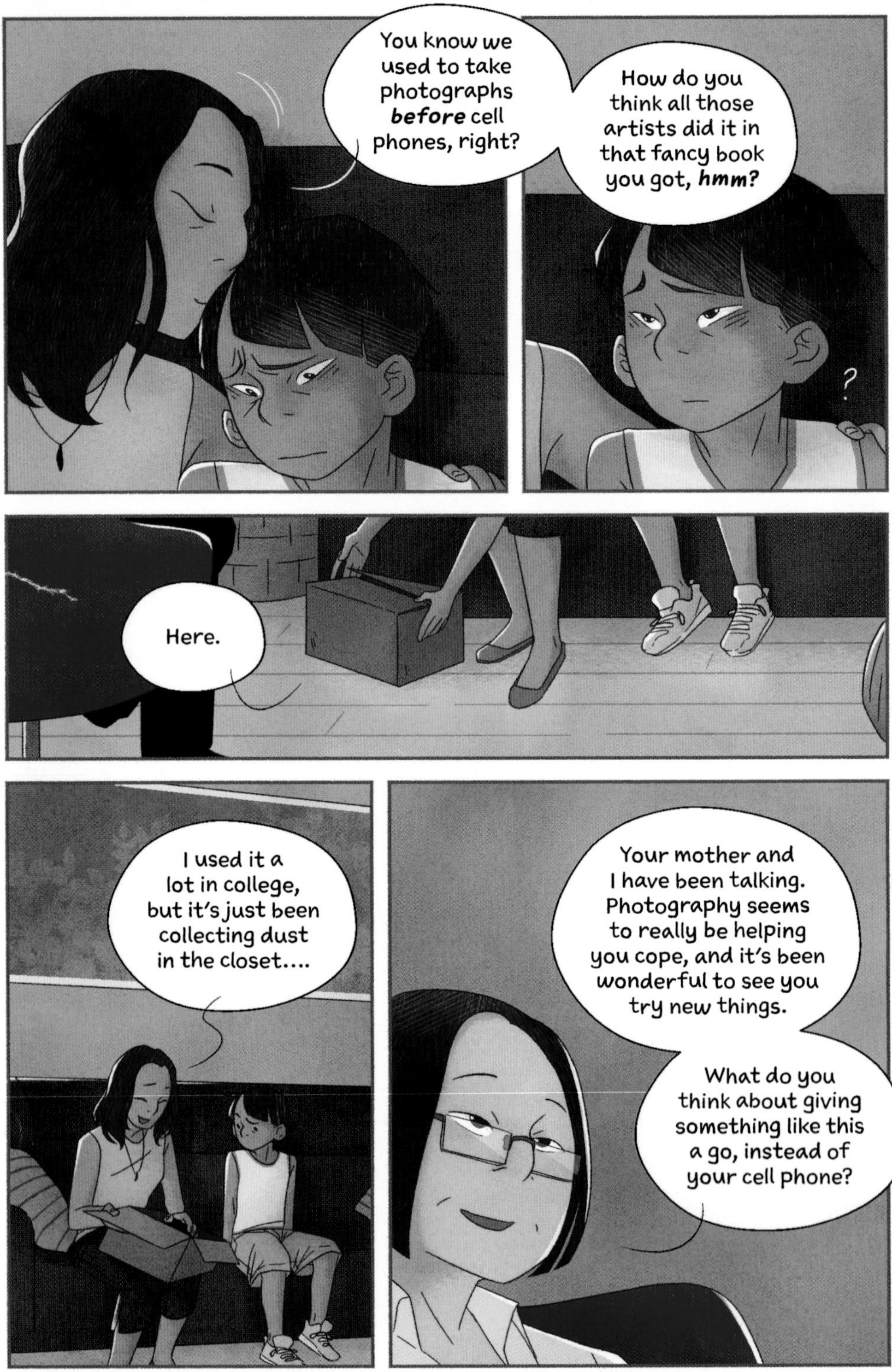
You know we used to take photographs *before* cell phones, right?
How do you think all those artists did it in that fancy book you got, *hmm?*
?
Here.
I used it a lot in college, but it's just been collecting dust in the closet....
Your mother and I have been talking. Photography seems to really be helping you cope, and it's been wonderful to see you try new things.
What do you think about giving something like this a go, instead of your cell phone?

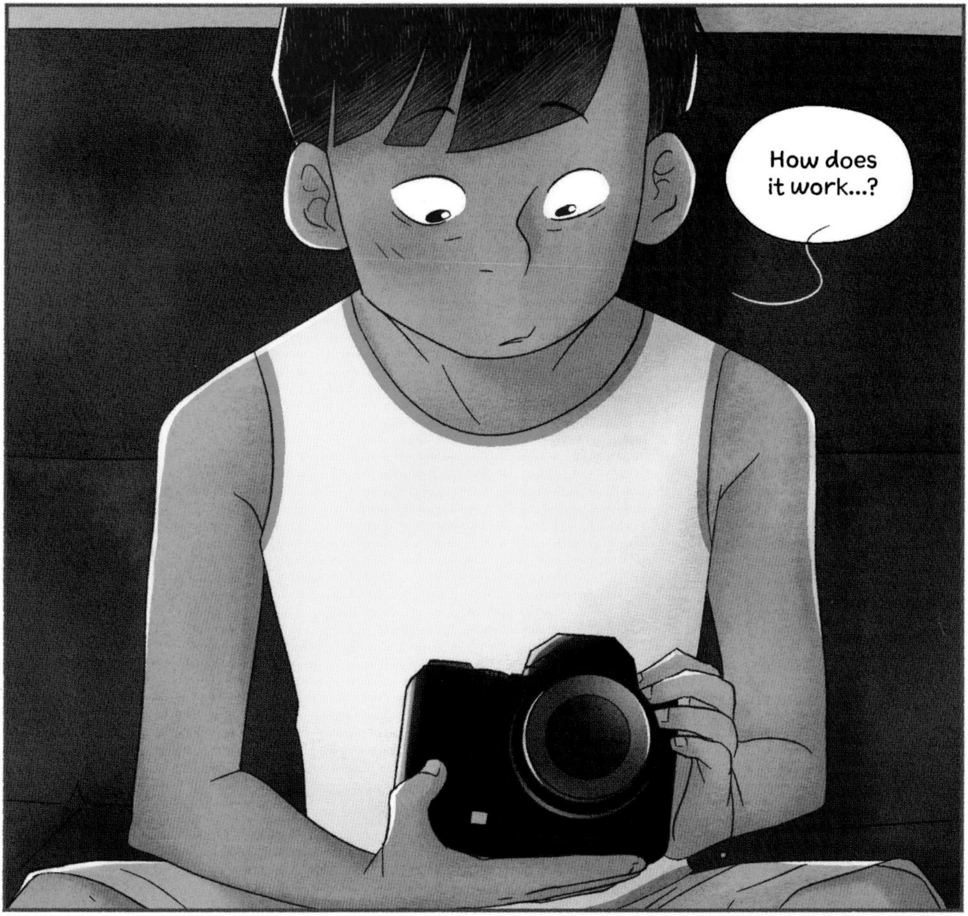
How does it work...?

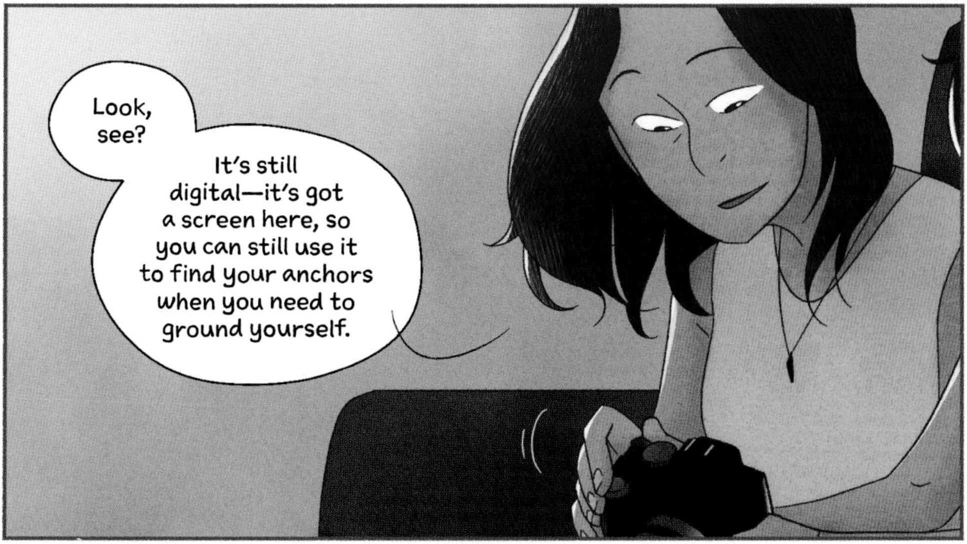
Look, see?
It's still digital—it's got a screen here, so you can still use it to find your anchors when you need to ground yourself.

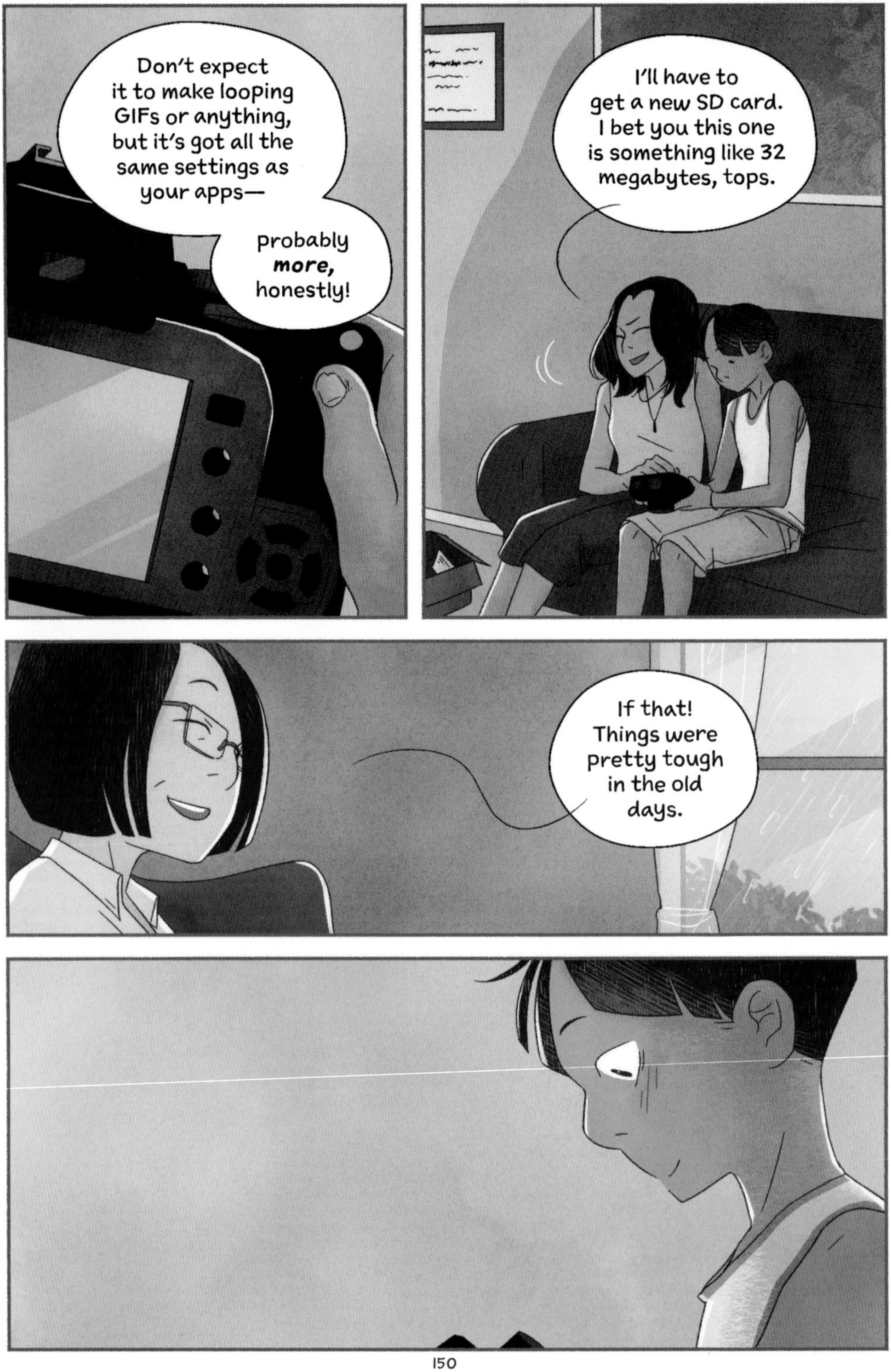
Don't expect it to make looping GIFs or anything, but it's got all the same settings as your apps—
probably **more,** honestly!
I'll have to get a new SD card. I bet you this one is something like 32 megabytes, tops.
If that! Things were pretty tough in the old days.

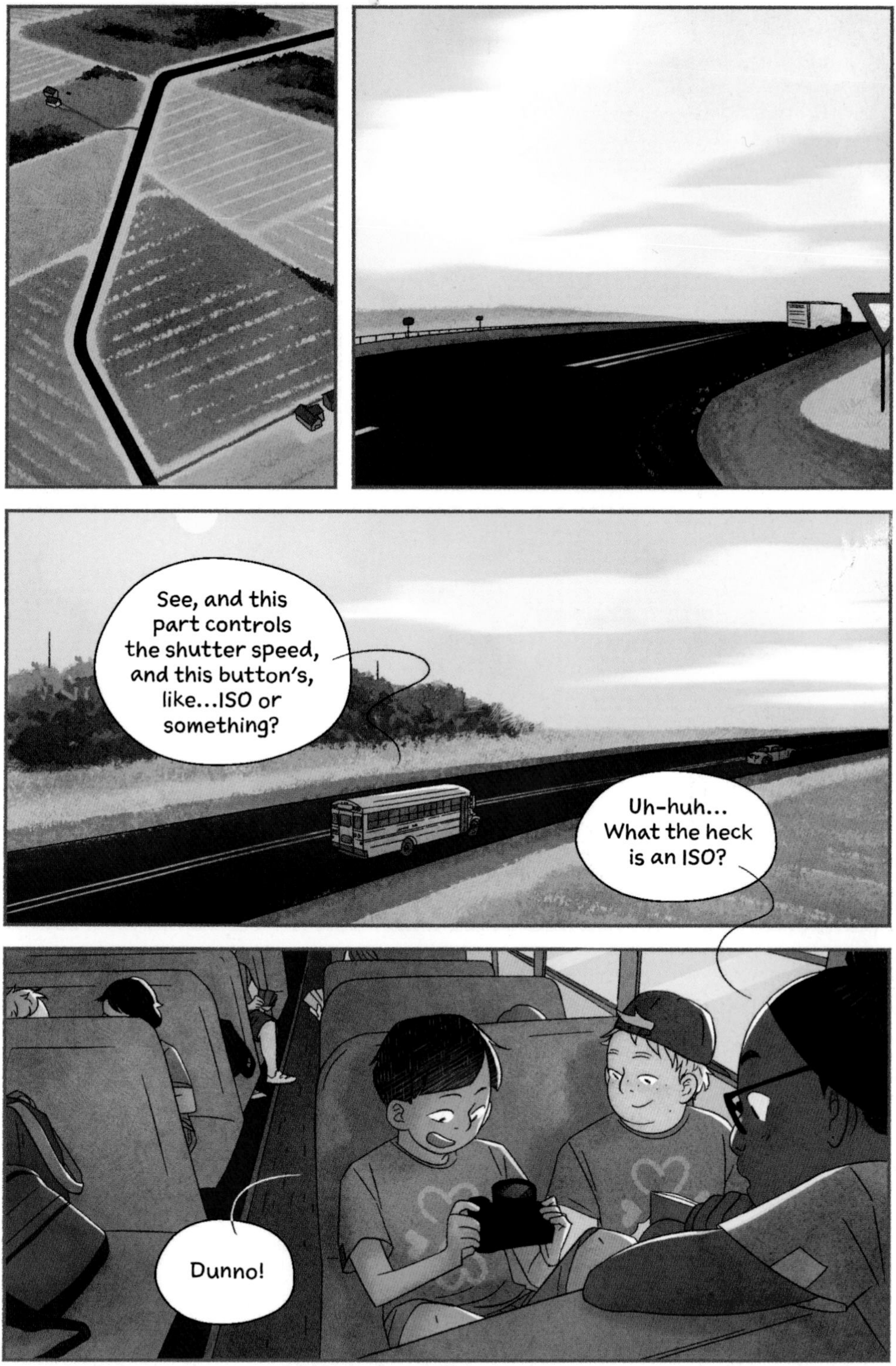
See, and this part controls the shutter speed, and this button's, like...ISO or something?
Uh-huh... What the heck is an ISO?
Dunno!

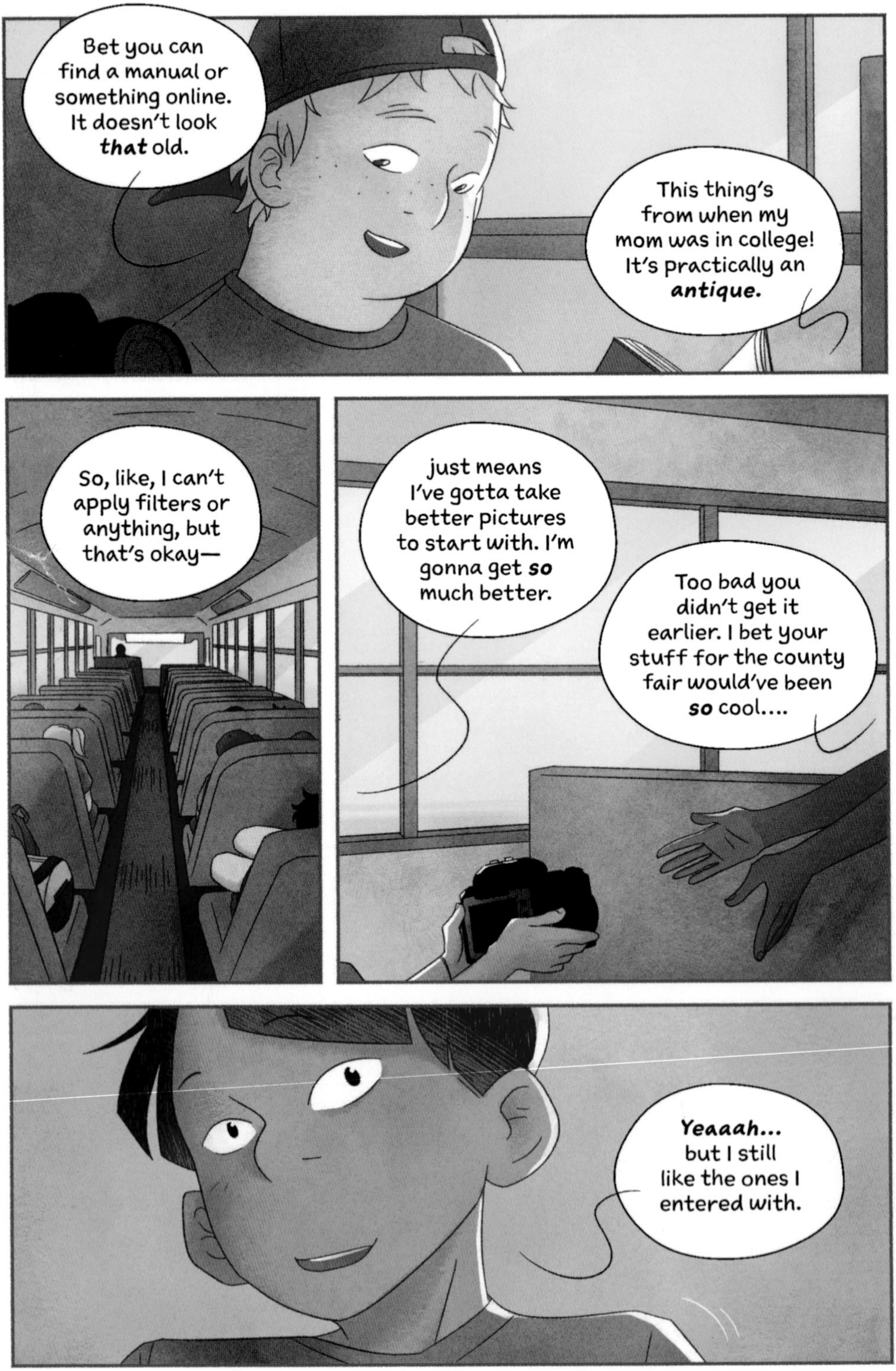
Bet you can find a manual or something online. It doesn't look ***that*** old.
This thing's from when my mom was in college! It's practically an ***antique.***
So, like, I can't apply filters or anything, but that's okay—
just means I've gotta take better pictures to start with. I'm gonna get ***so*** much better.
Too bad you didn't get it earlier. I bet your stuff for the county fair would've been ***so*** cool....
Yeaaah... but I still like the ones I entered with.

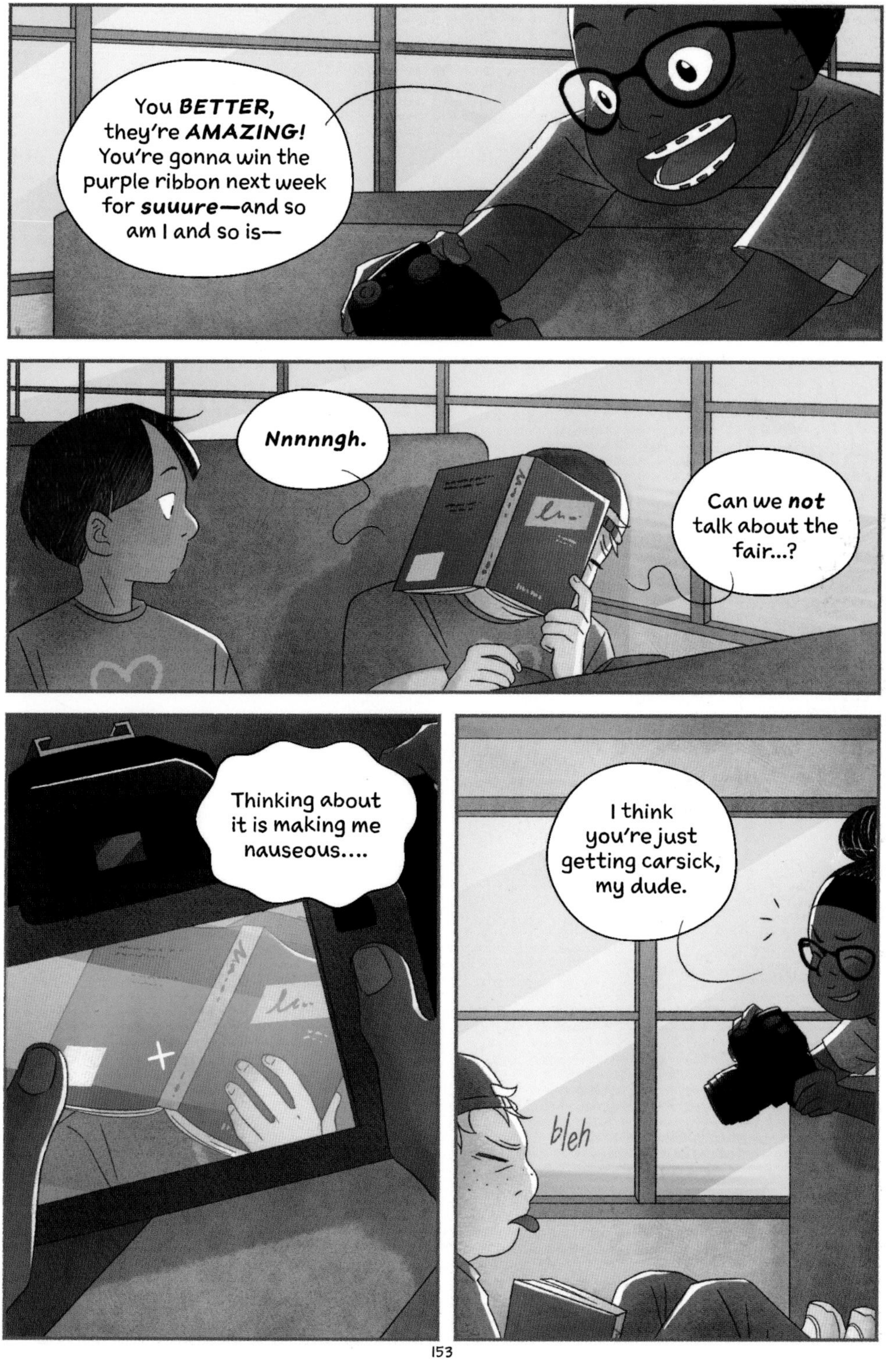
You **BETTER**, they're **AMAZING!** You're gonna win the purple ribbon next week for **suuure**—and so am I and so is—
Nnnnngh.
Can we **not** talk about the fair...?
Thinking about it is making me nauseous....
I think you're just getting carsick, my dude.
bleh

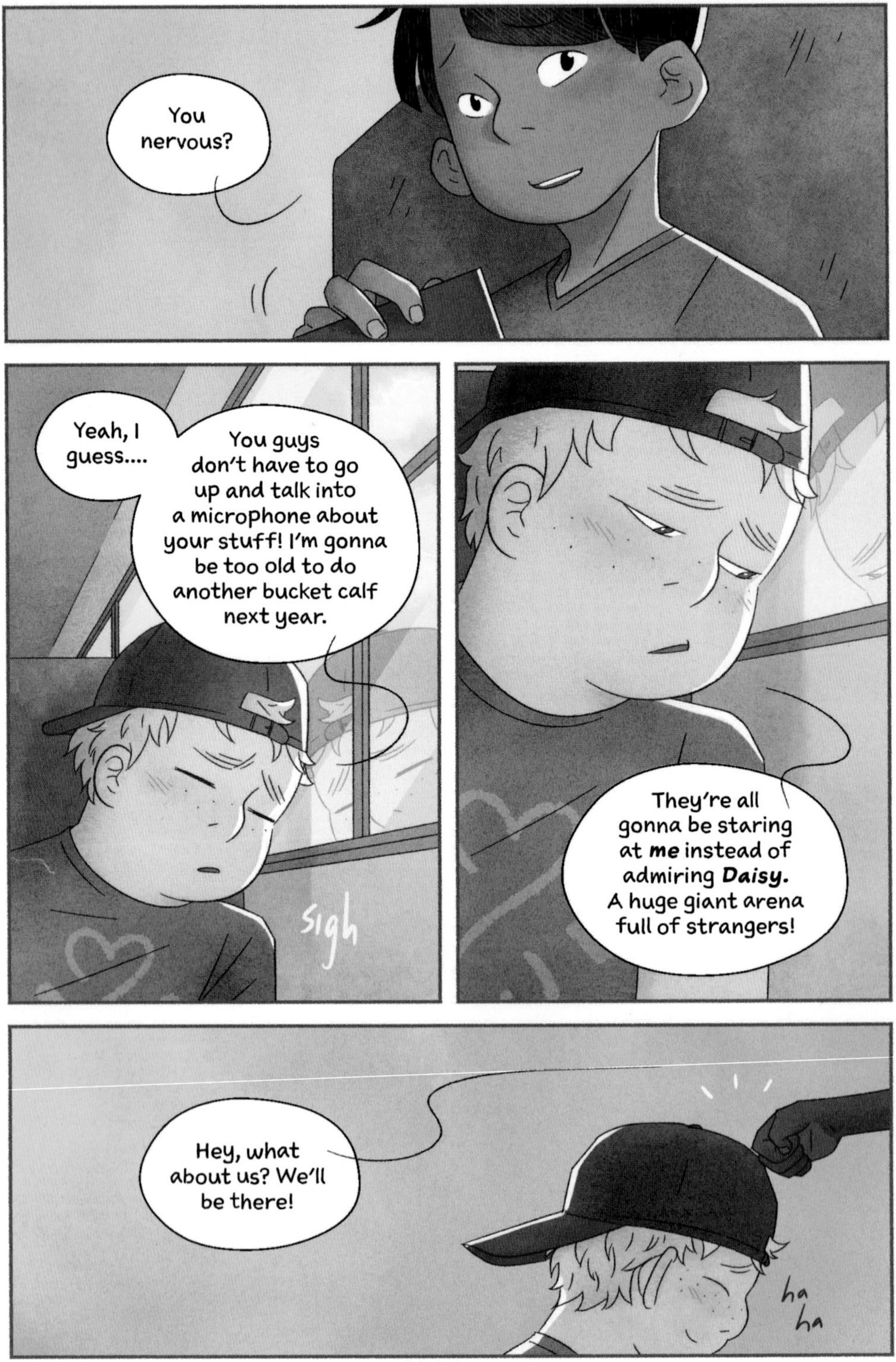
You nervous?
Yeah, I guess....
You guys don't have to go up and talk into a microphone about your stuff! I'm gonna be too old to do another bucket calf next year.
sigh
They're all gonna be staring at **me** instead of admiring **Daisy.** A huge giant arena full of strangers!
Hey, what about us? We'll be there!
ha ha

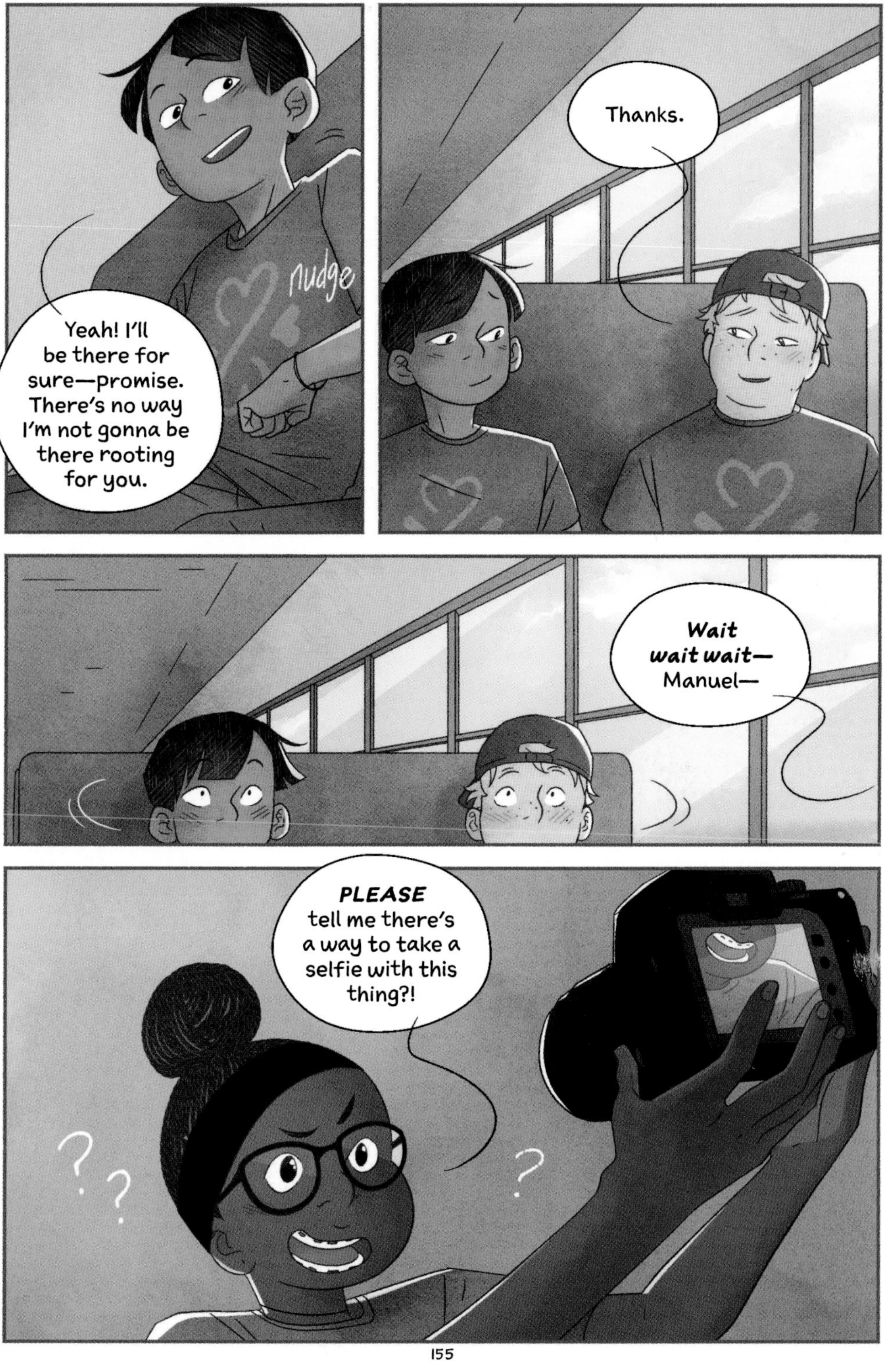
Yeah! I'll be there for sure—promise. There's no way I'm not gonna be there rooting for you.
nudge
Thanks.
Wait wait wait— Manuel—
PLEASE tell me there's a way to take a selfie with this thing?!
? ? ?

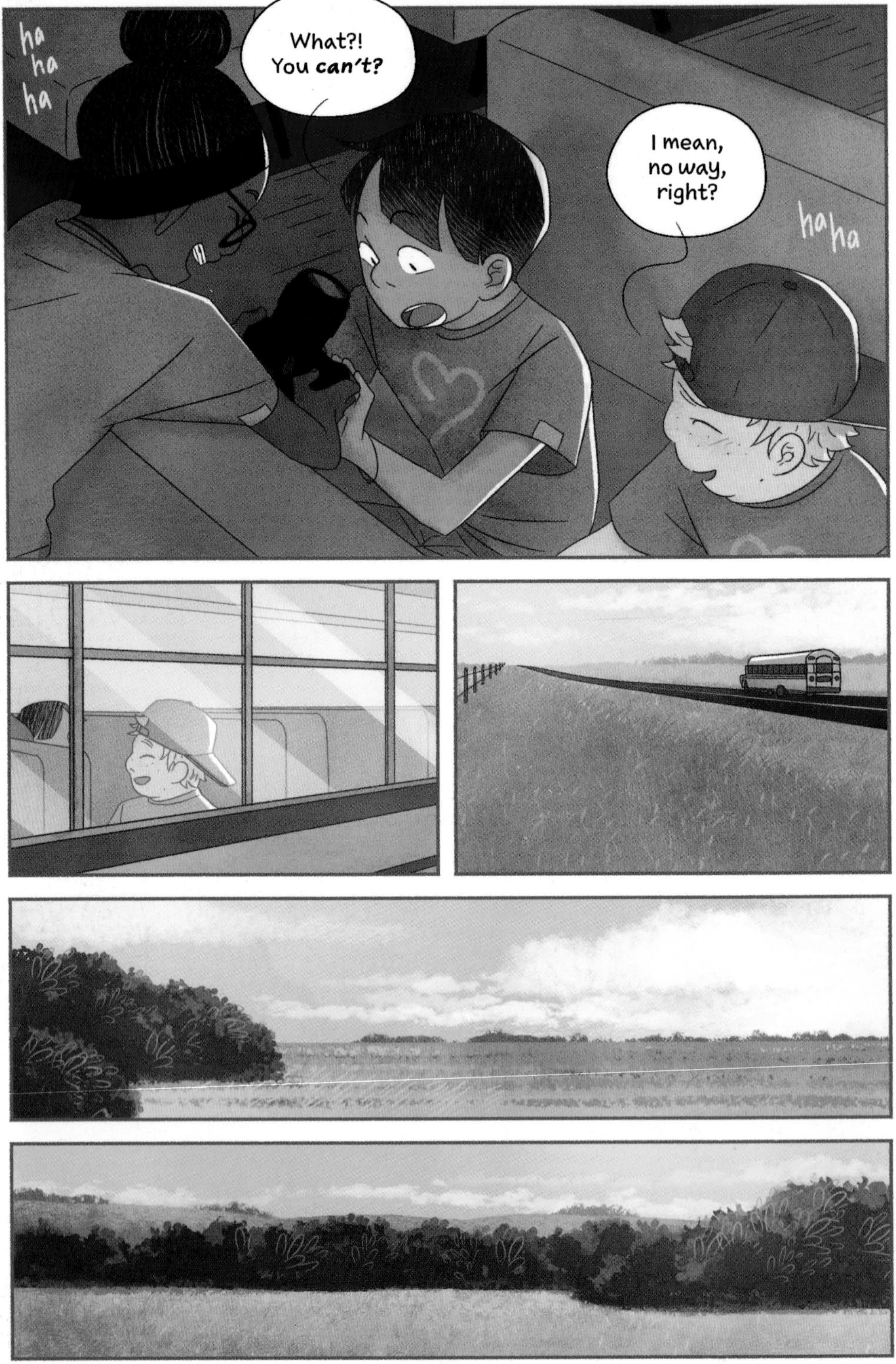
ha ha ha
What?! You can't?
I mean, no way, right?
haha

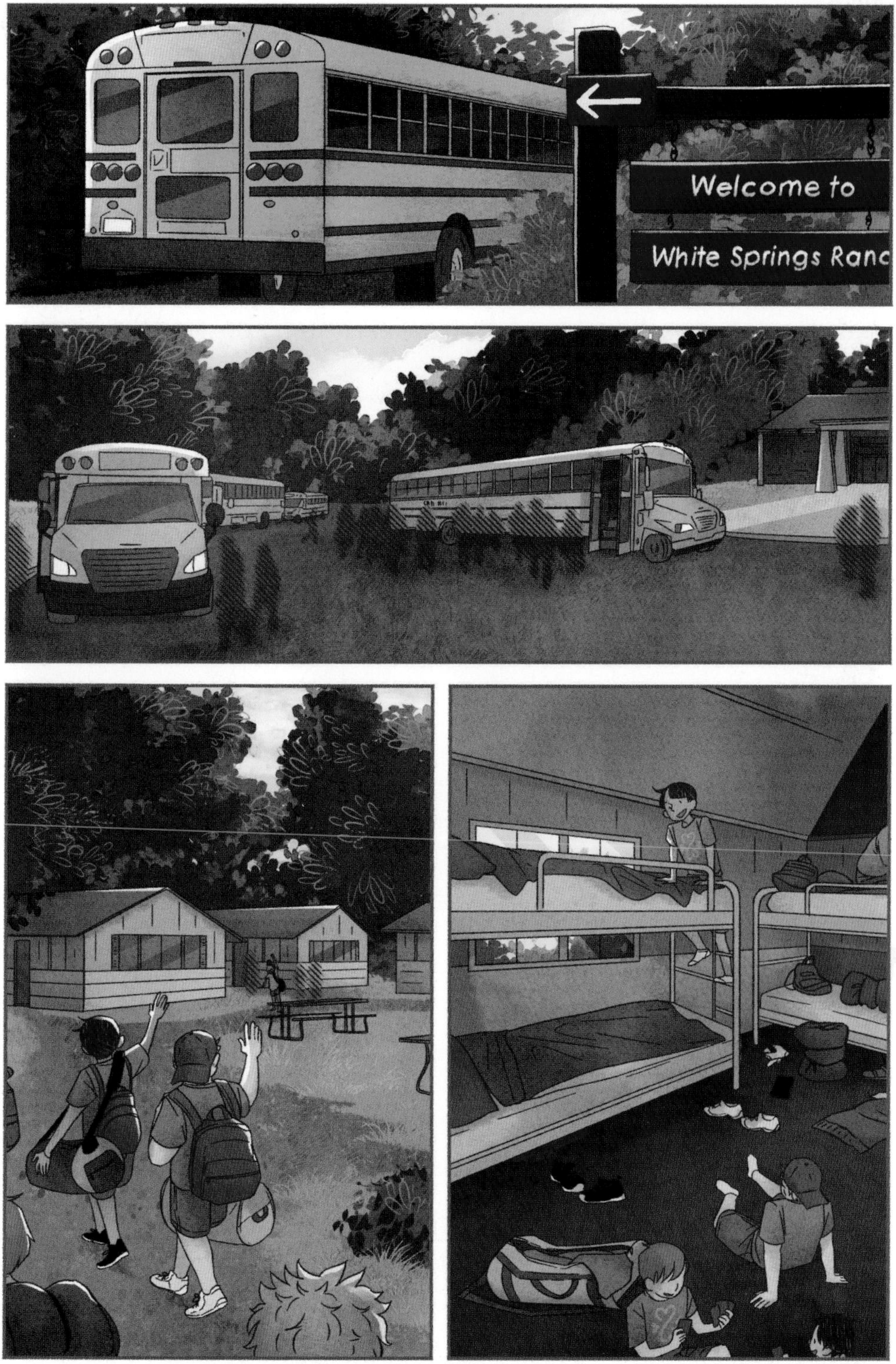
Welcome to
White Springs Ranc

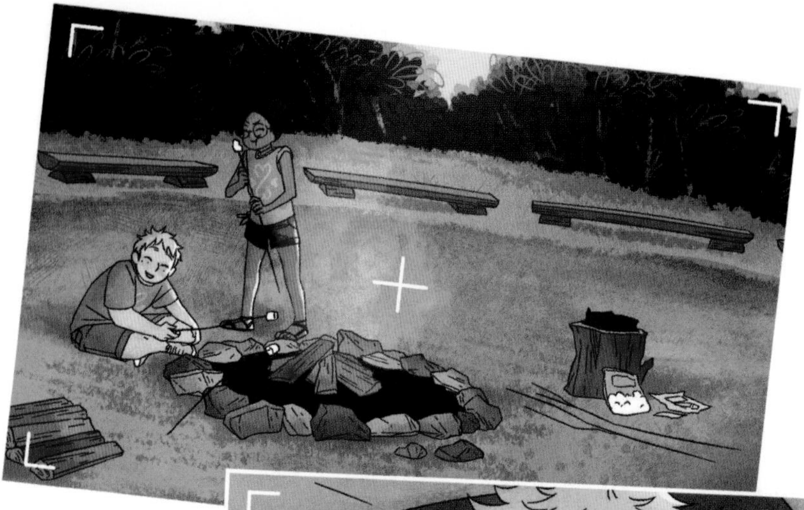

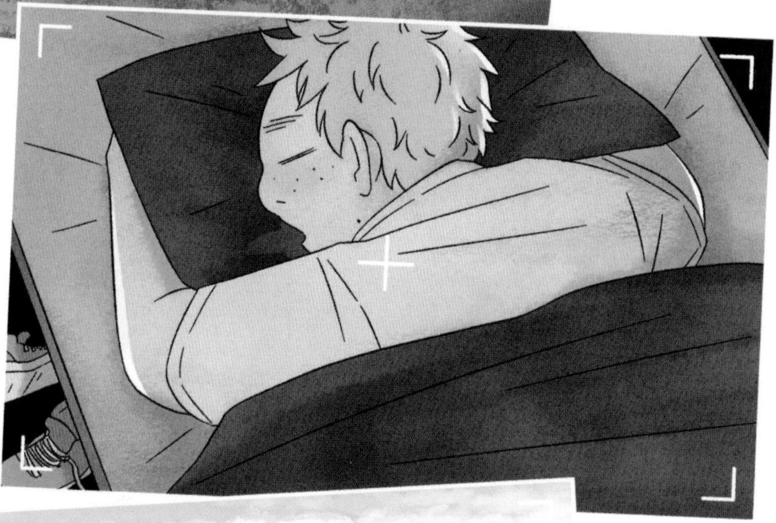

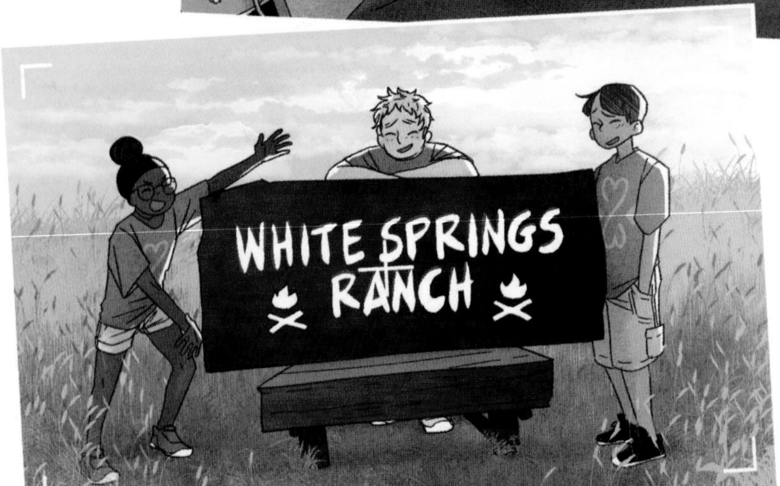
WHITE SPRINGS
RANCH

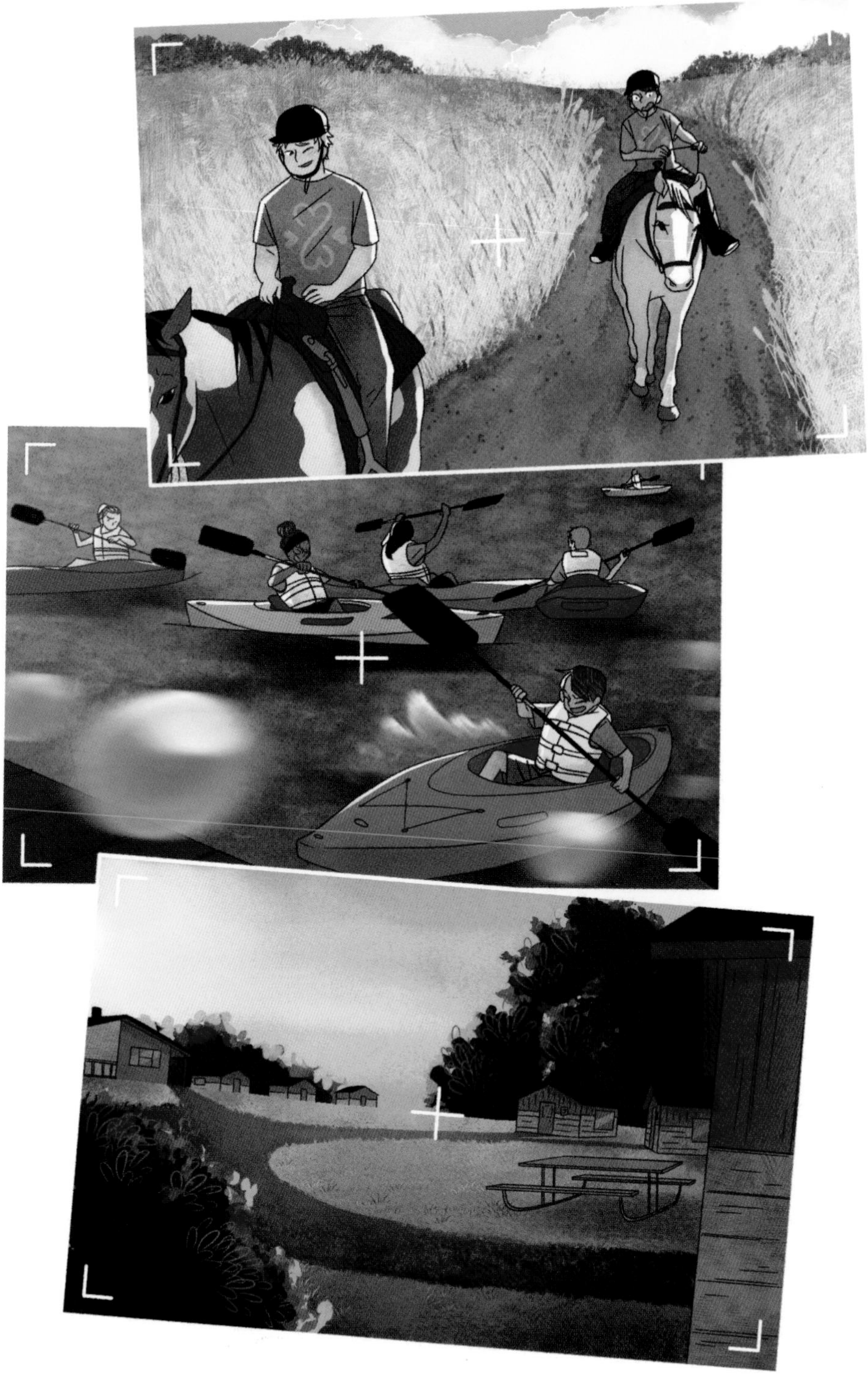

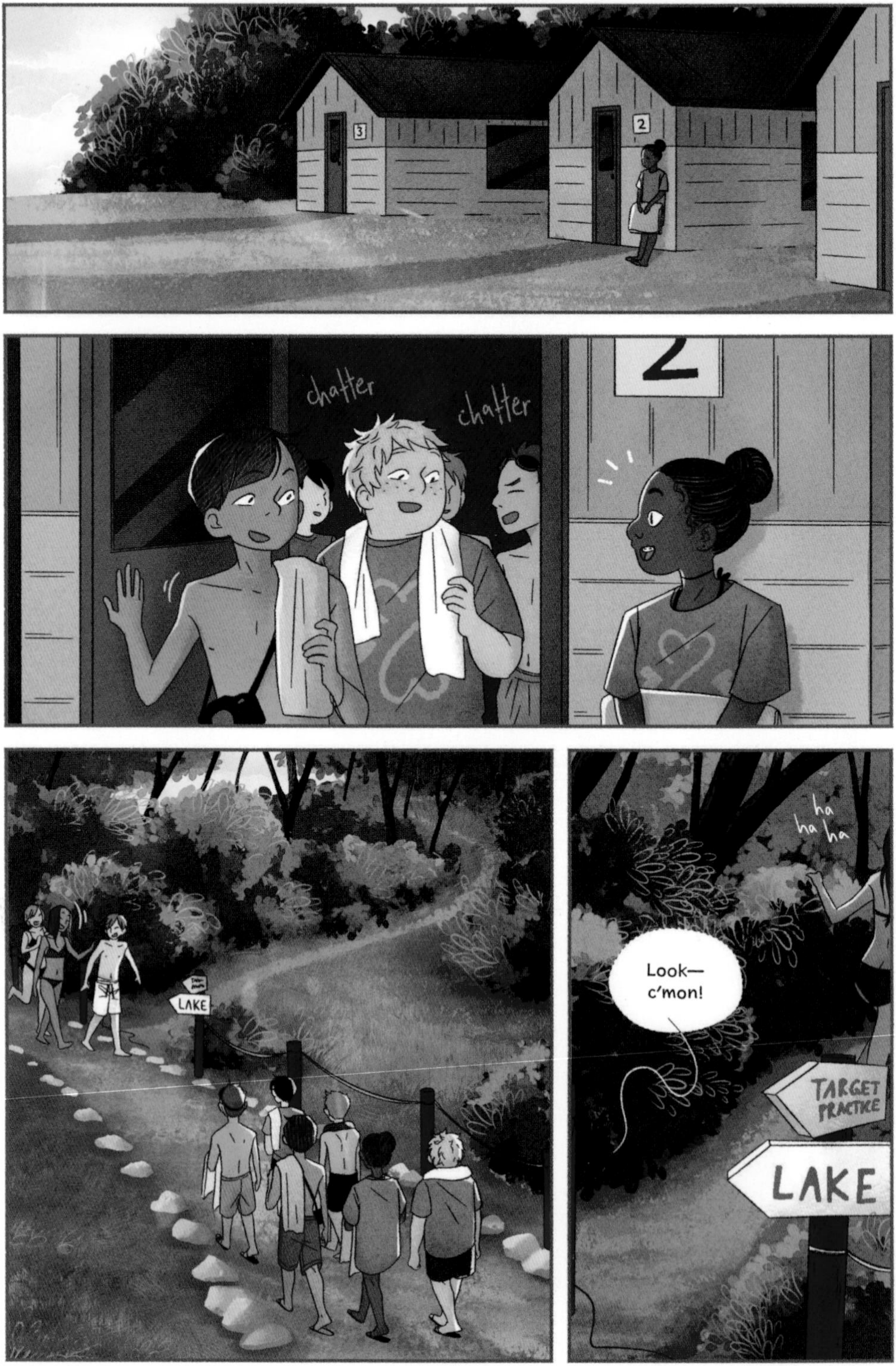
3
2
2
chatter
chatter
LAKE
ha
ha ha
Look—
c'mon!
TARGET PRACTICE
LAKE

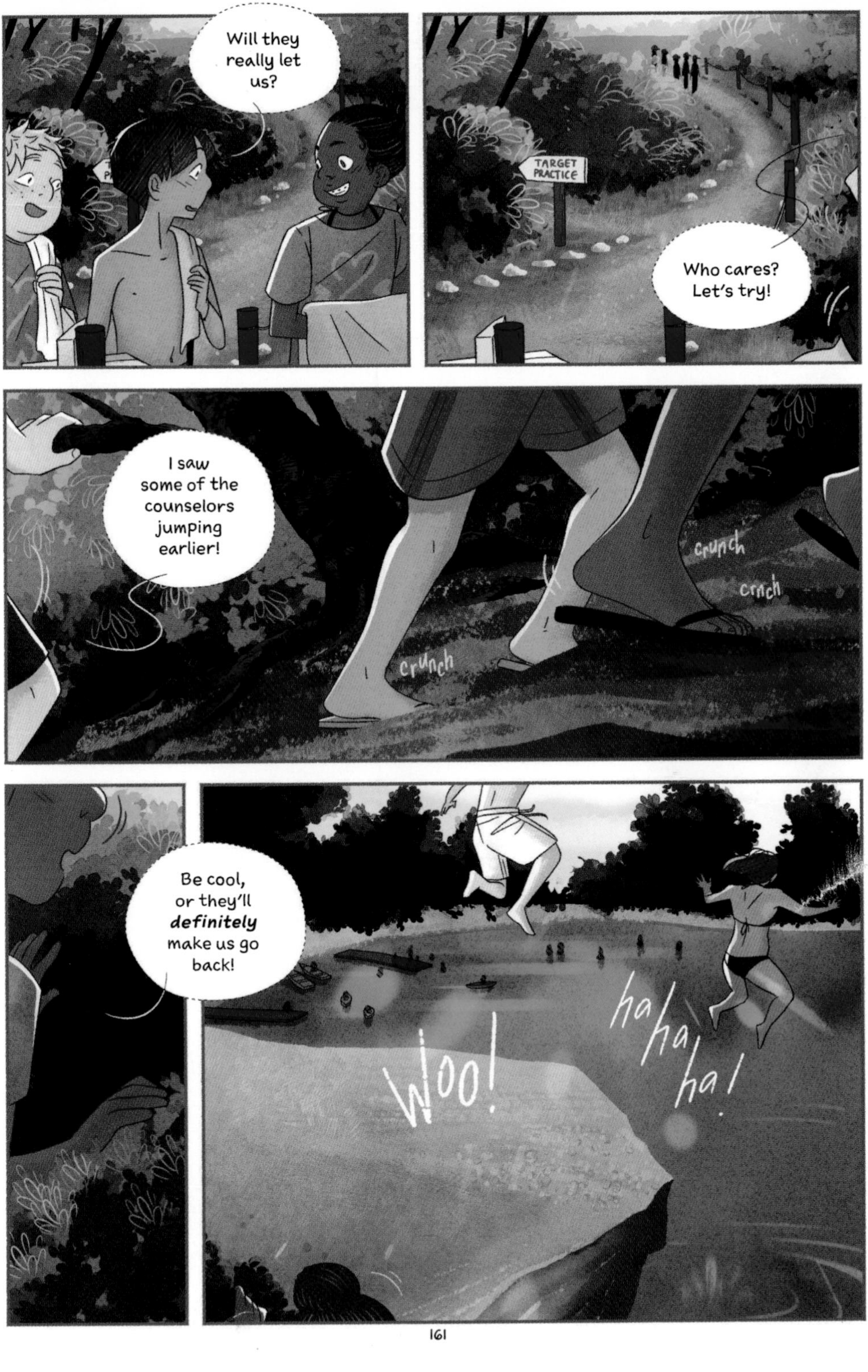
Will they really let us?
TARGET PRACTICE
Who cares? Let's try!
I saw some of the counselors jumping earlier!
crunch
crnch
crunch
Be cool, or they'll ***definitely*** make us go back!
Woo!
ha ha ha!

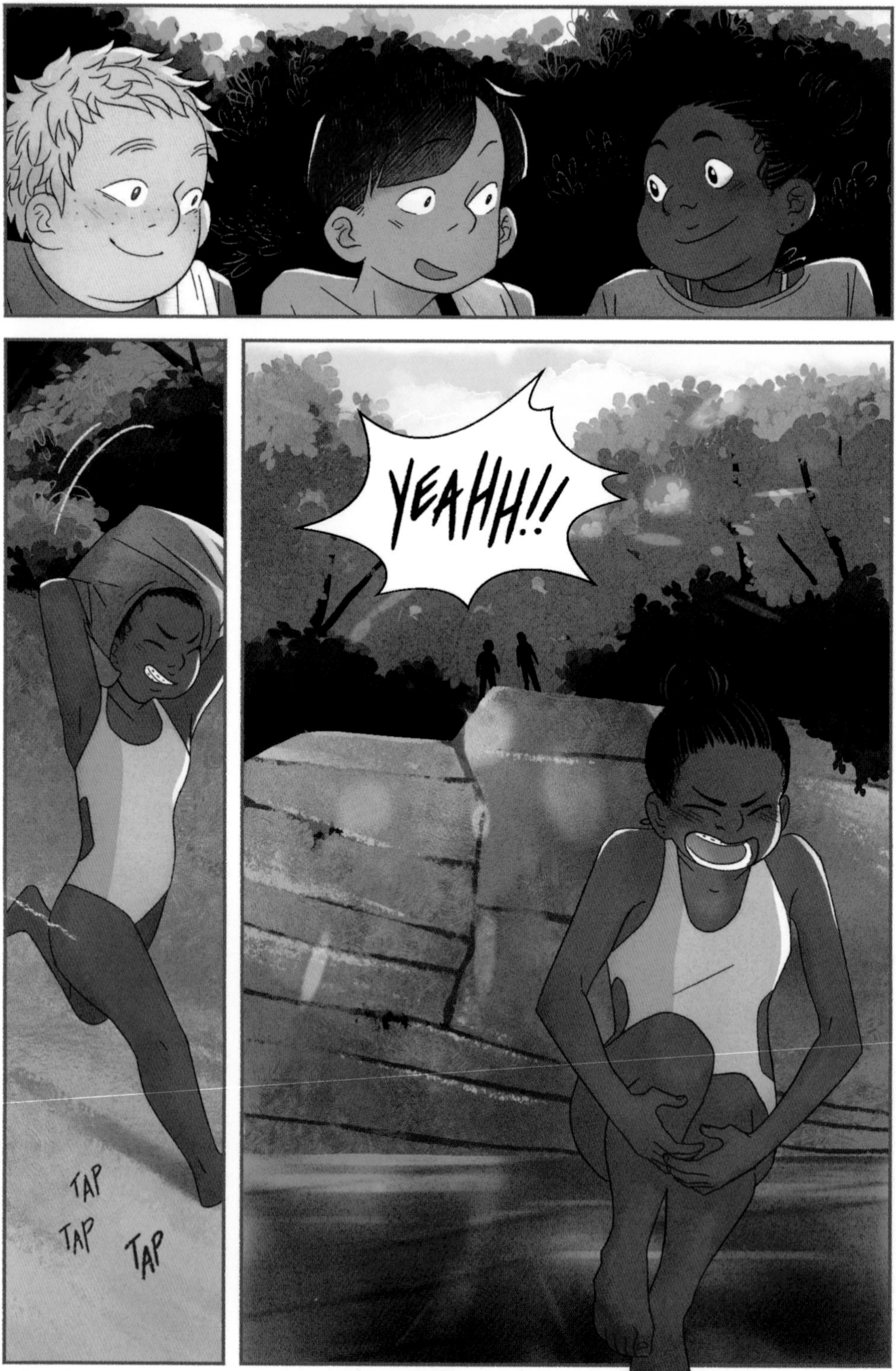
TAP
TAP
TAP
YEAHH!!

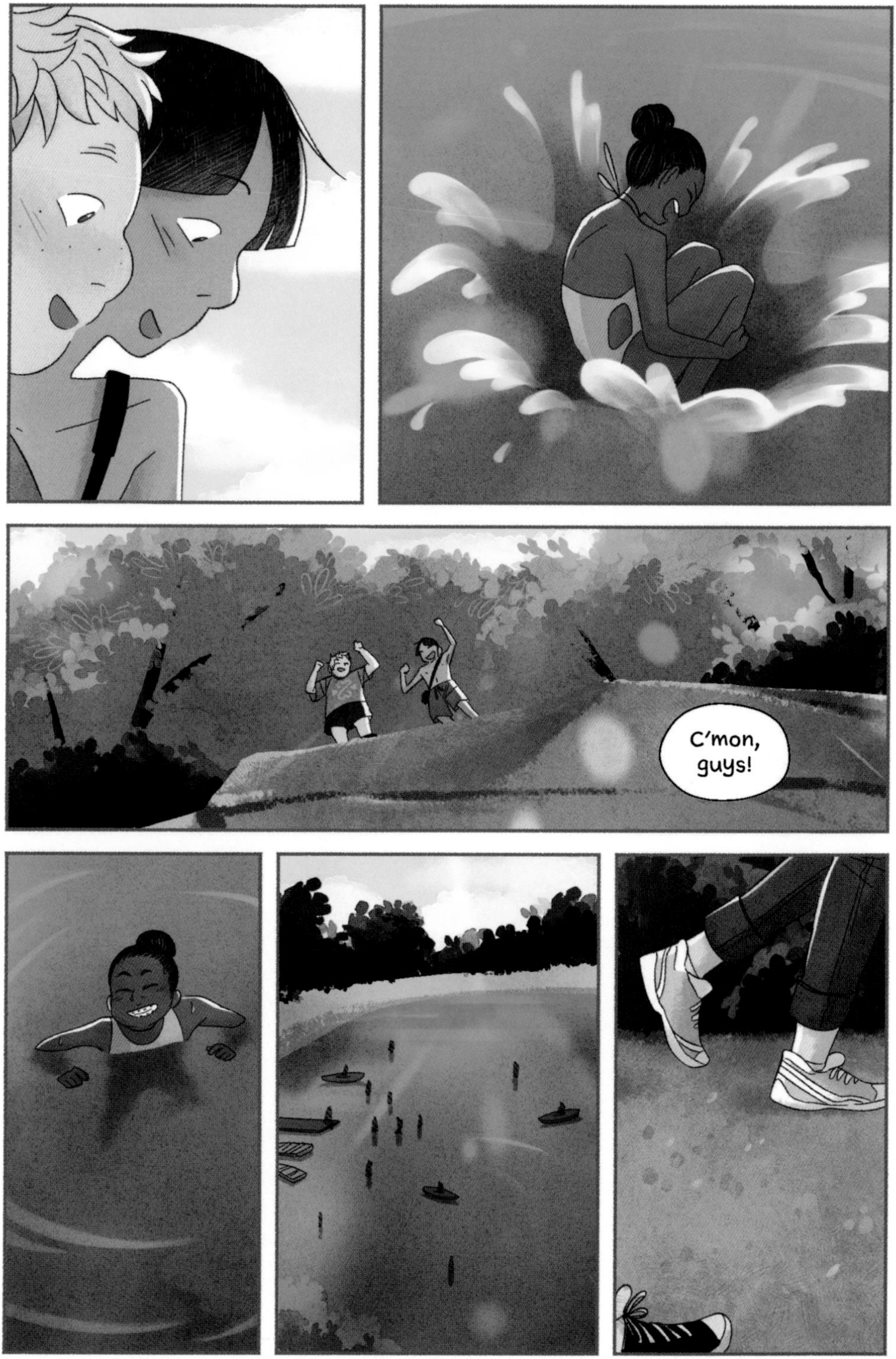
C'mon, guys!

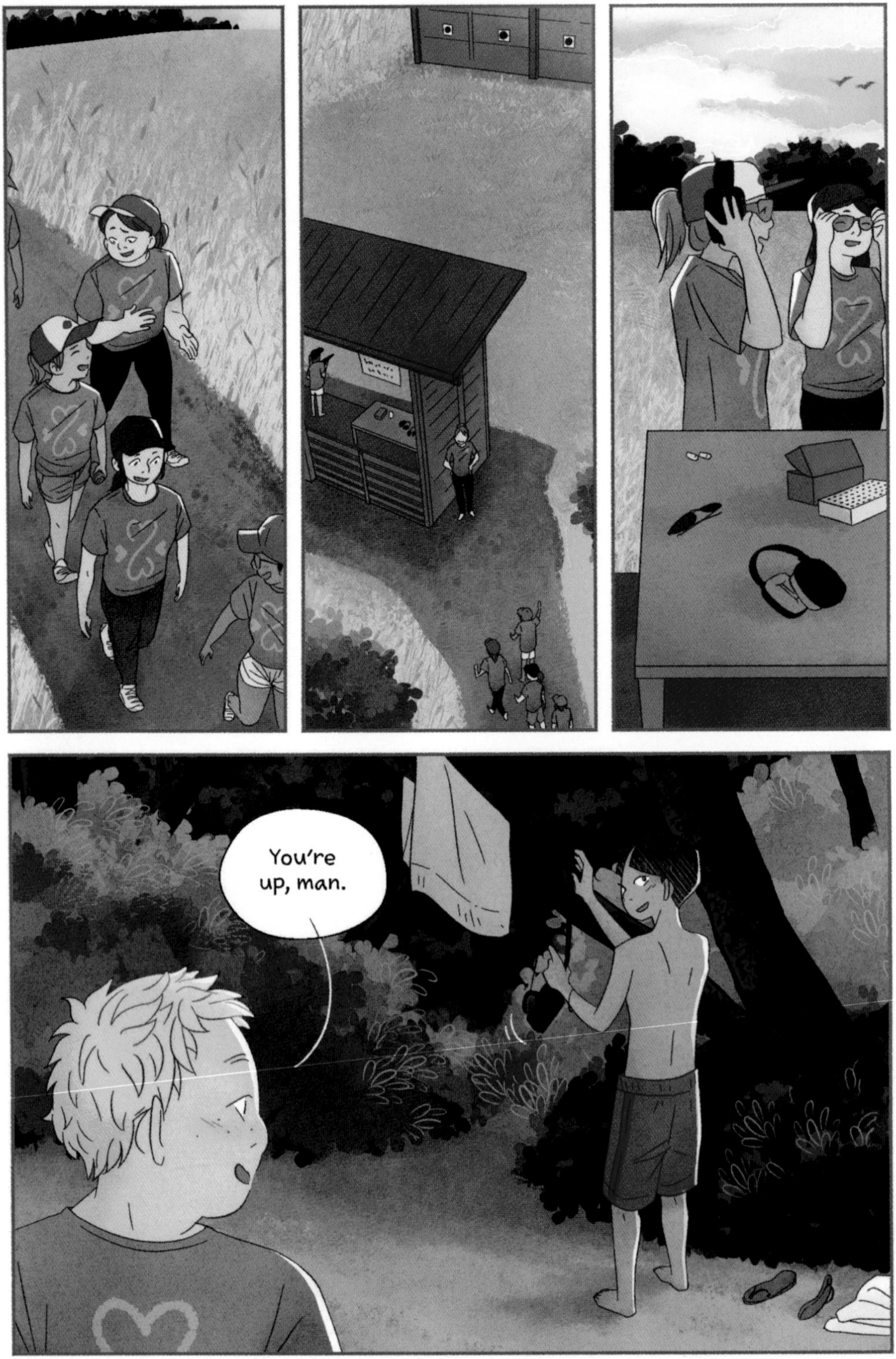
You're up, man.

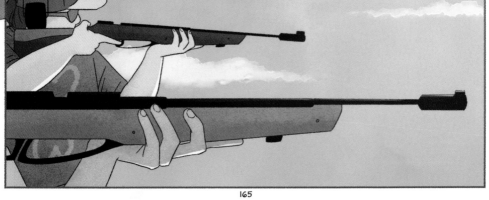

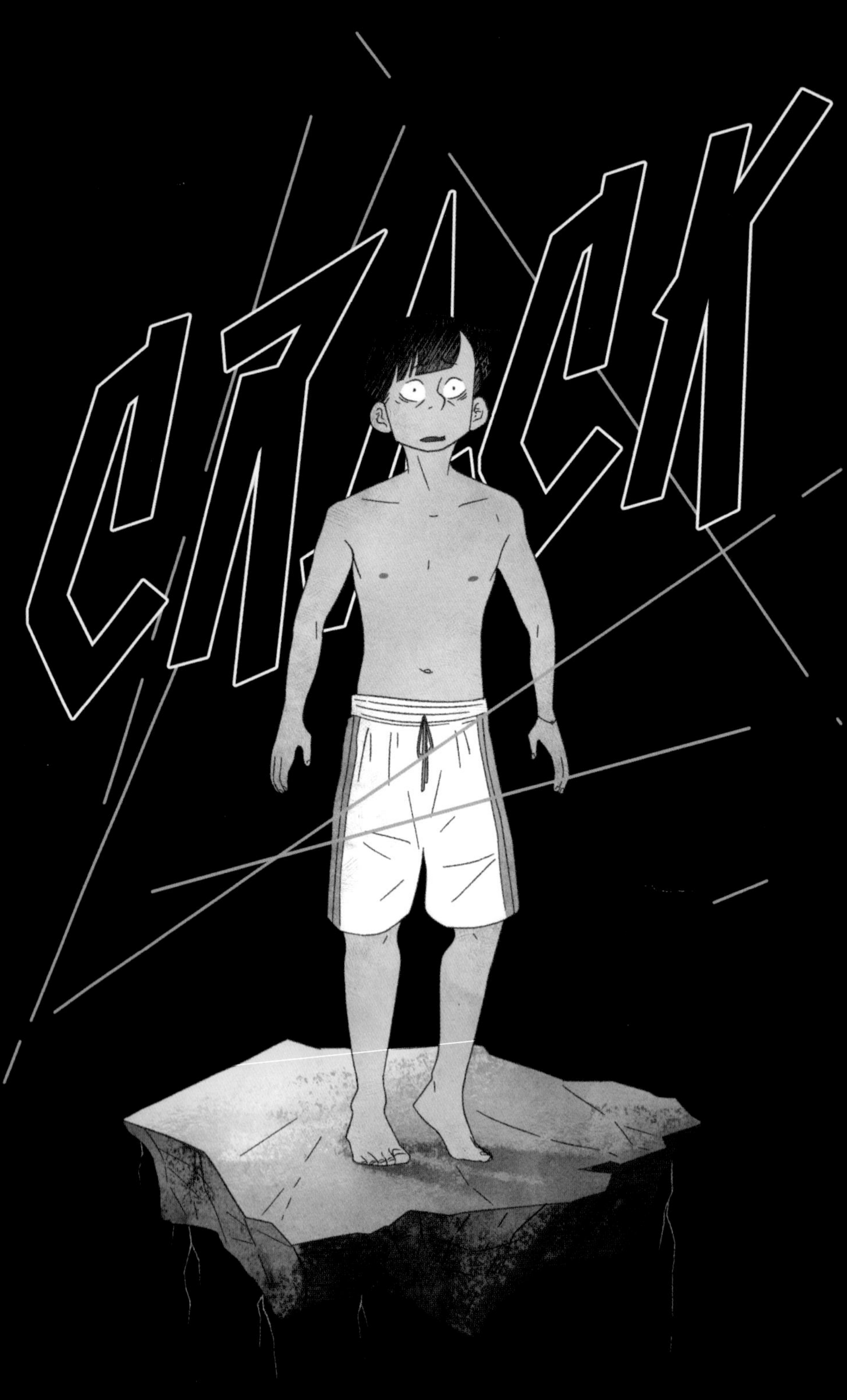
CRACK

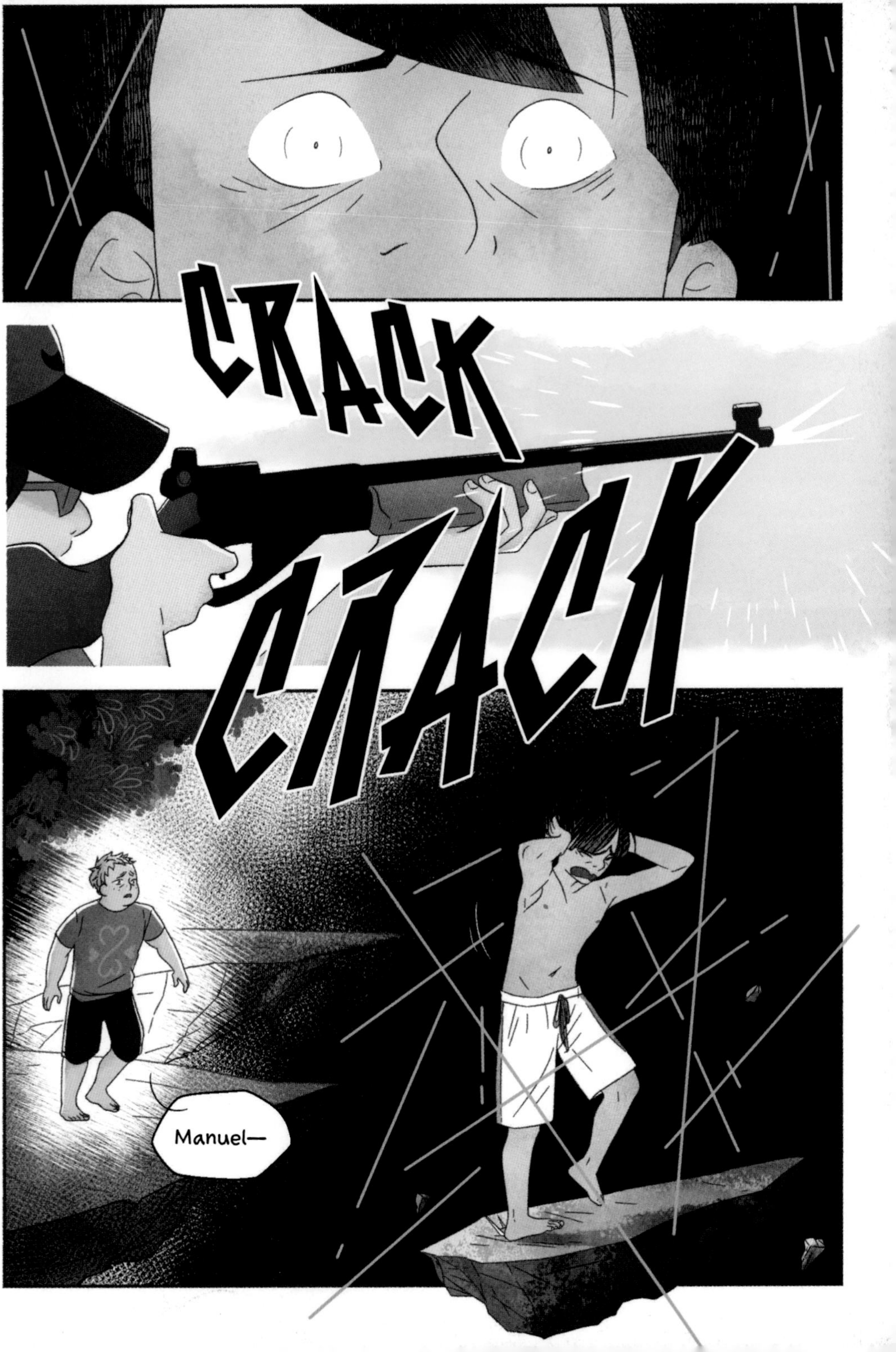
CRACK
CRACK
Manuel—

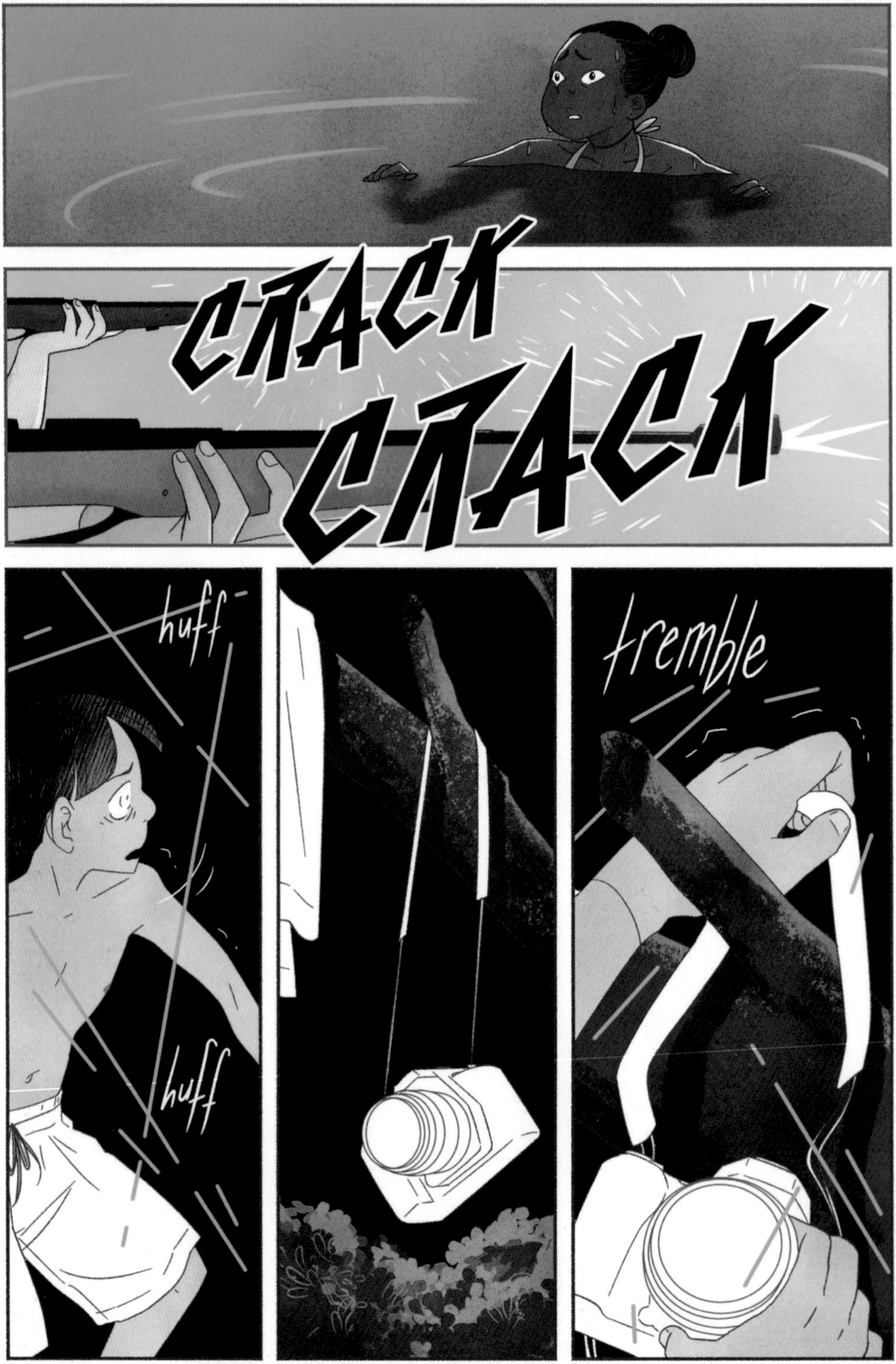
CRACK
CRACK
huff
huff
tremble

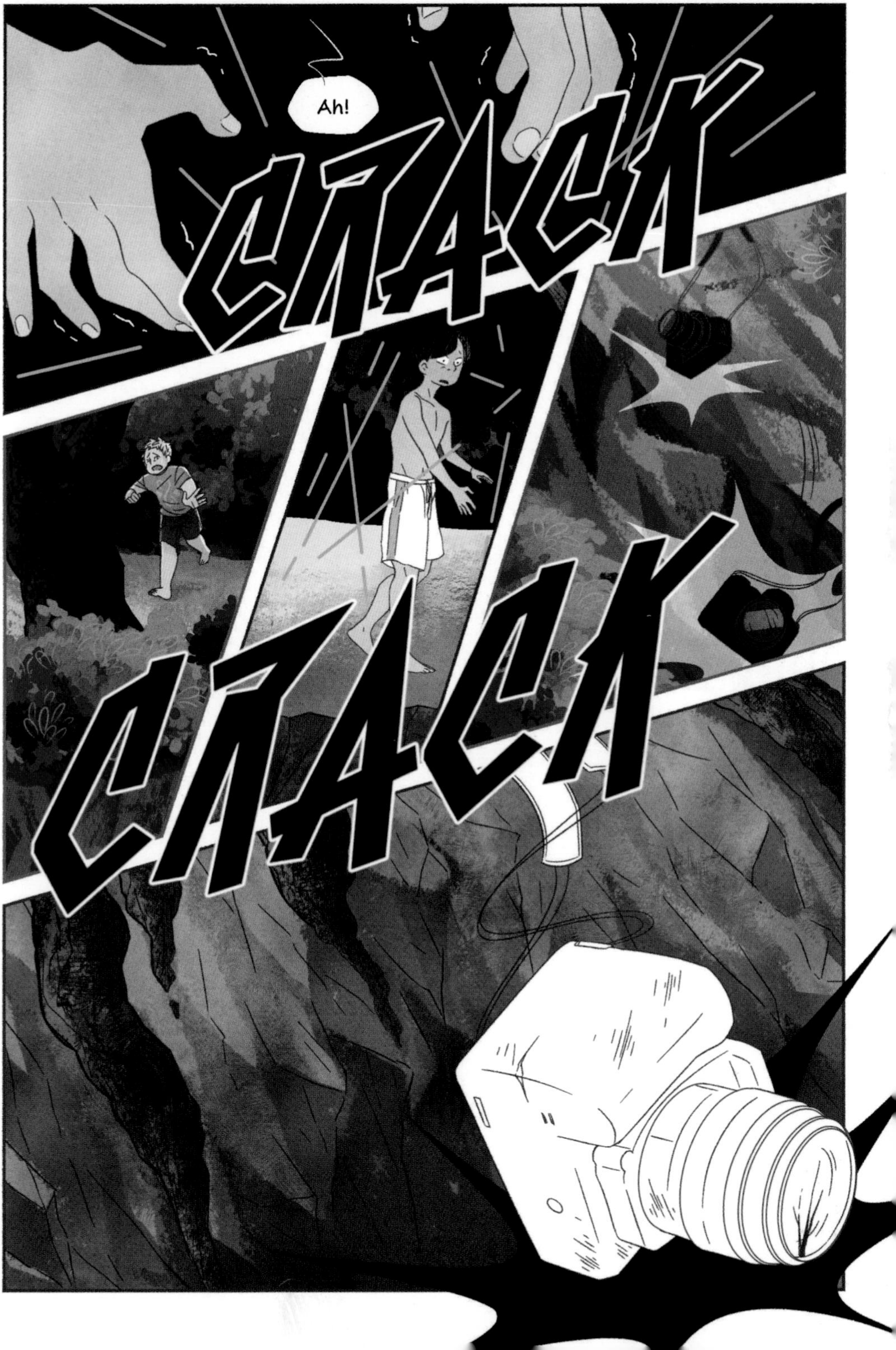
Ah!
CRACK
CRACK

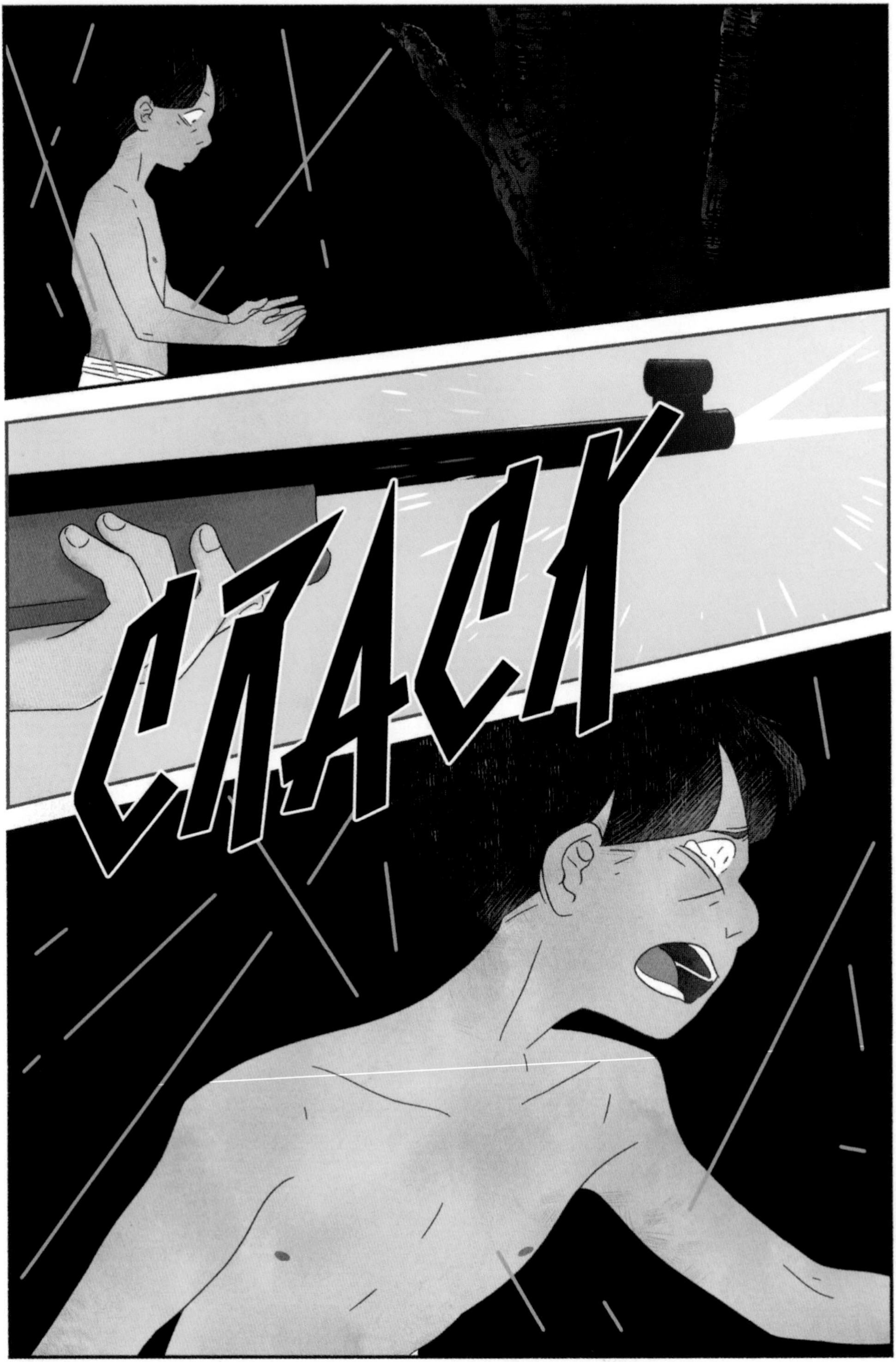
CRACK

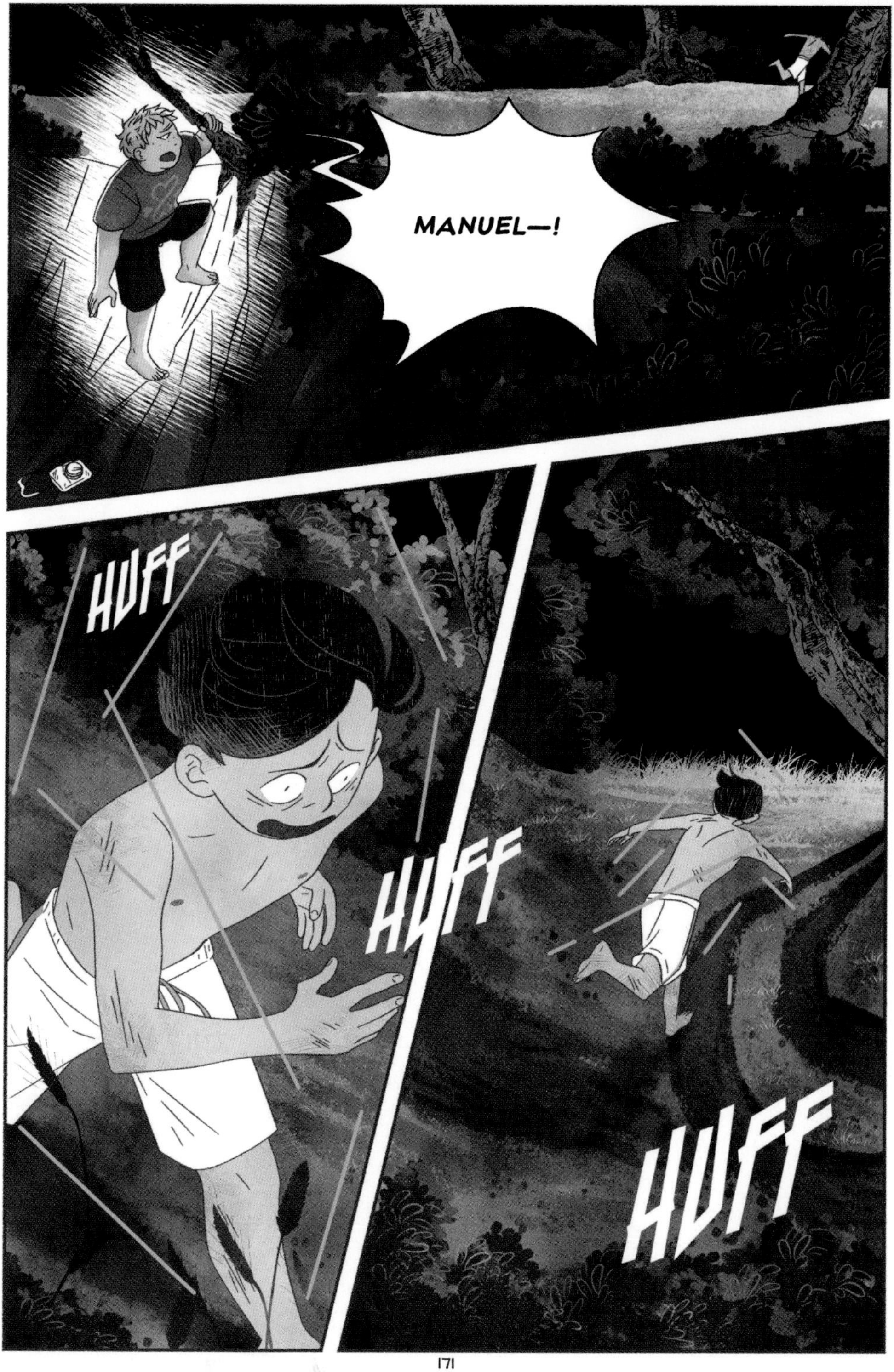
MANUEL—!
HUFF
HUFF
HUFF

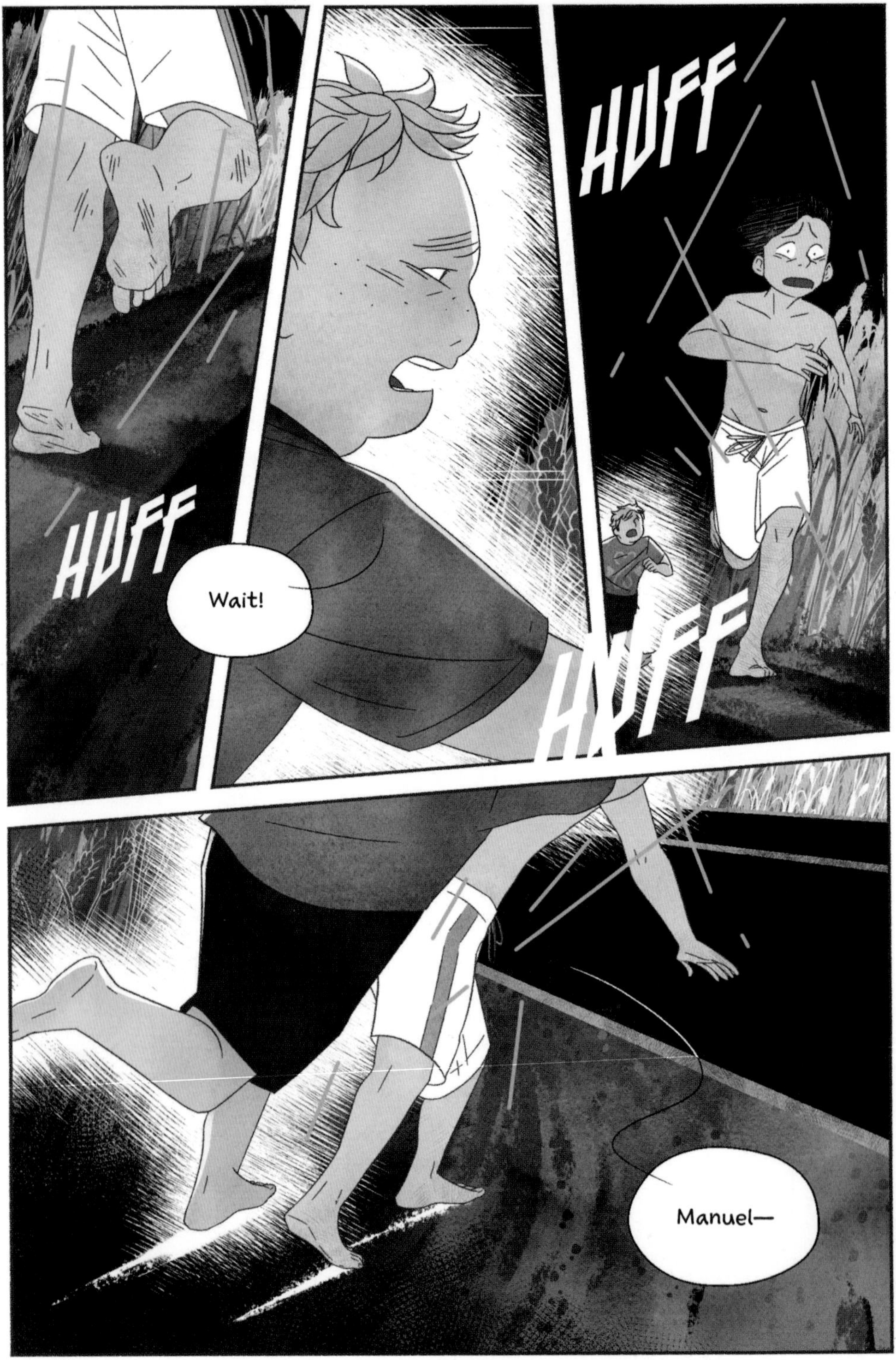
HUFF
Wait!
HUFF
HUFF
Manuel—

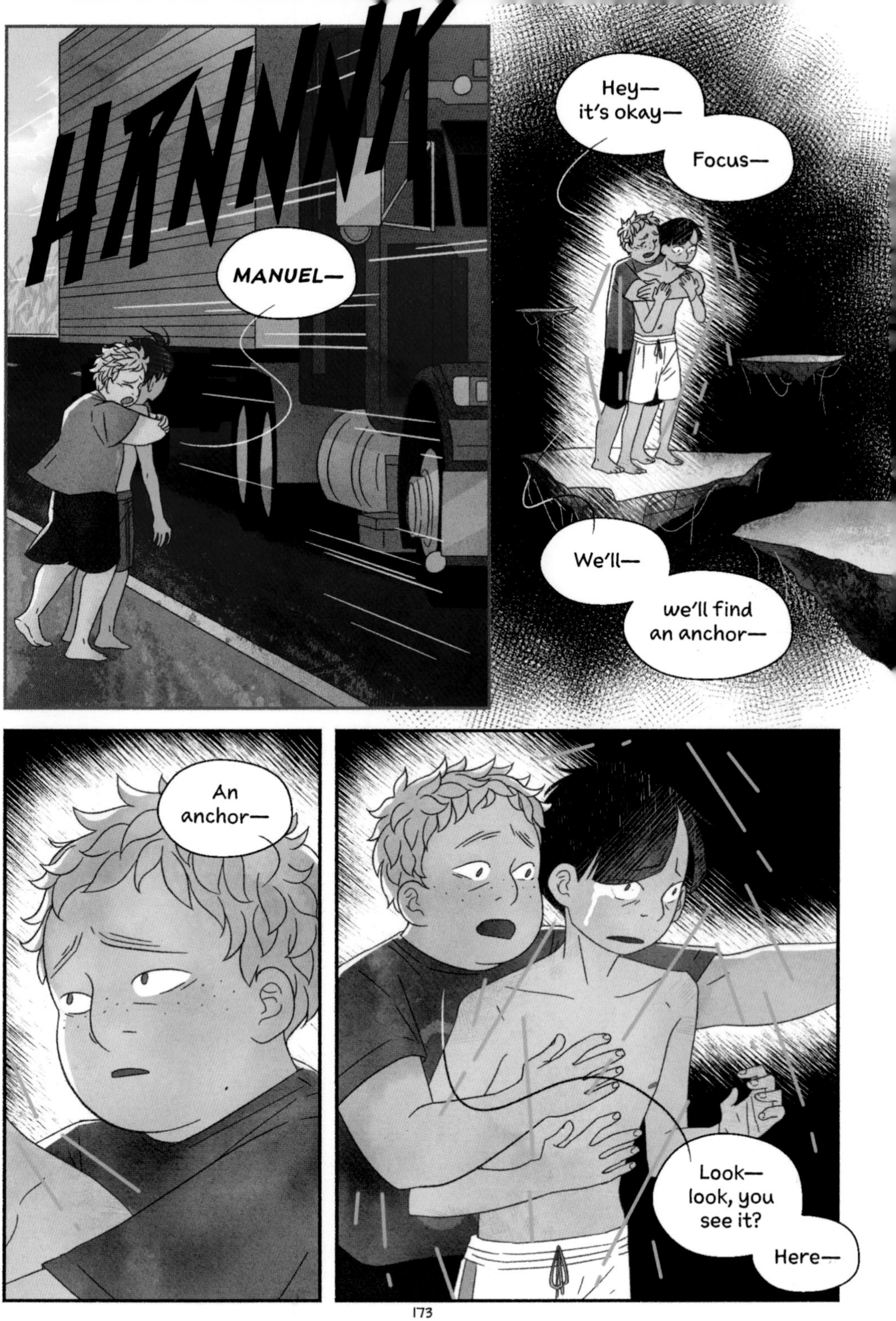
HRNNNK
MANUEL—
Hey— it's okay—
Focus—
We'll—
we'll find an anchor—
An anchor—
Look— look, you see it?
Here—

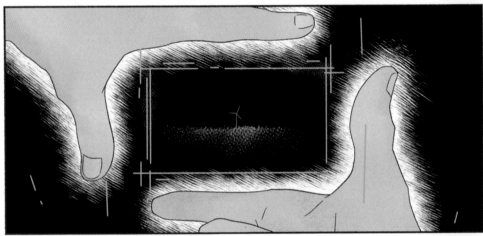

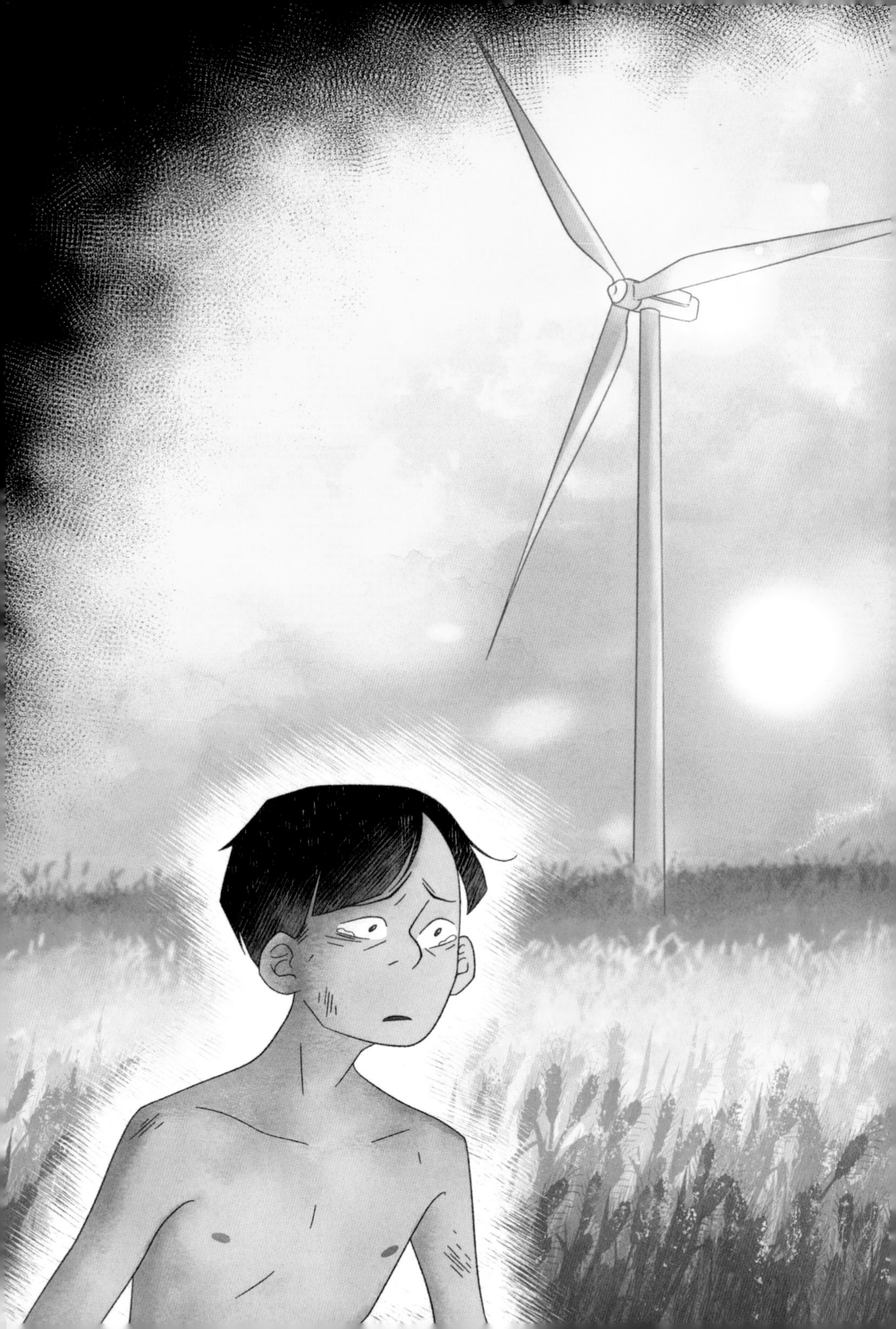

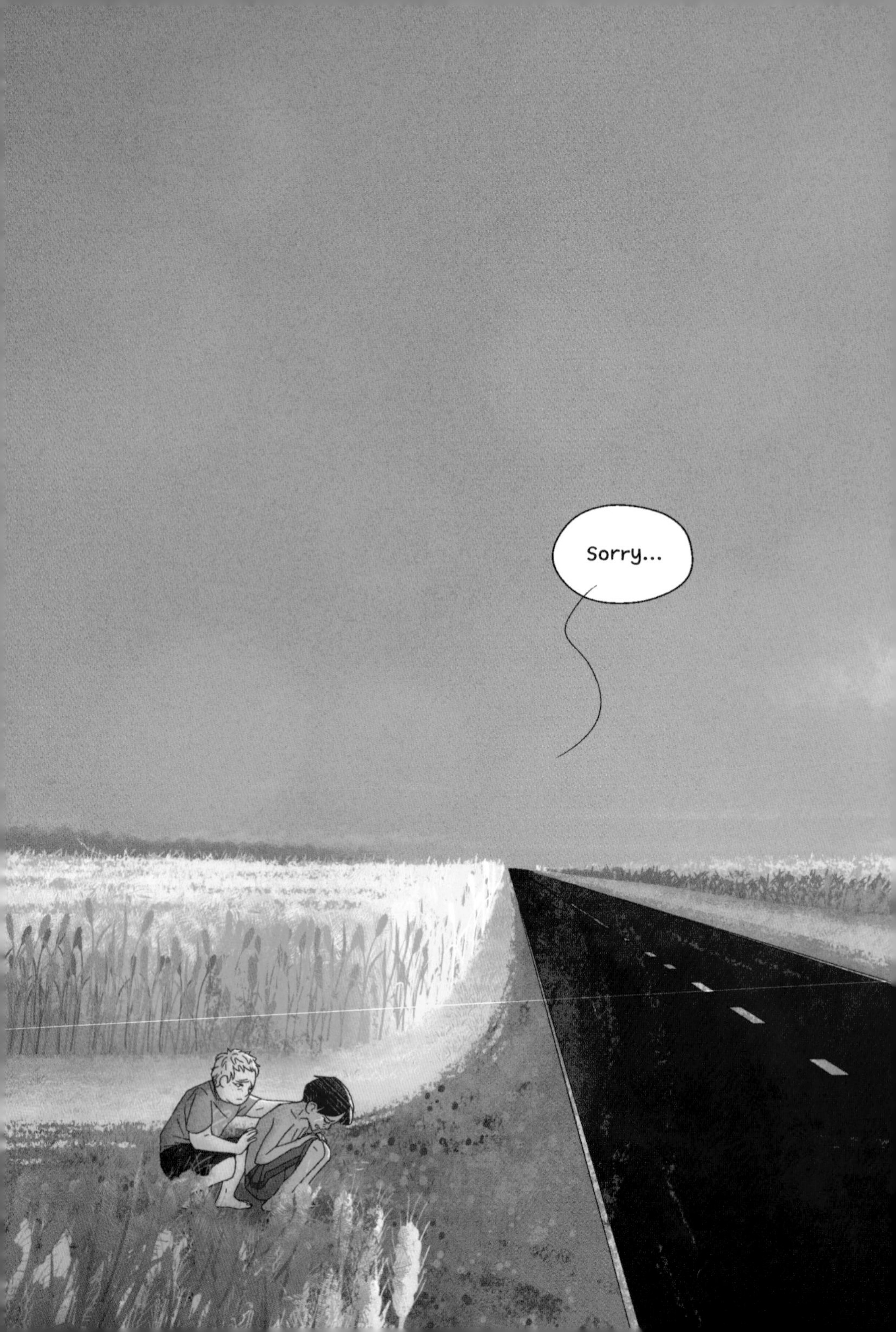
Sorry...

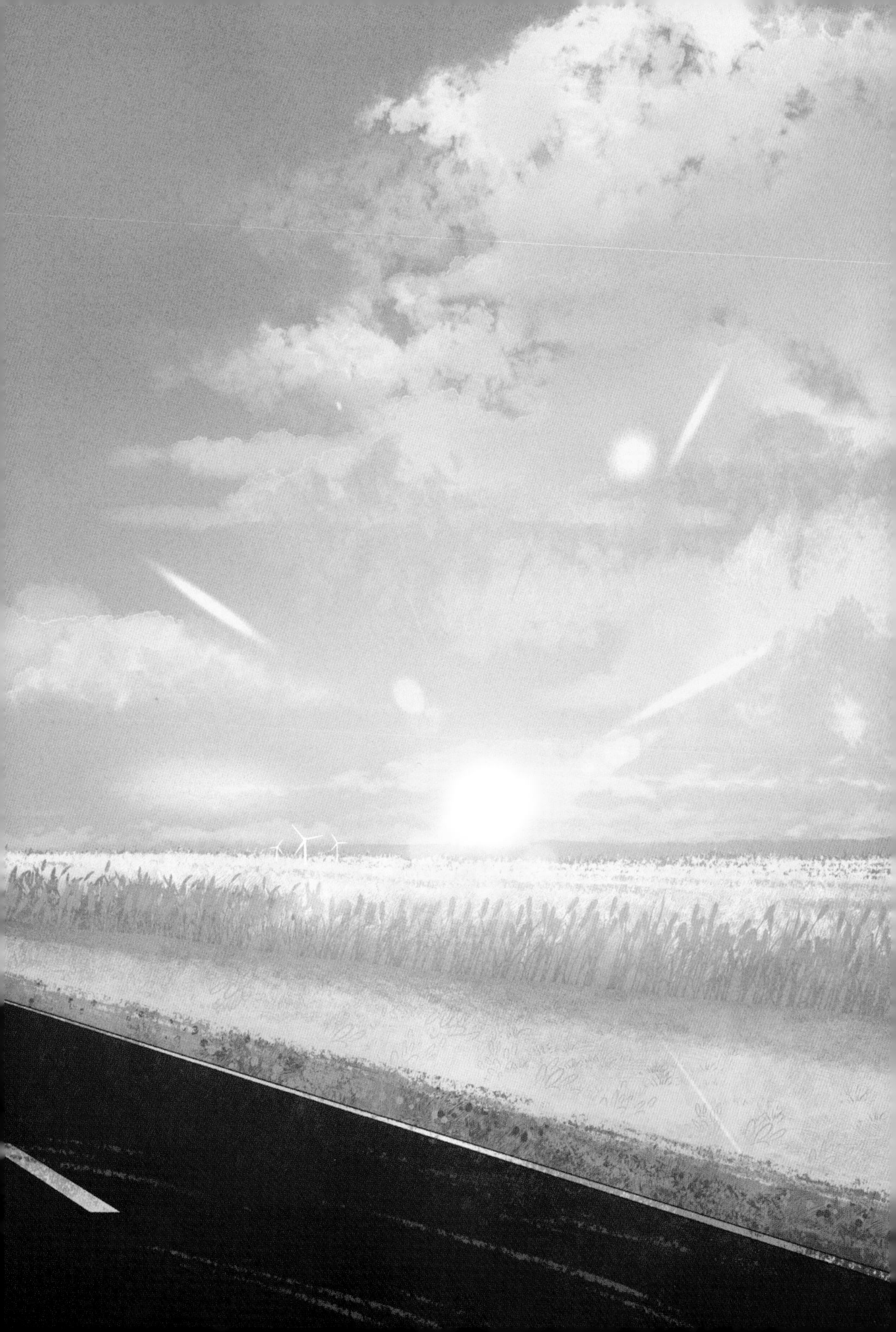

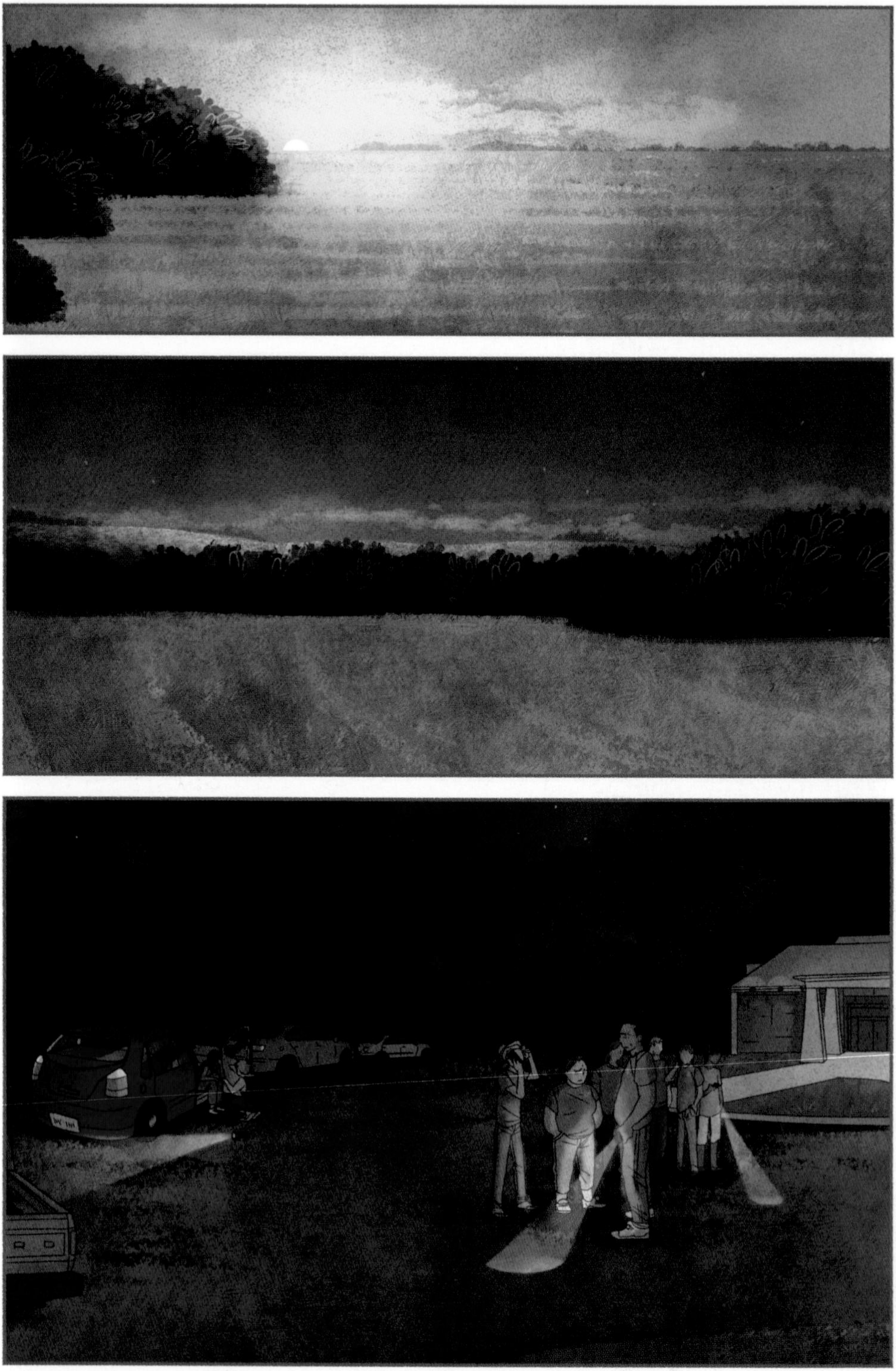

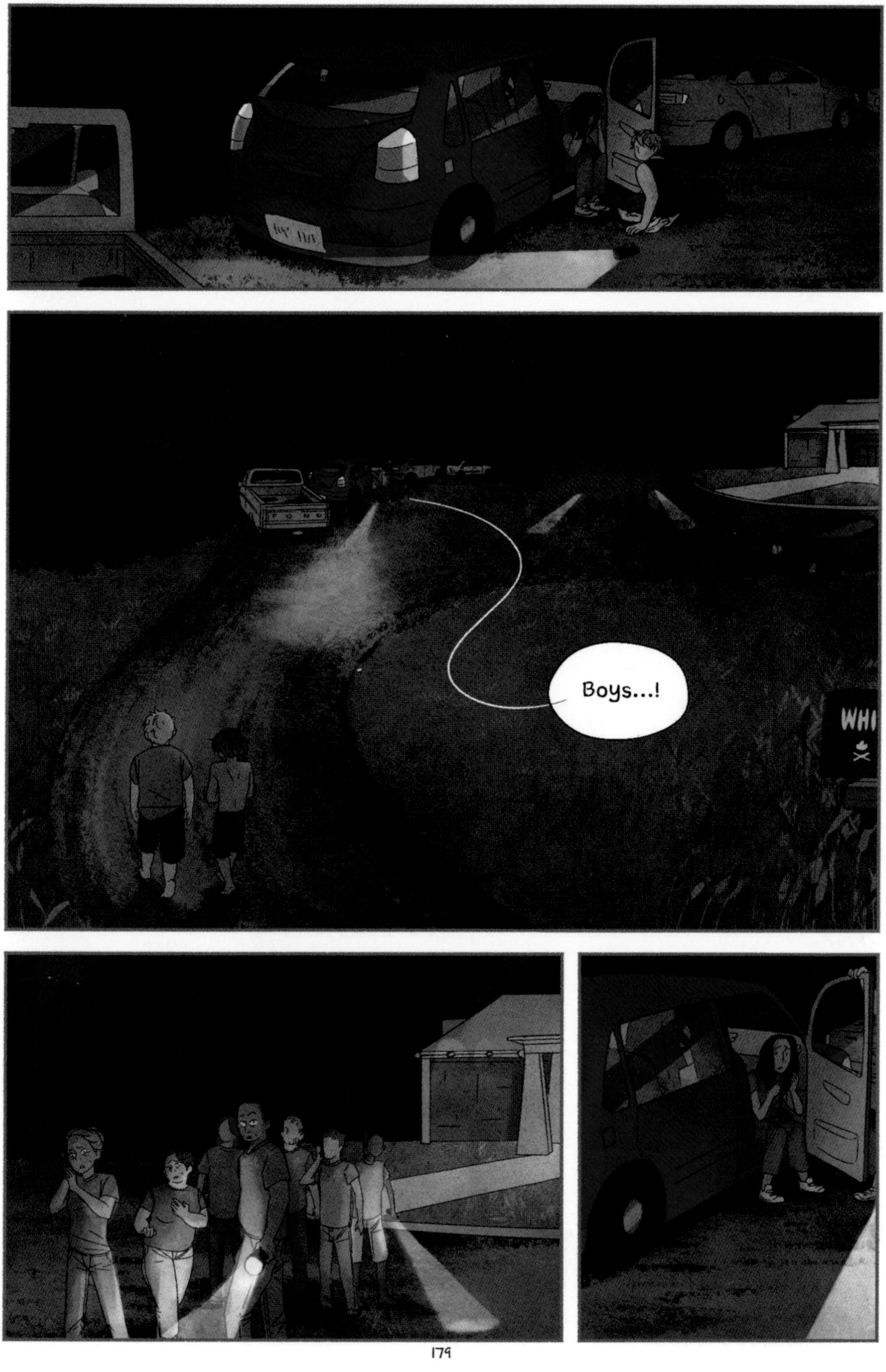
Boys...!

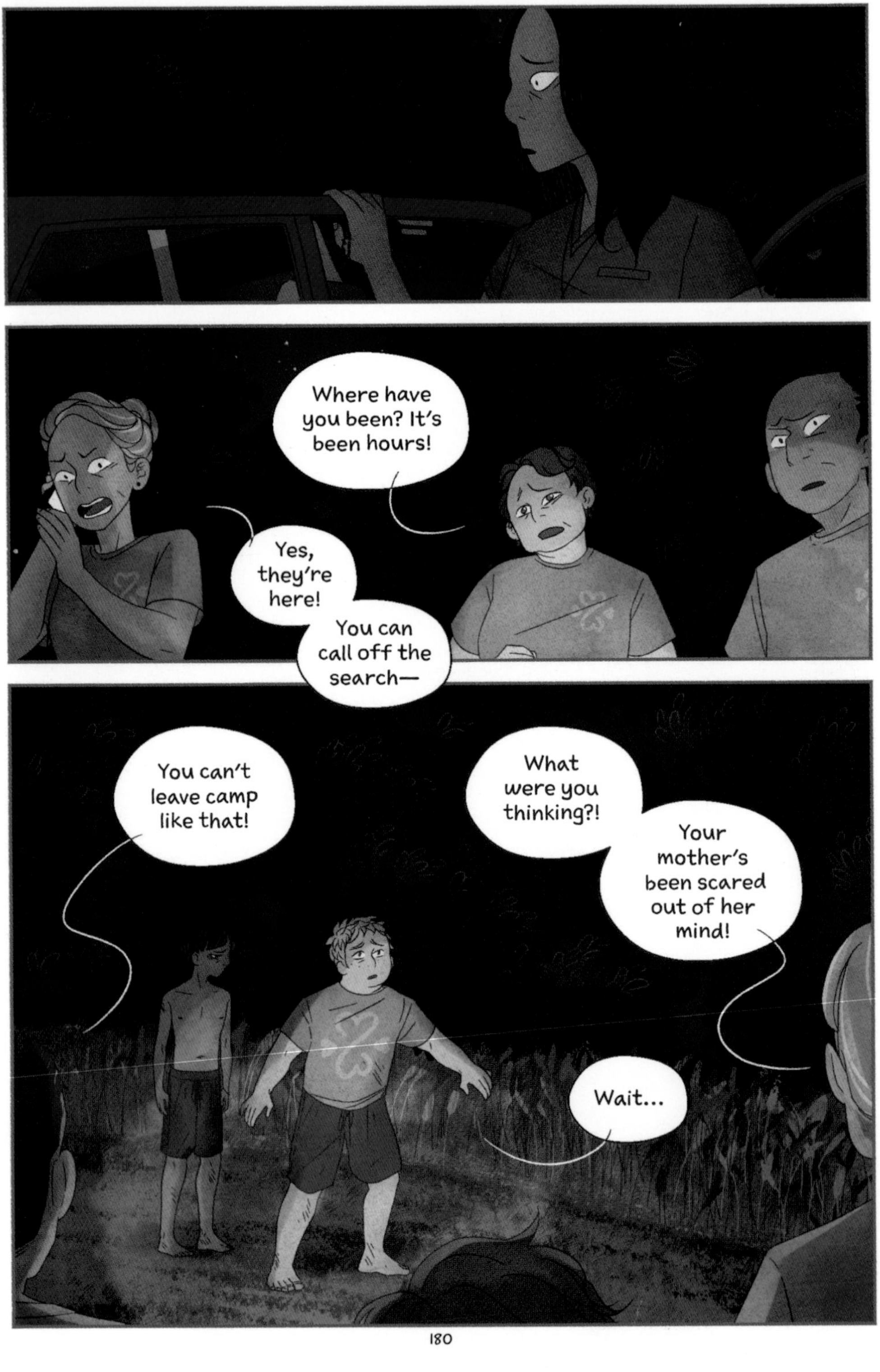

Where have you been? It's been hours!
Yes, they're here!
You can call off the search—
You can't leave camp like that!
What were you thinking?!
Your mother's been scared out of her mind!
Wait...

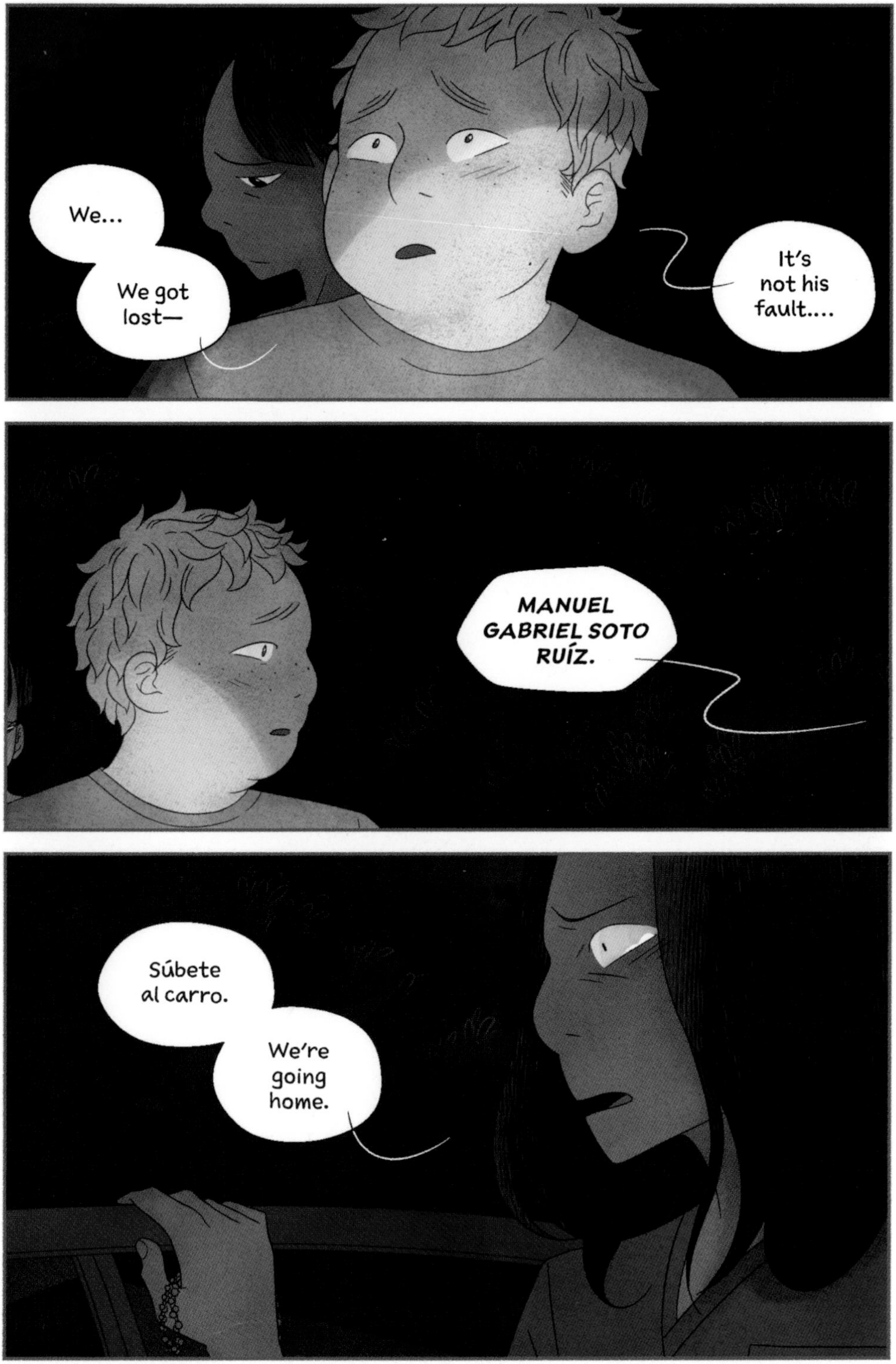
We...
We got lost—
It's not his fault....
MANUEL GABRIEL SOTO RUÍZ.
Súbete al carro.
We're going home.

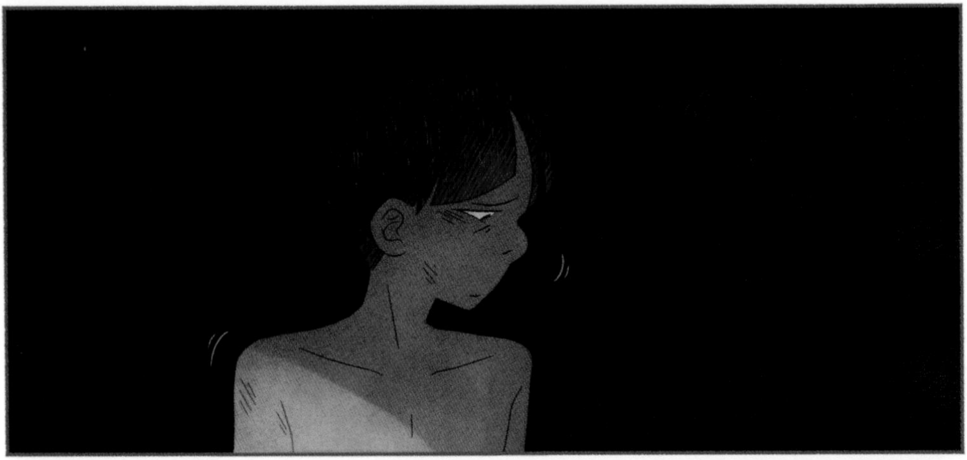

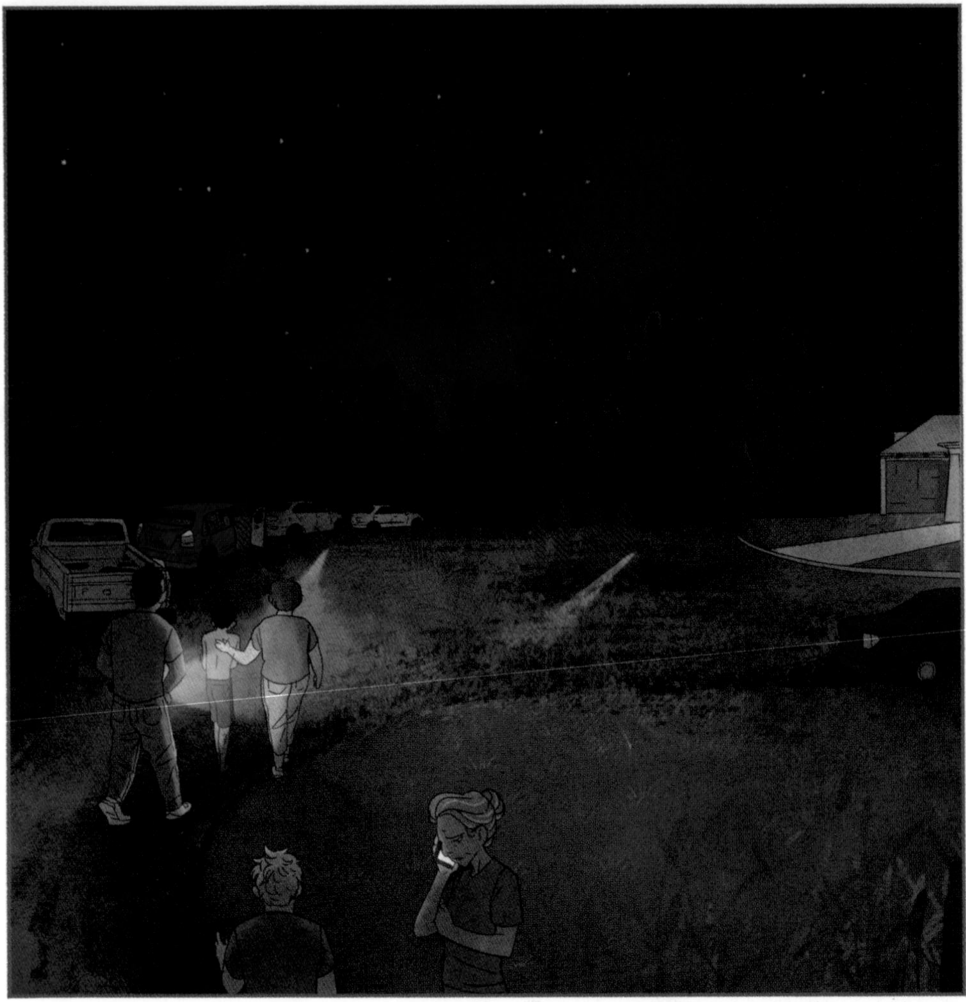

chapter five

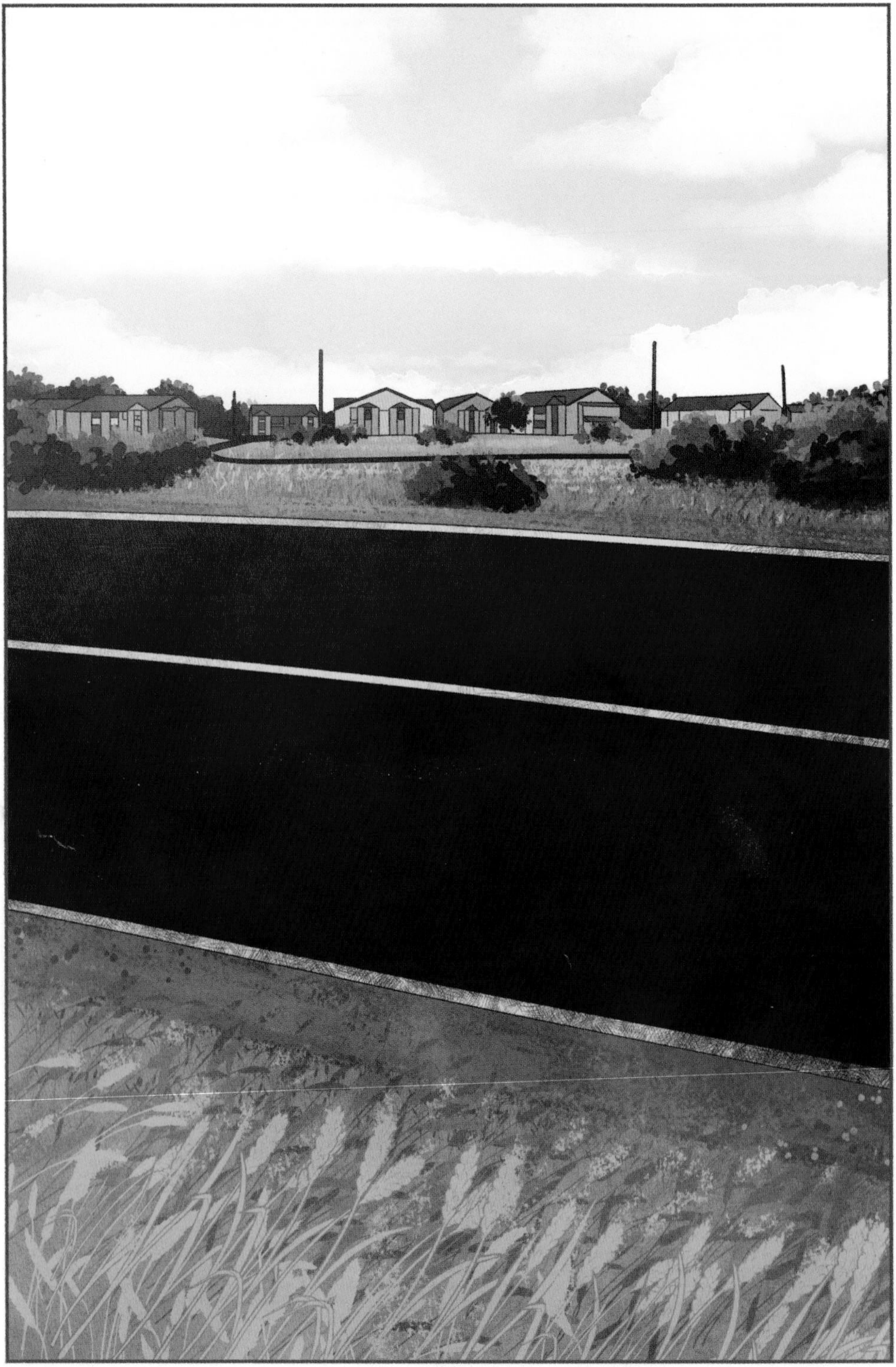

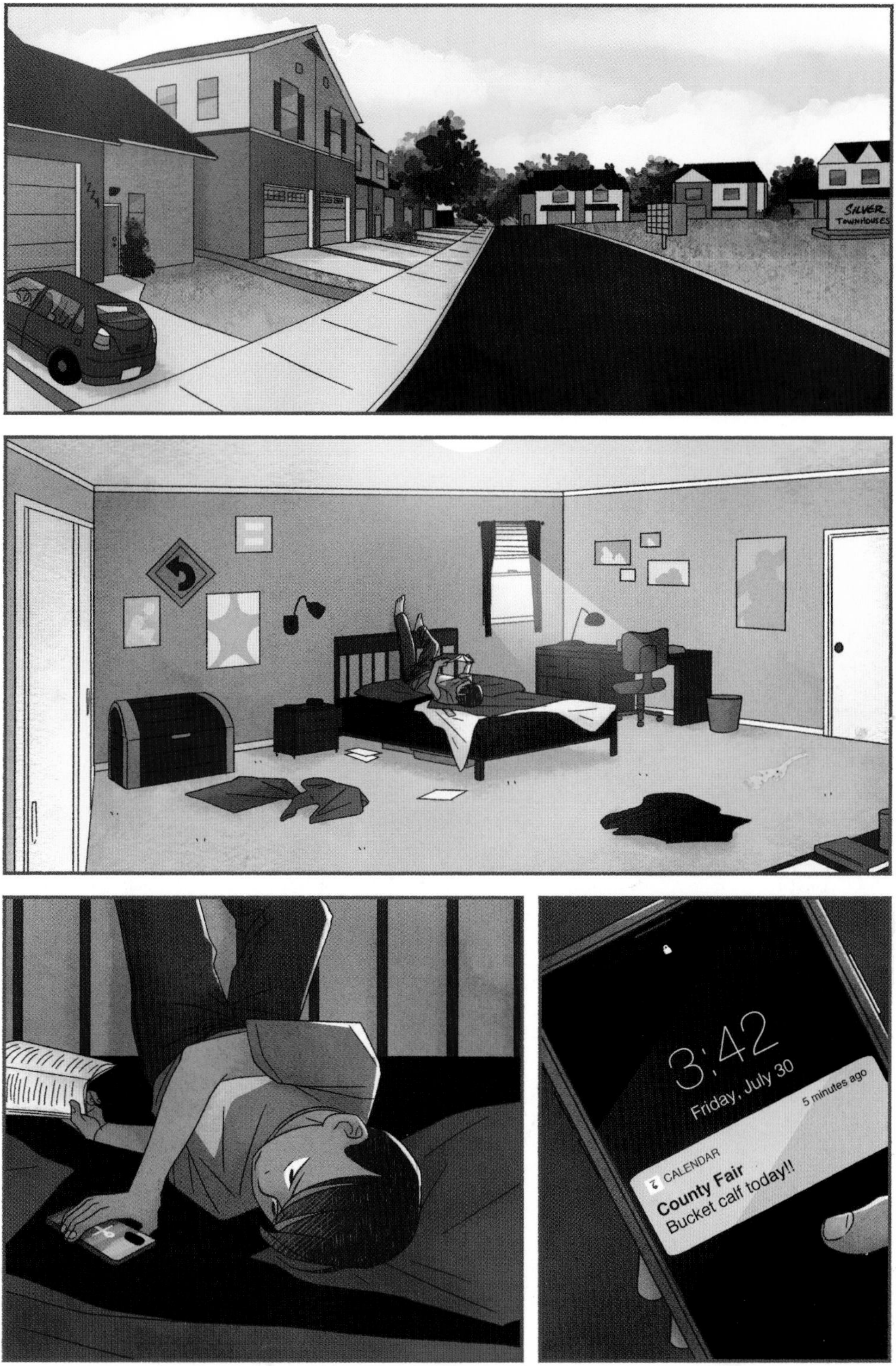
SILVER
TOWNHOUSES
3:42
Friday, July 30
5 minutes ago
CALENDAR
County Fair
Bucket calf today!!

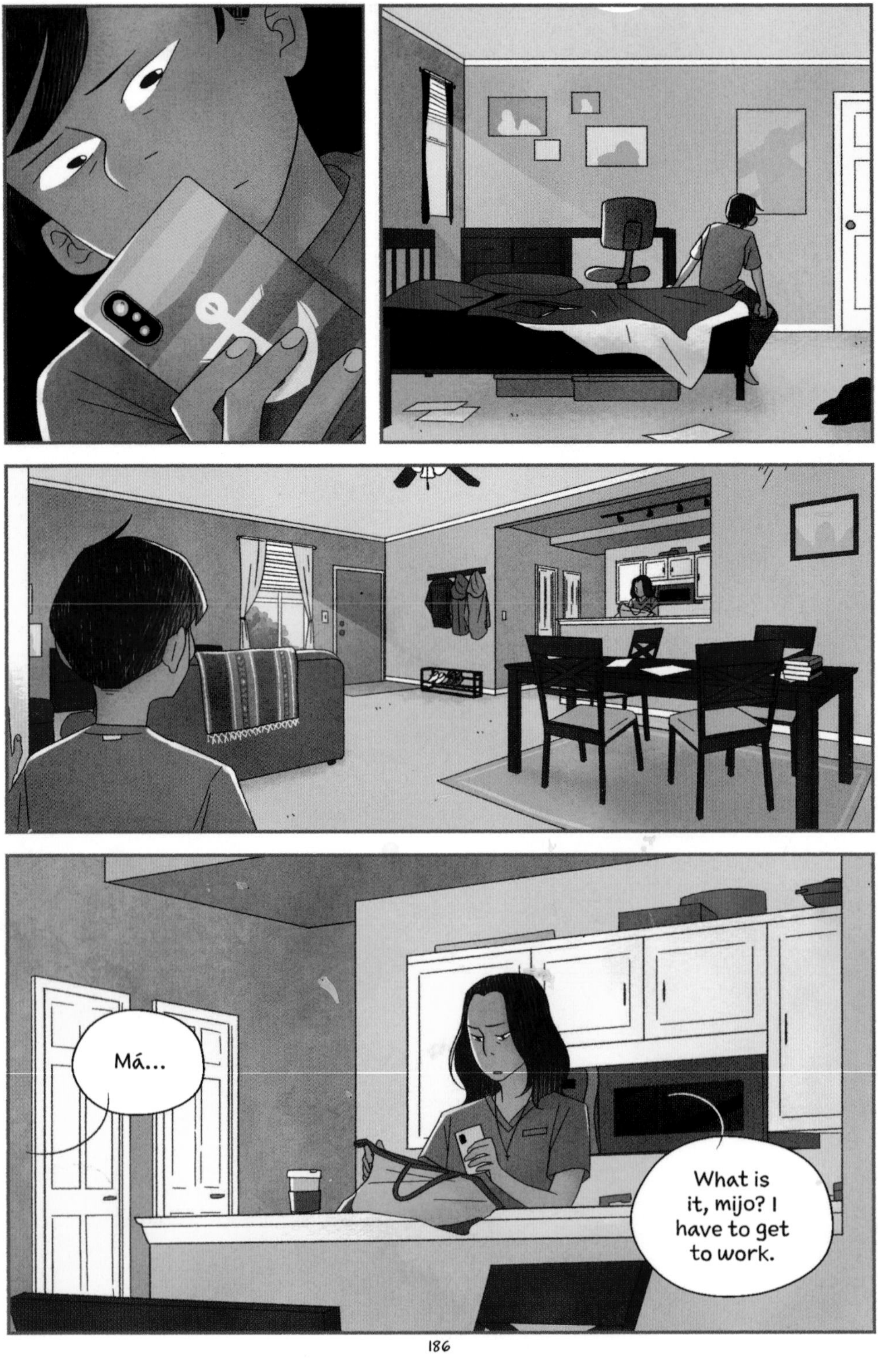
Má...
What is it, mijo? I have to get to work.

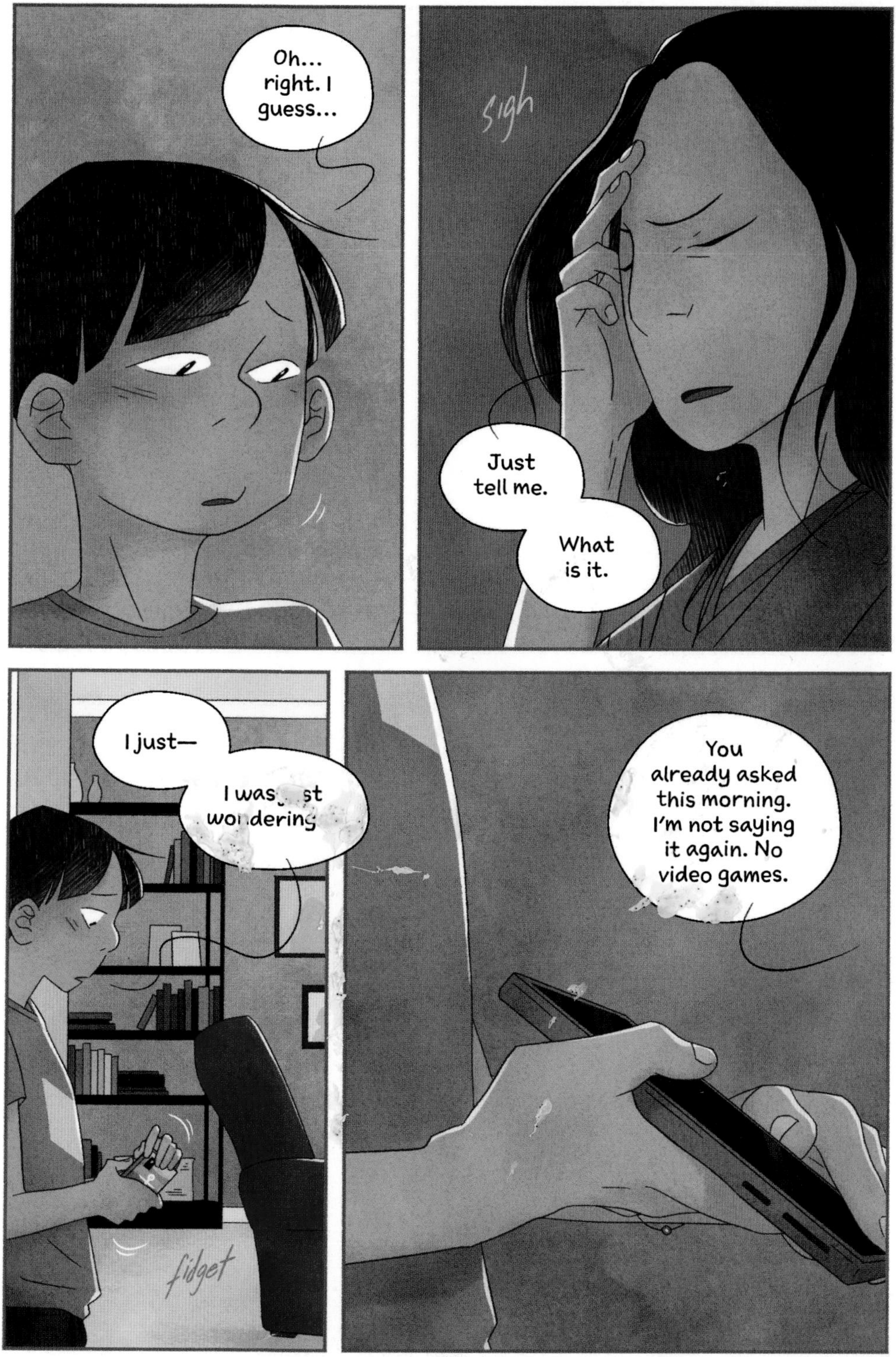
Oh... right. I guess...
sigh
Just tell me.
What is it.
I just—
I was just wondering
fidget
You already asked this morning. I'm not saying it again. No video games.

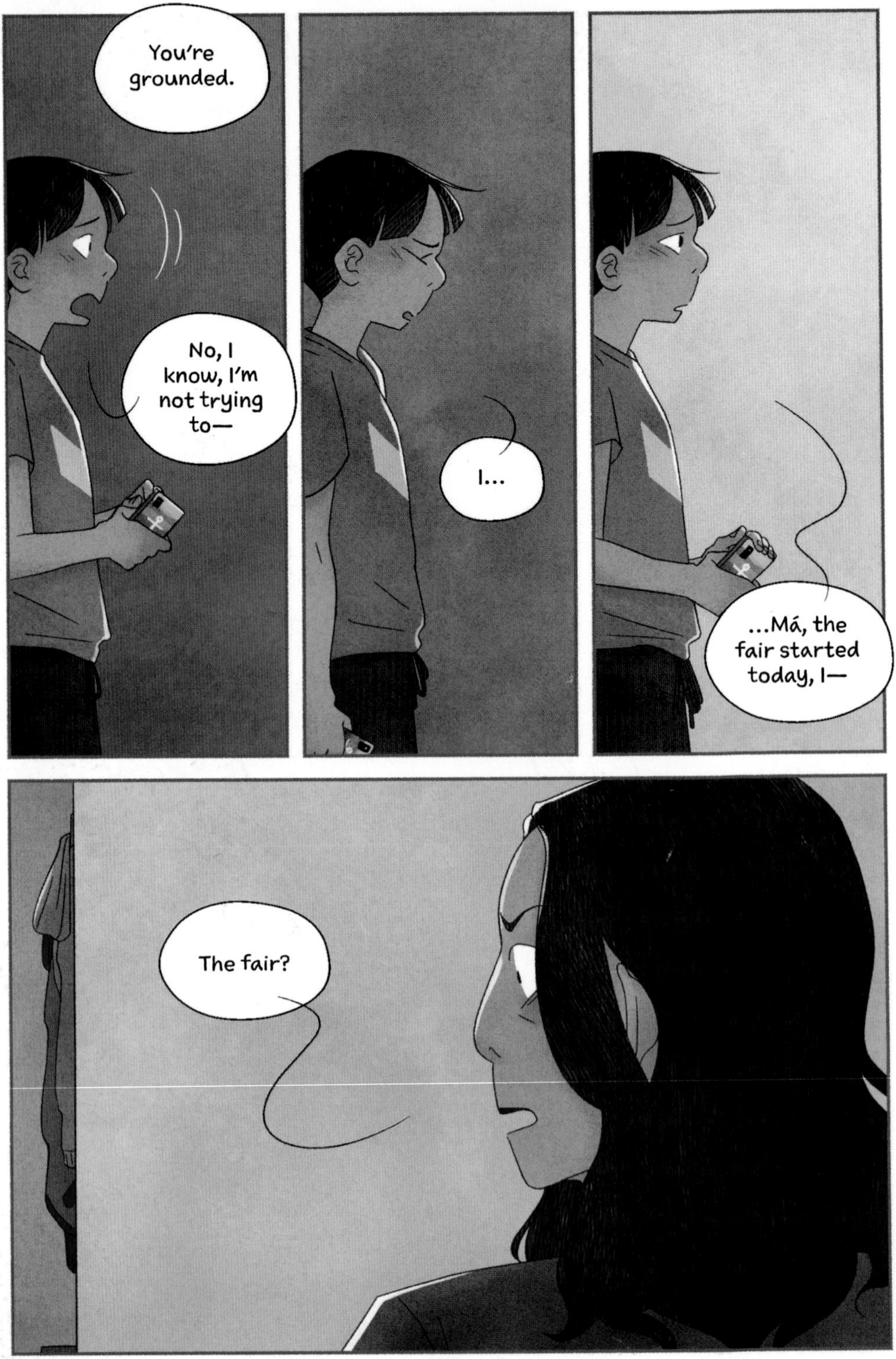
You're grounded.
No, I know, I'm not trying to—
I...
...Má, the fair started today, I—
The fair?

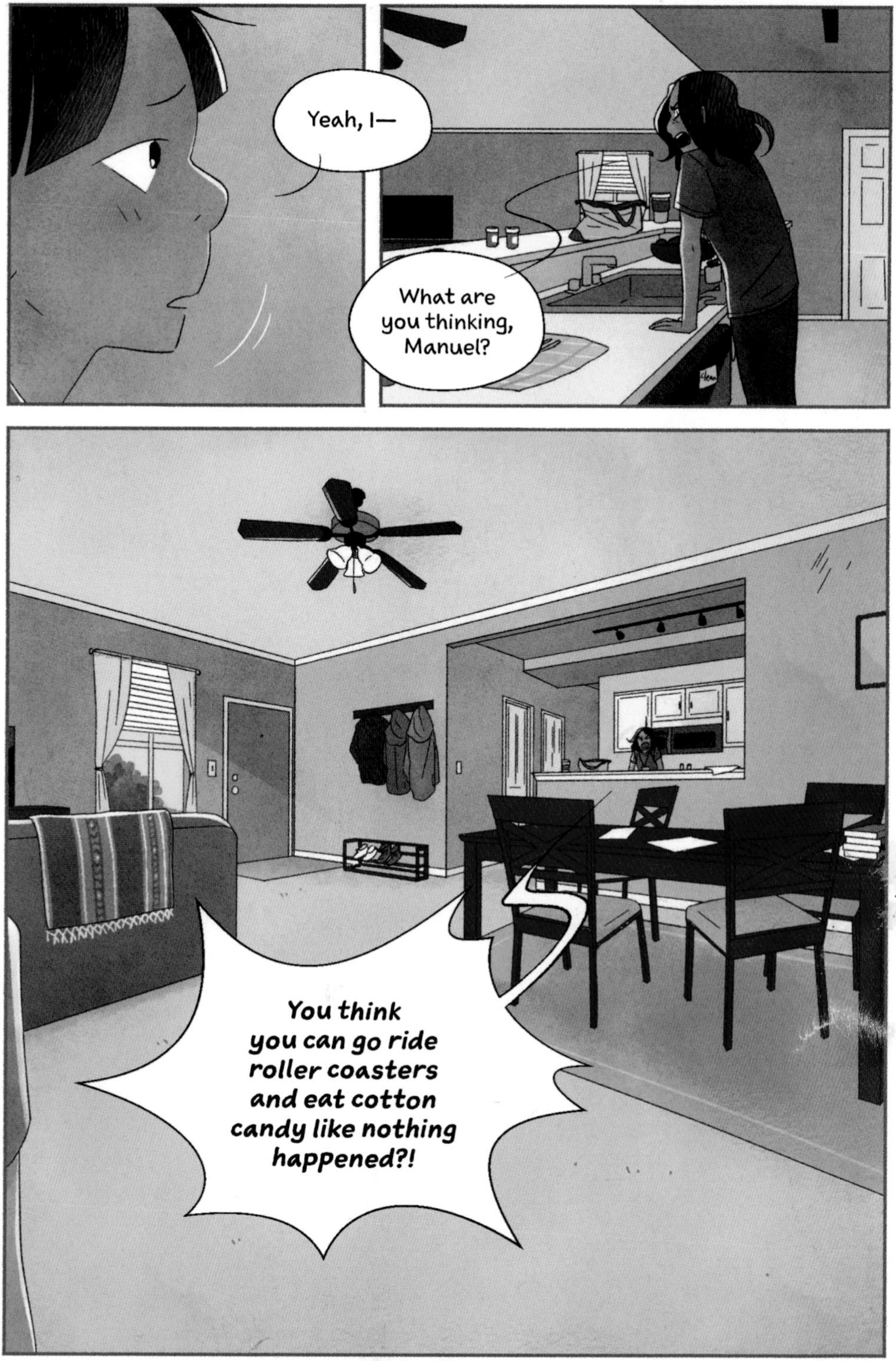
Yeah, I—
What are you thinking, Manuel?
You think you can go ride roller coasters and eat cotton candy like nothing happened?!

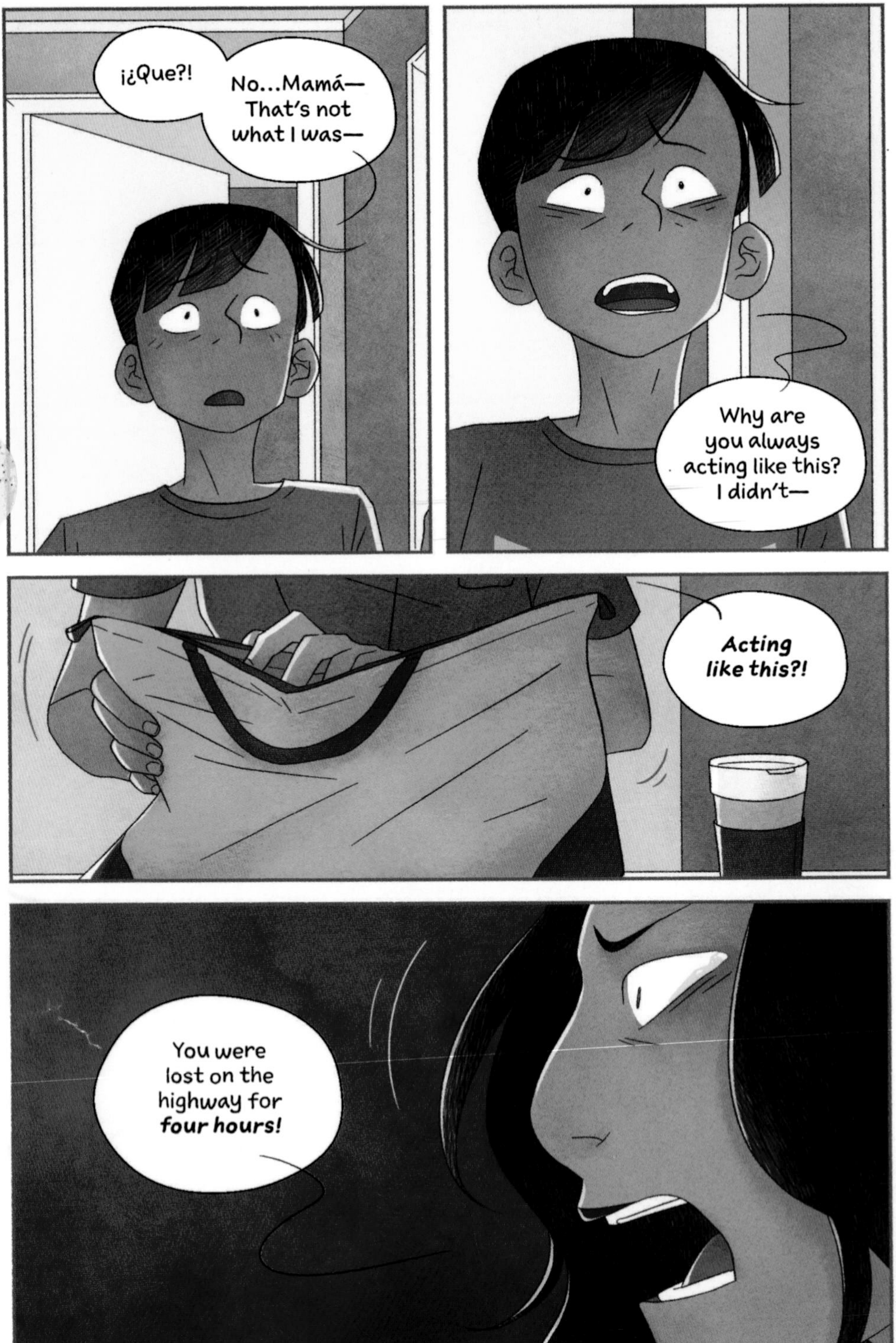

¡¿Que?!
No…Mamá—
That's not
what I was—
Why are
you always
acting like this?
I didn't—
Acting
like this?!
You were
lost on the
highway for
four hours!

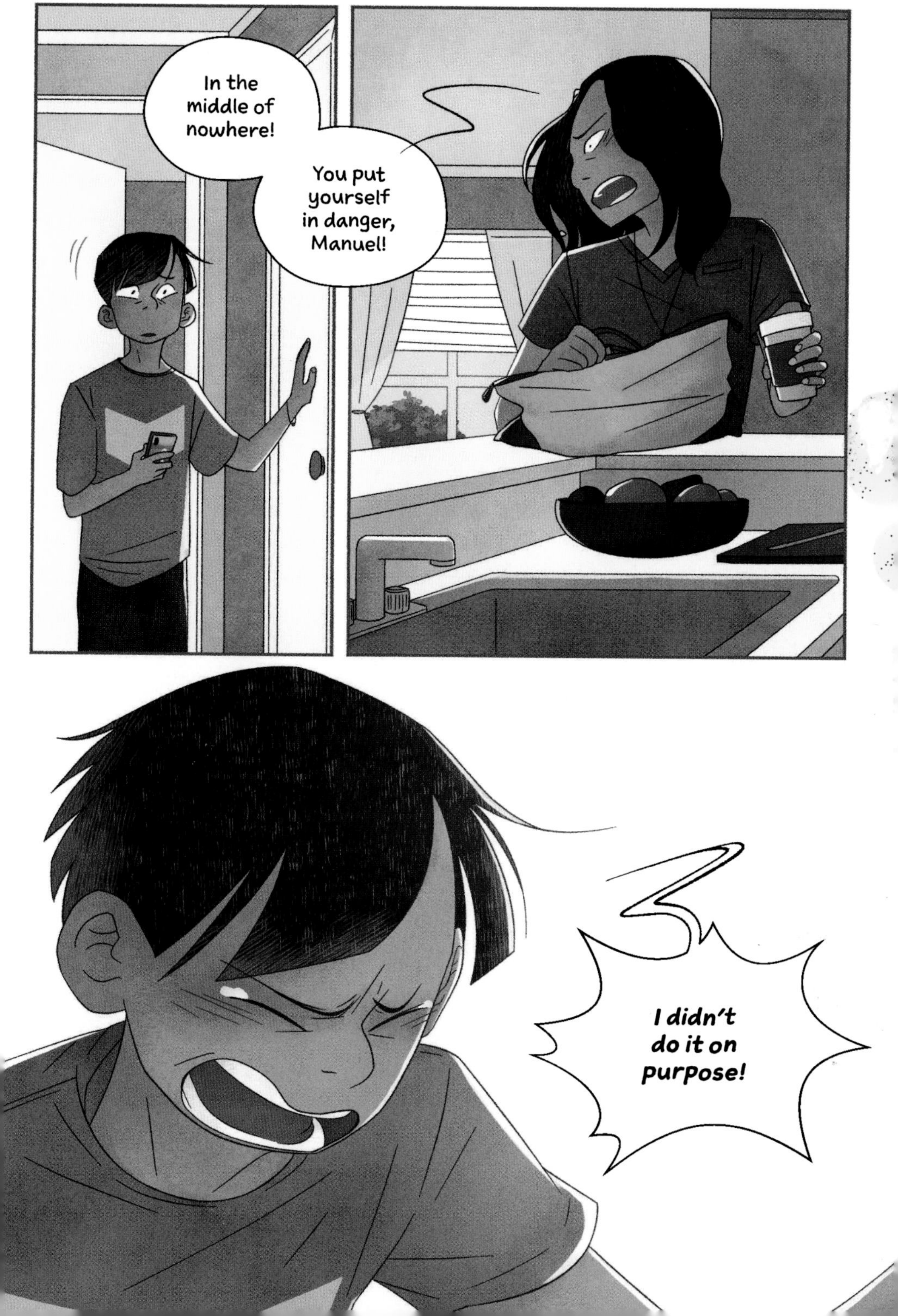
In the middle of nowhere!
You put yourself in danger, Manuel!
I didn't do it on purpose!

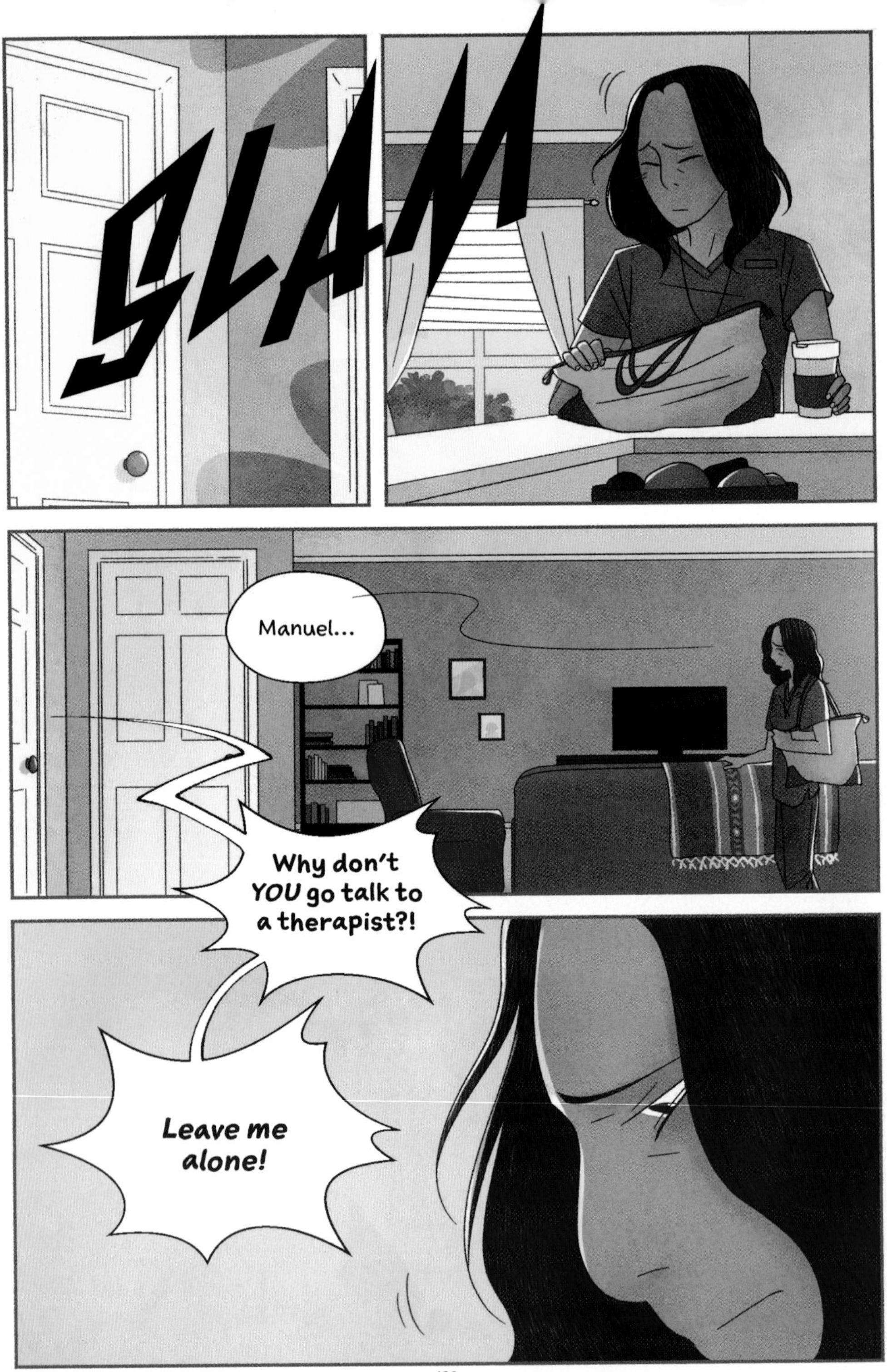
SLAM
Manuel...
Why don't YOU go talk to a therapist?!
Leave me alone!

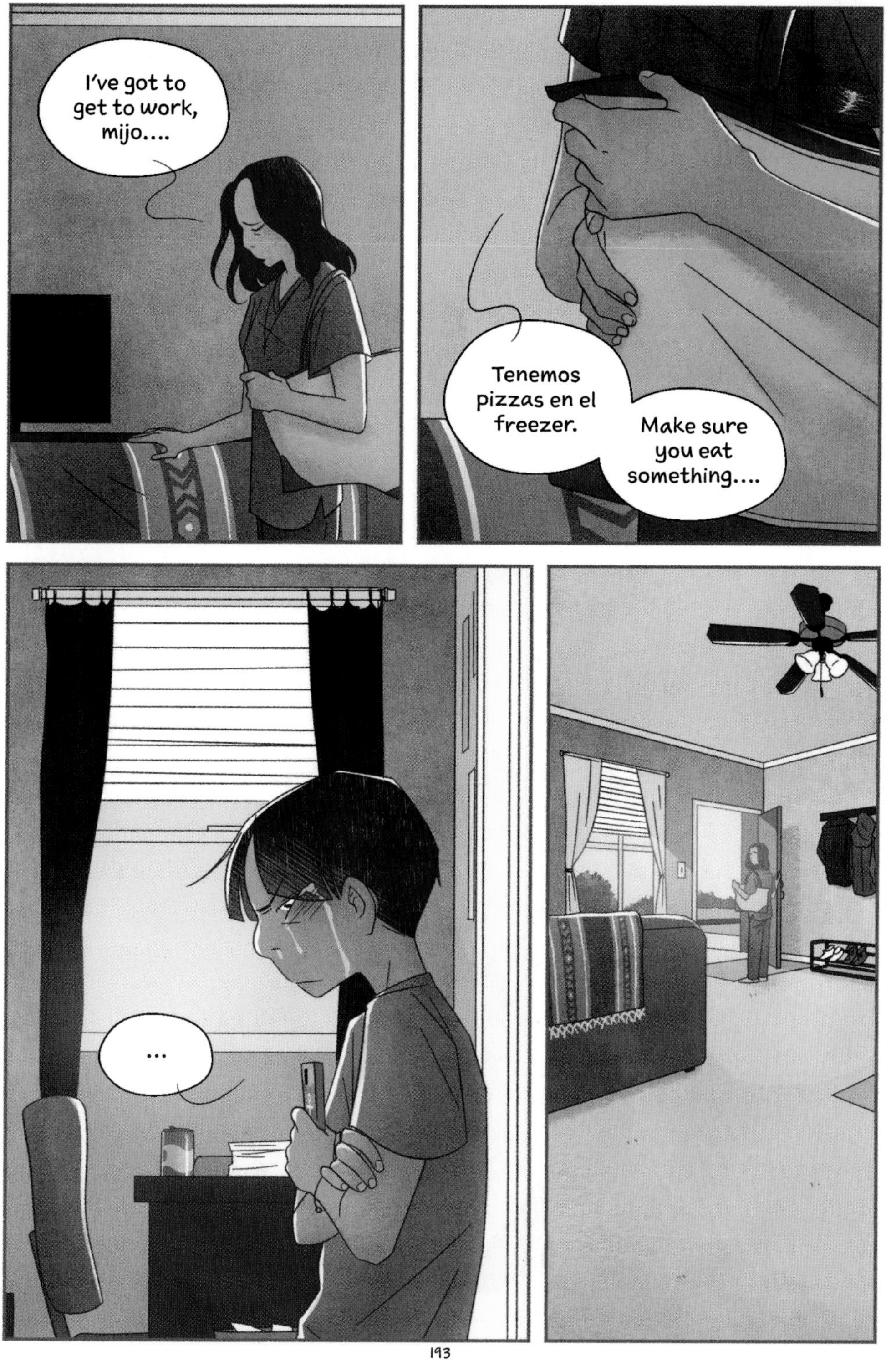
I've got to get to work, mijo....
Tenemos pizzas en el freezer.
Make sure you eat something....
...

clik

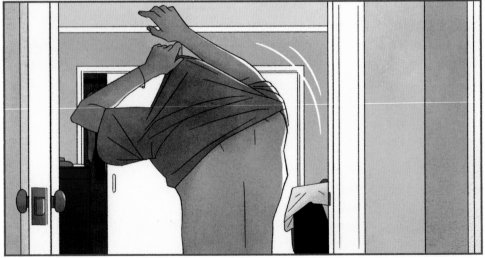

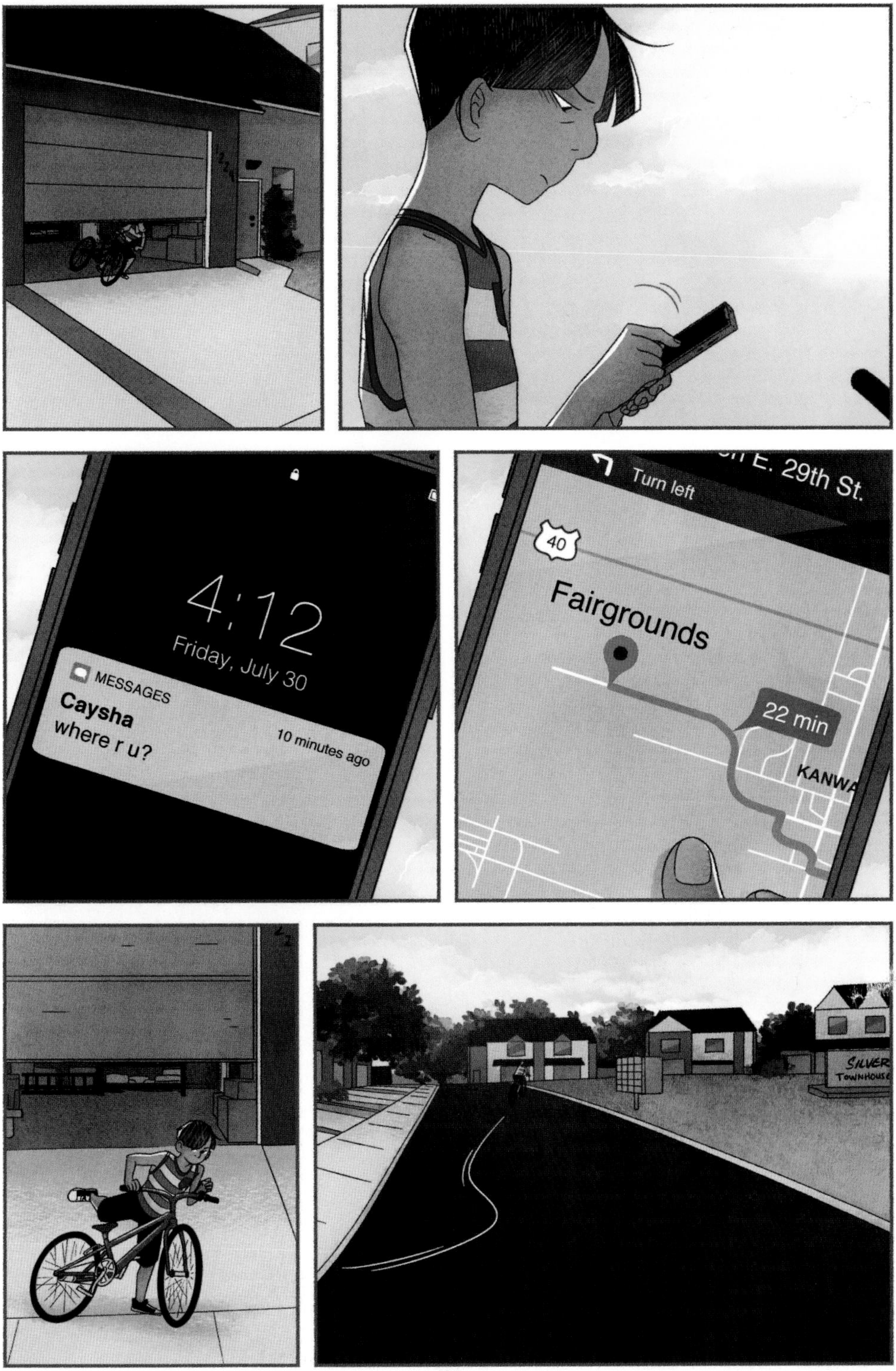
4:12
Friday, July 30
MESSAGES
Caysha
where r u?
10 minutes ago
E. 29th St.
Turn left
40
Fairgrounds
22 min
KANWA
SILVER
TOWNHOUSE

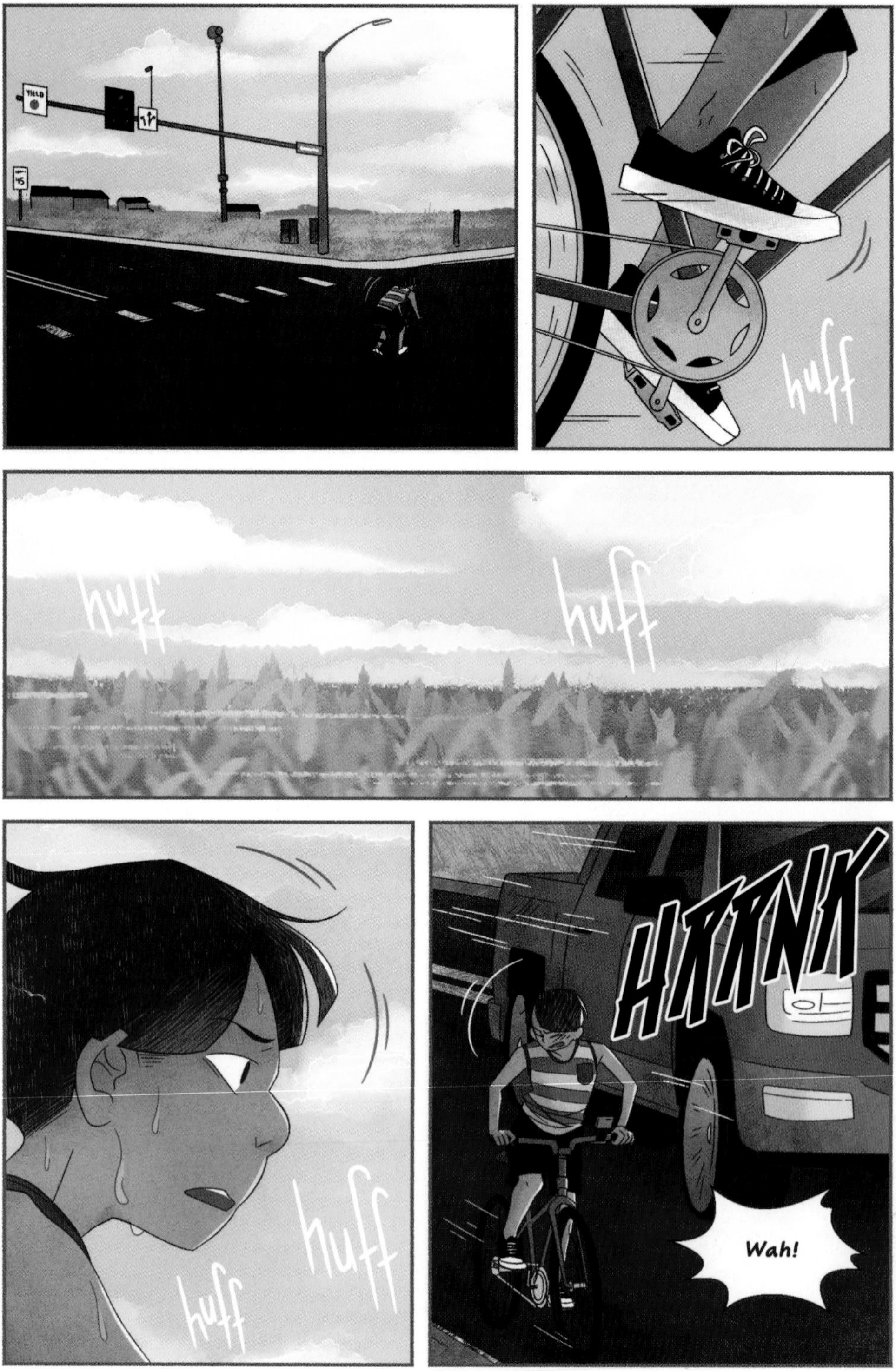
YIELD
45
huff
huff
huff
huff
huff
HRRNK
Wah!

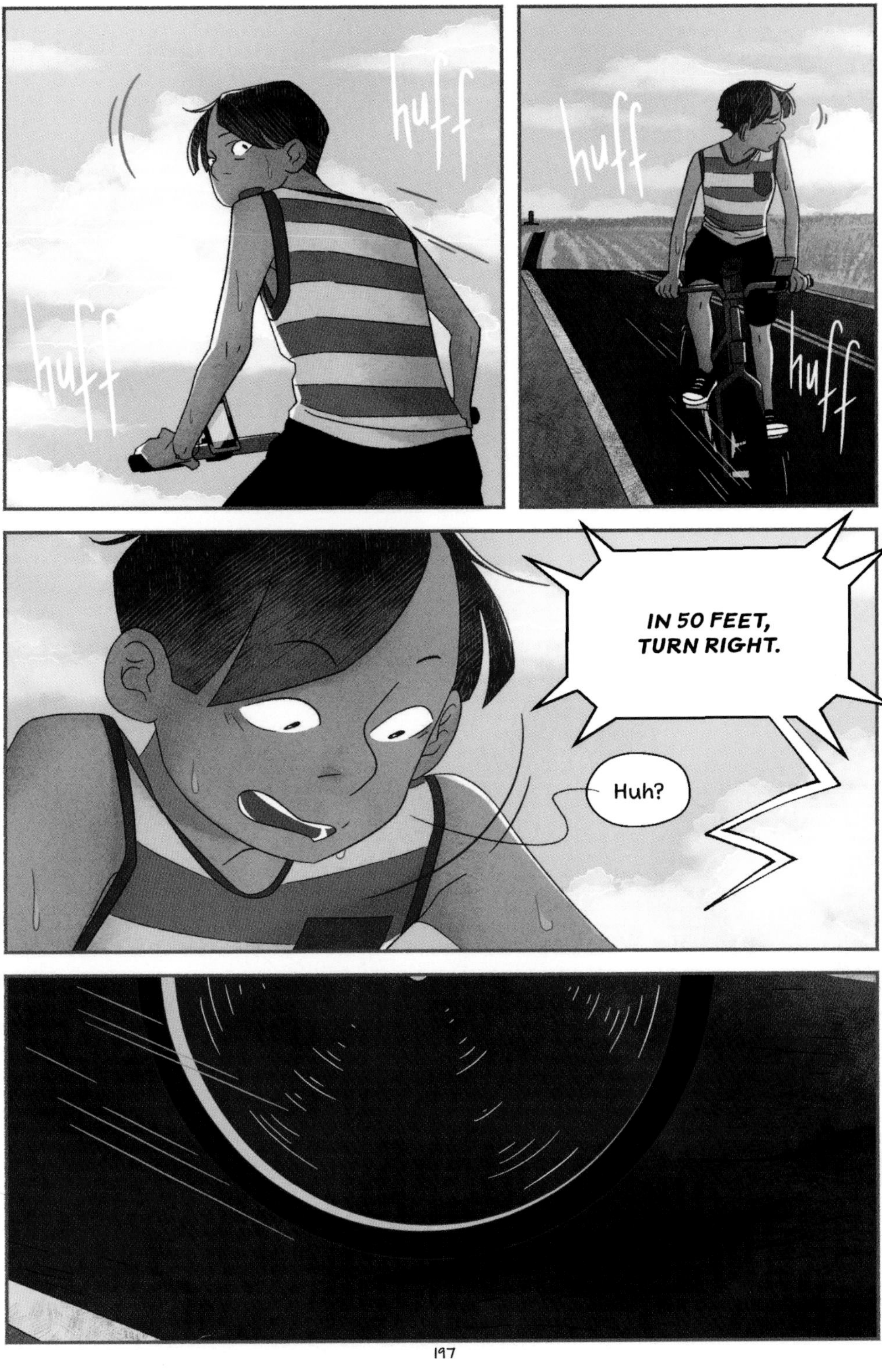
huff
huff
huff
huff
IN 50 FEET, TURN RIGHT.
Huh?

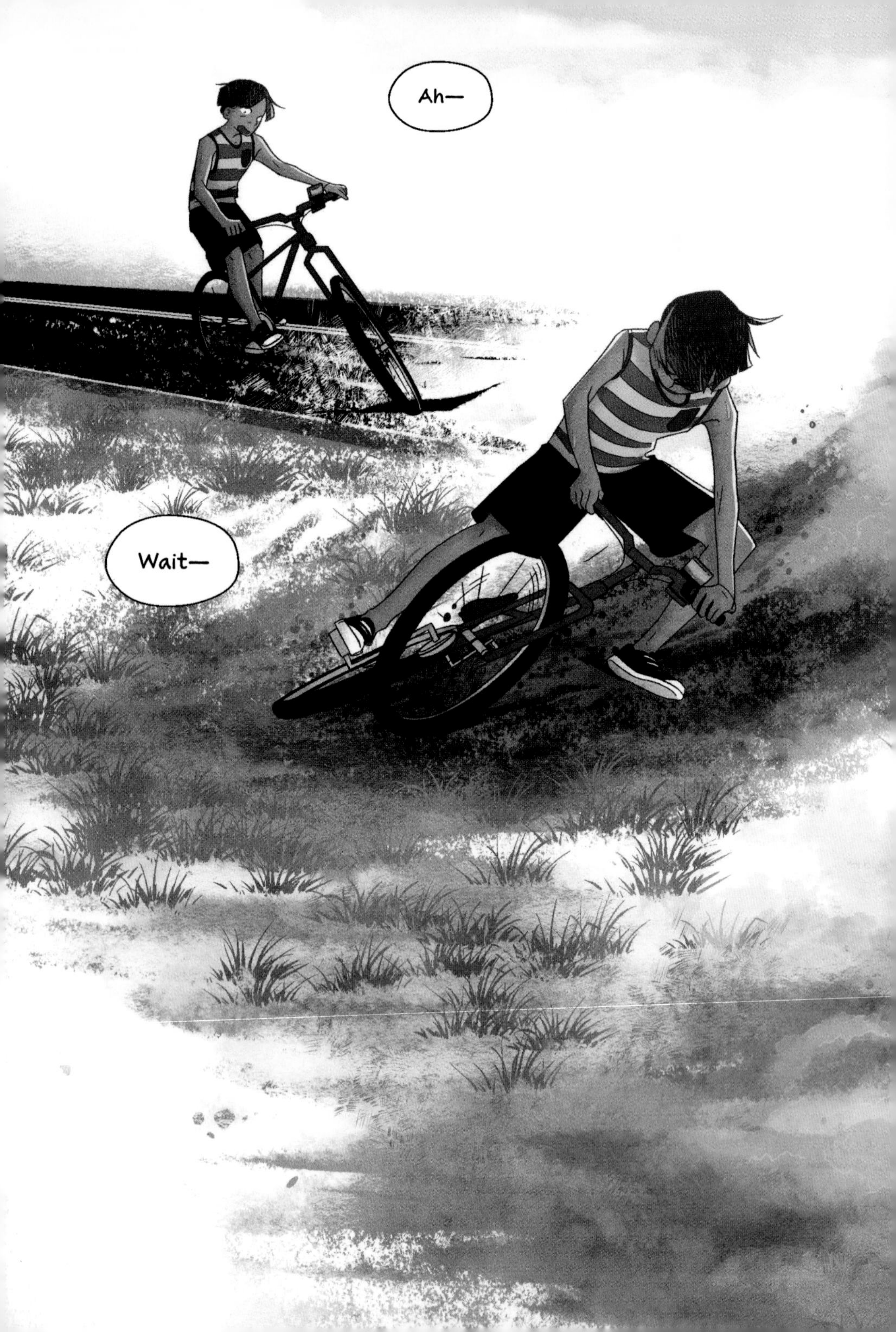
Ah—
Wait—

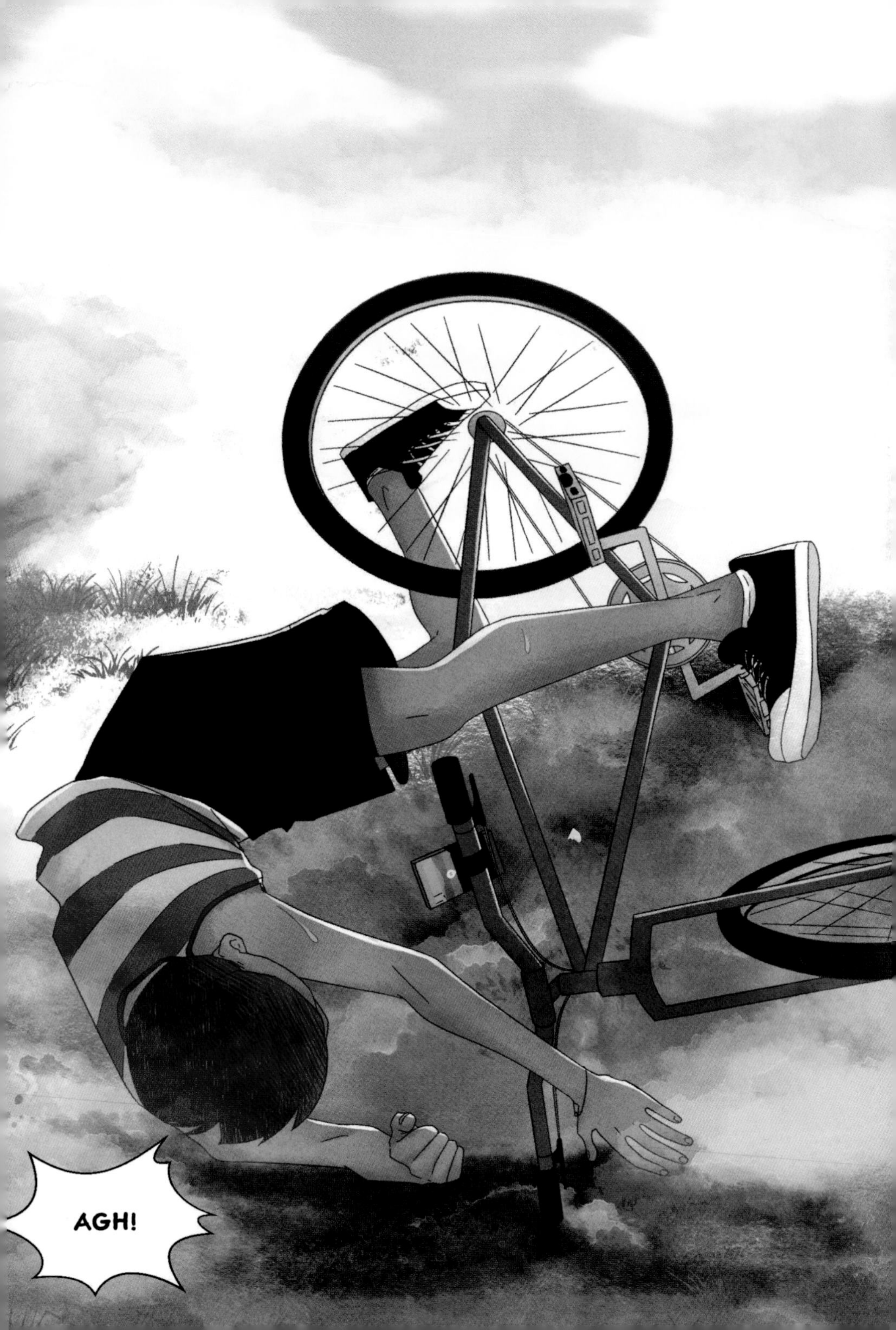
AGH!

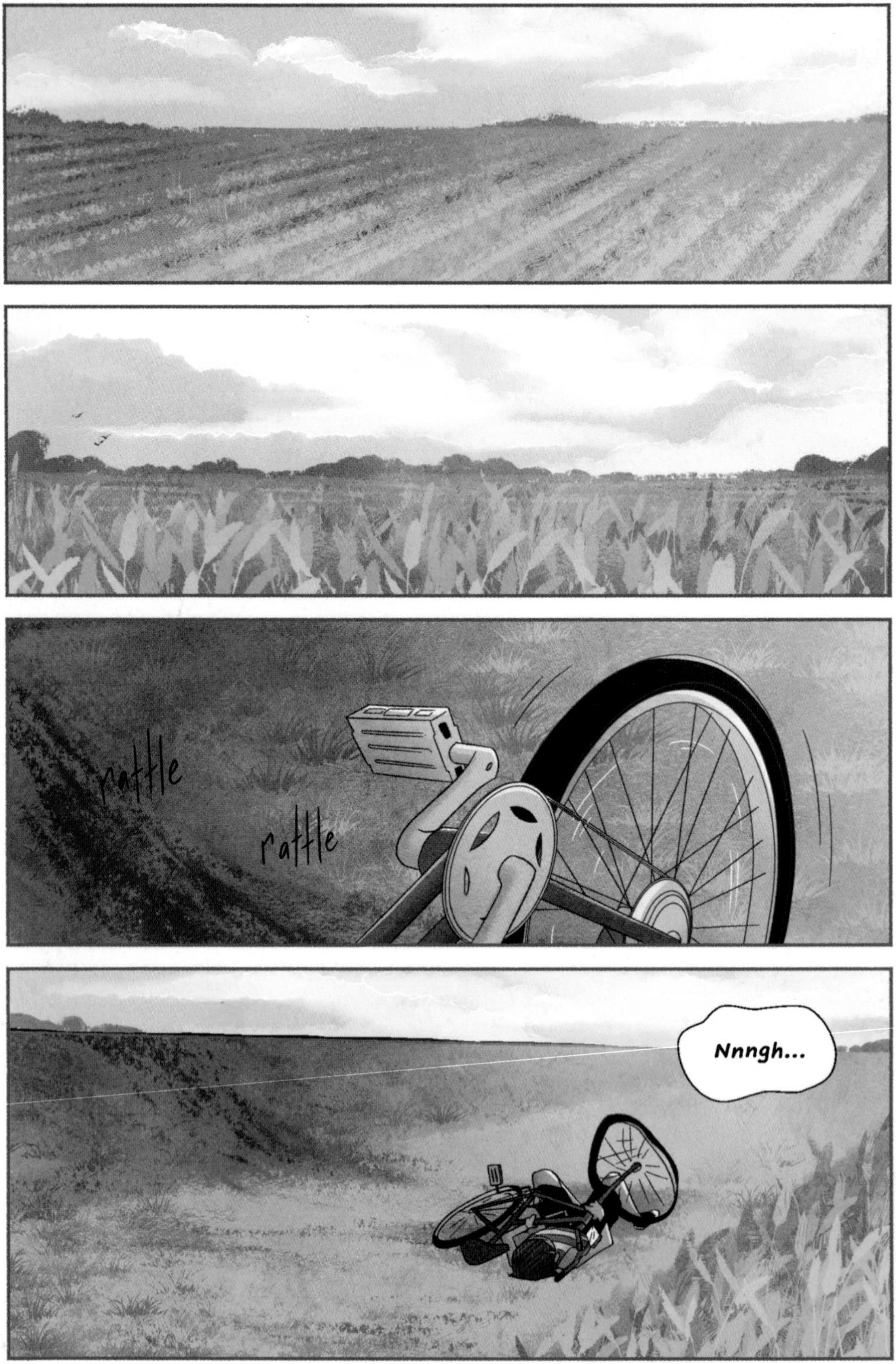
rattle
rattle
Nnngh...

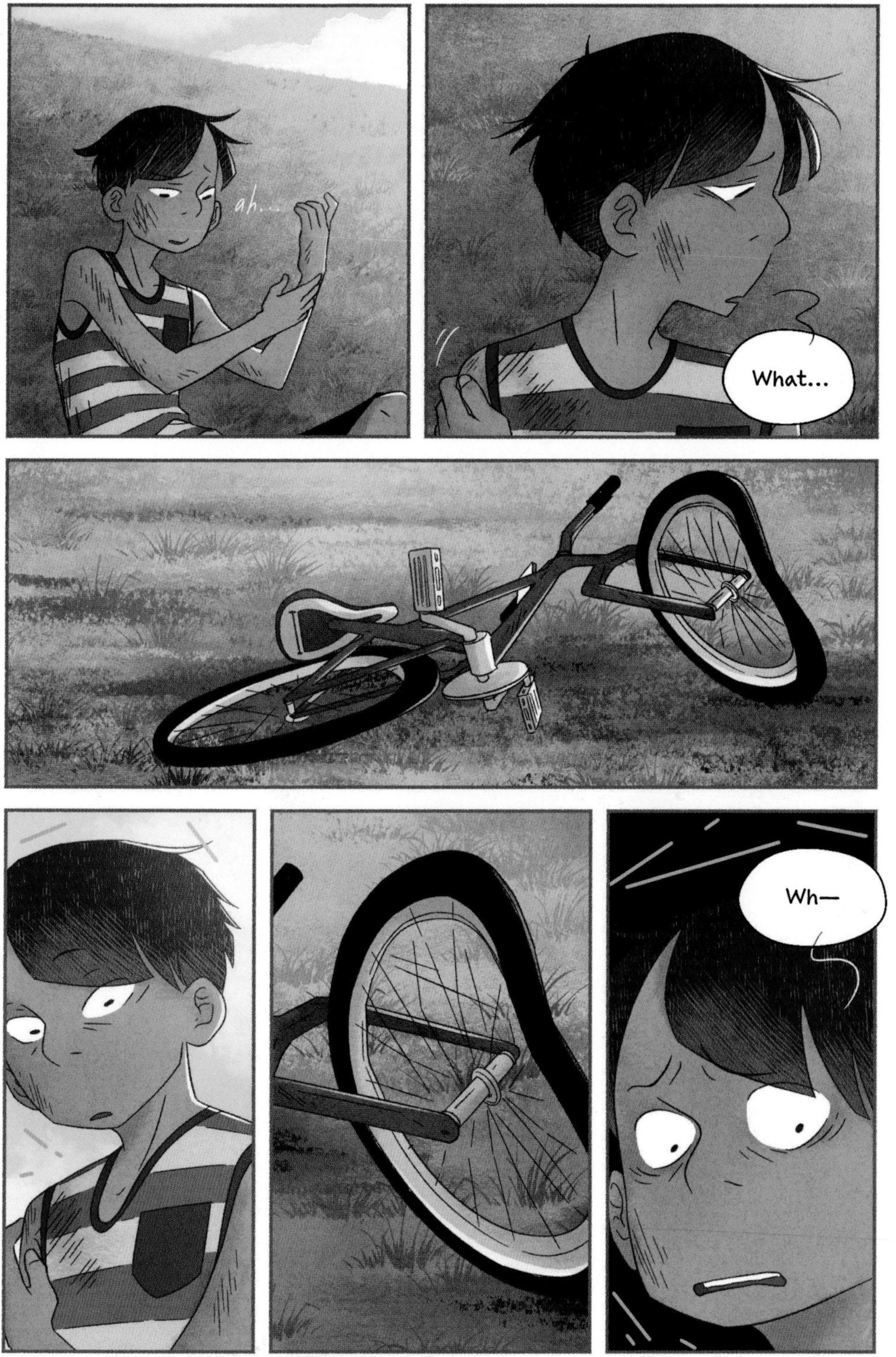
ah...
What...
Wh—

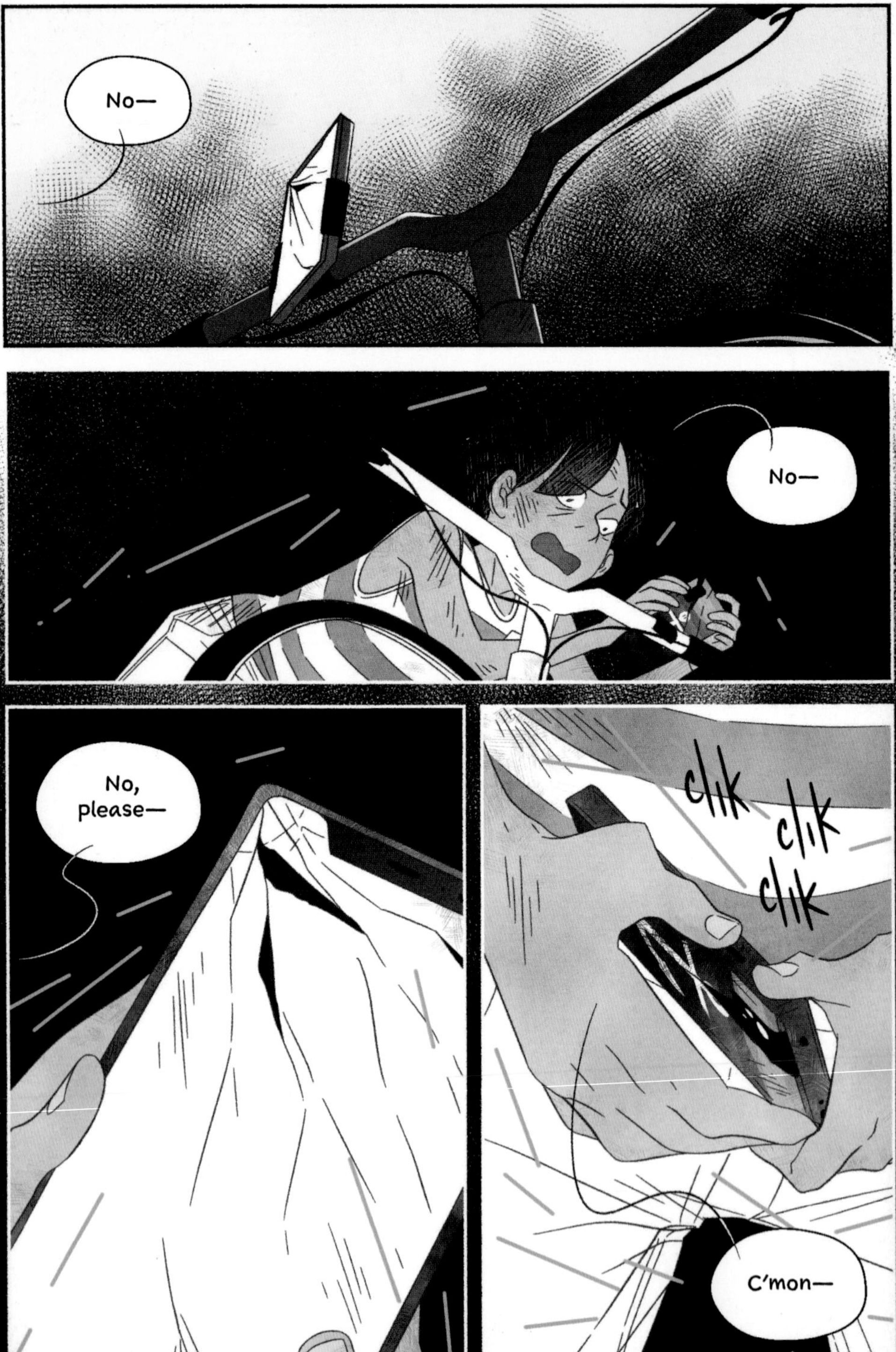
No—
No—
No, please—
clik
clik
clik
C'mon—

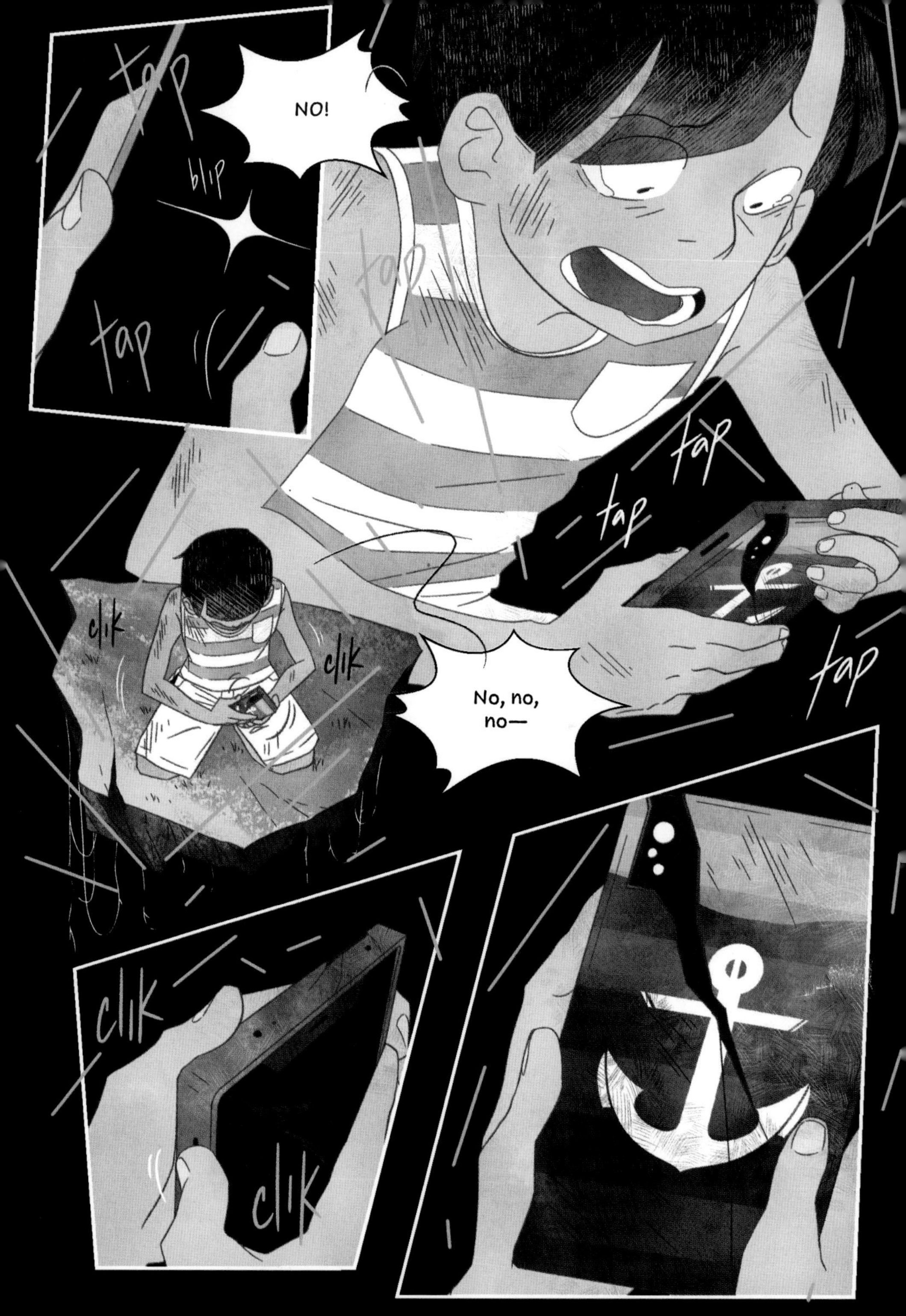

tap
blip
tap
NO!
tap
tap
tap
clik
clik
No, no,
no—
tap
clik
clik

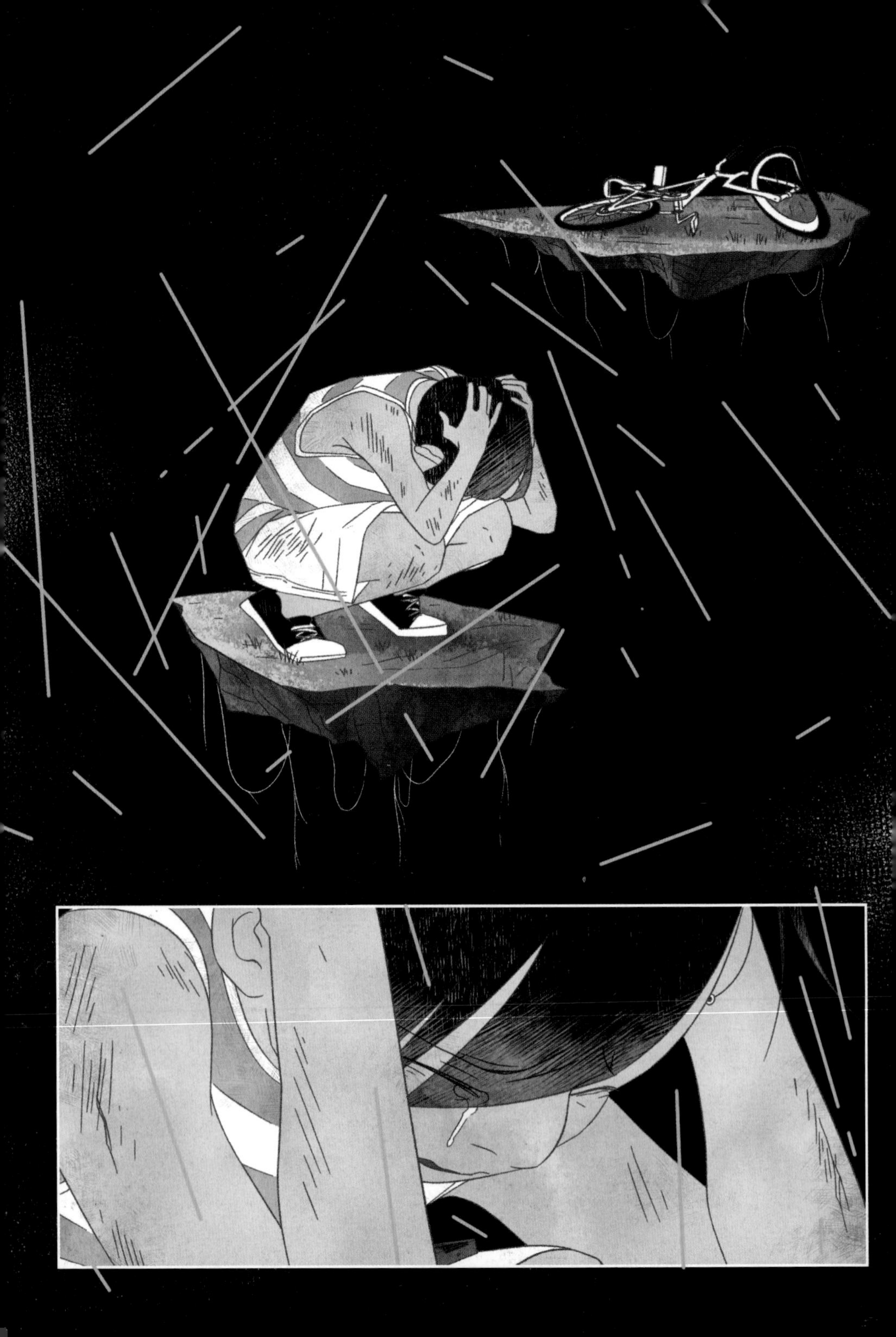

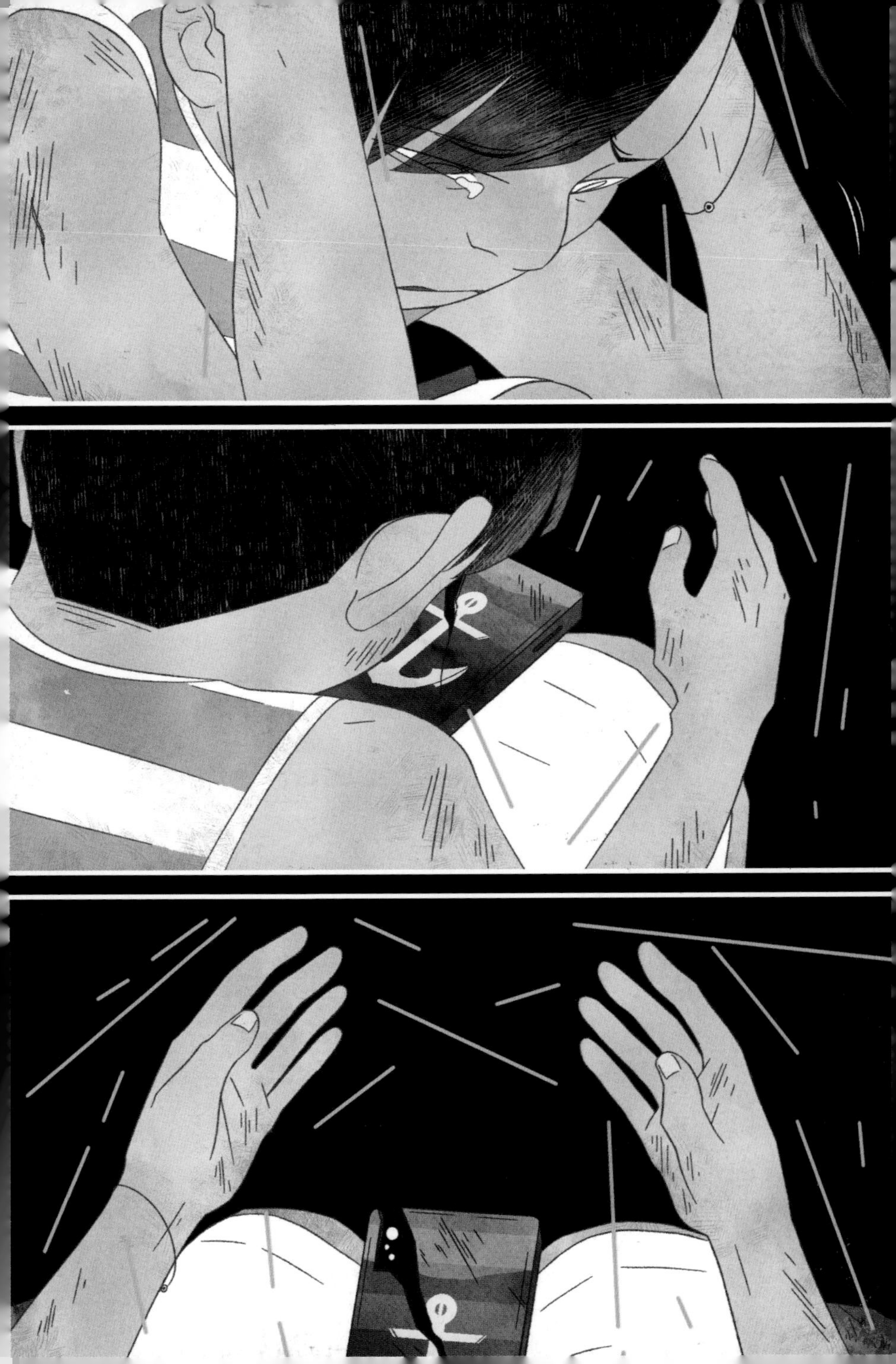

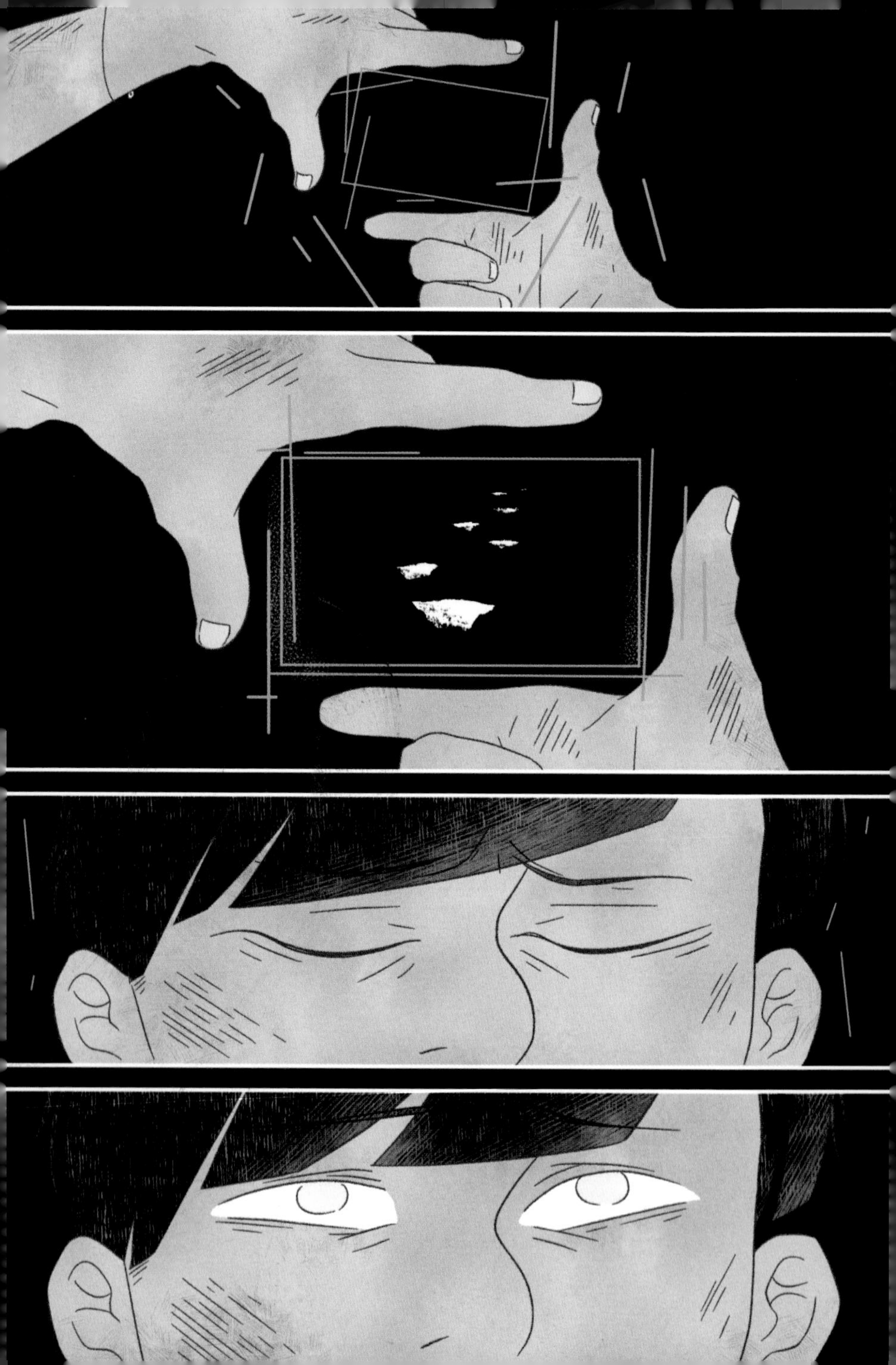

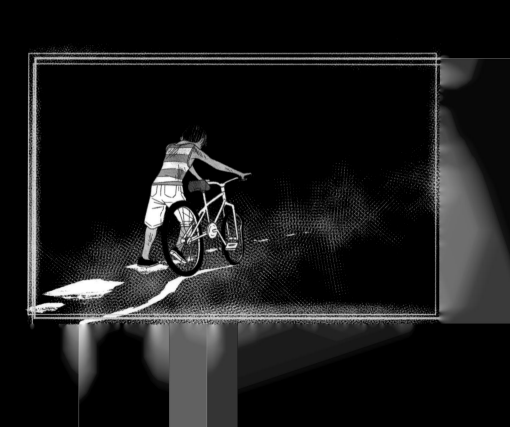

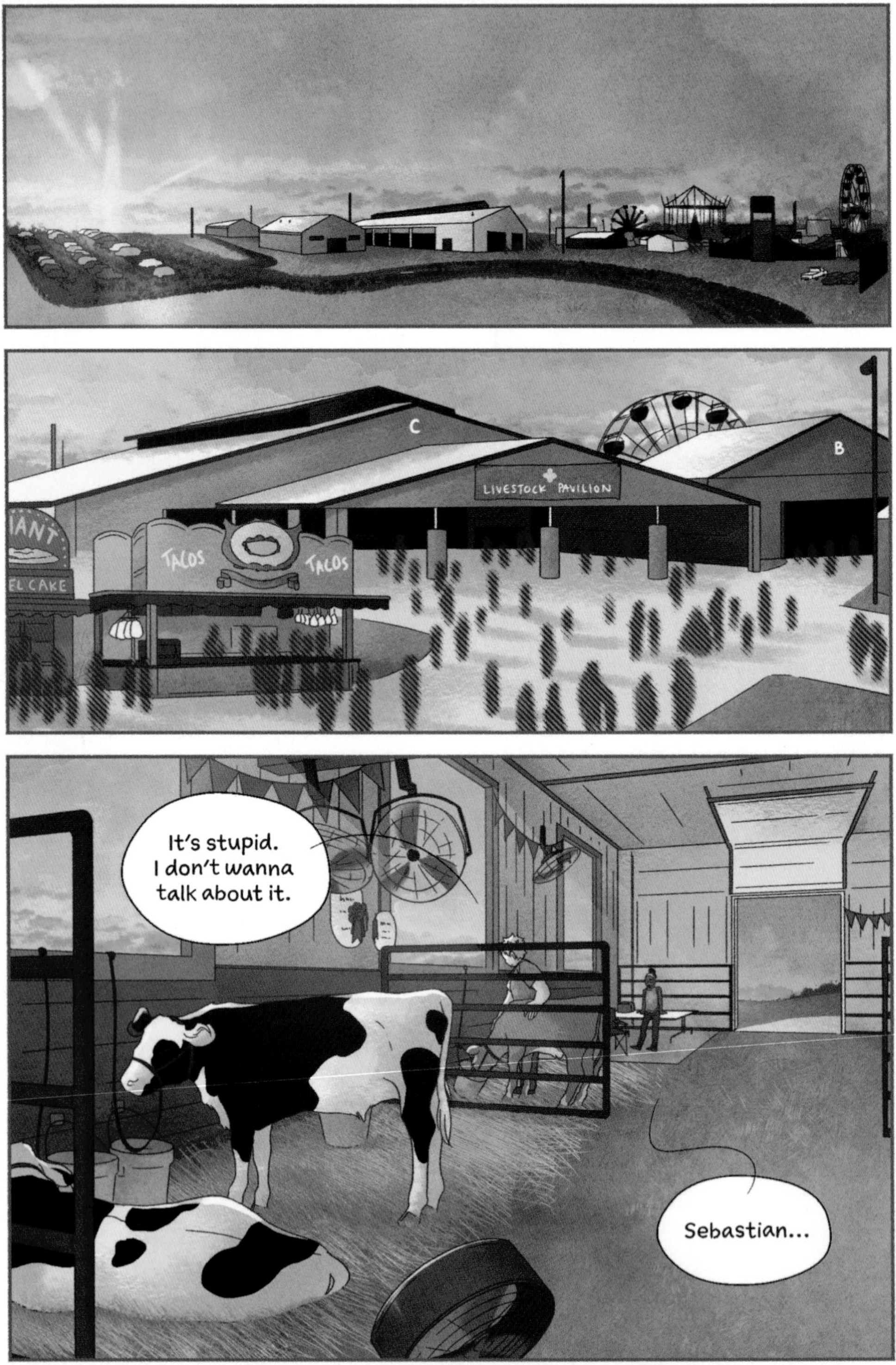
C
LIVESTOCK PAVILION
B
TACOS
TACOS
It's stupid. I don't wanna talk about it.
Sebastian...

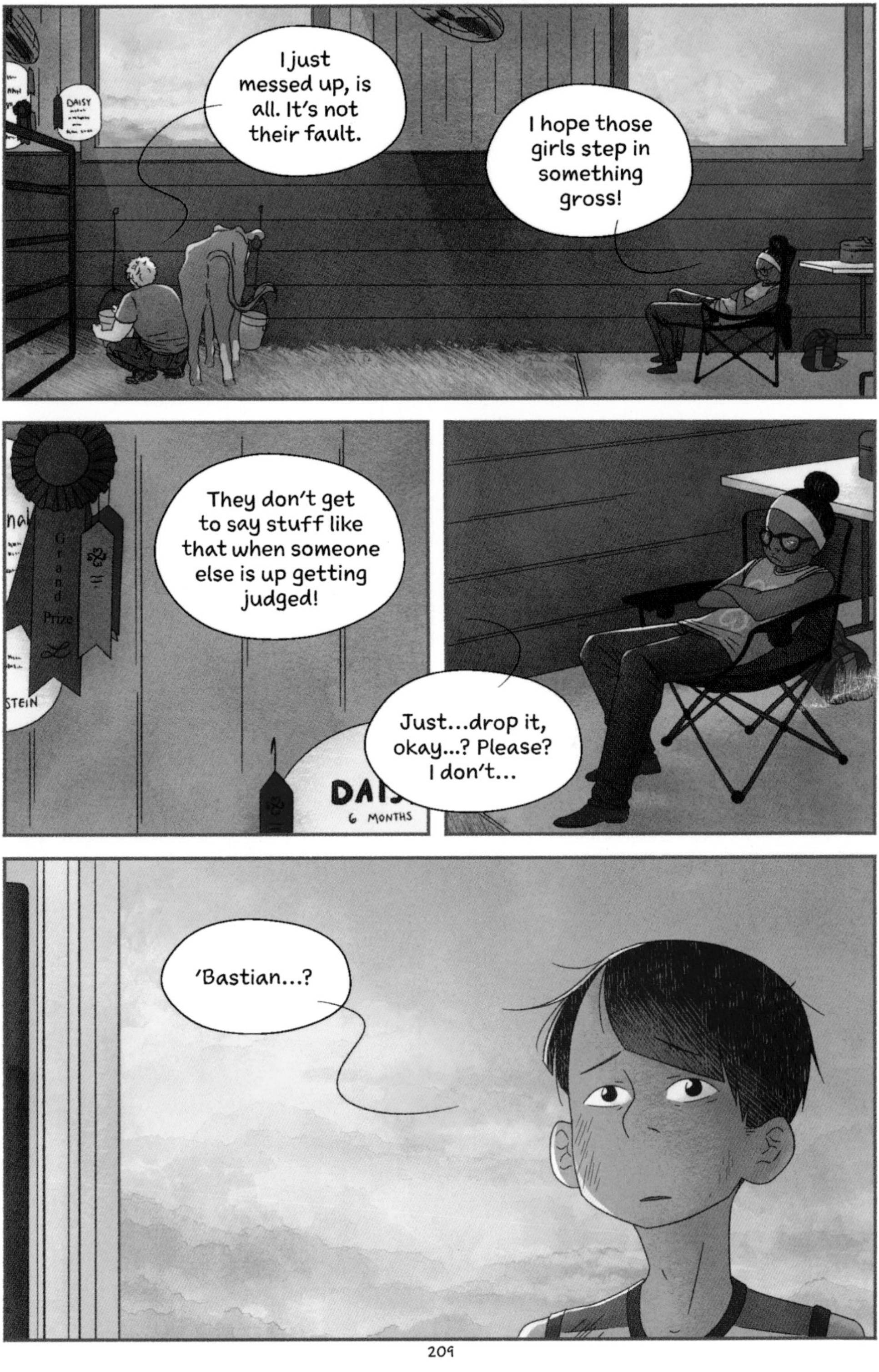

I just messed up, is all. It's not their fault.
I hope those girls step in something gross!
DAISY
Grand Prize
They don't get to say stuff like that when someone else is up getting judged!
6 MONTHS
Just...drop it, okay...? Please? I don't...
'Bastian...?

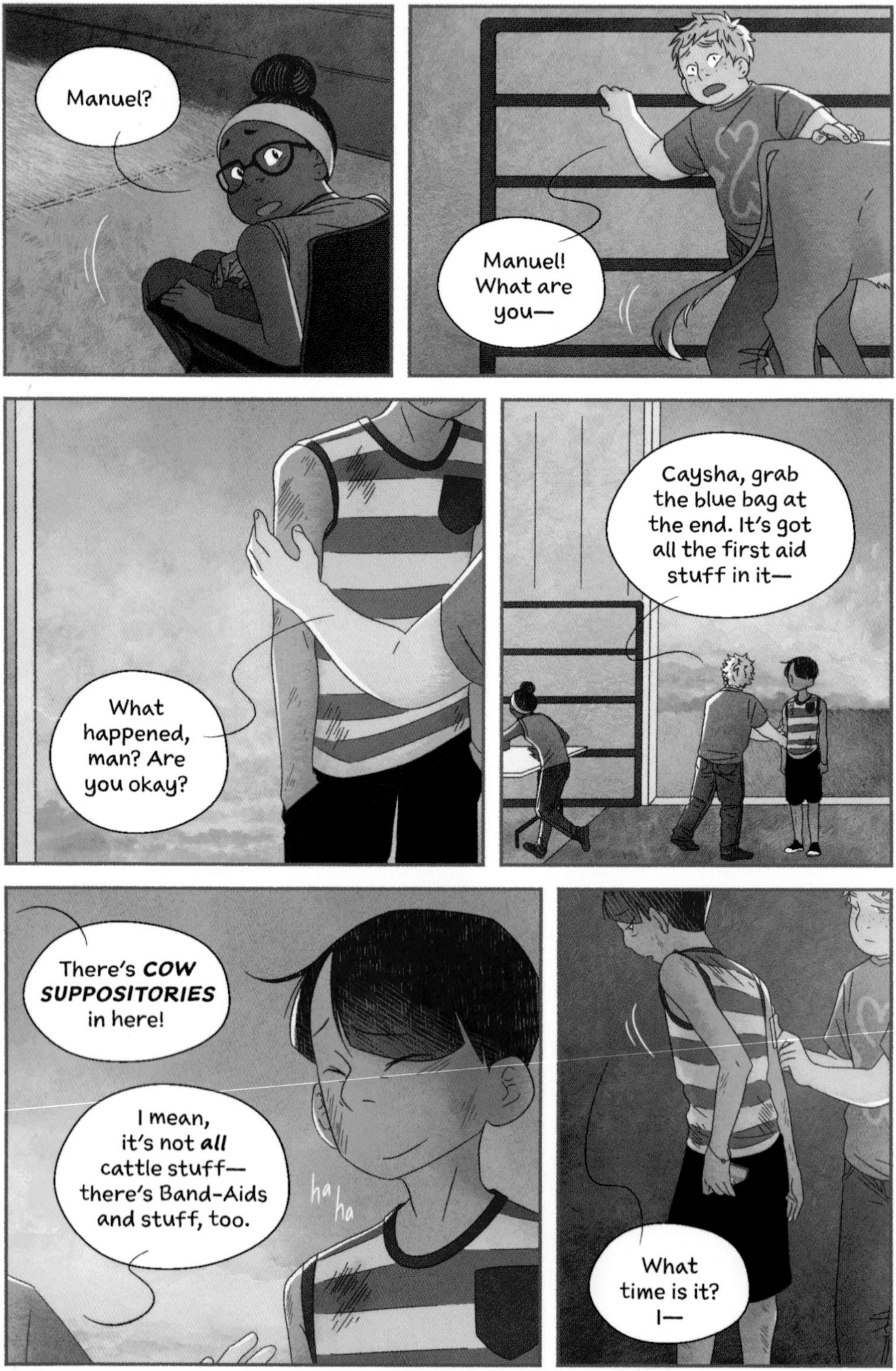
Manuel?
Manuel! What are you—
What happened, man? Are you okay?
Caysha, grab the blue bag at the end. It's got all the first aid stuff in it—
There's **COW SUPPOSITORIES** in here!
I mean, it's not ***all*** cattle stuff— there's Band-Aids and stuff, too.
ha ha
What time is it? I—

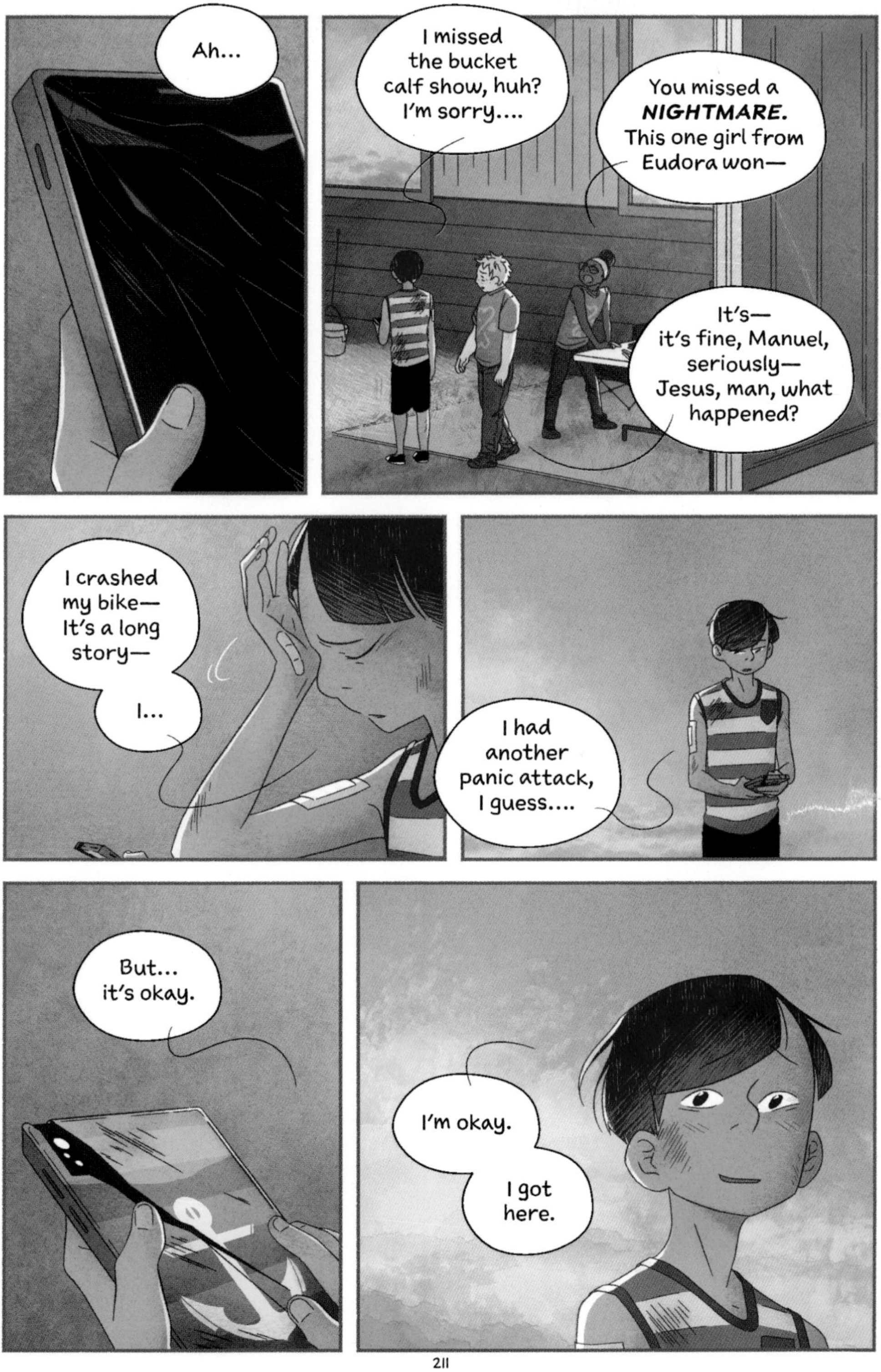
Ah...
I missed the bucket calf show, huh? I'm sorry....
You missed a ***NIGHTMARE.*** This one girl from Eudora won—
It's— it's fine, Manuel, seriously— Jesus, man, what happened?
I crashed my bike— It's a long story—
I...
I had another panic attack, I guess....
But... it's okay.
I'm okay.
I got here.

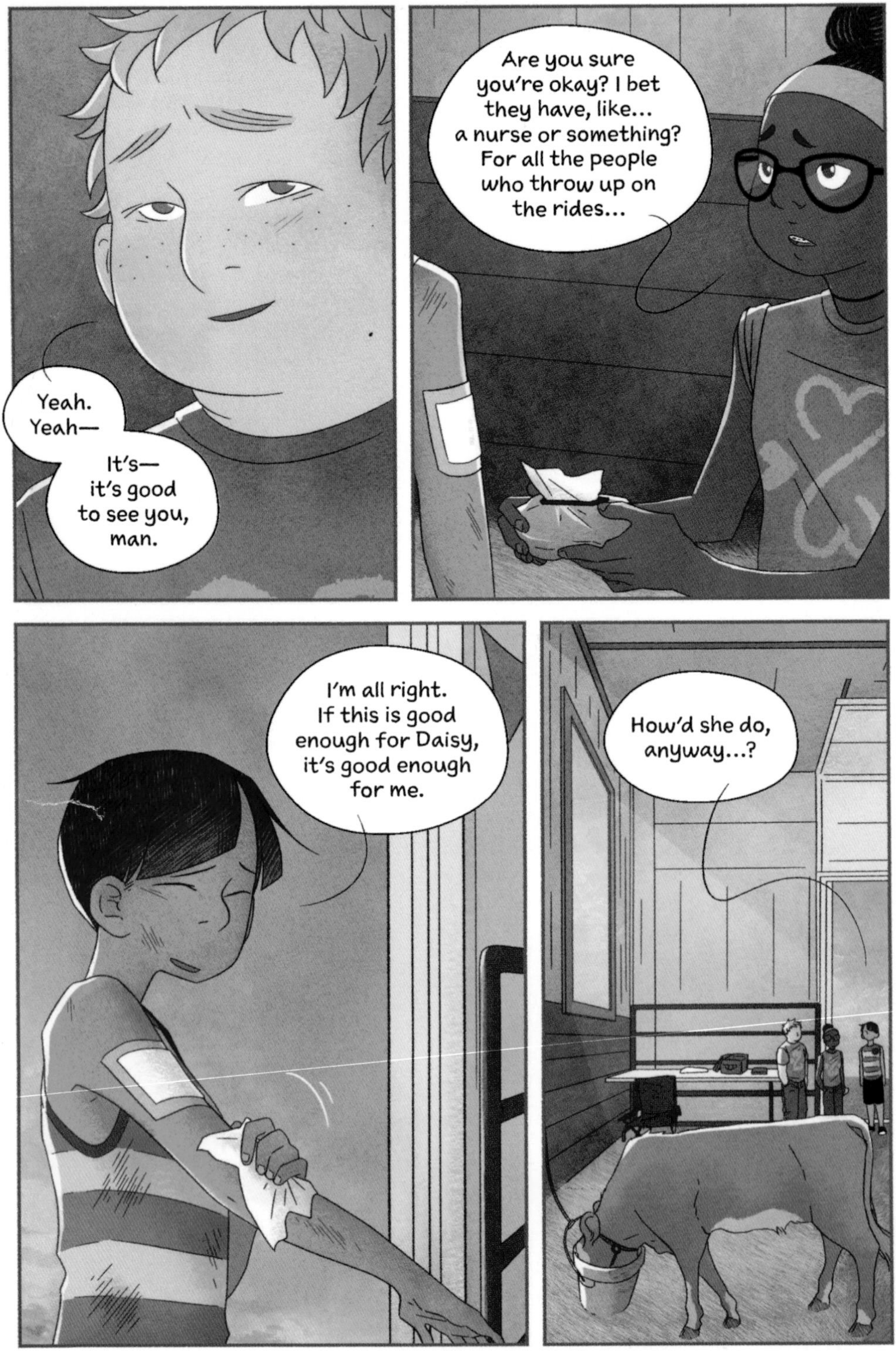
Yeah. Yeah—
It's— it's good to see you, man.
Are you sure you're okay? I bet they have, like… a nurse or something? For all the people who throw up on the rides…
I'm all right. If this is good enough for Daisy, it's good enough for me.
How'd she do, anyway…?

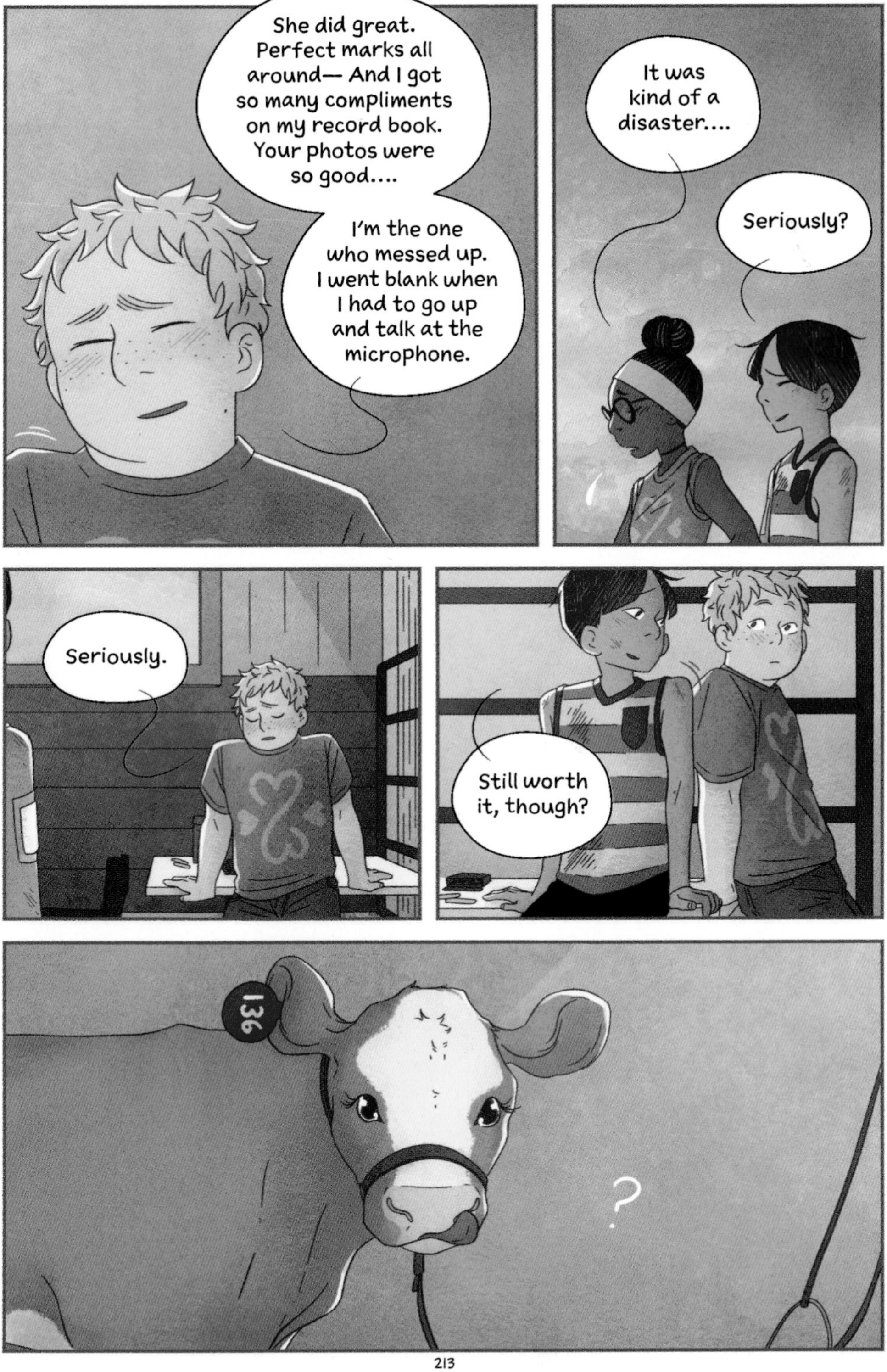
She did great. Perfect marks all around— And I got so many compliments on my record book. Your photos were so good....
I'm the one who messed up. I went blank when I had to go up and talk at the microphone.
It was kind of a disaster....
Seriously?
Seriously.
Still worth it, though?
136
?

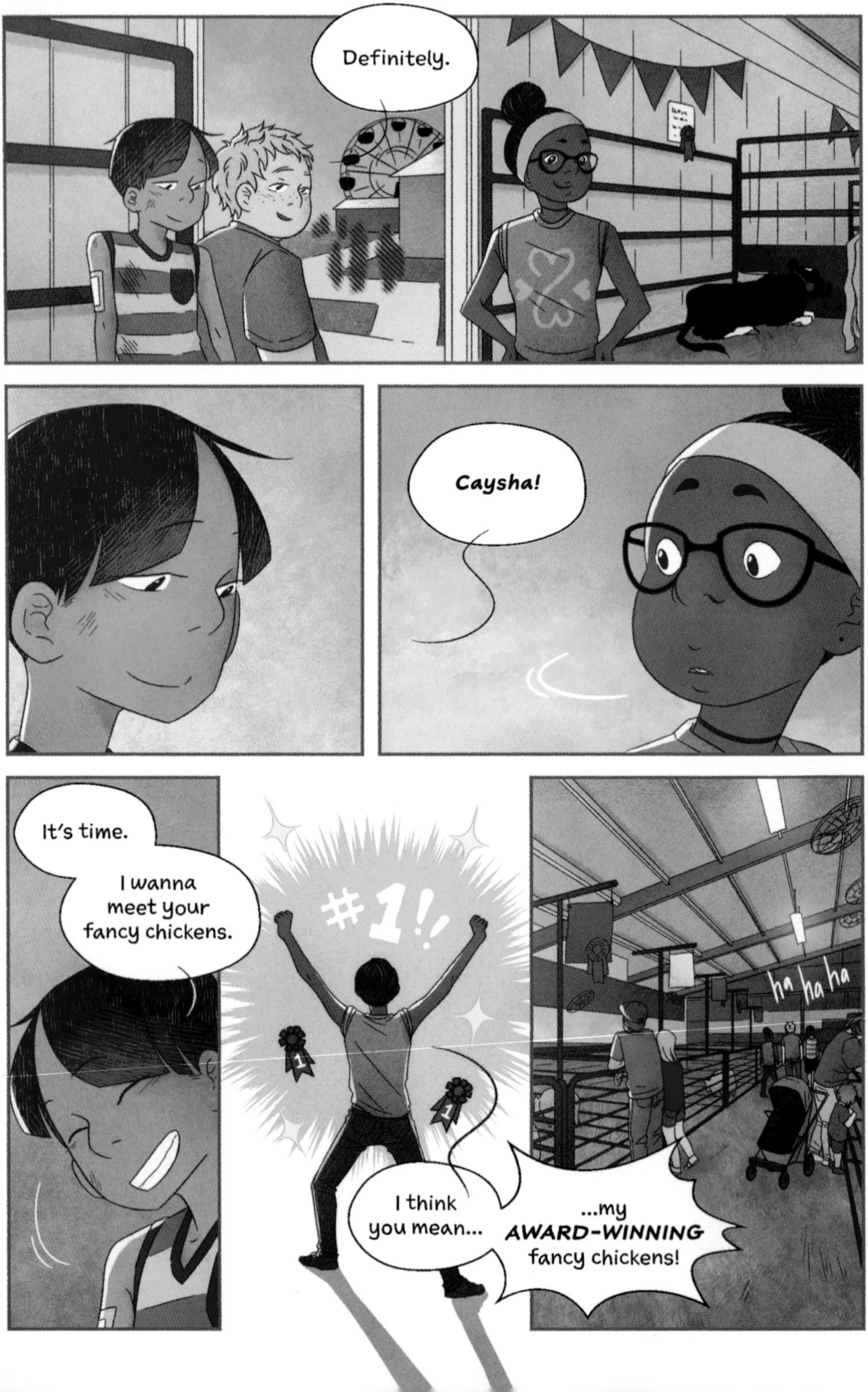
Definitely.
Caysha!
It's time.
I wanna meet your fancy chickens.
#1!!
I think you mean...
...my AWARD-WINNING fancy chickens!
ha ha ha

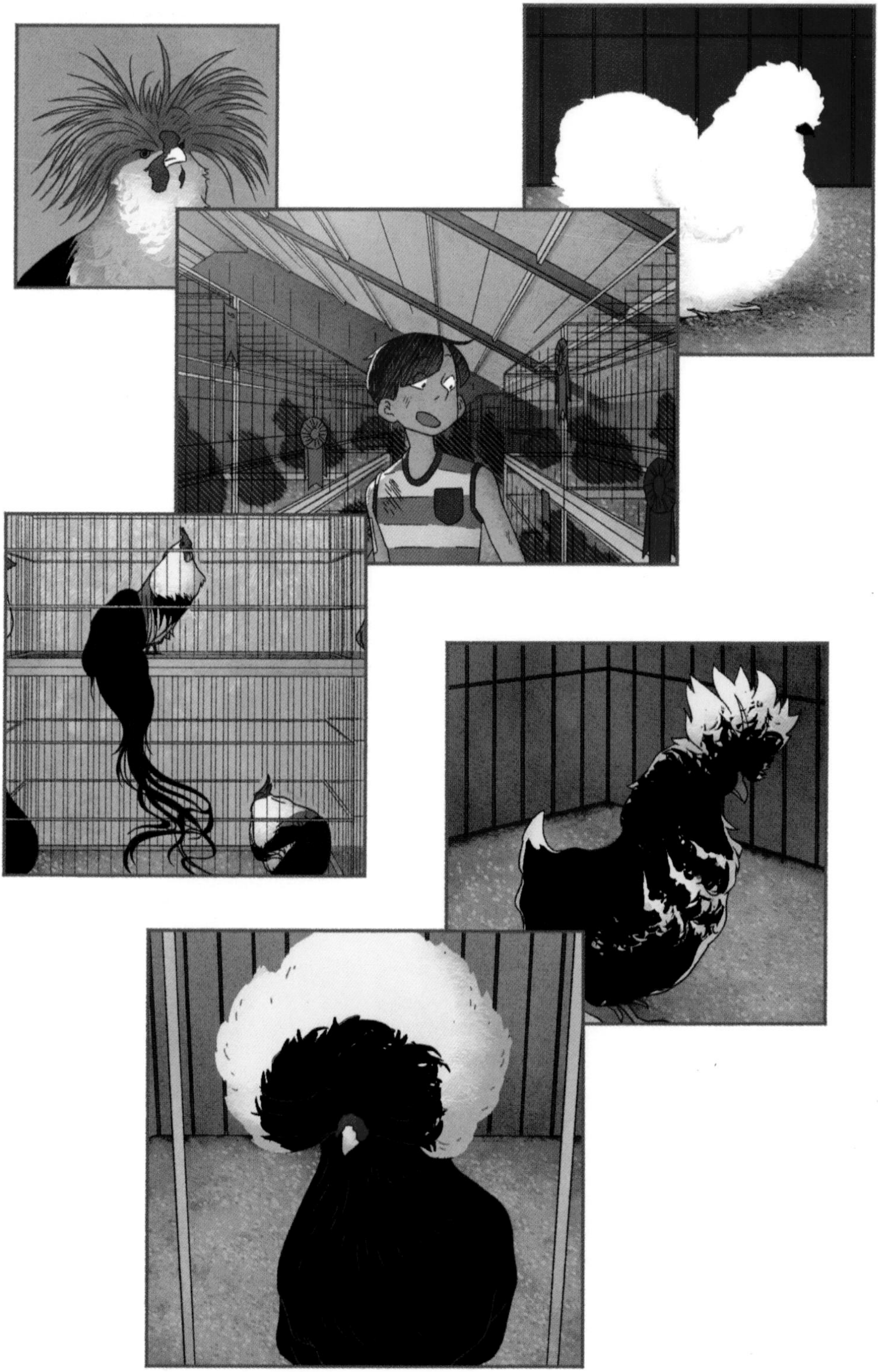

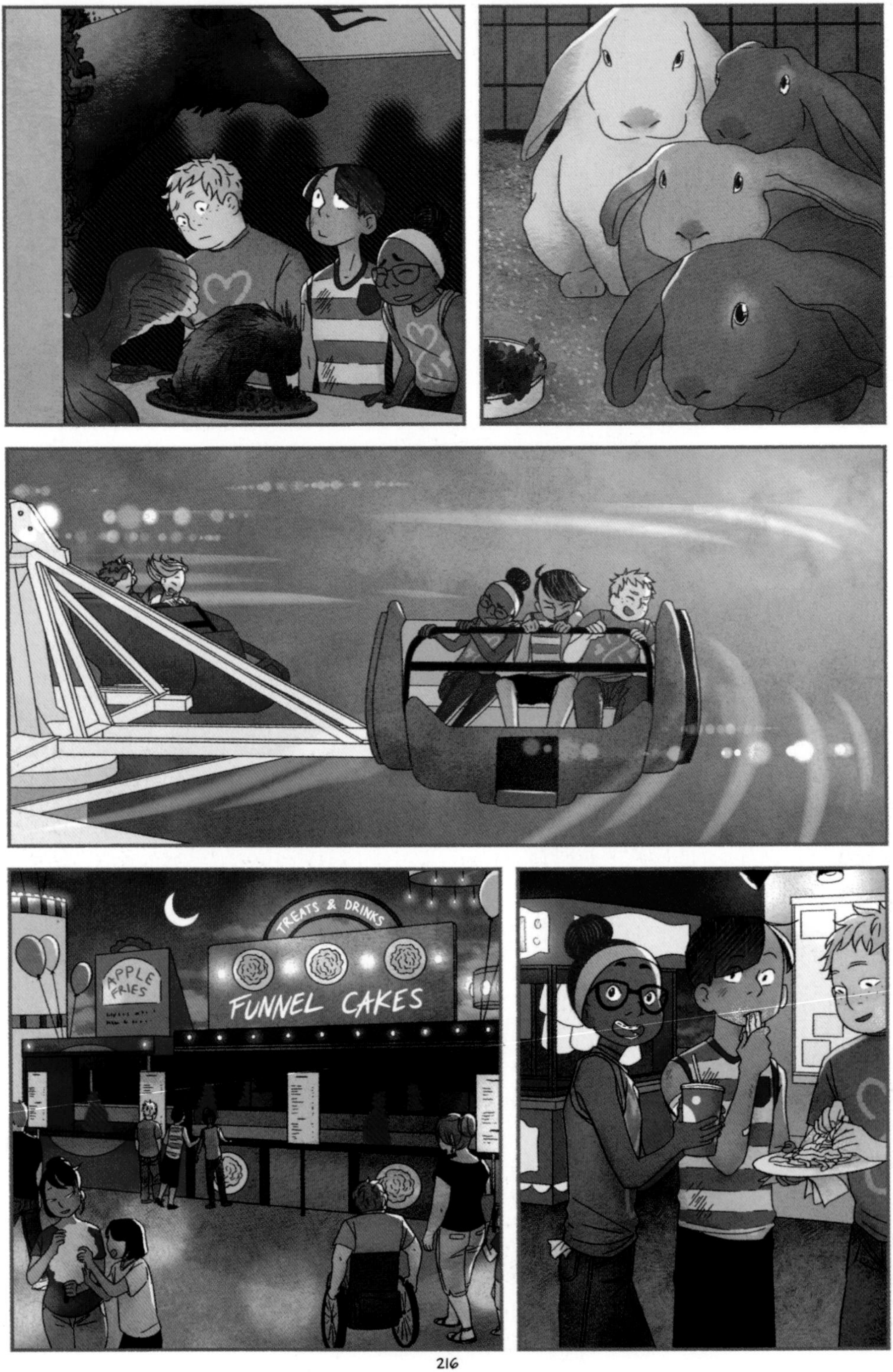
TREATS & DRINKS
APPLE FRIES
FUNNEL CAKES

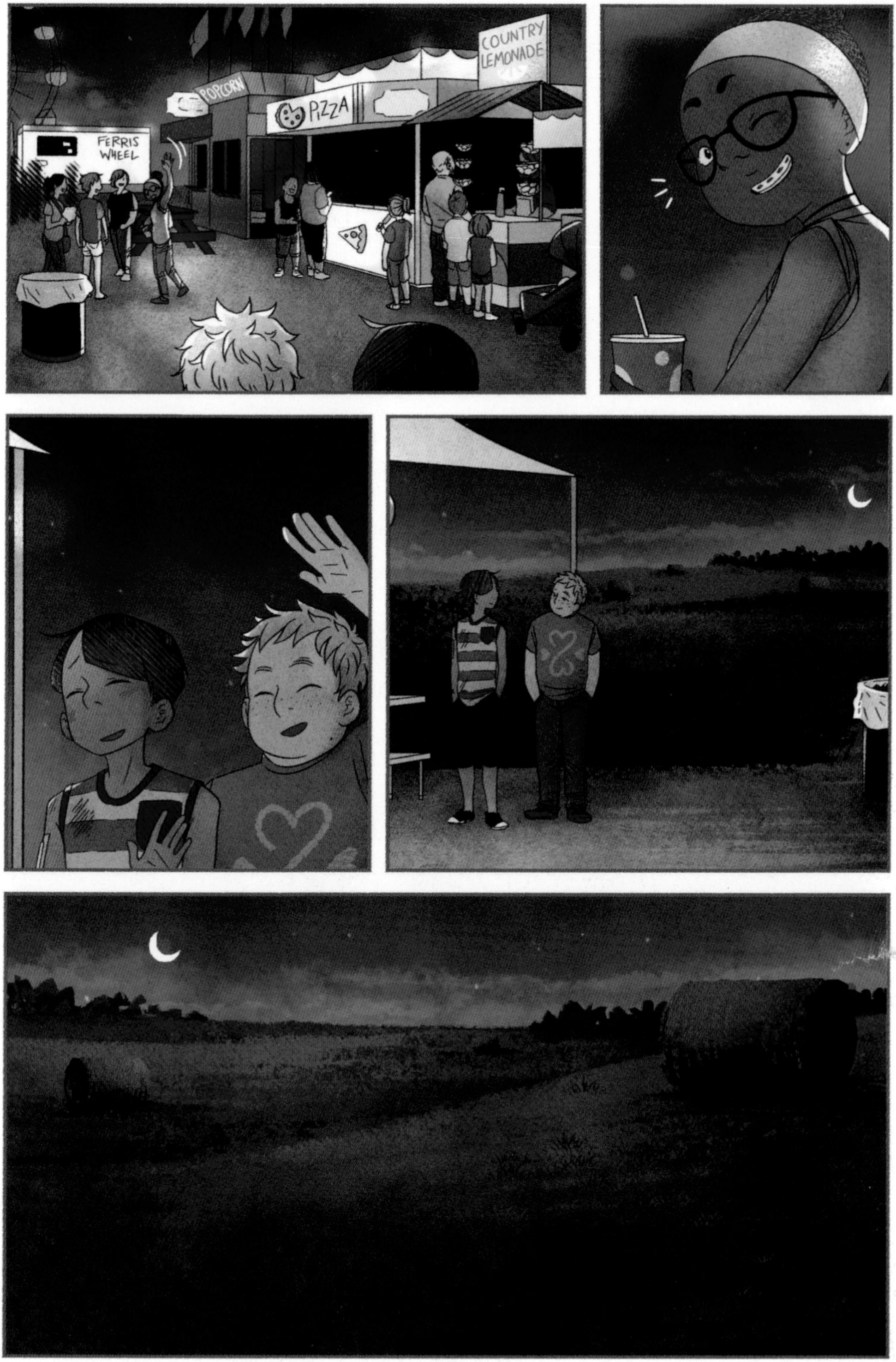
COUNTRY LEMONADE
POPCORN
PIZZA
FERRIS WHEEL

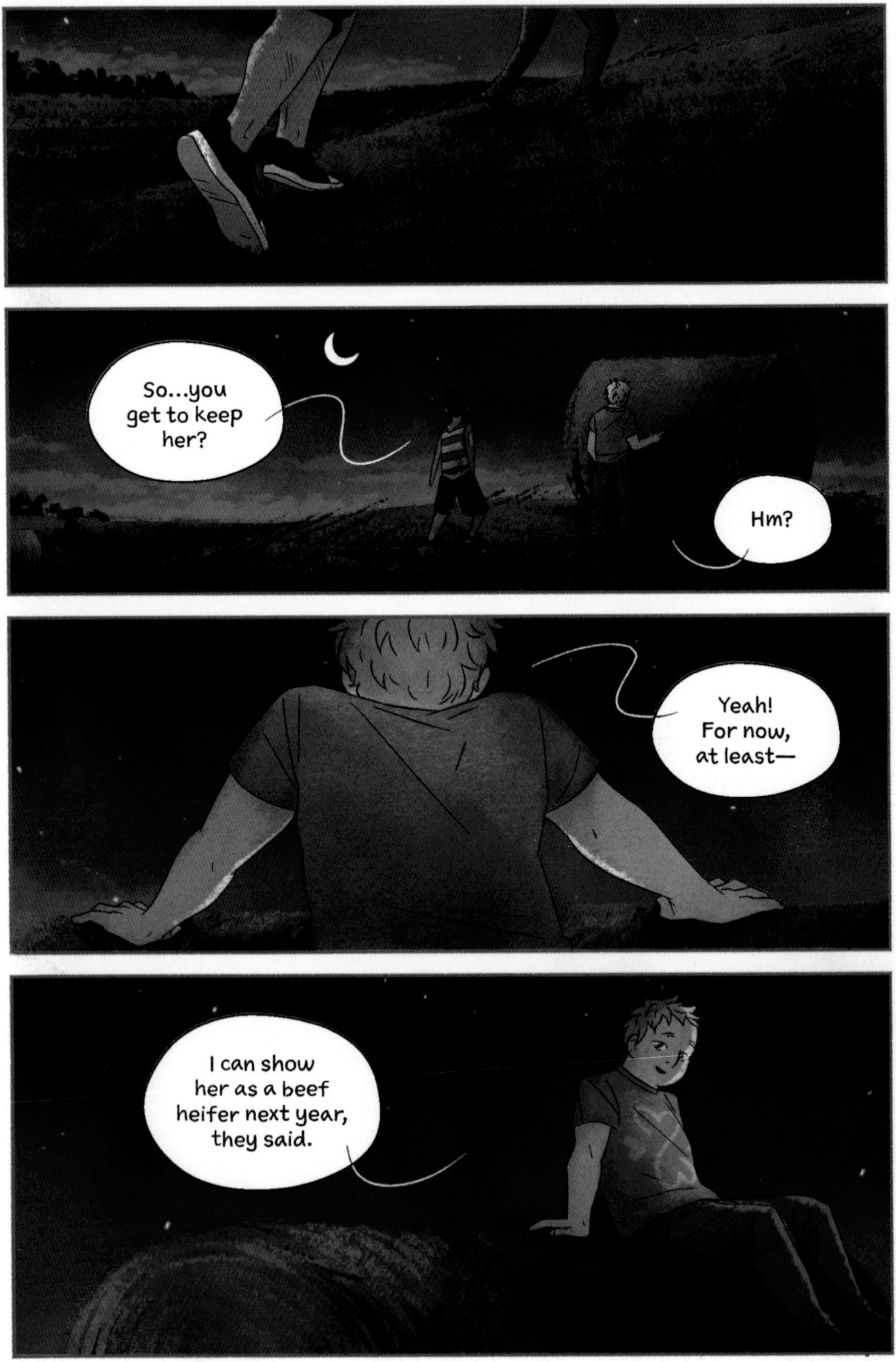
So...you get to keep her?
Hm?
Yeah! For now, at least—
I can show her as a beef heifer next year, they said.

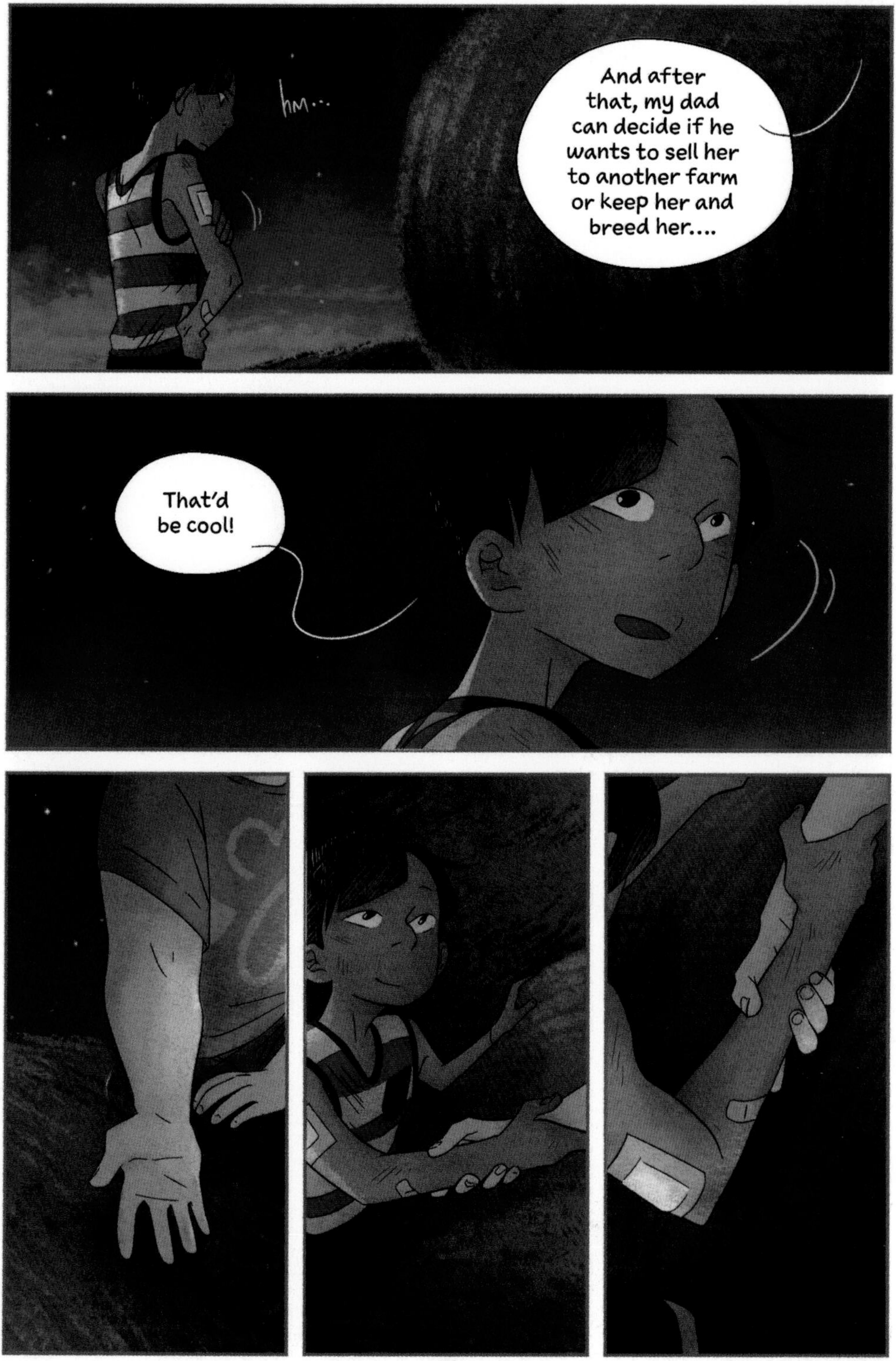
hm...
And after that, my dad can decide if he wants to sell her to another farm or keep her and breed her....
That'd be cool!

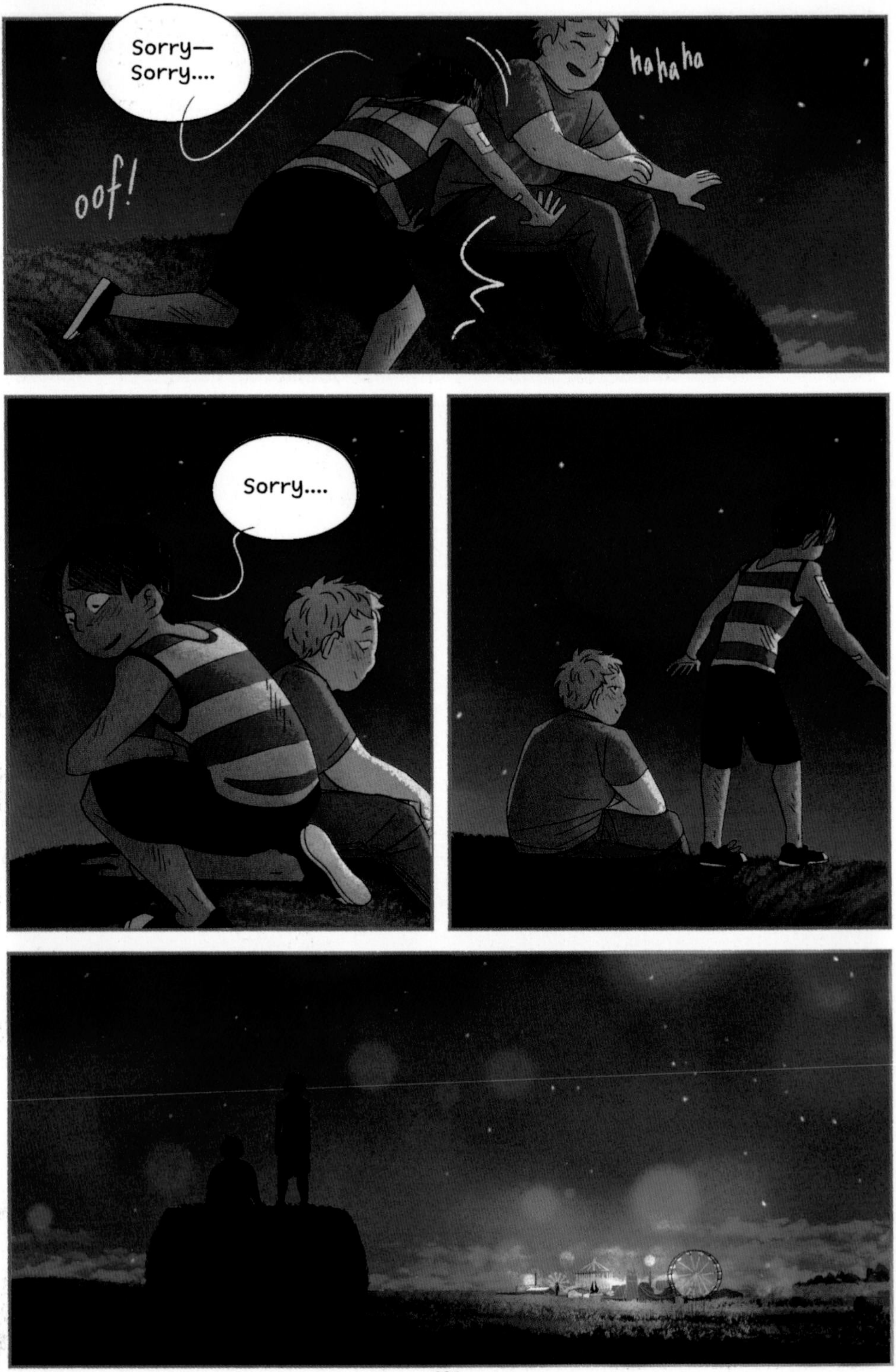
Sorry—
Sorry....
haha ha
oof!
Sorry....

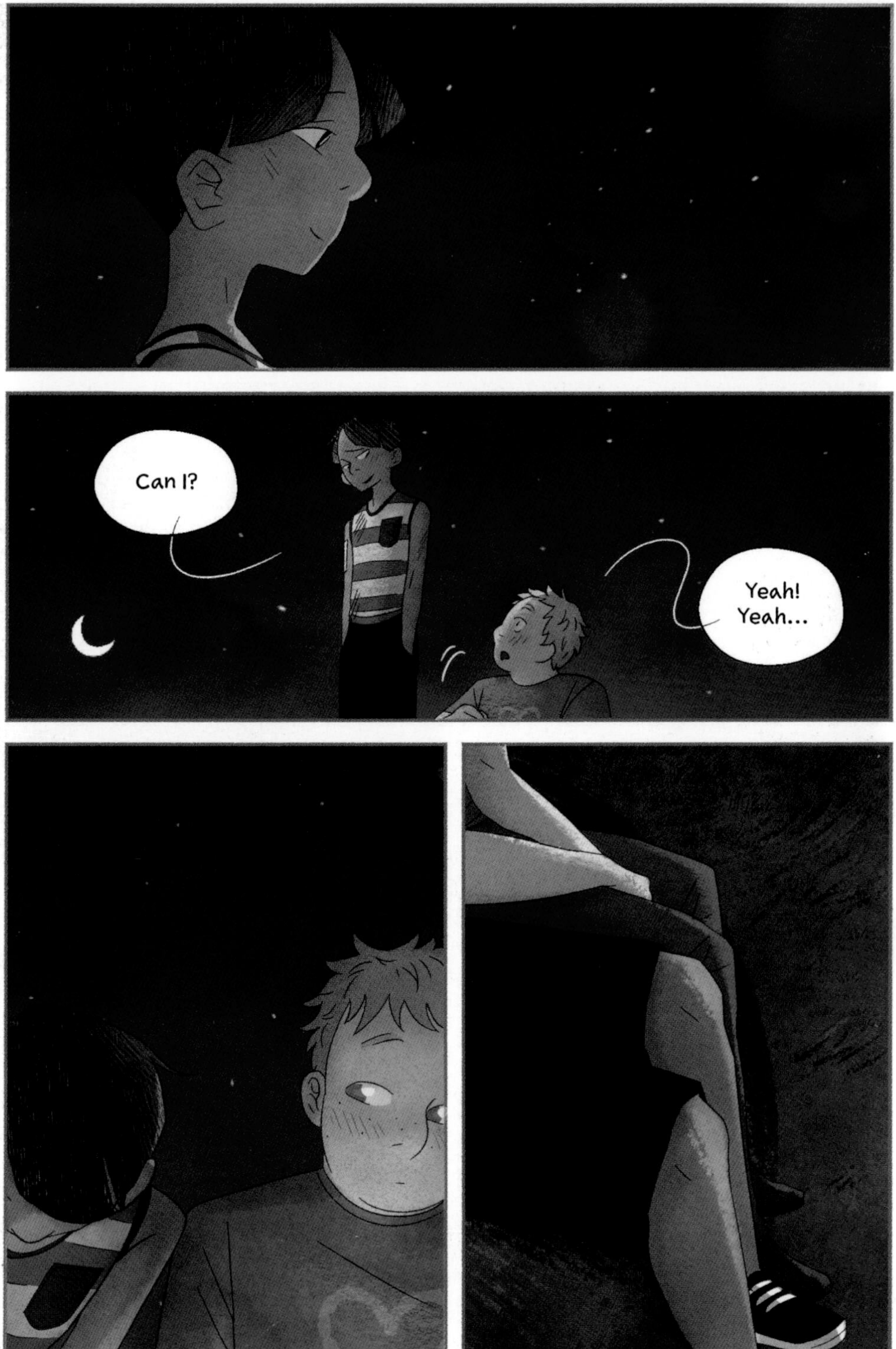
Can I?
Yeah!
Yeah...

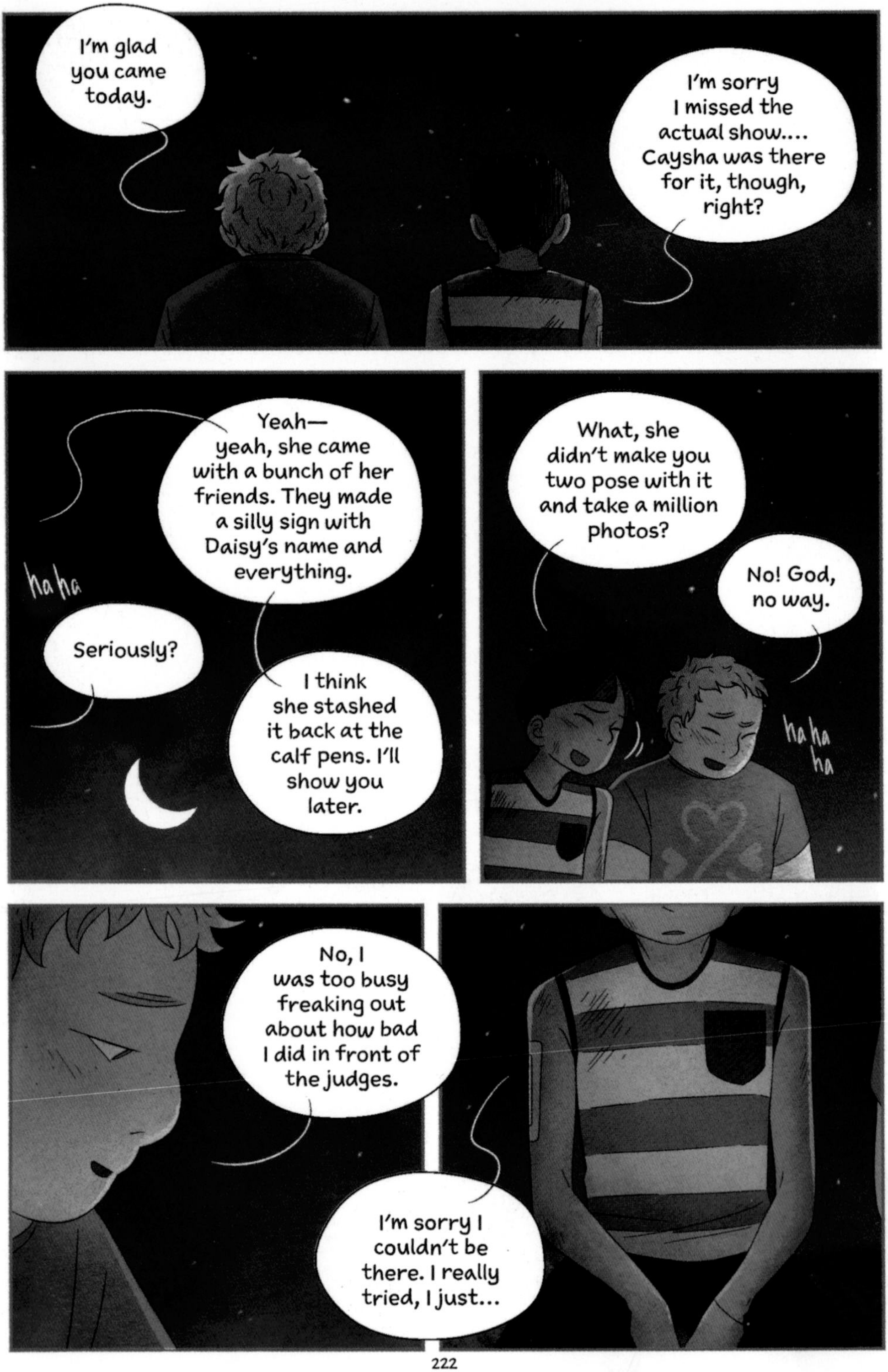
I'm glad you came today.
I'm sorry I missed the actual show…. Caysha was there for it, though, right?
Yeah— yeah, she came with a bunch of her friends. They made a silly sign with Daisy's name and everything.
ha ha
Seriously?
I think she stashed it back at the calf pens. I'll show you later.
What, she didn't make you two pose with it and take a million photos?
No! God, no way.
ha ha ha
No, I was too busy freaking out about how bad I did in front of the judges.
I'm sorry I couldn't be there. I really tried, I just…

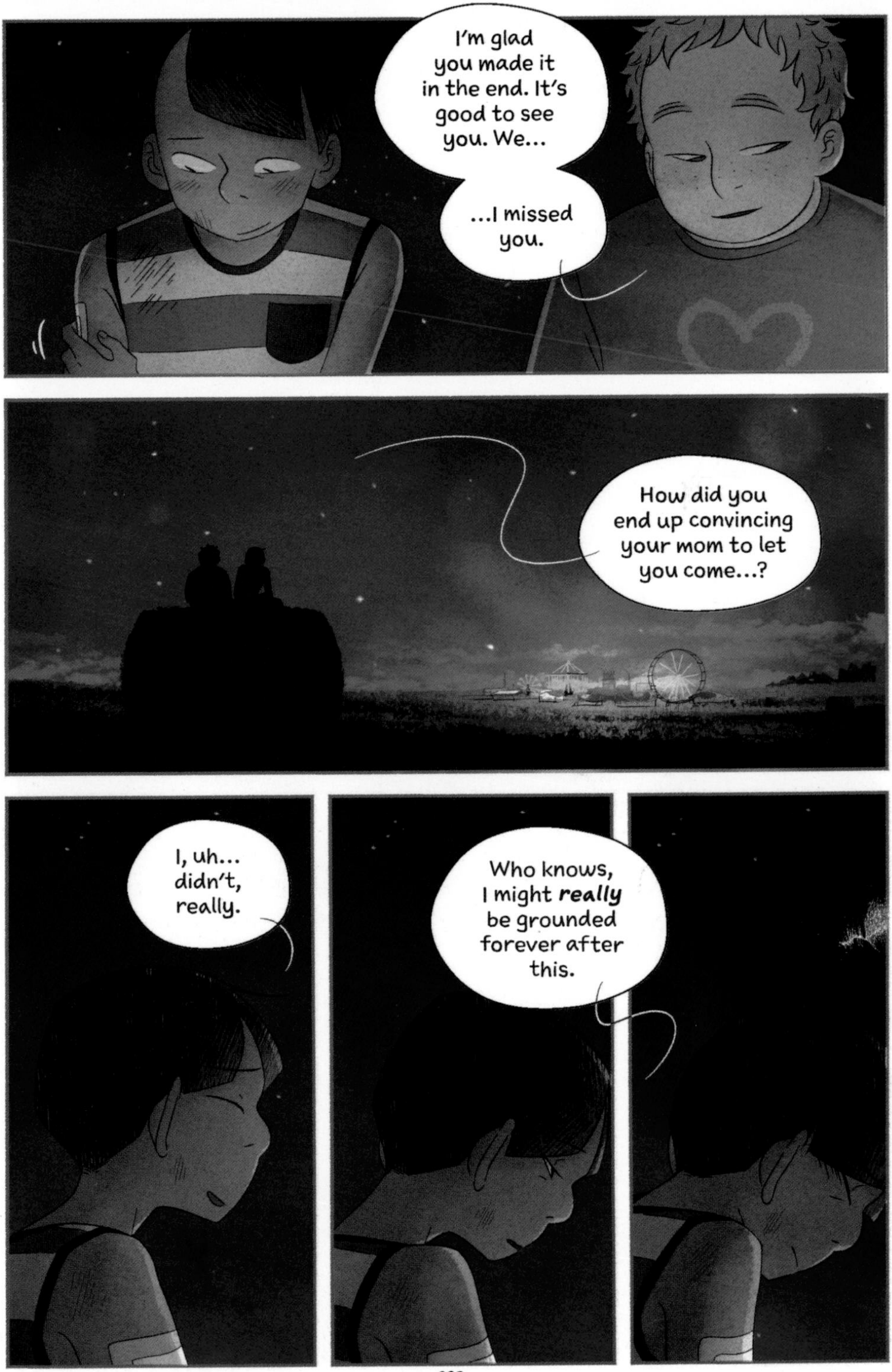
I'm glad you made it in the end. It's good to see you. We...
...I missed you.
How did you end up convincing your mom to let you come...?
I, uh... didn't, really.
Who knows, I might **really** be grounded forever after this.

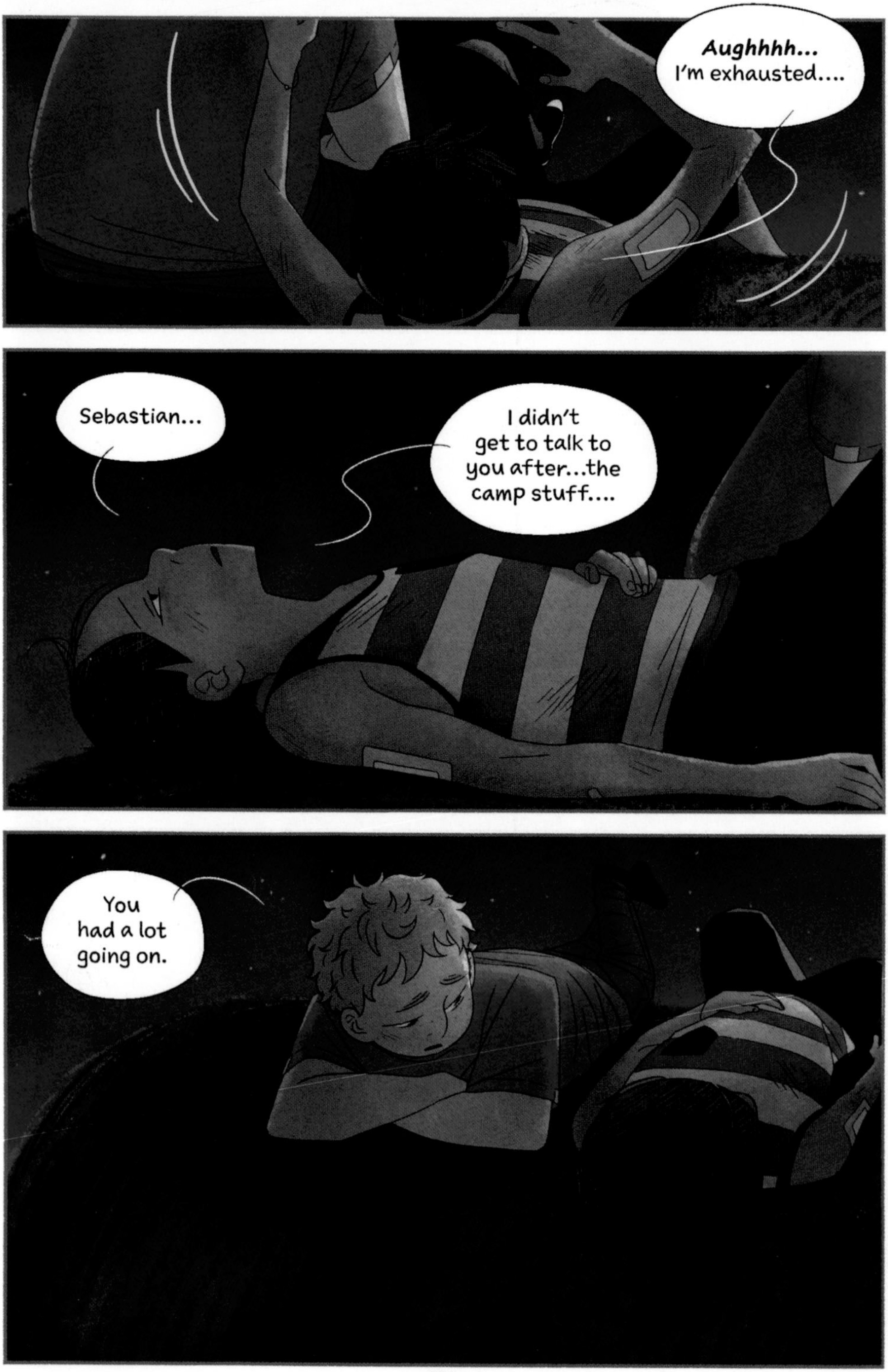
Aughhhh...
I'm exhausted....
Sebastian...
I didn't get to talk to you after...the camp stuff....
You had a lot going on.

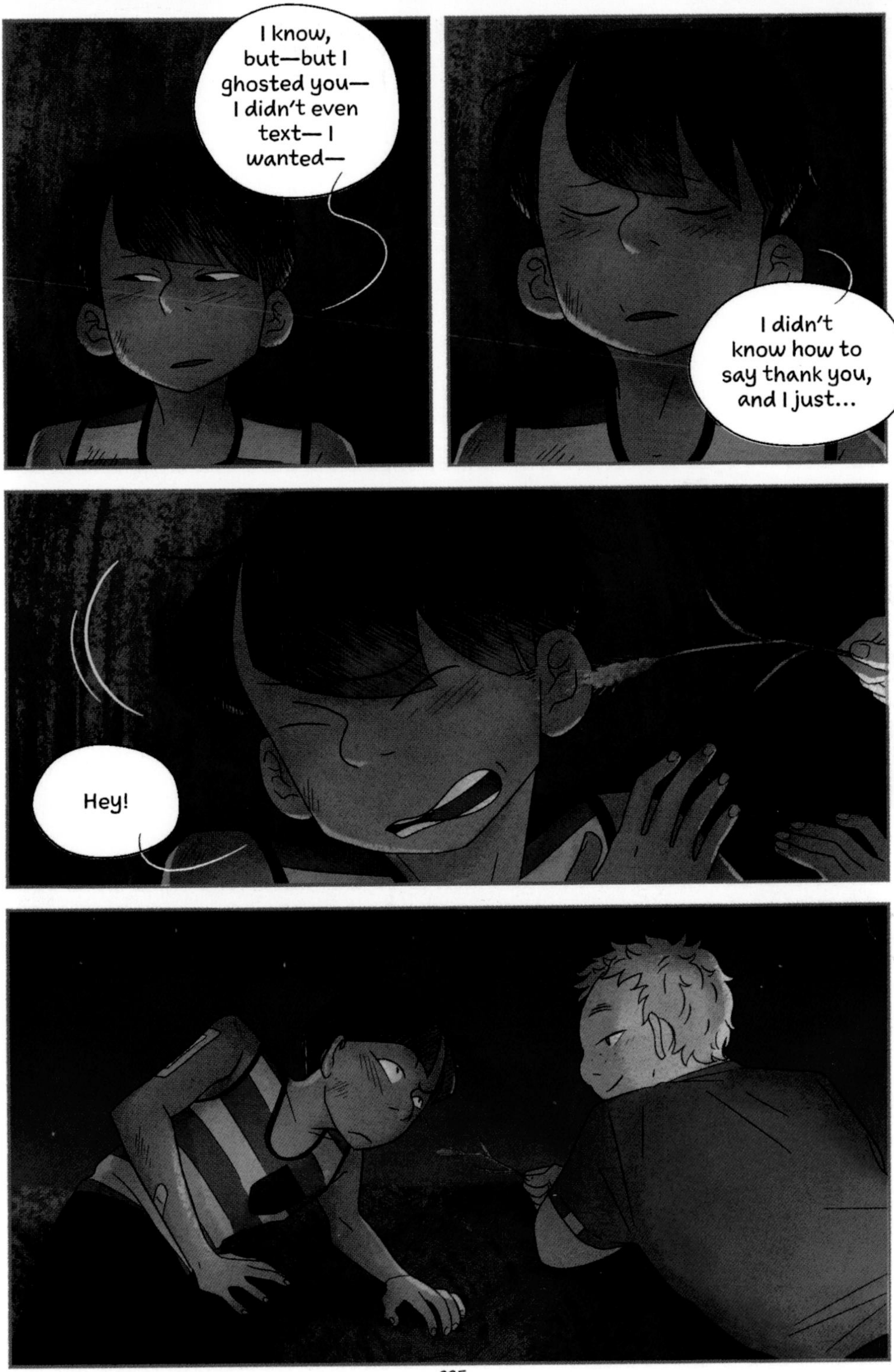
I know, but—but I ghosted you— I didn't even text— I wanted—
I didn't know how to say thank you, and I just...
Hey!

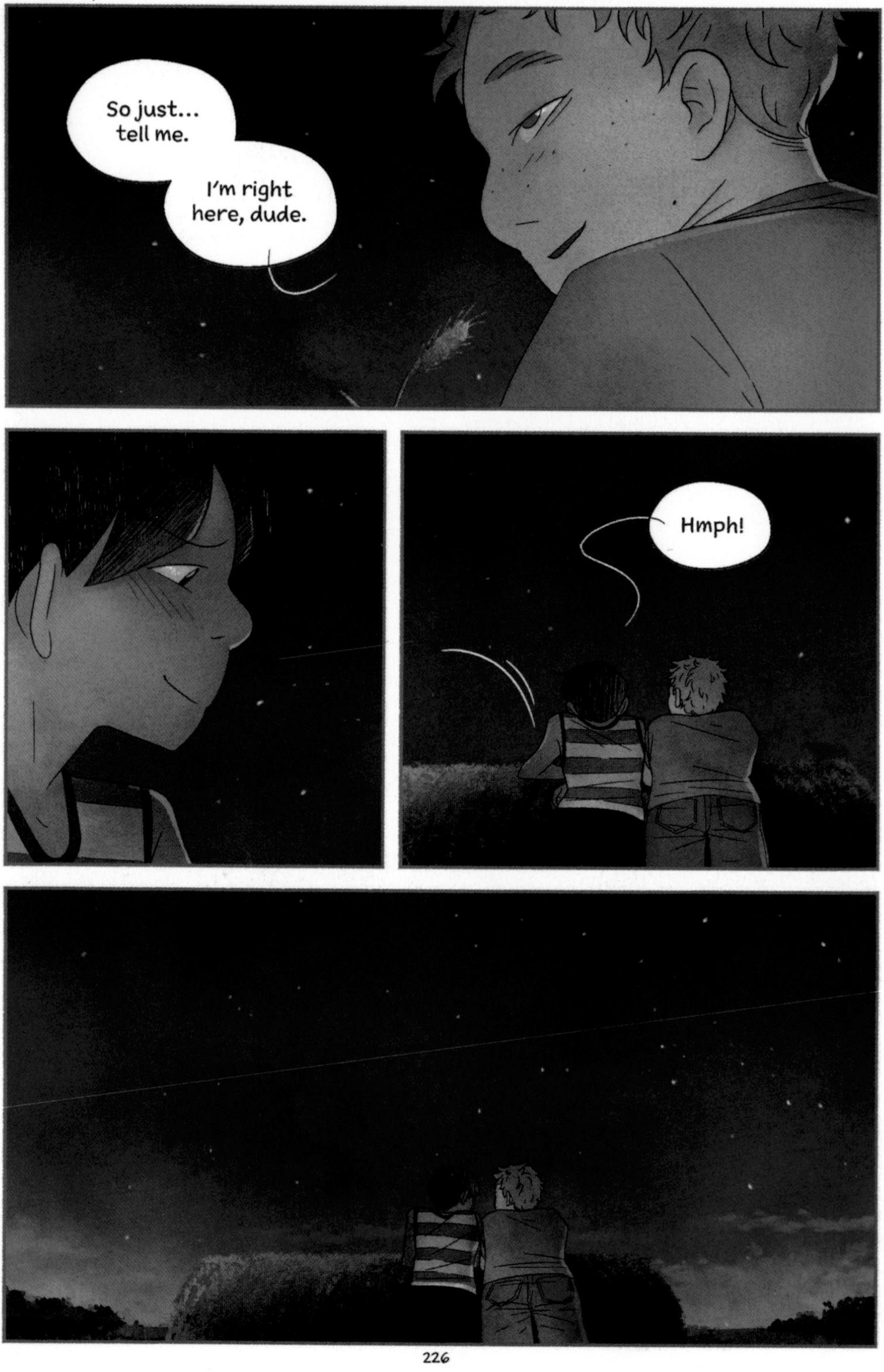
So just... tell me.
I'm right here, dude.
Hmph!

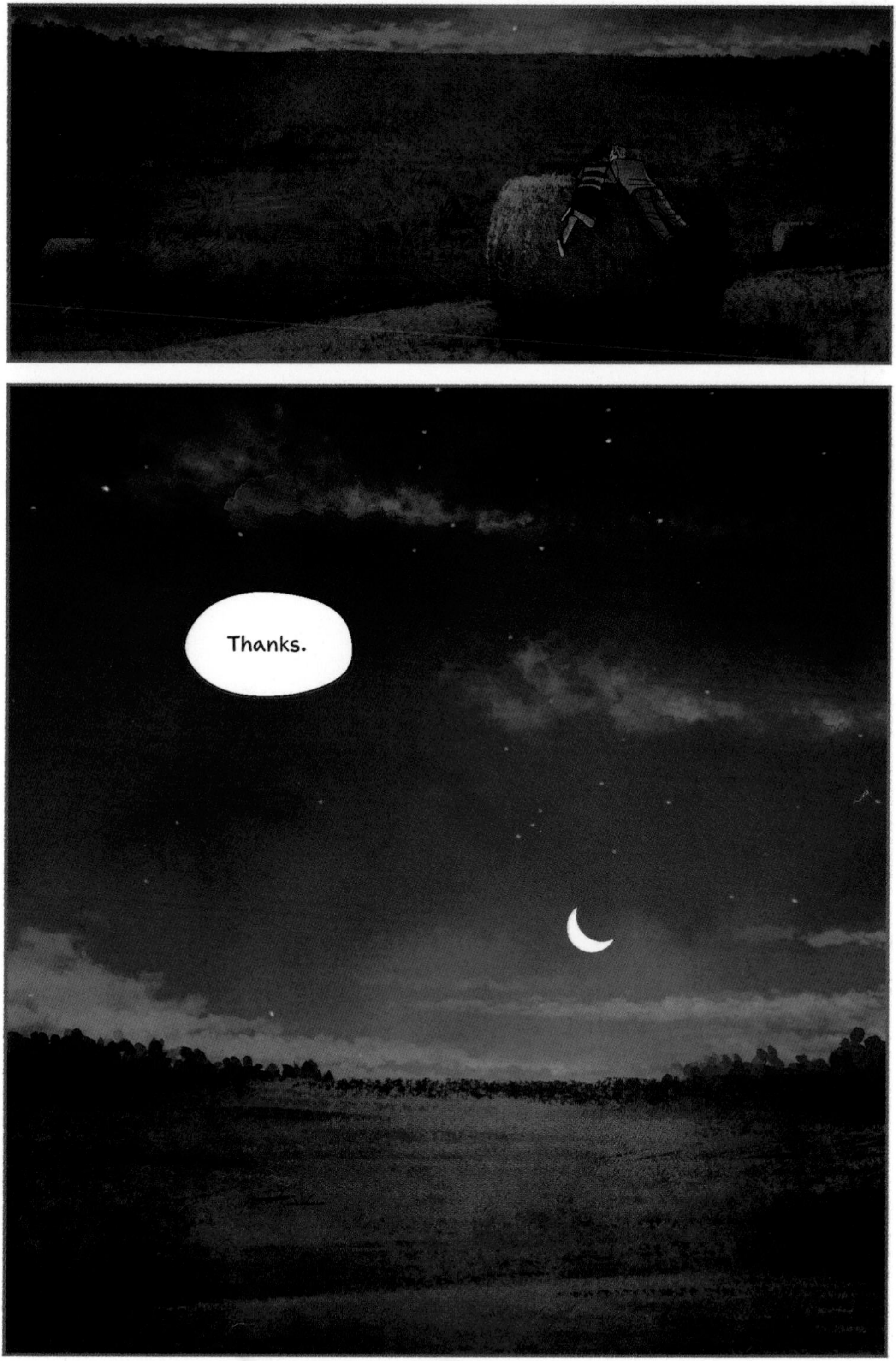
Thanks.

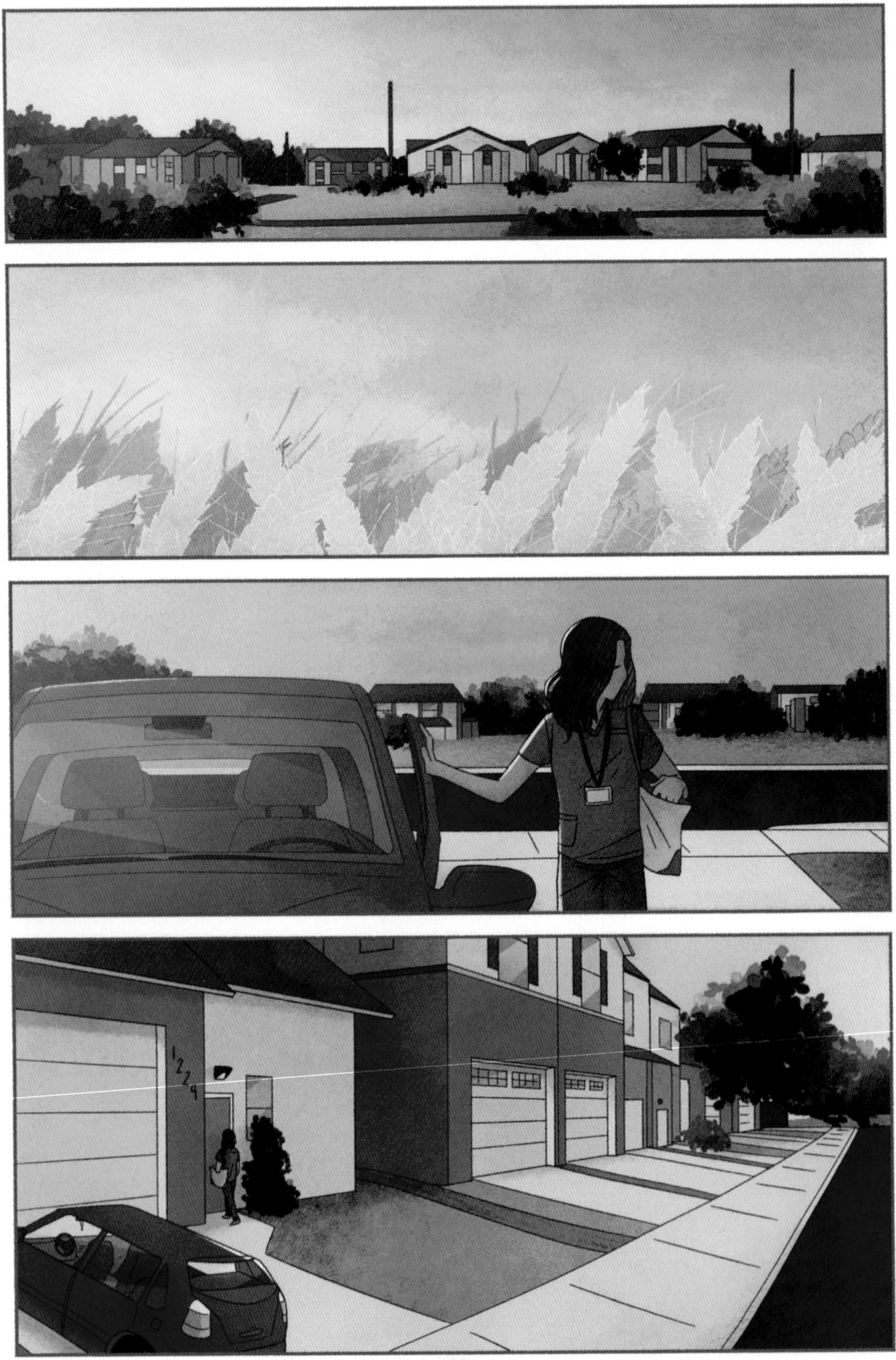
1224

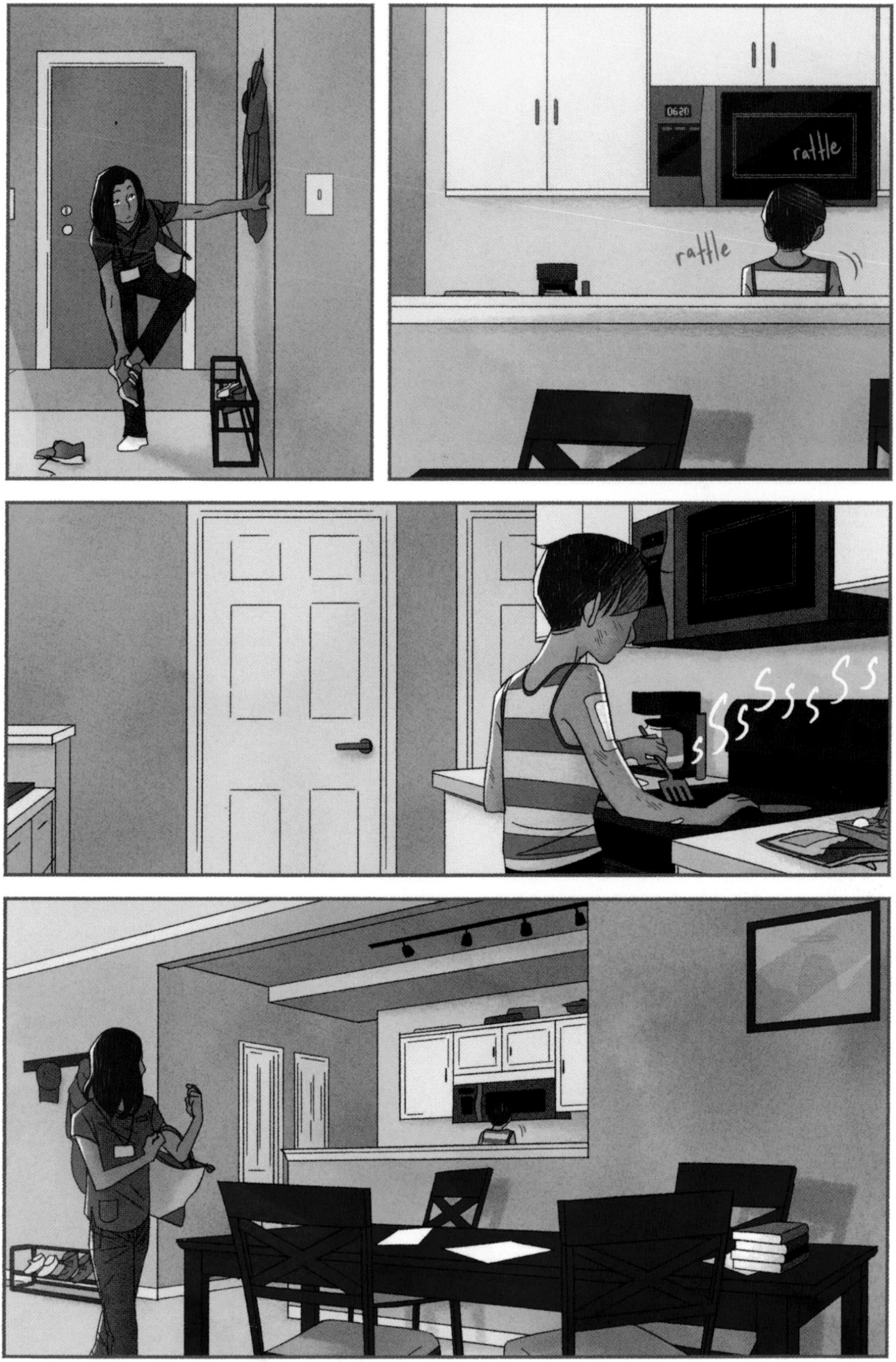
0620
rattle
rattle

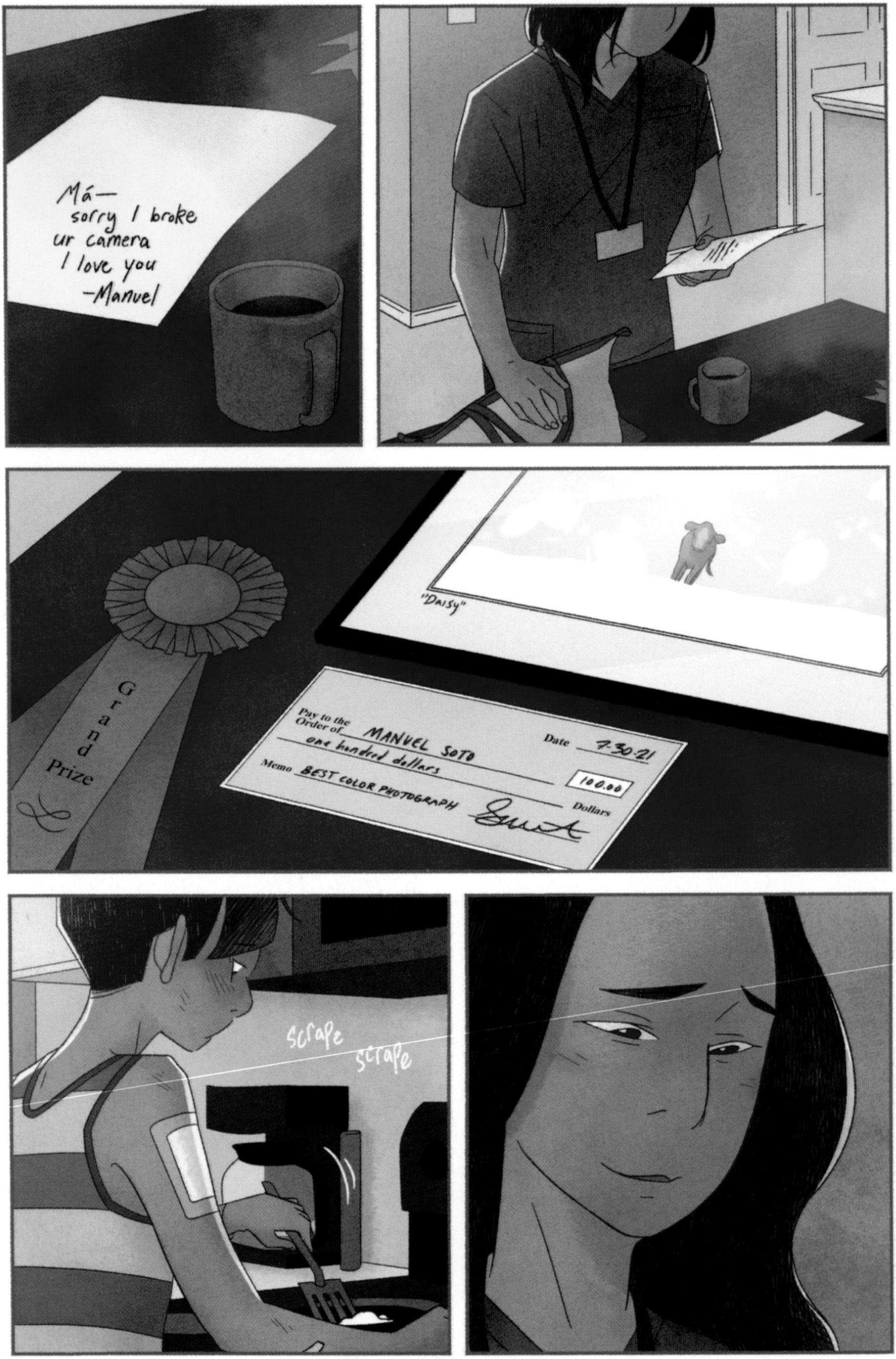
Má—
sorry I broke
ur camera
I love you
-Manuel
"Daisy"
Grand
Prize
Pay to the
Order of MANUEL SOTO
Date 7-30-21
one hundred dollars
100.00
Dollars
Memo BEST COLOR PHOTOGRAPH
scrape
scrape

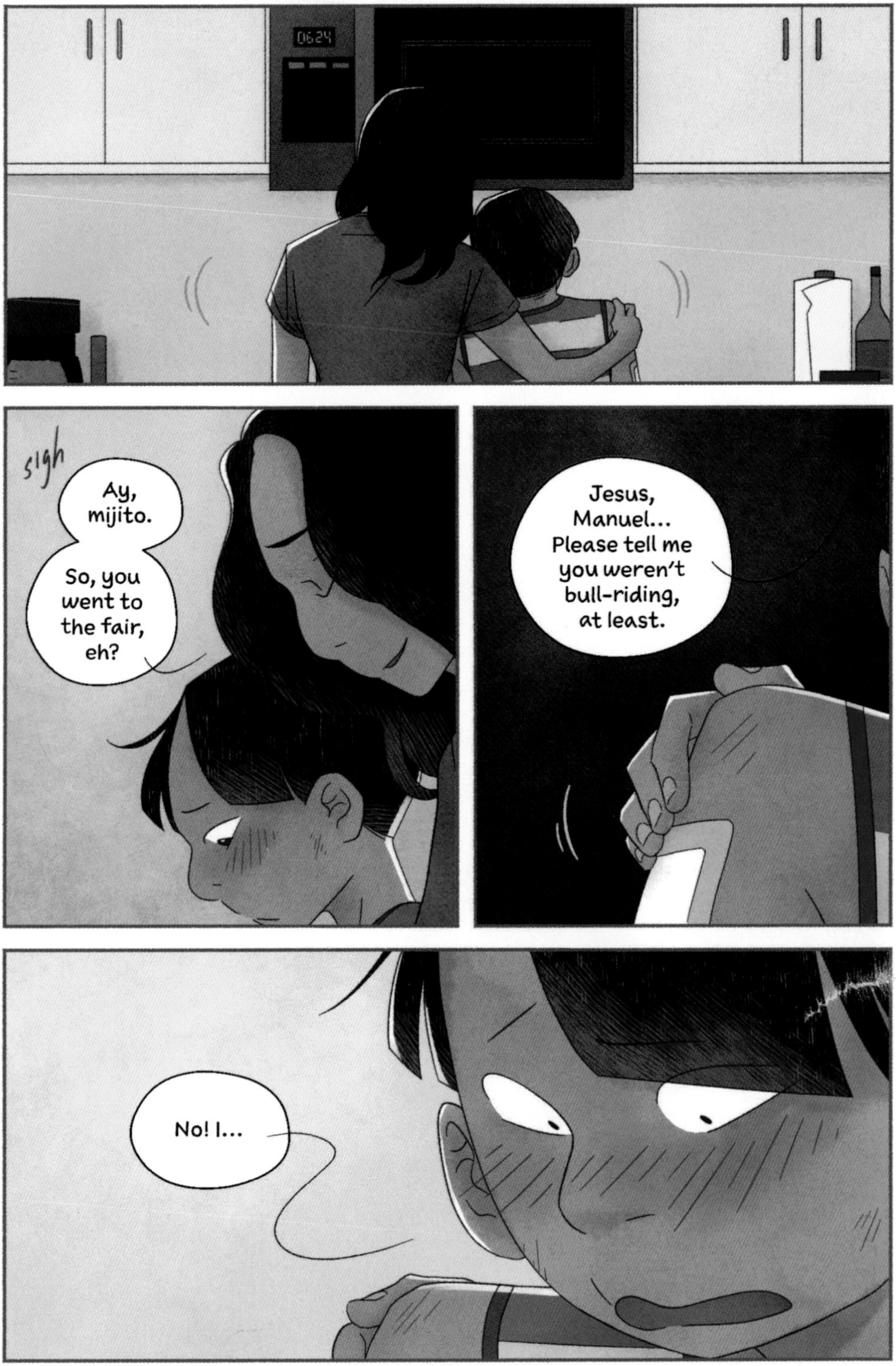
0624
sigh
Ay, mijito.
So, you went to the fair, eh?
Jesus, Manuel... Please tell me you weren't bull-riding, at least.
No! I...

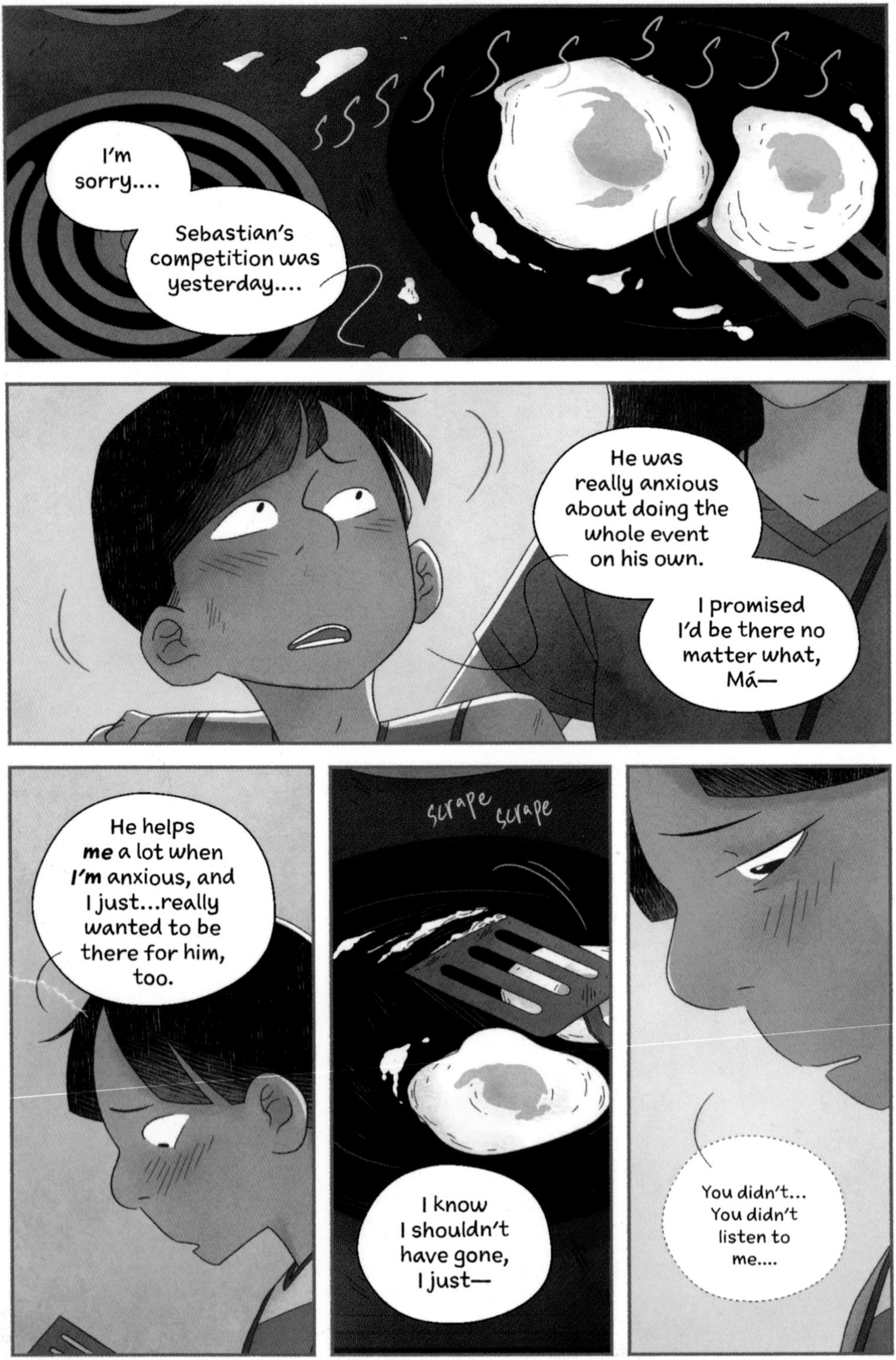
I'm sorry....
Sebastian's competition was yesterday....
He was really anxious about doing the whole event on his own.
I promised I'd be there no matter what, Má—
He helps **me** a lot when ***I'm*** anxious, and I just...really wanted to be there for him, too.
scrape scrape
I know I shouldn't have gone, I just—
You didn't... You didn't listen to me....

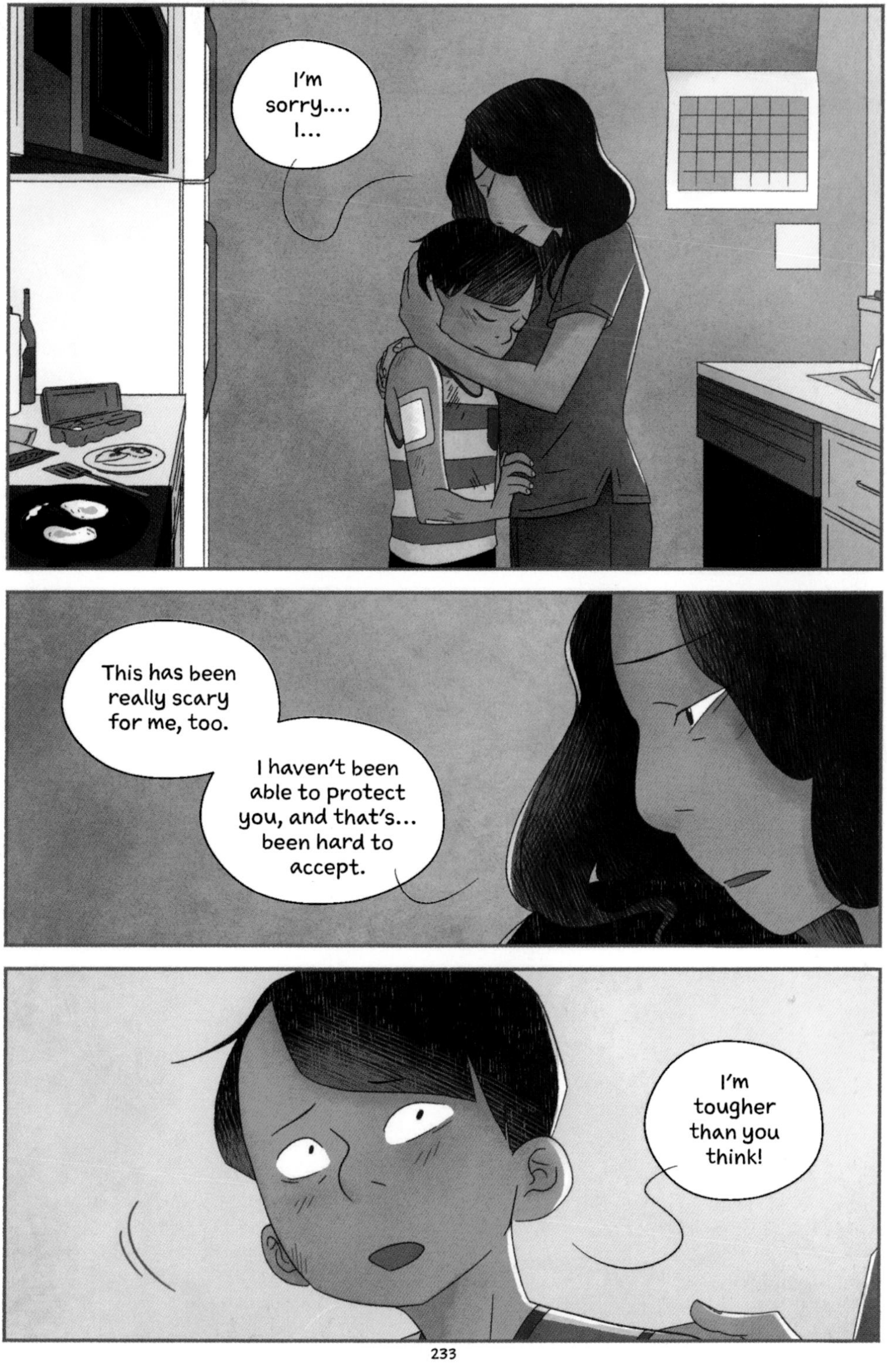
I'm sorry.... I...
This has been really scary for me, too.
I haven't been able to protect you, and that's... been hard to accept.
I'm tougher than you think!

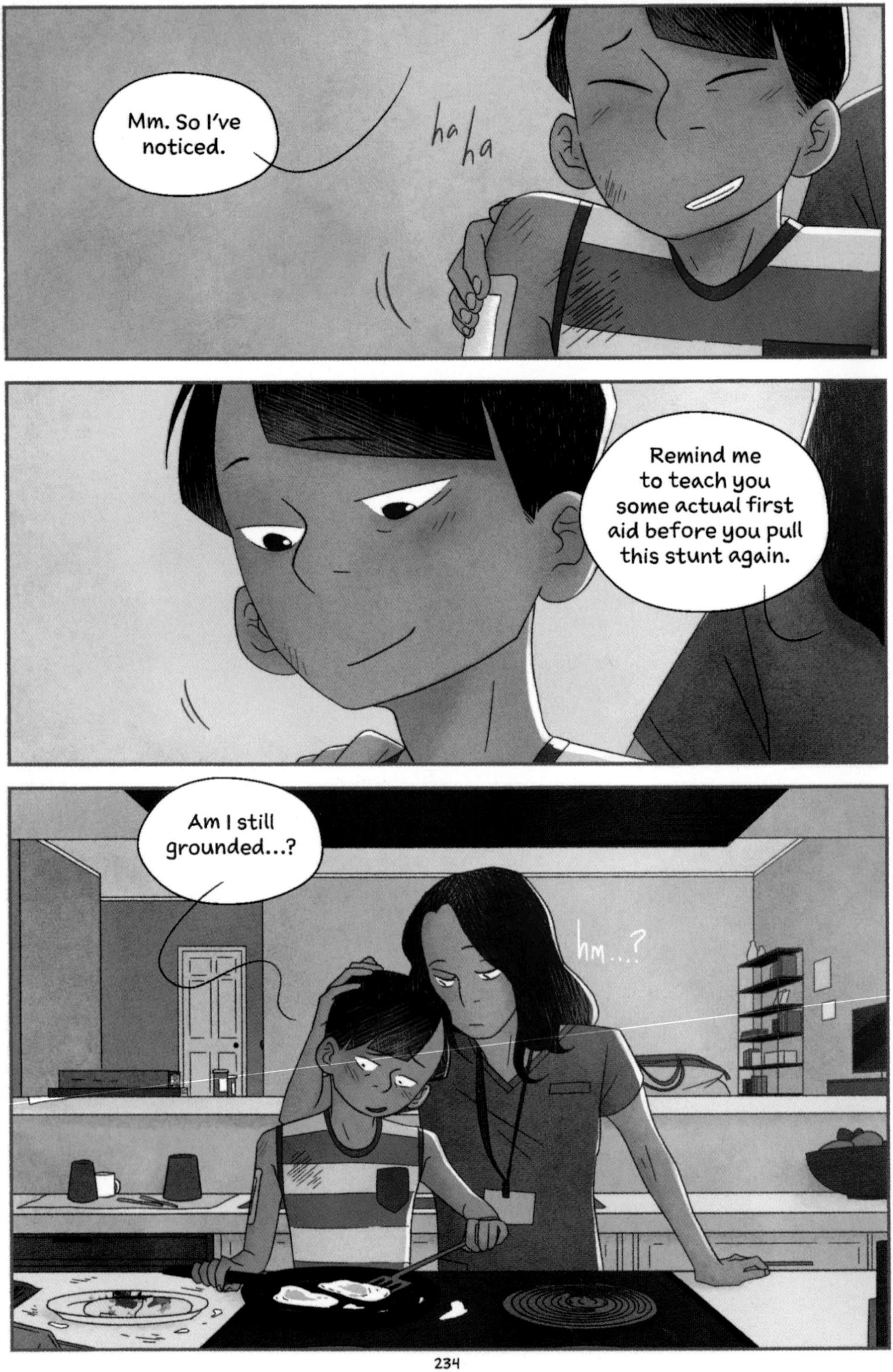
Mm. So I've noticed.
ha ha
Remind me to teach you some actual first aid before you pull this stunt again.
Am I still grounded...?
hm...?

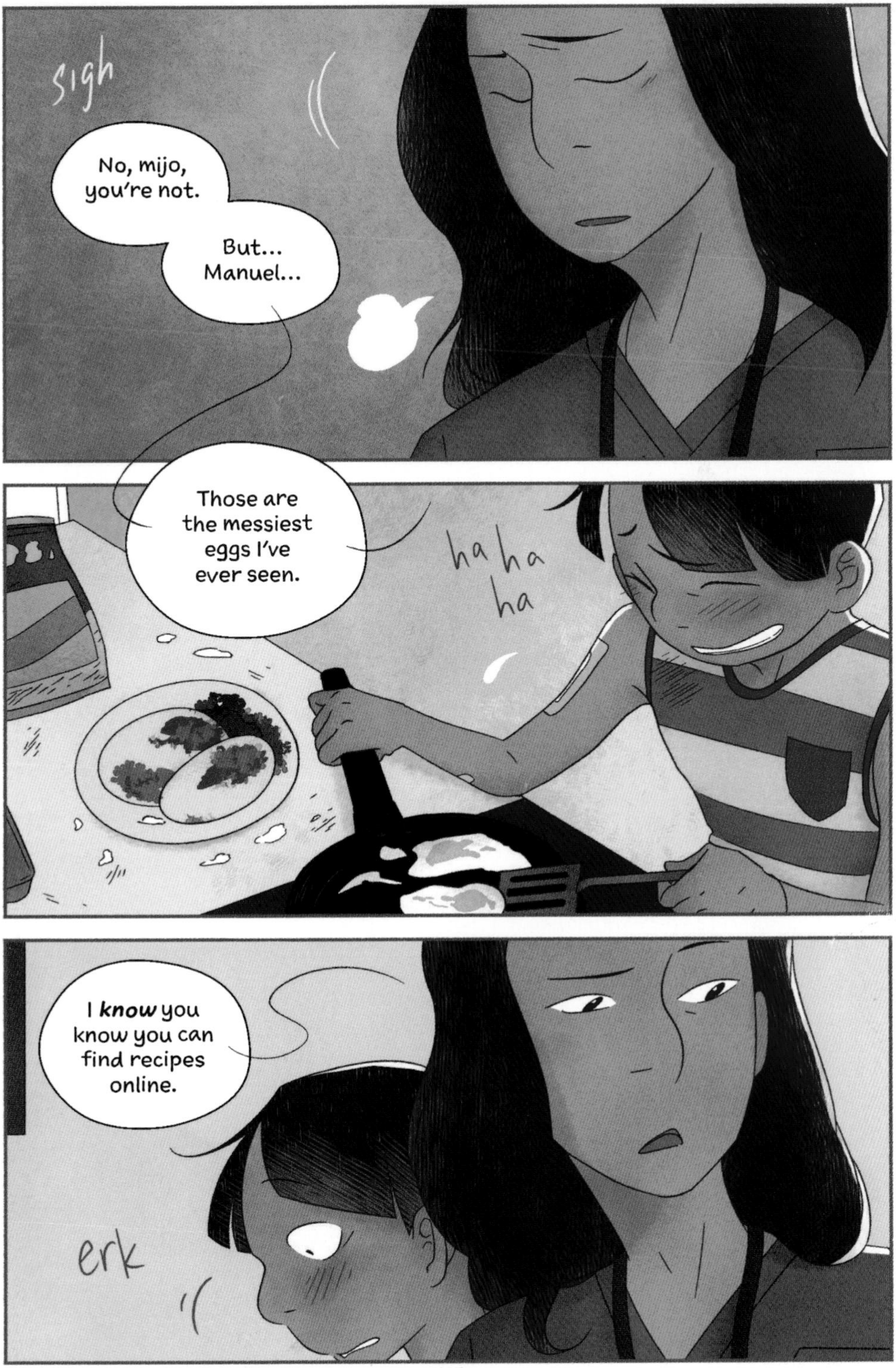
sigh
No, mijo, you're not.
But... Manuel...
Those are the messiest eggs I've ever seen.
ha ha ha
I **know** you know you can find recipes online.
erk

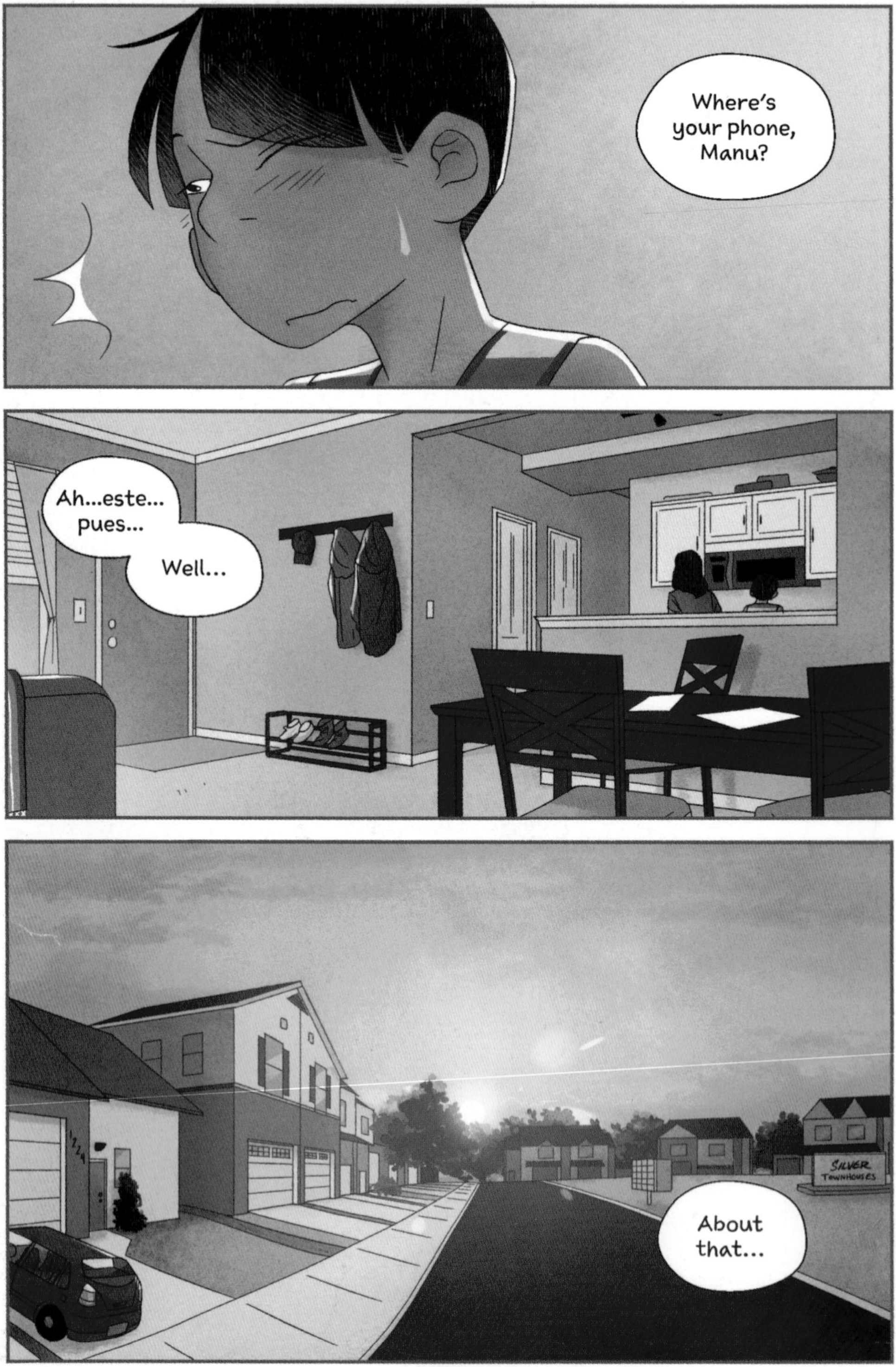
Where's your phone, Manu?
Ah...este... pues...
Well...
1224
SILVER TOWNHOUSES
About that...

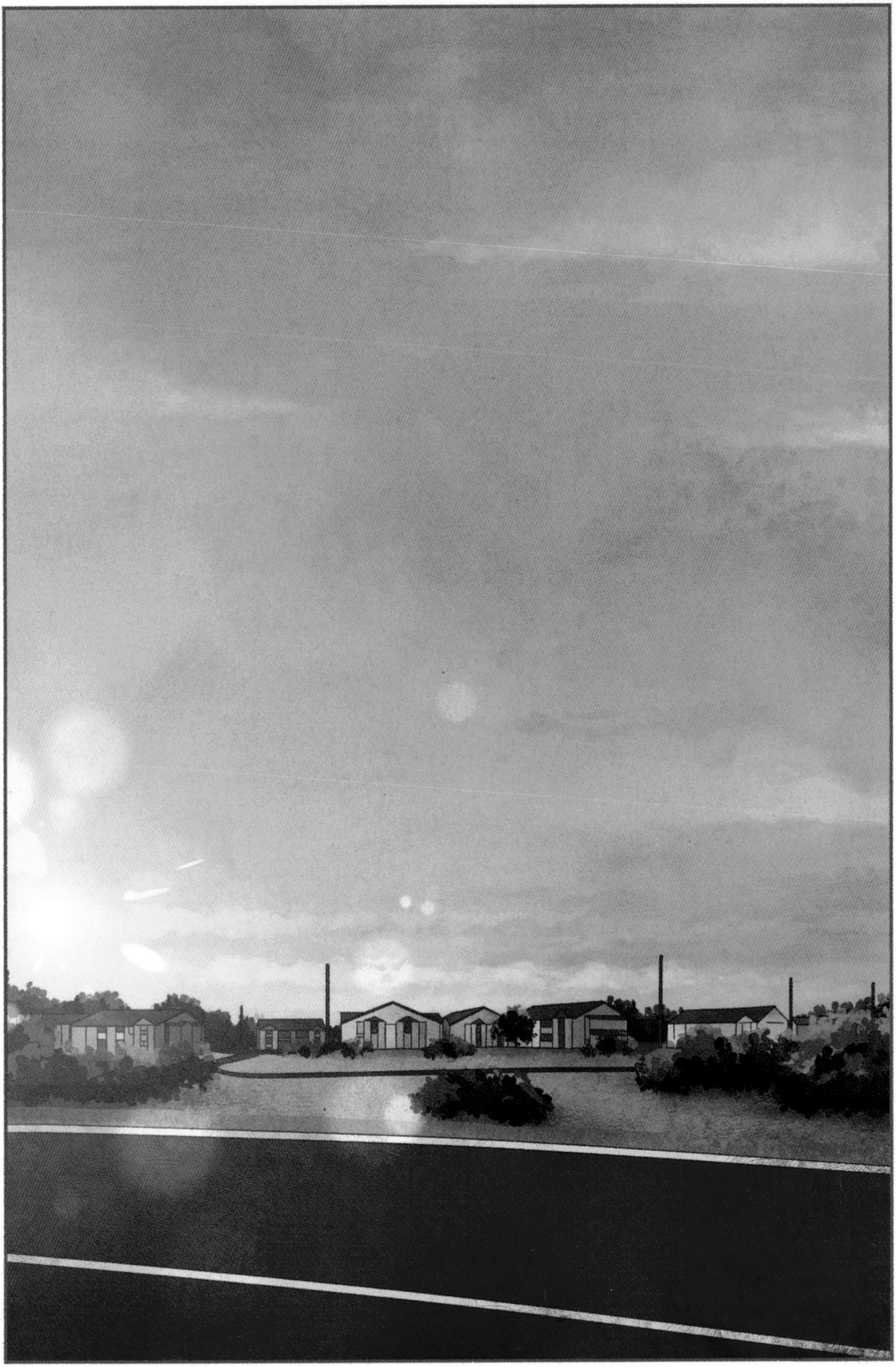

ACKNOWLEDGMENTS

The Golden Hour was in many ways inspired by my childhood in Kansas. Like Manuel, I was the "town kid" in my local 4-H chapter, and I spent many years earning ribbons of all colors for my drawings and photography. Thank you so much to Janelle Crawford-Hine and the entire Crawford family for letting me spend so many weekends on your cattle farm growing up.

I wouldn't be making graphic novels without all my wonderful art and English teachers over the years. Thank you especially to Angelia Perkins for your endless guidance and support, and for letting us spend so, so many high-school afternoons in your class darkroom. I don't do much photography anymore, but I think about your lessons on composition every time I draw a comic panel.

I couldn't have made this book without the tireless support of my agent, Charlie Olsen. And so many thank-yous to my wonderful editor, Rachel Poloski, who made sure I had a steady stream of calf and chicken GIFs to keep me going! *The Golden Hour* would still be an awkward mess without the incredible help of my art director, Ching Chan, and the rest of the amazing LBYR team.

Thank you so much to Belinda Kay Peñaloza Sloop, aka "Bee," and Andrea Melania Rodriguez Moon for your incredible help and translations, and for always letting me ask just one more thing—over and over again. And to my mental health consultants: Thank you; your feedback was invaluable.

Thank you to all the friends and family who were happy to read this book in its early awkward stages: Sarah, Kori, Sfé, and Jules. And to Bradley, who is always there when I need to wax nostalgic about the Kansas landscapes of our childhood!

And to Kiri...for everything.

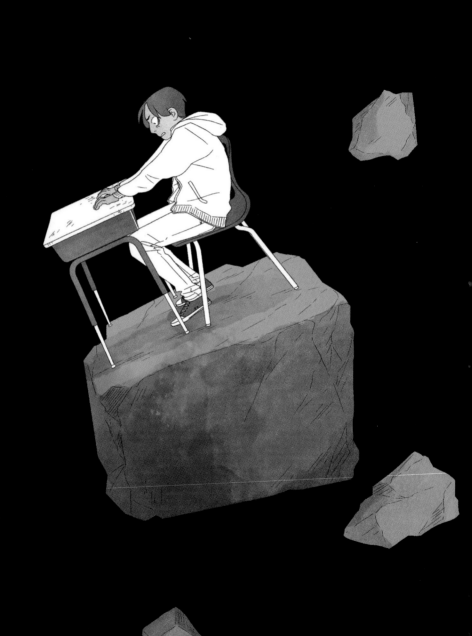

A Note from the Author

Post-traumatic stress disorder (PTSD) can be caused by many things, but it often affects people who have experienced a distressing or life-threatening event.

Throughout *The Golden Hour*, Manuel struggles with many lasting symptoms of PTSD: nightmares, invasive flashbacks, and anxiety. There are also physical symptoms, such as shortness of breath and shaking. In particular, Manuel experiences panic attacks and what is called "derealization": a state in which he feels detached and disconnected from his surroundings.

In working with his therapist, Manuel learns to practice grounding himself. Grounding can take many forms, such as focusing on your breathing, counting backward, reciting a mantra, or touching an ice cube. Manuel's therapist encourages him to use his cell-phone camera as an anchor when he feels himself begin to dissociate.

Everyone responds to trauma differently. If you or a loved one are struggling with anxiety, you can talk to your school counselor or doctor. They'll be able to help you obtain the right resources to find a way to cope with the symptoms.

Resources

ADAA.org: Anxiety and Depression Association of America

NCTSN.org: The National Child Traumatic Stress Network

TheTrevorProject.org: The Trevor Project, crisis intervention for LGBTQ youth

Manuel's art teacher gives him a book about the history of photography. As he flips through the pages, you can see a few famous pieces.

Boulevard du Temple
Louis Daguerre, 1838

Migrant Mother
Dorothea Lange, 1936
Library of Congress

The Tetons and the Snake River
Ansel Adams, 1942
National Archives

Heat Wave at Coney Island
© Weegee, 1940

taken with this kind of camera

Speed camera, 1943
National Archives

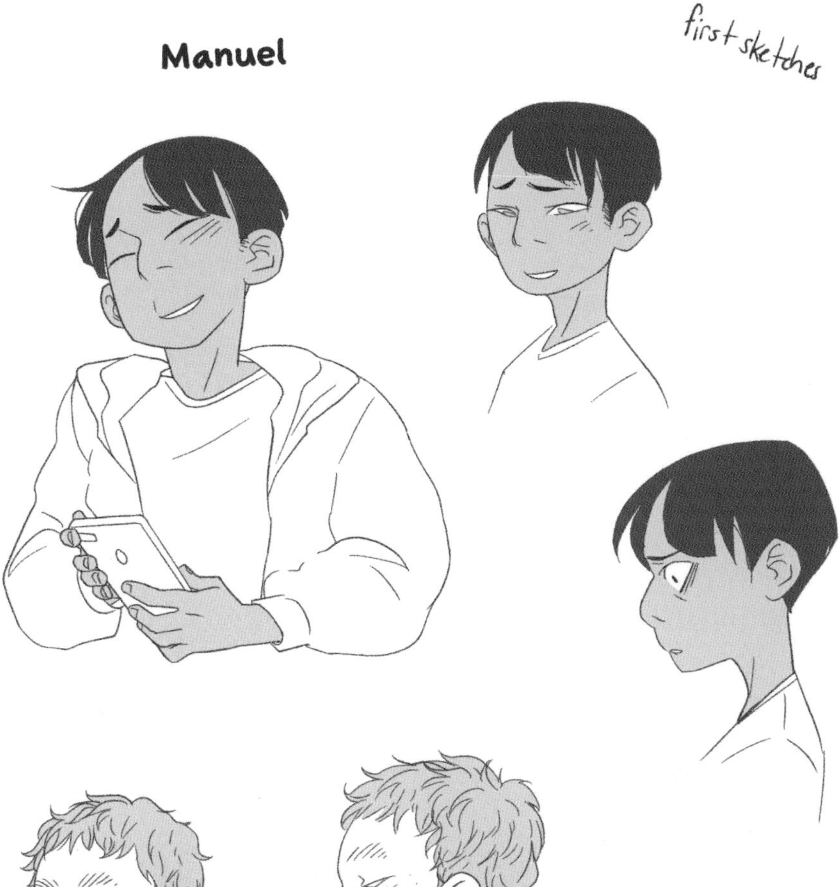
Manuel
first sketches

Sebastian

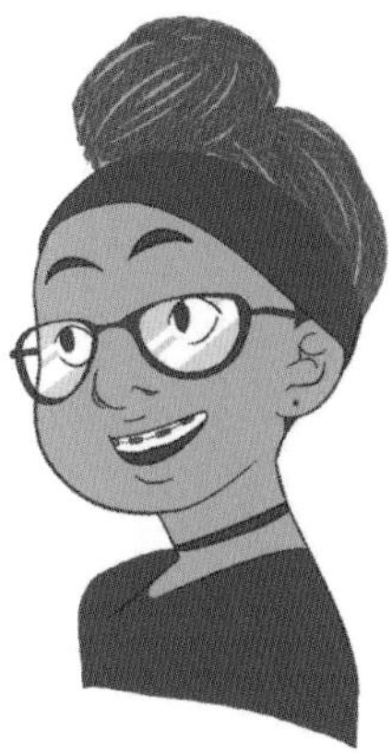

Caysha

The town *The Golden Hour* is set in
is made up, but I like to think it's near
where I grew up, in northeast Kansas.
I named it "Kanwaka" after my old 4-H club.

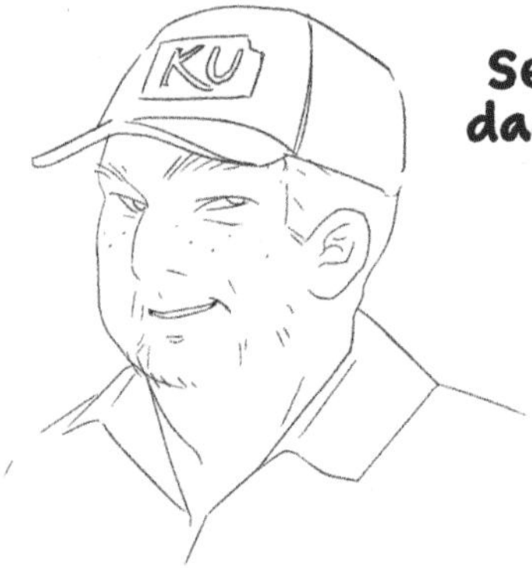

Sebastian's dad and mom

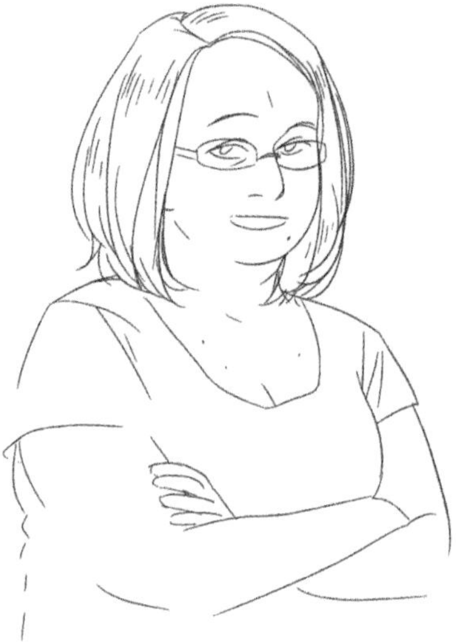

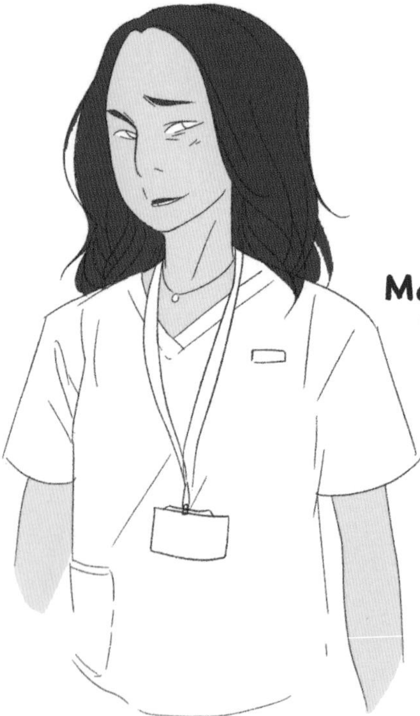

Manuel's mom

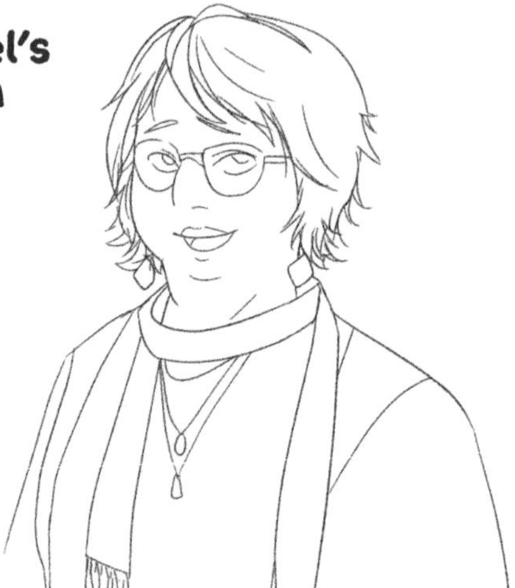

Ms. Winstone

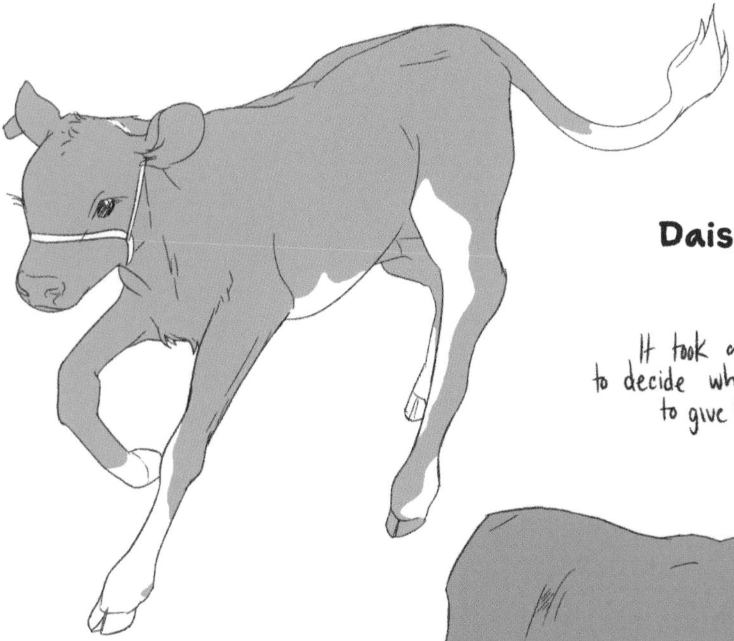

Daisy

It took a while
to decide what colors
to give her

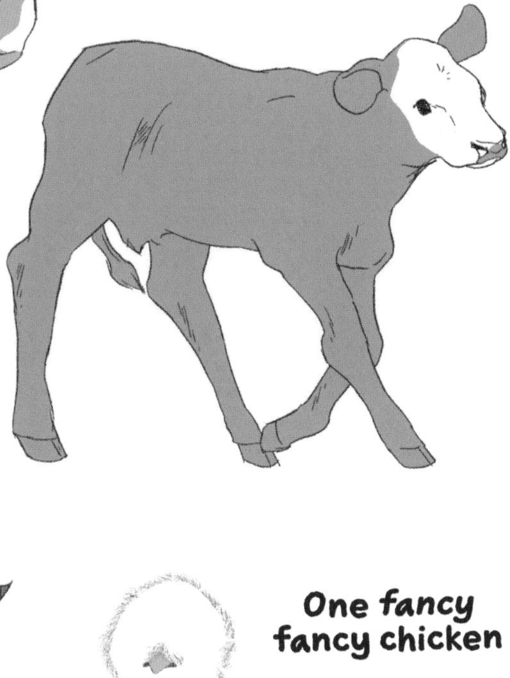

I looked at a lot of
photo references
in my early sketches
to help me figure out
calf anatomy

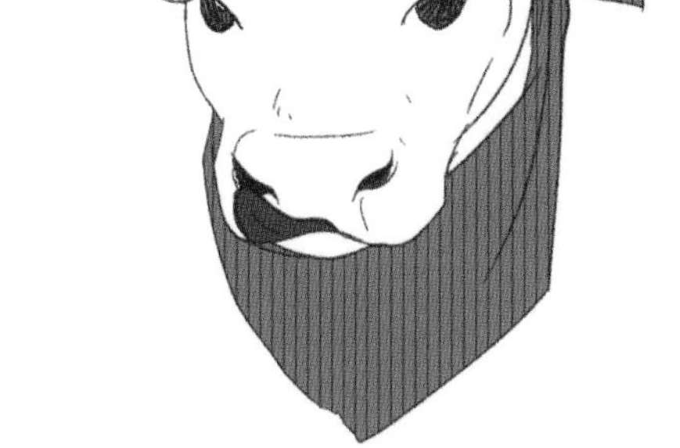

**One fancy
fancy chicken**

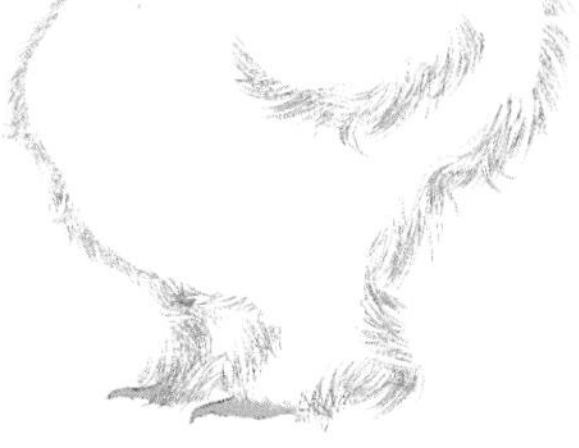

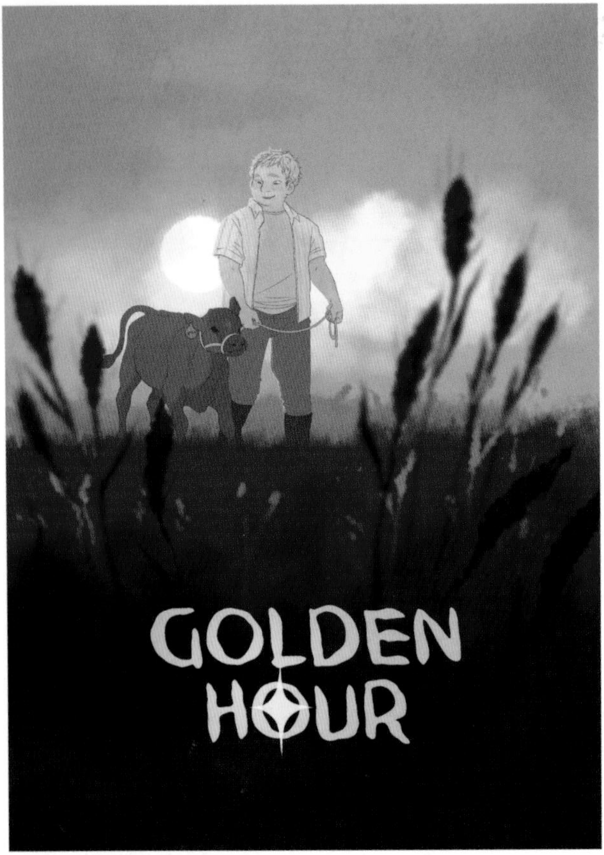
GOLDEN
HOUR

Another of my early drawings. I knew I wanted the backgrounds to look painted, so this was my first attempt at figuring that out.

This one was colored in Photoshop, but the final book was drawn and colored in Clip Studio Paint.

If you look closely, parts of the wheat + sky are in the final book cover

The "golden hour" is a special term in photography for the red-tinted light you see only at sunrise and sunset.

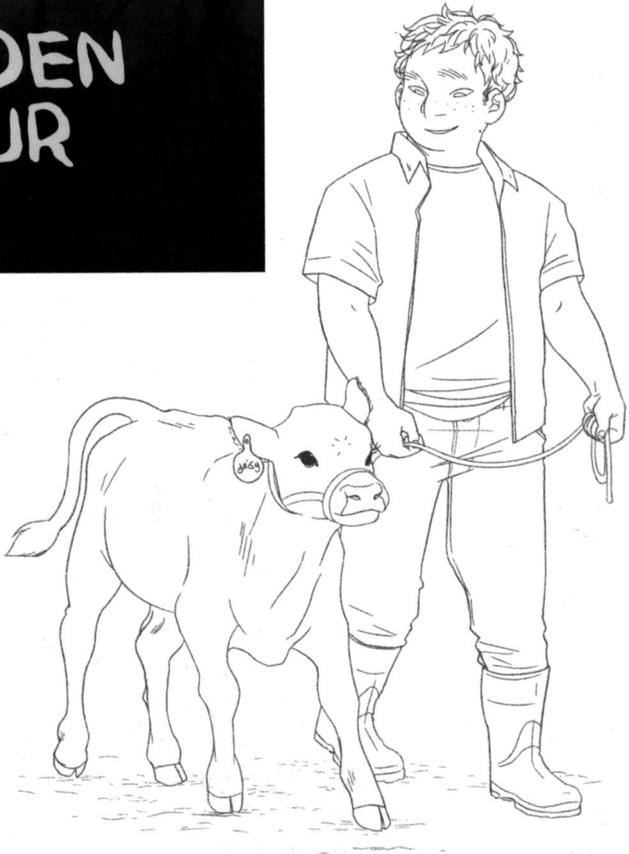
daisy

A PANEL FROM START TO FINISH

PAGE 204

Panel I

The county fairgrounds, the sun setting into evening, the light gold but fading. In front of the fairgrounds is a mile of mowed grass roped off and acting as parking lots. There are huge pavilions with exhibitions, and in the distance there are lights of the rides and food carts.

SCRIPT

This is written kind of like a movie script. I figure out pacing and how the story unfolds.

ROUGHS

I split the page into panels, add lettering, and do a quick sketch.

LINE ART

I carefully redraw each panel. The yellow lines are what I'll reference when I paint the background.

FLAT COLORS

This is when I figure out the color scheme for each scene.

FINAL COLORS

I add lighting, shading, and textures.

Kiri Wolff

NIKI SMITH no longer lives in the Sunflower State, but she will always call Kansas home. She is the author of the Lambda Literary Award—nominated graphic novels *The Deep & Dark Blue* and *Crossplay*. Niki now lives in Germany with her wife.